I0776940
AE

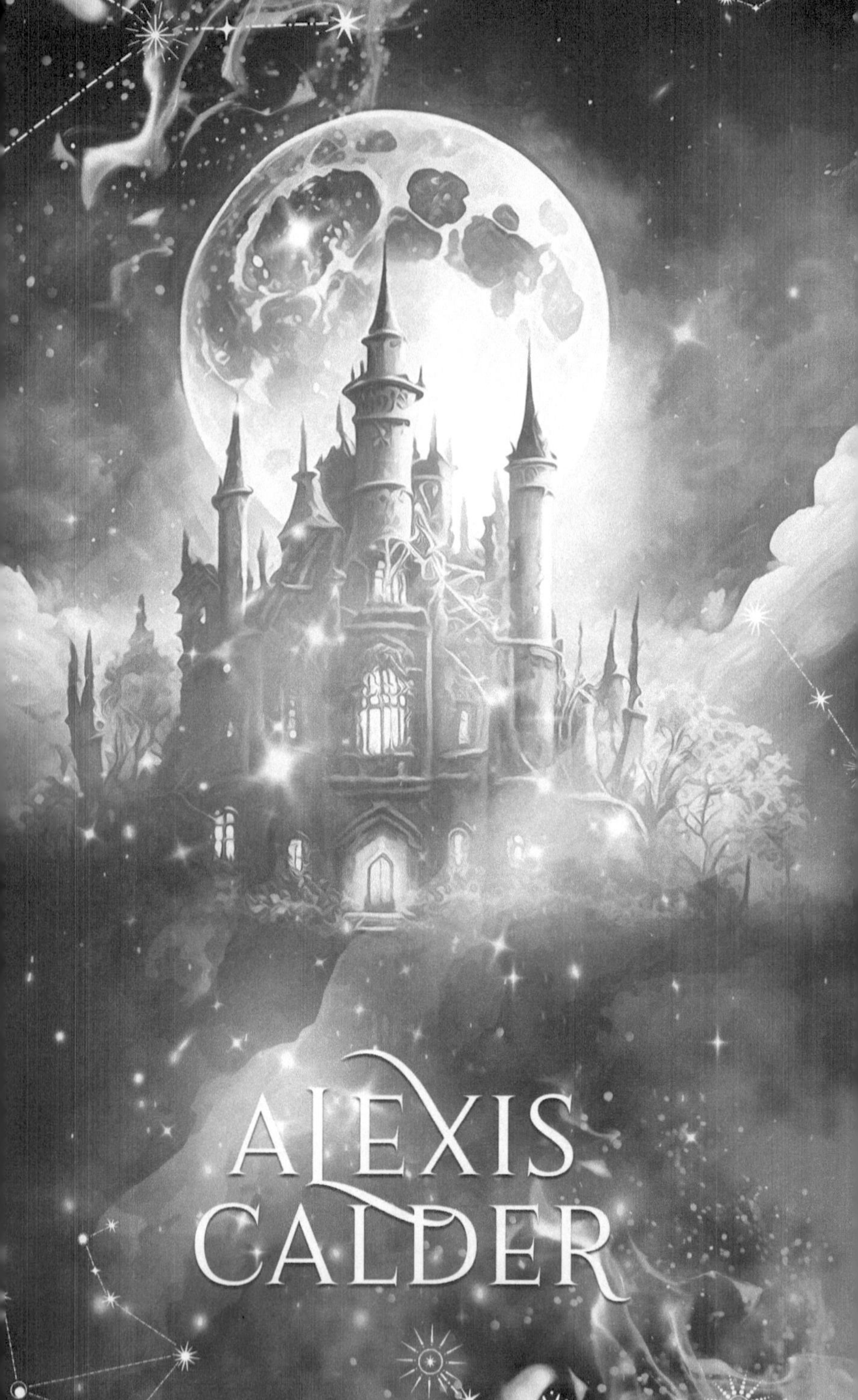

ALEXIS
CALDER

ACADEMY

OF THE

ELITES

SPECIAL EDITION COLLECTION
BOOKS 1-4

CONTENTS

FATED MAGIC

UNBOUND MAGIC

COPYRIGHTS

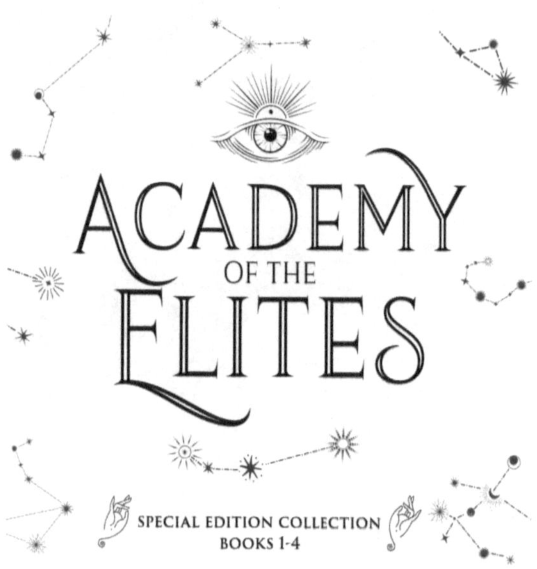

COPYRIGHTS

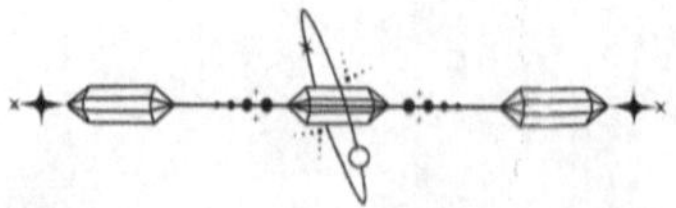

WRITTEN AS ALEXIS CALDER

<u>Blood and Salt Series</u>
Kingdom of Blood and Salt
Court of Vice and Death
Crown of Stars and Fate

<u>Royal Blood Series</u>
Obsession
Hunger

<u>Rejected Fate Series</u>
Darkest Mate
Forbidden Sin
Feral Queen

<u>Moon Cursed Series</u>

Wolf Marked
Wolf Untamed
Wolf Chosen

<u>Royal Mates Series</u>
Shifter Claimed
Shifter Fated
Shifter Rising

<u>Academy of Elites Series</u>
Academy of Elites: Untamed Magic
Academy of Elites: Broken Magic
Academy of Elites: Fated Magic
Academy of Elites: Unbound Magic

<u>Brimstone Academy Series</u>
Brimstone Academy: Semester One
Brimstone Academy: Semester Two

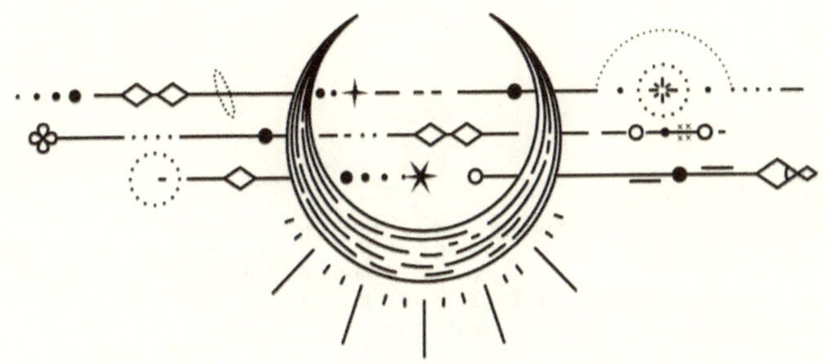

ROMCOM WRITTEN AS LEXI CALDER

In Hate With My Boss
Love to Hate You

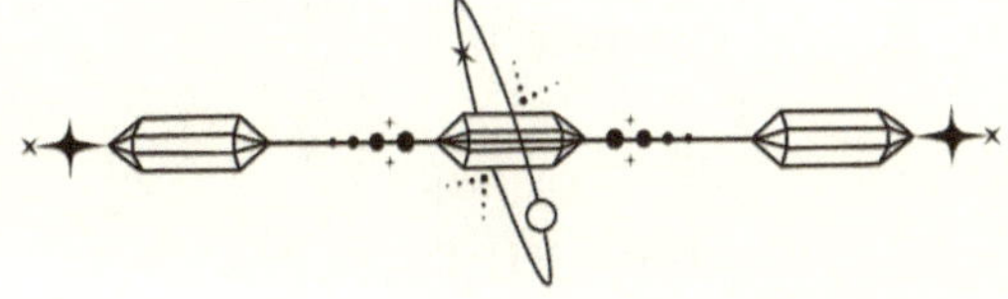

DESCRIPTION

**My name is Raven Winters and I'm a mage.
Who the hell knew?**

When I somehow summon fire in an act of self defense, I'm given two choices by the magic cops: attend some stuck-up magic school, or go to magic jail.

Well, shit. There go my plans for the next year. Apparently, I have Untamed Magic, whatever the hell that means. And I've got a year to get it under control at this magic academy that's basically a finishing school for the elite. Everyone here is somebody important. And rich. Except for me.

Which paints quite the target on my back. Being the token poor kid is bad enough. Throw in that I somehow form a mating bond with four of the school's most eligible bachelors. Oh yeah, and add in the fact that someone is trying to kill me. FML.

This is the complete four-book series that follows Raven's adventures at the Academy of the Elites. This is a steamy series where the heroine doesn't have to choose.

This edition contains all four books in Raven's story:
Untamed Magic, Book 1
Broken Magic, Book 2
Fated Magic, Book 3
Unbound Magic, Book 4

Acknŏledgments

Thank you to all the readers who took a chance with this series. This was my first book with my pen name after I decided I wanted to do something a little different than I had with my previous books.

This series means so much to me and I know it means a lot to many of you. Raven is tenacious and fights for herself and those around her. She's defiant and strong. She's like so many of my readers who have been through hell in their lives and despite the odds, have persevered.

This edition is for all of you. Keep fighting for yourself no matter what.

XO,
Alexis

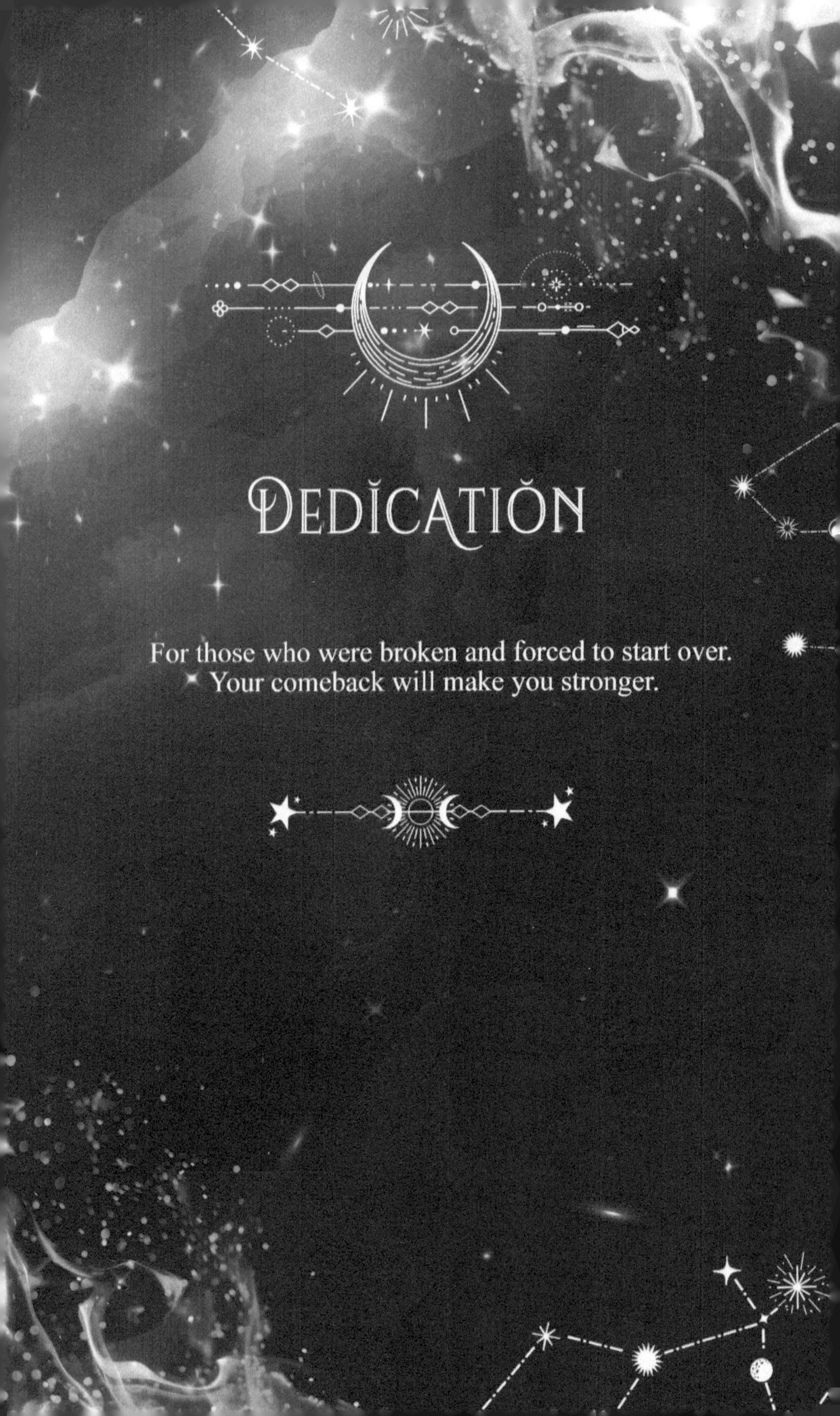

Dedĭcatiŏn

For those who were broken and forced to start over.
Your comeback will make you stronger.

UNTAMED MAGIC

SPECIAL EDITION COLLECTION
BOOK 1

ALEXIS CALDER

CHAPTER 1

RAVEN

The beads clicked together on the pendulum on the desk. *Click. Click. Click.* It was an odd choice of desk decoration in a place that supposedly had magic. I looked away from the toy and back at the headmaster sitting behind the desk.

The monster sitting in front of me should appease my disbelief. Dr. Green, the headmaster of the Academy of the Elites, was a demon. I think. He was huge. A hulking form squeezed into a suit and tie. His skin was a blushing shade of pink and his hands were covered in what could only be described as fur. Don't even get me started on his eyebrows. Or should I say eyebrow. One massive, bushy brow over both of his yellow eyes.

He frowned, his upper fangs hanging over his lower lip as he shuffled through a pile of papers on his desk.

"Like I said, you really can just call me an Uber. I'll find my way home on my own. None of this is necessary." I'd been saying it for hours but it was worth trying again.

He lifted his eyebrow and glanced up at me, then went back to the paperwork.

I let out a heavy sigh, clearly demonstrating my annoyance. All they'd told me was that I was in trouble and I had to come to this stupid school. I'd asked for a phone call, but to be honest, I didn't have anyone to call. That's what happened when you made sure you never stayed in one place for too long and never let anyone get close.

A grandfather clock chimed. Two times. It was already morning. Very fucking early in the morning. How the hell had the whole night gone by so quickly? I glared at the clock as if it were somehow responsible for my being here.

It was an odd creation. The clock itself was tall with branches that came off of it, making it look like a creepy Halloween decoration of a tree. It didn't help that it was painted black. The clock face had a pair of gold eyes on it, resembling an owl. I wasn't sure if it was the coolest clock in the world or if it was an ominous sign of things to come in this place.

The rest of the office was relatively unimpressive. Red carpet. Bookshelves lining the back wall. A bar to my right with glass decanters full of brown liquor. At least they didn't outlaw alcohol in this place.

"Ms. Winters," Dr. Green said.

I turned back to him, trying to make eye contact. You know, show that I wasn't afraid or some shit. It was nearly impossible to avoid my eyes lifting to the horns on top of his head. He looked like *Hellboy*. It was very distracting.

"Your little stunt is going to take days to clean up, you do realize that?" Dr. Green growled.

"I didn't do it on purpose," I said, exasperation evident in my tone. Hadn't we been through this already? The people who brought me here drilled me on this. He drilled me on this. We've already covered this.

"You roasted two human men alive," he said.

My stomach flipped. "In my defense, they did try to kill me."

He shook his head. "You're lucky you're under age or they'd toss you in a cell and throw away the key. You can't do magic in front of humans. And you certainly can't burn them alive in public."

I frowned. "I didn't even know I had magic." How many times was I going to have to tell him it was an accident? And it really was self defense. They were trying to kill me. Or worse. Who knows what they would have done to me if I hadn't defended myself. "So they're allowed to come at me with a gun and I do nothing?"

"No. You can and should defend yourself but you have to be smart about it. That's why you're here."

Here. At some magic school I didn't ask to attend. I sighed. My choices were clear. Attend this school, or go to magical juvie. Cause apparently, at twenty-one, I was still a minor according to magic law or some bullshit.

"I still don't understand why I'm here," I said.

He lifted his eyebrow. "You have to learn how to control your magic. Untamed magic is a danger to everyone. Magical and Human."

He wrote something down on a piece of paper, then slid it into a manila folder on his desk.

"Is that my file?" I asked. The idea that he was keeping notes on me made me uncomfortable.

He held up the folder and I saw my name, Raven Winters, written on the tab. My mouth twisted to the side at the sight of it.

"We keep a file on all of our students. It stays with you through your term here at the Academy of the Elites. When you graduate, you can take it with you. It's helpful when applying to jobs within the supernatural community."

I scrubbed my face with my hand. This was not how I expected today to go. I was supposed to be on my way to a friend's house for a party. "What about my life?"

I'd worked so hard to afford my tiny, run down apartment. Sure, my job was shit, but it was mine. And I was good at it.

"When you graduate, you can go back to getting humans drunk if you choose."

I scowled at him. Way to make my job as a bartender sound even less glamorous than it was. "Can't I just attend classes at night or something? Don't you have a community college version?"

One corner of his lips tugged into a smile. "You're going to be a handful, aren't you?"

"A handful? Look, I'm not a kid. I don't care what your laws say, I'm an adult and I get to make my own choices."

"Sure," he said. "Make your choice. Prison cell or dorm room."

Fuck. We were going around in circles. "I can't pay tuition."

"That's not a problem. We have generous donors and scholarship funds available for unique cases such as yours," he said.

"I'm a unique case?" I asked, lifting a skeptical eyebrow. Considering how everyone I knew was raised to believe that magic wasn't real, I couldn't be the only one to randomly create fire and throw their whole life into a tailspin.

"It's rare for a mage to be unaware of their powers." He frowned for a moment, then he returned to the impassive expression he'd maintained for most of our conversation. "You will be behind your classmates, but I imagine you'll catch up quickly. If you put the work into it."

"What if I don't want to?" I asked.

"Then you'll fail."

"And let me guess," I said. "If I fail, it's magic prison?" To be fair, I was starting to think this place was just as much of a prison as the mysterious threat.

"Or worse." He stood, then walked toward the door. "I'll have someone show you to your new room."

"What exactly does that mean?" I asked. "Are you threatening me? Are you allowed to do that? Aren't you an educator?"

He shook his head and turned to me. "The Academy of the Elites is the most prestigious graduate program for magic users in the country. It is a privilege to be here. You should be kissing the feet of whoever got you in here."

"I didn't ask to be here," I said.

"And yet, here you are. You want my advice, young mage?"

Not really. I bit down on the inside of my cheek to keep from saying what I really wanted to say.

"Appreciate your time here. Learn something. Don't fuck it up." He turned away from me and walked toward the door.

I slumped back against the chair feeling both called out and pissed. Who was he to decide what I did with my future? And if this place was so fucking great, why the hell was I here?

"You ready?" A silky male voice called out.

I turned and my jaw nearly hit the floor. Apparently, my guide was a fucking Greek god. The ideal specimen of man standing in front of the doorway was six feet of lean muscle. His sandy hair was a perfect mess, partially covering one eye. It was the kind of hairstyle you knew he'd spent ten minutes getting just right in the mirror.

He smiled at me, showing a row of straight white teeth. His square jaw was dusted with soft gold stubble. He tossed his head, sending his hair away from his eyes and I blinked in stunned silence as I caught his icy gaze. He had eyes like nothing I'd ever seen before. They were a stunning blue. Practically glowing. And they made me clench my thighs together right there in the chair. Talk about bedroom eyes. I was ready to get it on with him just from his stare.

Dr. Green cleared his throat, causing me to break free of those eyes. I looked down at my feet, trying to regain my composure. Then, I stood. "Let's get this over with."

"Aw, kitten, it's not that bad," the sexy stranger said.

I glared at him. "My name isn't kitten."

"I like Kitten." He shrugged. "My name's Luka. You want to know where your room is or not?"

"Some welcoming committee," I grumbled under my breath. I glanced over at Dr. Green, but he'd already left the office. I didn't even notice him go. Apparently, I was no longer his issue.

"Fine. Tell me where I'm supposed to go."

He lifted up an envelope. "In here you'll find all you need to get started. Class schedule, room assignment, key card, PIN number, all of that."

"Key card?"

"We might use magic, but we're not afraid of technology here. Other than cell phones. No matter what you do, there's just no service. Anyway, your card is everything. How you enter your room, how you get your meals, and how you get your weekly allowance."

"Oh, I'm sure that won't be a concern for me," I said. "Nobody's paying me an allowance."

He lifted an eyebrow. "What do you mean, nobody?"

"I'm a scholarship kid. They're forcing me to go here. Feel free to engage in the poor kid bullying now."

His brow furrowed. "The Academy doesn't really do scholarships."

I thought back to the conversation with the dean. He distinctly told me I had a scholarship. Maybe they didn't make it obvious to others. I wasn't sure what to say.

"You might want to keep that to yourself," Luka said. "This is a very exclusive school. Nearly impossible to get accepted into. People spend their whole lives saving money to send their kids here and there is no shortage of applicants."

If it was that exclusive, what the fuck was I doing here? Luka's expression told me I needed to take this warning seriously so I didn't ask any questions. "Thanks for the advice. Maybe I mis-heard Dr. Green."

"I'm sure you did." He tipped the envelope and pulled out the contents. He handed me the card. "You'll need this to get into your room."

He looked at the paperwork, then back up at me, his brow furrowed. "I thought for sure you were a mage. Your magic feels like mage magic."

"I am," I said. "At least that's what they said when they arrested me."

"When they arrested you?" Luka cocked a skeptical eyebrow. "Never met a felon before."

"Felon's a strong word. It was self-defense," I said.

"Curious," he said.

My brow furrowed. *Who the fuck uses that word?* "What's *curious?*"

"You're in the dungeon. It's not the usual dorm for mages. Most of them are in the tower."

"Dungeon? No, thanks." Though, come to think of it, a tower didn't sound much better. Both were used as ways to trap damsels in distress, weren't they? And though I'd never considered myself a damsel before, I was certainly being held against my will. This was going to be a long stay. "Wait, if mages are in the tower, what is in the dungeon?"

"Shifters," he said.

"Shifters," I repeated. "Like people who can turn into other things?"

"Yeah, that's the way shifters work." He narrowed his eyes at me. "You're new to all this, aren't you?"

"How can you tell?" I asked.

He shook his head. "You're going to have to learn fast or you're going to be eaten alive."

Luka

Her eyes traveled down then back up, checking me out while she sucked on her lower lip. It was probably her nerves but damn, she looked sexy when she was nervous. Her fire red hair was a mess, pulled back in a hasty bun. Makeup was smudged under her eyes. She looked like she just woke up after a long night out. Or a long night in someone's bed. I could picture those luscious lips closing around my cock.

"Stop it," she said.

"Stop what?" I asked.

"Stop looking at me like I'm a snack," she said.

I grinned. If she only knew exactly how much she looked like a snack to me.

She shivered and I looked at her torn clothes. No, not torn, burned. I smirked as my eyes traveled to the exposed flesh below her bra. My cock twitched. She was a mess. A fucking beautiful mess. I wondered how long it would be before I could get her to take off all of those clothes.

She crossed her arms over her chest. "You don't happen to have a new shirt in that envelope, do you?"

"Your uniform will be waiting for you in your room," I said.

"Uniforms? You're kidding, right. We're not kids."

"Afraid so," I said, lifting the breast pocket of my blazer, showing her the embroidered school logo.

She rolled her eyes. "Fine. Whatever. At least it'll be clean."

I swept my arm toward the door and she walked through. She looked defeated. Shoulders drooping, steps slow. She really had no idea how big of a deal this school was. My parents started writing seven-figure donation checks the moment they found out my mom was pregnant.

We walked out of the administrative offices toward the main hallway. "This is the Academy's main artery. You find this hall-way, you'll be able to get to wherever."

She paused and looked both ways as if committing the hallway to memory. "Which way is the exit?"

I grinned. "Already planning your escape?"

"Maybe," she said. "You going to tell on me?"

"Not my problem," I said. "You can do what you like."

"You're the teacher's pet, aren't you? One of those *yes sir* and *no sir* types."

"Kitten, you know nothing about me," I said.

"Why else would you be giving tours to the new kid?"

"Maybe I'm working off some debt, just like you," I said.

She looked up at me through her dark lashes and my breath

hitched. Damn she was beautiful. Those green eyes, those soft lips. My whole body felt hot. I was usually in full control of myself. Women didn't do this to me. I'm an incubus. I do this to them. Fuck, she was sexy.

"I doubt you have the same kind of debt as me," she said. "Which means you're trouble."

"I have a feeling you're a lot more trouble than me." For once, I wasn't being playful. With any other woman, this would be flirting. With her, I meant it. There was something about her, a force that I couldn't lock down. I had to get away from her before I fucked her in the middle of the hallway.

"Come on." I started walking down the hall before she could say anything else.

We walked past the commons. Even at this late hour, it was full of students. We had an unusual schedule here. Classes during the day and at night. Options for the variety of creatures that dwelled within our walls. Mostly, the room was full of those of us who thrived in the dark. Like me.

A table of vampires bared their teeth as we walked by, showing their fangs to the new girl. Stupid, cocky assholes.

Raven squeaked.

"Ignore them. The bagged blood makes them all a little nuts." The vamps around here think they're hot stuff ever since that whole Twilight phase. Just because they were trendy, didn't mean it made them interesting. Sure, they were strong, difficult to kill, and basically had eternal life, but they lived off of blood. I got my energy from sex. Between them and me, I was the cooler one by far.

"Bagged blood?" she asked.

"We can't exactly have them drinking from other students. Though some still do. Apparently, there are those who get off on that," I said.

Raven stopped walking, her gaze fixed on a long table in the back of the commons. Two dark haired mages sat on the top of the table, throwing a ball of fire back and forth between them. *Show offs.*

"Are they mages too?" she asked.

"Yeah, the twins. Fire elementals." My brow furrowed. "Is that what you are?"

"Maybe," she said. "I did roast a couple of dudes alive."

"Huh. Remind me not to piss you off."

"You think they could teach me that?" she asked.

"Probably," I said, then I glanced down at the envelope I was still holding and pulled out her schedule. "You've got beginning magical theory in a few hours. You'll get there."

She turned and snatched the schedule out of my hand. Her fingers brushed against mine and a wave of want rolled through me. Why the hell was I craving her so much? It hadn't been that long since I fed. I'd squeezed in a quickie after gym earlier today. It must not have been enough.

"Magical Theory, Spellcasting, Training Your Familiar, Diplomacy, and Gym." She looked up at me, her eyebrows high. "Gym? I'm twenty-fucking-one years old."

"Everyone takes gym," I said.

"I thought that was the perk of being an adult. No more gym class," she said.

"How else will they keep us humble?" I asked. "You get used to it."

Out of the corner of my eye, I noticed that the mage twins were looking over here. They were no longer juggling their fire-ball. If we waited any longer, they might walk over here. "Come on." I guided Raven back to the hallway. "You've got class in a few hours."

"Nine a.m.? Like tomorrow?" she asked, holding up the schedule in her hands.

"Yes," I said. "And the instructors don't like it when you're late."

We turned down a hall lined with doors. "Most of your classes will be in this hallway. They keep the beginner classes together."

"So how long have you been stuck here?" she asked.

"I'm a semester in. Probably going to give myself the full four semesters before I get stuck in the real world, you know? Prolong it a bit," I said.

"There are options?" she asked. "Like I could get out of here sooner?"

I shrugged. "Sure. You have to pass the trial and they consider you done. Usually students wait till at least their third semester before they take it."

"What if I just took it now? Can you pass on luck?" she asked.

"I don't recommend that," I said. "People die in the trial. It's not Star Trek. You don't just keep taking it until you pass."

She wrinkled her nose and I wasn't sure if it was because she got my obscure *Star Trek* reference or because I mentioned Star Trek at all. Either way, her judgy look was adorable. Once again, I felt the call of my cock. I wanted to be inside her so bad it was making me light headed. I needed to get her to her room and find a quick hook up. There was always someone up for some late night action. Maybe one of the sirens. They were usually a good fuck.

I picked up the pace through the classroom corridor. "Come on."

I could sense her behind me. Her body heat thrummed through me like a ball of energy waiting for release. She was sexual distraction personified. I glanced over my shoulder. "You sure you're a mage. You're not something else? Siren or succubus or something else from the deep?"

"Not that it matters, but all I know is what Dr. Hellboy told me. He says I'm a mage. So I guess I'm a mage."

"Huh." I wondered if the headmaster was off on his prediction. She was going to be fun to watch in the coming weeks as she started to figure out her magic.

Raven

"What are you? Can I ask that. I mean, are you a mage?"

He tossed his head back to look at me, his hair flipping with the movement. His smoldering gaze caught me like a cold wind, nearly knocking the breath from my lungs. Nobody had any business being this hot. And I had even less business being so fucking attracted to him. It was like suddenly, I was thinking with my hormones. I was twenty-one. I was supposed to be past this part of my life. Instead, I was getting physically warmer from looking at the beautiful man leading me down the hallway.

"I'm not sure you're ready for that answer yet, kitten," he said, winking.

I frowned, doing my best to pretend that I wasn't turning into a puddle of goo from his smile. I needed to get to my room. And fast. Maybe it was all the excitement. Or the magic. It had to be. I'd never used magic before. Of course there would be repercussions. What if using magic turned you into a horny teenager? I would have to be careful in this place. Sex made things complicated. While it was very enjoyable, it was not usually worth the strings that came attached. Even when guys told you they wanted a casual thing, they usually lied. What they really wanted was a girl to pine over them so they could shoot her down and lift their ego up. They hated it when you didn't pine.

We reached the end of the classroom hallway. I wished I could see inside the doors but unlike the high school I'd attended, none of the classrooms had windows facing the hallway. I guess they didn't like it when kids stopped in the hall to make faces at the people in the room. Though I supposed that might not be a problem here. People didn't still act that way in college, did they?

"This is the most direct route to the dungeons." Luka stopped in front of what looked like an emergency exit door. He pushed it open and took a few steps down a darkened stairwell.

The only light was the light pouring in from the hallway above into the darkness below. It was like a crime scene waiting to happen. "You're kidding me, right?"

"Don't worry, I'll hold your hand if you want."

Annoyed, I pushed past him, and took the steps as fast as I could. If this was the way to my dorm room, which hopefully had a working lock, I needed to suck it up.

As I brushed past Luka, I was hit with the overwhelming scent of leather and smoke with a hint of something else that I couldn't identify. Whatever it was, it was masculine as hell. Pure fuel for my sex drive. My belly clenched and I tried to ignore the growing dampness between my legs. What the hell was wrong with me?

Taking deep breaths in through my mouth, I tried to focus on the scent of the stairs. Damp, dusty, cold air filled my lungs. The cement under my feet felt slick, like someone poured water on the steps. I dragged my fingers along the wall and they were gritty and a little slimy. Like something was growing on them. Disgusted, I pulled my hand away and wiped it on my ruined pants. I wondered if I would have to sleep in the provided uniform or if there was even a shower available.

I opened my mouth to ask Luka about shower arrangements just as another wave of his scent rolled over me. I breathed it in as if it were fresh cinnamon rolls baking in the oven. My mind instantly flooded with an image of the two of us in the shower naked. Water beading up on our skin as his mouth and tongue explored my nipples. Shit. Shit. Shit. What the hell was wrong with me?

Thinking about a shower around Luka was a bad idea. In fact, thinking about Luka was a bad idea. Starting something with a stranger on my first night in my new school was a bad idea.

Finally, we reached the bottom of the stairs, emerging into a hallway of closed doors. The doors looked at home in a dorm titled *the dungeon.* They looked like they were made of metal and they were windowless, just like the classroom doors. Voices drifted from somewhere ahead. I craned my neck to see if I could find the source.

"Common room," Luka said as if he could read my mind.

He pushed past me and I held my breath, not making the mistake of breathing in the smell of pure sex his pheromones created. "Come on."

I followed him down the hall. Flickering torches - honest to fucking god torches - lined the walls. One between each of the metal doors. Two, four, six, eight, ten. Ten rooms before we reached the common area.

Several red velvet couches were arranged in a square around a low table. A group of six students in matching uniforms were laughing and talking, cards in their hands. I recognized the set up on the table. Good to know they played Texas Holdem in magic school. That was one of my few skills. Granted, I was better with a drink or two in my system but I could beat the pants off of most people I'd played against. Literally. We're talking strip poker champion.

The laughter died down and six pairs of gold eyes turned to face me. I froze, my moment of confidence stripped away in a single second.

One student stood and set his cards down on the table in almost slow motion. His body moved with a rippling power I'd never seen before. Making every movement intentional as his large form prowled gracefully toward me.

In the flickering torchlight, it was hard to make out details other than his sheer size. The man was a beast. A dark-haired, dark bearded beast. His tan skin took on a gold tone in the light. If there was an opposite for Luka's lean, fair beauty, this man was it.

He moved toward me, his gold eyes flickering along with the firelight. He smiled, his teeth catching the light, drawing me to his full lips, his hard jaw, his fangs. Shit. Dude had fangs.

My throat bobbed and my jaw tightened. They warned me about the other kinds of creatures in this world but seeing one up close was different than hearing they existed. I looked back up at his eyes and took in the rest of him as he came to a stop in front of me. His long dark hair hung loose around his face, settling in just below his shoulders.

Even through the uniform, I could tell he was cut. He wasn't large because he chugged too much beer. He was this size because he probably spent most of his down time lifting weights.

"Who'd you bring me, Luka?" His voice came out in a growl that made my toes curl.

Fuck.

I'd never heard such a sexy tone in my life. This man was bad news. I didn't even know his name yet, and I already knew that. Between Luka's scent making me want to rip his clothes off and this man's baritone, I was a useless, damp puddle. My whole not fucking a guy when I just met him thing was getting very tested tonight. Was every dude in this place like this? Honestly, with the way these guys made me feel, I was surprised I hadn't walked into an orgy down here.

"New student. Room Twelve," Luka said.

Sexy man leaned in to me until we were nearly touching. Tingles shot through my body just from his proximity. I held my breath.

And then he sniffed me.

He pushed his nose up against my neck and sniffed.

I should have been startled, I should have slapped him, I should have done anything except go weak in the knees. But that was what I did. Right there as he pressed his nose against me, I nearly fell over.

He caught me, a massive hand on my lower back while the other rested on my stomach. I had to force myself to keep from panting at the sensation of his touch. It was electric, sending a rush of pleasure through me that wasn't normal. I mean, normally a guy had to hit just the right place to make me feel that good. I bit down on the inside of my cheek to help contain myself. How would it look if I moaned in front of all these strangers?

Then again, he had growled at me. Maybe that was how we were supposed to communicate here.

"You don't smell like a shifter," he said the words softer, almost in a whisper.

"That's because I'm not." Finally, feeling like I'd regained control, I pushed his hands off of me. "They say I'm a mage."

He cocked an eyebrow. "Mages live in the tower. Shifters live in the dungeon."

"So I've been told," I said.

"Makayla," the brute said. "Show her to her room."

"I'm supposed to take her," Luka said.

The shifter in front of me let out a low growl, baring his teeth. His gold eyes flashed. "This isn't your domain, fallen one."

"Hey, no need for that," I said. "Luka has been helping me."

"I'm sure he has. That's what they do. They help you, then they get in your pants and steal your soul."

"That sounds a little dramatic, don't you think?" I said.

"He's an incubus. It's what he does," the shifter said.

I turned and glanced at my guide. "Is that true? You're an incubus? Isn't that like a sex demon?"

Luka's casual exterior seemed to harden in front of my eyes. His whole body tensed, and his blue eyes stormed over.

I took a step back, suddenly terrified by the man I'd been ready to pounce on a few minutes ago.

"You don't know anything about me, Ben." Luka shoved the papers he was holding into the shifter's chest. "She's your problem now."

Ben grabbed the papers while glaring at Luka. The incubus turned and headed down the dark hall.

"Luka, wait." I felt terrible for how I'd reacted to discovering what he was. Weren't we all monsters when it came to the tales humans were told? How was I any different than him? He'd been nothing but nice to me.

The incubus faded into the dark and I was left alone with the shifters.

Ben

"Come on, love. I'll show you to your room," Makayla said.

"No," I put my hand out, stopping my most trusted pack member. Makayla was a powerful wolf shifter, my right hand in this pack we'd created, but something wouldn't let me pass off this newcomer. "I'll take her."

I glanced back to the table where the others were sitting, tense and ready to attack if I asked them to. We'd formed a pack quickly, the six of us being the only wolf shifters on campus. I'd taken the alpha role seamlessly, something I hadn't expected but welcomed. "I'm out. Play without me."

Makayla hesitated, and I nodded to her, assuring her that everything was fine. She turned back to the table. "Who's ready to give me all their money?"

The sound of the others getting back to the game calmed me. It made me feel like I had a small amount of privacy with the newcomer. I wasn't sure why I wanted her to myself or why I wanted us to be away from the rest of the pack, but I couldn't shake it.

"Can I have my stuff?" She pointed to the envelope I was still clutching to my chest. I looked down at it and read her name. *Raven.* It was an unusual name, though there were weirder names here.

"Come on, Raven, I'll show you where your room is."

"I'm sure I can find it myself," she said.

"I told you I'd show you." I wasn't used to having people ignore my commands.

She reached for the envelope and I tugged it away. As she moved closer to me, I could smell the scent of her arousal. It made my cock twitch. She was either really into the incubus or she was feeling something for me. The thought of her with that pretty boy made me bare my teeth on reflex.

She took a step back. "No need for the tough guy act. I just need my schedule and shit."

I handed the envelope to her. "Fine. Come on."

This time, she followed me without argument. I sort of wished she'd push back. It had been a long time since anyone stood up to me and to be honest, it was hot.

We cut through the common room, heads turning to watch us as we walked by. I ignored the others and led her to the hallway on the other side. Six rooms lined this hall and the only vacant room was number twelve. Right next door to mine.

I leaned against the wall by the metal door labeled with a twelve. "Here it is, home sweet home."

"Maybe for you," she grumbled.

My brow furrowed. It wasn't the usual reaction to gaining your dorm room here. Most new students, even the most stoic, had at least a smile. "Homesick?"

"More than you could ever know," she said as she held up her key. "Do I just slide this in here?"

Our hands brushed as I pointed to the slot for the keycard. Chills ran up my arm and my breath caught. She was like a walking wet dream. There was no way I should be feeling like this about a woman I just met. There had to be some explanation. "What are you? You can't be a normal mage."

"They told me I'm a mage, so I suppose that's what I am," she said.

"What do you mean *they told you*?" There was something so unusual about her. She was different in so many ways.

She pressed her lips together and stood in silence for a moment as if trying to decide if she should say anything. I waited patiently, feeling an irresistible urge to know all I could about her.

"Why do you care?" she asked.

"I'm curious, what can I say. Besides, I'm in charge down here so it's good for me to know what to expect," I said.

She slid her key card into the door and the light flashed green. She turned the handle and pushed open the door. "Not tonight."

Then, she slipped inside and closed the door behind her. Heat welled up in the pit of my stomach. It was rare for someone to ignore my orders. It was even more rare for a woman to close the door on my face. In fact, I couldn't think of a single time that had ever happened. My reputation as a player was well deserved and none of the ladies I'd been with had ever complained. Now, there was some mage ignoring me and shutting the door on me?

If not for the throbbing of my cock, I might not have worried about it. But I wanted her. And not just me. My wolf wanted her. He wanted to taste her, to claim her. He wanted to mate her.

I held my breath, feeling hot sweat roll down my forehead. Where had those thoughts come from? My wolf had never had an interest in specific women. He just wanted to fuck as many as he could. Now, suddenly, there was this woman who he had to fuck.

I ran my hand through my hair, still staring at the closed door in front of me. It took every ounce of my willpower not to break the door down and take her right there in her room.

But I'd never begged for sex. And I'd never force myself on a woman.

Letting out a slow breath, I turned from the door and forced the feral part of me to comply. With a whimper, my wolf obeyed.

When I arrived back in the common room, I looked at the other women playing cards. Any of them would happily join me in my room. Normally, that was enough to satisfy both me and my inner wolf. Tonight, none of them would do. I only wanted Raven.

Raven

I leaned against the door, my wobbly legs almost giving out from under me. If I'd hesitated even a second longer, Ben would be in my room right now with his clothes on the floor and my thighs wrapped around him.

Why I was suddenly thinking about sex around the clock, I had no idea. It had to stop by the time I went to class tomorrow or it was going to be a very difficult day.

Peeling myself off the door, I felt for a light switch and flicked it on. A florescent light hummed to life above me and I squinted against the brightness of it. I made a note to invest in a lamp if that so-called allowance was actually worth anything.

Finally, adjusted to the light, I looked around my new living quarters. It was much nicer than I expected. A large four-poster bed with a fluffy white comforter and a dozen pillows took up one corner of the room. Along the back wall was a good-sized desk already lined with office supplies and a sleek black laptop. *Nice.* I wondered what kind of homework I'd end up doing on that little machine. Did magic schools make you write papers?

On the floor next to the desk was a navy blue backpack with the school's crest and my name embroidered under it. How the hell did they have time to get that ready for me? I wondered if there was a way to magically apply stitching to bags. That would come in handy for repairing ruined clothing.

Glancing to the other side, I saw a closed door. My brow furrowed as I walked toward it. I half expected it to be a door connecting to the adjoining room. Hoping it was locked, I turned the handle and stepped inside a massive bathroom. I switched on the lights and gasped. It was magazine gorgeous.

We're talking spa like.

Who puts a bathroom like this in a dorm room? Not that I was complaining, but it seemed excessive. A giant jetted tub, oversized shower, vanity with a stool and a separate sink filled the spacious room. To the right of the sink was another door.

Quickly, I walked toward it and opened it to find a walk-in closet that was nearly as large as my entire apartment. In fact, I was sure the bathroom and closet combo was larger than my apartment.

I turned on the light and discovered that the racks were already lined with clothes. Most of them were school uniforms. Variations of white-collared shirts: short-sleeved, long-sleeved, and sleeveless. Black skirts, shorts, and pants. Several black blazers and sweaters hung next to the pants. Some of them had the school crest embroidered on them and others were plain.

The other side of the closet had jeans, a variety of tee shirts, and a few black dresses. Next to those were several coats. A lightweight jacket, one made of leather that would cost more than I made in a year, a black peacoat, and a puffy black coat I was guessing would survive a winter in Alaska. It was literally more clothing in this one place than I had owned in the last decade. This had to have cost a fortune.

I turned again and found several red ties hanging on hooks next to a shelf full of shoes.

Eighteen pairs of shoes.

Who the hell needed so many shoes?

I knew lots of girls liked shoes, but I'd never thought of myself as one of those kinds of girls. But seeing the boots, heels, trainers, and flats lined up like this made me squeal.

Black matte, black shiny, soft black leather, fuzzy black something. All the shoes looked like they were designed to go with the largely black wardrobe I'd acquired.

There was no way I could afford any of this.

I set down the knee-high patent leather boot in my hand and took a step back from the gorgeous clothing. Was this really for me? Or was this some kind of trick to get me to screw up? Would they send me a bill if I touched any of it?

Feeling nervous, I wiped my damp palms on my tattered pants. This morning I'd been towed away in chains for accidentally incinerating two assholes who tried to kill me - or maybe do other things with me and then kill me. Either way, they deserved what they got, but that didn't make me feel okay about what I did. Maybe I should be in that magical prison Dr. Green warned me about. Because I certainly didn't feel like I belonged in here. This was so far above my station it wasn't even funny.

I felt uncomfortable. And like they were going to realize

what a mistake they'd made and drag me out of this place any minute.

I ran a hand through my hair and spun in a slow circle, taking in the massive closet. Funny, how something as simple as clothing could make me feel so insignificant.

I'd worn the same pair of jeans to work every day until they tore in the crotch, forcing me to get a new pair.

I slept naked because who had time or money to waste on washing clothes just for sleeping?

Brow furrowed, I approached the last part of the closet I hadn't investigated. Four drawers next to the rows of shoes.

Holding my breath, I pulled open the first drawer. I let out a relieved sigh. It was full of underwear and bras. That wasn't so bad. And it was kind of a necessity.

I picked up one of the black bras. Of course it was black. It was my exact size. How the hell did they guess on my bra size?

A chill ran down my spine. How did they know anything about me? It was so weird. But it made me think I was probably supposed to be here. This wasn't a mistake. They wanted me here.

It still didn't make sense, but I supposed it was better than the alternatives. Magic prison sounded scary as hell and to be fair, my shitty apartment and barely scraping by every month wasn't much better.

I opened the second drawer and found workout shorts and tee shirts folded in neat piles. Grumbling, I closed the drawer quickly, remembering that I had gym on my schedule.

The next drawer was full of pajamas. Matching shorts and tee shirts dotted with moons and stars. They were all unbelievably soft. I grabbed a set out and tossed them on the floor behind me.

The final drawer was full of neatly folded socks. For some

reason, that made me smile. Clean, matched socks with zero holes. When was the last time I'd seen that?

Going back to the first drawer, I grabbed a pair of the black underwear. It was time to test out the shower before collapsing into my princess-like bed. Tomorrow, if I was lucky, I could spend my whole evening in the bathtub.

My mind flashed to Ben and Luka. That bathtub was large enough for company and I was pretty sure either of them would accept an invitation.

I shook my head, trying to send the thought away. The last thing I needed while I was here was the complication of a relationship.

Letting the hot water wash away the blood and soot, I took a few calming breaths. Maybe this could be a fresh start. Maybe things would go well for me here. I could learn how to control whatever this power was and meet other people who were like me. Maybe I could find a job that wasn't as awful as the one I had where drunk men pawed at me while I delivered their drinks.

Feeling hopeful for the first time in years, I drifted into a peaceful sleep.

6

Raven

Suddenly, I was in a dark space I didn't recognize, and my chest tightened as panic took hold. This wasn't right. The floor was damp stone and I could barely see the walls in the dim light.

Glancing around I looked for the source of the light. I couldn't see any torches or lamps. It was just there. My brow furrowed, trying to make sense of this place.

Carefully, I walked forward, my bare feet stinging against the sharp stone floor. The walls on either side of me were made of the same stone as the floor but ahead I saw bars.

My heart raced and my breathing quickened. I was in a cell.

Locked up somewhere. Had the school lied to me? Had they sent me to the magic prison after all or had the school been a dream? It had seemed too good to be true.

"Calm down, kitten," a smooth sexy voice sounded from behind me.

I turned to see Luka, standing in the middle of the cell. "Where did you come from? How did you get in here?"

He smirked. "This is my domain. I can come and go as I please."

"Am I in hell?" I asked, remembering that Luka was a demon.

His smile faded. "Is that what you think of me?"

"No," I said. "I just don't understand what's going on here."

He moved closer to me, his lithe body moving with the grace of a cat.

That was when I realized he was naked.

Completely, totally, blissfully - oh my god he was gorgeous - naked.

Goosebumps fluttered over my skin and my breath caught. I wasn't scared anymore. Just wet. So wet. *WTF?* This had to be a dream.

"Okay, dream Luka, I don't know why my subconscious has sent you to me naked, but I'd like it to stop now."

"Do you, though?" He asked as he seemed to undress me with his eyes.

I gasped. I was naked now too. He'd literally undressed me with his eyes. Or had I just willed it as if I was in a dream? Embarrassed, I covered my chest and my lower bits as best I could. "Time to wake up. Wake up. Wake up. Wake up."

"Why wake up when you can enjoy yourself?" He moved closer. "After all, it's just a dream."

"But it's not. It feels so real," I said.

"Hey, I just visited your dream to check on you, make sure

you were alright after leaving you with that brute. You're the one who made us both naked. That wasn't me."

"You're kidding, right?" I didn't have that in me. Sure, I enjoyed sex as much as anyone, but I usually waited till I knew the guy for a few days at least. Even when I had a one-night stand, it wasn't a total stranger. I'd at least seen the guy around the bar a few times. I always wished I was brave enough to go for it with a guy I just met, but I wasn't.

Then, the rest of his words sank in. "Wait, you came here, into my dream on purpose?"

He shrugged. "Incubus. I can travel through and control dreams. But I promise you, I'm not calling the shots here. I just showed up. You created this room," he gestured around, "this prison cell."

I looked around the room again. The bars with the black void beyond, the cold, damp floors and walls. This wasn't a dream. This was a fucking nightmare.

"What if I fix this a little?"

Suddenly, the room blurred, as if I was driving past it at a hundred miles an hour. Dizzy, I closed my eyes for a second, then opened them up to see a new room.

We were in a massive temple. Tall white marble columns climbed skyward all around me. Above, the temple was open to a night sky of inky black full of diamond specks of stars. A full moon provided an otherworldly glow inside the minimal space.

The ground was white marble stones. Tiny plants grew in the cracks, green leaves and miniature purple flowers peeking through.

Nearby, was a pile of cushions and blankets set up as perfect space to lounge. It was pretty clear what that was for.

Though I was sure dream Luka was trying to get into dream me's pants, I felt the tension in my shoulders melt away. There was so much peace and simple beauty here. It was more beautiful than any dream I could conjure.

I took a few steps toward the center of the temple and felt fabric rustle against my legs. Looking down, I was surprised to see that I was clothed in a Roman style dress. Long white fabric draped down my body, cinched in with a gold belt. It was airy and comfortable and surprisingly elegant. A slight breeze rustled the fabric, bringing with it the scent of the sea. There was no way this was a dream. It felt so real. "How did you do this?"

"I told you, dreams are my domain." Luka walked over to me, wearing a shorter version of the dress I wore, an honest to god toga. I smirked. Even in a toga he looked sexy as hell. Though, part of me was disappointed that he wasn't naked anymore.

I clenched my thighs together at the thought. Why did he drive me so crazy?

"Better?" He asked. "I mean, it's no damp prison cell."

"It's gorgeous," I said, meaning it. "What is it? Is this a real place?"

"No, but it's based on some of the ancient architecture I studied as a kid. I grew up in Rome and it reminds me of home. Though, a much more romanticized and not at all historically accurate version."

"It's very peaceful," I said.

"I've never brought anyone here," he said.

"Really?" I asked. "Cause this is like the stuff of every girl's fantasy."

"I don't know," he said. "Most of the girls I've met would rather have a penthouse and Ferrari."

"Well, I like things simple," I said. "A penthouse sounds like too much work, too much responsibility."

He moved closer to me. "Who are you, really?"

"What do you mean?" I asked. "I told, you. Raven, reluctant mage."

He shook his head, stopping an inch from me. "The Academy doesn't let in just anybody. You're someone, you're just not telling me."

"If I'm someone, it would be news to me." I could feel his body heat and my own temperature seemed to rise just from being this close to him.

He brushed his fingers over my upper arm, sending shivers down my spine.

I leaned closer to him, my breathing shallow in response to his touch. "This doesn't feel like a dream."

"I assure you, it is." He leaned down, his lips pausing above mine as if giving me a chance to stop him.

I didn't want to stop him. My body called out to his, screaming internally for release. I lifted my chin and our lips met.

He wrapped his arms around me, pulling me to him. Our bodies pressed together as his mouth and mine moved in rhythm. Hungrily, I devoured him, unable to get enough of his kiss.

He slid his tongue past my lips, and I met it, massaging it with my own. Tightening his grip on me, his kiss grew more urgent. I moaned into his mouth, feeling the want of that kiss.

My hips pressed against him and I felt his erection against my stomach. He wanted me just as badly as I wanted him.

A warm hand cupped my cheek, then moved to my neck before resting on my shoulder. His fingers worked their way under the thin fabric that held up my toga.

I kissed him harder, my lips swollen, my heart racing. I didn't want him to stop.

Emboldened by my tempo, Luka slid the fabric of my tunic down my shoulder. Then, he moved to the other side, repeating the motion.

The fabric slid down my chest, practically melting away from skin until it pooled at my waist, held up by the gold belt.

He broke away from the kiss and took a step back from me, staring at me with his gorgeous eyes. I was naked in front of him. Well, half naked and all he did was look at me. His gaze didn't break from my face and despite the fact that my tits were on full display, he didn't look down.

There was something in that stare that reached down to my very core. It wasn't just lust, there was something else there. Some connection that I couldn't explain.

But then again, this was a dream. Maybe I was searching for a reason to justify how wet I was or how badly I wanted to feel this stranger's cock inside me.

Heat rushed through me in a rolling sensation that was familiar but difficult to pinpoint. Where had I felt that before? Then, I realized I felt something similar when I'd used my magic. Terrified I was about to burst into flame, I pushed the sensation away, and with it, the moment of connection.

This wasn't love. This wasn't personal. This was lust. Pure and simple. It was a dream and I deserved to do what I wanted, right?

A few hours ago, everything in my life had been ripped away from me and I was confused and scared and really fucking stressed out. I needed to get my mind off of everything. I needed release.

I needed to fuck this handsome man in front of me until I couldn't remember my own name. Because at least I still had myself and I might as well enjoy the ride.

Luka

All I could think about was getting Raven out of her dress and on top of me. Her scent alone was enough to make me hard and her kiss was like a force of nature, ready to consume me. Sex was a currency for me, a way of life. It was how I gained power and how I sustained myself. I lived for sex and I was good at it. The only thing all my partners had in common was that they were mine to claim; they bent to my will and gave me what I needed. I prided myself on being fair. My partners got off too. But it wasn't about them. It was about me.

With Raven, all I could think of was pleasing her. I wanted to yield to her, to let her win. To let her have all of me. This wasn't just sex. This was something else.

And it fucking terrified me.

I slid my fingers under the straps of her dress, ready for anything to distract me from the way I was feeling. I needed to get caught up in the moment itself, focus on the sex. My hands slid down her throat to her shoulders, the soft skin sending a rush of goosebumps down my arms. Trying to ignore the pounding of my heart, I pushed her strap down, then the other.

The only way to turn the tables on her was to take control the only way I knew how. I had to fuck her. It wasn't personal that way. It was my nature.

Breaking away from the kiss, I meant to grab her and carry her to the pile of pillows or bend her over. Either would suit me. But her eyes…

I locked in on her gaze, her green eyes staring at me with something different from the usual desire I saw in a woman's eyes. She wasn't hazy or unfocused. She wasn't thinking with her libido. She was seeing me. Really seeing me.

Women didn't see me like this. They saw a way to get off as I did with them. But this was Raven. I hardly knew her but when I stared at her, it was as if we'd simply been apart a while.

Suddenly, it was like I knew exactly what she needed from me. Raven didn't need me to coddle her. She didn't need me to sweep her off her feet in a romantic gesture. She was hurting, and she needed distraction.

I wasn't sure how I knew that or why, but I could sense it. And I was ready to deliver.

Raven broke eye contact first, and I made my move. With a wicked grin, I swept in, lifting her over my shoulder. She squealed, then laughed. Her bare tits pressed against my back and I growled at the sensation of her soft flesh against me.

I threw her down on the pile of pillows and she landed on her back, her red hair framing her face like a halo. She told me she was a mage but right now, she was sending a pulse my way that vibrated through me like a beacon. It wasn't normal for a mage. It was the way it felt when I connected with another creature of the underworld. When two demons fucked, it was euphoric, but also dangerous. The pleasure could be too much and it could ignite magic in unexpected ways.

For a moment, I considered stopping. But the pull to her was too strong. Quickly, I imagined the clothing gone from both of us, altering the dream to my will.

Raven gasped as the air made contact with her bare flesh. Then she smirked. A delicious, inviting, mischievous smirk that had my balls aching for release.

I kneeled down and spread her legs apart roughly, making room for myself. I could smell her arousal and her pussy glinted with wetness. The pulse between us intensified, linking us. Whatever she was, she wasn't a normal mage. It didn't matter, though. Risk or not, she would be worth it.

Settling between her thighs, I heard her hold her breath, and I plowed in without giving her time to adjust.

She cried out, a sound that was pain mixed with pleasure. It was a sound I knew well, and I lived for it.

"Oh my god," she breathed.

Leaning down, I silenced her with a kiss. Raven wrapped her arms around me, her nails digging into my back as I thrusted inside her. Her hips lifted and fell in rhythm, matching my movements, our bodies coming together as both of us began to pant.

Her tits pressed against my chest, sending shivers down my spine. I kissed her again, then bit down on her lower lip almost hard enough to draw blood. She moaned, then arched her back, lifting her hips just right. My cock tightened, nearly ready for release.

Startled at how quickly she'd brought me to this point, I

pulled out. For the first time in my life, I wondered what it would be like to be with Raven alone. I moved away from her, taking deep breaths. People like me didn't settle down with one woman. People like me lived in the shadows. We didn't get happily ever afters.

"Don't stop," she begged.

Her words were breathy, and her gaze hooded. She was nearly panting. This time, there was no pulse. No soul piercing stare. Just lust.

Growling, I grabbed her and threw her over so she was on her stomach. Pulling her hips to me, I entered her from behind. My fingers dug into her ass, keeping her in place as I thrust hard. Each thrust was like a test. How long could I go until I lost control?

She moaned, her skin hot under my touch. I leaned in until my lips touched her neck, kissing her while she squirmed under me. Her moans grew to cries and just when I thought I couldn't hold out anymore, she let out a scream of pleasure.

I gave in as her body pulsed under me, taking me deeper inside her as I released.

Raven rested her head on my arm as we collapsed in the pile of pillows. The salty scent of the sea hung in the air, a taste of memories long gone. I brushed the sweat-slicked hair away from her forehead and kissed her gently. She was perfect. Everything about her made me never want to leave this moment. I wanted to hold her and breathe her in. I wanted to protect her. I wanted to be with only her.

The thought was alarming, but it was worse to think of a life without her in it. Nothing made sense. But then again, this was all a dream.

Raven

Thud. Thud. Thud.

I groaned as I rolled over in the bed. "Go away! I'll pay you tomorrow."

"Raven, get up or you'll be late to class," a woman's voice called.

I opened my eyes and sat up so fast it made my head spin. Everything rushed in at once. I was at the Academy of the Elites. I was trying to avoid magic prison. Though right now, I was wondering if they got to sleep more in magic prison.

I had a very sexy dream last night.

My skin tingled at the memory of Luka's hands on my skin. I touched my lips, recalling the pressure of his kiss. They felt swollen. Had it been a dream? It all seemed so real.

"Get your ass up, princess. The alpha will have my skin if you're late to class."

Brow furrowed, I tossed aside the blankets and shuffled to the door. When I opened it, I was face to face with the woman who tried to help me last night. She was built like a gymnast. Small but fierce. Her dark hair was cut in a pixie cut and bright gold eyes stared back at me. She was deceivingly adorable. I knew girls like her and you only underestimated them once. "Makenzie? What are you doing here?"

"It's Makayla," she said. "And I told you, Ben is going to be pissed if you're late."

"Why is it your job? And why does *Ben* care if I'm late?" I asked as I walked back into the room.

"Hell if I know. He just said I had to make sure you were on time." She glanced at her watch. "And there's only thirty minutes left of breakfast, so you better change fast."

I noticed that Makayla was already in a school uniform. She wore a short-sleeved white button-up shirt with a red tie loosely tied around her neck. Black shorts and black combat boots completed her chosen outfit.

Makayla put her hands on her hips. "Do you need help getting dressed, or what?"

I glared at her. "What time is it, anyway?"

"Seven thirty."

"I don't even have class till nine, why are you here?" I glanced back to my bed longingly. It was so soft and warm, and the mountain of pillows had been like sleeping in a cloud.

"I already told you, breakfast ends at eight. Let's go, princess."

"Quit calling me that," I said. "You know, if you let me skip breakfast, I'd be able to sleep for another hour."

"No way, you gotta eat. You need your strength," she said.

My eyebrows lifted. "Your words, or Ben's?"

"Just hurry, okay."

Last night I had decided to make the best of this, but mornings were not my thing. Realizing it would be easier to just go with her, I let out a heavy sigh as I padded toward the bathroom.

After a quick use of the facilities, face wash, and teeth brushing, I headed to the giant closet. Part of me expected it to be gone as if I'd dreamed the whole thing. But it was still there, packed to the brim with clothes I could never afford.

Quickly, I tugged on a pair of black shorts and a sleeveless, white button-down shirt. I grabbed a tie and threw it over my neck untied. Finally, I grabbed a sweater and headed back to where Makayla was waiting for me.

She cocked an eyebrow. "That's how you're going to the first day of class?"

I looked down at my outfit, then back up at her. "What's wrong with it?"

She sighed then took a few steps closer to me, shaking her head. "Now I see why Ben sent me. You're useless."

"Hey," I said. "I've been dressing myself for nearly two decades, okay?"

She grabbed the tie around my neck, and I stepped back. She tugged on it, pulling me closer. "Hold still so I can tie this for you."

I had no idea how to tie a tie. It wasn't exactly a skill a chronically single girl working in a bar needed to learn. I'd untied my fair share from men's necks, but I'd never bothered to pay attention to the knots.

Makayla tightened it. "There." She took a step back. "You going to do anything about that hair?"

I frowned. I hadn't bothered with my hair - it definitely had that just-woke-up look. "Why do you care what I look like?"

"Because it's important to make a good impression. You must look like you belong here or the other students are going to single you out as the weakest link."

"So what?" I wasn't any stranger to bullying. I was the weird kid who lived with her alcoholic aunt growing up. When I said I'd been dressing myself for nearly two decades, I wasn't exaggerating. I'd also been cooking my own meals, doing my own laundry, and cleaning up after my aunt when she went on a bender. It wasn't a pretty way to live, and it had made me grow up fast.

"Look, I get that you're an unusual case. That's obvious. You were stuck down here with the riffraff instead of housed with the favored mages. That's already a strike against you. But if you want to survive, you'll have to fake it."

"It's school," I said. "I can handle it."

"It's not school like you're used to. Students graduate or they die here. There's no in between," she said, her expression deadly serious.

I stared at her for a moment, waiting for her to crack. Was this some kind of hazing?

"Just trust me. You're in no position to be turning down a friend."

"Oh, we're friends now?" I asked.

"Until Ben gives me the order to let you figure this shit out on your own, yeah, you're stuck with me. So you might as well make the best of it. And hurry. I'm starting to get hangry."

"Starting to?" I grumbled as I walked back to the bathroom. There were a million unanswered questions. Did students really die here? Why the hell did they care what I wore to class? I'd gotten away with wearing pajamas half the time my last year of high school cause I'd stopped giving any fucks. Now, I was in a preppy shirt with a fucking tie and that wasn't good enough?

I pulled open the drawers until I found a hairbrush and quickly ran it through my red hair. I looked tired. Dark circles were painted below my green eyes and my skin looked more pale than usual. I wasn't even sure if make up would have made me look rested. Brushed hair and a clean uniform would have to do. Maybe I could actually get some sleep tonight. I held my breath as my memory drifted back to my dream. Maybe sleeping wasn't the best way to get some rest around here.

"Hurry up," Makayla called.

I set down the hairbrush and left the bathroom. "Let's go."

She led me down the hall, past the empty common room, and back up the damp stairs. It was so creepy down here. Her comment about the shifters getting treated less than the mages came back to me.

"How come shifters are down here in the dark?" I asked.

She glanced over her shoulder but kept walking up the stairs. "Used to be for vampires."

"What happened to the vampires?" I asked.

"They formed their own academy and most of them left. The few who attend here are legacies and they have the nicer basement dorms."

"So now shifters are stuck in the dungeon while mages are in a tower?" I asked.

"Yep," she said. "And demons and fallen angels have the old dorms next door to the main building."

"Demons and fallen…." I said the words quietly, more to myself than to her. It was still hard to wrap my head around all of this.

"Fallen angels." She stopped to open the door to the main floor of the school. "There's other academies with other creatures, but they limit it here."

"Why did you say shifters were not treated as well?" I asked.

"Because they aren't," she said. "There's a hierarchy in the supernatural world. Old alliances and ancient grudges. Shifters used to be the protectors, the workers. Some of the community isn't happy that we want to be more than that."

I had a lot to learn. "It doesn't sound much different from the human world. Assholes who think they're better than other people for superficial reasons."

Makayla stopped outside the door as I walked through. She closed it behind me then turned to look at me. "You know, I was pissed when Ben charged me with watching after a mage. But I think you and I might get along just fine."

Raven

The cafeteria was a hum of conversation and seemed to vibrate with an energy unlike anything I'd ever felt in a human school. Though, sadly, the round tables with attached plastic chairs were just like the tables we had in my high school.

I hoped that didn't mean I was in for the same bullying and jabs at my self-esteem that high school brought me.

"Welcome to the jungle," Makayla said with a grin. "Otherwise known as the cafeteria."

I glanced from table to table, taking in the other students in uniforms. There was a good variety of clothing choices. Some students in shorts, some in pants, a few in skirts. They all had white shirts and a red tie. Some wore blazers or jackets or sweaters. But they were all a well matched group in red, white, and black. It was like walking into a cheesy nineties teen movie.

I hoped nobody broke out into a synchronized dance.

We walked a little farther into the room and as we passed the tables, the conversations died down. My cheeks heated as I felt the gaze of dozens of eyes on me. Fuck. Maybe this would be exactly like high school.

A table on my right had four girls seated at it and all of them were staring at me. I stopped in my tracks and stared back at them, entranced. They were the most beautiful beings I had ever seen.

Two had straight, dark hair down to their waist, while the other two had short natural curls that framed their faces like halos. All four of them had sea-green eyes. They were so soothing to stare into.

"Hey," Makayla grabbed my upper arm and tugged me away, "leave the new girl alone."

"We didn't do anything," one of the girls said.

"She was raised in a mage community. Give her a week to warm up to being out in the wild," Makayla said.

The girls broke their gaze on me and I stumbled forward, Makayla's hold keeping me upright.

"She's got a week, then she's fair game, puppy," the girl said.

Makayla growled, then guided me away from the table.

"What just happened?" I asked. "And why did you say I was raised in a mage community?"

"Shhhh," Makayla hissed. "You're here five minutes and you're already being charmed by the sirens."

"Sirens?" I asked. "I thought you said there were only four kinds of creatures here."

"Sirens are considered demons," she said. "And much like the incubus, they can get in your head quickly."

It was a good thing she didn't know just how much Luka had gotten inside my head.

"You're going to get eaten alive in here," Makayla whispered. "You're lucky Ben decided to make you honorary pack."

"What does that mean?" I asked.

"Exactly as it sounds," Makayla said. "Please tell me I don't have to explain everything."

"No, I get it, but I guess I want to know why."

"I suppose he felt sorry for you. A mage thrown in with the shifters is bound to have a harder time fitting in. Plus, none of us want to have to carry you back to your room after you get your ass kicked," she said.

I ignored the rest of the students as we walked toward the line for food. I could still feel their stares on me but I didn't want to risk another siren situation.

Delicious smells greeted me as we approached the food line.

Cheerful women with pink cheeks passed trays of food to each waiting student. My stomach rumbled in anticipation. It had been nearly a day since I last ate and even cafeteria food sounded good right now.

Makayla went first, grabbing a tray and silverware. I followed her and moved along behind her in the line. They set a heaping plate of eggs and bacon on my tray. Then a bowl of fruit joined the other plate. My mouth watered at the sight of the food. It looked delicious.

After stopping to grab what I hoped was a decent cup of coffee and a glass of orange juice, I joined Makayla at an empty table.

Before I even got my first bite, someone sat down next to me. Startled, I dropped my fork.

"Hey, new girl." The newcomer was a tall guy with a buzz

cut and a dark five o'clock shadow. He wasn't bad looking, but the sleazy grin on his face made me shudder at his closeness. Something about him didn't quite sit well with me.

I scooted over to the next seat, dragging my tray with me. "Personal space."

He scooted over to the seat I just left. "We're all family here, aren't we? I heard you joined the shifters. That makes you pack."

"Not your pack, Remi. She's under wolf protection." Makayla bared her teeth.

"I don't see how you get to judge that," he said. "Let the little mortal decide for herself."

"I'm a mage." As much as I'd been internally fighting the idea of magic and joining this world, I'd picked up on the fact that I had to act the part.

"You smell human, baby," he said.

"I'm not your baby," I said.

He leaned in closer to me, sniffing me. I leaned back and pushed myself away from him, knocking my tray to the ground in the process. Eggs and fruit landed all over my lap.

Remi laughed, clutching his gut.

I jumped up from my seat and brushed the food off of me while glaring at the obnoxious man who caused me to lose my breakfast.

He stood, and in a movement so fast I didn't see it coming, he grabbed hold of both of my wrists and pulled me against him so we were flush. I could feel his hard on through his pants. Gross.

I tugged my arms away from him, trying to break his grasp but he held me there, against him.

"Let me go, asshole," I said.

He grinned but didn't release his grip.

Gritting my teeth, I lifted my knee, making fast contact with his crotch. Remi let go of my wrists as he cried out in a shocked gasp. "You bitch!"

I scrambled away but Remi followed me. He shoved me to the ground, and I landed with a thud.

"The mages didn't want you but you're no shifter. We will make your life hell," he growled, still protecting his injured manhood with one hand.

"You don't scare me, asshole," I shouted.

"Just you wait until gym class, bitch," he said.

Suddenly, a massive form lunged into Remi, knocking him down. It took a moment for me to realize it was Ben, the shifter I'd met last night.

"Get out of the way," Makayla screamed at me.

I jumped to my feet and moved away from the fight. Remi and Ben rolled around on the ground for a moment before Ben pinned him. He pulled back his fist, then punched Remi in the jaw, the contact making a sickening crack.

Blood ran down Remi's mouth but he wasn't giving in. He kicked up his feet, pushing Ben off of him. The two of them were both on their feet now, circling like animals.

Remi charged Ben, landing a punch in Ben's stomach. Ben grunted but quickly regained control. He grabbed hold of Remi and threw him to the ground again. This time, Ben remained standing. He set his foot on Remi's throat.

"Stay away from her," Ben said.

"She doesn't belong to you," Remi said, straining against the foot on his vocal chords.

"Stay away from her or I'll fucking kill you," Ben said.

"Ben, stop!" I called out. "Stop it. You won, okay?"

To my surprise, he took his foot off of Remi. "He threatened you, Raven."

"Yeah, cause he's an immature asshole," I said. "That doesn't mean you should kick the shit out of him."

Remi sat up, coughing. He spit blood on the ground and I wrinkled my nose in disgust. He was a sleaze ball for sure but that didn't mean he deserved this. Ben had no reason to fight him. Was he trying to defend my honor or some shit? What was with this guy? He sent his friend to look after me, which was sweet and all, but this was too much.

I'd taken care of myself most of my life. I could handle a school bully and threats of gym class. What was he going to do, dodge ball me to death?

"He needs to learn his place," Ben said.

"His place?" I asked.

"He can't mess with something of mine," Ben said.

"I'm not yours," I said. This was getting scary. First day of school and I already had a bully, a group of mean girls, and a stalker. It was turning out far too similar to my high school experience. The only way I'd survived high school was by keeping to myself and avoiding everyone. It looked like I needed to reinstate that plan here.

"You stay away from me." I pointed to Ben, Makayla, and Remi. "All of you."

I ran from the cafeteria. I would figure this out on my own. It couldn't be that difficult, right?

Ben

My whole body shook with anger as Raven walked away from me. How could she not feel the connection between us? I had tried to stay away but I couldn't resist her pull. She seemed to call to me and I knew it was my job to keep her safe. I wanted to deny it, but the mage called to me in the way only a mate can call to a shifter. She was mine and I would protect her at all costs.

"Looks like your claim is going unrequited," Remi said.

I glared at him. "You want a formal challenge? Cause we both know how that will turn out."

Remi's upper lip curled. "Careful, dog. Just because you have a pack doesn't mean you're better than me."

"You want to try me?" My muscles tensed. If he wanted to keep fighting, I'd fight him. Human form or animal. Day or night. He threatened my mate, and he deserved whatever pain I could cause him.

"Why don't we let the girl decide for herself? First one to claim her wins," he said.

"You're both disgusting," Makayla said. "She's not a chew toy."

"She's my mate, I can feel it," I said.

Remi cocked an eyebrow. "If that's true, then why did she run off from you?"

"Because she doesn't know it yet," I said.

"Are you serious, Ben?" Makayla asked. "I've never heard of a shifter with a mage for a mate."

"I'm telling you, it's true," I said.

"What's all the commotion over here?" Dr. Green looked from me to Remi. "Looks like someone has earned some time in confinement."

"No," Remi and I both said at the same time.

"Just a misunderstanding," Remi said, wiping the blood from his mouth.

"Getting warmed up," I said.

Dr. Green lifted a skeptical brow. "Don't let me find you warming up in the cafeteria again or it's confinement for both of you."

"Yes, sir," I said.

"Yes, Dr. Green," Remi said.

The headmaster walked away, and I returned to glaring at Remi.

"Don't look at me like that," Remi said. "Until she's marked, you know she's fair game."

"She has zero interest in you," Makayla said.

"For now," he said. "I'll admit I came on a little strong."

"If you value your life, you'll stay away from her," I growled.

"Neither of you are getting this," Makayla said. "You're acting like cave men and you *both* scared her away. She doesn't want anything to do with either of you and it's not your choice anyway. It's hers."

She turned and walked out of the cafeteria. I almost called her back, but I knew she was right. That wasn't going to change anything, though. I felt the mating call when Raven was near and until she was marked as mine, I would have little control over how I responded. She called to me and she called to my wolf. When Raven was around, my wolf had more control than the human side. With her around, I wasn't stable - I was dangerous.

The bell rang and the remaining stragglers in the cafeteria headed toward the door. Class started in five minutes and it wasn't a good idea to be late. This school might be for the most talented supernaturals, those with the most money and power, but that meant the stakes were higher.

Any toe out of line resulted in confinement. And the horror stories about what happened in those hidden chambers were the stuff of nightmares. It wasn't that the time spent there resulted in your death, it was the fact that the students who ended up serving even one night in confinement had a history of gruesome accidents before they graduated. As if the punishment acted as a magnet for trouble.

I pushed the image of the mage who fell to his death last week out of my head. There was so much blood. So much screaming. It wasn't really a surprise, though. He'd spent a night in confinement the week before.

Some speculated that it drained your magic, making it harder for you to complete the tasks at the academy. Others said you emerged cursed. Either way, I didn't want to find out.

Without a word to Remi, I headed to my first period class. I'd have to deal with Raven later. Somehow, I had to get her alone. I had to get her out of that uniform and under me. I needed to feel my cock inside of her. I had to claim her. It was the only way to satisfy my wolf and the only way to keep myself from making another mistake.

My family pulled strings to get me in here and I owed them. I couldn't afford to end up in confinement.

Someone rolled a table out of the way and I glanced behind me to see the cleaning crew already clearing away the remains of breakfast. I bolted out of the cafeteria and hooked a right to dive into the nearest classroom, which just happened to be my first period class and took my seat with a minute to spare.

As soon as I settled in, I caught the unmistakable scent of Raven. She smelled like honeydew and rain. It was intoxicating. I didn't even need to turn around to know she was sitting behind me but I risked a glance anyway.

There she was, in the back row, three chairs behind me. Her gaze was fixed on the front of the room. She looked nervous. And sexy. Oh, so sexy. I gripped the edge of my desk. It was going to take a lot more willpower than I anticipated to stay away from her.

Professor Hurd, an aging mage with long silver hair walked into the room. He was carrying a stack of books in his arms, huffing with effort. One of the mages seated at the front jumped up and relieved him of his burden. I watched with narrowed eyes. This particular professor had never been kind to shifters and had made it clear he didn't think we belonged in this class. I should be pissed about it, but I had to agree.

Studying the theory of magic wasn't something that helped

us as our magic came from the animal inside each of us. It wasn't like I was going to cast a spell or something. Shifter magic was internal and unintentional. The only thing we could do was learn to control our inner animal so we could control when we shifted.

And when we fucked.

Because right now, my inner wolf was battling with me and if he had his way, Raven would be dragged out of this room into the woods behind campus and claimed.

The human part of me wasn't going to allow that but that didn't mean it was easy. The mating bond was a magic of its own. Something else we couldn't control. Maybe they should cover that in class.

"Thank you, Deanna," Professor Hurd said. He removed his glasses and cleaned them on his shirt.

Without them, his eyes were tiny, nearly hidden in the wrinkles on his face. He slid them back on which magnified them to the same size as the lenses. It was unnerving but so were the tiny eyes. There was no winning with this guy. Either way, he made you feel uncomfortable.

"Will you pass the books out to the class, Deanna?" Professor Hurd asked.

The mage, Deanna, nodded brightly and began to pass books. She paused in front of me and dropped one on my desk. I turned to see how she'd react to Raven. It wasn't often a new student was added to the Academy after the term was in session.

Deanna paused in front of Raven's desk. "You're new."

"Yes, I am. My name's Raven."

Deanna eyed her up and down. "You smell like a wet dog. Are you a shifter?"

I let out a low growl deep in my throat.

"You smell like a thirteen-year-old who just discovered Bath and Body Works. Do your parents know you're here?" Raven asked.

Deanna scoffed, then dropped the book on Raven's desk before turning on her heels and heading to the next seat.

I leaned back in my chair, a grin on my face. Maybe Raven can take care of herself. That's my girl.

Raven

My hand ached from all the notes I'd taken in Magical Theory. I felt like I had to write down everything since it was all new to me. While I didn't ask to be here, I knew I should get as much out of it as I could. After all, I had magic inside me, and I needed to learn how to control it at the very least.

The bell rang and the students got up, leaving their books on the table. I didn't want to leave my book. We'd started on chapter seven and I was way behind.

I gave the others a moment to shuffle toward the door, then I walked toward Professor Hurd, my book in hand. "Excuse me, professor?"

"Yes, Raven, is it?"

I nodded. "Yes. Um, can I borrow the book to read what I've missed?"

"You've missed in every class. Are you going to catch up on all of it tonight?"

"No, that's impossible," I said.

He chuckled. "Technically, with magic, it's not impossible. But I suppose you aren't there yet, are you?"

I winced. How much was I supposed to tell him? Luka had warned me about sharing that I was so different. But surely he didn't mean teachers? "I just found out I had magic yesterday so yeah, I'm not there yet."

He cocked a brow. "Really? That's very unusual. We occasionally get late starts but there's always an excuse. Travel, illness, something in the family."

"Nobody else has had this happen?" I asked.

"Most mages come into their power during puberty. It's very unusual to see repressed magic. Or magic that doesn't flare until later in life." He tapped his index finger on his chin. "Did you have an encounter or something that triggered the magic?"

"A couple of guys tried to kill me if that's what you're asking about."

"That would do it," he said. "You need to be careful while you figure out what you're capable of. Most mages who exhibit power later in life end up incarcerated."

My heart thumped against my ribs. I'd already had that threat leveled against me. "Why?"

"It's odd. You'd think the late bloomers would be less powerful, but that's not usually the case. More often than not, they're the dangerously powerful bunch."

The room seemed to spin. That couldn't be me. I'd used magic once, on accident. "I'm sure that's not me."

"Be careful, Raven. Mind your temper and pay attention to your studies. If you lose control here… Let's just say, you won't get a warning and you won't be going to magic prison."

Professor Hurd's words swam through my mind as I stumbled toward the door. I was only two steps out when a large figure stood in front of me.

My chest tightened in panic, then I let out a breath of relief that I didn't want to feel. I should be annoyed by Ben hulking outside the classroom waiting for me. Instead, I was flattered. Which pissed me the fuck off. I felt like my emotions betrayed me at every turn here. From the involuntary responses to Ben and Luka, to the hottest wet dream ever, to my heart pulsing like a schoolgirl with a crush as Ben looked at me, concern in his expression.

"You all right?" he asked.

"I'm fine. And like I told you earlier, I don't need your help." *Liar.* After everything I'd just heard, I needed help more than ever. But I wasn't about to let Mr. Possessive know that. He went from zero to sixty when he saw someone being rude to me. How would he respond if he knew what Professor Hurd said? *Wait.* "Were you spying on me?"

His cheeks flushed. "No, of course not. I - I thought you might need help finding your next class."

"Going to help me yourself this time instead of sending your minions?" I felt bad referring to Makayla as a minion, but I was pissed.

"You're right. I should have helped you myself this morning. Then that asshole panda wouldn't have bothered you."

"Panda?" I asked.

"Bear shifter insult," he said with a shrug.

The bell chimed.

"Shit, we're late. Come on, I'll show you to your class." He started walking, and I followed him, tugging my schedule out as we walked. I glanced down at it. My next class was Spellcasting. Room 122.

We stopped in front of a class. Room 122. I frowned. "You memorized my schedule?"

"I have a good memory. You better go. Maybe they'll go easy on you, first day and all," he said.

I gave Ben one last glance and my heart flipped and tingles ran up my thighs to my core. For some reason, after everything, I was still drawn to him. Terrified by my body's response to him, I ducked into the classroom without saying goodbye.

Spellcasting was nothing like Magical Theory.

The room was a huge circle with benches that wrapped around a platform in the middle, like an amphitheater. And like an amphitheater, I was in the center on full display of everyone looking down on the professor in the middle of the room.

The professor was a woman in a tight black dress that hugged her curves. Long dark curls tumbled down her back, past her waist. Completing the look were black stilettos that made me wonder how she was standing. I rarely saw women at parties dressed this well, let alone a teacher. All my high school teachers had worn jeans and tee shirts. This woman was something else.

Her hands were stretched up above her and a dozen glowing lightbulbs floated in the air.

The door closed and a dozen faces turned to me, including the professor. She dropped her hands and the light bulbs fell to the ground. The room echoed with the sound of shattering glass and the scent of burning electricity hung in the air.

"You must be Ms. Winters," the professor said. Her face was narrow, and she had huge, gorgeous eyes. Her nose and chin were as sharp as her cheekbones. She looked like she'd been airbrushed but this wasn't a magazine cover. It was real life. Nobody should look like this in real life.

She ran a hand through her hair and I caught sight of her ears. They were pointed. Fucking pointed. Like a Christmas elf. Was she some kind of demon or a shifter I hadn't met yet? I wished I knew more about this world.

"Have a seat." She gestured to an empty space on the first row. "If you're late again, you'll be sent to confinement."

"Thank you, sorry," I said as I walked across the entire stage area toward the empty seat. I could feel the eyes of my classmates boring into me but I didn't dare look up. Hell of a way to be introduced to the class. At least she didn't make me stand up and share my favorite television show or something equally cheesy. I hated when teachers did that shit.

Thankfully, the gorgeous professor went right back into teaching. It was like whiplash. Desperately, I looked around for a notebook or something I could write on. They'd been passed out in my last class but there was nothing on my desk. Internally, I cursed myself for not grabbing the backpack sitting in my room.

Trying to make the best of it, I looked back at the Professor and tried to memorize all of her words.

"Remember, all spell casting goes back to our primary four tenants. You keep those with you and you'll successfully cast your spell and limit the amount of," she chuckled and gave a knowing nod, "personal damage."

The rest of the class laughed, clearly in on the joke. I smiled awkwardly, wishing I could curl up in my bed and hide from the world. This was going to be a very long day.

"*Psst.*"

I glanced over to see one of the twins I'd seen earlier signaling to me. There were a few empty spaces worth of seats on the bench in between us and he stretched his arm toward me. In his hand was a notebook and pen.

Gratefully, I reached out and took the offered supplies. "Thank you," I whispered.

He winked and flutters filled my chest.

Quickly, I grabbed the notebook and turned back to the teacher. My face felt hot and I squirmed as my body fought to move closer to the attractive mage. Gritting my teeth, I opened the notebook and tried to think about the lecture and not my sex drive.

"Each of us has the possibility of finding untamed magic within us," she said.

That caught my attention. I straightened and listened, my pen hovering above the paper.

"Untamed magic is the most unstable but most powerful kind of magic. While you're learning to use your magic, you might find a skill you previously didn't know you had and it can flare out of control. Learning to recognize shifts and changes in your magic will prevent that from happening. You have to maintain control, explore any new magic as it arrives in calm, controlled steps. That's where spell casting comes in. You must learn control."

I was so entrained by her words about harnessing internal magic that I nearly jumped out of my seat when the bell rang. Quickly, I jumped up and walked over to where the twins were to return the notebook, but they were off the bench and out the door so fast, I didn't even get to ask about how to return it.

"Ms. Winters," the professor called.

I turned to her. "Yes?"

"You'll need to make some friends with other mages. You have a lot to learn."

"Thanks, I'll work on that," I said.

She nodded, then walked away. Deciding that meant I was dismissed, I headed to the door. So far, I'd been befriended by a possessive shifter, dream fucked by an incubus, threatened by a bear shifter, and hypnotized by some sirens. Making friends was not my strong point.

"Hey, princess, you still mad at me?" Makayla's voice called from outside the door.

I smiled. She wasn't a mage, but Makayla was a welcome presence right now. "Only if you're here because someone sent you."

"Nope, this time I'm here cause we girls need to stick together, you know?"

"Thanks," I said.

"Ready for lunch?" She asked.

My stomach growled. I had dumped my breakfast all over me this morning and I was going on day two of no food. "Please tell me we can eat somewhere other than the cafeteria."

"No such luck," she said. "But you'll be more prepared this time."

"Right." I said. "At this point, I'm hungry enough that I'll probably slug anyone who gets between me and my lunch."

"Hey, you're getting the hang of how to handle this place."

Raven

The cafeteria was already buzzing with students when we arrived, and I realized for the first time exactly how many people attended this school. While breakfast had been scattered with open tables and tables with lots of open seats, lunch was a different story.

My palms were sweaty as I gripped a plastic tray and followed Makayla through the line to get food. The kind looking women working behind the counter set a plate with a burger and fries on my tray. It wasn't my favorite meal, but my stomach still grumbled in appreciation at the prospect of food.

I grabbed a few paper cups full of fruit and followed Makayla out of the line. She led us through the maze of tables toward the back of the room.

"New girl, come sit with us," one of the sirens hissed.

I ignored her and kept walking.

Someone whistled at me and my cheeks burned. What was with this place? Did they all miss high school this much that they had to pretend they were back there?

A leg shot out in front of me and I stopped just in time to keep myself from landing face first on the ground. I bared my teeth and turned to find Remi, stretched out in his seat causally.

"Do you mind, asshole?" I nodded to his outstretched leg.

"Not at all," he said, pulling his leg back in.

I rolled my eyes and took a step forward.

"Hey, Raven," he called out.

I turned to look at him despite the fact that I knew I should ignore him.

"You and I got off on the wrong foot this morning. How about you let me make it up to you? I can pick you up tonight at seven and I'll show you a good time."

"She doesn't need to catch your fleas," Makayla growled.

"How about you play fair here, wolf," he said.

"Remi, I accept your apology, but I'm not dating anyone right now," I said. It wasn't what I wanted to say. I wanted to tell him that I wouldn't let him touch me if he was the last man alive but I knew I didn't need the extra enemies or the distractions of a bully. If I was really going to get through this school, I had a lot to catch up on. And I knew that despite the fact that my only friend was a wolf shifter, I had to find some mages to help me.

"Fair enough," he said, holding his hands up in mock surrender. "You know where to find me when you're ready."

"Come on," Makayla said.

I turned away from Remi and followed Makayla to a table at

the back of the cafeteria where Ben and three other students were sitting. She set down her tray and took one of the empty seats. I sat down next to her, trying to avoid eye contact with Ben. I wasn't ready for the flips I knew my stomach would make when I looked at him.

"You must be our resident mage," a girl with blonde curls said.

"That's me," I said, then I took a huge bite of my hamburger to prevent having to say anything else.

"Let the girl eat," Makayla said. "Remi knocked her breakfast all over the floor this morning."

"And he's still alive?" The blonde girl asked. "Wow, Ben, how did you hold back?" She had a strong southern drawl and came across as someone who was often the center of the gossip. I wasn't sure why I thought that, but I had a feeling if I wanted info about anyone, she was the girl to ask.

I lifted an eyebrow and risked a glance at the pack's alpha. For a moment, our eyes met and just as I expected, a rush of tingles shot through me like electricity sizzling down through my chest, low into my stomach. We both turned away.

"Never mind that," Makayla said. "What I want to know is why Cormac is in confinement. Who was in gym this morning? Did anyone see it?"

The table burst into conversation as one of the other shifters, a man with dreadlocks and a full beard explained how someone named Cormac had threatened the gym teacher this morning. "It was like he snapped."

I was grateful for the distraction away from me and used the time to eat all of my food quickly while I still had the chance.

Finally, feeling a little more like myself after the surprisingly good meal, I decided to join the conversation. These people seemed nice and I didn't really care what their magical power was. "Officially introducing myself now, thanks for letting me eat. I'm Raven, reluctant mage."

The blonde girl with the curls stretched her hand across the table, knocking over a bottle of iced tea that was thankfully empty. "Oops." She quickly righted it and extended her hand again. "Jenny, Missouri pack."

I accepted her hand. "Nice to meet you."

The man with the dreadlocks waved. "Jamal, from the 303."

"I have no idea what that is," I said.

He laughed. "Denver."

"Got it," I said.

"Sam," a woman with black hair cut in a bob said brightly. "I'm kind of a nomad. No pack affiliation."

"I don't think she cares," Makayla said.

"I care," I said. "It's interesting. So you all belong to a group of other shifters?"

Jamal laughed again. "Packs. We come from packs of wolf shifters."

"Right," I said.

"Aren't mages in covens?" Sam asked.

"Isn't that witches?" I asked.

"There's no such thing as witches. Well, none with actual magic," Jenny said. "You're a nomad too, then?"

"I guess so," I said.

"Imagine that, Ben. Your - ow, hey!" Jenny rubbed her side after Ben jabbed her with his elbow.

"What am I missing?" I asked.

"Nothing," Ben said. He looked around at everyone at the table. "Am I right?"

"Yeah, yeah," Jenny said. "We got it, boss."

Ben stood up and picked up his tray, leaving without another word.

I turned and watched him walk away. He'd been so nice to

me when he'd walked me to class. "Did I do something to piss him off?"

"Don't worry, he's a moody asshole," Makayla said. "But he's right, we should get going. What's your next class?"

"Gym," I said.

"Ugh, so sorry," she said. "You'll need to change out before you go. Don't go in your uniform. Coach sends more kids to confinement than any other teacher. Just go along with whatever till you get the hang of it."

"What if I don't go?" I asked, dread sinking into my gut like a weight. Gym hadn't been my strong suit in high school either. I nearly failed because I couldn't climb that damn rope. I had to run so many laps to make up for it that by the end of the semester, people were asking me to join the track team. As if I'd run for fun. What the fuck was wrong with those people?

"You have to go. Trust me, you learn ways to get through it quickly. Just don't do anything to stand out," Sam said.

"Well, it was nice meeting you all," I said as I left the table. I was still worried about the fact that I didn't know how to control my magic but I was starting to think that being sent to this school wasn't the worst possible thing that could happen to me.

Raven

Gym was just as awful as I remembered it. Coach Miller was like something out of a horror movie. His upper body was that of a man who worked out way too much. Bulgy and veiny in a too roided out to be attractive kind of way. His lower body was a massive, coiling snake tail. He even made a slithering sound when he moved.

The mere sight of him made my skin crawl.

"Six more laps, ladies," he called.

I picked up the pace, grateful for the excuse to round the curve on the track and be farther away from him.

The sexist prick had the girls working out on the track, running laps, while the guys were over on the other side of the gym pushing giant tires and whipping ropes around. Apparently, gym at a magical school was exactly the same as the gyms the rich people paid hundreds of dollars a month for. Except for the whole coached by a dude who might swallow you whole.

Panting, I waited till the coach had slithered away before I slowed down to a walk. All the other girls sped past me, not easing up on the running. Who knew magic academy students were in such good shape?

"You shouldn't stop to walk," a pale, fair-haired girl said as she slowed to join me. She glanced to her right then looked back at me. "If he catches you walking, he'll make an example of you."

"Why are we running so much? Isn't the point of having magic so you don't have to run? I mean, can't we just shoot fire at the bad guys?" I asked.

She laughed. "Well, maybe you can, but us vampires can't actually turn into bats and fly away."

"Oh." I wasn't sure what else to say. I'd never met a vampire before. Shit, I'd never met anyone or anything magical before today so that wasn't a surprise.

"I take it you're a mage," she said.

"Yeah," I said. "Guess it shows?"

"The whole throwing fire at them gave it away," she said.

"Right."

"Look, coach is an asshole, but he's right that we need to be stronger. Magic takes a lot out of you so the stronger your physical body is, the easier it is to recover when you use it. Even for the undead." She laughed. "We're not really dead. That was a joke."

I forced a laugh. What the hell were vampires if they weren't dead? Everything I'd learned from horror movies and books was wrong. So very, very wrong.

"I know I'm not seeing walking on the track," Coach Miller called.

Quickly, I started jogging, the vampire matching my pace. "Thanks."

"You're welcome, new girl," she said.

"I'm Raven," I said.

"Violet," she said.

The two of us jogged next to each other until the coach blew the whistle. I followed her off the track toward the locker room. As we walked, a familiar creature caught my eye, and I held my breath.

Luka stood in front of the entrance to the men's locker room, a grin on his handsome face.

I stopped short of the door to the women's locker room and stared at him.

"I'll leave you two alone," Violet said, then she disappeared through the door.

"You survived your first day at gym," he said.

"Barely," I said. "I'm sure I'll be paying for it tonight. I'm going to need to test out that giant tub."

"Want me to join you? I've been told I give the best back rubs." He winked.

Every part of my body seemed to be firing explosive tingles through me, urging me to grab hold of him and pull him against me here and now. I didn't even want to wait for tonight. I wanted him.

But there was one small part of me that resisted. Reminding me that I was serious when I said I wasn't dating anyone right now.

"I really need to focus on figuring all this shit out before I get involved with anyone," I said. Internally, my body was screaming. Before it could betray me, I pushed through the doors and headed for the first cold shower I could find.

"Wait," Luka called.

I turned to see the door closing behind him.

"The fuck, Luka!" Someone yelled.

"Hey, get out, incubus!" Someone else called.

"Luka, what the hell are you doing?" I asked.

"I'm not sure. Breaking all my own rules." He smirked.

Flutters filled my chest and my mind swirled back to the dream that didn't feel like a dream. Wasn't this every girl's fantasy? A sexy Greek-god of a man chasing her down and confessing… actually, I wasn't sure what he was doing, but it felt like it should be romantic.

Even my own body was betraying me as tingles started between my thighs. It was as if I reacted to him on instinct, with no free will of my own.

And that was fucking terrifying.

"You have to leave," I said. "I told you, I can't do this right now."

"Are you going to fuck her or what?" someone called.

I glanced behind me to see Violet standing with her hands on her hips.

"Because if you're not going to get it on, you're wasting all of our time. Hers, yours, and your audience," Violet said.

She was right, there was a group of girls gathered around her and all of their eyes were fixed on me. Most of them wore knowing glances.

"I mean, I don't blame you for sampling a demon but make sure you get him to wrap that thing. We all know where its been," a mousy girl with huge ears and light brown hair said.

The rest of the girls laughed and my cheeks burned. I knew I had to be as red as my hair. Had all of these women slept with

Luka? Had they done it in dreams or in real life? Either way, the implication made me furious. I didn't want to share him.

I shook my head, sending the insane thoughts away. We didn't even know each other. Our interaction last night wasn't real. I lowered my voice, trying to gain at least a little privacy. "Listen, the dream was nice, but it wasn't real."

"That's what I kept trying to tell myself," he said. "How's that lie working out for you?"

My jaw tightened, and I tried to think of something to say. "You need to go. We don't even know each other."

"Dude, she turned you down," Violet said.

He laughed. "Good thing I wasn't asking." He reached into his pocket and pulled something out, then held it up in the air. "I just came to drop this off."

I stared open-mouthed at a pair of black panties.

Behind me, the room burst into giggles.

"Those are not mine," I said.

"Are you sure? Because they smell like you."

I glared at him. After the dream and after the way he'd burst into the locker room, I had thought for a minute that he was different. But just like every other man I'd ever been with, it didn't last. He was just as cocky as the moment I met him. "You're an asshole."

"A busted asshole."

The room went silent, and I watched as Luka's expression of triumph melted away into a mask of seriousness.

Slowly, I turned to see the owner of the voice. My magical theory professor was standing in the middle of the lockers, silent students on either side of her.

"I was just leaving," Luka said.

"Wrong direction," she said. "This is the third time you've been busted in here. You know the rules."

I turned back to Luka, incredulous. Jealous heat flared in my chest that quickly turned to anger. "Three times?"

He shrugged.

"You really are an asshole," I said.

"Come on, lover boy, it's confinement time for you," she said.

I swallowed against the lump in my throat. Despite his brazen attitude, I couldn't help but feel bad for him.

And there was still that part of me that wanted him.

"Luka," I started but couldn't think of anything else to say.

He shoved the underwear into my chest and I automatically grabbed them, too dumbfounded by the situation to argue with him. Was he really going to confinement over this?

Luka paused next to me and leaned down to whisper in my ear. "They really are your panties."

I squeezed my hand around the fabric so tightly that my fingernails dug into my palms before I realized I was holding on to someone's underwear. Snapping out of it, I marched toward a trash can and tossed them in.

When I looked back to where Luka had been, he was gone. And so were most of the other students.

Violet stood alone in the center of the room. "You know, you might just bring the excitement I was craving to this school. Things have been too dull lately. Too normal, you know? I have a feeling you're going to shake all of that up."

"Ms. Winters," A male voice boomed into the locker room. "It's Dr. Green. When you're decent, you need to be in my office."

My insides twisted and the ground seemed a little unstable. This was it. He was going to send me to magic jail. I was so, so fucked.

"You better go," Violet said. "The longer you keep him waiting, the more pissed he gets."

"Hey, thanks for not trying to hypnotize me or threaten me or anything," I said.

"We just met," she said. "No promises I won't try something in the future."

I laughed, then headed toward my fate.

14

Raven

I knocked on Dr. Green's closed door and tried to swallow down my fear. Now that I'd had a taste of this place, I really didn't want to leave.

"Come in, Ms. Winters," he called.

I opened the door and stepped inside, pausing just beyond the threshold.

"Sit."

Swallowing against the lump in my throat, I complied. The room wasn't quite as creepy during the day. Sunlight streamed in through the open slats of the wood blinds, making a pattern on the dark red carpet.

The ominous clock even looked more subdued in the sunshine. The owl's eyes weren't glowing now, and the tree appeared more brown than black. I could have sworn it was as black as night last night.

The chair creaked as I settled into it and I kept my eyes on Dr. Green's massive hands.

"Raven," he said.

I looked up, startled by the causal use of my name. "I swear I didn't ask him to come in the bathroom." Suddenly, I felt like I was sixteen all over again, denying that I'd spray painted the boarded up temporary buildings in the back of the school. Of course, then I was lying. This time, I wasn't.

"I know," he said. "But you're on thin ice here. Do you know how many strings were pulled to get you into this school? How many phone calls were made on your behalf?"

Fire simmered in the pit of my stomach. "Of course, I don't know. I didn't even know this place existed until I was dragged here."

"Calm down," he said, his tone level.

I didn't want to calm down. "Why am I here? There's no such thing as a scholarship fund, and it's clear I don't fit in. I'm not wealthy and I'm not important. I don't belong here."

"Do you want to leave the school?" He asked.

"No," I said, startled at how quickly I answered. I knew I wanted to stay, but I usually wasn't so open with others until I knew their personal agendas better.

"You're here because you belong here. Even though you don't know it, you were meant to be here, so it was arranged for you to attend when you were found."

"Why?" I asked, desperation sinking into my tone.

"I'm not the right one to explain all this to you, but you'll have answers soon. I'm going to need you to trust me."

"I don't even know you," I said.

"I'm trying to protect you. Your options are limited. You stay here, you prove you're not dangerous and you can move on with your life after you pass the trials," he said.

"*If* I pass the trials," I said. "I keep hearing how dangerous this place really is. I'm not sure it's much better odds than prison."

"You're right, the trials have their own risks as all things with magic do. But I can assure you, it's a better place than magic prison. You have food and shelter and clothing, and you still have use of your magic here," he said.

My brow furrowed. What exactly was he saying? Would they take away my magic if I was sent away?

As much as I wanted to stay here, I'd clearly upset something or someone. I didn't want such a fuss made over me when I didn't even know why I was here in the first place. My skin crawled thinking of the fact that I owed a favor to strangers without even asking for the favor in the first place. "Look, if it's such a big deal, just send me back. I was making it just fine on my own."

He shook his head. "You can't go back. When you used your magic, you sent a signal into the world. A signal that many were tracking. You won't be safe until you can learn to control your magic. And even then, you're always going to be at risk."

"You're going to have to start giving me some answers," I said.

He sighed and picked up a folded piece of paper that was sitting on his desk and handed it to me. "You received a letter about an hour ago."

I lifted my eyebrow. "You read my mail?"

"You told me nobody knew you were here," he said. "So, who would know to send you a letter?"

"Touché," I said, taking the paper from him. I unfolded it and read quickly. The paper shook in my trembling hand. This had to be a joke. Some sort of hazing.

"This isn't real, right? It was probably sent by the sirens or one of the other students," I said.

He took the letter from me and set it flat on the desk so I could see the words. "I wish that were the case. But it was tested by Ms. Halifax."

My brow wrinkled as I tried to place the name.

"Our Spellcasting teacher," he added, "I believe you've met her. She's the best spell caster we have."

"Oh," I said, as it dawned on me that I never learned her name. "Right. She seems good."

"But why threaten me?" I looked at the note, reading it again. "They can't be serious, right?" I read the letter out loud. "*Your time is coming to an end, just like your brethren. Enjoy each breath as soon you'll breathe your last.*" It sounded sort of silly now. I mean, who writes threats like that?

"So this was sent by someone outside of the school?" I asked. "Nobody even knows I'm here aside from the cops that brought me in."

"Like I said, when you used your powers, you left your unique magical signature. It's possible you were being hunted, and it's possible, whoever is after you even suspected you before you released your magic."

I shook my head. "None of this makes sense. I'm nobody special and I'm not a threat to anyone."

"The two dead men in the alleyway would disagree."

"That's not fair," I said.

"Raven, you have magic that is different from most mages

and just as in the human world, some supernaturals have a difficult time accepting those who are different."

"You're kidding, right?" I couldn't believe we were having this conversation. "We're talking about a world where creatures suck blood, and get magic from sex, and can compel you to do things you don't want to do. What could I possibly have that would mark me as a threat to random strangers?"

"The basic term is Untamed Magic, as I mentioned before. It's not just about magic that's not controlled, but it's about magic that we don't understand. I'm not sure what yours is yet, but I have suspicions."

"Dr. Green, you gotta give me some answers here," I said.

He interlaced his large hands on the desk in front of him and leaned closer to me. "You are a mage. By any count, a powerful mage. It seems like you have an affinity for fire and I think you need to learn how to control that. As for whatever else you are, you're going to need to give me some time."

I felt trapped and even more confused than I was when I arrived last night. Some first day. "Fine."

"I expect you'll be focused and on your best behavior," he said. "You have no choice but to learn how to control your magic."

"What about the threat?" I asked. "Do you think I should worry? I mean, is someone going to sneak into my room while I'm sleeping?"

He shook his head. "Our grounds are warded. Only students and teachers can enter or exit. Anyone else must have permission from me. And I'm not about to let any threats to my students into this building."

I wasn't sure why, but for some reason I believed him.

"Now, go to class." Dr. Green looked back at the documents on his desk, as if I wasn't even in the room.

Just as abruptly as the meeting started, it was over. A heavy weight settled into my stomach as I left his office. Not only was there the Untamed Magic to deal with, which I still didn't even understand, there was someone hunting me. It had to be a mistake, right? Why would anyone care about some random mage without a penny to her name?

Luka

"Raven?" I whispered her name, afraid to startle her.

She looked up, her face tear streaked. We were in the dungeon cell again and she was wearing a filthy dress made of rags. She sniffed, then wiped the tears from her face.

Quietly, I walked toward her and sat down next to her. I'd planned on storming in, showing her how much I wanted her, making her toes curl.

But I couldn't bring myself to do it once I walked into her dream. "Is this recurring for you?"

She nodded. "I didn't want to tell you before. It's kind of my go to. But now that you're here, at least I know it's a dream."

I set my hand on hers. "It's just a dream. Want me to change it for you?"

She shook her head. "We can't keep doing this. I meant what I said. Dr. Green reminded me that this school is my only option."

I loved how vulnerable she was in her dreams. There was no way she'd open up like this to me in the real world. She was too tough on the exterior. Here, it was like she let her guard down. Or maybe she was willing to let her guard down with me.

My insides twisted with guilt. I'd barged in on her when she wasn't ready for me. I'd caused her pain, which was the last thing I ever wanted to do. Unless of course it was in the bedroom and she was into that. "I'm sorry. I shouldn't have pushed you."

"I can't be around you, you know," she said. "Not in real life."

I squeezed her hand as my whole body tensed. There was no way I could handle being tossed out of her life. I needed her. She needed me.

"I can't trust myself around you and I'm not ready to go that route," she said. "I'm going to need you to help me on this."

I slid my hand up to her arm. "I can do my best, but Raven, I have to admit, I've never felt a pull to another like what I feel to you."

She tugged her arm away and stood abruptly. "Something is wrong with me." She started to pace the room, her hands on top of her head, fingers woven into her hair.

I jumped to my feet. "What are you talking about? You're amazing. There's nothing wrong with you."

She stopped walking and dropped her hands to her side. "Luka, I'm dangerous. There's something inside me that shouldn't be."

"That's how we all feel. Look at me. If I don't get enough sex, I could take it from someone. I'm a fucking monster."

She shook her head. "No, don't say that. You have a gift. You give pleasure and happiness and make people feel good. So far, all I can do is destroy."

"You don't know that. You accidentally used your magic once, right?" I asked.

She nodded. "But Dr. Green says I'm dangerous. That if I don't get it under control, I could be locked up."

I took her hands in mine and tugged her closer to me. Staring down into those green eyes, I knew we were meant to be together. "Raven, you and I are going to figure this out together. If that means I wait for you in real life, I wait for you. But we have a bond. I need you and you need me. Can't you feel that?"

She let out a shaky breath. "I feel something for you, but it's not just you."

My brow furrowed.

She tugged her arms away from me and took a couple of steps away from me. "It's like my hormones are on overdrive since I arrived. It's like I'm craving sex all the time."

"Maybe because you're not getting what you need." I had every intention of respecting her boundaries, but I approached her anyway. My cock twitched at the sight of her round ass through the sheer fabric of her nightgown. It was transparent, showing me all of her curves.

She turned so she was facing me and I could see the mounds of her soft, round tits. Her pink nipples hard against the thin fabric. I groaned at the sight of her. The want in me making me feel nearly drunk. "Do you even know how sexy you are?"

She frowned. "I was trying to open up to you."

"I know," I said. "And I'll leave if you want me to. But have you considered that maybe you need the release? Maybe your body is craving this for a reason?"

Her eyes dropped, and I knew she was looking at the tent in my jeans. There wasn't any way to hide my arousal from her. Even with my ability to control dreams, I couldn't control my feelings for her.

"Dreams only," she said. "Never during the day."

I was willing to take what I could get, for now. As long as I could have her. "Agree."

Reaching for her, I cupped the side of her face, rubbing my thumb on her soft cheek, then down her lips.

She held her breath, then she batted my hand away. "Wait a minute, you're in confinement. You went there for me."

I shrugged. "It was my fault. I shouldn't have followed you."

Her eyebrows knitted together in a look of concern. "Are you okay? They say it's terrible."

"It's not so bad. Especially if you're someone like me, who can escape in a matter of speaking." I didn't want to go into the rumors about reduced magic and lower powers after a trip to confinement. It was too depressing and would definitely ruin the mood. Besides, I was able to get to Raven's dream. That was all I needed.

Taking a chance, I leaned in, hesitating only a second before I claimed her mouth with mine.

She wrapped her arms around me and I pulled her closer to me. Our lips moved together in ravenous, hungry fashion. Her fingers spread through my hair, tugging the strands as she pulled my head closer to hers.

My hands moved below her ass and I lifted her. She instantly wrapped her legs around my waist.

Tongue in her mouth, tangling with hers, I carried her toward the wall until her back was pressed against it. Using the wall as leverage, I let go with one hand so I could pull down my pants.

She lifted her dress so it was hiked up around her waist.

I didn't even bother to remove her panties. I just shifted them to the side before thrusting into her. Her head rolled back, breaking the kiss as she cried out at the force of my entry.

Moaning in pleasure, I pounded her as her fingernails dug into my back. It was fast and dirty and exactly what both of us needed.

As my cock thickened, I buried my face in her neck, nipping at the sensitive flesh. She let out a scream as wetness covered me from her orgasm. I released into her, my whole body feeling like an explosion went off inside me.

Panting, I rested my head on her shoulder.

She kissed the top of my head.

I didn't deserve her.

Raven

The next two weeks passed by in a blur as I focused on classes, not dying in gym, avoiding the awful girls in the cafeteria, and trying not to let my hormones get the better of me. I took Dr. Green's warning to heart and was a better student than I'd ever been in my whole life. I took notes, I studied, I practiced, and I avoided distractions. He still hadn't called me to his office to explain anything. But thankfully, nothing had come of the letter and I didn't receive any other threats.

Well, at least not from outside sources. This school had its share of bullies and assholes, but I avoided them and continued to hang out with the shifters who lived in the dungeon.

While I was finally starting to figure out how this place worked, I still hadn't managed to make any friends with any of the other mages.

Not that I was trying too hard.

I spent lunch with the wolf shifters and most of my free time with Makayla. The two of us had even spent a day off school at the nearest mall. It was ridiculously normal.

And it turns out I do have an allowance. A huge allowance. Part of me wanted to argue about it, but mostly I was thrilled with the new lamp and really amazing headphones I'd purchased.

Makayla shoved a bag in my hands as we stopped in front of the stairs leading to the dungeon. "I got this for you while you were distracted."

My brow furrowed. "You really didn't need to get me anything."

She shrugged. "I wanted to."

With a smile, I opened the bag. It had been years since anyone had got me a present. Inside was a pair of earrings in the shape of flames. They were silver and subtle and beautiful.

"Maybe they'll bring you luck," she said. "Since I know you haven't really tried using magic yet."

I frowned. The earrings suddenly felt like they weighed a ton. During lunch and down times, I saw other students use magic to create horses made of fire that could dance around the room and butterflies made of smoke that moved so effortlessly it seemed like they were breathing. Once, I'd even seen another mage draw a line of fire between himself and another mage in an act of self-defense. I knew I'd have to use my magic sooner or later and I knew fire was important to mages.

Even though we'd never talked about it, I had a feeling that

Makayla knew I was afraid. The men who'd attacked me died by my fire. What if I lost control again? Those men were monsters. The people here were students. I didn't want to hurt anyone or hurt myself. Plus, there was the whole Untamed Magic thing Dr. Green warned me about. I couldn't shake the part of our conversation about having power I didn't know about. The fire had been surprise enough. I wasn't sure I could handle any other new magic.

Worse, I didn't want to end up thrown out of here. I was worried that once I tried using magic, they'd learn what a fraud I was, or I'd do so much damage they'd kick me out.

I'd grown to like being here. The food was good and reliable. The water was never cut off and my room was never freezing so I could save money on heat. I had it good here.

"Don't worry," she said. "You'll know when the time is right to try your magic again."

I nodded, forcing a smile on my face. "Thank you."

The two of us were laughing over a shared joke when we reached the common room.

Out of the corner of my eye, I noticed Ben jump up from his seat. I'd only seen him in passing over the last two weeks. It was clear he'd been avoiding me.

The sexy wolf shifter glanced toward me and for a second, our eyes locked. My breath hitched and I felt warm all over. I still wasn't sure how he was able to do this to me with a look, but he seemed to have a hold on me that I couldn't shake.

It felt like we were alone in the room, just the two of us.

He broke the stare first, looking down with a nod. "Raven, Makayla."

"Hey, Ben," Makayla said. "What are you guys playing? Cause Raven here keeps saying she's a champion strip poker player but I'm not sure I believe her."

Makayla nudged me with her elbow playfully.

"It's been a while since I played," I said, still unable to take my eyes off of Ben.

"Come on, show us what you got, little mage," Jenny said, tapping the empty space on the couch next to her.

"I think I'll sit this one out," Ben said.

"That's probably smart," Makayla said. "We all know you can't handle losing well."

"Who says I'd lose?" He asked.

Makayla shrugged. "I mean, if you're afraid, sulk back to your room."

He looked back at the table, then turned his gaze back on me as if waiting for me to say something. Once again, my breath hitched, but this time, there was a twinge of sadness at the thought of him walking away.

While I knew he was expert level temptation, the thought of him leaving was worse than knowing I had to be on my best behavior. "Afraid you'll lose to a girl?"

He laughed, a rich, dark sound that filled my insides with flutters. How I wished he'd laugh for me. Just the two of us, naked and entwined in my bed.

Swallowing hard, I pushed the sexy thoughts away. "Or is it that you don't think you can beat a mage?"

"Oh, you're on, princess," he said.

Makayla grabbed my shopping bag. "I'll stash this in my room. You go get in on that game."

"You're not playing?" I asked.

"Oh no, I'd rather watch you kick his ass."

I cracked my knuckles playfully as I walked toward the low table. "Y'all ready to lose?"

Jenny shifted a little, making more room on the couch. I sat down next to her and looked across the table where Ben was settling back into his seat. I winked at him, suddenly feeling very emboldened by the familiar sound of cards being dealt. "You ready to lose that shirt?"

He lifted his eyebrows. "I don't lose at this game."

"You've never played against me." I took my cards from Jenny.

Trey was sitting next to her and called out his bet. "Let's start with shirts today."

"Call," Starla said.

"Call," Ben said.

"Call," I said, not taking my eyes off of Ben.

Jenny turned the cards and I smirked. I'd never been great with poker face, but I was incredibly lucky. There was no way I was going to lose this hand.

As we went through the game, the player with the lowest hand lost a piece of clothing. Trey was down to his boxers and Starla had lost her shirt. Jenny maintained her position as dealer, keeping all of her clothes just as Ben and I both had.

"I told you I was good at this game." I threw down my cards.

"Dammit," Trey said.

"Take it off!" Starla shouted.

Everyone laughed as Trey stood and started dancing. "Hey, if I'm going to strip for all of you, I might as well make it a show!"

I could feel Ben's gaze on me as I watched Trey shake his hips. It was strong enough to drag me away from the performance just as Trey hooked his thumbs under the waistband of his boxers.

Our eyes met and heat rushed to my cheeks. Ben was staring at me as if I was the only one in the room. The laughter around me sounded far away. I clenched my thighs together and tore my eyes from him. Without a word, Ben had managed, once again, to make me feel things I shouldn't.

Trying to ignore the intensity of our connection, I turned back to where Trey was shaking his bare ass for the whole group. Jenny reached up and slapped him and Trey howled. "Hey, that's unwanted touch."

"Right, that's exactly what you said last night," she said.

He turned back to the group, his large cock on full display. He had nothing to be ashamed of. "Ladies and gentlemen, I bid you farewell." He bowed low, then scooped up his clothes, using them to cover himself.

Then, he turned to Ben. "Take her out, will you? It's not right that she's sitting there fully clothed."

"You got it," Ben said.

"I wouldn't count on it," I said.

"We'll see," he said. "I'm sure I'm going to get you out of those clothes."

Wetness spread between my legs. If he only knew how badly I wanted him to make good on that threat.

Ben

It was down to the two of us. Starla took over dealing once Jenny followed Trey down the hall. The sounds of Jenny's screams reached the common room, amping up the sexual tension that was already filling the space.

I could smell Raven's arousal. I knew she wanted me. But I needed her to make the first move. There was no way I would be able to stop if we started so I had to make sure she wanted it as much as I wanted her.

She was my mate, I was certain of it so it was a matter of time until we made it official. I would feel my cock inside her. I would mark her as mine. And with every second that passed, I could feel us inching closer to that moment.

Starla turned the cards, and I maintained my stoic expression. I wasn't going to win this hand.

Drawing a few more cards would only delay the inevitable. Besides, maybe removing some of my clothing would help speed this process up. I wanted Raven. I needed her.

"Strip," she said.

"You sure you're ready for that?" I asked.

"I think I can handle it," she said.

I shrugged. "You asked for it." Slowly, I pulled my shirt over my head. I knew I looked good naked.

Tossing the shirt to the side, I watched Raven's face. She was terrible at hiding her emotions, which is why it was surprising she was doing so well at this game. She had zero poker face.

I smirked as she involuntarily licked her lower lip, her eyes traveling down my chest to my abs. Probably lower. "You like what you see?"

Her green eyes shot back up to mine. "I see another cocky asshole who spends more time in the gym than he does with a book."

"Ouch, burn." I laughed. "Are you calling me dumb?"

Her cheeks flushed. It was adorable.

"Just deal, okay. Unless you fold?" she asked.

"Never," I said.

Starla silently dealt the cards. I turned mine over and couldn't help but smile. No poker face this time. When you hold two aces, you're in good shape.

Starla turned over the cards on the table. Another ace.

I grinned. "Ready to take off that shirt?"

"Not so fast," she said.

But I could see it on her face.

A minute later, Raven scowled at me as she pulled her shirt

over her head. Her perky tits were sitting in a lacy black bra on full display for me. My cock hardened at the sight. Her body was even more beautiful than I'd imagined. And trust me, I'd imagined it a lot over the last few weeks.

"What no comment?" She said.

"Stunned silence from the alpha?" Starla said. "That's a mighty powerful rack you've got there. We're going to have to keep that in mind for when we want him to shut the fuck up."

I glared at Starla. "Deal."

She laughed as she dealt the next hand. This time, my shoes came off. Then, my socks.

Finally, I won a hand. Raven took off her shoes.

Then I won again. Raven's socks came off. All that was left was her pants to see what she was wearing over that pussy I'd fantasied about.

Another round and I was holding the winning cards. But I wasn't quite ready. This wasn't how I wanted to see Raven fully naked. I wanted her to myself - alone in my room. Or at least somewhere with a little privacy. My wolf growled internally, demanding I show my hand. He wanted her. All of her.

I knew the risk I would take if I got her down to her panties. I wasn't sure I could keep my wolf - or myself contained.

"I'm out." I threw my cards on the table, face down. Letting Raven win.

Raven cocked an eyebrow at me. It was the first time I hadn't shown my hand. I didn't have to show my cards, but I know she was suspicious.

"Pants, pants, pants," Starla chanted.

I stood. "You ready, princess? This is what you were waiting for, right?"

Raven rolled her eyes. "Trust me, I'm sure your underwear isn't any better than any of the others I've seen."

I unzipped my jeans and tugged them down. It was worth it

to see the wide-eyed response to my well fitted boxer briefs from Raven.

If I lost again, I'd bare it all. My wolf panted in agreement. It was a calculated risk. One I was willing to take to try to get her to act on her impulses. I knew she wanted me. I just needed to get her to admit it to herself.

"You lose this, and you're out, Ben," Starla said.

"Got it," I said. "Unless Raven wants to fold now?"

"Never," she said.

My cock twitched. God, I loved that stubborn streak. Did she even have any idea how fucking sexy she was?

Starla dealt.

I peeked at my cards. They were good, but I wasn't sure if they were good enough. Once again, I thought about Raven's pussy on full display. My cock twitched.

I wanted her. To be inside her.

But not like this.

"I fold," I said.

"Just like that?" She said. "Does that mean you don't want to show me what's under those boxers?"

"Oh, I want to show you," I said. "Just not here."

I could hear Raven's heart pounding. Her cheeks flushed pink and I could sense the change in her breathing. She was ready.

"You lost, Ben," Starla said. "Time to strip."

I looked at Raven. "Want me to do it here, or should we go somewhere more private?"

"Strip," Raven said, not missing a beat.

She was brutal. And I was pretty sure I was in love with her. Nobody pushed me around or stood up to me. She was exactly what I needed.

I stood, my eyes focused on hers. She didn't blink as I stared at her. Our connection sent a rush of fire though me, as if every part of me was lit up. My skin felt hot and my chest was tight. The only thing I could think of was Raven. Her lips pressed into mine so hard they came back bruised. Her nails digging into my back. My cock deep inside her as she moaned in pleasure.

Hooking my thumbs under the waistband, I tugged down my boxers. My erection sprung free, its full size clearly visible.

Raven's eyes lowered, and she took a deep breath, holding it. I watched as her fingers gripped the fabric of the couch. She squeezed her legs together, then she looked up at me. Our eyes met again.

"You like what you see?" I asked, taking a few steps toward her.

"It's impressive," she breathed.

"Raven," her name escaped my mouth like a prayer. How did I explain this to her? Did she know that she called to me? That we were meant to be together?

"Alright, you two," Starla said. "The common room is off limits for sex."

I turned to her, letting out a low growl.

"Not my rule," she said.

"I have to go," Raven said. She pushed past me, holding her clothes.

I watched her leave. Now wasn't the time, but we were close. Soon, she'd come to me.

Raven

"Good news, class," Professor Halifax said. "We are officially done with the technical preparations. Today, we begin the practical study."

The class cheered and my eyes widened. I knew at some point, I'd have to actually use magic but the last few weeks of learning about it from a safe distance had been just fine for me.

"Today's practical session will be a group study. Groups of three, make sure you have at least one newer student in your group. Choose one of the elemental spells to focus on today and work through it until you can safely cast."

Chatter sounded around me as my classmates stood and moved around the room, greeting their friends and quickly forming groups.

I turned to the person next to me just as she walked away to join another group. *Fuck.* It was like elementary school gym class square dancing. Nobody wanted to be my partner, so I had to dance with the teacher. I really hoped there was no square dancing in gym here.

"Need a partner, new girl?" someone asked.

I turned to see the twins from the first night smiling down at me. Up close, they were even more handsome than I'd realized. They were identical from their short brown wavy hair and dark eyes to their strong jaws and light stubble. They looked like they'd be more at home on a big screen than inside a magic school in matching uniforms.

Everyone at this school was like a fucking model. No pressure. I straightened my shirt and inwardly thanked Makayla for making me brush my hair. I mean, if I had to deal with this place, I might as well enjoy myself. And to be fair, I'd been left with lady blue balls from the dream with Luka. Either of these two would be a welcome substitute. For a second, I imagined them both naked and touching me.

I shook my head and tried to send the dirty thoughts away. Something was wrong with me. Very, very wrong. "Yeah, I need a partner." *In more ways than one.*

One of the twins lifted a knowing eyebrow and my cheeks heated. Did he know what I was thinking? Could mages do that?

"Come on, you can join us, new girl," he said.

"Raven," I said. "My name is Raven."

"Matt and Zach," the other twin said.

My brow furrowed as I searched their faces, trying to find anything that could identify them as individuals. Not seeing anything, I lowered my eyes to check out the rest of them.

Finally, I noticed that one of them had a freckle on his right hand while the other didn't. "Who is Matt and who is Zach?"

"I'm Matt," the one with the freckle pointed to himself.

"Zach," the other said.

"Got it," I said. "Thanks for inviting me to join your group."

"We've got to be the first to check out the new girl," Matt said.

"Unless Luka beat us to it," Zach said.

"I don't know what you're inferring but that's not how I roll," I said.

"Pity," Matt said. "I could have made you scream my name for hours."

"Doubt it," I said. "That takes skill."

"Solid burn," Zach said.

"I think I might want different partners," I said, glancing around the room. Everyone was already in groups. I was stuck with the cocky asshole and his twin.

"You're stuck with us, darling," Matt said.

"Fine, but I'm not your darling," I said.

"You will be," Matt said with a shrug.

I ignored his confident words. "Shouldn't we get to work?"

"Sure, you start," Zach said.

"I don't know how," I said.

Matt turned his hand and flames flickered to life in his palm. He grinned. "It's easy. Now you try."

"Don't I need to say some magic words or something?" I asked.

"Only in the movies," Zach said, turning his hand and creating his own flames. "If you have the magic, you call to it and bring it forth."

I looked down at my hands and frowned. I'd created fire once before and it ended in destruction and death. Balling my hands into fists I reminded myself again that I was in the right.

I shouldn't feel bad for what I did. And I did want to control it.

Blowing out a breath, I copied their hand movement, willing fire to come.

Nothing happened.

"Maybe you're not good with fire," Matt said. "We can try water."

I shook my head. "No, I know I have fire. At least I think I have fire."

Zach closed his hand around his flame. "Try this." He stretched his arm out and splayed his fingers wide. Then he turned his hand slowly, so it was palm up, then closed his hand into a fist. When he opened it, there was a tiny flame burning in his hand. "If you're a fire mage, you should manifest fire easily. The other elements are harder to create."

I can do this. I had to learn how to do this. It was the only way out of this place. If I could play along and graduate, I could move on with my life. Whatever the hell that looked like after walking away from what I'd left behind.

My hand shook as I stretched my arm out. I took a steadying breath as I turned my hand palm up. Squeezing my hand into a fist, I closed my eyes, imagining fire springing to life as if I held an invisible lighter. I opened my eyes and carefully opened my hand.

My heart skipped a beat as I watched a tiny flame breathe to life. It danced in my palm as if it had always been there. I laughed, my stomach twisting as relief mixed with disbelief. I'd had doubts before but here it was. Absolute proof that I could create magic.

Suddenly, the flame expanded, growing beyond my control. The fire spread as if my arm was kindling, working its way up. I screamed and shook my arm, trying to put the fire out.

"What the fuck?" Matt said.

"Stay calm, control it," Zach said.

In a matter of seconds, my entire body was alight with fire. I stood frozen, terrified, numb, confused. It didn't hurt but there was no escaping the fact that I was still engulfed in flames.

Zach slammed into me, throwing his arms around me, knocking me to the ground. I landed on my back so hard it sent white dots dancing in my vision.

Zach stood and dusted the soot from his burned clothes before offering a hand to me.

The flames were gone, but I was left smoking on the ground, my clothes burned away. None of my skin was injured, but I was naked. In front of my entire class. The whole room was silent.

The blush I felt was hotter than the flames that had burned up my clothes. I stood, doing my best to cover myself.

Matt threw his jacket around my shoulders. "Here."

I tugged it closed around me, my lower lip quivering in embarrassment.

"New girl's pretty hot," someone said.

Someone else whistled.

"Enough," the professor called. She marched over to me and glared, her expression cold. "You better get control of yourself or you'll never make it out of here alive."

"I didn't mean to," I said.

"No excuse," she said. "Matt, Zach, get her back to her room. She's in your group, she's your responsibility. She fails, you both fail, too. The rest of you, get back to work."

Matt

When I asked the new girl to join our group, I was hoping to score. As in, in bed, with her, naked. Not the kind of score where my grade and my whole future was now in jeopardy. I glanced over at Zach as we all silently made our way out of the classroom.

"Dad is going to kill us," I said through our telepathic bond.

"Mom would kill us if we didn't help her," Zach answered.

I frowned. Our mother was the type to take in strays. We had two dozen barn cats living on our country property because she was constantly caring for any abandoned creature she found. The vet was a regular visitor, always working on helping some poor flea-bitten, starving animal my mom took in.

"This isn't the same, though. She's a mage. Not an injured bird."

"Same thing, higher stakes," Zach answered.

"Hey, where are you going?" I asked, realizing that Raven had passed the hall that took us to the tower stairs.

"My room is in the dungeon." She blinked at us, her expression blank.

"For real?" I asked.

She rolled her eyes. "Look, you don't have to come with me. I get that I fucked up but I'll work on it, okay? Is there like a YouTube for mages or something where I can watch some videos?"

I smiled despite myself. "You'll find the internet isn't a thing here, so no, you won't find a blog or video to help you."

She cocked her eyebrow. "Does anybody read blogs anymore?"

"You're missing the point," I said.

"No, I get it." She pointed at me. "You wanted to fuck me." Then she pointed to Zach. "You might be a genuinely nice person, but you have an asshole brother." She pointed her finger at herself. "And I'm a colossal fuck up. Sound about right?"

There was something about her tone and the way she popped her hip when she put her hand there, that had me aching for her. There was no denying that I wanted to fuck her when we first met. But now, it wasn't just a way to pass the time. Now, I had to conquer her. I had to know what that attitude would be like in the bedroom.

She folded her arms over her chest. She looked damn sexy in just my jacket. My cock twitched at the thought that my jacket was all that stood between me and her naked body. Which, from the brief glance I got after she burned off all her clothes, was quite stunning.

"Quit smirking at me," she said.

"So sorry, princess, should I avert my gaze?" I asked.

"That's enough," Zach said. "It doesn't matter what any of us want. You have to get better and we have to help you."

"And how are you going to manage that? Last time you tried to help me I burned off all of my clothes," she said.

"Magic meld," Zach said.

I looked at him, my eyes widening in disbelief. *"No way. Too dangerous. Too many consequences."*

"We don't have a choice," Zach said.

Frustrated, I ran a hand through my hair. "Tell me, Raven, how was your training at home? Did your tutors focus on practical stuff?"

"I didn't have tutors," she said. "I…"

"Go on," Zach said.

Her eyes darted from side to side as if checking to see if we were alone. Then, she looked back at me. "Fine. I just found out I was a mage the day I arrived here, okay? I'm learning as I go. I used magic for the first time on accident and then they made me come here."

"That was not what I was expecting," Zach said.

"Me neither." I glanced at my twin. "You're right. We don't have a choice."

"Should I be worried?" Raven asked.

"About?" I asked.

"Whatever the fuck you two have been talking about with your secret twin magic," she said, dropping her hands to her side in frustration. The jacket opened, revealing her breasts and her soot covered skin. She quickly pulled it closed.

"You could tell we were communicating?" Zach asked.

"Yeah, it was obvious you were doing something. Plus, hello, this is magic school," she said.

"Right," Zach said.

The bell rang and the hum of conversation and footsteps of dozens of students moving to their next class filled the hall.

"Come on, we need to get out of here," I said, grabbing Raven's upper arm.

She tugged it away. "I've got another class after this."

"Don't worry, we'll get you excused," Zach said.

"You can do that?" I asked.

"For the money our parents are sending to this school, they should let us do whatever we damn well please," I said.

She licked her lips and looked down at the ground. I could tell she was nervous about something but now wasn't the time. We needed to get out of the hallway and somewhere quiet so we could try the magic meld.

"Come on," I said. "We'll go to our room."

She hesitated, and for a moment, I thought she wasn't going to follow. Then, she nodded and started moving.

We cut through the students and down the hall to the winding staircase that led up the tower. It was a wide column heading up ten levels above the rest of the building with platforms leading to rooms on each level. Each floor had 4 bedrooms with the exception of the seventh floor, which had only one massive set of rooms that wrapped all the way around the winding interior staircase. That was our stop.

Since our family started this whole place a hundred years ago and still made hefty donations every year, we were given what we affectionally called the sacred suite. In past generations, the massive suite had been used by one child at a time as our family had a strict one-kid policy. They had some weird belief about spreading the magic too thin and believed that having more kids could result in children with no magic, which were seen as lower than shifters to people like my parents. The whole lot of them were a bunch of assholes.

"Here we are," Zach said, sliding his keycard into the slot. "Home sweet home."

I gestured for Raven to enter the room and she stepped in, then froze in the foyer. "This is your room?"

"Rooms," I said. "It's a suite."

"Wow," she said.

I glanced around, taking in the space I rarely stopped to admire. To an outsider, it was probably over the top. The floors were made of gray marble streaked through with white. The walls were covered in black and white damask, textured wallpaper. As you looked into the space, you could see the rich wood floors of the living area and the high end, modern furniture.

Everything in here screamed wealth. Which was exactly what my family was going for when they remodeled it a few years ago.

"Doesn't exactly scream *college dorm*," Raven said. "But then again, the canopy bed in my room doesn't either. They really went all out when they decorated this place, didn't they?"

"Well, it's sort of our…" Zach began until I elbowed him in the side.

"They threw us in one room, twins, you know," I said.

"Right." She walked into the living area then stopped near an eighteenth-century globe shaped liquor cabinet. Her brow furrowed and she dragged her fingertips along the edge of the globe.

I swallowed hard, wishing those fingers were dragging along my skin. Shaking my head, I tried to push the thoughts of the two of us together away. She was hot for sure, but I had a feeling she was more trouble than she was worth.

Zach walked over to her and set his hand on top of hers, guiding it along the globe until they reached the seam.

Heat rose in my chest as jealousy flared. I didn't want him touching her. I wanted her to myself.

I took a step back, surprised by my reaction. I'd never cared which girls Zach fucked. Neither of us let girls stick around long enough to get attached. We'd passed off girls to each other enough times to have an understanding. When you had as much money as we did and you carried the *Obscura* name, things came easy. Even girls.

Zach opened the top of the globe, revealing the liquor and glasses inside.

"That's really cool," Raven said. "Right out of a movie."

"Want a drink?" Zach asked, lifting a bottle of brown liquor.

"It's like ten in the morning," she said. "Besides, I'd rather have something else to wear."

Zach set the bottle back down and closed the top. I took the opportunity to head to my room and grab an oversized gym shirt. It would probably fit her like a dress.

When I returned, Raven was giggling at something Zach said. Rage twisted my gut, and I threw the shirt at Zach, harder than I should have.

"What the fuck?" He caught it but nearly lost his balance. "Was that necessary?"

"We have things to do," I said. "We can get her excused for a while, but we don't have time for you to take her to your bedroom right now."

"Nobody is taking me to their bedroom, you get that, right?" Raven grabbed the shirt out of Zach's hands and marched down the hall.

As soon as she was out of sight, Zach stomped over to me. "What the hell, Mr. Cockblock?"

"Did you ever think about the fact that I saw her first?" I asked.

"So that's what this is about," he said. "Well, she thinks

you're a pig and she hates you so you have no shot. Why fuck it up for me?"

"You think you're going to have a shot if she hates someone who wears the same face?" I asked.

"How about you stop trying to decide who will get to fuck me and start being gentlemen who realize it's not your choice. I don't know what kind of women you're used to but you can't do this to people. It's wrong."

Her words made me feel like I'd been slapped in the face. I knew I wouldn't have said that if I thought she was back in the room. I wasn't good with people I wasn't paying and Raven wasn't one of the usual girls who would throw themselves at us.

"I'm sorry, Raven," Zach said. "It won't happen again."

"I'm sorry, too," I said.

"Look at that, maybe there is hope for both of you," she said. "As my class partners. Not as bedroom partners. Because that, boys, is never going to happen."

Raven

There was something different about these men. Granted, I didn't know any mages aside from myself and to be fair, I had always been different. But it wasn't the magic that made them seem different. It was something else. As if they'd never been told no in their lives. What kind of world had they grown up in where they thought it was okay to fight over women? Ugh. Whatever it was, I sure felt bad for whatever woman ended up with either of them. Or both of them. Maybe they were the sharing type.

"So what exactly was it that made you drag me to your mini mansion of a room and risk getting confinement?" I asked.

"We have to figure out what is going on with your magic. Find out if you're for sure a fire mage or if it's another element you connect with and then pinpoint your source," Zach said.

"Okay, pretty much none of that made sense," I said. "For real, I know zero about magic."

"We're going to connect our magic, all three of us, so we can find yours and help you reach it," Zach said.

"Okay, sounds harmless enough," I said. "How exactly?"

"It's not harmless," Matt said. "It can backfire or worse."

"What do you mean *backfire*?" I asked, not even wanting to get into the *worse* part of it.

"Connecting magic is something that's not done often. If we aren't careful, we could accidentally siphon the magic from one person and give to another. That's why we always do it in groups of three. Three is a sacred number for mages. It helps our magic to be stronger and keeps one mage from overpowering another," Zach said.

"Is that something that happens often? Someone overpowering someone else?" The magic world sounded more brutal with each new tidbit I learned.

"Not even phased by losing your magic?" Matt asked. "That's the part you should be focused on."

I shrugged. "Until recently, I didn't even know I had magic. As far as I can tell, it's more of an inconvenience than anything else. Sure, it helped me get away with my life but it landed me here. Away from my home and my job and my life."

"None of that makes sense," Matt said. "They don't just throw people who use magic in the human world into our school. It's not magic prison."

I blew out a breath. I was doing a terrible job of keeping the secret of how I'd arrived. At least I managed to skip the part about being a scholarship kid as Luka had suggested. My cheeks heated and an involuntary shiver ran down my spine at the thought of Luka. Was I ever going to be able to shake our dream from my memory?

"Look, I'm here now and I'm trying to make the best of it. Do you think you can help me?" I asked.

"You're sure you want to try this?" Zach asked.

"Do I have another choice?" I asked. "I can't afford to fail, I don't want to burn my clothes off again, and I definitely don't want either of you to fail despite your less than charming attitudes toward women."

Matt grumbled something under his breath and I ignored him.

"Are we going to do this or are we waiting for a full moon or some shit?" I asked.

Zach smirked. "You watch too much television."

"Yeah, cause I'm a normal twenty-one-year-old."

"No, you're not," Matt said. "You're a mage and it's time to tap into those powers."

"Let's do this," I said.

"Over here," Matt said, gesturing to the space in front of the black leather couch.

I followed him and then sat down next to him on top of the thick, ornate rug that probably cost more than I made in a year. What was with this place? Luka wasn't kidding when he said it was an expensive school. With each passing moment, I was feeling even more out of place. Maybe I should ask if they could take my powers. Then, I could go back to my normal life.

I thought of my shitty apartment with the bars on the windows and the heater that never worked. The threadbare sheets were nothing compared to the comfortable bedding I had here and my breakfasts of pop tarts and dinners of canned tuna were already dwarfed by the food here. Aside from the asshole I'd met in the cafeteria and the veiled death-threats, this place was a huge step up from what I had back home. Add in the fact that I knew, deep down, nobody missed me. That made giving all this up, this shot at something better, sound really, really stupid.

Zach was on one side of me, Matt on the other. We were sitting in a weird cross-legged circle. Three grown ass adults, well, if you consider us adults, which I barely did, sitting in a circle as if we were going to play duck-duck-goose. It was a bit ridiculous. But hey, we were talking about doing shit with magic so I guess it all sort of felt like make believe, anyway. "Now what?"

They reached their hands out and I set my hands in theirs without explanation. A jolt of electricity sizzled through my palms at the point of contact. "Ouch." It didn't actually hurt, but it was surprising. Like static electricity.

"That's the magic," Zach said.

"That's a good sign," Matt added. "We're already synched."

I lifted an eyebrow but didn't ask for clarification. This whole thing was mysterious enough and half the time I didn't understand the explanation. "Now what?"

"Close your eyes, and focus on your magic," Zach said.

I felt a little ridiculous sitting in a circle with my eyes closed. It struck me as odd that I never went through the Wiccan phase in high school like so many of the other girls I grew up with. Yet, here I was, sitting in a circle with a couple of mages trying to figure out my magic. If only those girls from high school could see me now. They'd be green with envy.

Something tickled in my gut, fluttering up through my chest. It was an odd sensation, weird enough to break me from my distractions and focus on myself. The fluttering grew until it felt like a bubble swelling inside me, threatening to pop.

Sweat formed on my brow, and my heart raced. The bubble

shifted, twisting until it felt like it was reaching toward all my limbs, as if it were composed of tentacles going in every direction inside of me. Something slithered down my back and I yelped.

"Hold on, don't let go of it. I can feel it," Matt said.

My breathing quickened as the slithering feeling continued. Then, it was as if something grabbed hold of the tendrils and pulled, tightening around them. I cried out as panic gripped me. Ice seemed to travel up the tendrils, silencing my cry.

I opened my eyes with a start and looked at Matt and Zach. The two of them were still next to me, still holding me but they were both staring at me.

As I met their eyes, shock waves of electric blue light ran up and down our arms, connecting us in a circle that I didn't want to break. The initial discomfort was gone, replaced by serenity, belonging, hope. It was like soaking in a warm bath, supported on all sides by the warm water.

Zach and Matt were the support. They were holding me here, keeping me calm, making me feel oddly comfortable. I'd never felt comfortable before. Not once. And now, I felt like I wanted to crawl in between them and let them hold me until I fell asleep. It didn't feel unusual to want to be with them. To touch them, taste them, smell them.

My senses began to fire on overdrive and suddenly the warmth spread to my belly, then lower to my core. I lifted my knees, squeezing my thighs together against the sudden arousal.

This wasn't happening. This couldn't happen.

Without thinking, I tugged my hands away, breaking the circle.

I shot backward, stopping when I hit the couch behind me. Dazed, I slowly looked up at the mages in the room with me. "What the hell was that?"

"The blue sparks or the sudden desire to fuck you right here even with my brother present," Zach said.

"Both, I guess," I said.

"You felt that, too?" Matt said. "Because I didn't think that was real."

"What are you talking about?" Zach asked.

"I read about a rare case when connecting magic formed a bond similar to a mating bond," Matt said.

"Mages don't feel mating bonds," Zach said. "That's a shifter and demon thing."

"Except for when it's forged by connecting magic," Matt said.

"What are you saying?" I asked. "That you just tricked me into falling in love with you or something?"

"No, it's not love, not really," Matt said. "Mating bonds are different. Animalistic. Possessive. Eternal."

"Okay, you two are nuts," I said as I stood up. It was bad enough that I had a broody shifter I had to avoid and a regular booty call with an incubus. I didn't need to be mated to a couple of mages on top of that.

"I'm sure it's nothing," Zach said. "I've never even heard of that."

"I think you're both fucking with me," I said.

"No, not at all," Matt said. "It was one study I read. I'm sure it's not what happened. It was probably just the power of the magic. I mean, some people say magic is an aphrodisiac."

"Well, not this person," I said, hands on my hips. "And I'm late for gym."

"Wait," Zach said. "I'll walk you there. It'll help you not get busted for being late."

"Fine," I said. "But we're never doing that connection thing again but you're both going to have to help me figure out how to make my magic work so I don't get kicked out of here."

"That sounds fair," Matt said. His hand brushed against mine as he walked past me toward the door.

His touch sent a shock wave through me, straight to my core and all I could think about was what it would be like to fuck him. Dammit. Whatever they did better be temporary.

Luka

My chest tightened as the bell rang and I still didn't see Raven. Over the last few weeks, I'd given her space in real life and while the late-night dream booty calls were nice, they weren't a substitute for the real thing. Every day when we had gym, I hoped it would be the day she'd decide to take things out of the dream realm.

It was hard to believe it had been nearly three weeks since she arrived. In all that time, I found that my appetite for other encounters had dwindled. It was as if she was the only thing I craved, and it was taking its toll on me. I needed to have some real-life action, but she was all I wanted.

Today was going to change that. I was going to get her alone. We had a connection, I knew we did. I just needed to talk to her. The whole day had dragged by so slowly as I waited for this moment. I'd been counting down, waiting for her.

And now it was time for gym, and she was nowhere in sight. I'd warned her about being on time to classes. She had to know by now how important it was to fall in line. This school might be the envy of all magic academies, but they were still practicing the old ways of punishment. Meaning, step a toe out of line and you'd pay with dire consequences that would be shocking to the members of the Spanish Inquisition. I should know, I'd had to listen to my family retell their take on the Inquisition every year on the Winter Solstice when we traveled between realms to visit those who had permanently crossed into hell.

"Demon, why the fuck aren't you warming up?" Coach Miller called.

I tore my eyes off the door and clenched my jaw as I turned to face the coach. Of all the teachers at the Academy, Coach Miller was the worst. He wasn't just a sadistic asshole, he was horrifying to look at. And I'm a fucking demon. I literally visit Hell every year. Coach Miller even freaked me out.

His lower half was a snake body, while his upper half was that of a man. A roided out man who spent too much time popping supplements and eating raw meat. The veins in his forehead were always bulging, but you were safe as long as the neck vein wasn't throbbing. Like it was starting to do now.

"On my way, coach," I said, trying to sound like I actually respected him. I didn't. Nobody did. That's why he was such a prick. Instead of earning respect, he made us suffer so we were all terrified of him. It was almost enough to sign up to take the trials now and avoid having to spend another hour with him.

I picked up my pace, running faster to meet up with the pack of students in the middle. We did the same warm up every day. Two miles around the track. It was tedious but it was the best part of class because at least while we were warming up, he wasn't trying to kill us.

With every lap, I glanced toward the door, hoping to catch a glimpse of Raven. But as I rounded the final lap, I started to hope she wouldn't arrive. The punishment for missing a class was probably the same as coming late but it would be determined by the dean instead of the coach so it was less likely you'd be fighting giant scorpions or something.

"Hey, Luka," James, the only other incubus at the Academy jogged over to me. "You had a shot with the new girl yet? I saw her at lunch today with the shifters. Whew, man, I'm telling you, I've never gotten such a high from a woman's scent as I have from that little mage. She's got to be a wild one in bed, don't you think?"

Everything inside me felt like it turned molten at James's words. I wanted to rip his throat out for talking about Raven that way. "She's taken."

He lifted a cocky brow and laughed. "Yeah, right. Like you already bagged that one. She's way out of your league. Besides, I'm pretty sure she's shacking up with the wolf's alpha."

"I can assure you, she's off the market. And not because she's fucking a dog," I said as I left the track and headed to the middle of the gym to wait for whatever today's fresh hell would be.

Suddenly, the doors opened and Raven walked in with the Mage twins behind her.

"Fuck, how do those assholes get all the pussy?" James asked.

"Because they're richer than god," another student said.

"Ms. Winters," Coach Miller boomed. "You're late. That was a stupid choice."

"It was my fault, Coach," Matt said. "We sort of caught her on fire last period."

The coach's eye twitched and one nostril flared. His upper lip curled, then he sucked in his lips as if he'd just eaten something sour. "Is that so, Mr. Obscura?"

"She was willing to come straight here and I made her get checked for injury. You know how it would look if an Obscura killed a student before the end of the first semester?"

"Yeah, they usually wait until the trials for that," someone called.

My stomach tightened. Had these two sunk their teeth into my Raven? We shared something. Our time in that dream wasn't just a dream; it was something bigger. When she was around, the whole world stopped.

I was pretty convinced we had a bond, though I wasn't ready to admit that to anyone. My grandparents had come together through a mating bond and when my grandmother died, it took my grandfather down with her. So my parents had been clear about their lack of interest in such a bond. For a demon, it was seen as weakness. But I didn't think I had a choice. The pull to her was too great. If she was my mate, I was willing to do whatever it took to spend as much time as I could with her. Today was supposed to be the day I made that leap. But I was going to have to get rid of the golden boys first.

"You missed warm up so you'll have to work cold," Coach Miller said.

"Thanks, coach," Matt said. "I'll pass your best along to my parents."

"Yeah, why don't you do that," he said. Then he turned to the rest of us. "Circle up. It's combat day."

I moved slowly, keeping an eye on the twins and Raven. The

mage boys left the gym and Raven slowly walked toward the group. I shifted so I could get closer to her but the coach moved next to her, cutting off my access. Frowning, I took a spot in the circle of students.

She was so close to me that I could feel her magic. It called to me like a ritual, sending me the scent of burning sage and garden roses. It didn't make sense how I knew, but I knew it was her. She didn't have this pull to her magic before. Something had changed. My nose twitched as I noticed another scent I was familiar with. Sex. The unmistakable scent of arousal and wetness.

I balled my hands into fists. Those mages were going to have to find their own toys. Raven wasn't one of their flavors of the month. She needed to be worshipped not used and tossed aside.

"Luka, you get to go first today," Coach Miller said. "And why don't you show the little mage how it's done. I don't think we've had a combat since you've arrived, have we?"

Raven shook her head. "No, coach."

Panic surged through me and my heart hammered in my chest. *No.* Combat was dangerous. It wasn't exactly fight to the death as most of us were immortal, but it was damn close. And I'd never fought a mage. I didn't know what they could take. "Coach, she's never even seen combat before."

The coach cocked his head to the side. "I've never known you to turn down a tumble with a member of the opposite sex. Isn't that what you shitty demons live for?"

I glared at him. Like he could talk. I got my magic from pleasure. My own and those I was with. I never forced anyone, and I was damn good at fucking. He was a half snake man with a steroid addiction. Did he even have a penis? Was that what this was? Penis envy?

"You won't do it, I'll find someone else who will," he threatened.

"I'll take a go at her," Remi called.

My insides rumbled in a low growl. I didn't like being threatened, and he knew exactly how to push my buttons. I swear, one day I was going to tear that grin off of his smug face. "Fine."

"Winters, in the ring," he called.

I stepped into the center of the circle of students, my heart falling to the pit of my stomach as Raven lifted her chin and stepped forward. Even as she approached the ring for an unknown combat test, she didn't waver. She didn't let her fear show. But I could smell it on her. And she had every right to be afraid. She should be very, very afraid.

Raven

I balled my hands into fists to keep from trembling, but I was sure they all knew how terrified I was. Lifting my chin high, I did my best to feign confidence as I stepped into the center of the circle.

There were twenty students in matching gym uniforms standing around me and all eyes were on me.

I glanced around, noting the different people. I'd gotten to know some of them during the last few weeks but it was mostly just introductions. Aside from Violet and Luka, there weren't any I'd consider friends. Violet was a gym class only friend and Luka was a dream booty call.

The students seemed to watch me with a bored detachment. Most of them would pass for human at first glance, but a few of them were obviously not human. I suppose I should be lucky that it's Luka I had to fight - at least I think this is a fight - rather than the kid with the spikes coming out of his head and mouth full of sharp fangs. In fact, there were at least six kids with visible fangs. And all of them were baring their teeth at me to show them off.

Coach Miller slithered closer to me and I shuddered. What the hell was he? I mean, a principal with the devil horns was the one thing but a snake man for a gym teacher was worse. Wasn't gym class bad enough as it was? Why throw in a dude who looked like the Rock from the awful *Scorpion King* movie? Except for this guy was half snake instead of half scorpion. It was enough to make you fight to hold down your lunch.

"Shirts or skins?" he asked. "Lady's choice."

"What?" I asked, startled by the question. We weren't playing basketball, and I obviously had breasts so why the hell would I take off my shirt? There were only two of us.

"She wants shirts," Luka said. "Right?"

"Um, yeah," I said, still in shock at the question.

"Next, choose your three," the gym teacher said.

"My three what?" I asked.

"Do I have to spoon feed it to you?" he asked.

"It's her first time," Luka said.

"Well, we all know who's trying to get into the new girls pants," the teacher said.

My cheeks heated. "What the fuck? You can't say shit like that. Besides, I'm not really new anymore."

He laughed. "I can say whatever I want. And you know, for that outburst, I'm going to pick your three."

"Give her a chance," Luka said.

"One more word from you and it's confinement," Coach said. Then he turned to the circle of students and pointed to three kids in front of him. "Garcia, Smith, and Hunt, you're with Ms. Winters."

The three students, all female and all petite like me, moved into the center of the circle. I should have asked for Violet. At least I knew she liked me.

"Lowell, Keller, and Sanchez, you join the Incubus."

Three huge boys moved into the circle. They looked at me as if they were starving and I was the main course. And not in a sexy way. In a they-were-going-to-kill-me way. "Fuck."

"Yeah, thanks a lot stupid mage," one girl behind me said.

"I'm so sorry," I said, not willing to look back at them. We were screwed. "How do we do this? Is it like a point per touch or something?"

"This isn't the human world, noob, it's last person standing."

Luka's brow was furrowed, and he mouthed the word, *sorry* to me. I could feel the tears already brewing behind my eyes. I didn't even know the rules but I had a feeling asking would be worse than just letting it happen, whatever it was.

Luka pulled his shirt off and tossed it aside. A warm flush rose through me and flutters filled my chest. I had almost forgotten how beautiful he was and how badly I wanted to finish what we had started in my dream. Did he remember that? Did he even care? Or was he visiting every woman he could find to fill his appetite?

I shook my head and forced the thought away. Now was not the time to focus on Luka's body. His amazingly chiseled abs or his unrealistically sculpted six-pack. Fuck. I needed to focus. Why was I doing this? The three guys behind Luka fanned out behind him. All of them flexing their biceps as they got into what I could only describe as ready positions. Ready for what though, I had no idea. All I knew was that I should embrace myself for pain.

"Go," the snake guy yelled.

I glanced behind me to see the three girls backing away from me and when I turned back to look at Luka, he was advancing.

The other three behind him waited, teeth bared. I could almost sense the bloodlust coming from them. It filled the air with a tension that was palpable. Everyone here wanted this. They wanted to see the fight. They were hungry for it.

Everyone except for me.

My heart pounded so loudly in my ears it nearly drowned out the cheers of the students gathered around me. Sweat formed on my brow. Everything seemed to be moving in slow motion.

No, strike that. Not seemed to be. It was.

Holding my breath, I focused on the sound. It had slowed to a roar like an ocean wave, the surrounding students nearly frozen in place as they moved so slowly I had to pay attention to notice it.

I moved my hand out in front of me. I was moving at normal speed. Or at least it appeared that way.

Luka was still moving toward me, though it would take him an hour to reach me at his current pace. Confused, I walked toward him and waved my hand in front of his face. He didn't react. He either wasn't aware of this happening or he was moving too slowly to register the change.

Why was this happening? Did I make this happen or was it someone else? It didn't seem to be Luka's doing since he was trapped in the same slow motion as everyone else.

What if I made this happen? What if we were stuck like this forever? My chest tightened and my tongue felt thick in my mouth. This wasn't supposed to happen. What if I fucked every-thing up?

I glanced around the room and then made a decision. As panic clawed its way through my insides, I raced toward the doors. I had to find out if the rest of the school was stuck like this or if it was only the gym class.

The halls were empty and all the classroom doors were closed. I hesitated in front of a classroom, wondering if I should open the door but fear prevented me from tugging it open. What if the professor wasn't moving in slow motion and they punished me for walking into their class?

Since I'd arrived, the threat of confinement had been dangled over me along with the looming sense of dread that I would fail and be sent somewhere worse than here.

Fuck. I had no good options.

Feeling defeated, I ran back toward the gym and burst through the doors to find everyone standing in a loose group, glaring at me.

"You. Confinement. Now." Coach Miller slithered toward me, a vein throbbing in his bulging neck.

I swallowed hard. "It was an accident, I swear."

"Manipulating time is forbidden," he said. "I don't even know how you managed it, but you'll wait in confinement until the enforcers arrive. With any luck, your magic will be removed by sunset."

"What?" I cried out. "I just got here. And I didn't even know that was a thing. The time thing or the magic removal or the whole fact that I could even do that."

"It was my fault," Luka said. "She didn't manipulate time, I did it."

"Nice try, Demon," Coach Miller said. He grabbed my arm and pulled me toward the door. "I knew there was something weird about you."

"It'll be okay," Luka said.

I wanted to believe him. I needed to believe him. But right now, I was having trouble seeing how that could happen. This had to be the worst gym class ever.

Raven

Confinement wasn't exactly what I expected after all the threats. I had imagined a dark cell lined with bars and the sound of dripping water.

What I hadn't imagined was a small white room with a single white upholstered chair. It was more like the waiting room of a hospital than the scary place they warned me about.

I paced the room for a bit, my hair blowing into my face every time I walked past the overly efficient air conditioner. Goosebumps rose on my legs from the chill in the air.

Every time I completed the tiny circle in the room, I passed the white chair. It seemed to call to me. As if it wanted me to sit on it, but something about it also repelled me. Warning me to avoid it. It was just a chair but then again, this place wasn't just a school. Now that I'd had a taste of magic, on several different levels, I was wary of everything.

Besides, if I didn't have my instincts, what else did I have?

The door opened, and I turned to see Dr. Green filling the doorframe. His fangs looked even more threatening when he was scowling.

"It was a mistake, I swear, I didn't even know I could do that let alone that it was illegal, I just didn't want to get my ass kicked, you know?" I said.

He held up his hand, and I stopped talking. He lingered in the doorway, not leaving the apparent safety of the open door. He looked even more uncomfortable than I felt.

"There's someone here to see you," he said. "I'm afraid this is out of my hands."

"But it was an accident, you have to believe me." I wasn't even sure why I was fighting so hard to keep my magic. I'd only had it for a short time and I didn't even know if I wanted it.

Something had shifted in me in that time. Now that I'd felt it, it was like another limb. The idea of it being cut from me was terrifying. I wasn't sure when the change happened or why I'd suddenly embraced it as part of me, but it was. It was part of me the same as my legs or arms or heart. Without it, I no longer knew who I was.

Granted, I didn't know who the hell I was with it, either. I just knew I had to defend it.

"Follow me," he said.

Without a word, I exited the strange room and as soon as I left, I felt like a weight had been lifted from me and I gasped. It was as if I had been under water and I finally got a breath of fresh air. It didn't feel that way inside the room, but now that I was out, I knew something had been restraining me.

"It's the magic in there," the dean said. "The longer you're in there, the longer your magic is quelled."

"What do you mean by that?" I asked.

"Ten minutes in there will result in no magic for about an hour after you leave the room. You can do the math from there," he said, not even turning to look back at me.

I felt for my magic, something I'd grown accustomed to doing over my time here at the academy. He was right, it wasn't there. Not even a shadow of my magic was there. My stomach twisted into knots as panic welled up inside me. I felt empty, different, fragile.

No wonder I didn't want my magic removed. It was an odd sensation. As if a hole was cut into you and part of your essence was just gone.

I shuddered. Not wanting to think about the possibility of this being my new normal.

We walked through the institutional hallways that made up the underbelly of the school. More white walls, more white tile, more florescent lights. Metal doors lined the hall not unlike the classrooms above but these maintained the hospital like feeling the rest of the detention area held.

Finally, we stopped in front of one of the doors and Dr. Green opened the door. "I'll collect you here when you're finished."

"You're not coming in with me?" I asked, feeling small. The imposing demon was the last person I'd expected to latch on to but at least he was somewhat familiar.

"I'll return for you," he said.

I nodded, then entered the room to find a square table with a folding chair on either side. It was a mother fucking interrogation room. Why the hell did they have this in a school?

Plain white walls surrounded us and I half expected to see a two-way mirror like in the movies. There wasn't one, but that didn't mean nobody was listening. I was sure there was magic that could eliminate the need for a human invention like a two-way mirror.

One chair was occupied by a rather severe looking woman. She had black hair pulled up into a sleek bun on top of her head. Her features were pointed and sharp. She didn't stand when I arrived, but I could tell from her stature in the chair that she was tiny. Probably not even five feet tall. "Sit."

Despite her small size, she packed an air of authority in her demeanor that made me comply.

I took the seat across from her and folded my arms on the table in front of me. My stomach felt like lead and waves of nausea rolled through me. I hadn't even been this nervous on the night I'd arrived and been stuck in Dr. Green's office.

"You're in big trouble, Ms. Winters," the woman said.

"That's what they keep telling me," I said.

She lifted her eyebrows. "You don't think you're in trouble?"

"Look." I set my hand down flat on the table. "I'm new to this whole magic thing. I'm still trying to figure this all out. And there's not exactly a guide book or list of rules somewhere to help me out."

"You're telling me that as a time wielder, you never knew your magic was illegal?" She leaned forward. "I thought for sure that was why you were in hiding."

"What are you talking about? You can't hide from something you don't even know exists."

"You're very good," she said. "I almost believe you. And I almost feel bad."

"Feel bad for what?" I asked as my heart picked up pace.

Something was going on here. Something very, very bad. I scooted the chair back a little, suddenly not wanting to be so close to this tiny woman.

She stood and locked her eyes on me. She was even shorter than I originally thought. Suddenly, she began mumbling words I couldn't make out and her hair lifted as if drawn away from her head by static electricity. Her eyes glowed blue and tiny bursts of lightning traveled down her arms.

"What the fuck?" I scrambled off the chair so quickly I knocked it over and it clattered to the ground.

"By the sacred service of the hunters, I sentence you to death," she said.

Instinctively, I tried to summon fire the way I had last time I'd been threatened. Nothing happened. Of course nothing happened. The stupid confinement room had drained everything.

I backed toward the wall as the woman moved closer to me. "I promise I won't do it again."

"I can't afford to have you ruining my plans." Her voice came out fuzzy and crackling with electricity. She was like a storm in the flesh.

My hair stood on end, rising from my arms and floating around my head. The whole room felt like it was charged and ready to explode. This was not how I imagined I'd die. A surge of fear spiked through me, sending my adrenaline into overdrive and I felt a sudden burst of energy. *Not today.*

I shifted to the side of the room, moving out of her path.

The woman's eyes turned to me and she adjusted her position, moving toward me with slow purpose. "You're only delaying the inevitable. I killed your parents and I'll kill you, too."

"You're insane. My parents died in a car accident." I moved again, into the corner, slowly sidestepping toward the door.

"That's what they told that mundane aunt of yours. I wasn't

sure you'd survived until I felt the surge of your magic. It's a shame that your bloodline must end."

This woman was bat shit crazy. And apparently, she was also a mass murderer. I inched toward the door, getting closer with every step. She wasn't in a hurry to kill me, apparently as she continued to move toward me with her slow, careful steps. I wondered if it was taking all of her energy to channel the lightning that was now encasing her whole body. She was like a walking science experiment. A woman trapped in a ball of unstable electricity. I had a feeling it wouldn't end well for me if the two of us made contact. Especially while my magic was absent.

I was finally at the door and slowly I moved my hand to the doorknob and turned. To my surprise, the door opened a crack. I threw it open and took a breath of freedom before a jolt shot through me sending pain into every part of my body. I fell to the ground, screaming.

The stranger was looking down on me now, a wicked smile on her lips. "You thought you could flee? Your parents were the most powerful mages in a century and I bested them. You're untrained with untamed magic. You don't stand a chance."

Blackness blurred around the edges of my vision and my breathing was ragged and difficult. Everything hurt. I tried to move, but I wasn't able to control my limbs. I turned my head to the side and realized I was partially in the hallway. I'd been so close to freedom.

I screamed as bursts of sharp pain circled my ankles and I was dragged back into the room. I heard the door slam behind me. Fighting to gain control of my body, I gritted my teeth and tried to move. Nothing happened.

Tears rolled down my cheeks. I wasn't ready to die. Especially not by a monster that had just confessed that she had killed my parents. Heat surged through my chest, fueled by anger. I embraced it, willing it to grow. I was not going to die lying down. I was not going to die by a madwoman's magic. I had to live.

Ben

Professor Luna droned on and on until the words were just a hum of noise inside my head. Usually, I was interested in the hunting and survival techniques we learned about in class, but today I couldn't focus. All I could think of was Raven's long hair, her soft skin, her warm mouth…

My wolf let out a low growl that vibrated deep in my chest. He wanted her too. Somehow, I was going to have to convince her I wasn't an asshole. I didn't know anything about romance or how to woo a woman. They usually came to me, we had our fun, and we went our separate ways. Sex wasn't a big deal. It was stress relief, a way to pass the time. But Raven, she wasn't a way to pass the time. She was the one I wanted to spend all my time with.

Suddenly, a scream broke through the room. Shrill and laced with pure fear. It shot right through me, sending a jolt of terror deep into my soul. My wolf prickled inside me, poised for an attack.

I jumped up and looked around, trying to find the source of the sound.

The class looked at me, confusion painted on their expressions.

"Nobody else heard that?" I asked.

"Mr. Lucia, please have a seat," Professor Luna said.

I tensed, my whole body on alert. "I heard a scream."

Suddenly, another scream broke through the silence, vibrating within me. I watched the unchanged expression on my professor's face. He really couldn't hear it.

My chest tightened as realization snapped into place. The scream was meant for me. Raven was in trouble. "I'm sorry. I have to go."

I knocked over my chair in my rush out of the room but didn't stop to pick it up. Running at full pace, I exploded out of the door, hitting the hallway at a sprint.

My wolf howled in anger as he clawed at my insides. With every step, I could feel Raven's pain, her fear. I pushed harder, pumping my arms. When my wolf fought to break free, I didn't resist.

I ran on all fours, my wolf leading the way toward Raven, following her scent and the pull of her fear. The hallway flew by in a blur and I didn't let thinking get in the way of the turns and twists my wolf made. We were sometimes at odds, but not when it came to her. Raven called to both of us and if I had any hope of getting to her in time, I had to give in to my wolf.

In my wolf form, my ears prickled as another scream broke through the silence of the halls. I wasn't sure if I was hearing her for real or through the bond we held. I didn't really care as long as I could find her.

Lifting my nose into the air, I sniffed, searching for any traces of her scent. My fur stood on end when I caught it and I lunged down the hall. Everything passed in a blur as I wound down stairs and through hallways toward my mate.

I couldn't hear her anymore and the silence was more painful than listening to her scream. At least if she was screaming, I knew she was alive. The silence was deafening.

A coppery scent filled my nose. Blood. Raven's blood. It didn't matter how I knew but I did. Baring my teeth, I growled as I charged toward the scent.

As I turned the corner, I caught sight of an open door and Raven on the ground. A woman I didn't recognize was standing over her.

I charged.

The stranger hit me with a bolt of electricity that sizzled through me, sending me flying backward away from Raven. I landed hard on the ground, smacking my head on the tile floor. Stunned, I stood up on shaky legs. The blast had sent my wolf away somehow. That shouldn't be possible. What magic was she using?

The room swayed or maybe I did. But I wasn't about to quit on her. "Leave her alone."

"My fight is not with you, shifter," the woman said.

"A fight with my mate is a fight with me," I said.

The woman's brow furrowed. "Foolish child, you don't understand what you're saying. You hit your head too hard."

I growled, clenching my hands into fists. She could say all she wanted, but it didn't excuse the fact that she'd tried to hurt Raven. For that, she was going to die.

I ran toward her, emitting a war cry as I charged her.

Blue sparks flashed across my vision before they hit me. I screamed in agony. It felt like every nerve was on fire. Panting, I fought against the onslaught. She wasn't going to bring me down. I could fight her.

My knees gave, and I fell to the ground. The edges of my vision went black, and I struggled to remain upright. "Run, Raven." I wasn't sure if I said the words aloud or if they were in my head.

Then, everything went still, the blue sparks hitting my chest were frozen in place. No, not frozen, they moved slightly just as I was moving slightly. I could think and feel, but I couldn't make myself move.

In a blink of an eye, I hit the ground, the blue sparks gone.

Raven

Her attention was on Ben instead of me. Using all of my strength, I tried to call to him, to tell him to flee, but I couldn't make words form.

Desperate, I rolled to my stomach and pushed myself up. Anger seethed in my gut, swirling and twisting like an old friend. I welcomed it, called to it, encouraged it. The feeling bloomed into my chest, filling me with throbbing power unlike anything I had ever felt before. It came as a comfort and it came with a request. It wanted to be unleashed.

The crazy mage ignited her sparks and Ben fell to his knees.

"No!" The energy swirling in me propelled me to my feet, moving me forward, beckoning me. Extending my arms, I released it, aiming the full force of it at Ben's attacker.

Once again, time slowed to a near stop.

But there was something else happening this time.

I could feel a sense of control I hadn't last time. Something had shifted. Lifting my hand into the air, I imagined controlling the other mage. Turning her so her vile blue lightning struck the wall instead of Ben.

Her body shifted, turning as if she were a pawn on a chess board, moving to my will.

The dark, swirling anger inside jumped a little, thrilled by the new discovery. But it wasn't enough.

Imagining I was holding a pop can, I closed my hand, as if to crush it with the motion. The mage crumpled to the ground, her lightening cut off by my action. She was helpless now. She couldn't hurt anyone anymore.

Dizzy, I let up on the magic, letting go of the power as I leaned against a wall. I squinted toward Ben, who was starting to move on the floor. He was okay.

Letting out a strained breath, I slid down the wall until I was on the cold ground. Ben scrambled toward the fallen mage and pressed his fingers to her neck. He looked up at me. "She's got a pulse."

"What happened?" Dr. Green was in the hallway, taking in the aftermath with wide eyes.

"She attacked us," I said.

He shook his head. "That doesn't make any sense."

"Well, she told me she'd killed my parents for their magic and then she tried to kill me."

Dr. Green's hands balled into fists and his jaw tensed. If I weren't so tired, I might have been concerned about his body language. But there wasn't enough energy left for me to move, let alone worry about what was going to happen from here. Maybe he'd ship me away to that prison they threatened me with. Maybe they'd just kill me on the spot. Who knows, maybe he'd even called this crazy bitch here to kill me.

The dean turned to Ben. "You should shift. You'll heal faster."

Ben's throat bobbed. "I can't."

"What do you mean, you can't?" Dr. Green asked.

He shook his head. "I tried that already. Whatever she did to me, it must have done something to my wolf. I can't shift."

Dr. Green turned to look at me. "What did she do?"

"Me? I stopped time again. I didn't have a choice. And I'd do it again," I said.

"Wait, you can control time?" Ben asked. "That was you?"

I nodded.

"No, not that. What did this," Dr. Green tapped his toe on her side, "mage do?"

"She had lightning of some kind. It was blue," I said. "Hurt like hell."

"She got me with it, too," Ben said.

Dr. Green let out a heavy sigh. "She's a thief."

"Please tell me you mean she's here to steal a painting," Ben said.

Dr. Green shook his head. "No."

"What's a thief doing here? And how did she get in?" Ben asked.

"Someone clue me in here," I said.

Ben turned to me. "It's a creature we don't like to talk about."

"Half mage, half demon. It has the ability to siphon off and build complex magic from other creatures," Dr. Green added.

"She said she killed my parents." I looked up at the Dean, fresh anger growing in the pit of my stomach. "Did she take their magic?"

A vein in Dr. Green's forehead throbbed. "I'm guessing she did. And it's probably how she was able to trace you here."

"So that's it, though, right? She's caught and she'll be executed," Ben said. "Then we get our magic back?"

"What do you mean *back*?" I asked. "I used magic."

"Shadow magic," Ben said. "I saw it. It's broken, unstable."

I scrubbed my face with my hand. Just when I thought I was starting to figure this all out, it got even more complicated.

"So now what?" I asked.

"Now we begin the healing process," Dr. Green said. "And we train you on your time magic without you getting caught. You're going to attract a whole lot of thieves if word is out about you. You'll need to be able to defend yourself."

Several men dressed in black ran down the corridor. I flinched, recognizing those uniforms. The people who arrested me and dragged me here wore those uniforms.

"I'm not going to magic jail," I said, forcing myself to standing with a groan.

"You're not leaving here," Dr. Green said. "You were sent as my charge by someone with more clearance than I have. That means, there's someone else out there who knows you're here and is looking out for you."

"My scholarship?" I asked. "Where was this mysterious benefactor when I was struggling to survive?"

The magic cops stopped in front of Dr. Green and saluted. That was new. Who the hell was this headmaster to get them to treat him like that?

"Sir, we await your orders," one of them called.

Dr. Green pointed to my attacker. "We've got ourselves a thief. A powerful one as far as I can tell. Question her. Find out everything she knows. How she got in here, who her contacts are. Get everything you can from her by any means necessary."

I shivered at the tone in his voice. It reminded me never to cross Dr. Green again. There was a lot more to him than I originally thought.

"You two, back to your rooms. I'll deal with both of you later," Dr. Green said.

"I'll walk you back," Ben said, offering his hand.

Still feeling uneasy on my feet, I accepted it. As soon as our fingers touched, heat surged through me and tingles spread up my thighs. My breath hitched and I turned to him in surprise. Despite my exhaustion, I was half tempted to take his clothes off right here.

Startled, I let go of his hand.

Ben smirked. "Now you know how I've been feeling around you."

"Why did you come for me?" I asked.

"Because you were in trouble," he said.

"How did you know?" I asked.

"We have a bond," he said. "A connection."

"What does that mean, exactly?" I asked.

"It means that one day soon, I'm going to claim you as mine."

My cheeks heated and I could almost feel what it would be like to have his hot breath on my skin.

"All that's going to have to wait," Dr. Green said. "We have bigger problems."

In front of us, the room flickered as if it weren't real. As if it were on a bad television screen.

"What's going on?" I asked.

"This is what happens when an entire building is held in a time stop and they didn't know it had a basement."

The flickering stopped abruptly and the three of us darted down the hall. Ahead, the magic police were on the ground.

The thief was gone.

To Be Continued

BROKEN
MAGIC

SPECIAL EDITION COLLECTION
BOOK 2

ALEXIS CALDER

CHAPTER 1

RAVEN

Nobody even tried to mask their whispers as I slowly entered the cafeteria. The nurse in the school clinic had insisted on keeping me for observation until the end of the week. They had hoped my magic would return by Monday.

Here we were, Monday morning.

No magic.

I've been dreading this since last night when I realized I'd have to return here to try to figure this out. The only thing that kept me going was seeing Makayla and finding out how Ben was doing. They'd kept me locked down in the hospital wing. And they didn't even have television. It was three days with textbooks as my only company.

My whole body relaxed as I saw Makayla and I flagged her down, a smile on my face. At least she looked the same. Hopefully none of this impacted her. I could deal with the rumors, whatever they were, and the stares, if I had a few people in my corner.

Makayla sprinted toward me, pulling me into an unexpected hug.

"I was so worried about you, and they wouldn't let me in to visit. The rumors are crazy. Did you really break out of confinement and kill a school guard?"

I broke away from the embrace and stared at her wide eyed. "Seriously? Kill a guard?"

She shrugged. "Wouldn't be the first time."

"I knew this place was dangerous, but students have killed guards?"

"Once or twice," she said. "They said it was an accident."

"Well, I didn't kill a guard," I said.

"So, the other rumor is true?" She lowered her voice. "The one about the magic thief?" She shuddered. "I was hoping that wasn't the case. They creep me the fuck out."

"Didn't Ben talk to you?" I asked.

"He's kept to himself. He's not really talking to anyone, I mean, he's really being hard on himself about you getting hurt."

"That wasn't his fault. If anything, he's the one who saved me from worse. I lost my magic, but I'm alive." My throat bobbed as I realized I wasn't sure how much worse it could be. I was stuck in a magic school without magic. Just the hope that it would return *soon.* Whatever that meant.

"Hey, little mage," Remi said as he strode up to me. "I heard you took out a magic thief or a guard. Either way, you're more of a badass than I thought. Hope there's no hard feelings about the other day."

"Um, sure, yeah," I said.

He winked. "Looking forward to seeing you around."

"Alright, enough of that," Makayla said. "Come on."

She grabbed my upper arm and dragged me toward the food line. "I'm sure you need something to eat. Full day of classes ahead and all."

I walked with her but looked over my shoulder at Remi.

He was still smiling at me. It was an odd turn of events. A few weeks ago, he was threatening me. Now he was offering to be my friend. This really was a weird school. The fact that I'd beat someone up had gained me some positive attention. I guess it wasn't all that different from prison in that sense.

The only difference was, it wasn't how I wanted to gain attention. And at this moment, I knew my magic wasn't responding. So, for now, I was a badass but as soon as I had to demonstrate something, everyone would know I was a fraud.

I had to figure out a way to get my magic back.

"Welcome back, little mage," one of the sirens called as I walked past their table. I could feel their eyes boring into me, but I kept my gaze on my tray of food.

"Thanks," I said, without turning back to them.

Makayla took us to the usual table but none of the others were here. Just us. "Where is everyone? I asked.

"They already ate. I waited. Hoping you'd come," she said.

She was a good friend. Possibly the best I'd ever had, which didn't say much for my life prior to this place.

"Thank god you're back," a female voice called.

I turned away from my eggs to see Violet walking toward me, another female vampire behind her. Both were dressed in matching black skirts and white shirts, their ties hanging loosely around their necks.

Violet's nearly white hair was pulled into a ponytail high on her head. She'd lined her eyes with dark eyeliner and wore bright red lipstick. It made her pale skin look almost translucent. She had an ethereal kind of beauty I imagined was only possible for a vampire to achieve.

The woman behind her had tan skin and wide, deep brown eyes. Her short black hair was in a perfect bob that looked like it belonged in a rendition of *The Great Gatsby*. Just like Violet, she was equally stunning.

Everyone here was gorgeous. Was that another thing that magic did? I thought back to my own teenage years. I'd literally never had a single pimple. Had to be the magic. And, honestly, as superficial as it was, it was another good reason to get it back.

"Gym class has been the absolute worst without you," Violet said.

I groaned. I forgot that I had to go to gym today. I'd been so fixated on not having any magic and wondering what everyone else was doing while I was stuck in the hospital that I didn't think about it. I guess it was better that way. All my time was focused on other things besides the new ways Coach Miller would try to kill me.

How was he going to react to me returning after he's the one who sent me to confinement in the first place? Was that going to make it even worse?

"I really don't want to go back to that class," I said.

"Eh, I don't even think he noticed you we're missing. He's had us running laps every day since then while he lifts in the corner. I think he's bulking up for some Mr. Universe or something."

"They have that here?" I asked.

"Oh yeah, you should see some of the shifters and other creatures bulked up," Violet said. "It's bizarre and hard to look away."

"And incredibly unattractive," Scarlett added. "Can we not discuss this before we've had our blood?"

"Fine," Violet said. "Bae gets cranky when she's hungry."

"Ugh," Scarlett rolled her eyes, "I hate it when you call me that."

"You're cute when you're mad, though," Violet said.

"Alright, the rest of us are trying to eat without having a healthy relationship thrown in our faces," Makayla said.

"See you later, Raven," Violet said.

I waved as the two vampires wandered away. "They're adorable in a terrifying way."

"Yes, they are," Makayla agreed. "You going to eat your bacon?"

"Hell yes, I am," I said, grabbing it off my plate. "Do you know what they fed me in the hospital? Oatmeal. Three days of oatmeal for breakfast and broth for dinner."

Makayla laughed. "I remember that. I was in there once when I broke my arm. Doesn't seem to matter why you're in there, it's all treated the same. Do some magic to heal you, give you oatmeal for breakfast."

"Hopefully, I'll stay out of there from now on," I said.

"Don't count on it," Makayla said. "Come finals at the end of the semester, most of us will spend at least one night there."

"How come?" I knew it was generally dangerous at this school, but what exactly did I have to look forward to for finals?

"Mock trials," she said. "Every year before the Yule Ball they set up a practice trial and we all test it out. If you fail, you're probably not ready for the real deal. If you pass, they expect you to sign up for the trial in the spring. When you fail, usually it's because something is broken. That's how I snapped my arm last year."

My stomach flipped as a wave of queasiness rolled through my gut. *Snapped.* That wasn't a word one used lightly. "What happened to *snap* your arm?"

"Climbing over a pit full of jagged rocks. You'd think the rocks were the real issue, but I made it over those. Got a little cocky and took the downhill too fast. Tumbled and fell all the way to the soft grass on the other side." She shook her head. "I basically celebrated that I finished too early and got cocky. Not going to happen this year, though. I should pass it. And when I do, I'm signing up for the spring trials. I'll be out of here by June if I play my cards right."

"Then what? Where will you go next?" I realized I didn't know anything about what life for a supernatural was like beyond these walls. Dr. Green had mentioned that my file would help me find jobs but what the hell did that mean?

"My parents own a gem supplier. We own some mines and import and sell diamonds and precious stones to some of the most prestigious jewelers in the world. It's not the most exciting, but I'll probably step in line and join the family business." She shrugged.

"Diamonds?" My jaw dropped. I knew the students here were loaded but if her family owned mines and sold gems, they were probably the wealthiest people I had ever met. I'd never even touched an actual diamond aside from my mom's engagement ring. Of course, it never made it to me. My aunt hawked it at a pawn shop within a few years of me moving in with her.

I shook my head, not wanting to think about my past. My parents were gone, my aunt was gone. I didn't have to deal with that part of my life anymore.

"It sounds glamorous, but I promise you, it's not," she said. "Hey, if you need a job after school, I'm sure I can hook you up. We employ several mages. They help us know which land to buy and where to dig."

"Wow," I said, a flicker of hope filling my chest. It was dashed quickly, and I frowned. "Though, I have to get my magic back first."

"It'll come back," Makayla said. "Have faith."

Ben

I wanted nothing more than to know that Raven was safe, but I was dreading seeing her in class today. My wolf wasn't responding and I was worried about what the thief had done to her.

They sent me to the hospital after the incident but kicked me out after a few hours. No matter what I did, I couldn't get in to see Raven. The last several days had been non-stop research into what to do about a shifter who can't shift.

It was terrifying not feeling my inner wolf. It was as if it was completely gone. The emptiness was awful. Like part of me died and yet I had to stay living with both the guilt and emptiness of that vacancy.

Raven had to be going through the same thing if her magic was also missing. But I didn't know yet. Nobody would tell me. So here I was, sitting and waiting in Magical Theory, hoping for some sign that she was okay.

When she walked through the door, her scent hit me like a slap on the face. I didn't even have to look up to see her. I knew it was her. My heart leaped and breathed a sigh of relief. She was safe, at least that I knew.

I still wanted her, with everything I was, but I couldn't have her.

I knew I had to resist. I wasn't good for her. I wasn't good for anyone. The visit from my father the night after the Thief attacked was reminder enough of why I needed to stay away from her.

My family was rich and powerful, that was true. But I was the first student in my family to gain entry to this school. Partially because they didn't used to allow shifters but mostly because the work my family did wasn't legal. None of it. Even the legit businesses were fronts for shady things.

But somehow, my dad had managed to pull strings. And he was deadly serious about me being the upstanding representative of the family he needed. With me gaining a diploma from the Academy of the Elites, it raised our status. Gave him entry to things he was previously barred from.

Plus, it was my only shot at getting away from the family and following my own path. Me going full legit made my dad look better so he was on board. But for that to happen, I couldn't afford to get kicked out. I had to pass the trials and I had to graduate.

If I didn't, well, my dad had a way of making things that hurt his business disappear and I wasn't so sure being his only son was protection enough for me.

I couldn't add that to Raven's plate. I couldn't drag her into all of this. Especially if I went down. My dad was already blaming her enough as it was. I'd chased after some girl and it cost me the ability to shift.

The only way I got him to stop threatening her was to agree to avoid her. There was no way I was going to tell him she was my mate. And mate or no, I couldn't be with her.

Raven's eyes locked on mine and a smile formed on her lips. My heart pounded against my ribs. It would have been easier if she was mad at me. Easier if she yelled at me and told me to stay away. Instead, she was walking right toward me.

"Ben, I was so worried," she said.

I waved my hand. "Nothing to worry about here."

Her brow furrowed, clearly reading my attempt at nonchalance. I wasn't doing the best job of not letting her get to me. Her honeydew scent made my temperature rise and my pulse raced. I shouldn't be feeling this kind of a reaction to her with my wolf dormant. How was she getting to me this much?

"Thank you for what you did in there," she said. "I'm so glad you weren't hurt."

"I was in the right place at the right time," I said, the words killing me. I wanted to touch her, pull her against me, check her body for any damage done by the Thief's lightning. I could feel my desire clawing against my chest, begging for release.

"You came for me," she said. "I know you did, and I don't know how I can repay you."

"No need," I said. "Class is going to start."

She frowned, a look of heartbreak in her eyes. It made my chest tighten. It took all of my willpower not to take it all back. I'd dismissed her heartlessly. She'd never forgive me for this. But it was better than her life being in danger. It was the only way.

Raven

I blinked back the stinging tears as I turned away from Ben. He had to be facing the loss of his shifter magic. There was no way he'd act this way toward me if not for that. He must hate me. If not for me, he'd be whole. Complete. I'd caused too much damage. I wasn't worth it.

I sat in the desk a few seats away from him and tugged my notebook out of my backpack. Going through the motions of taking notes and focusing on the lecture might help. At least it would get my mind off the heartache that weighed on my chest.

Somehow, I had to make it up to him but right now, I didn't

know how to do that. I'd give him space, and in time, maybe he'd forgive me. There was no other option. I couldn't imagine a life without him in it. He had to forgive me. Without him, it felt like there was an empty place inside of me that I couldn't explain.

Guilt. It had to be, right? Because we hardly knew each other and yet, he'd risked his life for me. And now he wasn't talking to me. I wiped a stray tear and opened my notebook.

"Hey, Raven, how was confinement? Did they do things to you down there?" someone called.

I looked up, brow furrowed, trying to find the offender.

"Hey, leave the girl alone. She's not worth your time. We all know any mage worth her salt wouldn't be slumming it with the shifters," a male voice called.

I spun around to find a guy I didn't know, feet up on his desk, a lazy smile on his lips.

"Any of those shifters are worth more than you any day," I said.

"We all know you're staying in the shifter dorm," A girl nearby said. "We've heard all about their weird orgies. I'm sure you're tainted by now."

"Um, what?" My brow furrowed. "You can't be serious."

"Shifter whore," someone called.

Rage simmered inside, the pulsing fiery kind of rage that previously would have resulted in me risking my magic. But nothing came. I reached for it, wanting nothing more than to throw a ball of fire. I wanted to shut them up. But my magic wasn't there.

Gritting my teeth, I turned to find whoever had said that, ready to give them a piece of my mind if nothing else.

A growl sounded behind me and a flash of fur passed alongside me as a massive wolf leaped over the desks.

It stopped in front of the male mage, hackles back, teeth bared. Low, threatening growls emanated from the beast.

The mage cowered. "I'm so sorry. I didn't mean it. I was just messing with her, you know, haze the new kid."

My nostrils flared as I took deep breaths. A mixture of rage and panic warred within me, each fighting for dominance. Trying to channel more of the rage, I clenched my fists and walked toward the offending mage. "You had no right. You don't even know me and I'm not even that new anymore."

The wolf growled and I could sense Ben under the fur and teeth. He felt a little different, but he was still in there. I set my hand on his side, feeling the wiry yet soft fur under my fingertips. "It's okay. He's not worth it. I don't want you in confinement for a worm like him."

"She's right," the mage was shaking now. "I'm not worth it."

The wolf snapped at him and the mage screamed. Then I noticed the front of his pants were wet.

"He pissed himself," someone called. The whole class started laughing and the mage bolted, nearly running into Professor Hurd on his way out.

The professor spun around, following the mage out the door. "Martin?"

"Shift back," I urged. Professor Hurd was distracted. "Shift back before he sees you, please."

I stroked the wolf's fur and tried to model calm for him. The creature whined and looked at me, pleading in its eyes.

My brow furrowed. I could almost see Ben in those eyes. "Shift back."

The wolf relaxed and then shook his head. A moment later, Ben was laying where the wolf had been.

I let out a sigh of relief.

Ben's uniform was disheveled, but at least he was clothed. I wasn't sure how that all worked until just then. Everything the night the thief attacked had happened so quickly the details blurred together.

"Why are we not in our seats and ready to learn?" Professor Hurd asked.

"You okay?" I asked Ben.

He nodded, then turned away from me, his expression impassive.

My heart ached at how quickly I'd been dismissed. How impersonal that expression was. But he'd shifted to come to my rescue. That had to mean he didn't really want to cut me out, right?

I shouldn't feel so worried about him not wanting to be my friend, but it hurt thinking he didn't want me around. I couldn't explain it. I needed him. At least there was a flicker of hope in his fast shift and rush to my defense.

It was like the Thief's attack all over again. I guess some girls had guardian angels looking after them. I had a broody, angry wolf shifter.

As I settled into my seat, I smiled to myself. Something told me he'd be there for me when I really needed him. Whatever he was going through, he needed time and space. I'd give him that and soon enough, he'd come around.

I tried not to think about Ben while Professor Hurd droned on and on about the theory of using portals for transportation to other realms. I still hadn't quite wrapped my head around the fact that there was magic in the realm I did live in. I wasn't sure I was ready to think about other realms with other kinds of magic.

"Before all of you were born, the realm to Faerie was sealed and any of the Fair Folk who lived in our realm were forced to choose between staying here with the lives they'd created or returning back to Faerie. That's why so few Fae remain in our realm and why their magic is so prized," Professor Hurd said.

I tried to take notes, I tried to focus but my head was spinning. Ben kept finding his way into my thoughts. Especially the image of him on the night we played strip poker. Why had I turned him down? I was seriously regretting that now.

It seemed if I wanted to get in his pants, I was going to have to wait for him to figure out whatever he was dealing with. Which was fine. I'd sworn off men for now, right?

"Portals can be dangerous for even the most experienced magic user and they should never be attempted by a beginner. I'd say usually they require a few centuries of practice before someone is really ready so if anyone ever invites you to join them though a portal, check their credentials," Professor Hurd said.

I wrote down *portals bad* in my notebook. This wasn't helpful. I wanted to learn how to get my magic back and unless a portal was going to get me there, I wasn't interested.

That's when it struck me. Ben had shifted. His shifter magic was back. Just like that, it came back to him. How did he do that? What changed? Or had he never lost his magic at all? I had to talk to him. I had to know.

I scribbled random words on the page until the end of class, not even hearing anything. My focus on Ben had shifted too. Instead of wondering about him in inappropriate ways, I had to find out how he'd used his magic.

"Don't forget, we'll have a quiz over portals on Friday so start reviewing your notes right away. Study session Wednesday night after dinner," Professor Hurd called.

The sound of zippers and shuffling papers filled the room as everyone prepared to go to their next class. I tossed my stuff in my backpack and turned back to where Ben was sitting but he'd already left. I looked toward the door and he was in the line of students pushing their way out.

"Ben, hold up," I called.

I darted between the desks trying to catch him.

"Ms. Winters, wait please," Professor Hurd said as he locked his eyes on mine.

Shit. If I wasn't making eye contact, I could have pretended I hadn't heard him, but I wasn't going to be able to pull that off. Forcing a smile on my lips I walked over to his desk. "Yes, professor?"

He adjusted his glasses, his huge eyes staring back at me. It was unnerving and a chill ran down my spine. Something about him just never sat right with me. He seemed harmless enough. Aside from being old and having no concept of modern reality, he couldn't possibly cause me any damage. He was frail and his face looked like worn leather. His hands were lined with blue veins, clearly visible through his paper-thin skin.

"I've been meaning to talk to you," he said. "I know you were in confinement, which can result in a dulling of a mage's magic. Are you experiencing any symptoms?"

I frowned. Surely the nurse had communicated my total lack of magic to my teachers. "There was more than just the confinement. Did you not hear?"

He adjusted his glasses. "Oh yes, the thief. Very exciting stuff, that. I would have liked to meet one in real life. The way they draw their power from others is fascinating." He paused as his brows lifted. "Oh."

"Yeah, oh," I said.

He leaned against the desk. "How much did she take?"

My throat bobbed. "All of it."

"Fascinating." He leaned closer to me, eyes narrowed as if he could see the remnants of the Thief's magic on me.

I took a step back. "Listen, you don't have any way to fix this, do you?"

"In theory, time will repair your magic. Eat a balanced diet, drink lots of water, and get extra sleep."

"So, treat it as if I have a cold?" I asked.

He smiled. "Exactly. Should be right as rain in a matter of days. Weeks, perhaps depending on how strong the magic thief was."

"Weeks?" I felt like a weight knocked the air from my lungs. How was I supposed to wait weeks? I'd already waited long enough to learn how to use my magic. Weeks longer?

He took his glasses off and his eyes shrunk down to the size of tiny dots on either side of his nose. I couldn't believe how small they were. He pinched the bridge of his nose, then put the glasses back on. His huge eyes looked back at me, his brow furrowed in concern. "Of course, there's a chance it'll never come back."

"What do you mean? What kind of chance?" I asked.

"It's hard to tell. So many that have an encounter with a Thief don't survive to tell the tale. I know of at least one case where the magic from a survivor never returned."

I shook my head. "That can't be. I can't have that happen." Feeling dizzy, I reached for a desk behind me to steady myself.

"We'll know soon enough, I suppose," he said. "In the meantime, try not to worry about it."

I cocked an eyebrow. "Not worry about it?"

"I know, but that's all you can do. Test it out, it'll either come back or it won't."

With his words ringing in my ears, I walked on autopilot out the door toward my next class. The students around me sounded like they were so far away. It was like walking in a weird tunnel where all I could sense was my own two feet stepping on the stone floor.

I was worried before but now I was terrified.

Raven

Spellcasting was going to be interesting. I fidgeted in the seat, trying not to recall the accident I'd had last time I was here. At least there was no risk of me setting myself on fire.

As the class took their seats around me, I kept glancing toward the door, hoping to see the twins. I kept telling myself it was because we were a group and our grades were connected but I knew that was a lie.

I'd thought about them more often than I wanted to admit over the last few days. Including one very delicious dream I was grateful Luka had not walked in on.

I frowned. Luka hadn't been in any of my dreams since my confinement.

"Class, take your seats. Notebooks away. It's another practical day," Professor Halifax called.

My grip tightened around the backpack in my lap. How was I going to get through this? I glanced around again, desperately looking for my partners. Their usual place was empty.

Footsteps and chatter floated around me as everyone moved into their groups. My pulse raced as I considered the fact that I could be thrown into another group. Or worse, stuck with the teacher.

"Ms. Winters."

I looked over at my professor. She was in red today. A tight Chinese inspired dress with a slit that was scandalously high on her thigh. Her dark hair was pulled into a bun with a pair of chopsticks sticking out of it. It was an unusual outfit for her. "Yes, Professor?"

"Your partners had a family emergency and will return soon. In the meantime, I suggest you spend your time in the library researching any solutions to your current problem."

My throat bobbed. I guess she knew there wasn't any magic for me to use. Both embarrassed and relieved, I ignored the heat in my cheeks and grabbed my backpack. Alone time in the library was a gift right now. Time to sort out my thoughts and maybe even find some answers. "Thanks."

She nodded, then turned away from me. "Today we're focusing on summoning spells. Each of you will demonstrate your progress by the end of the week. Pass or fail on this."

Blowing out a relieved breath, I pushed open the door and stepped into the empty hallway. All the classroom doors were closed. Everyone else was where they were supposed to be. Their magic in tact. Even Ben.

I forced my feet to move one in front of the other down the hall toward the library.

I'd only been there a handful of times, but it was a large room with lots of private corners. I could easily hide out in there for the whole period without having to speak to anyone.

I walked through the wooden door into the dark, musty smelling library. The few windows in the large irregularly shaped room were stained glass and caked in ages of grime. I often wondered what they'd look like if someone cleaned them. Maybe they liked it dark.

Rows of tables were lit with individual orange lamps and several corners were set with squishy chairs or benches. The library was filled with books as high as the ceiling and the rows of books around the space created lots of nooks and crannies. There wasn't any actual order to the organization. Some of the shelves were spaced wide with dead ends created by walls or more shelves. When you found these enclaves, it gave the impression of a private room. That's what I was looking for today.

I wandered, ducking into corners and checking spaces. I didn't have it memorized yet, so it was always a bit of a guessing game to find a place to sit and set up camp.

Turning a promising corner, I realized I wasn't the first to arrive. A couple of students were already occupying the space, clothing littering the floor as they rolled around. I nearly yelped in surprise and embarrassment heated my face.

Quietly, I backed away, not wanting them to see me. If it was awkward for me to see them, I could only imagine how much worse it would be for them to get caught.

Using a bit more caution as I turned every corner, I peeked first before entering. The next few were open on both ends, then I found another one where a student was taking a nap.

I backed away, wondering if I should just grab a chair in a

corner. Then I realized the napping student was familiar. I turned back and moved a little closer.

His sweater was thrown over his head, but I had almost memorized the taught muscles in his body, which were not well hidden by the tight white tee-shirt he had on. "Luka?"

The incubus shifted, moving the sweater away from his face. At first, he looked irritated, but his expression softened almost instantly. He sat up, setting his sweater down. "Kitten."

I sat down on the ground next to him, feeling eased just by being in his presence. Luka always had a way of comforting me and getting me to express how I really felt in my dreams with him. Until just now, I didn't realize that same feeling carried over to real life.

My shoulders dropped as everything swirling around in my head seemed to weigh even more heavily on me. I leaned on his shoulder and he put his arm around me.

"Hey, it's okay," he said. "Tell me everything."

So I did. I spilled it all. The thief, Ben rushing in then rejecting me, my magic not working, my worry that I'd never get it back. I told him how scared I was that I'd be kicked out and how empty I felt inside without my magic.

He pulled me in for a hug as tears streamed down my cheeks. "It's going to be alright."

"How?" I asked.

"Cause you have me," he said. "And you have Makayla. And Violet and people that want you to be here. You're not alone here."

My brow furrowed as I took in the deeper meaning of his words. It was as if I knew he was referring to my life before the Academy. A time when I always felt alone. When I had to do everything myself because I couldn't count on people to step up.

"Come on." He let go of me, then stood. "We have a little bit of time before lunch, right? Let's see what we can find."

He offered his hand. I took it, feeling like maybe I could figure this out.

Hand in hand, we walked to the librarian's desk. The librarian, a squat gray troll with mossy green hair glared at us. Luka let go of my hand.

I grabbed it back, squeezing it tighter.

For a second, I swore I almost felt a flicker of magic, but it was gone before I could be sure.

"Can you help us find some books on broken magic?" Luka asked.

The troll sized me up, looking at me over her wire framed glasses. "You lost your magic, mage?"

"Maybe," I said.

She frowned. "I can't help you narrow your search if I don't know the details."

I sighed. "Fine. Yes. I lost my magic. A thief got a hold of me."

She pursed her lips making her hot pink lipstick look even more bright against her stone colored skin.

"Do you have anything that might help us?" I asked, trying to be nice.

She sighed. "Follow me."

The librarian led us through the maze-like library until we reached a small shelf with about a dozen books. The empty space on the shelf was covered in a thick layer of dust. It didn't look like anyone had used these books in a long time.

"This is everything we have on thieves," she said. "Not much research on the topic as few live long after their encounter."

My throat felt tight, but I managed to squeak out, "Thank you."

She nodded and walked away, leaving Luka and I with the sparse resources.

"Well, there's ten books here and the check-out limit is five, so I think we're going to take all of these with us," he said.

I nodded. "Good plan." Some of the books were thick and were going to take time to read.

We each grabbed our five books, then I turned to look at him. "Thanks for your help."

"Any time." He looked like he wanted to say more so I waited.

"Was there something else?" I asked.

"Yeah," he said. "I know you're not doing the dating thing right now and I have to admit, that's what I really want from you. But there's no reason I can't be your friend. Just because I get my magic from sex doesn't mean I have to do it all the time."

"I've been meaning to ask you about that," I said. "Is it just sex that powers you? Do the dreams do anything or can other things do something?"

He smirked. "Well, sex is the best, for a lot of reasons, of course. But it is the strongest way to charge my magic. Dreams don't do much, but I get a little." He leaned in closer to me and lowered his voice. "Believe it or not, I don't do dream sex with every girl I meet. That's for fun, not magic."

My cheeks heated as he backed away. "What about other things?"

"Like oral?" he asked.

I shrugged. "Sure. Or kissing or touching."

"I get a charge from anything that's rooted in sex. Depending on the passion and lust behind it, the levels vary."

That was the answer I wanted to hear. I wasn't ready to hop in bed with him, but I wanted to give him something to show him how I felt. Rising to my tiptoes, I pressed my lips to his.

Luka moaned in surprise as I moved my lips in harmony with his. It was a bit of an awkward position with a ton of books in my arms, but the kiss felt right. Just like everything else with Luka, it was comforting and safe.

I pulled away from the kiss and stared into his blue eyes. "Thank you."

"You have no idea how much I want you," he said.

"Soon," I said, allowing myself to finally admit it out loud. It was a matter of time before I caved to my desires. But I wanted to do it for the right reasons. Luka deserved that. He acted tough, but I knew he deserved someone who wanted to be with him for him. Not just for his magic fingers.

Raven

Luka and I walked into the cafeteria together and were barely in when I noticed we were getting stares from some of our classmates.

"Hey look, the incubus has a new favorite," someone called.

I glanced over to see one of the sirens just as she cat-called us. "Jealous?"

She grinned. "Oh, sweetie, we've all sampled that. And trust me, you can do better."

"Ouch, Delores," Luka called. "That's not what your mom said."

I rolled my eyes and kept walking. "Seriously? A mom joke?" I glanced at Luka. "It was a joke, right?"

He laughed. "Yeah, it was a joke. Delores and I go way back. She's not as bad as she comes across. And no, I've never actually fucked her. We have made out a few times when we were drunk."

"You know, you don't have to give me your sexual history," I said. "We're not a couple and to be honest, I don't really want to know anyway."

I navigated toward my usual table with the shifters and set my tray down next to Makayla.

"How was your first day back?" She asked.

"Fine so far." I turned to see Luka standing behind me, his tray in his hands. "You going to sit?"

"We're doing this now?" Starla asked. "We're friends with the incubus?"

"Hey, you're friends with a mage, aren't you?" I asked.

"Any friend of Raven's is welcome here," Makayla said. "Right?"

"Sure," Jamal said through a mouth full of food.

"They're not so bad," I said to Luka.

He set his tray down next to mine and took one of the plastic circles that barely passed for seats at the round lunch table.

"I always wondered if incubi ate real food," Jessica said. "Or if sex was enough."

"Sex just powers our magic," Luka said. "We need food to live and stuff."

"See, not much different than us," I said.

"What drives a mage's magic?" Jamal asked.

"You know, I have no idea," I said, feeling stupid. It seemed like a simple question, something I should know considering I was a mage. But once again, I was reminded of how little I knew despite the fact that I'd now been here a while.

"No Ben again?" I asked, changing the subject. Makayla knew most of the details about my past, but nobody else did.

"He's probably at the gym." Jamal stood, picking up his now empty tray. "And I really should be too. Only a couple months till the Wolf Moon. Gotta bulk up before the big night."

"Wolf Moon?" I asked.

Jamal shook his head. "You have so much to learn, little mage."

"I got this. You go lift those weights. I can still see some of your neck so you're not full Coach Miller level of beefcake yet," Makayla said.

Jessica lifted her shoulders to her ears and put on her best angry Coach Miller expression. "You dumbasses have no discipline. You're all soft."

Everyone laughed.

"Joke's on you," Jamal said. "You'll see, come Wolf Moon, you'll all be blinded by my sexiness."

He winked and walked away while the rest of the table laughed again.

Luka set his fruit cup on my tray. "Since you love strawberries."

My brow furrowed and I turned to him. "I never told you that. How'd you know?"

He shrugged. "Lucky guess."

I accepted the fruit. The lunch lady had given me a paper cup of grapes instead. "Want mine?"

"Sure," he said.

I passed my grapes to him. "Thanks."

"You two kind of make me want to throw up," Jessica said. "Are you officially a couple then?"

"Um no," I said. "We're friends."

"Well I don't see you batting your eyelashes at Makayla," Jessica said, eyebrows raised.

"You don't see us in private," Makayla said, sweeping me into a hug. She planted a kiss on my cheek. "We're very close."

We all laughed again. For the first time in my life, I felt like I fit in someplace. Was this what other girls felt like growing up? It was nice to have friends. Though, I couldn't help but miss Ben. Why would he tell me he doesn't want to see me one minute then jump to protect me the next?

"What's wrong?" Makayla asked as she let go of me.

"Just worried about Ben," I said. "He doesn't seem happy right now."

"He did meet with his dad last week. Don't worry, he'll come around. He does this every time his dad visits. He'll be back to normal soon," she said.

I could appreciate that. My aunt was toxic enough to throw me into a tailspin every time she was around. When she passed, I spent weeks wrestling with the fact that the only emotion I felt was relief. She'd had a hard life and despite my attempts to help, she never overcame her addiction. Though, the alcohol wasn't what did her in, technically. She'd stepped in front of a bus on her way home from church. She didn't drink before church, but the reports said she was drunk.

I didn't want to think about the fact that it might not have been an accident now that I knew the truth about my parents. She had treated me terribly but at least she managed to keep a roof over our heads until she passed.

I shook the thought away. I hated thinking about my life before the Academy. Now that I was here, things were easier in some ways and harder in others. But unlike my life before here, I wasn't alone.

"So tell me about this Wolf Moon thing," I said, changing the subject.

"Are you Raven Winters?" Someone asked from behind me.

I turned to see a brunette with pigtails holding a piece of

paper. She blew a bubble of bright pink bubblegum and it popped before she sucked it back in and chewed it. "Well?"

"Yeah, I'm Raven," I said.

She snapped her gum as she passed me the paper. "They sent me to give you this."

I took the paper from her and glanced down at it. When I looked back up, she was already walking away.

Luka snagged the letter out of my hands. "What's this?"

I grabbed it back. "I haven't even read it yet."

"Report to Dr. Green's office," Makayla said, reading it over me.

"Hey!" I said. "Can you two let me read my own mail?"

"You get out of gym class again?" Luka asked.

"Lucky girl," Makayla said.

"I don't know about that," I said as I skimmed the note. "Apparently, I'm meeting my parole officer."

My stomach twisted as apprehension mixed with fear. Last time an authority figure aside from the staff at this school met with me, I'd nearly died. What if this parole officer was another attempt on my life?

"It'll be alright," Luka said.

"I'm sure it will be," I said, feigning nonchalance. "Hey, look at that. From a double murder where my punishment is this school to fighting for my life where I get my very own parole officer."

"They have seriously messed up priorities," Makayla said.

"That about sums up the way it works around here," Luka said.

"You'll be in the main office this time, though," Luka said. "Not hidden away in the basement."

I nodded, feeling comforted by his words. He was right. There would actually be people around to hear me scream if the parole officer tried to attack me.

"Well, us non criminals have to go to class," Makayla said, nudging me with her elbow playfully. "You need me to walk you to the office?"

"Nah, you guys should go, I don't want you to be late. Especially not to gym."

"I'll send your best to Coach Miller," Luka said.

"Oh, do not do that," I said. "With any luck, he won't notice I'm missing."

"He'll notice. And I'm sure he'll have lots of laps for you to make up tomorrow."

"Can't wait," I said.

"I'm sure it'll be over before you notice," Luka said. "Meet you in the common area after last period?"

"It's a date," I said.

Raven

Dr. Green stood outside his office when I arrived which totally threw me off guard. From what I knew of him so far, he loved that office. I wondered if him standing out here meant that he'd been kicked out by my parole officer or if something else was going on. Was he going to let me be alone with this person? After what happened with the last official visitor I had, I didn't trust anyone.

"Ms. Winters." Dr. Green inclined his chin. His fangs were showing clearly today over the slight scowl on his face. I had to hope that it was better than a full scowl.

"Dr. Green," I said.

He opened the door and gestured for me to enter. I followed and after taking a few steps, I stopped walking to take in the large man sitting at Dr. Green's desk.

The visitor was a pale, balding man with a red face and a bulbous nose. He had squinty eyes so pale blue they were nearly white. I balled my hands into fists, forcing myself to go tense rather than shudder at the odd, uncomfortable feeling the stranger gave me.

The man, if he was a man, slid a pair of circular wire rimmed glasses onto his face. He smiled, showing a row of sharp, yellow teeth. He definitely wasn't human.

"Ms. Winters, how lovely of you to join us," he said with a wheeze.

"Hello," I said, doing my best to be polite.

"Come in, please," the man said.

I inched toward him, surprised that he didn't stand to greet me. My aunt may have been shit in terms of raising me but at least I'd learned basic etiquette over the years spent in public school thanks to a few well meaning, old school teachers.

Once I was in front of the desk, I extended my hand. "Raven Winters."

The man behind the desk glared at my hand as if it were something dirty. "Have a seat, Ms. Winters."

I lowered my hand and glanced back at Dr. Green for confirmation. Go figure I looked to the massive demon with the horns on his head for comfort. When I'm telling my friends about this later, I'll be sure to let them know that I'd rather be spooning Dr. Green in a twin bed than sitting in a chair across the desk from this - whatever he was.

Dr. Green nodded.

Slowly, I took a seat in one of the two empty chairs in front of Dr. Green's desk. I looked over at the tree clock and noticed that it now had several bright orange leaves on its branches. I was sure it had been bare of leaves before.

"You may go, Dr. Green," the stranger said.

"No, I'll stay," he said.

"That's not necessary."

"Under the articles of this institution, I am the legal guardian of all students under my care until they graduate or reach the age of maturity, whichever comes first. Given that, I am permitted to be present at any and all meetings that pertain to their wellbeing."

The red-faced man's brow furrowed, and I could see perspiration beading on his shiny head. He was flustered by Dr. Green and he didn't want him in here. I wanted to give Dr. Green a high five. Something told me this man was rarely made to feel uncomfortable and rather enjoyed being the one to do it to others.

I pressed my lips together, trying to avoid the smile forcing its way out.

"Fine, you may stay," he said. "Sit."

To my surprise, Dr. Green took the seat next to mine. He barely fit in the chair, his hips expanding beyond the seat and his knees nearly up in his chest. It was easy to forget just how large he was compared to the human men I'd grown up with. Dr. Green wasn't fat by any means, he was just twice the size of a normal human man.

"Well, now that that's settled," the stranger said. "We should get to business." He looked at me as he opened a folder in front of him.

"Raven Winters, underage mage, student at the Academy of the Elites. Classified as a fire elemental mage. Is that correct?"

"Yes, I think," I said.

Dr. Green cleared his throat. It was as if he was telling me not to argue.

"I mean, yes," I said. "Sorry, I'm nervous. Last time I met someone official they tried to kill me." I laughed.

The man in front of me scowled. "This is not a laughing matter."

"Of course not," I said.

"You have a formal charge against you of using time magic illegally," he said. "Because you are a minor, instead of serving time, you are on probation with a warning. You are my responsibility now,"

I opened my mouth to say something but felt a jab in my knee. I glanced over to see Dr. Green bouncing his foot and staring at the clock.

Taking the hint, I kept my mouth shut.

"My name is Officer M and we're going to see a lot of each other over the next six months."

I nodded, keeping my thoughts about how insane this whole thing was to myself.

"You will meet with me weekly for the next month. I will be in contact with Dr. Green regarding your use of magic and keeping tabs on you," he said.

"I don't even have any magic right now," I blurted out.

Officer M cocked an eyebrow. "What do you mean that you have no magic?"

"The time thief seems to have temporarily halted her magic," Dr. Green said.

"So you can't do any magic?" Officer M asked, looking skeptical.

I shook my head. "None."

"That's not what I was told on my briefing," he said.

"Were you told that a government official was the one who took my magic?" I asked.

"Raven," Dr. Green chided.

"I'm sorry, Dr. Green, but how the hell did she even get in here?" I asked.

"I'm afraid that's a rather gruesome tale," Officer M said.

"What do you mean?" I asked.

"We found the real agent dead in her home. The thief broke in and stole her identification documents and her magic. We suspect she then shifted into her appearance before coming here," he said.

It felt like the air had been knocked from my lungs. I blinked at the officer as I tried to process what he just said. Not only was this psychopath after me, she was able to shift into other people's forms?

"Why wasn't the school informed of this attack so we could have increased security?" Dr. Green asked.

"I'm afraid that's above your clearance level," Officer M sneered.

Dr. Green stood so quickly I thought he might attack the other man. Instead, he set his hands on the desk and leaned over until he was inches away from his face. "These students are my responsibility and you will inform me if something like this happens again."

"Just because you used to be someone important doesn't mean you always get your way. I know what you did to get sent here. Your glory days are long gone, *sir*."

Tension hung thick in the air and I held my breath. My fingers hurt from the grip I had on the arm rests but I didn't ease up. I was ready to jump out of this chair and run if these two got into a brawl. I didn't have any magic and I sure as hell wasn't going to get into the middle of a scuffle between them. Dr. Green could probably crush a skull with his bare hands, and I didn't want to think about the sharp teeth on the other guy.

"That may be the case, *Officer*, but this is my school and here, I call the shots. And if any of my students are attacked because of your agency's inadequacy, it will be publicly announced when our board meets.

"You can't say a word," Officer M said through clenched teeth. "You know this is confidential."

"There are ways around every rule, you know that, don't you?" Dr. Green said.

Officer M looked back at me. "Ms. Winters, if you are caught using time magic again, you will not have a warning. You will go right to prison. No matter who is paying your tuition."

He stood, then slammed the folder closed. "Dr. Green, keep your students in line."

Dr. Green didn't say anything, but he took his hands off the desk and walked to the back of the room. He opened the door and held it, clearly signaling that the meeting was over.

I stood and waited for the officer to go first. He walked out from behind the desk and paused in front of me. He smelled awful and my nose wrinkled.

Officer M leaned so close to me, I could feel his warm breath on my cheek. I shuddered but didn't back down. After watching how Dr. Green stood up to him, I had a feeling that was the only thing this putrid man responded to.

"I look forward to our next meeting," he whispered.

I tensed, gritting my teeth. "I'm sure you are."

I held my ground as he backed away from me.

Officer M inclined his chin and walked past me, so close his body pressed against my ass. He paused, leaning closer to me, obviously copping a feel. Gross. I fought the urge to vomit as I took a step away from him. "Until next week, Ms. Winters."

The disgusting man walked out the door and as soon as Dr. Green closed it behind him, I let out a sigh of relief. "He's a piece of work."

"Careful," Dr. Green said. "He might be a waste of skin and bones, but he's got more authority over you than you know."

"Thanks for standing up for me," I said. "And everyone else."

"It's my job, Ms. Winters," he said.

I had a feeling it was a little more than just about a job. He might come across as scary, but he at least cared enough to want to keep me alive.

"Ms. Winters, I've been thinking a lot about your lack of magic."

"Right back at you," I said.

Dr. Green frowned briefly then his expression settled. "It doesn't do for a mage with no magic to be attending this school."

My heart hammered against my ribs and I held my breath. This was it. He was tired of me. Whoever was funding all this was sick of paying for someone to attend a magic school who couldn't do magic. They were going to kick me out.

Magic jail, magic sweatshop, back in the human world? I had no idea where I would go.

"I think it's time we take your training to the next level."

My jaw dropped open. That was not what I was expecting. "What do you mean?" I asked. I had no magic. Which meant I wasn't even at a level to start with. Unless zero was a level.

"From now on, you will have private lessons with Professor Halifax. Your other activities will cease until your magic returns."

I scrubbed my face with my hand. She was the one who sent me to the library to research on my own. "I don't think it's going to help."

"It has to help. You don't have a choice. You came in untrained. If you can't get control of your magic, you're considered too high of a risk..."

I waited for him to finish the thought. I could tell there was more he wanted to say but he just sighed and looked at the desk.

"What do you mean *I'm too much of a risk*?" I asked.

"Once before we had a student here who was like you. Untrained but powerful. She never gained full use of her magic. They worried she'd come into her full power one day unexpectedly. Much the way you did when you were attacked."

"What happened to her?" I asked, not sure I wanted to hear the answer.

"They came for her and I never heard from her again." He pressed his lips together, brow furrowed. It was the most concern I'd ever seen on his face. Whatever had happened to this girl, it was bad. And he was worried the same thing would happen to me.

I swallowed hard. I couldn't let that happen. I wouldn't. I had to fix this. I had to get my magic back. "You think it'll be enough? Working on extra lessons?"

"I hope so," he said, his expression returning to stoic disinterest, "for your sake. You start tomorrow. Eight in the morning."

Raven

Saturday should be for sleeping till noon then lounging with Makayla or Luka. Not this Saturday.

Last night Luka had returned to my dreams. He'd shown me how much he missed me. And he definitely made me want him more than I already did. I knew I needed to sort through this missing magic thing a little more before I complicated one of my few friendships at this school. But I wasn't going to last much longer at this rate.

At least I could carry the memory of the dream with me as I suffered through my first private tutoring session with Professor

Halifax. I glanced at the clock. "Fuck." I had ten minutes and was in desperate need of a shower.

As I padded into the bathroom, I flicked on the lights and caught sight of myself in the mirror. My tousled hair screamed *I just got laid* and I smirked as I stripped off my pajamas. Even in my dreams, he left me feeling like the real thing.

The hot water rolled down my body, reminding me of the feel of Luka's skin against mine. Everything with him was so much more intense than it was with any other partner. It was like he was made to make me feel good. He knew exactly where to touch and tease. His hands moved on my skin like a familiar comfort while his mouth made me feel things that shouldn't be possible. He was everything I was promised that sex should be from movies and television and then some.

I squeezed my thighs together and tried to shake the spiking desire coursing through me. It wasn't even real, yet it left me feeling shaken.

Quickly, I soaped up my hair with shampoo and used the lather to clean everywhere else. As I rinsed off, I wondered what Luka was doing right now. Was he thinking about me? He was an incubus, after all. Was he off with another partner?

I frowned as I squirted conditioner into my hand. We hadn't talked about what our relationship was. I just knew I needed him, but I didn't know what he needed. Could an incubus even be satisfied from one partner?

Clean enough, I climbed out of the shower and dried off. Without brushing, I threw my hair into a sopping wet bun on top of my head. It would have to do.

I ran into the massive closet and froze. It was Saturday, which meant I should be able to wear my regular clothes. But then again, I was going to meet a professor.

Shit. The clock was ticking. As it was, I was going to have to skip breakfast and coffee.

Deciding to go halfway, I grabbed a pair of black pants and a white shirt. The tie could wait till Monday.

Swinging by my desk, I grabbed my still packed backpack. I had no idea what private lessons were going to entail. Would I need to take notes? Would I need my books? Was she going to stare at me while I didn't do magic?

Cause so far, every time I'd tried, nothing happened. I failed every time. My gut twisted as nerves churned. I guess it was better that I didn't have time to eat. Right now, I wasn't sure I could keep anything down anyway.

Professor Halifax was amazing. She was sort of a minor hero of mine. She didn't put up with shit from students and she didn't mince her words. She had zero filter and never assigned busy work. Professor Halifax meant business. Which both amazed me and fucking terrified me.

Rumor was that she was fae. She never mentioned it, but it did explain her stunning looks and her pointed ears. I was still figuring all of this out, but I had read through every book I could find on supernatural cultures. From what I'd read, fae were rare here as they preferred to stay in their own realm with their own laws. Some books even mentioned that if they crossed over to our realm, there was a possibility they could get stuck here. I wanted to ask her about fae, but I was terrified of pissing her off. So, I stuck to keeping my mouth shut.

That wasn't going to work today.

As I approached her classroom, I saw her framed by the doorway, waiting for me.

"You're late," she said.

"I'm sorry," I said, lowering my gaze. Maybe the shower wasn't necessary.

"Well, let's get on with it," she said, sounding annoyed.

I walked past her into the empty classroom. "I'm so sorry Dr. Green is making you do this. I swear I didn't ask.

"That's why I'm mad," she said. "I had to wait for him to make you come. You should have been working with me since the beginning. Especially once that wolf got his magic back."

I wasn't sure what to say to that. I mean, she was the spell-casting professor so in theory, she knew more about this than anyone else. But I didn't want to be a burden. I stood in the middle of the room, looking up into the empty seats where I sat with my classmates every day for class. The room looked so much larger without the students to fill the amphitheater benches that circled around the lower stage floor. I shivered, feeling small and on display despite the fact that there wasn't anyone else in here besides the two of us.

"I wasn't sure if your magic was gone forever but once that mutt got his back, I knew yours had to be close behind. When it didn't return, I asked Dr. Green to send you my way. I'm going to force the magic out of you if I have to."

My throat bobbed and my chest felt heavy. Her words should have comforted me, she wanted to help, but they sounded more like a threat than a way to fix whatever was wrong.

The door closed and I heard her heels clicking across the stone floor.

I turned to face her, honestly terrified about what she was going to make me do. "How are you going to bring my magic back?"

"There are things we can try that aren't typically used," she said. "How badly do you want it back?"

I hesitated, considering the weight of her question. It was clear she wasn't asking this lightly. I knew whatever she was getting at was something big. And based on what I already knew about this world, it was likely dangerous. I thought back to my old life. Kegs popping and sending beer all over my shoes. Lugging bottles to the bar from the back storage room, slapping my boss for grabbing my ass. The real world, the human world, wasn't a good place for me. I'd struggled. More than I realized until I was given a chance here.

On top of how awful the human world was, add in how amazing this place could be. Sure, someone had tried to kill me, and some bitchy girls tried to make me feel bad about myself. I might get picked on, but it was nothing compared to eating ramen noodles every night for the rest of my life. Plus, there was Luka. The things that incubus could do with his fingers... and his tongue...

I couldn't walk away from all of this.

"I need my magic back. Whatever it takes," I said.

She grinned, making her features look even sharper than usual. "That's what I was hoping you'd say."

Raven

"Professor Hurd seemed to think it would come back on its own." A wave of nausea rolled through me as I stood rooted to the spot where Professor Halifax had directed me.

She lifted a perfect brow in annoyance. "I thought you said you were willing to try anything?"

My throat bobbed. "Yes, I did say that. But this is like the stuff out of horror movies, you do realize that?"

"Where do you think they got their ideas?" she asked.

I stood there, in the center of a circle of shiny pink stones.

Professor Halifax went back to setting candles up around me. So close that if I moved, I'd risk knocking them over.

"What exactly are we doing?" I asked.

She set down the last candle then stepped over the stones to leave me standing in the circle. "I know you did a magic meld with the Obscura brothers. This will reactivate it."

"But they're not even here," I said.

"I know, that's why we have the stones, they'll give us a little more distance on the spell," she said.

"They said the meld was dangerous," I said.

"I'm hearing a lot of complaining about someone who wants to get her magic back."

I covered my face with my hands and closed my eyes. She was right. What choice did I have? Wait and hope my magic came back or go along with this crazy ass plan. Honestly, I wasn't even sure what her plan was. And she was a professor and Dr. Green trusted her, right?

Dropping my hands to my side I looked up at her. "What do you need me to do."

She stood in front of me, outside of the circle of stones. Her arms were out on either side of her, fingers splayed. "I'm going to cast the spell, you have to lean into it when you feel the magic surge. Your goal is to light the candles."

"Alright, I can do that." It sounded harmless enough. No touching like I'd done with the magic meld before. It was just lighting a few candles. I tried not to think about how I'd set myself on fire last time I'd worked with fire. "Let's try it."

"You have to give me more confidence than that," she said.

"Okay, let's light some candles," I said with feigned confidence.

She lifted her arms and closed her eyes. I took deep breaths, concentrating on how I felt, searching for any flicker of magic.

I thought about the twins and the way we'd connected our

magic. The memory came flooding back to me, the sensation of the light that connected us shooting through my legs and up into my chest. Reacting on instinct, I called it to my hands and felt it rush to my fingertips. I had to harness this. I wasn't sure if it was a memory or if it was real, but I needed to embrace it just in case it was real. If this was my magic returning, I had to hang on to it.

Light the candles.

The words came from nowhere. I wasn't sure if they were mine or someone else's but I knew I had to try. I looked down at the ring of candles circling me and sent the sparks I felt toward them, urging them to ignite.

One of the wicks flickered to life as a tiny but steady flame bloomed from the candle. A rush of relief surged through me and I laughed.

Just as quickly as the magic had arrived, it faded. I stumbled forward as exhaustion set in. Dizzy and lightheaded, I managed to avoid knocking down the single lit candle as I stepped outside of the circle.

"That was a good start," Professor Halifax said.

The room was spinning and my pulse raced. I felt like I'd just run ten miles. Everything felt surreal and uneven. I wasn't even sure what was real and what wasn't. The whole room had a dream like haze around it. "What happened?"

"You found your magic," she said.

My heart leaped and I smiled and hope expanded in my chest. "Does that mean it's back?"

"It means it's ready for us to tap back into it. I'm guessing a few more weeks of practice and training and you'll be back at full power."

That was the best news I'd heard since I arrived here. "How do I practice?"

"You can continue to meet with me, but you'll do better with the twins," she said. "Since you melded your magic, yours will probably respond to theirs. You three are connected."

I still didn't understand all of that but all I could think about was that I had a path toward getting my magic back. "When are they returning?"

"I'm not sure," she said. "I believe their great-grandfather passed. Mages can only extend their lives for so long. He founded this school, you know."

My lips parted as her words sunk in. The fancy suite, the ability to be late to class while everyone else was punished. They mentioned that their parents donated a lot but left out the fact that their family started the whole thing. "That explains a lot."

Professor Halifax smiled. "You didn't know."

"They told me their parents donated to the school," I said.

"They are also paying your tuition," she said.

My breath caught and I blinked at her in stunned silence. Did Matt and Zach know that? "I don't understand. I mean, I'm grateful, but why me?"

"The Obscura family comes from a long line of pure blood mages. They aren't all that different from most of the high fae families in the sense that they believe that magic shouldn't be diluted or mixed. Though, with fae, the reasons are due to giving too much power to other supernaturals. Like you. You shouldn't have the abilities you do. But with the fae blood, you're more powerful than average mages. With them, they feel that it reduces mage power."

"Does it?" I asked.

She shook her head. "Of course not."

"They mentioned something about that to me. Something about the one-kid policy in their family," I said.

"I still don't see why they'd cover my tuition," I said.

"Because of your parents," she said. "You come from a long

line of famous mages. I wouldn't be surprised if the family is already planning on you joining them in one way or another."

"Joining them? Please tell me you're talking about a job offer and not an old school betrothal kind of thing."

She shrugged. "You'll have a lot more options once you get your magic up and running so try not to worry too much. Appreciate the gift you were given."

"I do," I said. "I'm grateful but I don't know what I got myself into."

"Don't worry," she said. "It'll all make sense soon enough."

My brow furrowed as I tried to discern what her words meant. I was tired and didn't want to think any more about the complicated relationship I was in with the Obscura twins. We had a bond of some sort through our magic and apparently their parents were trying to push us together because of who my parents were. None of it made sense. It was too much.

"What about my parents?" I asked.

"Not today," she said. "You need to rest. The magic you just performed was more taxing than you realize."

"What exactly did I do?" I asked. "In all my research, I couldn't find anything that sounded like it would work."

"You managed to call some of your magic through a small tear," she said.

"A tear?" I asked, completely lost.

"A mini-portal, essentially," she said.

"I thought portals were nearly impossible and super dangerous." Wasn't that what we'd heard in class?

"They are," she said. "But you're a time magic user, which means you have fae blood in there somewhere. It gives you the ability to use portals unlike any other supernatural. Nearly as good as the fae themselves."

"Wait, what?" I asked. "Did you just say *fae blood*?"

She smiled. "Probably. It might not be much, but most of the time magic mages I've met over the centuries were of fae origin. Someone in your family history got it on with one of the fair folk. It's what gives you your unusual magical signature."

"How come nobody told me this before?" I asked.

"It's not widely taught," she said. "And if I were you, I'd keep it to yourself. The fae are not treated well in this realm." She frowned for a moment, then her face returned to normal.

"Are you treated poorly?" I asked, my brow furrowed. She might have unorthodox methods, but Dr. Green trusted her to help me and she had brought back some of my magic. Her talents were incredible. I would think everyone would want to be on her good side.

"That's a story for another day," she said. "Today we confirmed that your magic still exists, it's there, but it's broken."

"So what does that mean?" I asked.

"It means we have work to do."

Raven

The next two weeks flew by as I tried to make good on my agreement with Dr. Green. I knew he was still keeping things from me, but I had a feeling he was on my side. And I couldn't say that of everyone.

My days were the same. Meals with Makayla and the other shifters while Ben was who knew where. Luka was actually fitting in with them after the first few days. They opened up around him now, having our usual conversations about the drama going on at school or which teachers were giving pop quizzes.

Even gym had been tolerable. I couldn't prove it, but based

on the way Coach Miller avoided eye contact with me, I was pretty sure someone said something to him. My money was on Dr. Green.

The highlight of every day was my time in the library with Luka. Each day, we poured through a new book, taking notes of anything that might give us any clues as to what the thief's magic had done to me.

So far, I'd learned that thieves were only second in their power to those with time magic. Which made sense why one of them was after me. Their magic was largely unstudied in formal studies and most of the books gave us summaries and observations. Some of them dating back hundreds of years.

All creatures seemed to fear thieves. They were capable of removing even the smallest amount of magic. And as I'd already learned from Ben, they could remove a shifter's ability to shift.

"Did you see this part?" Luka asked, pushing the latest book toward me, his finger pointing to a passage in the middle of the page.

I tugged the book closer and read where he was pointing. "When a thief removes the magic of a demon, the creature will be prevented from ever transitioning between realms."

I looked up at Luka. "Does that mean dreams?"

"Maybe," he said. "But it could also mean between the other realms. Like the underworld."

"Like Hell?" I asked. Luka had been pretty private about his life outside of school and I wasn't sure how much he wanted to talk about.

"Yes, that's one of the names," he said.

"Do you travel there?" I asked, fascinated by the topic. When he visited my dreams, it felt so real. Was that what it felt like to visit Hell, too?

"Every year," he said. "You know how humans visit family for Christmas?"

I nodded. "I never really celebrated Christmas, but I knew a lot of others who traveled."

"That's sort of what it's like for us around the Solstice. We visit every year to see anyone who is locked in that realm," he said. "But to be honest, I never really worried about how they got there. I wonder if anyone in there was trapped by a thief."

"Wouldn't they get stuck in our realm?" I asked.

"Not sure," he said. "You can send a demon to hell with certain spells. They aren't pretty and they have a high cost to the caster, but it's possible."

I smirked. "So, I could send you to hell?"

He elbowed me playfully. "You'll have to get your magic back first."

"You're funny," I said.

He closed up the book. "Come on, class is about over, and I have to run back to my room before lunch."

I grabbed the book. "I'll take this to my room and meet you at lunch."

He grinned. "Want me to go with you to your room?"

"So polite," I said as I stood. "But no, thanks. I got it."

"You say the word, and I'll be there," he said, as he did almost every day.

"I know," I said as I turned away from him.

I felt bad because I wasn't sure why I kept turning him down. I liked Luka. I wanted to have sex with him. For real, in the real-world sex. Not just in my dreams. A rush of heat spread low in my belly at the thought of our last dream encounter. It had been a while, but like he said, he'd respected my boundaries.

Soon, whatever it was that was making me say no despite my body's desires, would cave. And I had a feeling the wait would be worth it.

Quickly, I used my key card to get into my room and pushed open the door. I flipped on the light switch and caught a glimpse of a book sitting on the middle of my floor. Brow furrowed, I walked around it and set my backpack and the book I was carrying on the bed.

I swore I hadn't left anything on the floor when I left. Bending down, I picked up the book. My fingers left marks on the thick layer of dust. It looked like it hadn't been touched in years. Careful not to move the dust around, I looked at both sides of the book. It appeared that either I was the only one to handle it or I had touched it in the same exact place as whoever had brought it into my room.

I knew it wasn't my book. I'd have remembered if I had a book like this. The binding was dark brown leather, cracked in places from age. Gold trim bordered the cover and two words were printed on the cover. I squinted at them, unsure if I was seeing what I wanted to see or what it actually said.

Carefully, I carried the book to my desk and set it down. Using a tissue, I wiped the cover to reveal the title. It really did say what I hoped it said. The words seemed to call to me. *Broken Magic.* I had no idea how this book got here, but if it was about broken magic, I was grateful that it was here.

Carefully, I opened the cover. It cracked as I lifted it and I winced at the sound, hoping I wasn't damaging the ancient text. The interior looked surprisingly new compared to the worn cover, but I'd learned to stop questioning things too much. After all, we were in a school filled with magic.

Turning past the cover pages and the title page, I skimmed through the table of contents. A chill ran down my spine as I traced my fingers down the list. It was everything I needed. Chapters on how to repair broken magic and chapters on how to heal the body and mind. It even had several chapters on surviving and coping with a thief attack.

I glanced back to my closed door as if whoever had left this here would show up and tell me how they'd gotten into my room and how they'd found this book. Why wasn't this in the library? Or maybe it was and I looked in the wrong place?

This book could be the key to getting my magic back. I glanced at the clock on my wall and noted that I only had a short time until class. It was either reading now or lunch.

Making a choice, I took a seat at my desk and started to read. My pulse raced as I turned the pages. I'd been wondering about my lost magic and finally, maybe I had some answers.

Flipping ahead, I stopped on a chapter titled *Stolen Magic*. I skimmed the lines, looking for anything mentioning a Thief. Frowning, I kept skimming, not finding what I was hoping for.

Then, something caught my eye. I read the paragraph four times, getting more hopeful with each read. According to the book, I didn't need all my magic to come back, I just needed a piece of it. Any piece of it. If any kind of magic was able to be ignited inside me, it would unlock the rest of the missing magic.

Last time I needed to access my magic, I'd had some help from two other mages. We'd joined hands and they'd sent magic through me. Surely, if we did the same thing we had a chance of turning it back on, right? Was that part of what Professor Halifax had been talking about?

Quickly, I closed the book and grabbed my backpack. The twins were supposed to be back soon, but I didn't have classes with them till tomorrow. Hopefully they'd be there when I got to class. For now, I'd have to deal with gym and the rest of my afternoon. It wasn't much, but there was hope.

Luka

Raven never came to lunch. I tried to laugh with her friends and pretend it wasn't bothering me, but since her time in the hospital she'd been like clockwork. She attended all her classes, she did her homework, she studied in the library with me, she joined her friends for lunch. Even her weekends were boring. She was a model student. The only thing she lacked was her ability to use magic.

Frowning, I glanced toward the door again.

"She's a big girl," Makayla said.

"I know," I said. "It's just not like her."

"Maybe she got called in to her parole meeting?" Makayla suggested.

"She went a few days ago," I said. "She only has to go once a week."

"Maybe she wasn't hungry," she said.

"Maybe." I knew something was going on, but I didn't know what it was. But I wasn't too worried. Despite her lack of magic, I could still feel her through our bond. I was certain of it now. The two of us shared that bond. I knew when she was anxious or scared. Right now, I didn't feel any of that.

I blew out a frustrated breath. Even knowing she was probably safe, it was still difficult to be away from her. Especially since we hadn't consummated our bond. It was painful to be so close to her all the time without touching her. Without being inside her. But it was more painful to be away from her. And with a bond between the two of us, it was only a matter of when. So, I waited. Each day, I felt my magic dwindle, but I waited. She was going to come to me sooner rather than later. And when she did, it would be worth the wait, that much I knew.

Quickly, I finished my last bite of food and picked up my tray. "See you guys later."

Makayla and the other shifters waved as I walked away from their table. It was an odd thing to sit at a table with a bunch of shifters. Some of the other demons had given me strange looks the first few days but now they didn't even glance my way. Unlike the shifters, we didn't really care what the others were doing. There was no pack for demons. We had families, sure, but mine wasn't here and mine wasn't the kind of family you crossed.

The others here knew I liked to be alone. I wasn't a people person unless I was fucking said person. So my sitting with a group of shifters was so far out of the norm for me, I was sure it raised some questions. But you didn't mess with my family. In the other realm, my mother was one of the few people who could determine your whole fate with the stroke of her pen. Sometimes I hated the power she held, the power she'd pass to me if I wanted it. Other days, like today, I didn't mind too much. At least it kept my classmates at a distance.

Though I had to admit, I wasn't looking forward to seeing her in a few weeks at parent's day. She was bound to catch the weakness of my magic. I wasn't even sure how much longer I could go before I'd be struggling in classes.

I picked up the pace as I headed toward the locker room. I wanted to wait for Raven, and I knew she was worth the wait, but I might have to start thinking of another way to recharge.

The thought made my stomach twist into uncomfortable knots. It literally made me sick to think of fucking someone else. My pull to Raven was so great, it had to be her. How was that for a sick twist of fate? As an incubus, sex was never personal. Now, that was all I wanted.

I was going to need a very cold shower after gym.

Thankfully, Raven was already stretching with the other girls in the class when I got into the gymnasium. I waved to her, hoping she'd notice me.

She waved back.

I jogged over to her. "Hey, you alright?"

"Yeah, I'm good. Just got stuck reading one of those books," she said.

Her answer surprised me, but she seemed fine.

"Hey, demon, you want to run laps till dinner?" Coach Miller called.

I rolled my eyes. "See you later, Raven."

One of these days, I'd love to see someone stand up to him but I wasn't willing to risk confinement again.

Raven

The locker room was a buzz of conversation as everyone finished changing after another grueling day of gym. Today's class had been the same as the last several - running intervals with breaks for planks and pushups. To be fair, I was probably in the best shape of my life, but it didn't come without a price.

I groaned as I lifted my shirt off over my head. My arms were not used to this much work.

"That was brutal today," Violet said.

"I know," I said. "I keep hoping we can go back to those long runs where he just ignored us."

"Same," Violet said as she tugged off her gym clothes. "Hey, you want to come to a party tonight?"

Her question surprised me. Violet and I were gym class friends and greeted each other in the halls and cafeteria for occasional conversation. We'd never hung out outside of school before.

She laughed. "I promise that Scarlett will be on her best behavior."

I smiled. "Okay, sure. Sounds fun."

"You know where the basement dorms are?" She asked.

I nodded. I'd never been down in the dorms where the few resident vampires lived, but I'd passed by the entry a few times.

"You really should come. Our parties are the best." She turned and took a few steps away then looked over her shoulder. "Bring that delicious incubus of yours. I'm sure he'd be up for some fun."

"He's not exactly mine," I said.

"Right," she said, not hiding the sarcasm. "That's why the school's biggest slut hasn't slept with anyone since he started following you around like a faithful hound."

My throat bobbed as guilt weighed heavy in the pit of my stomach. Was I stringing him along? Was he losing out on fun with others because of me? I pushed the thought away. He was a big boy. He could make his own decisions. Besides, I wasn't ever going to let guilt pressure me into something I didn't want to do. I'd gone down that route before and it hadn't turned out well.

But I did like the idea of taking him out for a night. Luka and I had spent most of our free time reading old books lately. Getting out to do something fun probably wasn't a bad idea. It wasn't like my magic was going to mysteriously reappear out of the blue. Based on everything I'd read, there was always something that brought it back.

Quickly, I finished changing and ducked out of the locker

room. If I hurried, I could catch Luka before dinner.

I'd only been to Luka's room once before. We'd kept our meetings to shared spaces like the library and cafeteria. Once, though, I'd walked back here with him while he changed clothes after he'd encountered a bad spell in the hallway that left his uniform covered in red spots. He was lucky it hadn't stuck to his skin.

The demons were housed in the old dorms next to the main building. Really, I should call it a castle. Apparently, the dorms were off campus when the school was just getting started and still housed a few government offices and other odds and ends of things. Eventually, the school grew large enough to take over everything. Plus, as more famous and wealthy families started sending their kids here, the competition to get in grew. They took over the whole thing and added dorms inside the building to make room for all the new students. At least that was what I'd learned flipping through one of my books.

You'd think a magic academy would have a more interesting back story than a small elite school for rich kids that started alongside a bunch of government offices but I was learning that there were a lot of things the supernatural world had in common with the human world. Money and politics seemed to be similar. Though, I still hadn't wrapped my head fully around the politics and systems of this community outside of the school.

If I ever got my magic back, I supposed I'd have to do that. I pushed open the doors and stepped into the brisk night air.

It was nearly November and the nights were long. Stars twinkled overhead, brighter than usual because of the tiny sliver of a moon that kept the sky dark. My breath came out in clouds and I tugged my sweater closed around me to keep warm.

Thankfully, the dorms were only a few steps away. I paused outside the door, unsure of how I'd be greeted by the demons I encountered in the common room. When I'd walked through with Luka, it was the middle of the day and most students were at class.

Now, it was that gap between classes and dinner and it was prime time to gather in public spaces.

Blowing out a long breath, I lifted my chin and tried to pretend that I belonged here. Then I pushed open the door and stepped inside.

Heat blew into my face from a vent right in front of the door and I was instantly warm. The demon and fallen angel dorm was kept at a balmy eighty degrees at all times according to Luka. Made it cozier for those who were used to living in the underworld.

I tugged off my sweater and tossed it over my shoulder so I wouldn't have to carry it.

"Take the rest of it off, it's hot in here," someone called.

I lifted an eyebrow as I turned to face the gathered group of demons in the common area. Six of them were lounging on chairs or couches. Two of them were sitting in chairs in front of a large television, gaming controllers in their hands.

The sounds of battle and explosions filled the room, the two gamers not even turning my way.

"I'm visiting Luka," I said.

"Man, that incubus gets all the good ones," someone said.

"You don't even know good until you've been with a guy with wings," an angel with huge black wings tucked behind his back said.

"Aren't you sweet," I said, the sarcasm heavy.

Trying to ignore them, I walked forward, right for the staircase. For a second, panic made my chest tighten. I'd only been to his room once and I hadn't paid much attention to where it was.

I knew we went up the stairs. Second floor, maybe? I walked up, hoping for something that looked familiar.

As soon as I stepped into the hallway, I knew I was in the

right place. It didn't make sense, but I felt Luka calling to me. It was as if I could smell him. That scent of smoke and something that was distinctly him.

Feeling confident, despite the fact that I couldn't explain any of this, I stopped in front of a door in the middle of the hallway and knocked.

The door opened and Luka's lips turned upward into a grin. He wasn't wearing a shirt and his belt hung unbuckled from his pants. I must have caught him as he was undressing.

Heat burned in my face as I stared at his muscular chest and his hard, broad shoulders. His abs were right out of a catalogue for male perfection. I was fiercely reminded of why I'd likened him to a Greek god when we'd first met. Then I realized this was the first time I'd seen him without his clothes on in real life. He was even sexier than he was in my dreams.

My core heated and I felt a tingle between my thighs. This wasn't why I was here. I was here to invite him to a party. Not for sex. *Don't think about sex.* My eyes traveled down to his pants and I could see the bulge. He wasn't exaggerating in our dreams.

"Hey, kitten."

"Hey, yourself," I said, forcing my eyes up to his.

"Like what you see?" he asked.

"Of course, I do," I said.

He smirked. "But that's not why you're here."

I squeezed my thighs together, urging my body to behave. I wasn't sure what I was waiting for with Luka. Why had I put it off so long?

We were both adults. We both wanted this.

I wanted this.

I wanted him.

Before I lost my courage, I moved closer to him and set my palm on his bare chest. Gently, I pushed him into the room until I could close the door behind us. There was no reason to keep denying how much I wanted him.

His lips parted and I could feel his temperature rise as he connected the dots. But he waited for me to make the first move.

My breathing was already shallow as I stood on my tiptoes and threw my arms over his shoulders.

His arms wrapped around me, pulling me closer to him until our bodies were connected, pressed together as one.

Lifting my chin, our lips met. The kiss was hot and hungry as weeks of frustration poured out of both of us. Luka grabbed hold of my hips and lifted me while our kiss deepened.

I wrapped my legs around his waist and ran my hands through his hair. As he carried me, I slid my tongue into his mouth, meeting his in a playful exchange.

He broke away from the kiss, giving me a smirk before letting go of me. I fell to the bed, sinking into a giant pile of pillows and soft blankets. It reminded me of the corner in his dream world, though his dorm room wasn't nearly as appealing.

Our dream place was open to the stars. His room was full of the orange glow of a salt lamp in one corner and the white light of a small lamp on his desk. The room was neat and spacious, much like all the rooms here.

I could care less about where we were. Everything about this felt right. I propped myself up with my elbows and watched as Luka slid his pants off.

His impressive erection sprung free and I knew that every-thing about our dreams had been just the way it would be in the real world. Which meant I was in for a dozen orgasms. Wetness spread between my thighs just from thinking about our dream sessions.

Luka leaned down over me and slid his hands under my shirt. His touch was rough but welcome and he slid his hands around my back to unsnap my bra without any trouble.

I sat up a little more, making it easier for him to slide my shirt off. He tossed my shirt aside while I threw off my bra. His hands were on my breasts in a heartbeat, caressing them.

I moaned as he sucked one of my nipples into his mouth. With expert strokes of his tongue, he kissed and licked each nipple as he settled in between my thighs.

Squirming, I shifted so I could work my skirt up around my waist, giving him better access. Suddenly, his hand was in my panties, his fingers working around the sensitive nub. Then he inserted a finger, instantly finding the place inside that made me gasp.

All thoughts left my mind. I couldn't concentrate on anything other than the feel of Luka's fingers. I moaned, tossing my head back, enjoying every touch.

Luka's lips pressed against my neck, sending a shiver of tingles down my spine. His every touch was electric.

I could feel little sparks traveling up and down my skin as if I was covered in static electricity. My body tensed, heating as I gasped for air. Pleasure built low in my belly, working its way to a crescendo as Luka continued to pleasure me.

Just as I was about to come, an alarm blared. I jumped back and Luka stopped what he was doing.

Covering my ears against the wailing tone, I looked to Luka.

"Fire alarm," he yelled as he tossed me my shirt.

I threw it on and then re-covered my ears. Luka tugged on his pants and pulled a shirt over his head. Then he reached for my hand and led me out of his room.

The hall was full of bewildered students. Each of them pausing outside their rooms to look down the hall. Finally, someone started walking toward the stairway and they all followed. Luka and I joined the crowd.

All I could think was that there better be a damn fire.

Luka

We'd been so close. So, so close. My cock ached, begging for release as I pulled Raven closer to me. A small crowd had gathered outside the dorms and surprisingly, I could see smoke coming from one of the upper floors.

Even the vampires had crawled out of the basement. I shuddered at the sight of them. All dressed up for something in the depths. You'd think that vampires wouldn't bother me. I'd seen my share of scary shit in the depths of the underworld, but they didn't feed on death the way the vampires did.

When I was young, I'd once walked in on a vampire as she

was draining a victim. Unfortunately, for the vampire, the victim was a demon. I was accompanying my mom on a visit to a reform house for demons. One of her many charity projects that she ran to make her look better than she was. I was a kid, but already being groomed for the family business.

When reports of a disturbance came from the landlord, my mom figured it would be a good learning experience.

I never expected to find a blood covered naked vampire feeding on a sprawled out dead demon. It was weird shit. Especially for a kid.

My mom hadn't hesitated in convicting and sentencing the vampire. She was staked right there in front of me.

I thought about the stake I kept in my room. My mom had insisted I bring it with me. She wasn't fond of the fact that our dorms were in the same building as what she referred to as *the leeches of the supernatural world* but there wasn't much choice. This was the top school and if you got in, and you could afford it, you went.

While I wanted to gain power and make my family proud, I knew I'd be handling things differently if I did accept the position. Being a prince in the underworld was hard enough without accepting the title. Once I stepped up into the role officially, I'd have the same authority my mother did. Judge, jury, and executioner all rolled into one.

I glanced around and found Violet. I knew she spent time with Raven, and I knew Raven liked her. In fact, I'd made friends with several of the vampires here. I just didn't want to be in their dark basement ever. That was too much. I didn't want to know if they were doing anything illegal down there.

Violet caught my eye and waved in our direction. I felt Raven turn toward her. She shifted in my arms, then looked up at me. "Let's go see if Violet knows what's going on."

"Sure," I said.

Raven slid out of my grip and I instantly felt like part of me had been cut out and removed. Every piece of my instincts was fighting me to grab her and drag her back to me.

But she'd come to me tonight and she was ready. I'd waited this long. All I needed was a quiet space to be alone with her and we could finally be together as we both wanted.

I could finally get my cock inside of her.

The thought made me clench my teeth. It was taking everything I had to force myself to wait. The scent of arousal still clung to her from our interlude and she'd felt so good under my touch.

I needed her. As soon as they cleared the building, I had to get her back into my room.

"You still coming to the party?" Violet asked.

"What party?" I asked.

Raven turned to me. "Violet invited me to a vampire party tonight. You should come with me. We can hang out together."

"I'd rather hang out with just you," I said.

She grinned. "I know. But we can finish what we started later."

"Oh, did the fire alarm interrupt something?" Violet asked. "About damn time."

I cocked an eyebrow. Was Raven talking about me to other girls? That had to be a good sign, right?

"What's with this alarm anyway?" she asked.

I glanced toward the building. The smoke I'd seen moments before was gone.

"No idea," Violet said.

"Hey, lover," Scarlett called. "They're saying we can go back in."

"Come to the party, please," Violet said.

I looked back at Raven. She seemed so happy about being invited to a party. Who was I to freak out about it? I mean, that crazy vamp encounter happened when I was a kid. I was sure they weren't hiding chained up humans in the basement. Probably.

"Alright everyone, that's enough excitement for tonight," Dr. Green called out.

I turned to see him coming out of the dorms. I didn't even know he was in there. My brow furrowed. He must have gone in to check out the fire alarm.

Professor Halifax walked out behind him, her chin high and her sharp eyes darting around at all the gathered students.

"You may go back to your rooms," Dr. Green said. "Except for Raven Winters."

"What do you think happened?" she asked, looking up at me.

My chest tightened as I noticed the flicker of fear in her bright green eyes. "I don't know."

She took a deep breath and blew it out. "I really wish we were back in your room right now."

I groaned, unable to control myself. "So do I."

"Raincheck?" she asked.

"Any time. Any place." I was trying to be playful, but I meant it. I was so ready to finish what we started.

Dr. Green walked toward us as the students around us darted toward the door. I glanced down at Raven, who had to be freezing. Her nipples were showing through her white shirt. Fuck. I didn't grab her bra on her way out. I wished I had my sweater but giving her a tee shirt wasn't going to do much good.

"Ms. Winters," Dr. Green said. "Sorry to interrupt your evening plans, but I'm afraid we have to have a chat."

"What happened?" she asked.

Dr. Green glanced over at me, then back at Raven.

"You might as well just say it," she said. "I'll tell him whatever it is anyway."

Dr. Green frowned. "Fine. The alarm that went off was set off by someone inside the demon dorm manually."

"Sounds like someone pulling a prank," I said.

Dr. Green shook his head. "Professor Halifax couldn't match the magic with any species of supernatural we have on campus. It came back as fae magic."

My brow furrowed. "Isn't Professor Halifax fae?" I asked. It had never been said out loud but that was the only explanation for her appearance and her abilities.

Dr. Green cocked an eyebrow. "Are you suggesting one of our faculty came into a student dorm and pulled the fire alarm?"

My face heated. "No, that doesn't make any sense."

"I don't understand what all this has to do with me," Raven said.

Dr. Green sighed. "We have reports of several more government officials who have been found dead, all their magic drained. One of them was fae."

Raven looked like she'd seen a ghost. Her already pale features washed out completely. She honestly looked like she was going to throw up.

"Raven?" I asked.

"You're saying the thief was here, aren't you?" Raven asked, finally.

"It can't be," I said. "How would she get in? Don't you have security at this school?"

"Watch your tone, Mr. Drake."

I pressed my lips into an angry line. They were supposed to be protecting Raven, not letting the crazy Thief who was trying to kill her gain entry to our school. This place was supposed to be the best there was.

"How did she get in?" Raven asked.

Dr. Green shifted, his gaze downcast.

"How?" Raven repeated.

"One of our guards left his post ten minutes before the alarm was pulled. He left the gate open and removed the wards," Dr. Green said.

I felt numb and betrayed. Grabbing hold of Raven's hand, I pulled her closer to me. She didn't resist and leaned up against my chest.

"What does that mean?" she asked.

"It means you're no longer leaving the main building. You have to stay in the castle all the time. The wards on that building can only be broken by me. You'll be safe there."

"That's what you said last time," I mumbled.

Dr. Green shot me a glare. "She will be safe."

I swallowed hard. This changed things. "You have to get your magic back now."

She nodded. "I need to see Zach and Matt. They might be able to help me."

"The Obscura twins?" Dr. Green asked.

"We did a magic meld before and we connected somehow. I think maybe they could help me bring it back," she said.

"I should have known there was something going on with you and that family," Dr. Green said.

"What do you mean?" Raven asked.

"They're the ones who have been paying your tuition." Dr. Green started to walk away, then stopped and looked back at us. "Get in the building. And stay there."

Raven

I paced my room as a rush of tangled emotions flooded through me. I was stuck here, without my magic and without any way out. It was possible my magic could return on its own. It was possible it would never return. Add in the fact that the thief was still after me and when I could defend myself, I was punished for doing so.

I stopped walking and glared at the book on my desk. It had told me that if I could unlock any of my magic, it could all come back. I wished I'd shown the book to Luka. Maybe he could have found something in there that I'd missed.

I was seriously regretting telling him I wanted to be alone.

If the thief was on campus, if she'd broken into the demon dorm, I was pretty much screwed anyway. Plus, there was that whole thing about one of the school's guards letting her in. I had my doubts that the wards at the school would keep me safe.

And why the hell would she pull the fire alarm? What if she wasn't here and it was some kid with fae heritage who pulled it?

I ran a hand through my hair and worked my fingers through the tangles. None of this made sense. And I was getting frustrated.

I should be at a party right now. Making friends and trying to fit in to this place. Instead, I was pouting alone in my room.

Doing what I was supposed to do hadn't helped. Going to classes hadn't helped. I was getting tired of always doing the right thing. Besides, I was starting to think I was screwed no matter what I did. The two times I'd used magic to defend myself, I'd gotten in trouble. Now that I didn't have magic, I was defenseless. I was fucked either way.

Before I could change my mind, I ran into my giant closet and tugged one of the little black dresses off the hanger. Quickly, I changed clothes and pulled on some knee-high boots.

As soon as I shrugged on the black leather jacket all of my worries slipped away. If I was going down anyway, I might as well have some fun before I did.

I felt like a spring wound too tight. And I knew if I didn't let off some steam, I was going to snap. A party with a bunch of vampires sounded like just the right amount of debauchery to get this out of my system. Nobody expected me to leave the school. I could sneak out and sneak back in two hours. Get it out of my system and settle into my house arrest tomorrow.

Feeling confident in my decision, I left my room and quietly walked down the hall. Thankfully, the common room was empty. Everyone was probably out doing fun things. Or at dinner.

I wondered if I was going to be too early for the party but now wasn't the time to second guess that. Worst case, I'd hang out with Violet a bit then come back here.

As I walked through the halls of the school, I passed students who were on their way to various Friday night activities or heading into town. Nobody stopped to ask me where I was going. Keeping my chin up, I powered through as if I was on a mission. I'd learned over the years that you got a lot less questions if you pretended you knew exactly what you were doing.

As soon as I slipped through the main doors and the cold air greeted me, I felt liberated. I took a deep breath, the cool air sending a welcome shiver. I was out and I was free, for now. Tonight, I just wanted to be a normal student, whatever that meant.

I wanted to forget about the thief, forget about my missing magic, and forget about my past. I wanted to embrace the present and live my life without worry.

I'd never been in the vampire dorm, but I knew they had a basement entrance on the opposite end of the demon dorm. Their entrance went straight down to the basement from what I'd heard.

I slipped into the door and found myself on a dark staircase much like the one that led to my dorm in the dungeon. Like the dungeon, the hallway was lined with flickering magical torches.

Their wall was finished, beautiful brick, though. Whereas the walls on our stairs were coarse, damp rock.

I frowned at the reminder of how poorly the shifters were treated. The thought solidified the fact that I didn't want to spend time with the other mages on campus. Aside from the twins, none of them had been welcoming. Plus, there was that whole shifter whore thing that was going around.

The thought of Ben made my throat tighten. He still wasn't talking to me and when we passed in the halls or saw each other in class, he ignored me. It was like a knife to the heart every time I saw him. I kept hoping he'd get over whatever anger he had toward me with time, but it had been weeks.

If not for the distractions with Luka and the research, I'd have probably barged in on him in his room and demanded answers. It was only a matter of time at this point, though. I was feeling reckless and that streak of rebellion rising up in me felt good.

If I was facing another upcoming attack without any magic, what the hell did I have to lose? Maybe I'd go pound on his door when I left here. Or maybe I'd go right to Luka's room instead and finish what we started earlier.

For a second, my memory flashed to Luka and me in his bed. His mouth on my nipple, his fingers inside me. Then, the mental image shifted and instead of Luka, it was Ben.

My eyes widened in surprise and I shook the thought from my head. I hadn't even spoken to him in weeks, where had that come from?

The stairs ended in a long, dark hallway. Thumping bass vibrated the ground and I knew I wasn't too early for the party. Ahead, I could see colored lights dancing on the walls.

I moved toward the sights and sounds of the party and ended up in a large room that was probably their common room. Only they didn't have any couches or chairs. Instead, it was a massive open space. Other than the green and purple lights that moved along the walls, the room was as dark as a night club. And the music was just as loud.

Probably a hundred people filled the room, moving and dancing to the music. Most of the ladies were dressed like me in little black dresses. Some of them were in bras and underwear. A couple were wearing nothing at all.

There was a rhythm to the movement I'd never seen at a club or party before. Nobody seemed to be in couples. The dancing was free flowing, with people moving from partner to partner without regard for who they were dancing with. A man in cutoff jeans shorts grinded against a woman in a pink bunny onesie. A woman in a bra and underwear was chest to chest with a woman in a little black dress. A couple of men in school uniforms slow danced with their arms around each other.

As I watched, the music changed rhythm and everyone moved, finding a new partner and resumed their dance, unfazed by the change. It was freeing to see. Nobody here was worried about the details. They only wanted to dance.

"You made it!"

I looked over to see a breathless Violet in a black slip dress. A streak of red was smeared on her mouth and cheek and her fangs, which were usually retracted, were on full display.

"I made it." I gestured to her face. "Looks like you already had dinner."

Her eyes widened and she quickly retracted her fangs then wiped her face with the back of her hand. "I'm so sorry you had to see that."

I shrugged. "It's not like I don't know what you eat."

"Well, you don't," she said. "Not really."

"What do you mean? Don't you drink blood?"

"Sure," she said. "But we're supposed to stick to the synthetic stuff from Japan or the donor bags."

I glanced around the room again as realization dawned on me. Sure enough in the back of the room, along the wall were several couches I'd missed at first glance. People were making out on them. Only, I was pretty sure they weren't actually making out. When I looked closer, I could tell they were feeding.

"They're all willing, I assure you," Violet said. "And I'm told it's actually very pleasurable. Most of them sit there and orgasm the whole time we feed."

"I'll have to take your word for it," I said, suddenly feeling very self-conscious about the amount of bare skin I'd show if I took off my jacket.

"Don't worry," she said. "You're off limits. We have a rule here. Willing only. And guests are never to be propositioned. Ever."

Before I could consider how I actually felt about the whole thing, Violet pulled my jacket off and tossed it to someone. Scarlett maybe?

The next thing I knew, I was on the dance floor with Violet, moving to the beat of the music. As soon as I started moving, my body took over, feeling the music on instinct.

"Have fun," Violet said just as the music changed.

Without thinking, I moved until I was facing a new partner. I didn't even realize I'd turned to someone else. It was as if the music was driving my movements.

A tall, thin blonde vampire wrapped his arms around my waist and the two of us danced together as if we had been a couple for years. We anticipated the other's move, dancing in time as if we'd rehearsed the steps. I laughed. "This is wild."

"First time?" he asked.

"Yes," I said. "How does it do this?"

"It's the music," he said. "Siren magic. They might be crazy creatures, but they sure know how to make a killer playlist."

Just then, the music shifted again, and I turned to my next partner.

Luka smiled at me. "Wanna dance?"

I narrowed my eyes. "I thought you didn't do vampire parties?"

He shrugged. "I want to be where you are."

How could I resist that? I took his hands. "How about we get out of here and finish where we left off?"

He grinned. "I like that even better."

Raven

Luka's hands slid up my dress before the door even closed behind us. I lifted my arms, encouraging him to get the dress off me faster.

As he tossed it to the ground, I pulled up his shirt. He took over and finished taking it off. It joined my dress on the floor.

His mouth found mine in a hungry, passionate kiss with so much heat behind it that my skin felt like it was on fire. As his lips and mine moved in unison, I reached for his fly.

Luka's hands wrapped around my back, finding my bra strap. Just as he released the clasp, I had his fly open.

Breathless, I stepped away from the kiss and slid my bra off of my shoulders. Then I hooked my thumbs under the waistband of my panties and pulled them down.

I stood there completely naked but felt like I was burning up. I wanted Luka so bad it was as if my body and his were magnetically attracted to each other.

He stepped out of his jeans and I glanced down to see that he wasn't wearing any underwear. I smirked. He was prepared for tonight.

I admired him for a moment. His lean, chiseled form. His strong chest that led down to washboard abs. Below that, the V of his hips pointed straight to his large erection.

I didn't stand a chance. He was a perfect male. The kind of partner I would have thought only existed in my dreams.

Turns out, I was the lucky one who got to have him in my dreams, and I was about to finally have him in real life.

Unable to wait any longer, I moved to him and took his hand. He grinned, that cocky playful grin of his that made my heart flutter. I'd made him wait and I was ready to make it up to him.

When we reached his bed, I pushed him down.

"Oh, I like where this is going," he said.

"Just wait," I said.

I crawled onto the bed, between his legs, then lowered my head. Using my tongue, I licked his cock from base to tip before pulling it into my mouth.

Luka groaned and fell to his back on the bed.

Gripping his upper thighs, I continued to lick and suck until his hips bucked and his moans grew more rapid.

There was no way in hell I was going to stop here. I wanted more than this.

I lifted my head and climbed over him so I was straddling his hips.

"You are so fucking sexy," he said.

"Have you seen yourself in the mirror?" I asked.

He laughed. "I'm not really my type if you know what I mean."

"I'm pretty sure you're everyone's type," I said.

"Well, that's high praise, especially from you. The one who kept me waiting." He sat up and wrapped his arms around me, pulling me on top of him.

I could feel the head of his cock at my entrance and I held my breath in anticipation. After all this time, all this wait, it was finally real.

Slowly, I lowered myself onto him, letting myself adjust as he filled me. When he was deep inside me, I leaned forward and the top of his cock hit me in just the right place.

We both moaned at the same time and sparks seemed to explode across my skin. It was as if little bursts of electricity sizzled around us. Then, just as soon as it started, it stopped, and I was hit instead with the pleasure of his cock inside me.

I leaned forward, pinning his shoulders down with my chest. My breasts pressed against his bare chest as my lips made contact with his.

Slowly, I lifted and lowered my hips. The friction making me moan into his mouth.

Luka slid his tongue into my mouth and I had to brace myself with my hands on the bed to keep from losing control. All the sensations combined were pushing me closer and closer to climax.

I leaned back up so I was sitting on him and continued to thrust with my hips. When Luka's fingers found my clit, I cried out as an orgasm crashed through me.

Breathless, I didn't even resist as he lifted me off him and rotated us so I was now on the bottom.

He looked down at me with those blue eyes and I felt like I'd turned into a puddle. The man had a hold on me, that was for damn sure. He could probably do just about anything to me and I'd go along for the ride.

Smirking, he parted my thighs and slid his hips in between them. Still holding my thighs, he lifted them so my legs were in the air. I could feel his cock at my entrance, and I held my breath in anticipation.

He didn't enter me right away, though. Instead he rubbed his cock against my clit, teasing me. Wetness grew between my legs and I whined. "Please."

"Wait," he said, letting go of my thighs. He leaned forward and kissed me, sucking my lower lip into his mouth.

I moaned again and bucked my hips against him. His mouth moved to my jaw, then down to my neck. He trailed kisses along my collar bone and then moved back up my neck to my ear. When his tongue hit my earlobe, I gasped. I had no idea that was a turn on.

Again, I lifted my hips and this time, I was met with his cock sliding easily into me.

He thrust slowly at first, then grabbed my legs, holding them up again. He picked up speed, pounding me hard.

Grabbing fistfuls of sheets to hang on, I cried out with each thrust. The pressure kept building and I gasped for breath as I got closer to climax with each thrust.

Finally, I tossed my head back and screamed as an explosive orgasm rippled through my body.

Luka finished in the next thrust and then he collapsed, resting his head on my breasts.

His warm breath came out as rapid as my own. I ran my fingers through his golden hair. It was damp with sweat and still sexy as hell.

Sex in my dreams had always been amazing with him but this blew that away.

He lifted his chin and smiled at me; his eyes hooded with desire. I knew exactly how he felt. The post orgasm haze had me feeling like I was drunk, but I was totally sober.

He was just that good.

Ben

Each time I saw Raven, it got harder to keep my wolf in check. She wasn't even in the classroom yet but walking by her usual desk was enough to send an involuntary growl into my throat. She wasn't even sitting there but her scent still hung in the air.

I forced down the beast inside, maintaining control as best as I could. As we got closer to the wolf moon, I was struggling to contain it. I'd had to let my wolf run in the woods outside the school every night this week and it still wasn't enough.

The human part of me was exhausted and losing focus with each passing day as the power of my wolf grew. I just had to make it to the wolf moon. It was the strongest moon of the year. The one that gave us shifters the most power. Our creatures within were at their peak on that night and gained power leading up to it. Once I survived that night, I was in the clear. I could control myself. Control my wolf. But it wasn't easy.

We'd learned so little about mating bonds because it was rare. Most of us never came in contact with our mate. I'd heard the stories. Tales of forbidden love that usually ended in tragedy. I'd also heard how incredible sex was with your mate. Apparently, it was so amazing there was an ancient shifter word used to describe the orgasm that came with it. *Furor*. From the Latin word for *Frenzy*.

My wolf rumbled low in my chest and I knew what that meant. Raven was here.

I looked up to see her walking into the classroom, her backpack slung on one shoulder. She was in a white long sleeve shirt and a short black skirt today. All I wanted to do was push that skirt up around her waist and claim her.

But I had to resist.

My dad was still breathing down my neck and I knew he was paying at least one professor to keep an eye on me. If I made a move on Raven, he'd know.

And as much as I wanted her, I needed her to be safe even more. Especially since she was without her magic. Thankfully, Makayla kept me updated on her progress. Or lack of progress.

Part of me wondered if we could get away with hiding in a dark corner. But this was my mate, not some one-night stand.

She waved to me and smiled. It was a smile she didn't use anywhere else. It was my smile and I knew it. Despite my ignoring her, she hadn't stopped being kind to me. It made me feel even worse.

I inclined my head, acknowledging her but looking away quickly so I didn't invite her to come over.

A rush of her honeydew scent filled my nostrils and I knew she took her seat nearby. I didn't have to look up to feel her gaze on me. She was probably waiting for me to give in. Even if she didn't know what we were, she had to be feeling a pull to me. I was lucky she'd been raised in the human world and didn't know the mating bond when she felt it stir inside her. If she came to me, I wouldn't be able to stop myself.

My wolf growled again and my cock twitched, he wanted to claim his mate. And I couldn't blame him.

I'd have to run again tonight. It was the only way to try to wear down my wolf. Keep it distracted. Give it some freedom while denying the only thing both of us wanted.

Once class started, I risked a few glances at her. She was as stunning as ever. Her long red hair hung down to the middle of her back. I wanted to run my fingers through it. I wanted to grab it and tug her to me. I wanted to do everything to her.

Breaking myself away from the thoughts of her lips around my cock, I looked up at Professor Hurd. He was droning on and on about portals and magic history. I couldn't concentrate. All I could think about was Raven.

The Wolf Moon couldn't come soon enough. I just had to make it through and then things could return to normal.

Raven

Ben still wasn't talking to me but at least he wasn't pretending I wasn't here. His little nods hurt, though. We'd been at the start of something good, I knew it. That night playing strip poker wasn't an accident. And somehow, I knew he still wanted to get to know me better.

I sure did.

I was pretty sure that if he walked up to me and kissed me, I'd kiss him right back. And we wouldn't stop there.

None of it made sense. He'd been ignoring me for weeks, but I couldn't help but feel like I broke him. Something happened that night with the thief when he saved me. Whatever he was working out needed more time, but I hoped it wasn't much longer.

If not for the distractions of tutoring and researching with Luka, I'd probably be driving Ben crazy with questions. It wasn't like me to let something go this easily, but I somehow knew he needed the time and space. There was a part of me that wanted him to heal, no matter what the cost was to me. We hardly knew each other, but I was pretty sure that I would sacrifice my own happiness if it meant he could recover from whatever he was going through.

I glanced behind me to get another look at him. He was facing the professor, seemingly interested in the lesson. We were still learning about portals, despite the fact that we'd been told to never use them. It seemed like a waste of time to me, but I guess it must be on some supernatural curriculum check-list or something. One of those things they make you learn even if they have zero real life applications. Like existential poetry.

With a sigh, I turned back to the lesson, trying to get anything I could. Nothing stuck. Instead, I doodled flowers and vines all over my notebook till the bell rang.

As usual, Ben was out the door before I even zipped up my backpack. Feeling a bit defeated, I left the classroom. I wanted to catch him to tell him my magic was starting to return, but I knew he'd just avoid me.

I hadn't told anyone yet, but I thought Ben would understand what I was going through. He'd been without his ability to shift for a few days. He knew what it felt like to have your magic stolen.

Soon I'd tell Makayla and Luka. But right now, I was still a little too nervous that the candle had been a fluke.

I walked into Spellcasting, expecting to check in before

going to the library but as soon as I saw the familiar faces next to my seat, I realized plans were about to change.

Matt and Zach both wore grins on their identical, handsome faces when they saw me. "Hey, little mage," one of them called.

As I got closer, I checked for the freckle. "Hi, Zach." Then I turned to the other twin, "hi, Matt."

"I told you she can tell us apart," Zach said.

"It's impressive for sure," Matt said.

"Did you miss us terribly?" Zach asked.

"I actually did," I said, feeling a comforting warmth spread through me. I was really, really glad they were back. I didn't realize how much I'd missed them until now. I wondered if it was the bond we'd forged from our magic meld that made me feel that way.

"It seems we missed some action," Matt said, his brow furrowed in concern. "Are you okay?"

"I guess," I said, not really sure how to answer. I'd repeated the story so many times I wasn't in the mood to tell it again. "I'm sorry about your grandfather."

"Great-grandfather," Matt said.

"He was a dick," Zach said.

"He was still family," Matt said.

"Which is why we couldn't get out of the twenty-one days of mourning. I think I'm good with family visits for the next decade or so," Zach said.

"Until parent's weekend," Matt said.

"Shit," Zach said.

"Speaking of parents," I said. "You two want to tell me something?"

Both of them pressed their lips together, obviously aware of what I was asking.

"You'll have to thank your mother for me," I said. "For paying my tuition and all."

"You'll be able to thank her yourself," Zach said. "She wants us to invite you to tea on parent's weekend. Thankfully, you have a few months to prepare for that."

"Huh. No denial. So you both knew but didn't think I'd be interested to know your parents were footing the bill?" I put my hands on my hips, annoyed.

"Just our mom," Matt said. "Our dad passed when we were babies."

I dropped my hands to my sides. "Sorry."

They shrugged.

"Class, in your seats," Professor Halifax said.

We quickly sat down and I faced the professor. Today she was wearing a pair of tight black slacks and a gray sweater. It was by far the most causal thing I'd ever seen her wear. Her hair was pulled up in a hasty ponytail and she didn't have her usual impeccable air about her. I wondered if she'd overslept. The thought made me smile. I supposed professors weren't that different from us.

"Today is your last day to prepare for the group presentations," she said. "You'll begin presenting tomorrow, beginning with Malakai's group. Wednesday will be Joanna's group, and Thursday is Hunter's group."

She moved closer to us and locked her eyes on me. "Your group will present on Friday, so I suggest you three figure out how to demonstrate your use of elemental fire magic before then."

My jaw dropped open. I had managed to make one candle light with the help of some kind of weird fae portal magic. How the hell was I supposed to do anything more exciting than that? "Professor, I..."

She stared at me, her eyebrows raised. "You have a week."

The whole thing seemed completely unfair. She'd worked with me on Saturday. She knew my magic wasn't there.

Suddenly I remembered what she'd said, and I glanced at the twins sitting next to me. She was pushing us all and forcing us to use that bond to bring my magic back.

"Guess we have some work to do," Matt said, then he lowered his voice. "I heard your magic was taken that night."

I swallowed then nodded. "It was but I worked with Professor Halifax on Saturday and she got some of it to come back. And she told me you two might be able to help me."

"The magic meld," Zach said.

I nodded again. "Yes. I'm not sure how, but I think it might work."

"We connected our magic when we did that," Matt said. "If we try it again, it could jumpstart yours."

"It's worth trying," Zach said. He shot his hand into the air.

Professor Halifax walked over to us. The rest of the room was a hum of conversation as students talked through their projects and practiced their magic. I felt so out of place, like I didn't belong here. It was an awful feeling.

"Yes, Mr. Obscura?"

"Permission to go somewhere more private to practice?" he asked with a cheeky grin.

"Fine," she said, almost too quickly. It was as if this was what she expected. Without another word, she turned and walked away from us.

"Our room?" Zach asked.

I shook my head. "Not this time. My turn for the home turf."

"In the shifter dorm?" Zach asked. "You can't be serious."

"Why not?" I asked. "It's where I sleep every night."

"They hate us, you know that right?" Zach asked.

"They don't hate me," I said.

"True," Zach said. "So they'll just shift and bite our heads off and leave you be."

I narrowed my eyes. "You don't really think they'd do that?"

He shrugged. "You don't know all the things my mom has said publicly over the years."

"If there's one thing I'm starting to notice it's that everyone hates their parents. And none of us are our parents. If we were who raised us, I'd be a crazy alcoholic living off government assistance."

Zach's brow furrowed. "I thought your parents were dead."

"My aunt raised me. If you can call what she did raising me. Basically, she kept me clothed, fed, and a roof over my head. Most of the time," I said.

"I'm so sorry," Matt said.

"I know, poor little troubled mage," I said, rolling my eyes. "I really don't want sympathy from the rich kids."

"Hey, we get that same thing on us, you know?" Matt said. "Just because we were raised with money doesn't mean our lives were easy."

"I'll take your word for it," I said.

"I'm serious," he said. "We didn't struggle, that's true. But I wouldn't wish our life on anyone."

"You mean that?" I asked, thinking back to Professor Halifax's comment about why my tuition was being paid.

"I do," he said.

"Sorry," I said. "You didn't get to choose your parents any more than I did."

"It's okay," Zach said. "We get that a lot. Spoiled rich kids, which we are."

"Time's ticking," Professor Halifax said.

"Come on, I've always wanted to see the shifter dorm," Matt said.

Zach

Raven seemed confident as she led us down the dingy stairs to the dungeon. It was hard to believe that a mage of her abilities had been thrown down here with the shifters. She could have thrown a fit and demanded a different room. But the whole thing made no sense to begin with. Why had they put her down here?

While we'd been with our family, I'd discovered that my mom had been paying her tuition. Something about a favor she owed her parents. I didn't get more details than that from her but I did know she was interested in meeting Raven. How was I supposed to drop that truth-bomb on her? It was bad enough that she was dealing with all of this right now. No magic, dorm in the shifter dungeon. She didn't need the most powerful mage in the supernatural world nagging her about her grades or her life. Though, I knew it was inevitable. My mother got whatever she wanted.

Torches flickered along the stairway and my fingers traced over the damp walls. Nothing about this was what I expected. Sure, it was called the dungeon, but I thought it was a clever nick name since it was in the basement. I'd been in the vampire dorm a few times and theirs was almost as nice as the mage dorms.

We left the stairs and passed through a common room. A couple of students were sprawled out on the couches, but we didn't linger. Ignoring their inquisitive looks, we moved on, following Raven.

Finally, we stopped outside of a door and she used her key card to enter.

She flipped on a light then walked over to a lamp and turned it on. "Can you turn that one off?" She pointed to the light switch by the door. I flipped it down and the blinding fluorescent lights went out leaving us in a dim room lit by her small lamp.

"It's not as nice as the Obscura suite," she said, "but it's far superior to anywhere I've ever lived before."

She picked up some laundry off the floor and tossed it into the bathroom. "Sorry for the mess."

"Don't worry," Matt said. "I'm guessing you don't get maid service down here?"

She lifted an eyebrow and glared at Matt, her green eyes flashing. "Seriously? You need a maid? You can't even take care of your own room?"

"We can, we just don't have to," Matt said with a cocky grin.

I knew that wasn't going to work on her. She wasn't the kind of girl who was impressed by our wealth. In fact, I think it had the opposite effect on her. I tried not to grin too much knowing that all Matt was doing was killing any chance he had of scoring with her.

"Your room is great," I said. "Thanks for letting us use the space to try this."

She turned her gaze on me, her stance tense. She ran a hand through her hair and let out a frustrated sigh. "I'm sorry. I should be thanking you both for helping with this. Professor Halifax said you can probably help bring more of my magic back."

"What have you done so far?" I asked.

"She worked with me to get me to light a candle. Some kind of fae magic involving portals, I think."

"Portals?" Matt asked. "That's dangerous stuff."

"So are magic melds," I reminded him.

"Yeah, but we've already done it once, right?" he asked.

"True," I said, then I turned to Raven. "Where do you want to sit?"

"I guess right here," she pointed to the floor.

I extended my hand, offering it to her. "Ready?"

To my surprise, she took my hand. "I don't really have a choice."

I hated that she viewed us as a necessity. I wondered if I'd ever get a shot at her if not for this. For a brief moment, I was thankful she'd lost her magic. I needed more time with her. Guilt swam through me at the thought. I knew she was going through a terrible time but the selfish part of me that wanted her seemed to take over.

She sat cross-legged on the ground and I followed her lead. Matt sat next to her close enough that his thigh touched hers. Heat filled my chest as jealousy flared. I wanted to be alone with her. I didn't want him here.

Taking a deep breath, I pushed the thoughts away. This wasn't like me at all. I'd never felt this way about a woman. Especially a woman I hardly knew. Sure, she was sexy as hell, and I knew she was a knockout even under her clothes, thanks to her setting herself on fire. But I typically had more self-control than this.

"So last time we did this, we were trying to find out about your magic," Matt said.

"Which we never really did," she responded. "Cause the whole using time magic thing would have been helpful."

"Yeah, sorry," he said.

"Today, let's focus on trying to find your magic and coax it out. Once we find it, we can see if we can learn more about it," I suggested.

"Alright," she said, extending her hands on either side.

I pushed down the jealous thoughts as Matt took hold of her and grabbed his other hand, not letting go of hers.

"Close your eyes," I said. "Deep breaths."

I closed my eyes and sent my magic toward Raven, urging it to find hers and connect us the way it had last time. I didn't have to wait long.

Tiny pinpricks of pain traveled up my arm. They were so sudden and intense that I nearly cried out. None of them stayed in one place long enough to cause lingering pain but they were annoying. Sort of like when your foot falls asleep. Though, instead of staying in one area, the pain traveled up my arm, across my shoulders and down my back.

As the pain eased, I could feel her. It was impossible to explain, but there was something there that wasn't just my magic. It called to me, urging me toward it. Internally, I encouraged my magic to go to it.

A rush of overwhelming emotion surged through me as if I'd been given a shot of adrenaline after jumping off a cliff. It was surprise mixed with fear and awe. I couldn't fully explain it, but I wanted it. I craved it.

Then, just as quickly as it had arrived, it left, and Raven tugged her hand away breaking the connection.

I looked over at her. She was gasping for breath and her hair was standing on edge as if she'd walked through a static field. Her eyes were wide and her full lips were parted. I never wanted to tear someone's clothes off more.

"What the hell was that?" Matt asked. "Did you feel that?"

"I don't know what happened. It was right there. I could feel my magic. It was right there and then it was gone." Raven's brow furrowed and I was pretty sure I could see tears pooling in her eyes.

"I felt something," I said. "It was like it was calling to me."

"More like dragging me in," Matt said. "Was that your magic?"

"I think so," she said. "Maybe."

"Try to make fire," I said.

"I don't know," she said. "That didn't go so well for me last time."

"We found your magic," Matt said. "It's still there or it's coming back or something. You should try it."

She nodded and then extended her hand, going through the motions of the trick we'd taught her to make fire.

For a moment, nothing happened. Then a tiny blue flame flickered to life in her palm.

I leaned closer to her. "Blue."

She looked up at me, locking those green eyes on me. I felt like my insides turned to goo. She could throw that fire at me and I wouldn't even move away from her. She had me completely under her spell. I would do anything to be with her.

"Your magic is still in there," Matt said.

She tore her gaze off me and closed her hand, extinguishing the flame. "It doesn't feel the same as it did before."

"It's probably still healing," I said. "We can try again." All I wanted to do was touch her. Even if it was just holding her hand as we attempted a magic meld. I just needed her. Any part of her would do. For now.

"No," Matt said. "We're lucky nothing bad happened. You need to recover. We can try again later."

Raven stood and I quickly got to my feet. I wanted to grab her and drag her to my bed.

"Thank you both," she said. "Hopefully I'll be fixed by Friday when we give our presentation."

"Don't worry about that," I said. "We'll be fine."

"Not all of us have rich parents to bail us out," she said.

"Well, actually, you kind of do," I said.

"I know your mom is paying my tuition," she said.

"That kind of makes you honorary Obsucra," Matt said.

I wrinkled my nose. I didn't want to think about her like that. I wanted to fuck her not adopt her.

"I still need to be able to defend myself," she said.

"You know, there's enough room in our room for company," Matt said.

She glared at him.

He put his hands up in mock surrender. "Just saying it can't hurt to have some people nearby who can help you if needed."

"It's not a bad idea," I said.

"I think I'm fine here," she said.

A knock sounded on the door and she walked over to answer it.

"Ben," she said, sounding surprised.

I turned to see the huge shifter standing in her doorway. I knew the expression on my face made it clear he was unwelcome. I didn't care. I didn't want him sniffing around my girl.

"Study session?" he asked.

"Something like that," she said. "Trying to get my magic back."

The shifter's expression softened. "It still hasn't returned?"

"No," she said.

Ben looked at me then at Matt. He quickly returned his attention to Raven. "I heard there were some people in your room and I wanted to make sure you were safe."

"I'm fine," she said. "Thank you for checking on me."

He stepped back from the door. "I'm going back to my room," he looked up at me and Matt, "next door. Let me know if you need anything."

"I guess you do have help around if you need it," Matt said.

"Yeah," she said, sounding surprised. "I guess I do."

Raven

Things seemed to be going up for the first time in a long time. I was still confined to the main building and I was still spending several days a week in private lessons with Professor Halifax. But Ben was speaking to me again. And the twins helped me learn how to demonstrate fire. My magic was finally returning and while Professor Halifax said it wasn't fully back, it was good enough to fake my way through the presentation so I didn't fuck over Matt and Zach's grades.

Plus, tonight there was going to be a rather epic party. All week, Makayla had been telling me how amazing the wolf moon party was. All the shifters would be there. They'd take over the entire common room and flood into the dorm rooms.

I was looking forward to a night of drinking too much and honestly, I was hoping Ben would be there. Now that we were talking again, maybe we could do something besides just talk.

Because to be honest, I was finding him sexier and more irresistible every time he smiled at me. The thought of that smile made me weak in the knees. I had a serious problem.

I should be satisfied with my incubus, but I couldn't keep my head out of the gutter when it came to Ben.

That was the one bad thing about my life right now, though. There hadn't been any time to connect with Luka in real life. My after school and weekend tutoring sessions along with studying for the upcoming exams was making my social life nonexistent.

But tonight was a holiday so there was no homework given. And the party of the year was taking place in my dorm. There was no way I was going to be able to skip it even if I wanted to.

"Ms. Winters, can you tell me the formula for the spell?" Professor Halifax asked.

I shook myself out of my distraction. I'd been so busy thinking about the fun I was going to have tonight that I hadn't heard a word she said.

Zach pushed his notebook over to me and I glanced down at the word he'd circled.

"Two candles, a full moon, and a live fern?" I asked.

She pursed her lips. "It's lucky for you that your lab partner is paying attention."

I swallowed hard and ignored the heat in my cheeks. I could feel the eyes of my classmates boring into the back of my head. "Sorry, Professor."

She shook her head then went back to teaching.

I tried to pay better attention the rest of the period. It was painful. I'd been so focused on being a good student the last couple of months that I'd rarely let go. I needed this party. I needed to feel normal.

Finally, it was time to pack up.

"You want to practice again tonight?" Zach asked.

We'd worked on bringing my magic back every night this week. Every time we melded our magic, I felt a little stronger after. I also felt a deeper connection to both twins after, too. Though, I was trying to ignore that. It was complicated enough as it was balancing the feelings I had for both Luka and Ben.

"Not tonight," I said. "It's the Wolf Moon."

"But you're not a shifter," Matt said.

"All her friends are," Zach said.

"Most of my friends are," I said. "But it is in my dorm so I might as well go. Besides, I haven't been to a party in a long time."

"And you won't be attending tonight, Ms. Winters," Professor Halifax cut in.

I turned around to stare at her, my mouth open, ready to protest.

"Your magic is not fully functioning yet and Dr. Green wants you ready to take the practice trials before Yule. You don't have time to go to a party." She crossed her arms over her chest.

"Surely one night off won't kill me," I said.

"Won't it?" she asked. "I'm not the one who has a thief hunting me."

I scowled. She had me there. It was irresponsible of me to go to a party when the alternative was staying alive. *Fuck.* "Fine."

"In here right after dinner," she glanced at Matt and Zach, "you two can join her."

"They don't have to do that," I said.

"We don't mind," Zach said.

"Really, you don't need to give up your Friday night," I said.

"Raven, it's fine," Matt said.

A rush of warmth spread low in my belly as he locked his gaze on me. His smile was confident and warm. There was not even a slight sense of being upset about being asked to help me. How were these two so selfless? I hadn't stopped to really think about it before. Professor Halifax had threatened their grade but now that I knew who their mother was, I knew that was never a valid threat. They were helping me because they wanted to.

None of the other mages wanted anything to do with me. They went out of their way to help. *Shit.* The thought brought me right back to the crazy dream I'd had last night. With both of them. At the same time.

For a second, I was back in that dream. Matt's tongue in my mouth as Zach's tongue was in a far more intimate place. I shivered, sending the memory of the dream away.

I did not have the emotional energy to be thinking about them like this. I knew there was a connection between the three of us from the magic meld, but I kept trying to tell myself it wasn't real. It was the magic that bonded us, not anything else. It wasn't the same way I was attracted to Luka or Ben. Was it?

"I'll see you all here after dinner," Professor Halifax said.

I forced a smile on my face as I tossed my backpack over my shoulder. "Can't wait."

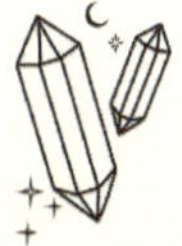

The rest of the day dragged by. The worst part had been telling Makayla that I wasn't going to make it to the party.

"She can't keep you all night," Makayla said as she took a bite of her hamburger.

"That's true," I said. "How late do you usually go for this party?"

"Oh, easily till dawn," she said.

I straightened in my chair, feeling a resurgence of joy. There was no way our tutoring session would go all night. "I'm sure I'll make it then. I just won't be there right away."

"Fashionably late," Makayla said. "Like the mysterious mage you are."

I laughed. "Right. I'm super mysterious."

"You really are, though," she said. "Think about it. You live in the shifter dorm, you had it out with a magic thief, you don't know your parents..."

"I get it," I said. I was still annoyed about the parents thing. It seemed Dr. Green and Ms. Obscura both knew my parents. The Obscura family well enough to feel like they owed a favor in the form of my tuition. Yet, no matter what I asked, I didn't get any information. It was beyond frustrating.

"Go to your tutoring. I'll stash a bottle of vodka in the back somewhere so we can do shots when you join us," she said.

"Better make it tequila," I said with a grin.

"Perfect. I'll hide a couple of limes and we'll be good to go." She leaned in closer to me and lowered her voice. "Hey, maybe you can ask Ben if he wants to lick the salt off of you."

I laughed with Makayla, trying to blow it off but my mind had already gone to picturing Ben's tongue on my neck. I squeezed my thighs together. I wasn't the only one thinking that maybe this party could be the one where we finally break the sexual tension between the two of us.

"Well, you get him a few drinks to lower his inhibitions first," I joked.

"Raven Winters, are you trying to take advantage of my alpha?" she asked.

"Maybe I am." I laughed and Makayla joined in. I might be attending the party late, but I'd still get to go, and I knew that no matter what happened, I'd have a good time.

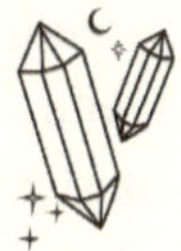

Professor Halifax was waiting for me when I walked into her classroom. I set my backpack down in my usual spot out of habit despite the fact that it was just the two of us.

"Where are your partners?" she asked.

"I'm not sure," I said. "I didn't see them at dinner."

"You must start spending more time with mages," she said. "I do think it'll help your power return to full strength. We fae do better around our own. We feed from their power. That's part of why fae are so much more powerful in their realm."

"Do you miss it?" I asked.

She blinked, her large eyes searching my face in silence for a moment. "Of course. But there's no point in worrying over things you can't control."

It was the first time I'd ever heard her speak about Faerie or about being fae. With her appearance, there was no way she could disguise what she was, but she had never come out and said it. This was the most personal she'd ever been with me.

"Do you think you'll ever go back one day?" I asked.

"Perhaps," she said. She looked like she was going to add something more but turned toward the door just as it opened.

Matt and Zach walked in. They were both in jeans and tee shirts, having shed their school uniforms. And damn, they both looked amazing in their tight jeans.

I pulled my gaze up from their jeans and looked at their faces. Their identical, handsome faces. They were both smiling, but Zach's smile was a bit more crooked than Matt's.

I looked down for the freckle, and realized that for the first time, I'd identified them correctly without my cheat. The more I got to know them, the more I noticed their subtle differences. Matt was cockier and walked with a swagger that was different from Zach. Not that Zach wasn't cocky, he was. Just in a different way than his brother.

"What are we working on tonight?" Matt asked.

"I want to see what the three of you can do together with portal magic," she said.

"Really?" Matt asked.

Professor Halifax lifted her brows and gave him a look that seemed to dare him to question her.

"Alright, let us know what to do," Zach said.

Raven

"You two here," Professor Halifax pointed, "one on each side of her."

The twins moved to either side of me. Zach on my right and Matt on my left. I wasn't sure where she was going with this, but I'd had some luck with lessons so far. If this was going to be the thing that finally unlocked my magic, I would go for it.

"Stones?" Matt asked. "What are those for?"

"Conduction," Professor Halifax said as she set the stones in a circle around the three of us.

"Conducting what?" he asked.

She set down a stone and looked up at him. "Do you want to help her get her magic back or not?"

"I do," he said.

"Then don't question the process," she said.

"There's a process, Matt," Zach said, not hiding the sarcasm.

"Your family might not allow us to fail you, but I can assure you that your mother would not be happy to hear you are not living up to her high standards," she said.

"Can you two just trust her?" I asked. "When we tried this last time, she was able to find some of my magic. I even got a candle to light."

"Without setting yourself on fire?" Zach asked.

"What is with you today?" I asked.

"Nothing," he said.

"He's jealous," Matt said.

"Of what?" I asked.

"You sure spend a lot of time with that incubus," he said.

"So?" I asked. "He's my friend. And you don't have any say over who I spend time with."

"Can we get back to the lover's quarrel later?" Professor Halifax asked.

"There's no lover's quarrel here," Zach and I said at the same time.

Brow furrowed I looked on either side of me, wondering why the twins were being so strange today.

That's when I noticed that there was a blue glow around the three of us. I'd been so busy watching Professor Halifax set up the stones that I didn't even notice that our magic had activated. Was the magic doing something to the twins?

"Go ahead and hold hands," the professor said.

Matt and Zach grabbed my hands and a rush of heat shot up my arms from the point of contact. My skin tingled and I felt more alive than I ever had before. Then the tingling sensation traveled to my core and I sucked in my lower lip, biting down to keep from moaning. What the hell?

"Just as I suspected," Professor Halifax said. "The three of you formed a mage bond. You really shouldn't mess with magic you're not prepared for. I suppose we should be grateful for the fact that you did considering it's the best chance at helping Raven retrieve her magic, but it's going to keep you three bonded for the rest of your lives."

"So it's real?" Matt asked.

"It's real," she said.

"What does that mean for us?" I asked, fighting against the sensual sensation of the twins' magic caressing me.

"It means you're experiencing a bond similar to a mating bond. It's rare in mages. The three of you are going to have a lot to talk about after this," she said. "For now, keep those libidos in check. Focus on the candles."

I took a deep breath in, trying not to be too overwhelmed by all the sensations in my body. Apparently magic and sexual attraction were a dangerous combination. But there was no way in hell I was going to let it get to me while standing in a classroom.

I looked at the candles in front of us. There were eight of them in a line at Professor Halifax's feet.

"Raven needs to light these candles but she'll need your help. However, you need to focus on connecting to her magic and sending it through her. Don't use yours," Professor Halifax said.

"Got it," Matt said.

"Can do," Zach said.

The warmth intensified in my hands and I felt the familiar shockwaves of magic as it filled my veins. Narrowing my eyes, I focused on the candles on the ground. I needed to find my magic and light them all.

Behind the candles, I was vaguely aware of a sizzling sound but I ignored it, focusing on the wicks.

Trying to send all other distractions away, I focused on the sound of my breathing and the feeling of my chest rising and falling. The harder I focused, the more clear things became. I felt like I was alone. Just me and the candles. Nothing else mattered. I couldn't hear anything else. I couldn't see anything else. I felt magic flowing through me, my hands acting as a conductor for the power.

Urging the magic forward, I imagined the flames rising from each of the wicks, one at a time, down the row.

Suddenly, the whole room went dark and I fell to the ground. Slowly, I blinked, adjusting to an odd weightless sensation. It was as if I was in a swimming pool, suspended in liquid.

As my eyes adjusted, I noticed a row of lit candles in front of me. From somewhere far away, someone called my name.

I looked up just as a hand grabbed me and pulled me up.

All at once, the lights returned and I could breathe normally again. "What happened?"

"You nearly opened the portal," Professor Halifax said.

"I don't understand," I said.

She smiled. "I made a tiny tear again to pull in some extra magic. It was too much. You're almost too strong with your mates."

Brow furrowed, I looked at the row of candles. They were all happily flickering away. "I did that?"

She nodded. "You did."

"Does that mean her magic is back?" Zach asked.

"It's close," she said. "I can feel it just below the surface. She'll need something big to push her over that last edge to bring it out."

"Like what?" I asked.

"I have a few things in mind that we can try," Professor

Halifax said. "But for now, you should get some rest. While your friends were supporting you, that was your magic being used."

"She's right," Zach said. "I don't even feel like I used any magic."

"You're helping her find hers," Professor Halifax said.

"Thank you both," I said.

"Maybe you should come back to our room with us for a while and rest where we can keep an eye on you," Matt said.

"I don't think so," I said. "We might have some kind of bond, but it'll take more than that to get into my pants."

"That's fair," Zach said.

I smirked at him, reading between the lines. He was looking at me as a challenge and part of me was looking forward to making him work for it. Just because they were spoiled and cocky, didn't mean they didn't have a chance. Especially given that our magic was practically begging us to get it on. If anything, it would be a test of how long I could go before I broke.

Ben

The Wolf Moon party was in full swing. Tomorrow night, we'd all be running in the woods in our shifted forms. It was the biggest night of the year for shifters. The Wolf Moon was almost impossible to resist. Many of us had our first shift on that night and as we got older, we still felt the pull. It was the one night of the year when shifters yielded to their feral side and ran free.

It's probably where all the werewolf myths came from. The forced shifting on the full moon and all. Most of us had control, but the Wolf Moon could break the control of even the most reserved shifter.

I had always credited myself on my ability to keep my emotions in check. The last few months had challenged me in ways I'd never experienced before with Raven.

Leaving class to go to her aid, nearly attacking a student who insulted her, none of that was like me. And tonight, I was on edge. With the moon nearly full, it called to me. It called to my wolf. I knew I was the closest I'd been since I was a kid to losing myself to the monster within.

I took a deep breath, trying to push the thoughts of Raven from my head. The school was empty tonight. Everyone was either at the party in the dungeons or out doing normal Friday night activities.

Tomorrow, only the shifters would be out. It was too dangerous for non-shifters.

I'd ducked out of the dorms so quickly, I didn't even catch wind of Raven's scent, but she had to be there. Where else would she be tonight? I was sure Makayla was with her and I was sure they were having a great time. Thank gods for Makayla. I'd trust her with my life and since she and Raven were inseparable, I knew she'd keep Raven safe.

My wolf growled sending a low rumbling vibration through my chest. He wanted out. He felt the pull of the moon already. *Not yet.* That was the other part of Wolf Moon. We held off on shifting for the five nights prior. It was challenging, but that shift tomorrow night would be the most liberating feeling in the world.

He growled again and my skin prickled as if someone was nearby. I glanced around the empty hallway. Dark classroom doors and a few emergency lights were all I saw.

It was probably just the pull of the nearly full moon. I glanced at a clock on the wall. I had a few more hours to kill. Maybe I should go to the library. The trolls running it kept it open round the clock.

I turned around and headed back the opposite direction. If nothing else, I could find a spot to take a nap. It might make the night go faster.

Just when I'd convinced myself that a nap in a quiet corner was the perfect solution, I caught the distinct scent of honeydew laced with hints of burning sage. As soon as the roses hit me, I knew I was in trouble.

There was only one person in the world who carried that scent and as I turned the corner, I was face to face with her.

Raven's lips parted in surprise and she jumped. "You scared me."

I could hear her heart racing. "I'm sorry."

"It's okay, I'm glad it's you and not someone else," she said.

"Were you expecting someone?" My wolf tensed, ready to take out any other male who might be a threat to our mate.

"No," she said. "I was just walking back to my room."

"You smell like magic," I said, then regretted it. Who says that?

She smiled and cocked her head to the side. "You can smell my magic?"

"Wolf thing," I said.

"Wow," she said.

"You're out late." I could smell another male on her. Two if I wasn't mistaken. It was taking every ounce of control I had to keep myself from pushing her up against the wall and taking her right here.

"They're making me take extra lessons to get my magic back," she said. "Actually, I've been wanting to talk to you about that but you've been avoiding me."

"I haven't been avoiding you," I said.

"Liar," she said.

"Fine," I said. "What did you want to know?"

"How did you shift again?" She combed her fingers through her hair, a trait I'd noticed she did when she was nervous.

I didn't like that I made her nervous. I was supposed to protect her. I was supposed to make her feel safe. I took a step back from her in case I was too close.

"You did lose your magic for a while, right?" she asked, taking a step closer to me.

My wolf clawed at my insides, desperate for release. Begging me to move closer to her. I wanted to feel her warm skin under my hands and my lips on hers. I wanted to slide my cock inside her. I wanted to claim her.

Swallowing, I tried to ignore my desires. "Yes. I couldn't shift until that day in class. When I felt like you were in danger. I had to respond."

"Why?" she asked, moving closer to me again.

I could feel her body heat from here. She was too close. I was going to lose control.

"Why did you do that and then stop talking to me?" She moved closer again. We were nearly touching now.

I could smell her arousal. She was just as drawn to me as I was to her.

"Raven, I can't," I said.

She didn't respond, she stood there, staring at me with those green eyes. I couldn't take it anymore.

With a growl, I advanced on her, pushing her up against the wall and boxing her in with my arms.

I didn't wait. My body took over. All I could think about was making her mine.

Raven

He moved so fast I didn't have time to react. Suddenly, I was against the wall and his mouth was on mine.

Matching his force, I pressed my lips into his, my breathing already shallow. Everything about the kiss was passion laced with desperation. It was hungry and brutal and holy shit I was wet already.

I couldn't deny that I'd wanted Ben from the moment I saw him. Everything felt so right. Our breaths in synch, our lips moving in rhythm, everything felt just as it should be.

I felt one of his hands on the side of my head, pulling me

even deeper into the kiss. I pressed my body against him, wanting more.

He shoved me back against the wall, pinning me there with his hips. I could feel his erection through our clothes. The feel of him against me made my breathing even more rapid and I slid my tongue into his mouth, hungry for more.

I laced my fingers in the tangles of his dark hair, pulling him down a little lower. He grabbed my wrist and tugged it away, moving it to the wall.

Breaking free of the kiss, he pulled back so he could look at me. Using my free arm, I reached for him to bring his lips back to me. He grabbed my other wrist and held it against the wall, keeping me pinned in place.

Panting, I looked up at him. "Why'd you stop?"

He smirked, then he moved my wrists in front of me and used one hand to hold them in place. "I'm just getting started."

His mouth was on mine again. His kisses almost painful. I welcomed it, pressing back harder. My lips were swollen and his stubble scratched my face, but I couldn't stop. I didn't want to stop.

Dropping my hands, he moved his hands around my waist, then lower to my ass. Without breaking the kiss, he lifted me and I wrapped my legs around his waist.

Effortlessly, he carried me to the nearest classroom door, using one of his huge shoulders to push it open.

He dropped me on the teacher's desk.

My ass hit the desk hard, but I didn't care, I was already reaching for Ben's fly. He batted my hand away, grabbing hold of my wrists again and this time, pinning me down on the desk.

I groaned in protest, lifting my head to try to nip at Ben's lips. He smirked down at me, unyielding in his hold on me. "You're not getting away this time."

"I don't want to get away," I said.

"That's what you say now," he said.

"I think I can handle it," I said.

He climbed on top of the desk, straddling me. Then he lowered his face and kissed my neck. He nipped me and I moaned. I never thought I'd be into that. In fact, this whole thing was something I never thought I'd be into, but I was up for him holding me down any time.

I tried to lift myself enough to kiss him, but he pulled away again, sending a surge of frustration through me.

"Not yet," he said.

Still holding my wrists with one of his huge hands, he slid the other down my chest and down my hips to my upper thighs. Goosebumps spread across my skin as he tugged the skirt up around my waist.

His fingers slid under the waistband of my black panties and he stopped before he got any deeper.

I whined in frustration, bucking my hips in encouragement. In a single motion, he tore my panties off and tossed them aside.

I gasped in surprise but it turned into another moan as his fingers found my clit. I lifted my hips, enjoying the sensation of his fingers on my body.

Just as a finger entered me, he silenced my moans with a kiss. I pressed into him, my bruised lips still sore from the hallway. Releasing my arms, he started working on the buttons on my shirt.

I took the opportunity to feel for his buttons and fumbled with them while he slid his tongue into my mouth.

He broke away from me, then climbed off the desk. I sat up, watching him though an intoxicated haze. I felt almost drunk on desire. Practically panting, I scooted toward the end of the desk, not wanting to be too far from him. I had to have his hands on me. I had to feel his skin against mine. I needed him inside me.

He locked his gaze on me, drawing me into him as if he were a hypnotist. I couldn't look away. He grinned, an expression that made my heart soar. After weeks of him pulling away from me and avoiding me, I hadn't realized how starved I'd been for him.

It was like he was the only sustenance I needed. I had to have him. "Ben," I whispered.

He slid his pants down, freeing his erection.

My eyes traveled down and my lips parted in surprise. He was a huge man, he towered above me and he was solid muscle, and oh so sexy. I shouldn't have been surprised that his cock matched the rest of him. Especially considering his hand was the size of my whole face.

He tossed his shirt aside and moved closer to me, setting his huge hands on my upper thighs.

My heart raced in anticipation, my breathing shallow. I'd never been with anyone this big before and I was a little nervous, but I wasn't going to let that stop me. Somehow, I knew this was supposed to happen. We were supposed to be together.

He pulled me to the edge of the desk so my ass was barely on it and I wrapped my thighs around his waist.

Leaning down, he slid his hands up my stomach toward my breasts, cupping each with his hands gently. Then he lowered his lips to my right nipple, pulling it into his mouth and sucking. At the same time, he pressed his cock to my entrance, teasing me.

I gasped as tingles shot through me, all the way down to my center. Wetness grew between my thighs.

He moved to the other nipple and I threaded my hand into his dark hair. I tossed my head back as I gasped in pleasure. Between the feeling of his cock pressed against me and his tongue expertly caressing my nipple, I was already nearing climax.

Leaving the nipple, his lips traveled up to my neck, kissing along the way. He stopped, his face above mine. Panting he locked his gaze on me again and I felt like I was being pulled into those dark eyes. I never wanted to leave.

We didn't need words. I could feel his want and I knew he could tell how much I needed him.

He moved slowly, entering me a little, then pausing. I gasped as I adjusted to his large size. He moved in more and my pulse raced in anticipation. I'd never been filled this much before.

His gentle tempo was excruciating after everything else. I wanted him now. I didn't want him to be gentle.

I sat up a little, which moved my hips closer, and I grabbed his back, pulling him to me.

He thrust in completely and I cried out, at first, in pain, but he thrust a few more times and I adjusted until the pain was replaced by gasps of pleasure.

Digging my fingernails into his back, I held him close to me as he continued to thrust. Both of us were damp with sweat, breathing heavy in unison. My back arched as the pleasure increased with each thrust. Unable to contain it any longer, I cried out as an orgasm burst through me.

Ben pressed his lips to mine, claiming my mouth as I came again, moaning into the kiss.

He wrapped his arms around my back and lifted me so I was sitting, the two of us pressed together as he continued to thrust.

As a third climax simmered I dug my fingernails into his back as I tossed my head back, gasping for air.

Ben buried his face into my shoulder and just as I cried out with another orgasm, he bit down on me, sending shooting pain into my shoulder that mixed with the pleasure in a way that made my eyes roll into the back of my head. Gasping, I fought to take breaths so I didn't pass out.

Ben leaned his head on my chest, breathing just as heavy as

me. I kissed the top of his head. He looked up at me and when our eyes met, something changed.

Something snapped into place and suddenly, it all made sense. All of my feelings for him rushed through me at once. None of it was logical but every primal thought I'd had about him seemed validated.

"Raven," he whispered.

I brushed his hair away from his eyes, taking in his handsome face. "I know."

"I wanted to tell you," he said. "I was trying to protect you."

"I don't care what you were doing, please just don't ever do it again," I said.

He stood, backing away from me. "We shouldn't have done this."

"I don't think we had a choice, unless I'm reading this wrong," I said.

He moved closer to me and took my hands in his. "I've put you in danger by claiming you."

"I don't care," I said, knowing it was true. I slid off the desk and my skirt fell back down around my legs.

"You don't know what I just did," he said. "But I swear on my life, I'll keep you safe."

I smirked. "You do realize I'm the one who has a thief after me."

He smiled. "We make quite the pair."

I touched his cheek and he looked down at me. I could tell from his expression that he was still conflicted.

"What is it?" I asked.

"My father," he said. "He blamed you for my loss of magic."

"But your magic isn't gone anymore," I said.

He pressed his hand on top of mine against his cheek. "That's true." Then his brow furrowed and he lowered my hand. "What about yours? I could smell it on you when we met in the hallway."

"I was working on it with Professor Halifax and the twins," I said.

He growled a little.

"Jealousy isn't a good look on you," I said.

"You're mine," he said.

"I am," I said. "But you don't own me."

"You might be the most difficult mate of all time." He set his hands on my upper arms, then pulled me closer to him. "But I have a feeling you're worth it."

"I assure you, I am," I said with more confidence than I realized I had.

He leaned down to kiss me and as soon as our lips met, I felt sparks shooting through my body. It was the same way I felt when my magic was activated.

Gasping, I pulled away from him.

"What is it?" Ben asked.

I looked down at my hands and quickly moved through the motions for creating fire.

A little flame burned in my palm. Orange and gold flickered in my hand, steady and soothing.

"Does that mean?" Ben laughed.

I closed my hand around the flame before it could go out of control. "My magic. That's the first time I've used it on my own."

Brow furrowed, I looked at Ben. "When you shifted, you said it was because of me?"

"Our mating bond, I've been feeling it for a while, but it flared, then all I could do was protect you at any cost," he said.

"You bit me," I said.

"It sealed the bond," he said.

I laughed. "We used magic when you did that, I suppose?"

He nodded. "Don't ask me how, but I know there's magic involved."

"Ben, you freed my magic. I just needed to tap into it to unlock it all." This whole time, I thought it would be the magic meld with the twins. Who knew sex was the answer?

Raven

I woke up in Ben's arms, still not believing that last night had been real. I got my magic back and I Ben and I made up. Twice.

I turned so I was facing him. His dark hair hung over his eyes and he was breathing slow and steady. In the time I'd known him, I'd never seen him look this peaceful.

As I watched him, his eyes fluttered open and a lazy smile spread on his lips. "I wondered if I was dreaming."

"I thought the same thing," I said.

He tugged me closer and I breathed him in, memorizing the feel of his strong arms around me. We had a bond, that was clear.

And apparently, he'd been feeling it for a while, but I still didn't know exactly what that meant for me. Ben wasn't the only one I'd felt a pull to.

Plus, there was that whole avoiding me thing and the veiled warnings about his father. "Ben, how long have you known?"

"That you were my mate?" he asked.

I nodded.

"Almost since the day we met," he said.

"Why didn't you tell me?" I asked.

"Would you have believed me? You just found out magic was real," he said.

That was true. "You have a point. But why did you wait? After poker that night..."

"I was trying to have you come to me," he said. "You can see how well that worked."

This was the most open I'd ever seen him. Hell, it was the most open anyone had really been with me since I got here. I had to take advantage of it. "What about your dad?"

He frowned and I could feel his muscles tense. "He's bad news, Raven. We're going to have to keep this between us."

"Everyone saw us walk through the party toward my room last night," I said.

"Everyone saw us walk toward *our* rooms," he said. "We are right next door."

"True, but how are you going to get out of here?" I asked.

"One at a time," he said.

I shook my head. "We're both adults. How bad can it really be?"

He laughed. "You've seen *The Godfather*?"

"Yeah," I said.

"You won't get a horse head as a warning. He'd just kill you and probably me. Give me some time to figure this out before we go public, okay?"

"Okay," I said. For once, I found myself fully trusting a man who asked me to do something for him. There were no warning bells, no intuition screaming at me. Things with Ben felt right.

I wasn't looking forward to going back to not speaking to each other, but it helped knowing that I had him in my corner. I sat up, my body instantly protesting against leaving his warm embrace. I knew we couldn't stay here all day.

"You in a hurry?" he asked, sitting up next to me.

"My magic came back last night, I'm officially obligated to inform Dr. Green when that happens. I have no intention of giving my PO anything else against me."

"Go figure that the son of the biggest mob boss in the supernatural world tries to go legit and ends up mated with a criminal," he said.

"You know it turns you on," I said, giving him a wink.

He lunged toward me, knocking me back onto the bed. I squealed in surprise but he quickly silenced me with a kiss.

Dr. Green could wait.

Raven

I should have taken a shower before I headed to Dr. Green's office. At least I was in fresh clothes. That was going to have to do.

Ben bolted from my room right after I left, and it was heartbreaking listening to him walk away from me without turning around to say one last goodbye. Though, we'd definitely made up for it in our morning tumble.

Three times in less than twelve hours. Ben was going to keep me on my toes. In the best possible way.

I moved through the nearly empty halls toward Dr. Green's

office. I'd been here every week over the last few months to see my parole officer and I wasn't looking forward to having to explain my returned magic to him. However, returned magic was my ticket out of here, eventually. And surely, they wouldn't make me continue to meet with him once I was a graduate, right?

The thought of no longer having meetings with the sweaty, pink-faced whatever-the-hell-he-was made me walk a little straighter. Now that my magic was back, I could prepare for the practice trials. I could move on with my life. I didn't realize how much of a holding pattern I'd been in. It was a liberating feeling.

Plus, I felt more like myself again. I'd missed the hum of my magic just below the surface. It was comforting and reassuring to have it back.

I passed a few students in last night's clothes, likely walking back from a late-night rendezvous in a different dorm than their own. We greeted each other with silent nods of understanding. Though, I was far more put together than them.

The main office was empty, Dr. Green's secretary missing from her usual post at the front desk. I should have expected that. It was a weekend after all. I frowned, wondering if I wasn't going to find anyone here at all.

Taking a chance, I knocked on Dr. Green's door. Then I waited.

Noises came from behind the door and I knew it was occupied. Then more noises. The sounds of shuffling and hurried footsteps. Something fell to the ground with a thud.

My heart raced and I grabbed the door handle, worried that something was wrong. "Dr. Green? You okay?"

I turned the handle, prepared to enter if he didn't respond.

"Wait," he called.

I let go of the handle and stepped back. A second later, he opened the door, his pink face nearly red from exertion. His hair was mussed and his shirt was buttoned unevenly.

Out of the corner of my eye, I noticed a female sitting in one of the chairs facing his desk. Her back was to me but she was smoothing her own disheveled hair.

I pressed my lips together, trying to keep from laughing awkwardly. I'd clearly interrupted something. My cheeks burned in embarrassment. The last thing anyone wanted to do was walk in on their dean getting busy. I silently thanked whoever was watching out for me for making me drop my hand from that door handle.

I couldn't even imagine the therapy I'd need if I had seen my demon dean getting it on.

"Ms. Winters, what can I do for you?" He cleared his throat.

"I'm sorry to interrupt," I said. "You told me to come to see you if my powers returned."

"Your magic has returned?" A woman's voice asked.

I looked from Dr. Green to the woman and then back again. He didn't seem to object to her asking the question. "Um, yes."

"Well, well," the woman said. "That is reassuring to hear."

My brow furrowed. Who the hell was this woman? She looked like she was in her mid-forties, though with magic, I was learning that age was a tricky thing to pin down. She was wearing a black pencil skirt and a white blouse. Her long brown hair hung loose around her face and had probably been sleek and straight before her activities with Dr. Green.

"Raven Winters, I'd like you to meet Madeline Obscura, your benefactor," he said.

My jaw dropped open and I quickly recovered, forcing a smile on my face. Now I really wished I had taken a shower. Though, from the looks of it, Ms. Obscura was in the same position as me.

"It's lovely to meet you," I said.

"You too, dear," she replied as she walked closer to me. "And might I add that you are even more beautiful in person. My sons have told me a lot about you, but I thought they were exaggerating. I'm thrilled to know they were not."

Uncomfortable with her compliment, I shifted on my feet and tried to maintain my smile. "Thank you."

"Why don't you come in, Ms. Winters?" Dr. Green asked.

Relieved to have a reason to break eye contact with Ms. Obscura, I stepped into the room and settled into the chair next to the one she'd been occupying. She sat down next to me and Dr. Green took his place behind his desk.

"Explain what happened," Dr. Green said. "Was it something from your session with Professor Halifax?"

"Not exactly," I said. There was no way I was going to tell them I'd unlocked my magic by having sex. That was not the conversation you wanted to have with your friend's mom. Especially when you were *interested* in your friends. As it was, it was going to be hard enough if they ever found out the truth. I didn't need it to come from their mom.

"So how did you do it?" Ms. Obscura pressed.

"It was shortly after my training session last night," I said. "It sort of just returned."

"Just returned?" Dr. Green said, lifting a skeptical eyebrow.

"Yes," I said.

"Ms. Winters, please, I've come to know when you're withholding," he said.

"Seriously?" I said. "Can't we just be cool with the fact that it came back?"

They both looked at me, unspeaking, waiting for an answer. The silence was heavy, weighing on me.

Fuck.

"Fine. I had sex, okay?"

Dr. Green's face turned crimson. "You're right, we didn't need to know that."

"Not with that incubus, I hope," Ms. Obscura said, her nose wrinkling.

"Madeline, I don't think we need the details."

"Of course, Max," she said.

I lifted an eyebrow. "Max?"

"Dr. Green," he said.

"Got it," I said. "The point is, I'm here to tell you that my magic is back so I'm not violating my parole."

"Thank you, Ms. Winters. I'll send a message along to Officer M."

I sat in the chair for a second as another round of awkward silence filled the room. "Well, if that's all, I can go."

"Wait a moment, Ms. Winters," Ms. Obscura said. "Dr. Green, would you mind if the two of us had a chat?"

My pulse quickened. I didn't really want to be alone with her in here, though I knew I owed her everything. If not for her paying my tuition, I wouldn't even be here.

"Of course," he said. "I'll wait outside if either of you need anything, let me know."

Ms. Obscura sat quietly while Dr. Green walked away from his desk. I heard the door shut and knew the two of us were alone.

She leaned closer to me. "By now, I'm sure you've learned that I'm paying your tuition, yes?"

"Yes, and thank you," I said. "It's beyond generous and I want you to know that I'll do what I can to pay you back one day."

"I'm sure you will, dear," she said, her voice saccharine sweet. "However, I think it will be a different way that you envision."

"Oh?"

"I know you're close with my sons," she said.

I swallowed, bracing for the *stay away from my kids* talk. I was from the wrong side of the tracks, for sure. They were practically royalty and I was like the hired help.

"I want you to know that you have my full support with whichever son you choose to be with. In fact, I'd be happy to see you with both, if that's your preference."

"I'm sorry, what?" My words weren't polite, but I was honestly lost.

"As you know, finding pure blood mages is rare, especially in this day and age. Your parents were both mages. That makes you quite the find."

My lips parted but I couldn't think of what to say to her.

"You're still new to this world, but you'll soon learn, this is how we keep magic alive. If my sons were to join our house with a human family or with another supernatural, our magic would fade. Mages are dying," she said.

"Is that why you're paying my tuition? So I'd marry one of your sons?" I couldn't believe that was what the reason was. It seemed insane.

"Among other things," she said. "Your mother and I were close when we attended the academy in our youth. When Dr. Green passed along that you'd been found alive, well, I wanted to pay tribute to her in the only way I could."

Her and my mom as friends was all I could think of now. "Can you tell me more about her?"

She smiled, her face softening for the first time. I could actually see some resemblance to her sons now.

"I'd be happy to tell you anything you want to know. I even have photos of us together. Don't you see? Her death is part of why it's so important for us to keep the mage bloodline alive. She was hunted for her magic, killed in cold blood as was your father."

My gut twisted at her words. She was so much more candid than anyone I'd met so far.

"I thought it was for the time magic," I said.

She frowned. "I suppose so. But your parents weren't the first to be taken down by a magic thief and they won't be the last."

"Well shouldn't we be focusing on that then instead of making more mages as the solution?" I asked.

"Of course, and we are. But there's no reason not to consider the future of our family. A future I'd very much like you to be a part of."

Her words struck a chord with me. *Family.* Wasn't that what I wanted? A place to belong? People to love me and support me?

Her sons and I did share a bond. I probably could be happy with them. Then my thoughts traveled to Ben and Luka. I wasn't about to walk away from either of them.

Besides, her obsession with a pure blood line was gross. Even her own sons didn't seem to support it. And there was the whole thing about having fae blood.

"Thank you for your kind offer, but I have to be honest with you," I said.

"Please don't tell me you're pregnant from one of the other boys you've been seeing," she said.

My eyes widened. "How did you know I was seeing anyone? Never mind, don't answer that. I don't want to know. And no, I'm not pregnant."

"What is it, then?" She leaned closer to me. "Did one of my sons do something? I swear, I will set them straight. They can be cocky little assholes."

"Well, that's true, but also not what I was getting at," I said.

She leaned back, her lips pursed.

"I'm not full mage, at least, I don't think I am," I said. "Professor Halifax says I have fae blood."

Her eyes widened. "Are you sure?"

I nodded. "I mean, that's what she said."

"Welcome to the family," she said, leaning in and wrapping her arms around me. "You have a place with us anytime."

What the hell just happened? I tensed under her embrace.

Deciding that going with it was the best way to end this awkwardness, I patted her on the back before pulling away from the hug.

"When you're ready, you let me know," she said. "And if you need anything, you tell Max and he'll connect us."

I forced a smile. "Thanks."

Finally, Dr. Green came back in the room. He looked just as uncomfortable as I was, but I doubted it had anything to do with having someone's mom proposition you on behalf of their son. Ugh.

"I want you to meet with Professor Halifax. She'll run a few tests to see if you're ready," he said.

"Ready for what?" I asked. "I've been doing classes for months now without magic."

"Yes, but the trials are something else, even if they are practice," he said.

"You can't be serious about making her go through those?" Ms. Obscura said. "What if she gets hurt? What if she dies?"

I would have been flattered if I thought she was concerned about me for any reason other than breeding. "I'm sure I'll be fine. I need to see what I can do and I still have a few weeks, right?"

"Right, but straight to Professor Halifax. She's waiting for you."

I nodded, grateful for the dismissal. This had been the strangest conversation of my life and I was ready to leave the room.

As I pulled open the door, Ms. Obscura called to me. "Don't forget what I said, dear."

I lifted a hand to wave to her. "I won't forget."

Raven

"This better be good," Professor Halifax said as I walked into her classroom.

"I got my magic back," I said.

She scoffed. "Just like that?"

"I guess," I said, not sure what to say. She was wearing sweatpants and a hoodie and her hair was in a messy bun. I'd never seen her look so normal. Usually she was dressed like she was ready to walk the runway. This morning, she looked like she was getting over the flu.

"Are you feeling okay?" I asked her.

"I'm hung over, if you must know," she said. "Weekends are supposed to be my days off."

Wow. Okay. That wasn't what I expected. Especially not from a teacher. Though, I supposed it wasn't high school like I was used to in the human world. "I'm sorry, this wasn't my decision."

"No, but it took you long enough to put two and two together from the book I left in your room," she said.

My brow furrowed. "You left that book in my room? Why?"

"I wanted you to figure it out on your own," she said. "I can't exactly go around suggesting a student get it on with another student."

Again, speechless.

Professor Halifax let out a sigh. "Look, I knew there was a chance that if you explored that mating bond with one of the twins, you'd unlock all your magic."

"I didn't have sex with one of the twins." And while the idea *was* appealing, meeting their mother had taken off some of the allure.

She cocked her head to the side and narrowed her eyes. "But you did have sex with someone."

"Why is everyone here so obsessed with who I'm having sex with?" I asked.

"Interesting," she said. "The incubus?"

Now that she mentioned it, I had felt something when I was with Luka. Like part of my magic had unlocked. Then, when I was with Ben, it was like a floodgate.

"Well, not just him," I said.

She pinched the bridge of her nose. "Oh, Raven. You're getting in over your head, aren't you."

"Look, I didn't ask for any of this," I said.

"I don't think I want to hear any more," she said. "I'm your teacher. Not your friend."

"Tell me about it," I mumbled.

She ignored my comment though I was sure she'd heard me. "Let's try the candles again. See what you can do without the help of the twins or the portal."

She set the candles out in front of me, then looked up at me, brow furrowed. "Not the twins?"

"No," I said. "Not the twins."

"Huh," she said. "Not yet, then."

"Can we not?" I said. Getting it from their mom was bad enough. Throwing in a teacher on top of it was too much. I knew there was attraction there. I knew my body was drawn to them. And if I was being honest, I knew it was a matter of time before I caved. But today was not that day.

She smirked. "Magic. Just the magic."

"Thank you," I said.

"Go ahead," she said.

I looked at the candles. "Just like that? Just light them?"

"You're a mage with a fire affinity. You don't just light them, you command them," she said.

I wasn't feeling very much in command of anything at the moment, but those candles were starting to feel like a taunt. Like they were judging me. And I had just about enough of that for today.

Reaching within, I felt for the spark of my magic. It came to me quicker now that it was easier to recognize. It was as if the time spent without it had helped me to realize what I'd missed. I suppose it had always been there with me, even when I didn't know what it was. It wasn't until it was stripped from me that I even knew what to look for.

Pulling from that source, I went on instinct, reaching my right hand out in front of me toward the candles. I wanted them all to light up. Not explode, just flicker on.

Tempering the urge to throw everything I had at the candles,

I held my breath, holding back on the magic and sending a small portion of it. Somehow, I was able to control it better now.

The candles in front of me flickered to life, a dozen dancing flames winking back at me all at once.

I dropped my hand and laughed at the sight. It was amazing that something so simple sent such a huge rush of joy through me.

"Well, it seems that you've found your magic. And you've gained some control." Professor Halifax stood behind the candles, looking down at them. Then she looked up at me. "You didn't by chance find a partner you bonded with, did you?"

More questions about my sex life? "Maybe."

"You must have more fae blood than I gave you credit for," she said. "I know you were raised human, where talking about these things seems taboo, but it's normal for us. Most mages don't form mating bonds, that's the fae side that's bonding with someone else."

"What does that have to do with my magic?" I asked.

"Aside from helping it find its way back to you, mating bonds are a unique kind of magic in their own right. When you open that source of magic, you strengthen your base magic. In your case, your elemental mage magic."

"What if I have more than one mate?" I asked.

She lifted an eyebrow. "Then I'd say you are about to become a very, very powerful mage."

I thought back to Dr. Green and Ms. Obscura discussing the practice trials. "Do you think I can pass the practice trials?"

"If you work on your magic over the next few weeks, it's possible you'd be ready to pass the actual trials," she said.

"In weeks?" I was surprised that she thought I could learn that quickly.

"You have an advantage that others don't with your time magic," she said. "And before you object, hear me out. Learning

to use it in subtle ways is going to help you learn to not accidentally unleash it. You have to be able to tame it and control it."

"How?"

She sighed. "I suppose you'll have to keep working with me.
But this can't go anywhere else. Nobody can know."

"What if I get caught?" I wasn't keen on risking a trip to
prison. "I've got a parole officer breathing down my neck."

"Like I said, you either learn how to control it in small, unde-
tectable ways, or you eventually lose control and end up in
prison anyway."

When she put it like that, it didn't sound like I had much of a
choice. "What am I supposed to tell people?"

She shrugged. "That's your call." She walked toward the door
and opened it, holding it for me. "I'll see you tomorrow after
dinner, Ms. Winters."

During our short session, I went from thrilled that my magic
was back to crushed and overwhelmed. There were so many
things to consider and so many ways this could go wrong.

I walked down the hall, absorbed in my own thoughts. What
was I going to tell Luka or Ben? What would I tell the twins?
They'd all want to know. Then there was Makayla who'd been
cheering me on the whole time. And Violet and all the shifters I
ate lunch with. They'd all want to know about my magic and
wonder why I was still in sessions.

Professor Halifax had a point, though. I had no control of the
time magic. While I'd somehow developed at least enough
control of fire to not light myself on fire, I didn't have any clue
how to tap into the time magic, let alone control it.

I had to be able to manage the magic I held.

"Raven," someone called my name.

I turned to see the twins walking toward me. My insides
squirmed. I was not ready to talk to them yet. The discussion
with their mother was too fresh in my mind.

"We are so sorry," Zach said.

"For real, if we knew our mom was here, we would have hidden you away," Matt said.

I relaxed a little, relieved that they were likely just as embarrassed as I was about their mom. "So I take it that my name has come up at home?"

"She's super old fashioned. They used to do the whole matchmaker thing in the mage community and if she had her way, she still would," Matt said.

"We shot her down," Zach said.

"Well, she's ready for me to have babies with one of you. Or both of you," I said.

"While I wouldn't turn down some alone time with you, I can assure you, I'm not ready to have kids," Matt said with a smirk.

Zach elbowed him.

I chuckled despite myself. "While I appreciate the offer, I'm not in the right place for anything like that."

"We heard you got your magic back," Zach said.

"Yeah," I said. "Looks like I won't be holding back our group anymore."

"You were never holding back the group," Matt said.

"And you're still trying to get into my pants," I said.

"Always," Matt said.

Raven

Spellcasting class was a lot more fun when you could use your magic. I went through the exercises with Zach and Matt, practicing turning water to ice to steam. The three of us all identified with fire, but we were responsible for demonstrating at least basic levels of working with the other elements.

I was amazed how quickly the magic came to me, though it wasn't any different than it was for Matt and Zach. I supposed I was finally using my magic correctly. Whatever the mating bond magic had done to me, it had an incredible impact on my magic. Though, I wasn't about to tell Matt and Zach the details.

They didn't mention it and I wondered if their mom left that part out so they would keep hitting on me. Which they did, relentlessly.

I kind of liked it.

"Very good, Ms. Winters," Professor Halifax said as she walked by our group. My cup of water had a massive inverted icicle sticking out of it after I successfully turned the water to ice.

"You think that's good," Matt said, "check this out." He threw the cup of water at Professor Halifax and froze it mid pour. The water hardened into a frozen splash before it could hit the professor. The ice fell to the ground, cracking into dozens of pieces.

"Impressive, Mr. Obscura," Professor Halifax said.

"Lucky, more like," Zach said.

The professor smirked, then turned away from us to visit another group.

"That was ballsy," I said. "What if you didn't freeze it in time?"

He shrugged. "Worth it if it impressed you."

"You're not going to give up, are you?" I asked.

"No way," he said. "When you give in, you'll get to experience just how incredible sex can be. You can't connect magic with a shifter the way you can with a mage."

My cheeks burned. He'd never given any sign that he knew I'd been with Ben, but now I knew. "I'm sure there are plenty of mages here who would happily take you up on the offer. Mages who weren't set up by your mom."

"Burn," Zach said.

"Class, please clean up your supplies before you go," Professor Halifax said just as the bell rang.

Quickly, we cleaned up everything and I grabbed my backpack and walked toward the door. Luka was standing in the hallway waiting for me.

"I was going to ask if you wanted to meet up later but I can see that you're busy," Matt said darkly.

I didn't get a chance to respond before he and his brother took off down the hall. I turned back to Luka. "That was weird."

"Not really," he said. "There's some bad blood between our families."

"Seriously?" I asked. "Why is everything in this world so fucking complicated?"

"It can't be that much different from the human world, can it?" Luka asked. "How was your first day back?"

"Having my magic back is so, so good," I said.

"I do miss you in the library," Luka said. "But I'm glad you got your magic back."

"At least we have gym together," he said, his voice heavy with sarcasm.

"*You* have gym. I have to meet my parole officer," I said.

"Lucky girl," he said.

"Right, so lucky." I honestly think I'd prefer gym to the conversation I was in for today.

"Meet me in the library after dinner?"

I groaned. "I can't. I have to meet with Professor Halifax."

His brow furrowed. "I thought you were done with that."

I shook my head. "I've got catching up to do."

"Alright. I'll wait till you're done. Find me in our usual place?" he asked.

"Sounds good," I said, expectant flutters swimming in my chest. Time with Luka was always good.

He pressed his lips to mine, then flicked my upper lip with his tongue as he pulled away from the kiss. "See you later, kitten."

Tingles spread low in my belly just from his kiss. I couldn't wait for our time together tonight. "See you then."

My next few classes seemed to crawl by as I counted down

to lunch. Usually, I looked forward to seeing my friends, but today was going to be a quick bite and straight to Dr. Green's office.

My stomach twisted into knots at the thought of how Officer M would glare at me once he knew my magic was back. Would it change anything for my meetings? Would he come more often or make me keep meeting with him? Would he make me show him what I could do?

The whole thing made me beyond uncomfortable.

I could barely taste my food and lost the thread of the conversation at lunch.

"You okay, Raven?" Makayla asked.

"Yeah, just dreading this meeting," I said.

"I'm sure it's just worse in your head," she said.

"I hope so," I said.

I fidgeted in the chair, wondering what was taking them so long. Dr. Green had let me in his office to wait while he spoke with my parole officer in the hall.

I stared at the tree clock. The leaves were gone now. It was back to its usual dead, black branches. The owl face seemed to stare out at me, and I could hear the gentle *tick, tick, tick* of the second hand as it moved around the numbers.

After six minutes, which felt much longer, the door opened and Dr. Green walked in. He gave me a look that made me shrink in my chair. Like I'd done something terribly wrong.

He settled into the chair next to me, which surprised me. He hadn't been in attendance for my last several meetings. Why today?

Officer Malone waddled over to the chair, setting a briefcase on the desk before settling into Dr. Green's usual place.

"I hear some of your magic has returned," he said without preamble.

"Um, yes," I said, risking a glance at Dr. Green.

He was staring straight ahead, not looking at me.

"Dr. Green says you're working with an instructor after classes to bring it up to full strength. How are those sessions going?" he asked as he opened his briefcase.

"Good," I said.

"Good?"

"Yes, it's basically just extra class time, you know?" I said.

"Sure," Officer Malone said. He scribbled something on a notepad. "And at this time, are you planning to attempt the practice trials?"

I glanced at Dr. Green again, hoping for some support here. Something was obviously going on, but I wasn't getting it. He didn't look at me, so I turned back to my parole officer and tried to get a read on him.

His face was flushed as usual and he was breathing through his mouth, his sharp yellow teeth clearly visible. I still had no idea what he was. All I wanted was for him to stay as far away from me as possible.

"If my professors think I can safely participate, I'll join my classmates," I said. "Honestly, it's up to them."

"Good. You've learned your place, it seems," he said.

I gripped the armrests of the chair, squeezing them to prevent myself from saying something I'd regret. The sooner I got through this meeting, the sooner he'd be gone. And I'd have another whole week before I had to put up with him again.

"And your extracurricular activities?" he asked.

I lifted an eyebrow. Here came the part where he tried to find out about my personal life. It was so creepy. Why the hell did he care what a twenty-one-year-old girl was doing or who she was doing it with?

"Same as last week," I said. "I rarely do anything other than schoolwork."

"Ms. Winters is a model student, as I told you before," Dr. Green said.

"We received reports that she's recently been spending time with the Obscura twins and time in the demon dorm," he said, keeping his beady eyes on me.

I nearly choked in surprise. "You're spying on me?"

"I told you, we are keeping a very close eye on you," he said. "If you so much as use one ounce of time magic, we'll know."

"I told *you* that I'm not doing anything wrong. Is it illegal for me to have friends?" I asked.

"It's not illegal but it is suspicious considering the attack on campus resulting in a dead guard and a possible intruder in the demon dorm the same time you were there," he said.

My mouth dropped open in surprise. "Are you accusing me of something?"

"Should I be?" he asked.

"As I told you before," Dr. Green said. "Raven is not a suspect in that attack."

"That's not for you to decide," Officer Malone said.

"I was with a friend during that incident," I said. "I wasn't prowling around outside."

"What were you doing with your friend?" he asked.

I swear his breathing quickened. It was like he already knew and wanted me to say it out loud. Pervert. "I don't think that's any of your business."

"As I told you before, we have witnesses who place her nowhere near the incident," Dr. Green said.

"I've heard stories like this before," Officer Malone said.

"Don't think that you're above the law just because the Obscura family is paying your tuition."

"I don't think that," I said.

"You're on strike two, Ms. Winters," he said.

"What?" I scoffed. "That isn't even fair. I didn't do anything wrong."

"That's my decision. As far as I'm concerned, your alibi lines up too nicely. You even think about time magic and I'll get you locked up for not just illegal magic but for murder as well."

"Wait a minute," I said. "I had nothing to do with all of that. You can't do that."

"I can and I will," he said. "Do you want to test me?"

I opened my mouth to object but wasn't sure what to say. Somehow this had gone from a typical meeting to me being accused of murdering a guard. It didn't even make sense. Why would he jump to that? Especially since we'd met since it happened? Why bring it up now?

I closed my mouth and clenched my teeth. Something must have happened. Something shifted, someone somewhere wanted to hurt me or get me in trouble for something. I didn't get it, but I had to hope Dr. Green had my back.

"Any other questions, Ms. Winters?" Officer Malone asked.

"No," I said, the word coming out more defiant than I meant.

"Good. Now play the game like you should and everyone will be fine," he said.

My brow furrowed. I had no idea what he was talking about, but I stayed in my seat as he walked out the door. I wasn't about to leave this office till Dr. Green gave me an explanation.

As soon as the door closed, I turned to see Dr. Green walking back toward me.

"What the hell was that?" I asked.

He frowned. "Careful, Ms. Winters, I am still the dean."

I blew out a frustrated breath. "Fine. What just happened in here?"

"Apparently, someone isn't happy that you're cozying up with the Obscuras."

"So they want to pin a murder on me?" I asked. "That's insane."

He shook his head. "I think it means our thief has infiltrated the justice system."

"What do you mean?" I asked, my heart suddenly pounding against my ribcage.

"If you get kicked out of here, it's easy for you to disappear. But with the Obscura family watching over you, they'd have to make it look legit. Someone is calling the shots and they want you out of here. You better keep your nose clean. I'm doing the best I can but there are certain things I can't save you from," he said.

"If she's impersonating someone high up, can't they just catch her? I mean, doesn't anyone notice?" I asked.

"She's got decades worth of stolen magic. Including the magic from both of your parents. I'm pretty sure she's capable of convincing anyone of anything at this point," he said.

I looked back to the office door. "Do you think that was her?"

"Officer Malone?" he asked.

I nodded, feeling the blood drain from my face as I turned back to Dr. Green.

"It's possible, but I have a feeling she's replaced someone higher up. He's always been a weasel, willing to do whatever they tell him. He wouldn't need much convincing to do someone else's dirty work."

"So what do I do?" I asked.

"Stay in the castle, keep working on your magic and don't do anything stupid. They have no reason to arrest you if you do what you're supposed to do," he said.

Raven

Nervously, I entered the classroom. Somehow, I had to tell Professor Halifax that I couldn't risk using my time magic. Not now that I knew the thief was monitoring me so closely.

Her classroom was lit only by the emergency light. Empty and desolate. It was creepy as hell in the dark. "Professor?"

I heard some noises from the back of the room and there was a stripe of light on the floor coming from a closet door. "Professor, is that you?"

The door opened and Professor Halifax stepped out, a huge bundle of black fabric in her arms. "I'm here."

"Professor, I can't do this," I said before I lost my nerve. "My parole officer threatened me today and they're watching me more than I realized."

"Which is exactly why you have to be able to control your magic," she said. "If you let it slip, you're screwed."

That was true. But how was I supposed to practice it if the use of it set off something they could track? Officer Malone seemed confident that he could trace even the smallest time magic. "I don't want to go to jail."

"That's why we're doing this," she said with a sigh. "I always thought you were one of my smarter students."

"Wow, thanks for that," I said. "Look, I get why this is important, but they said they can track it."

"I suppose, in theory, they could." She set the bundle of fabric down on her desk. "Though, I haven't met anyone who could track magic from a distance in the last century. They'd have to actually be in the room where the spell was cast to trace it. And they'd have to be there within twelve hours of the casting."

"Really?" I asked.

She nodded. "Like I said, it's possible, but if they had people with that skill working for them, they wouldn't need to send people like your Mr. Malone to make threats. They could just sit back and monitor you from a distance."

Her words didn't make me feel more confident about messing with time magic. But I knew there was probably more of a risk of me screwing up big, possibly in front of people if I didn't learn to control it. Last time I'd used it, I was in a life or death situation. The time before it felt like a life or death situation.

What was to stop someone from pushing me too far just to see if they could get a rise from me? Or worse, what if I got scared during the practice trials?

Professor Halifax smoothed out the fabric on her desk so it draped over it like a tablecloth. It was black and looked soft. Velvet maybe. My brow furrowed as I watched her tugging on it to even the sides. I wasn't sure what it had to do with our lesson, but I had a feeling she had a reason for it.

"Okay," I said. "Just enough to learn how to keep me from using it accidentally. Nothing more."

"Of course," she said. "I wouldn't dream of teaching you how to actually *use* your time magic. That would be illegal. Teaching you how to *contain* it, however, is my duty as your instructor. I'm morally obligated, right?"

"Uh, sure," I said.

"Over here," she said as she placed her palms flat on the velvet fabric. "Like this."

I walked over to the desk and set my hands down on top of the fabric, copying her. My hands tingled instantly from contact. It felt similar to the way my own magic felt, but this wasn't mine. It was different. "What is this?"

"It's my last connection to Faerie," she said. "It's woven with fae magic and will make our session easier to complete."

"How is that even possible?" I asked.

"The magic there far surpasses what is possible here," she said. "Compared to the Fae realm, this place is stuck in the stone ages when magic is concerned."

"You must miss it terribly." I was guessing it was like us going to a place where cell phones and television didn't exist. Not that I had time or use for those things here, but I did miss them.

"Let's just focus on the magic," she said.

"Alright," I said. "What do you want me to do?"

"You're going to attempt to call your time magic, but I can't have you slowing the time around us or risking a time bubble," she said.

"A time bubble?" I repeated.

"That's a lesson for another time," she said.

"So if I'm not slowing time, what am I going to do?"

"You're going to create a tear," she said. "A portion of a portal."

"I thought portals were crazy dangerous for people who don't know what they're doing," I said.

"We've been through this," she said. "Your magic is basically a portal key. Besides, you have me to help. I wouldn't ask you try it alone."

"I have no idea how to open a tear," I said.

"Close your eyes and concentrate on the magic you feel in the room. My magic will be amplified by the fabric. I'm going to guide you for this first time."

I closed my eyes and focused on the tingling in my hands. As I did, it intensified until it was nearly a burning sensation that didn't cause pain. It was an odd feeling, uncomfortable, but tolerable. Was that from the fabric or was that Professor Halifax's magic? "I feel something."

"Good, concentrate on connecting to that feeling. You need to be able to channel it through your veins. Pull it into your own magic, weave them together."

I took a deep breath and focused on the unfamiliar magic, urging it to come into me. Slowly, I felt it seeping up my arms, toward my chest. My own magic flickered like a pilot light deep in my belly.

Then I felt something else. Another magic that I didn't recognize. It felt like it was pulling me toward it, somewhere beyond the black cloth my hands were on.

"Don't fight it," Professor Halifax said. "Embrace it."

I steadied myself, leaning into the new magic, letting it mingle with mine the way I had with the twins. But this felt cold and dark and foreign. It wasn't familiar and welcoming the way the magic meld had been.

"That's your time magic coming to the surface," she said. "Feel that? You have to harness it, control it. Don't lose focus."

I held the magic, following the other magic's lead, urging it downward into the cloth.

Suddenly a bright light split the fabric and I could see what could only be described as a tear. It opened in the fabric, a blue light around the seams. Inside was a black void. Nothingness staring back at me.

It was cold and terrifying, sending a rush of ice through my veins.

Gasping, I let go of the magic and in a burst of energy, I was thrown from the table. I landed on my ass nearby, panting and sweaty.

"What was that?" I asked.

"You created a tear," she said. "You held your magic and channeled it successfully. Without stopping time, I might add."

"So what does this mean? How does this help me?' I asked.

"That feeling you had when it called to you, how was it?" She asked.

"Uncomfortable," I said. "Dark and unwelcome."

"Interesting." She walked over to me and offered her hand.

I took it and pushed myself off the ground with her help. Her hand was like ice. As cold as the magic that had run through me. "When you felt that, though, instead of panicking, you embraced it. You controlled it. You didn't succumb to fear."

She walked back to the black fabric and started to fold it up. "Next time you feel the time magic threatening to rise, you embrace it and command it until you can send it away."

I nodded, the exercise finally making sense. It wasn't about opening the portal, it was about control. "I can do that."

"Good. We'll keep working on it, but in the meantime, remember if you feel it coming, embrace it, don't fight it."

Raven

The next two weeks were a blur of learning how to use my magic and fitting in sessions with Professor Halifax.

I was getting stronger. Keeping up with the twins during class and holding on to my time magic for longer when I practiced with the portal tear.

Even my meeting with my parole officer couldn't bring me down. I was feeling like I finally had some control over how things were going in my own life.

The only downside was sneaking around with Luka and Ben. Since I couldn't leave the school to go to the demon dorms, and I didn't want to bring Luka to my room - where I shared a wall with Ben - the two of us had been creative in our meetings.

The library was our usual meeting place, but we'd even ducked into a few classrooms from time to time.

Ben on the other hand, was completely different. With him, it was late night sneaking around because he was so worried one of the other shifters would see us.

In fact, he'd been so worried about it, the two of us hadn't seen each other in days.

And I was getting antsy.

I mean, it wasn't like I wasn't getting action, but every time I walked past him in the common room or saw him in class, my sex drive went into high gear. I needed him. Bad.

There had to be a better way.

As I was leaving the office from another round of threats by my parole officer, I stopped at the secretary's desk.

She looked over her reading glasses at me. "Yes?"

"Is there any way I could get a new keycard for my room?" I asked.

She pursed her lips. "What happened to your old key card?"

"I thought it was in my backpack, but I must have left it in my room this morning."

She scowled at me. It was as if no student had ever left their key card in their room before.

Finally, after what felt like minutes of silence, she pushed herself away from her desk on her wheeled desk chair and opened a file cabinet behind her. After a moment of digging through the drawer, she rolled back to her desk, a card in hand.

She lifted the card to me. "Don't lose it."

"I won't, thank you," I said.

Her lips were still puckered as if she'd eaten something sour when I took the card from her hand. I wasn't sure why she worked here. She certainly seemed to hate people. Then again, I supposed working at a school could do that to you. Maybe she'd been a people person when she started here and was stuck here.

I shuddered and silently vowed to cross teaching or customer service off my list of post academy occupations. All day interacting with people was enough to leave anyone jaded and angry.

Quickly, I shoved the card in the pocket of my black pants and left the office before anyone could say anything else to me.

I didn't actually lose my card. In fact, it was safely tucked away in my backpack. And I had a sneaky suspicion she knew that. But I had a plan.

Beelining it to class, I hurried to get to my seat before the rest of the students settled. This was my only class with Ben and if I played my cards right, I could get this to him without drawing attention.

He entered with another shifter, the two of them chatting as they came through the door. He glanced toward me, his eyes lingering on mine a second longer than they should have before he looked away.

My chest hurt every time he did that. I knew we had to keep everything a secret. At least until we figured something else out, but it was wearing on me.

He took his seat and I kept my gaze forward, not wanting to draw attention to myself. It took all my willpower to keep from looking back at him.

Finally, Professor Hurd walked into the room, carrying a stack of blue exam books.

I bit down on the inside of my cheek as I braced for what I was about to do. I still wasn't great at magic, but I was pretty sure I could cause a distraction.

We'd been working on air all week in Spellcasting and I was okay at it. Decent enough that I could probably send a gust to blow the books out of his hands.

Silently, I called to my magic, letting it flood through me, gaining in momentum as I pushed it out toward Professor Hurd in a rush of wind.

To my surprise, it worked, the books went flying, pages open all over the room.

The students near the front jumped up and started helping while the rest of the class either moved to help or laughed at the situation. Quickly, I left my seat and casually walked toward Ben, picking up a book that had fallen right at his feet.

He bent down, his fingers brushing mine as we both picked up the book. Quickly, I slipped my key card into his hand. He closed his fingers around it.

"I got it," I said, taking the book.

He took his hand away and sat back in his chair.

I carried the book to the front of the room and handed it to Professor Hurd.

"Very funny, whoever did that," he said with a frown. "Whoever it was, you cost your classmates an essay. You no longer get to choose from one of the three essays, you'll now complete them all."

I winced as I walked back to my chair. The class booed around me and I quickly joined in, trying to cover up my own involvement.

"That's not fair. Just make the mages do it," one of the shifters said.

"You'll all do it," he said.

I settled into my seat, feeling guilty. Though, knowing that I might have a visitor later tonight made it all worth it.

Raven

It was cold and dark. Water dripped somewhere nearby. My bare feet were freezing against the cold stone floor.

Wake up, wake up. I was back in the dungeon of my dreams and I knew it was a dream this time, but I couldn't get myself to wake up. Shivering, I dropped to the ground and pulled my knees to my chest. I had to wake up since I knew it was a dream, right? Wasn't that how it worked?

Leaning my forehead on my knees, I took deep breaths. I pictured meadows full of sunshine and sunflowers. I imagined sitting at the beach and feeling the sand under my toes.

Fear crept down my spine in icy tendrils. I was stuck here in this dream. How long would I have to wait until I woke up? It was the same dream I'd been having since I was a kid. Nobody ever came. I was always alone. And terrified.

Trying to distract myself again, I thought of Luka's dream world. The temple with a roof of starlight. The soft pillows and cushions where we'd had our first romantic interlude, even though it hadn't been real.

For the first time, I found myself wishing I had his magic. If I could control dreams, I could get out of this one. I wondered how he did it.

"Did you call for me?" Luka's voice came from behind me and I turned to see him standing in the dungeon with me.

He was dressed in his uniform, his hair in that perfect mussed look that made him look like he woke up looking that good.

I stood and turned to face him. "Are you really here or am I imagining you?"

"I'm here," he said. "I could hear you thinking about me."

"Thanks," I said. "I hate this dream."

"Should we improve it?" The room spun around me and when it stopped, I was in Luka's temple. It was just as beautiful as I remembered.

Suddenly, his brow furrowed. "You're not alone."

"What do you mean?" I asked.

"Someone else is in your room, I can feel them. Wake up, Raven."

Luka vanished and I was left alone and terrified in the dream temple. It didn't last long, though. Before I could even process what just happened, I was back in the cell.

I started screaming.

"Raven, wake up." Ben's touch on my arm was gentle as he shook me awake.

I sat up, gasping.

"You were having a nightmare," he said.

"Yeah, I guess I was," I said.

Ben put his arms around me and pulled me close. "Come here."

I snuggled into him, feeling my heartbeat slow as I settled into his embrace.

Suddenly, a loud thumping sounded on my door. "Raven, open up."

"Oh, shit," I said.

"Who is that?" Ben asked.

I ran to the door and opened it before Luka could wake the whole dorm.

"Raven!" Ben whispered behind me.

Luka stood in the doorway, his gaze quickly moving away from me to where I could only assume Ben was standing behind me.

"I was right, you weren't alone," he said.

"Luka, I can explain," I said.

"She's busy tonight, demon," Ben said.

He wrapped a protective arm around me and I shrugged it off. "Hold on now."

"Did you try to slip into her dreams?" Ben asked.

"I've been in more than just her dreams," Luka said with a grin.

I could feel the temperature in the room rising and I knew Ben was pissed. It was like his emotions were vibrating through me. He felt hurt and jealous and a little murderous.

On the other hand, I could practically feel Luka's *come at me* thoughts. His cocky grin was just the right kind of ammo. He was doing exactly what he needed to piss off Ben.

Shit. This wasn't going to end well if I didn't do something quickly.

"Okay, first you need to get in here." I grabbed Luka and dragged him into my room. Then I peeked out into the hallway to make sure we didn't have an audience. Thankfully, the coast was clear. I closed the door, then flipped on the light before I stepped in between the two of them.

"First of all, you both need to calm down," I said.

"I'm calm," Luka said.

I glared at him. He really was calm. None of this seemed to bother him.

"Now that I know you're not in here with a killer, I'm good," he said. "Well, that's not true, I'd be better if I was in Raven's bed, but I suppose it's not my turn."

Ben growled, and I turned toward him and set my hands on his chest. "Ben, don't do anything stupid."

He looked down at me. "Have you been with the demon?"

"I thought you knew that," I said.

"I didn't know for sure," he said.

"Ben, I share a bond with both of you," I said.

"Wait, you have a bond with him too?" Luka asked.

I looked over at the incubus and saw the first sign of concern on his expression since he realized I wasn't in danger. "I do."

"Wow. I've never heard of that before, have you?" He was looking at Ben, waiting for him to respond.

"No," Ben said.

"Then again," he said, "You rarely hear of a mage having a mating bond at all. Especially not with a shifter or an incubus."

"I'm sorry I didn't tell you," I said, looking from Luka to Ben. "I need you both."

"We haven't been exactly keeping things a secret," Luka said. "Why hide the shifter? Are you embarrassed that you're with a wolf?"

Ben growled again.

"I'm serious, I'm not trying to insult you," he said. "I never thought of Raven as the type to hide things unless there's a good reason."

"My father can't know about this," Ben said.

"Your father?" Luka's brow furrowed, then his eyes widened as realization dawned on him. He took a step closer to Ben. "What have you done?"

"He didn't do anything," I said.

Luka wasn't listening to me. He moved closer again. "You're putting her in danger. Did you think about anything other than your cock?"

"Hey, stop." Now I had to diffuse Luka. And to be honest, seeing him mad was a little scary. He was standing tall, his upper body tense, his hands balled into fists. Flames danced in his eyes. *What the fuck?*

Shaking off my own fear, I grabbed Luka's arms, squeezing gently. "It's okay. I'm safe."

He looked down at me, his eyes returning to normal. He still looked pissed, but he looked calmer. "It's not okay, Raven. Do you know who his father is? Do you know what he does to people?"

"Yes," I said. To be fair, I didn't fully know, but I had a general idea. And I knew it still didn't matter. I didn't have a choice. Ben was mine and I was his. The same as it was with Luka. I couldn't walk away from either of them even if I wanted to. And I didn't want to. I needed them. We were bonded in a way I couldn't explain.

"Listen," I said, rubbing my palms up and down his upper arm. "I didn't get to choose him any more than I chose you. But I'm glad for it. I need you. I need him too."

Luka's eyes flicked past me. I could feel Ben's body heat moving closer to me. I turned so I could see them both, releasing my hands from Luka. "You two don't have to like each other, but you're both going to be in my life and you're going to have to at least pretend to get along."

Both males let out low growls.

"That doesn't sound like pretending to get along," I said.

The growling stopped.

"Look, you know none of us chose this. But you both have to know that I wouldn't trade either of you for anything. You're going to have to be okay with this." I held my breath as I waited for them to respond.

"At least he can be out with you in public," Ben said. "He can keep you safe when I'm not able to."

"You know I will," Luka said.

"See? We can make this work," I said.

"I'll play nice if he does," Luka said.

"Ben." I looked over at my handsome shifter, wondering if he was going to go along with it. "I need you."

He reached his hand out toward me and I took it in mine. He squeezed my hand. "I need you too."

"Well, I suppose since it's your turn tonight, I'll be on my way," Luka said.

My face heated. I never imagined I'd be in a position where I was juggling two males. At least it was all out in the open now.

Ben pulled me closer to him, wrapping his arms around me. "You can show yourself out."

"See you in the morning, Kitten," Luka said as he slipped out the door.

Raven

Makayla was waiting for me outside the cafeteria and I hurried to meet her. I'd skipped breakfast this morning. Luka had joined me in a dream, and I didn't want to wake up.

My stomach grumbled at the smell of food. "I hope it's good today, I'm starving."

"Yeah, I wondered where you were during breakfast," she said. "Ben seemed to be looking for you too."

"Sorry, I overslept. Those magic sessions with Professor Halifax wear me out." I ignored the comment about Ben. The two of us managed to get quality time a few times a week at least. Yesterday, we'd skipped lunch together and met for a quickie in his room. Between him and Luka, I was getting quite the workout.

"How come you have to keep doing that now that your magic is back?" she asked.

"Just helping me catch up," I said. "I did miss quite a bit while my magic wasn't working."

"That's true," she said. "Hey, pizza day."

I grabbed a tray and pulled two plates of pizza slices onto it. The cafeteria made the best pizza I'd ever had. After picking up a bowl of salad and a bottle of iced tea, I left the line and followed Makayla to our usual table.

Ben was sitting with us again, though the two of us never sat next to each other. He smiled at me quickly, then went back to his conversation with Jessica.

I was pretty sure all the shifters at the table had figured out what was going on between us, but they never said a word. I didn't know if he'd talked to them and asked them to keep quiet or if they were just following our lead. I wasn't sure I wanted to know. It was almost easier to feel like I had to hide it from them too. If I got used to being open about our relationship in front of them, I might slip in front of someone I shouldn't.

Just as I took my first bite, Luka slid onto the seat next to me. He planted a kiss on my cheek as he did every day. At this point, the fact that Luka and I were an item was old news around the school. Though, I knew Ben hated every second of Luka's affections. I felt bad about it, but I tried to make it up to Ben in our private time.

"Hey, I have something lined up for tonight. All of you should come," Luka said to the table.

"What is it?" I asked. "I still can't leave the main building."

"You won't have to leave." He lowered his tone, making

everyone have to lean in to hear him. "But meet at the gym at midnight."

"Why?" Jamal asked.

"Or don't, your choice." He shrugged, then took a bite of his pizza. "Hey, did you all hear about Remi and Dolores?"

"What about them?" Jessica asked.

"I guess someone walked in on the two of them in a classroom last night and they were not studying," he said.

"I knew it," Jessica said. "I knew those two were sneaking around campus. Students always try to hide it, but their relationships come out into the public sooner or later."

My stomach churned and suddenly I wasn't as hungry as I was before. She was right. It was difficult to hide anything at this school.

"I'm sure there are lots of secrets at this school," Luka said. "That's what makes it so much juicier when one breaks."

The table broke into conversation about past rumors and secrets that had come out. Most of the stories were new to me and they helped take my mind off of Ben and me. I knew I didn't want to keep our relationship hidden forever, but until we had a better way of dealing with it, this was how it was.

The rest of the day flew by. Even gym was tolerable today. I'd gotten pretty good at running laps on days when Coach Miller ignored us while he lifted in the corner. He recruited some of the larger shifters to lift with him or spot him and seemed to be enjoying their sessions. I was happy to run around the circle with Violet.

"How are things with the demon?" she asked.

"Good," I said.

"Good, that's all I get?" she asked.

"How are things with you and Scarlett?" I asked.

"Let me tell you, the things that woman can do with her tongue. I mean, she's a handful and sometimes I wonder why I put up with her shit, but once we get naked, I stop thinking completely."

"Oh, that's what you were looking for," I said.

"Of course," she said. "Like I could give two shits about how you feel or what your bond is or whatever. I just want to know how he is in bed. I hooked up with a succubus once. Best night of my life. Wasn't sure if the male version was the same way."

"Well, I've never been with a succubus, but I can confirm that Luka is incredible. In my dreams and in the real world."

"Dream sex, I'm jealous. That means you could literally doze off in class and have the most amazing wet dream ever," she said.

I laughed. "I hadn't thought about it like that, but I guess I could."

After class, as I changed in the locker room, I couldn't help but wonder what Luka had planned for tonight. He'd never invited the whole group to anything before. In fact, the only time he was part of the shifter group was at meals. When I hung out with them, it was usually in the common room.

I left the locker room thinking about how I'd pass the time till dinner when I ran smack into one of the twins. It took me a second to shake off the surprise to realize I was staring at Matt. "Hey, what's up?"

I'd been avoiding them lately, which I felt bad about after all they'd done to help me. But their mom freaked me the fuck out. It was one thing to be interested in someone, it was another thing to have their mom ready to throw you a baby shower before you've even decided you want to have sex with her kid.

"I heard a rumor," he said.

My heart raced. How did he find out about Ben?

"I heard you and your friends have some plans for tonight and frankly, I'm hurt." He frowned in a playful, exaggerated way.

"What are you talking about?" I asked.

"Word travels," he said. "Gym at midnight?"

"Oh, that," I said. "I don't even know what Luka is planning."

He frowned again briefly but this one wasn't forced. It was real. And I had a feeling it was in response to me dropping Luka's name. Since I'd been more public in my affections with the incubus, Matt slowed on his flirting with me. There was a part of me that missed it.

"We want in," he said. "I thought we were friends."

"We are," I said. "But I feel like I'm missing something here. What do you think we'll be doing?"

"The gym is being set up as we speak for the practice trials. If your friend wants you to meet here tonight, my guess is he figured out a way to get a preview. We want in."

"Oh, yeah." I hadn't even thought about the fact that they might set up for the trials early. We took them Monday.

"Any peek is going to help," he said. "I take mine Monday. I drew the first position."

"You must be so nervous," I said. "I'm so sorry."

He shrugged. "Someone has to be first. But I'm not thrilled that it's me. It gives me a huge disadvantage. I don't get to ask anyone about it before my turn."

"Of course you can come with us," I said.

He smirked. "Nice to see you still care about me even if you're spending all your time with that incubus."

I winced. His words hurt. Just because I'd been avoiding him didn't mean I didn't still feel drawn to him and Zach. I just wasn't ready for the pressure of his family. And I couldn't afford to mess things up. His mom was paying for me to be here. What if we hooked up and he dumped me? What if he decided he didn't want his family helping me anymore?

Also, right now, his mom's help was charity. Granted, I knew she had ulterior motives, but I could try to ignore that. If

I started sleeping with her son, there was so much more pressure.

"I do care about you," I said. "But things are complicated right now."

"I worry about you, Raven," he said.

"Why?" I asked. "I'm fine."

He shook his head. "It's not just jealousy that I'm not in your bed, which, trust me, is a thing. I do want to be in your bed. But Ben isn't exactly the type of guy you should be sneaking around with."

I felt like a bucket of cold water had been thrown on me. He knew. Which meant other people had to know too.

"You don't need to deny it or tell me anything, really," he said. "I won't say anything."

"Matt, there's a lot going on," I said.

"I'm sure," he said. "But his father isn't a joke. People say my mom's bad, or that Luka's mom is bad. I mean, she is a princess of hell."

My eyes widened. I'd never discussed Luka's family with him but now I was thinking I needed to. If his mom was royalty, didn't that make him the same? What had I gotten myself into? Luka and I needed to have a serious talk. Soon.

I sighed. It didn't change anything. I knew I'd be with both of them no matter what their parents were like.

Matt leaned closer. "Ben's dad is so much worse than either of them. You need to be careful."

My throat bobbed. Ben himself had tried to warn me but I'd blown it off. Now that we were sneaking around the school and people were starting to find out, I was a little nervous.

"Thanks for looking out for me," I said.

"You know where to find us if you ever need anything," he said, a forced smile on his lips. "I can't say I'm happy that you chose someone else over me, but I'm still here if you need me."

It was a rare, real moment with Matt. Usually, he was all self-confidence and laughter. I'd never seen this side of him before. And honestly, it was both terrifying and sexy as hell.

"See you later tonight." He turned and walked away before I could process what just happened.

It seemed the word was getting out about me and Ben. And that Matt was still interested in me even after I'd been blowing him off.

Things at the Academy were never easy. Complicated was a way of life here.

Raven

I skipped dinner that night. I wasn't sure yet how to handle the Ben situation until I knew how many people were on to us. Instead, I grabbed a few snacks from the stash in my desk drawer.

Swiss cake rolls and beef jerky sure weren't healthy, but they were perfect when you were trying to work out what the hell you'd gotten yourself into.

I knew I couldn't walk away from Luka or Ben. Ever. We were connected, bonded in a supernatural way that I didn't want to break. But that didn't make it easier to comprehend. I'd been raised in the human world with most of the world telling me I got one partner.

It was odd because the concern from Matt wasn't over the fact that I was with two males, it was regarding the dangerous family one of them came from. Though, it turned out Luka's mom was apparently pretty badass. I sure hoped she liked mages.

Even Ben and Luka, who hated each other, were going along with it. For me. It was a lot to wrap my head around.

I woke with a start to someone pounding on my door. My room was dark and I knocked the box of cake rolls to the ground when I crawled off my bed.

Running a hand through my hair, I walked toward the door. "Who is it?"

"Makayla," she hissed in a loud whisper. "Raven, open up."

I flipped on the light and then opened the door, letting my friend in.

"You look like hell," she said. "What happened? Did one of those assholes say something to you?"

"I fell asleep. Wait, what assholes?" I asked.

"The Obscura twins stopped by the common room after dinner and asked to talk to Ben," she said.

I lifted my eyebrows in surprise. "Seriously?"

She nodded. "I didn't get to hear the conversation, but Ben was pissed when they left. I was surprised he didn't shift and chase them down."

I scrubbed my face with my hand. "Fuck."

"You weren't in here because of them, were you?" she asked. "Oh, love, the snack cakes? What happened?"

I walked over to the box and scooped the fallen cellophane wrapped cakes back into it and then offered the box to Makayla. "Want one?"

She held up a hand. "No, thank you."

I set the box on my desk. "Matt stopped by after gym."

"And?"

"And he told me he knew about Ben," I said.

"That asshole," Makayla said. "You can't trust those mages."

I cleared my throat.

"Present company excepted," she said.

"He didn't threaten anything and I don't think he'd tell people, but if he figured it out, everyone probably has." I narrowed my eyes at her. "Wait, I never told *you* about Ben."

She smiled sheepishly. "He told me."

"Of course, he did," I said.

"But just because I'm his best friend, doesn't mean I'm not yours, too," she said.

"I don't want to put you in the middle of anything," I said.

"You're not," she said. "Ben didn't even tell me what the twins told him."

"It probably had to do with the fact that they're worried about me," I said.

"Worried? Ben could kick anyone's ass who tried to hurt you," I said.

"Except his father, apparently," I said.

She was quiet for a moment. "Yeah, there is that."

"Is he really that bad?" I asked.

She nodded, her expression grim.

I supposed there were perks to not being plugged into the supernatural world. If I knew everything about Ben's dad, would I have tried to stay away from him? Would it have even worked? Somehow, I doubted it.

"Well, I guess we'll have to figure out how to deal with that once we get there." I glanced at my clock. It was almost midnight. "But now, I guess we should get going before everyone else comes looking for me."

"Just be careful around the twins," she said. "I don't trust mages."

"Again, mage here," I said.

She winced. "I always forget you're a mage. You're not like the rest of them."

"Yet, Ben's murderous dad is oaky?"

"No, he's not," she said. "But none of us are our parents."

"True," I said. Those were heavy words. I didn't remember my parents, but they were apparently very powerful and well liked. I wish I knew them. I'd been left instead with someone I very much didn't ever want to be like.

I grabbed a hair tie and pulled my hair into a messy bun. "Ready?"

"Let's go." Makayla opened the door for us.

We walked quietly through the dungeon and crept through the silent halls of the school. Occasionally, I heard the sound of students talking in the distance, but we never encountered anyone on our walk to the gym.

The gym was on the opposite end of the school from the cafeteria, common room and other social gathering places. This time of day, it was a ghost town.

Luka, Jessica, and Starla were already waiting for us.

"Hey, kitten, you okay?" Luka asked.

"Yeah, I decided to rest for a minute on my bed..." I let the words trail off.

"Took a nap, huh?" Jessica asked.

"Yep. Thankfully Makayla came to get me."

I heard the sound of footsteps and turned to see Ben walking over to us with Jamal. He avoided eye contact with me which told me the twins had probably talked about our relationship with him.

With the practice trials hanging over our heads, dealing with relationship issues was the last thing I wanted to think about. I pushed the thought away and turned away from Ben. I would deal with it later.

Out of the corner of my eye, I noticed more people walking toward us. I looked up to see the twins.

"You invited them?" Luka asked.

"They heard about it somehow," I said. "Better to have them in on it than telling others, right?"

"Did they threaten that?" Luka asked without taking his eyes off of them. He didn't look happy.

"No, they didn't, they just asked to come. They're my friends and they have helped me a lot."

Luka blew out a breath and then turned to look at me. "You're right. I'm grateful to them for helping you with your magic."

"Is that everyone?" Makayla asked.

"I think so," I said.

"No more surprise guests?" Luka asked.

"Not from me," I said.

"Well, here goes," Luka said, holding up a key card. "I'm guessing you all figured out why we're here. I swiped this from the office. Figured it wouldn't hurt to get a peek at what they had in store for us."

"You know this will get us kicked out if we're caught," Makayla said.

"You want to fail the trials again at the last minute?" Jessica said.

"No, I'm just reminding you all. If we get caught, get yourself out. Nobody try to be a hero," she said.

"Good point," I said. "Don't linger, just run."

"Here we go." Luka slid the card into the slot by the door and the light turned green.

All of us filed into the gym and my jaw dropped open in surprise as I stared at the transformation. It no longer looked like a gym. Instead, it was like something out of a reality television show. Climbing walls and zip lines and tunnels filled with who knew what.

In the dim light of the emergency lights, the whole thing looked like something humans would do to prove their athletic prowess. The thing was, on top of that, there would be magical elements added.

From somewhere in the back of the room, something growled. Low and threatening, the sound was joined by several more growls.

And it wasn't coming from any of my friends.

We weren't alone.

Raven

"Please tell me that was one of you wolves," Luka said.

"You know it wasn't," Ben said.

"Are there usually other creatures in the trials?" I asked. "Or guards?"

"There weren't last year," Luka said.

"You snuck in here last year and still didn't pass," Makayla said.

"Hey, some of us didn't want to graduate right away," he said.

"Alright, everyone stop arguing. We should go before whatever it is finds us," I said in a loud whisper.

"Too late," Starla said. "Run."

I turned toward her voice and my mouth dropped open in shock. There was a dragon looking down at us. *A fucking dragon.* It opened its mouth and roared.

Someone grabbed my arm and pulled. I turned and ran, Ben dragging me along with him.

We raced toward the door we'd come in. A rush of air passed overhead and the dragon landed in front of the door, roaring again. The sound made every hair on my body stand on edge.

"Dragons are fucking real?" I screamed as we took off running in the opposite direction.

Nobody answered and I didn't really expect them to. It was obvious from our current situation that dragons were fucking real, but it was still a lot to take in. You'd think humans would know if dragons existed. How the fuck did they keep them hidden all this time?

I risked a glance behind me and saw a second dragon swoop in and join the first. They both screeched in unison as if communicating something. I wasn't sure I wanted to know what it was.

Grateful for all the running I'd been doing the last few months, I kept pace with Ben as we bolted around a climbing wall and around a few platforms.

I caught a glimpse of the rest of our friends as they dove under a structure. Tugging Ben's hand, I dragged him in that direction so we could catch up to the others.

We slid under a platform structure just as the first round of fire blasted the gym floor. I tucked my legs under me to move farther into the back of the little enclosure.

Panting, I looked around at the terrified faces of my friends. "Anyone got a plan?"

"Can't you use fire?" Makayla asked.

"Yeah, but that's a dragon," I said.

"I'm going to cause a distraction," Luka said. "The rest of you, run."

"Luka!" I shouted after him as he darted toward the dragon.

"Come on," Ben said, grabbing my arm.

The dragons flapped their wings, sending stray hair flying into my face. I turned toward them staring in horror as they followed Luka.

"Run, Raven," Ben pulled me toward him but I was paralyzed. I couldn't leave Luka like that.

The rest of the group ran toward the door, reaching it before I even moved.

"We can't leave him, Ben," I said.

"Fuck." Ben dropped my arm. "Come on, then."

The two of us raced toward the dragons. Luka was running up a ramp, ducking from another round of fire. He disappeared and I screamed. "Luka!"

My heart pounded against my ribs and I felt my own magic rising to the threat. It surged through me, demanding that I release it. I breathed in through my nose, doing my best to keep the time magic contained. At least my lessons with Professor Halifax had helped me with that. A few weeks ago, I would have already frozen time on instinct.

Next to me, I heard a familiar growl and I turned to see a huge wolf where Ben had been. He took off, moving faster than I ever could even with all the running practice I'd had lately.

He charged one of the dragons, snapping at its leg.

"Ben, be careful," I yelled. My heart felt like it was splitting in two. On one hand, I had Luka somewhere nearby, possibly hurt. On the other hand there was Ben actively chasing down a fucking dragon.

I stopped moving, trying to decide where to go next. I couldn't choose between them any more than I could choose to breathe.

Suddenly, a fireball shot past me and I lunged to the side, risking a glance behind me. I expected a dragon, but what I got instead was the twins.

Both of them were facing down the dragon that had turned on Ben.

"Go get Luka," Matt said. "We've got the dragons."

I nodded. At least Ben was getting help.

The second dragon flew over me, joining his friend just as Matt and Zach arrived next to Ben. The three of them had a chance, I supposed.

Moving fast again, I raced toward the drop off where I'd last seen Luka.

It didn't take long to find him. He was on the ground and he wasn't moving. A pool of blood was spreading away from him, leaving a red stain on the floor.

"No." I felt like my heart had been ripped out through my chest. He had to be okay. He just had to be.

I ran to him, collapsing onto my knees at his side. "Luka, say something. Please be alive. You have to be alive."

He didn't move.

I pressed my fingertips to his neck, feeling for a pulse as I watched his chest for signs of breathing. His pulse was weak, but it was there.

Leaning down, I moved my ear above his mouth, listening for breath. It came, but it was strained and rattling. I wasn't a doctor but even I knew he was running out of time.

"Raven."

I turned to see Ben. He was covered in blood and his clothes were burned and falling apart. But he was standing and he was taking to me. I allowed myself a second of relief for his safety before turning back to Luka.

"We have to get out of here," Ben said. "The twins got the

dragons back in their pen. We have to go now before they break out again."

"He's dying, Ben," I said. "I don't know what to do."

Ben dropped down next to Luka and pressed his fingers to his neck. "He still has a pulse. He probably needs to feed."

"Like sex?" I asked.

Ben slid his arms under Luka and lifted him. Luka's head rolled back, his eyes still closed.

"Ben we can't let him die, please, you have to help me," I said, tears welling up in my eyes.

"Come on," he said. "I have an idea."

I followed Ben to the gym doors where Matt and Zach were holding them open for us.

"Is he?" Matt asked.

"Not yet," Ben said. "But he doesn't have long."

Ben turned and walked toward the nearest door, the women's locker room. "Open the door."

I opened the door and held it while Ben carried Luka in. He paused just inside the room and turned back to the twins. "I need you two to let us know if anyone shows up."

"You got it," Matt said.

My heart swelled as I looked at the twins. They'd come back for us and they were still helping. I owed them more than they'd ever know.

"Thank you," I said.

"Go, help your friend," Zach said. "We've got this."

I nodded then followed Ben into the locker room.

He set Luka down on the ground inside the massive group shower, then he turned to me. "You're going to need to get him some magic."

I looked at Luka. He was laying there unresponsive. How was I supposed to do anything to help him?

"Kiss him," Ben said.

Leaning over the injured demon, I pressed my lips to his. Then, I cupped his cheeks and gently kissed his forehead. He took a breath and it sounded better than it had before.

I looked up at Ben. "I think it helped."

"He needs more." Ben moved closer to me and then grabbed the back of my head, pulling me in for a kiss.

I broke away from him and looked at him, my eyes wide. "Now is not the time."

"It's exactly the time," Ben said. "He feeds off sexual energy. Not just his. But those around him. You want to save him?"

"Of course I do."

"Then kiss me." Ben pulled me into another kiss, pressing his lips hard against mine.

My body responded almost instantly as tingles shot right to my core. I leaned into him and weaved my fingers into his hair.

Raven

Ben's hand slid up under my shirt and my skin felt like it was on fire from his touch. Heat spread through me and my desperation climbed. Just from his touch.

Quickly, I worked the buttons of my shirt and shrugged it off, leaving me sitting there on the shower floor in my bra. Ben's large hands cupped my breasts. One of his hands traveled up to my neck then went around to the back of my head, pushing me deeper into the kiss.

His other hand left my breast, and I whined into his mouth,

missing his touch. He grabbed hold of my hand and guided it to Luka, then he broke away from the kiss.

"Kiss him," Ben said.

Panting and already wet from Ben, I turned back to Luka and lowered my mouth to his.

This time, he stirred under my kiss, turning slightly toward me. I moved my hand to his chest, then lower until I reached his cock. It was already hard through his pants.

I pulled away and Luka blinked up at me. Laughing, I planted another kiss on him.

"Easy, kitten," he said.

Slowly, he sat up and I could see the wound on his head where the blood had come from. His blonde hair was matted and filthy.

Gently, I touched the injury. "We need to get you to the hospital."

"No need," he said. "You keep doing what you were doing and I'll heal just fine."

A hand grabbed mine and I turned toward Ben. He pulled me into him and pressed his lips against my shoulder, then up to my neck. His tongue teased my earlobe as his hands went around my back to my bra.

In a flick of motion, my bra was unsnapped and Ben leaned back, pulling the lacy garment off of me and tossing it aside.

Luka's hands came around from behind me and he caressed my exposed breasts. He squeezed my nipples before going back to feeling my body. A moment later, his lips gently brushed against the back of my neck.

I gasped as a shiver of pleasure moved down my spine.

Ben stood, then held his hand out to me just as Luka's touch left my body. I took Ben's offered hand and he pulled me to standing. Without waiting, he unbuttoned my pants and slid them down my hips.

I stepped out of them.

From behind, I felt Luka's fingers hook under the waistband of my panties and he slid them down.

I was naked now. Vulnerable and completely exposed. I should have been terrified but everything felt so right.

Standing on my tiptoes, I tilted my face so I could reach Ben's mouth. I gave him a quick kiss, then I turned back to Luka.

He looked better now but was still more pale than I'd like to see him. Plus, there was all that blood.

I went to work on his clothing, removing his soiled garments. Then I walked over to one of the showers and turned it on. I turned the next two showers on also. While they warmed up, I walked over to Ben and quickly stripped him of his destroyed clothing. To my surprise, he didn't object.

I guided him to the middle shower which was now nice and hot. A cloud of steam rose around our feet.

Filling my hand with soap from the dispenser, I went to work lathering up Luka's hair. He grabbed my arm, kissing the inside of my wrist. "Thank you."

"You're the one who charged after the dragon to save us all," I reminded him.

"Yeah, but I'm the asshole who took you all there in the first place," he said.

"We're okay, though," I said. "We're all okay."

He let go of my hand and leaned back in the hot water, rinsing the suds from his hair.

I turned to Ben, my hands still full of soapy bubbles and I spread the lather on his firm chest. He grinned and scooped the bubbles off of himself and rubbed them onto my breasts.

I grabbed more soap and got to work lathering up every inch of exposed skin I could find on him.

He laughed, doing the same to me.

When I bent down to get soap on his lower legs, I felt

someone come up behind me. A hard cock pressed into my ass cheek and I stood quickly, startled.

Luka's arms wrapped around me and I looked over my shoulder at him. His head wasn't covered in blood anymore and his color had returned.

"You look better," I said.

"I feel better," he said.

His hard cock pressed against my hip as he held me in his embrace. I felt tension I didn't even know I was holding release. I'd been so worried about him and now I could relax. He was going to be okay.

Just then, Ben moved forward, the bubbles on his rock-hard body washing away under the running water of the shower. His huge cock pressed against my stomach.

Wetness spread between my legs as my body reacted to being between two sexy men.

He leaned down and kissed me. I moaned into his mouth, feeling intoxicated with lust. I didn't even care what they did to me. I just wanted them both.

Ben broke free of the kiss and Luka's mouth replaced his. I could feel the sexual energy radiating from him, filling the shower room. It was as if the three of us were in a spell we couldn't break free of.

Ben's mouth found my nipples and someone's fingers teased my clit. I gasped into Luka's kiss as an orgasm threatened.

A finger slid inside me, but I was too far gone to even notice who was doing what. Hands explored my breasts, while another hand cupped my ass.

A second finger joined, and I gasped as my pleasure peaked with each pulsing moment.

I came hard, breaking away from Luka's kiss to cry out. But they weren't about to let me have time to rest.

Suddenly, Ben lifted me up and I wrapped my legs around

his waist. Slowly, he lowered me enough to enter me. I bit down on my lower lip as I held my breath in anticipation. His huge cock slid into me quickly. "Fuck!" He felt so good inside me, hitting in just the right place to nearly take me to climax again.

Luka's hands caressed my ass and I panted hard as the little movements from Ben's cock sent me closer and closer to orgasm.

Then I felt pressure at my asshole and my eyes widened. I'd never done that before. Despite all my experimenting with sex, the back door wasn't something I'd ever explored. I wasn't sure it was a good idea and was just about to say so when Ben adjusted his position, thrusting in a way that sent chills through my whole body as I cried out in ecstasy.

That's when Luka's cock slid into my ass.

I gasped, feeling fuller than I ever had before. I turned so I could look back at Luka and he leaned closer, kissing my cheek. I rested my head on his shoulder for a second as I adjusted to the new sensation. Both males were still, breathing in time with me, as if waiting for my queue.

For a moment, I felt like I couldn't handle it. It was too much. Then just before I thought I couldn't take any more, my body adjusted. Taking a deep breath, I leaned forward, and kissed Ben.

Both males began to thrust slowly and the pleasure began to build again. I gripped Ben's back, digging my nails into him as I fought against the intensity as a rush of heat low in my belly began to surge through me.

It didn't take long before it exploded, making me scream as both males continued to thrust.

The orgasm rolled through me in waves, over and over. I'd never felt anything like it. Intense and overpowering, I was useless against it.

Finally, both males joined me in their release and they set me back down on the ground.

My legs wobbled and the room was spinning. I lost track of how many times I'd come. "Wow."

"I get that a lot," Luka said.

"Don't think it'll ever happen again," Ben said.

I knew Ben had done this for me and I knew how hard it must have been for him to do considering the way he felt about Luka. But I had to admit, I was hoping it would happen again.

Raven

Despite the excitement the night before, the practice trials were going on as planned.

I paced the locker room, waiting for my turn. Makayla and Violet had both already taken their turns, making my wait feel even longer.

"Hey, little mage," Delores called.

I let out a sigh as I turned to face her. I wasn't in the mood today. "What?"

"You have a plan to get through this thing alive?" she asked.

"Same as you," I said. "Go through it and do my best."

"Right," she moved closer to me, "except for the fact that you saw it last night. I know you did. Zach may have mentioned it. You know, pillow talk."

My insides tensed, then twisted until I felt like I was going to throw up. I couldn't stand the thought of Zach curled up with this bitch. "You're bluffing."

"Wanna try me?" she asked. "You do know what my magic does, right? I have the ability to get people to sing."

"You wouldn't," I said.

"Not if you give me something I can work with. Otherwise, you'll be confessing your sins to Coach Miller," she said with a grin.

I rolled my eyes. What did Zach see in her? And how was I ever going to look at him the same way again?

Really, all I wanted to do was claw her eyes out but that was irrational. I had zero claim on Zach. If anything, I should be thrilled that he was done flirting with me. Instead it felt like a punch in the gut.

"What do you have for me, little mage?" she asked.

"Fine," I said.

She leaned in so her ear was near my lips. "I'm waiting."

"There are two dragons out there," I said.

She pulled away, her eyes wide. "Are you serious?"

I nodded. "We nearly died. Did Zach fail to mention that part?"

Her brow furrowed. "He might have."

"Well, now you know."

"Raven Winters, it's your turn," Professor Halifax called from the doorway.

"Good luck," Delores said.

"You too," I said, calling it out on reflex. I kind of hoped the dragon swallowed her whole.

Professor Halifax closed the door behind me, and I stood

next to her facing the gym. The scorch marks from last night were gone.

"I'm proud of you," Professor Halifax said.

I turned to look at her, confused. "I haven't done anything yet."

She smirked. "Last night you faced down a dragon and you didn't resort to your time magic. Do that again today. You can get through this while keeping yourself in check."

My cheeks heated. Did everyone know about last night?

"Go on," she said. "You have to ring the bell on the other end. However you get there is up to you."

Taking a deep breath in through my nose, I squared my shoulders, staring out at the ladders and ramps and rock walls ahead of me. The whole room was a mess of obstacles.

However, she didn't tell me I had to use them. She just said I had to get to the bell. "Just ring the bell?"

She nodded. "That's the only rule."

It seemed too easy. Why the hell would anyone choose to climb all the obstacles if they didn't have to? Feeling like I was missing something, I walked out onto the gym floor.

A low rumbling sounded behind me and I knew the dragon was on its way. I didn't look back. I ran.

Going around the climbing wall, I ducked under a bridge just as a wall of fire hit the ground next to me.

The room smelled like burning paint and campfire. Did they clean it up after every candidate? It seemed like a lot of work to go through every year. But then again, they had magic.

The dragon swooped past my hiding spot, then landed nearby. Its claws tapped along the wood floor as it moved closer to me. In a few seconds, it would sniff me out.

I glanced behind me to find that I was in an enclosed space. *Fuck*. I might have been spared for a few minutes, but now I was totally screwed.

I needed a plan.

My magic seemed to respond to my being trapped here. Heat flowed through my veins, reminding me of the way I'd summoned fire in the past. But would fire be helpful against a dragon?

Thinking fast, I remembered how I'd knocked the test booklets out of Professor Hurd's hands. It wasn't enough to do damage, but it had sure given me a distraction.

Channeling air, I pulled all my magic inside and held it tight like a spring ready to explode.

The dragon stuck its large head into my hiding space and blew out a burst of air from its nostrils. It smelled like brimstone. I honestly wasn't sure what brimstone even was, but I was sure it smelled like dragon breath.

With a yell, I released the magic, sending a huge rush of wind right in the dragon's face.

The creature roared and pulled its head back. Then, it stumbled and landed on its back. It howled.

It was pissed.

Really. Really. Pissed.

But it was down.

Not waiting to see if a dragon on its back could get up quickly, I ran from my hiding spot and darted around a few more obstacles.

I could see the bell.

It was on the top of a tower that was connected to a second tower via a zipline.

There was no way up except for the zipline. *Fuck*. I cursed under my breath and spun around to follow the zipline.

And there was dragon number two.

This one was quiet, creeping on all fours toward me like a fucking cat. "What the hell?"

Whoever heard of a stealthy dragon.

My magic bubbled below the surface, calling to me. It wasn't the same magic I'd used before. This was darker magic. Something that was urging me to claim its power.

I'd used this magic once before when I attacked the thief. I didn't know how it worked or what it was, but I was pretty sure it was connected to my time magic. Which meant, it was off limits.

Pushing the magic back down, I looked around for somewhere to go. The dragon growled and broke into a run.

Time's up.

Running as hard as I could, I race toward the tower.

Ring the bell.

Ring the bell.

Reaching inside, I called to whatever magic I could find. The dark magic happily rose up to the challenge. I didn't care. I didn't want to be eaten. Or burned alive.

I threw the magic at the bell, urging it to ring.

Like an invisible curve ball, something hit the bell and it sounded clear and strong, ringing out through the gym.

I dove behind the bell tower, panting.

Other than the sound of the bell, the gym was silent.

I wiped the sweat off my brow then risked a glance around the tower. No dragons.

My heart was racing and my breathing was still too fast, but I was alive. For now.

"She didn't ring it herself, it's not over," Coach Miller said.

"The rules are clear, she has to ring the bell, she rang it," Professor Halifax said.

I walked toward the sound of their arguing, still breathing too fast to speak.

"She cheated. That's never been the intention of the trials. Otherwise a student could use magic to ring the bell the second they step foot in the gym," he said.

"And there's no rule that says they can't," Professor Halifax said.

"She's right," Dr. Green said. "Congratulations, Raven. You passed the practice trial."

The whole thing felt surreal. I did it? I passed? I had to admit, I sort of agreed with Coach Miller. I did feel like I cheated, but I wasn't about to look a gift horse in the mouth.

"Thanks," I breathed.

"You won't get so lucky at the real trials," Coach Miller said.

"I guess we'll see, won't we?" I asked, then I turned and walked away before he could say anything else. I probably just ensured that my next week in gym was going to be hell, but it was worth it.

Raven

I knocked on Makayla's Door. "You ready?"

The door opened and Makayla stepped back, spinning in a slow circle. "What do you think?"

Her long, red dress hugged her curves in all the right places. Her cropped brown hair was dusted with something that sparkled in the light and her fire engine red lipstick was perfect.

"You look amazing. Jonah isn't even going to know what hit him," I said.

"I'm still mad as hell that he didn't ask me," she said as she walked out of the door. "But at least I know he's going alone so he has a chance to make it up to me."

She stopped in the hall and put her hands on her hips. "Did you even attempt to make yourself look good?"

I scoffed. "Wow. You're the best ego boost I've ever had."

"No, seriously. The dress is perfect. I told you you'd be hot as hell in it. But the makeup and hair are just sad. It's a ball, not a trip to a bowling alley or whatever the hell you did in the human world."

"I haven't been to a bowling alley since I was a kid," I said defensively.

"Well, lucky for you, I'm here to help." She swiped her key card then pushed me toward her door. "Come on."

Knowing it was easier to just go along with her, I let her push me into her room. Makayla's room looked like a tornado had torn through it. There were shoes and clothes all over her floor and bed.

She steered me toward her bathroom. The counter was covered in round powder compacts, lipstick tubes, liner pencils, brushes, and liquids I didn't recognize.

I took in my reflection. I didn't think I'd done too bad. I had pulled half of my hair up and pinned it with a sparkly clip. I'd even put on some blush and lip gloss. Wasn't that enough?

"Sit," Makayla commanded.

I took the chair facing the mirror. "I'm not a big makeup person."

"I know, but it's the Yule Ball. It's once a year. And it's a big deal. Besides, it might be your only one if you pass the trials in the spring."

"I doubt I'll be that lucky twice," I said.

She laughed. "None of us would survive if you got that lucky twice. I'm so tired of running up and down that tower."

"Same." Coach Miller had made us run the obstacle course

the way he wanted it to go all week for gym. That final tower to get to the zip line was only accessible through a hanging rope. You had to climb it while sliding down the glossy tower if you tried to use it for leverage. People who had better upper body strength just climbed the rope. I had to use the side of the tower and ended up falling on my ass more times than I could count.

"I sure hope he's over that by Monday," I said.

"That's the best part," she said. "Monday starts the holiday break. Solstice. Some of the students go home and others hang out here. It's basically a week of nonstop parties."

I sunk a little deeper into the chair as relief washed over me. I could use the break.

Makayla sprayed something in my hair then went to work with a brush and a curling iron. Ten minutes later, I had to admit, my hair was a gorgeous cascade of loose curls. "That looks amazing."

"You're welcome," she said cheerfully. Then she spun me around so I was facing her. "Now close your eyes."

I obeyed, nervous about what she was going to do. She didn't spend long applying makeup, but it was more than I usually did.

"All done," she said. "Now that date of yours is going to lose it when he sees you."

I turned to look at myself in the mirror. She'd kept the makeup subtle compared to hers, but gave me a muted smoky eye and a pink lipstick that enhanced the color of my lips. I looked like a better version of myself and I felt beautiful. "Wow. Thanks, Makayla."

"Now, we're ready," she said.

I stood and admired the finished product. I'd stuck to my standard black dress but this time, I'd gone a bit more dramatic in the cut. It was long and form fitting with an open back. A strand of rhinestones across my shoulder blades kept the straps from falling down. It belonged to Makayla and I had a feeling she'd ordered it for me and pretended it was hers. I was several inches taller than her and wore a size larger, but this dress fit me like a glove.

I didn't question it, though. She was delighted that I agreed to be her date. It worked well for both of us because while her potential date never gathered the courage to ask her, mine was far too complicated.

I'd seen both Ben and Luka separately in the days leading up to the ball and neither of them brought it up.

I supposed it was hard to navigate when you were dating two males but one of them was a secret.

The ballroom was only used for special occasions and as we climbed the stairs to the rarely used fourth floor, I wondered what it would look like. Most of our classes were on the first two floors and I'd been on the third floor once or twice to look around when I first arrived. The fourth floor was the ballroom, and guest suites for when people visited. Which, I supposed would be full come parent's day in the new year.

I shuddered at the thought of having to see Ms. Obscura again. Hopefully, things would be less complicated between me and her sons by then.

Music wafted down the stairway as we climbed higher. It wasn't the usual party music with its loud, thumping bass. This was sweet and dreamy and a little bit sad.

We arrived on the fourth floor and I saw several students milling about in the hallway outside of the massive double doors that led to the ballroom. Makayla slid her arm into mine and we walked inside, arms linked.

A string quartet greeted us, their music filling the room louder than should be possible. It took on an eerie quality that reminded me slightly of the siren music I'd heard at the vampire party. But it didn't have quite the same pull to it.

The dance floor was full of students moving to the music.

They seemed to know the steps to a formal dance I wasn't familiar with. I wondered if I could spend the evening at one of the round tables along the wall.

"Come on," Makayla said. "Let's grab a drink."

We walked over to a bar and each of us took a glass of champagne. Sipping the bubbly, I looked around for any signs of Luka or Ben. The first people I spotted were Zach and Matt. I frowned, trying to tell myself that I wasn't looking for them or that I didn't care what they were doing, but I did. They were both dancing with other mages. Jealousy rolled through me and I forced myself to look away. I had no right to feel like that. They were free to dance with anyone they wanted. Besides, I was already in a complicated relationship with two males. I didn't need to add more to my dance card.

"Do you see Luka or Ben?" I asked quietly.

"Not yet, but I'm sure they'll be here soon," she said.

"Hey, beautiful," a smooth male voice said.

Makayla and I both turned and as soon as I saw who it was, I glanced at her in time to see her expression light up.

"Jonah," she said. "You sure clean up well."

"And you look good enough to eat," he said.

"Just think, you could have had all of this if you'd bothered to ask me to the dance," she said.

"I didn't ask you to the dance because Ben told me not to," he said. "But he didn't say anything about me not asking you *to dance*."

"Wait, what?" she passed her champagne glass to me and I took it from her.

"Ben asked you to?" I asked.

He shrugged. "Guess he wanted to make sure his mage had company."

Makayla scowled then turned to me. "It was his suggestion that I ask you."

"I see." I threw back the champagne in one swig and then drank Makayla's glass too. "Seems he didn't want anyone else to ask me."

I set the glasses on the bar. "If you'll excuse me, I have a wolf to find."

Ben

I expected Raven to be upset when she found me. I didn't expect her to look as sexy as she did.

My inner wolf growled low as she approached. Raven was always hot as hell. She always made me want to tear her clothes off. But tonight she took that to the next level.

It was taking all of my will power not to run to her and throw her over my shoulder and carry her out of here.

She stopped in front of me with a hand on her hip. "For some reason you decided that if you couldn't be my date to the dance, nobody could? Did you tell Luka not to ask me too?"

"Not exactly," I said.

She lifted an eyebrow, clearly annoyed. "I'm waiting."

"I might have called in a favor with him," I said.

"You saved his life and your favor is for him to not ask me to a dance?" She shook her head. "You wasted your favor."

I reached for her hand and was pleasantly surprised that she didn't pull away from my touch. "I don't think of it as a waste. It's time we make this official."

Her brow furrowed. "What are you talking about?" She pulled her hand away. "We can't do that. You said so yourself."

"I had a chat with my dad," I said, waiting for the realization to dawn on her.

"So we went from *my dad is going to kill us both* to my dad is fine?" she asked.

He laughed. "Turns out the only thing he wants more than his son being legit is a connection to the underworld."

"How does that help us?" she asked. Then her eyes widened. "Luka."

"Turns out having a mating bond with a girl who also has a mating bond with the most powerful demon in Hell is a good thing."

"A good thing for whom?" She glanced around, probably looking for Luka. "Seems to me your dad and Luka's mom shouldn't be anywhere near each other for the sake of the world."

"Normally, I'd agree with you." I took hold of her other hand and gently urged her closer to me. "But I'm willing to let them hash things out among themselves if it means I get to have you."

"I'm not sure I'm worth it," she said.

"You are, trust me," I said.

"Please tell me you didn't cause the end of the world or something," she said.

I laughed. "They might have a lot of power, but my dad is only interested in money, I doubt we've ushered in the apocalypse with their introduction. Besides, I just arranged for them to meet. They still have to get along on their own."

"And if they do?" She bit down on her lip, a nervous habit of hers.

"Then they'll figure out a way to form a business relationship." I shrugged.

"And if they don't?"

"We'll cross that bridge when we get there. But I don't want to talk about my dad tonight. Or Luka's mom. Or Luka." I slid my arms around her waist. "I want to have a dance with the most beautiful girl at the ball."

She smirked and I could feel the tension releasing from her. She was probably still worried but like me, the pull toward her mate was overpowering her better judgement.

She had a point that it might have been dangerous to introduce those two, but I wasn't worried about them. They'd figure it out. If anything, they were dangerous to each other. And if it allowed me to be with Raven, to really be with her, it was worth it.

I led Raven onto the dance floor.

"I don't know the steps," she said. "In the human world we just grind on each other."

"Wow, never thought I'd be jealous of the human world," I said.

"You'll have to come to the next vampire party with me," she said.

"Sounds like a date." I led her through the motions, guiding her steps. After a few rounds, she had the dance down. She was graceful and a natural dancer.

In this moment, I knew my favor with Luka and the agreement with my father had been worth it. Raven was everything I ever wanted. And she didn't know that my favor meant I got her for the whole night. Luka even promised to stay out of her dreams.

Though, he did offer to join us if I wanted him there.

I frowned momentarily and shook the thought away. Sharing Raven was the one thing I didn't like. But if that demon played fair, I'd do it for her.

Suddenly, an ear-piercing scream broke through the ballroom and the music came to a halt.

Mumbled chatter filled the room as everyone looked around in confusion.

"What was that?" Raven asked.

"I don't know." The two of us moved with the motion of the crowd, toward whatever the issue was. My heart pounded harder and I kept Raven slightly behind me, ready to protect her if needed.

"Where is that time mage?" A female voice called.

"Raven, get out of here. Run," another female voice called. It sent chills through me as soon as I realized who it was.

"Makayla," Raven said, dropping my hand. She pushed through the crowd toward the voices and I ran after her, shoving people out the way to keep up with her.

"Raven, get back here," I hissed. What the hell was she doing? Whatever was going on up ahead was a trap.

I caught up to her and grabbed her arm, pulling her toward me. "We have to get out of here."

"Run, Raven," Makayla said again. Her voice was shaky, and she sounded like she was fighting tears.

"I won't run," Raven said. "I will never run."

My jaw tensed as I stared at the determined expression on her face. "Then we go together. And you let me help."

She nodded.

As we moved forward, the crowd parted for us.

Finally we reached the edge of the crowd and I dug my fingers into Raven's upper arm to keep her from running.

In front of us, the time thief held Makayla in front of her. She had a blade on Makayla's throat. I could see a silver band on Makayla's wrist that looked like a magic lock. The kind they gave shifters to keep them from shifting. She was helpless to fight back, likely weakened from the magic lock.

"Makayla, hang on," Raven said.

"Well, well, how nice to see you again, Raven." The time thief flicked her eyes to me. "And you brought your pet dog."

I growled, my free hand clenched into a fist. I was ready to shift. I wanted to rip that woman's throat out but I had to be careful not to hurt Makayla.

"Before you complete that thought," the time thief said, "consider your friend here."

She pressed the tip of the blade into Makayla's throat, drawing blood.

Makayla gasped and then quickly locked her gaze on me. "Don't even think about it. That's what she wants. Don't let her win."

"Let her go," Raven said. "Your fight is with me."

"I have no fight with you, little girl," she said. "I simply want your magic."

"You can't have it," I said, stepping in front of Raven.

"Aw, aren't you the adorable protective pup," she said.

"Ben, stay back." Raven set her hands on my back. "Let me handle this."

"No," I said. "She's not getting you or your magic."

The crowd shifted again and I saw Luka making his way toward us. I lifted my chin in greeting. I might not like the guy, but I knew he'd do anything he could to protect Raven, just as I would.

What surprised me was that following behind him were the

mage twins. I knew they were friends with Raven, but I didn't know they'd be willing to face a thief on her behalf.

"You're going to have to go through all of us to get to her," Luka said.

The thief shrugged. "As you wish."

Then she dragged the knife across Makayla's neck.

Raven

I leaned into Ben, my hands on his back for support. I knew the thief was strong. I knew her magic was likely even stronger than it had been last time we'd met. I also wasn't sure if I was strong enough to get my magic back again if she took it from me.

I needed a plan.

There had to be a way to outsmart her.

Like the bell. I didn't have to go through the extra obstacles, I just had to ring the bell.

This time, I had to save Makayla. Whatever else happened didn't matter. I just had to keep my magic long enough to get

Makayla away from her. I'd fought her before, but not while she was holding a weapon against one of my friends.

A flicker of hope rose in my chest when I watched Luka and the twins break through the crowd. Maybe there was a way we could take her down together. Maybe between the five of us we could even catch this mad woman.

My brain whirred, trying to come up with a plan as Luka faced the thief.

"You're going to have to go through all of us to get to her," Luka said.

The thief shrugged. "As you wish."

Then she dragged the knife across Makayla's neck.

My magic flared to life and I didn't fight it. I didn't care if it wasn't allowed. I embraced it, letting it explode out of me.

And like before, time stopped.

Before I lost control, I pushed past Ben and walked up to the thief. To my surprise, she lowered the knife.

I risked a glance at Makayla. The cut didn't look too deep and I had to hope they'd get her medical attention as soon as time started again.

"Your magic doesn't work on me," she said. "But I'm glad you froze your helpers. It'll be so much more satisfying to have them enter time again to see you dead on the ground."

"I don't think so." I kicked her hand, sending the knife skidding across the floor.

Then, I channeled my magic the way Professor Halifax had taught me. Holding onto it, I broke the time stop.

"How?" the thief asked, her eyes wide.

Ben, Luka, and the twins all slammed into her, wrestling her to the ground.

I stepped back and ran to Makayla.

Tears streamed down her cheeks and she held her hand to her injured neck.

"Are you okay?" I asked, gently moving her hand so I could look at her cut.

"I think so," she said. "I'm still alive so that's good."

Dr. Green cut through the crowd. "Everyone back to their dorms."

The students protested in grumbled murmurs.

"Anyone who is still in the ballroom in two minutes will be sent to confinement," he said.

The students shifted, moving away from us.

Dr. Green stopped next to Makayla and looked at her injury. He frowned. "Head to the hospital wing. They'll get you cleaned up."

She nodded.

"I'll go with her," I said.

"No, you stay," he said. "Matthew Obscura, please make yourself useful and accompany her to the hospital."

"I'm fine," Makayla protested.

"Just let him help," I said.

Matt squeezed my hand on his way past me to Makayla and the two of them walked away.

I turned my attention back to the pile of bodies that was pinning down the thief.

To my great surprise, she wasn't fighting back.

Several security guards circled the thief and Luka, Ben, and Zach stepped away.

"You think this is over, time mage?" The thief asked as one of the security guards snapped silver bracelets on her wrists.

"You've lost, you sick bitch," I said.

"That's what you think," she said. "But I always win."

My pulse raced but I tried not to show her that I was afraid of her.

"Get her out of here," Dr. Green said. "And don't let her escape this time."

Ben wrapped his arm around me and pulled me next to him as we stood in silence watching the guards walk her to the doors.

Then the lights flickered. *No. Not again.*

I broke free of Ben's grip and ran toward the thief. "You are not getting away this time."

In a burst of blue light, I was knocked backward onto my ass. Quickly, I righted myself and blinked to clear my vision.

The guards were on the ground and the thief was bolting toward the door.

"No! Someone stop her!" I ran after her. I was not going to go through this all over again.

The thief ran right into Professor Halifax. In another burst of blue light, the thief was on the ground.

I stopped just short of the fallen female.

Professor Halifax glared down at her. "How dare you."

"You," the time thief gasped up at her. "You traitor."

Professor Halifax leaned down, sending another round of blue light through her hands onto the thief.

When she stood, the thief was no longer moving.

I stared at Professor Halifax in horror. I'd never seen anyone use that kind of magic before except for the time thief. "What are you?"

I backed away, terrified that I'd traded one monster for another. "What did you do?"

"She was never going to stop hunting you, and now we know how she kept evading them." She squatted down to the dead thief and brushed her hair away from her ears.

My eyes widened as I watched the thief transform right there. Her body seeming to melt away into another form.

She was tall and thin, with high cheekbones. And her ears were just as pointed as Professor Halifax's.

"She was fae?" I asked.

The professor stood. "She was. Which is why none of their weapons could hold her. I didn't have a choice."

I was surrounded now by guards who quickly moved to the body.

"So it's over, then?" Ben asked.

"I guess so," I said.

"Professor Halifax," Dr. Green called. "You'll need to come to my office. I'm sure the authorities will have a lot of questions for you."

"Did she kill her?" Ben asked.

"Yes," I said.

"The thief looks fae," Luka said.

"Apparently she was," I said.

"That explains why they couldn't hold her," he said.

"I'm glad she's dead," Ben said. "She can't hurt you anymore."

He pulled me into an embrace and kissed the top of my head. "You're safe now."

I took a deep breath, trying to let myself feel safe but it wouldn't come. I couldn't help but think there was more to this story. Maybe I needed some time.

"I'm sorry I ruined your night," I said to Ben.

"Are you kidding?" He kissed my head again. "I don't care what happens as long as you're safe."

Suddenly, another set of arms wrapped around me. I didn't even need to see him to know it was Luka.

Ben grunted as Luka squeezed harder.

"We're doing group hugs now?" Zach called as he crashed into us.

I laughed as the three of them squeezed me. I didn't get the night I expected, but this was a pretty good way to end it.

Raven

Tick. Tick. Tick.

The tree clock was starting to become more of a comfort to me than it used to. I think that meant I spent too much time in this office. It was nearly midnight and I should be taking off my formal dress and crawling in between the sheets with my shifter.

Instead, I was waiting for my parole officer.

Talk about a mood killer.

The door opened and I turned to see Dr. Green, followed by Professor Halifax and both of the Obscura twins. Nobody made eye contact with me.

All of them looked the way I felt. Exhausted, a little broken, and really ready for this night to be over.

The twins settled in on a bench in the back of the office. I wondered if it had been added recently as I didn't remember it being there before.

Professor Halifax settled into the chair next to me. She looked over at me. "It's going to be fine."

"Don't argue," Dr. Green said from behind me. "I know that will be a challenge, but you need to trust us."

My brow furrowed. "Trust you?"

"Raven, please," Matt said.

"Just for once," Zach added.

Something was going on and I was missing it.

Before I could ask another question, the door opened again and Officer M walked in.

An involuntary chill ran though me at the sight of him. Despite our weekly meetings, he still made me uncomfortable.

"We've got quite the crowd gathered tonight." He set his briefcase down on the desk and settled into Dr. Green's chair as if he owned the place.

I pressed my lips together to keep from scowling at him. Everything about him put me on edge. Tonight, he was wearing a button-down shirt but he'd left the first several buttons open. Tufts of chest hair filed the gap in his shirt. It looked more like fur.

What the fuck was he?

Whatever it was, it wasn't attractive.

He dabbed his sweaty bald head with a handkerchief then turned his beady little eyes on me. "I guess tonight's the night, isn't it, darling?"

I winced at *darling*. Ew. "The night I stop worrying about the thief?"

He grinned, showing his yellow fangs. "No, the night I arrest you and pull you away from this cushy existence and toss you into a cell."

Ice cold fear filled my veins. "What?"

"The time magic used here tonight is so thick I could feel it just walking through the door." His smile didn't waver. He was enjoying every second of this.

"That's why we're here, actually," Matt said. He stood and walked toward the desk.

"Officer, I'm afraid I have to make a confession," he said.

Officer M gave an amused smirk. "Oh?"

"Raven didn't use the time magic," he said. "I did."

"What?" I asked, staring at him in disbelief.

"Please don't try to cover up for me," Matt said.

Professor Halifax squeezed my leg and I glanced at her. She gave me a tiny nod and I held my breath, remembering what they had said when they entered the room.

"Young man, that's a heavy confession, and I have to say I don't buy it for a minute," he said.

"It's true," Professor Halifax said. "The three of them completed a magic meld and I'm afraid some of her time magic was transferred to them. We've been working after hours to remove it as you'll see from my classroom logs."

She kept classroom logs? That was news to me.

"Dr. Green, can you confirm this?" Officer M asked.

"I'm afraid so," Dr. Green said. "We've kept it quiet as you know how the Obscura family prefers to avoid the spotlight with unfavorable news."

"Quite," Officer M said. "Though, I'll have to investigate this, you realize?"

"I understand," Dr. Green said. "Ms. Obscura was here not long ago to discuss the additional training sessions for her sons. I'm sure she'll be happy to speak with you about it."

Officer M tensed. I sort of knew how he felt. Thinking about

Ms. Obscura did that to me too. She wasn't a woman you crossed.

"Son, are you prepared to accept a punishment for what you did?" My parole officer wore a look of concern on his face. "You realize that if she takes the blame, she goes to prison. If you do, you're on parole and anything you do will get you tossed in prison."

I glared at him. Was he really giving Matt the option to throw me under the bus? *What an asshole.*

"We Obscuras hold to a strict code of honor," Matt said. "I must take responsibility for my own actions."

The room was silent for a moment and I could hear my heart beating.

"Very well," Officer M said. He turned to me. "Ms. Winters, you are dismissed. We will convene our meetings after the holidays."

I hesitated, not ready to leave the others in this room with him. But he wasn't taking his gaze off of me.

"Ms. Winters, you may go back to your dorm room," Dr. Green said.

I glanced over at the twins, torn over what they were doing. Matt was going to be stuck in here with meetings every week. He was going to have this on his record, the same as me. Why would he do that for me?

Part of me wanted to argue. To take responsibility. I was the one who had used the magic.

But then again, I really, really didn't want to go to prison.

"Ms. Winters," Professor Halifax said, "Makayla asked me to pass along a message."

I turned to her.

"She asked if you can sneak some real food into the hospital for her so she's not stuck with oatmeal."

I laughed. "I doubt they'll let me in."

"No, they won't, but I assured her I'd pass along the message so you knew she was safe." Professor Halifax's words were exactly what I needed to hear. It wasn't about oatmeal. It was about the fact that I'd made the right choice. Because I'd used my magic, Makayla was alive and the Thief was dead.

It wasn't just me they were protecting. They were standing up for the good my magic had done.

Finally getting it, I stood. "Thank you for letting me know."

I glanced at Matt and Zach, giving them a small smile before I left the room. I had no idea how I was going to repay them for this.

As I walked back to my room, a rush of gratitude washed over me. I had passed the practice trials, survived another thief attack, and successfully used and controlled my time magic.

Things were looking up for me. But there was always next semester to consider. And I knew better than to get too comfortable when things seemed up.

It was only a matter of time before the next crisis arrived.

For now, though, I had a wolf to find. Or maybe a demon. Or maybe, if I was really lucky, I could have both.

To Be Continued

FATED MAGIC

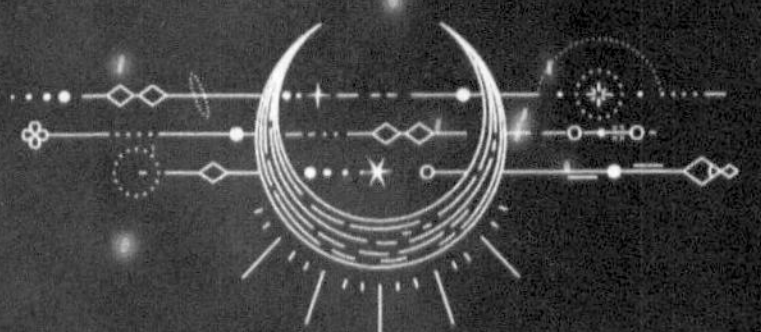

SPECIAL EDITION COLLECTION
BOOK 3

ALEXIS CALDER

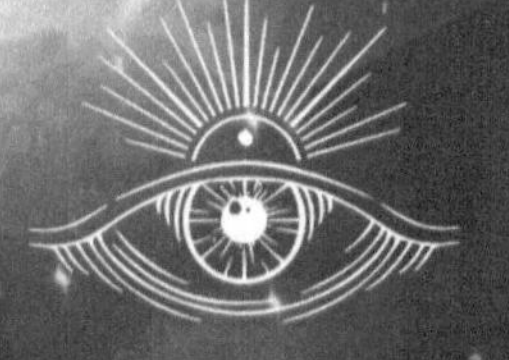

CHAPTER 1

RAVEN

Ben grabbed my hand and pulled me down onto the couch next to him. I snuggled in, enjoying the fact that we didn't have to hide our relationship anymore.

The common room was crowded tonight. Classes started back up tomorrow and everyone who had left campus to go visit family were back at school.

A few of the shifters raised their eyebrows at the sight of me and Ben snuggled up together, but nobody questioned it. Most of them had figured it out long before we started showing affection in public.

"It was nice to visit my family, but I sure missed hanging out without any expectations," Makayla said. She was stretched out across an entire couch and looked like she'd melted into the furniture.

"It was quiet here with you gone," Ben said.

"Aren't you sweet?" Makayla said with a grin.

"It was too quiet," I said.

"See, I know who appreciates me," she said.

"Schedules came out," someone called. We all turned to look toward the stairs. Jamal waved a pile of papers in his hand. "Who wants one and what are you going to give me for it?"

Starla jumped up from her seat nearby. "I'll take that challenge." She growled and then charged Jamal.

He let out a surprised sound as she knocked him to the ground. The papers went flying.

Makayla got up faster than I thought possible and grabbed them off the ground.

"No fair, I wasn't ready," Jamal said.

"Want to try again?" Starla asked. "In my room?"

"Yes, I do," he said.

Starla headed down the hall at a run and Jamal followed her. I heard the door slam behind them and knew they'd be there the rest of the night. Things seemed to be returning to normal. Nobody was worried about the thief or about the practice trials. And right now, the formal trials seemed so far away. Life was good.

Makayla stopped in front of me and held out a piece of paper. "Raven."

I sat up and took the paper from her.

"Ben," she said, holding up another sheet.

Ben lowered the arm that had been over my shoulders and reached for his schedule.

Makayla walked away, passing out the rest of the schedules. I looked down at mine and frowned. Gym first period. Yuck. Then Magical Theory, followed by Spellcasting. My brow furrowed when I read the next class. *Independent Study* with Professor Halifax. What did that mean?

Hadn't I spent enough time with her? I wondered if this was her way of making me continue working on controlling my time magic.

I looked over my remaining classes and noted that I'd been added to History of Magic instead of Training Your Familiar. I had been rubbish with the animals in that class anyway. Guess it was obvious to my professor.

"What do you have?" Ben asked, passing his schedule to me. We exchanged schedules and I quickly read through his.

"We have nothing together this semester," I said. "But it looks like you got out of Magical Theory."

"I hated that class but it was nice to see you during the day," he said.

"Don't worry," I said, snuggling back against his chest, "you'll get to see lots of me at night."

He grabbed our schedules and set them on the table in front of us. Then he pulled me into him and pressed his lips to mine.

Warmth spread through me and I clenched my thighs together against the wetness that came so easily from being with Ben. He had a way of getting me from zero to sixty in seconds.

"Get a room," Makayla said. "Some of us are still pissed that our Yule Ball dates didn't pan out."

I broke away from the kiss, feeling bad for Makayla. "Sorry."

"If you want, I'm available," Remi said as he walked into the common room.

I bit down on my lip to keep from laughing. Remi was trying to make nice lately but the thought of him and Makayla together was amusing.

"I think you can do better, Makayla," Ben said.

"She probably can." Remi shrugged. "But the offer stands."

"Thanks, Remi, I'll keep that in mind," she said.

"You know where to find me if you want some action." He winked then headed down the hall toward his room.

I held my breath waiting until I heard the sound of his door closing. Then I burst out laughing.

Makayla threw a pillow at my face and I laughed even harder.

"Hey, just because you're the luckiest girl alive and have *two* mates doesn't mean you can make fun of the rest of us."

I wiped a tear off my cheek. "You're right, I'm sorry. And Remi's not so bad, I mean if you're feeling tense."

"Yeah, my parents would love that. *Hey, Mom and Dad, I hooked up with a bear shifter. Surprise!*" She frowned.

"Do you think they'd care?" I asked.

She sighed. "Probably. We're a wolf family."

"My family was like that for the longest time," Ben said. "Then my cousin married a lion shifter. Everyone thought it would be this huge scandal and kept waiting for someone to say or do something at the wedding. The wedding came and went. Nobody said anything. Either nobody cared or they all kept their mouths shut."

Are you trying to talk me into fucking a bear shifter?" Makayla asked.

"I'm just saying, we all have our kinks," Ben said.

"He's an asshole, but sometimes assholes are the best in the sack," I added, playfully elbowing Ben.

Makayla rolled her eyes. "I never thought I'd see the day when my two best friends try to talk me into getting it on with a guy who was our mortal enemy until a few weeks ago."

"Hey, he was never our mortal enemy. We just think he's an asshat," Ben said.

"I'm going back to my room, *alone*, before the two of you get it on or before you talk me into doing something stupid," she said.

"Goodnight," Ben called. "Say hi to Remi for us."

Makayla walked down the hall, flipping the bird on her way.

I laughed again but felt a little bad. "Were we too hard on her?"

"Nah," Ben said. "They've been secretly fucking for about a week now."

"What?" I turned so I was facing him. "Are you serious?"

"Yep. Figured if we were cool about it, maybe she'd come clean to us," he said.

"Wow. You think you know a girl." I shook my head. "Hey, now I'm pissed. She should tell me these kinds of things. That's what friends do."

"We didn't tell her," he said.

"So this is revenge?" I asked. "That seems kind of petty."

"I think it's more likely that she's having fun with him but isn't sure she actually likes him."

"Huh." Part of me wanted to sneak past her room to listen. I still wasn't sure I believed it. But I was more interested in going to my room with Ben. "Well, if everyone else is in their rooms getting it on, shouldn't we give it a shot?"

He stood and then scooped me up into a bridal hold. I squealed as I threw my arms around his neck. Without any words, he ran toward his room, stopping short of the door.

The last few nights had been spent in either my room or his, but I was already ready for more.

Raven

Parents day. I hadn't realized just how hard this was going to be on me until the day arrived. Today, most of my classmates would be showing their family around campus and sitting down to a meal with them.

I had agreed to meet with the twins' mom before the Yule ball and Luka invited me to dinner with his mom. So in addition to feeling sorry for myself and my lack of parents, I was scared to death about meeting with Ms. Obscura after her son took the fall for me. Luka's mom didn't make me feel any better, either. She was a literal princess of hell.

I thought having a magic thief after me was the worst thing that could happen, but I had to admit, I was even more nervous about meeting my mates' parents.

I paused in front of the door to the twins' suite. We hadn't had a chance to talk after everything happened since they went home for the holidays. But I knew they got back late last night.

The door opened while my fist was poised to knock.

"I thought I could feel you out there," Matt said, grinning.

"You could feel me?" I lifted a surprised eyebrow.

"Magic bond, you should start paying more attention to your senses. Especially since you've got those mates of yours." He frowned for a moment but his lips returned to a smirk quickly. "What brings you to our humble abode?"

I laughed. "Nothing humble about your abode."

"True," he said, stepping back so I could enter the room.

I walked in and he closed the door behind me. "I never got a chance to thank you. Or tell you how incredibly stupid you were for doing that."

"Way to get right to insulting the guy who saved your life," he said.

I glanced around and was surprised Zach hadn't joined us. "Where's your brother?"

"Picking our darling mother up from the airport. Want to sit?" He walked toward the couch.

I followed him and took a seat, leaving a cushion between the two of us. Even with the space, I could feel my body reacting to him. My temperature rose with every breath. It was dangerous to be in here alone with him.

"You know you didn't need to do that," I said.

"I know, but my family can throw money at lawyers. You can't," he said.

My shoulders dipped and I felt small. It wasn't like I did any of it on purpose. Okay, maybe that wasn't true. I was fully aware that I was stopping time when Makayla was threatened. And I knew I'd do it again if I was in the same situation. It was the only way I could save her.

"Listen, friends help each other," he said.

"Friends shouldn't have to take the fall," I said.

"Hey, all I got was weekly meetings with a creepy parole officer so it's not all bad," he said with a grin.

"He is creepy, isn't he?" I asked.

"What is with those teeth?" he asked. "I swear I worry he'll bite my toes off."

I laughed. "I know! And he's always so red and sweaty. Like he runs a few miles before he comes to the meetings."

"Right? Even Dr. Green is grossed out by him," Matt said.

"I'm guessing it takes a lot to get to Dr. Green," I said.

"That's true. Did you know he used to be the head of the Supernatural Defense Department?" Matt asked.

My eyes widened. I'd heard some hints that he'd had a previous job of importance but I didn't see that coming. "What happened that got him sent here?"

"It was a huge scandal," Matt said. "He was caught tampering with evidence they said."

My brow furrowed. I didn't like the sound of that. Especially considering we'd just done something similar. "Like what we did?"

He shrugged. "We told a white lie. Not the same."

"Do you think he did it?" I asked.

"The evidence thing?" he asked.

I nodded.

"I know he did," he said. "My parents were involved somehow but I never got the details. I was really young when it all went down. All I know is that whatever went down, it was messy and dragged a bunch of the big families into the mess. When it was over, he was out of a job and sent here."

"Huh." I wasn't sure how I felt about that. So far, Dr. Green had been a surprising ally. "Well, I guess I should be grateful that he's here. If someone like Officer M had been in charge, I'd be screwed."

"That's true," Matt said.

"Which brings us back to this whole thing," I said. "I owe you. Big time. Even though I don't want to owe you."

"Hey, we're even," he said. "You don't owe me anything."

"Yes, I do. I'd be in prison right now if not for you."

He frowned. "I'm serious, Raven. I didn't even think twice about it. I couldn't bear to have them take you away from me. It was completely self-serving."

My brow furrowed as I studied his expression. He was sincere. "It's the magic bond. We created it with the meld. You and Zach have done so much to help me. It's not fair that you feel so connected to me because I couldn't figure out my magic."

"Is that what you think?" he asked. "That we don't want to have you around?"

"Well, it's not real, right? It was the magic that bonded us," I said. Not the way I bonded with Ben or Luka. It wasn't the same, was it?

"Oh, Raven." Matt scooted to the cushion in between us. "Why don't you see how amazing you are?"

"I know I'm amazing," I said. "I have zero issues with my self-confidence. It's the whole making other people feel beholden to me when it was manufactured by magic."

"You do realize we wouldn't be able to feel this way if there wasn't something between us to begin with, don't you?"

"Well, I know you've been trying to get into my pants since we met if that's what you're taking about," I said.

"That's exactly what I'm talking about," he leaned a little closer.

I held my breath, my body responding to his, wetness already between my thighs. I couldn't do this, could I?

"I'm not saying you're not attractive," I said.

"Then what are you waiting for?" He leaned even closer until his lips were right over mine. I could feel his warm breath on my face.

I could get up and walk away. I didn't have to do this. I could stop everything right now.

But I didn't want to.

Fuck it.

I leaned toward him, pressing my lips to his. His kiss was electric, sizzling into my lips and all the way down to my core.

His tongue slid into my mouth and he grabbed the back of my head, pulling me deeper into the kiss.

My body responded, my hips already rocking toward him. It was as if I'd lost control of myself. All I wanted was to get him naked.

I reached for his shirt, working the buttons one at a time while his lips continued their assault on mine. It was delicious and my whole body felt like it was on fire.

His shirt was finally open and I rubbed my hands across his bare chest. He was solid muscle and taught abs. I moved up to the curves of his shoulders and down his arms, sliding the shirt off him as I went. His biceps were flexed and I moaned into his mouth. Every firm inch of him had my panties soaked.

Matt broke away from the kiss and climbed off the couch. I whimpered, annoyed that he'd stopped now that I'd finally succumbed to him.

He smirked and I knew he wasn't walking away from me. Instead, he took off his pants, tossing them to the side.

I started working on my own buttons, slowly taking off the shirt I was wearing while he watched me. I smiled at him, knowing I was driving him crazy with each button I removed.

Finally, my shirt was open and I followed his example, throwing it to the ground. Then I stood and tugged off my skirt.

I was standing there in my underwear, waiting for him to make the next move.

He lunged for me, throwing me to the couch. I squealed as his lips found my neck. He kissed then nibbled my neck and then up to my ears. His hips settled in between my thighs and I grinned against him, feeling his hard cock pressing against the lace of my soaked panties.

Grabbing his back, I pulled him closer to me, repositioning so I could kiss him again. Stubble rubbed against my skin and his lips continued to explore my mouth and my neck.

I moaned again, still thrusting my hips into his cock. I was so ready. Why had I waited so long for this? Everything about it felt right. Suddenly, I knew that everything I felt for him was real. It wasn't about the magic meld. He was mine and I was his. Magic or no, the connection was there. I could feel his magic rising as if reaching for mine.

I reached for his boxers, trying to get my fingers under the waistband to pull them free. He shifted his position so it was easier for me to gain access and as he did, we both tumbled to the ground.

I landed on top of him, and for a moment I was concerned that I'd hurt him, but after a brief pause, his hands found the back of my bra and unhooked it. I shrugged off the straps and tossed the bra aside. His hands covered my breasts and he groaned as he teased my nipples with his thumb.

I adjusted so I was straddling him, then I leaned forward and set my palms on the floor bracketing his head. He moved his hands from my breasts, sliding them around to my back. With gentle pressure, he pulled me closer to him so my chest was pressed against his.

His mouth found mine again and as we kissed, my hips took

on a mind of their own, grinding against his rock-hard cock. Tingles shot through my body as I felt our magic connecting, mingling and intertwining in a way I'd never felt before. It was as if the magic inside us was urging us forward. Every nerve in my body was firing on overdrive.

Finally, Matt's fingers hooked under the waistband of my panties and I lifted my hips to help him pull them off. I was soaked between my thighs. I was ready to feel his cock inside me. I needed him and I knew he needed me.

As soon as I was free of the restriction of the underwear, I lowered my hips onto his cock. I gasped as he stretched me. I lowered slowly on to him until I had his full length inside of me. A rush of pleasure coursed through me, making me gasp, then hold my breath. Tiny bursts of magic sent a shiver down my spine. It was as if our magic was working together to push me closer to climax.

His hands were on my hips now, guiding me up and down. I started slowly, pushing my hips forward and back as I rode his cock. The pressure of my orgasm built quickly and I picked up the pace, learning the angles that made the tip of his penis hit my g spot. Each thrust inside me was like hitting a pleasure button, sending little shocks of sensation through me. I moaned with each thrust, getting closer and closer to climax.

Matt pulled me down to him, then sat up so I was in his lap. He helped with the motion, lifting and lowering his hips. He groaned, digging his fingers into my back as he increased the speed.

Every touch, every movement, every breath was inching me closer to losing control. It was as if all sensations were magnified. The intensity was driving me insane. My breathing grew rapid and it was impossible to concentrate. All I wanted was more of his cock inside me. More. So much more.

I felt Matt's warm breath on me, the two of us breathing

heavy in unison. All at once, climax took me and I cried out as wetness dripped down my thighs. Matt cried out, finishing right behind me. He pulled me tight against him and his whole body shook as he came.

We sat there, his arms wrapped around me, catching our breath for a good minute before either of us moved.

Matt cupped the side of my face with his hand. Our eyes met and I felt something snap into place. The bond, the connection that had always been there. Only, now it wasn't in the background. He was part of me and I was part of him.

"What just happened?" I asked.

"I think our magic bonded," he said.

"Not just our magic," I said. "You were right. It was never about the magic meld. It's always been about us."

"The magic meld might have solidified it, but you and me would have a bond no matter what," he said.

I pressed my lips to his again. Now that we'd found our connection, I knew I'd never let it go.

Raven

A maid - an honest to god maid dressed in a little black dress with an apron - set trays of food on the table in front of us. I wanted to believe that when the twins had mentioned maid service that they were joking.

Yet here we were, sitting down to lunch with a maid delivering the food. I wasn't sure where the food was coming from or where the maid stayed during the week but I wasn't sure I was ready to know those kinds of things

The Obscura suite was huge and I'd only seen the living

room area and now the large dining room that was down the hall from the living room.

I wondered what their bedrooms looked like. I took a sip from the ice water in front of me to quench the instant heat that shot through me at the thought.

I was still recovering from my tumble with Matt and hadn't been able to make eye contact with him while his mom engaged us in small talk about our schedules and which classes we liked best. I wasn't sure I could trust myself if I looked into his eyes. Just being this close to him was making my libido beg for more.

So far, we'd been here nearly ten minutes and the fact that I'd gotten her kid his very own one on one time with Officer M hadn't been mentioned.

It was like waiting for an explosion you knew was coming.

"Raven, dear," Ms. Obscura turned her gaze on me, "tell me, do you find Officer M just as insufferable as Matthew does?"

I nearly choked on the water in my mouth. Quickly, I swallowed it and coughed as quietly as I could to clear the water. "He's not my favorite person."

"That's a diplomatic answer," she said. "Matthew was telling me how much he seems to enjoy his tiny slice of power. I wonder if I should make some calls. Send him back to the cesspool he crawled out of."

"Mom, you do realize they could send someone worse," Matt said. "I mean, he's terrible, but he's also terrible at his job. So he's all empty threats."

"Fair point," she said.

"So what's with this independent study the two of you have together?" Zach asked.

I looked from Matt to Zach. "What do you mean?"

"Both of you have an independent study scheduled," he said. "During the same period. I assume that means it's together. Not much of an *independent* study when it's done that way."

I'd been so focused on not thinking about my interlude with Matt while he was talking about his new class schedule that I didn't even pay attention to which classes he had. "You're with Professor Halifax too?"

"Yes," he said. "I'm guessing it has something to do with our parole."

"I should have stepped up and taken the fall," Zach said, shaking his head.

"No," I said. "I'm glad you didn't. I'm still not happy that your brother did."

"But it kept us from having to go through so much red tape to get you out of prison," Ms. Obscura said. "I'm glad he thought of it so quickly." She smiled proudly at her son.

"Wait, you're okay with all of this?"

"Of course, dear. Like I said, we're family." She lifted a small bowl and held it up. "Sugar?"

I blinked at her and managed to shake my head. That word was getting thrown around a lot lately. For a girl who was raised with basically no family to suddenly be welcomed into multiple families, it was a lot.

Ms. Obscura set down the sugar bowl.

"Mom, can you ease off of her, please?" Zach asked. "She's kind of seeing two males right now and neither of them are your sons."

She narrowed her eyes and I could almost feel her judgement boring into me. *She totally knows.* Matt and I hadn't discussed our tumble on the couch. We'd barely had time to get dressed before his mom and Zach had arrived. I knew I had to have him in my life, but I wasn't sure how he felt about being with me.

"Regardless, we took her in when we started paying her tuition," she said, taking a sip of her tea.

"You said you knew my mom, right?" I was ready for a change of subject. I wanted to stop alluding to my sex life in front of my - well, I wasn't sure what Matt was - but I didn't want to discuss my relationship with her son - or her other son.

"I did," she said with a smile. "We were very close. In fact, I have something for you."

I straightened, feeling hopeful and curious. *This* was a conversation I wanted to have with her.

"Jenny, can you please bring the box that's on the guest bed?" Ms. Obscura called in the direction of what I assumed was the kitchen.

This place has a guest bed? I wondered if she spent overnights here with her sons. Or if it was for the maid. A brief flicker of jealousy flared through me. I didn't like the idea of the attractive maid spending the night so close to either of the twins.

What the hell? I knew they'd been with other girls while I'd been here and it never really bothered me. Okay, maybe it bothered me a little, but not like this. I sort of wanted to knock the maid's teeth in.

Jenny, the way too attractive maid, walked into the room and set a box down in front of Ms. Obscura.

"What is that?" Zach asked.

"Some things I saved from when I was in school," she said.

For a moment, I saw a sweet, nostalgic gaze from Ms. Obscura. It faded quickly and she cleared her throat. "I thought Raven might be interested."

"Yes, of course," I said.

Zach reached across the table and grabbed a basket of rolls. He set one on his plate then passed the basket to me. Feeling obligated, I took one and set it on my plate. Then I took the basket and passed it to Matt. Our fingers brushed for an instant and a burst of electricity shot through my hand and up my arm. I gasped, caught off guard. It wasn't painful. In fact, it was pleasurable. And terrifying.

Quickly, I adjusted my grip and set the basket on the table

next to him. *Note to self, don't touch Matt again in public.*

I turned my attention back to Ms. Obscura. She'd opened the box and pulled out a small stack of photographs. She flipped through them, a smile on her face. Then she looked up at me. "These are mostly from our last semester. I'm not sure why there aren't more from earlier."

She passed the photos to me and I took them from her. The top photo was a young Ms. Obscura and a red-haired woman in jean jackets leaning against a brick wall. I'd never seen a photo of my mom from before I was born. All I had seen were her wedding photos and a couple of photos of her holding me at the hospital. After my aunt passed, they were the only thing I went to look for in the apartment we'd shared.

But I hadn't been the first to arrive and her place was trashed. The landlord had told me it was debt collectors looking for valuables. I told him to sell anything that was left to cover the cost of disposing of the junk. He'd assured me he'd keep an eye out for photos. I never heard back.

My eyes blurred as I flipped through the photos. My mom and Ms. Obscura were in photos at the pool in their bikinis, at an amusement park, and in their school uniforms. In another photo, my mom was surrounded by cats in what looked like ancient ruins.

"Is that why you take in all the strays?" Matt asked, pointing to the picture. "Raven's mom seemed to love cats."

Ms. Obscura chuckled. "That was in Rome. Cats everywhere. And yes, Raven's mother was an animal lover. And they loved her back. She always said she was going to raise all the neighborhood strays like a crazy cat lady in her old age."

I looked up at Ms. Obscura. She looked sad and far away. As if caught in her own memories. Then, she turned her gaze to me and smiled. "But I get to honor her even more now by helping you, Raven."

"Does that mean you'll stop taking in strays?" Zach asked.

"Of course not." Ms. Obscura said. "But now you know why I do it."

I smiled. It was nice to know that my mother's memory had been carried by someone besides just me.

I turned to the next one and tears rolled down my cheeks. There were four people in this photo. My mom and Ms. Obscura with their dates. I recognized the face of my mom's date right away. I knew they'd dated in college, I just never realized that when my aunt had referred to my mom and dad's college days, she was talking about them being *here*. At the Academy of the Elites.

I looked up at Ms. Obscura as something occurred to me. If they'd met here, they'd had powerful parents to get them in. And if that was the case, why was my aunt practically destitute?

"Oh yes, the Yule ball. Your mother almost didn't go with him, you know. He asked her every day for a month and she finally caved," Ms. Obscura said.

I smiled. That wasn't a story I'd heard. *Of course it wasn't.* I didn't know any stories. "Ms. Obscura, do you know who my grandparents were? My aunt just said they were dead and that was that."

"She didn't talk about her parents," Ms. Obscura said. "I always sort of thought maybe they were dead."

"Oh," I said, feeling a bit defeated. That made more sense. If they were still alive, you'd think they would have come for me.

I passed the pictures back to Ms. Obscura. "Thank you for showing these to me."

"Everything in the box is for you," she said as she took the pictures and set them back in the box. "I imagine you'll want to go through it all. It's everything I could find that related to your mom."

"Thank you," I said. Maybe I had things all wrong about her.

She certainly had been close with my mom. Aside from the very outdated ideas about pure mage blood and all that, she seemed like she might be okay. I wondered if I could help her see how outdated her thoughts were. I could see us spending more time together if it meant getting more stories about my mom's life.

"I'll be happy to meet with you to talk about your mom when you're ready," she said. "Besides, we'll need to discuss your post-graduation plans and housing arrangements."

"Mom, please don't finish that thought," Matt said.

"Why not," Ms. Obscura said. "I understand that it's a complicated relationship with so many mates, but it's not unheard of. And just because she has other mates, that doesn't mean she has to live with them. There's nothing wrong with her living with one or both of you."

And just like that, she was back to the crazy matchmaker who wanted to be my mother-in-law. "I still have to pass the trials before I can decide anything."

"You'll pass them," Zach said. "I overheard Coach Miller talking about how he was going to have to make the course harder because you passed the practice trials faster than anyone ever had."

"Really?" That surprised me. I didn't feel like I'd done anything all that spectacular.

"Way to go, Raven. Making it harder for all of us," Matt said teasingly. He bumped me with his elbow and that shock of pleasure shot through me again.

This time, I managed not to moan at the table, but I did have to press my thighs together. *What the hell was wrong with me?*

I glanced over at Matt, already imagining getting him alone again. We'd been rushed last time, but next time, I was going to take my time with him.

Matt

Every time I brushed against Raven, it sent a surge of desire right through me to my cock. What had she done to me? I felt like a teenager discovering sex for the first time. It was all I could think about. Fucking Raven.

Of course, I had a healthy sex drive. Who didn't love sex? But this was so much more than that. I *needed* her. And that was fucking terrifying.

The bond we'd formed seemed to click into place when we finally gave in. Okay, when she finally gave in. I'd wanted to fuck her since the first moment I saw her. That hair, those lips.

Her curves were those of a goddess. And damn, she was just as good in the sack as I hoped. Actually, she was better.

I could hardly focus on the conversation during lunch. But I suppose that wasn't so new. I tried to zone out whatever my mother said when she was around. She was old fashioned and had zero filter. Half of what she said when I did listen didn't affect me.

Zach was the smarter one. We both knew it. He picked everything up first. From reading to magic. He was wicked smart. I was smart, too, but not the same kind of smart.

I was pretty sure my mom's will was only in his name. And that was fine with me. That meant I wouldn't have to deal with the money hungry relatives or the lawyers after she passed. I'd go live in a hut somewhere and let Zach deal with the fallout.

"Matthew," my mother called my name and I looked at her, plugging myself back into the conversation.

"Sorry, what was that?" I asked.

She pursed her lips and gave me her signature disappointed look. It didn't scare me the same way it had when I was a kid. "I asked you, when is your next meeting with your parole officer?"

"Oh, tomorrow," I said.

"I get to skip that one," Raven said. "Good behavior and all."

"Keep rubbing it in," I said.

"I'm still mad at you for taking the fall like that, but I guess when it comes with me only having to see Officer M once a month, I'm glad you did," she said.

I smiled. It was the first time she'd really seemed to appreciate my admission of guilt. While she'd thanked me, her words always seemed to be followed by comments that I shouldn't have done it. I wanted her to appreciate what I did. Besides, it wasn't that big of a deal.

So what if I have to meet with a creepy PO once a week? I'd

be out of here by June and I was sure my mom would find a way to end my meetings once I graduated.

"Well, I'd like to have a conversation with Dr. Green about all of this before I leave," she said.

"I'm not sure what good that will do," I said. "They're pretty excited that they get to corner an Obscure."

"Nobody corners us, ever," she said. "You played them. And you should be proud of that."

I wasn't sure how to respond to that. Being part of such a well-connected family meant that we got away with things. Even when we shouldn't. It was something that used to bother me more. As I got older, I learned that with wealth came certain privileges. It was a matter of telling myself that eventually, I'd have to pay for what I'd been given.

I was hoping Raven could help me with that. Seeing her reaction to the things that were handed to me made me start to question things again. It made me want to be a better person.

My mother set her napkin on her plate and Jenny swooped in to take the dishes away.

"The food was delicious," Raven said. "Thank you for inviting me. And thank you for the box of memories. It means the world to me."

"I'm glad you like it, dear," she said, in that false mothering tone she used when she was trying to impress people.

I had to fight not to frown at her. She was my mom, but we'd mostly been raised by the staff at the various houses we were dragged to as kids.

Our father had been more involved in our lives, but he passed two years ago. It still hurt.

"I'd like a tour," my mom announced. "Which of my sons will escort me around the school?"

"It can't have changed all that much," I said.

She lifted an eyebrow. "Well then, I think I know who will be giving me that tour."

I resisted rolling my eyes. She was so dramatic.

"I'll go with you," Raven said. "I honestly haven't seen all of the school yet. Maybe you could give me the tour."

I glanced at her, surprised. She had to be over my mother just as much as I was, but I could tell she was grateful. This was her way of saying thank you. She was such a better person than I was. I didn't deserve her.

"I'd love to have you along, Raven," my mother said. "I'm glad to see you were raised with some manners."

"Why don't we all go?" Zach said.

"No," my mother responded quickly. "I'd like some girl talk for a change. I'm surrounded by males all day. It'll be a nice change."

I clenched my jaw, trying not to overthink what her intentions were for this private chat with Raven. I was pretty sure this was her plan the whole time.

The woman was crafty.

Well played, Mom. Well played.

"Want me to take that to your room for you?" I asked, pointing to the box in Raven's hand.

"Sure." She handed it to me, then dug her keycard out of her pocket. "You can leave the key in my room. Ben has a spare."

The table got very quiet and Raven's face turned crimson.

"I lost my key once and got a new one. I gave it to him when I found my old one since he's my neighbor," she said quickly.

"That makes sense," I said, trying to help her. We all knew why he had a key. Though it wasn't like their relationship was a secret.

A flicker of jealousy rose into my chest but I quelled it quickly, reminding myself that this morning, it was my cock inside her. Not Ben's.

Raven

I was surprised that the tour ended up being solo with Ms. Obscura. I had a feeling she was looking for a way to get one on one time with me but I wasn't sure why.

As we walked down the stairs of the mage dorm, I couldn't help but notice that she was limping a little. I wondered if she'd had an accident or if she had a health condition. Suddenly, I felt bad for freaking out about her wanting to see her sons married off. Maybe she just wanted to see her kids happy. She was very difficult to get a read on. One minute, she was kind and helpful, the next she seemed to be plotting something. All I knew was that I needed to be careful around her.

"This place always takes me back," she said as we walked across the main hall. "I had a lot of great memories here. It's where I met my husband and where I met my best friends, your mother included."

"It's a good school," I said, not sure how to answer her. I liked it much better than being in a shitty apartment without heat. But there was the whole thing with a magic thief trying to kill me.

"It's more than that," she said. "It's a way of life. A network that you establish and will utilize for the rest of your life."

She led us to the stairs that went up to the fourth floor where the ball had been a couple of weeks ago. I followed her.

"You know, when I first married into the Obscura family, they were about to go under. Most of their businesses were failing and they were nearly bankrupt."

"Really?" That was surprising based on what I saw of their wealth now.

"They had invested in several human tech companies that were going belly up." She turned and glanced at me. "Never invest in human businesses. They are short-sighted and they rarely plan for the future properly."

"Good tip, thanks," I said. Not that I'd ever have the kind of money she's talking about.

"So I reached out to the connections I'd made as a student here and I scheduled meetings and introduced the Obscuras to some of the other great families."

We were standing in front of the ballroom now. The double doors were closed. She leaned against them, pushing them open.

The room was missing some of its magic today. It was huge and the shiny wood floor was beautiful, but without the light from the sparkling chandeliers or the chatter of people, it was kind of sad.

"So many memories," she said.

"I wish my memory of this room was better," I said.

She turned to me, a frown on her face. "You'll make a better memory here. They'll hold a ball for the students who pass the trials. I expect you'll be there. With both of my sons."

I tensed, still not sure how to navigate her. "Ms. Obscura, you should know…"

She lifted a hand, stopping me from continuing. "I know. You've mated with two others. You haven't decided if you want to be with my sons. But I'm confident that you will make smart decisions. You're an intelligent woman. A survivor. Like me. The right choices aren't always easy. You must be savage in your decisions if you want to succeed. And you have that streak. Even if you don't see it yet."

"I don't know about that," I said.

"Your mother didn't have it. She was a hopeless romantic. Ran off with your father, got herself cut off from the family fortune."

"Wait, what?" I blinked at her, shocked by this revelation. "I thought you said they were dead."

"Better that my sons didn't know this part," she said. "Nobody should know this part."

What could possibly be so bad that she didn't want her own children to know?

She took a deep breath and then glanced around the room again before turning her gaze back on me.

"I can't speak to your father's side, but your mother's parents disowned her for marrying your dad. A few years later, they were killed in an accident. They didn't include your mother in their will."

"They sound like they were total assholes," I said without thinking.

She smirked. "They were. I can honestly tell you very few people missed them but there was a lot of drama around their money."

"People get weird about money after someone dies," I said.

She cocked an eyebrow. "Don't you want to know where it went?"

I shook my head. "Not really. It sounds complicated and like it was a long time ago."

"You are unusual, Raven," she said. "I'm glad Dr. Green called me when they brought you to him and I'm happy I can repay my friend's kindness through you."

"I really appreciate it," I said. "I am glad I'm here."

"So am I," she said. "Want to see the secret passage I found with your mom?"

I perked up. "That sounds awesome."

She smiled and started walking across the ballroom. I followed her, watching as she dragged her fingertips along the wallpaper covered wall.

She stopped and turned to look at me. "Right here. See this?"

I looked where she was pointing. There was a tiny star in the floral pattern that wasn't on the rest of the wall. "How did you find that?"

"We used to study in this room since it's almost always empty. Practice spells and such. It's a good space for it. Found it on accident one day and then spent weeks trying to figure out how to open it."

She took my hand and moved it over the tiny star. "Here. Press down."

I did and then I gasped as a door slid open in the wall. "How many people know about this?"

"I doubt anyone here does anymore. Your mom and I never told anyone. Not even your dad. I haven't even told my sons."

"How come?" I asked, feeling guilty.

"Well, after what you just went through, I figured it might come in handy for you to have a safe place to hide."

"I sure hope not," I said. "I'd really like this semester to be normal."

"Nothing is ever normal here," she said, leading the way down a hallway.

The door closed behind us and it suddenly got very dark. My heart raced and suddenly, I worried that I'd walked into some kind of trap. What if this wasn't even Ms. Obscura? What if the thief wasn't really dead and she'd transformed into her likeness?

A light flickered on in front of me and I saw a few magical torches light on the wall.

"You coming?" Ms. Obscura was ahead of me now.

I tried to push the thoughts away. I saw the thief dead. I watched as security carried her body away. She wasn't coming back.

Taking a few deep breaths, I followed behind Ms. Obscura until we came to a room filled with bookshelves and a few very dusty chairs.

"Looks like nobody's been here in a while," I said.

"I'd guess it's still a secret, then." She turned in a slow circle, taking in the room. "It's not glamorous, but it was a good place to get away from everyone when needed."

"What do you think it was originally?" I asked.

"I'm guessing it was some professor's office." She pointed to two doors in the back of the room. "One of those takes you to the Spellcasting auditorium. The other to the creature den."

I'd been to the creature den a few times. It was full of cats, and mice, and birds. Mostly animals we worked with in our *Training Your Familiars* class. It was an uneventful class for me.

Turns out, I'm not very good with animals. Apparently, that skill skipped a generation. Though, I hadn't had any magic for most of the class, so it was hard to say if it was me or just shit timing.

"Thanks for showing me this," I said.

"I know I come across as harsh," she said. "But I'm a woman in a position of power. I fight every day for my company and for my place in this world. And I want a woman like that keeping my sons in check. I think that could be you."

"I appreciate your vote of confidence," I said.

"I may be old fashioned, but I'm not inflexible. Keep that in mind." She walked past me toward the tunnel that led out of the room.

I followed her, grateful that our chat was over. Tea with Ms. Obscura hadn't been what I expected, but it was still a pretty intense morning. I wondered if I'd have time for a nap before I met Luka's mom.

I also wondered what a princess of hell had in store for me.

Raven

The day seemed to spin by without any time to stop and think. We weren't even back in classes yet, but the semester was starting off well. I'd had an interesting meeting with the twins' mom.

And there was the solo time I got with Matt.

My face heated just thinking of it and how much I wanted to do it again.

Shaking the thought from my mind, I focused on myself in the mirror. Out of all my mates' parents, Luka's mom scared me the most.

What did that even mean?

I wasn't religious but I'd always thought hell was the place where evil people went after they died to burn forever. Well, I wasn't sure I believed it actually existed before all of this, but now that I found out it did, I wondered if the stories were true.

Was it really full of humans who had done bad things? Was Luka's mom in charge of something there? And if she was a princess was there a king?

I had a million questions but I was afraid to ask any of them. It made me feel like I didn't know as much as I should. Was her job common knowledge to the people around here?

Luka didn't like talking about his life outside of school and I'd respected that. But now that I was faced with meeting his mom, I wished I'd pushed back a little. I felt like I was walking into a gunfight unarmed.

And my makeup skills sucked. I looked worse with my attempt at trying to doll myself up than I did without anything.

Quickly, I scrubbed the makeup off my face. I was in big trouble. I needed Luka's mom to like me.

Hoping Makayla wasn't out with her parents, I left my room and headed to hers.

She answered on the first knock and I blew out a relieved breath.

"Don't you have dinner with royalty?" she asked, a hand on her hip.

"I need help," I said.

"What is it?" Her eyes widened and she tensed.

"Nothing's wrong," I said. "Other than the fact that I'm terrible at makeup and I know nothing about Luka's mom or hell or anything."

"Ohhhh," Makayla dragged the word out, then she opened the door wider. "Come on in. Let your fairy godmother help you out."

"Thank you," I said as I entered her room. "I'm sure you have places to be and I'm so sorry."

"My family already left." She shrugged. "Stopped by for a quick breakfast then heading to some new mines they're investigating in Argentina."

"That sounds exciting," I said.

She pushed me into a chair in front of her bathroom mirror. "Not really. It's all soil samples and negotiations with lawyers and government officials."

Her bathroom counter was covered in makeup just as it had been before the Yule ball. I was grateful that I had a friend who knew how to use all this stuff. I could pretty much only be counted on to use mascara properly.

"Sit still," Makayla instructed as she got to work.

She applied various creams and powders. Then she added eyeliner and mascara. "I'm keeping it simple today. Despite the reputation hell has, I think the princess will appreciate you going for a more natural look."

"What do you know about hell or about Luka's mom? Anything you can tell me?" I asked.

"Well, it's not like humans think of it. It's just another realm. It's where demons come from and is mostly inhabited by demons and fallen angels from what I hear. From time to time, mages will move down there, but it's pretty warm and I don't think it would be fun to live somewhere without sunshine."

I took a deep breath. It didn't sound as bad as the human stories made it seem. "And Luka's mom?"

"Oh, she's a legit badass. Royalty in the underworld is absolute. So she has all the power. They divide it between six royals and they each govern their own territory, but I think they can still act as the law when they visit other territories. I've always been a little fuzzy on their exact rules. I never figured I'd need the info since it wasn't on my bucket list of places to visit," she said. "Now, press your lips together."

I did as she instructed, rubbing the light nude lipstick on my lips. "Are there any customs or things I should know before I meet her?"

She set the lipstick tube on the counter. "Luka didn't give you anything?"

I shook my head. "I should probably be pissed, but we haven't done a lot of talking in the last few weeks."

"Got it. Booty calls round the clock," she said with a laugh.

"Speaking of booty calls…" I let the words hang in the air.

"We're not going to talk about that right now," she said. "We all get lonely sometimes."

"I'm not judging," I said. "Well, I'm not judging much."

She gave me a gentle push. "We can't all be as lucky as you."

"Hey, as long as he makes you happy," I said.

"Well, he's an asshole, but he's a beast in the sack," she said. "So for now, it works."

She looked happy and I was grateful she'd found someone to keep her company. My evenings had been very busy lately between Luka and Ben. Now that the holidays were over, it was time for homework and there was also Matt. And Zach.

My life had not gone the direction I expected it to go but I was grateful. "I'm happy for you."

"Yeah, yeah," she said. "Now, go impress a princess."

I smiled and admired her work in the mirror. Makayla had a gift for sure. "Thank you."

"I want all the details when you're done, though," she said.

"I promise," I said.

"I'll be here waiting. But you'll probably want to knock."

I laughed. "I've learned knocking is very important around here."

Luka

I hated that Raven was going to meet my mom this way. It was so public and would result in a lot more attention than I wanted.

Last year on parent's day, I'd managed to get my mom to agree to a tour and breakfast without all the fanfare of the parent's dinner.

I felt bad for Raven. She didn't have any parents coming to this and I knew it would be harder on her. Plus, there was my mother to endure.

"Should we get going?" my mother asked from the chair in the corner of my room.

She looked so out of place here. My room wasn't anything like the opulence she was usually surrounded by. I kept things simple here. Basic furniture, simple fixtures. I didn't like all the grandeur that accompanied life in the mansion I'd grown up in. Though, I suppose that just made me another whiny rich kid. Like everyone else here.

Except Raven.

I didn't like talking about my past with her. One, because my mother was intimidating and two, because I knew she'd had a rough childhood. I hated that she'd been through so much while the rest of us never had to lift a finger. It wasn't right. Especially given that her parents held enough clout to get her tuition covered.

"Yeah," I pulled my blazer on and turned to my mom, "Raven will meet us at the cafeteria."

"Oh yes, dinner at the cafeteria. Adorable."

"You're the one who wanted to experience parent's day," I reminded her.

"Mostly because I want to meet this girl who has you wrapped around her little finger." She wrinkled her nose. "It's unusual for an incubus to be so focused on one partner. I'm not sure I like it."

I still hadn't told my mom that Raven was my mate. I was hoping she'd love Raven and find her as endearing as I did and not sense the bond between us. It was a gamble, but it was better than having my mom go in already prepared to hate her.

"Just wait till you get to know her," I said. "Besides, it's not like she'd care if I was with others. She's seeing other males."

My mother lifted an eyebrow. "Oh? Yet you feel obligated to her alone?"

"I told you, it's still new and she's super hot," I said. "Besides, I did get it on with her and a wolf shifter a few weeks back."

My mom's shoulders seemed to relax at that statement. I had to be the only student here reassuring his mother about his life choices by talking about how much sex I was having. While I knew the other supernaturals here were pretty open about sex, for us, it was part of life.

My mom was a succubus so she also fed off sexual energy to fuel her magic. It was part of why I wasn't sure who my real father was. I'd met the three men who were the most likely candidates, and they were all involved in our lives, but it was a different kind of family.

I didn't call any of them *dad*, but I knew I could count on any of them to have my back. And we all shared the same table at holidays. Then my mom and one or all of them would retreat to her room and I would get the fuck out of the house before I had to hear anything.

It wasn't until I started leaving the underworld, and visiting other realms, that I realized just how different I was.

"She's meeting us at the cafeteria?" my mom asked as I closed the door behind us.

"Yes," I said. "Her room is in the shifter dorm and it's not my favorite place to go."

"Why is she with the shifters? I thought you said she was a mage?"

"Honestly, I still don't know why she's down there." It was something I'd wondered from time to time but it never made much of a difference overall. I didn't like going in the mage dorms, either.

"Her parents must have done something to piss off the other mages," my mother said.

"You think? I always heard how great they were."

"It's not like it matters to us, but some of those mages are still stuck in the fourteenth century," my mother said.

I rolled my eyes, not looking forward to another lecture

about the good old days. You could only hear about how glorious it was living during the Black Death so many times.

"You know, back then mages were feared, but not like us demons," my mother said. "Oh, no. All we had to do was bare our teeth and the humans went running. Now they just want to fuck us. I remember the good old days. Before *Twilight* made having sex with monsters so cool."

"I know, Mom, I know," I said, trying to zone her out.

As we neared the cafeteria, I stopped in my tracks as soon as I saw Raven. She was in her school uniform as we all were for this event, but she'd never made it look as good as it did tonight.

She was in a sleek black pencil skirt and a tight button up white shirt with the red tie hanging down over the buttons. A black short sleeve sweater made her look like the stereotypical sexy librarian. And I was in desperate need of checking out some books.

She'd applied some makeup and wore her long red hair straight down her back. She looked good enough to eat.

"You must be Raven," my mother said, stopping in front of her.

"Hi, I mean, hello, yes, I'm Raven. And you are Ms. Drake?" Raven seemed nervous and I nearly groaned as she sucked her lower lip in between her teeth. She had the sexiest nervous traits ever.

"Yes, Ms. Drake, or Princess Arianna, whatever you prefer."

"Oh, um." She glanced to me, her eyes begging for me to interfere.

"Mom, please," I said. "Do we need the titles?"

"You are the only one in hell who doesn't like the titles," she said with a sigh. "If it makes you feel better, you can call me Arianna."

"Ms. Drake is fine," Raven said.

"Let's grab a table," I said.

My mother took my arm and I led her into the room, wishing I was holding Raven instead. I wanted to know what she was thinking and feeling. I wanted to be inside her head right now. But I also had to play the dutiful son. The more attention I gave my mom, the less time she'd have to ask questions or assess the magic that connected me to Raven.

The cafeteria was festive tonight for the occasion. All of the tables were covered in white tablecloths and the usual round plastic seats were replaced with real chairs.

Instead of the normal cafeteria line with the kind ladies in their hairnets, two long buffet tables with a variety of food lined the back wall.

Most of the tables were already full, including the back table I usually sat at with Raven and our shifter friends. I knew that wouldn't go over well with my mother tonight.

I led us through the room to an empty table and pulled out the chair for my mom. Raven was already seated before I could do the same for her. She'd left an empty chair between herself and my mom. *Smart.*

One of the cafeteria ladies stopped by our table with a pitcher of water and filled the glasses. "Look at you two all cleaned up."

"They are a handsome couple," my mom said, forcing one of her signature fake smiles on her face.

This meal could not be over fast enough.

Raven

Luka's mom was terrifying if only in the way she carried herself. Like Luka, she was tall and lean with a graceful build. Her fair hair and soft features made her look like a goddess carved from marble.

Now I knew where Luka got his good looks.

Her blonde hair was pinned up in a neat twist on the back of her head and she looked perfectly put together in a black dress with her pointed stilettos. She was a knockout and she was quite possibly now my style icon. I wished I could pull off her look.

I smirked, knowing if I tried to wear those shoes, I'd be flat on my face before we even reached the table.

Luka pulled out the chair for his mom and I quickly settled in one chair away, making it so Luka would need to be next to her. I knew this dinner was supposed to be for me to get to know her but there was no way I was sitting next to her.

"I'll save our seats if you two want to go get food," I suggested.

"Nonsense," Ms. Drake said. "Luka will wait. Ladies first, isn't that right, son?"

"Always," he said, flashing a wide grin.

"Alright," I pushed back my chair, "let's grab some dinner."

My stomach grumbled as I walked toward the buffet. I'd been so distracted during tea with Ms. Obscura that I hardly ate anything. Now that there was food in sight, I was starving.

"Tell me, Raven," Ms. Drake said, passing me a plate. "How long have you and my son been fucking?"

Well, we were starting the TMI conversation early tonight. It seemed to be an ongoing trend with my mate's parents. "Well, we have been friends since my first day here and we got closer during that time."

She scooped mashed potatoes on her plate. "Save me the Puritanical human views on sex."

She passed me the spoon. "You've been fucking for, what a couple of months now?"

"I guess so," I said, adding mashed potatoes to my plate. "I didn't write down the exact date."

"Thank gods for that," she said. "I was worried you'd be a clingy one. Especially since you two seem to have formed a mating bond."

My face heated and I knew I'd gone crimson. *Shit*. That was the one thing I *had* talked about with Luka. He didn't want his mom knowing about our bond.

"Don't worry, I won't tell him that I know," she said. "But his magic flared as soon as he saw you and he gave the whole thing away. You, on the other hand, kept your control. There might be hope for you. That and the whole fae thing."

"Word travels fast," I mumbled.

She filled up her plate with more food and stopped at the end of the line. "Word?"

"About the time magic and all of that," I said, figuring she'd heard it all.

"Oh no, I wasn't talking about that. I was talking about your father."

My eyes widened as I stared at her in surprise. *Did she just say what I thought she said?*

She grabbed a roll of silverware and walked back toward the table.

Coming to my senses, I grabbed my own silverware and hustled back to the table. This time, I took the spot next to her rather than sitting by Luka.

"Did you just say *my father*?" I asked.

"What's going on here?" Luka asked.

His mother turned to him. "Your turn to get your food, dear."

Luka frowned, but stood and walked away from the table. I didn't even watch him go. My attention was already back on his mom.

Earlier today, I'd learned a little about my mother but I never thought I'd get anything more about my father aside from a few old photos and some memories of him in school from Ms. Obscura.

"Did you know him?" I asked.

"Of course, I did," she said. "His family was one of the first to open trade routes between our realm and theirs."

"I didn't know that," I said.

"Of course not," she said. "They don't teach anything about

fae history anymore. Not since they made it illegal to open any portals to their realm. It was a great loss for us, but the alliances with this realm were worth more than our alliances to Faerie. It wasn't worth a war, that's for sure."

I stared at her, trying to process everything she'd just said. Had she just said my father was *fae*? Like not just a trickle of fae blood, like full on fae?

She took a bite and chewed thoughtfully. "The food is still pretty good here."

"Are you sure it was my father's family?" I asked.

"Of course. He was very young when I met him and it was only once, but I met with his family from time to time. Last I heard, he'd moved here before they closed the portals. The fae age much slower than us, which could explain how he ended up here and met your mom."

"Wait, fae, like full fae?" I asked, my heart racing.

"What did I miss?" Luka asked, settling down next to me.

I turned to look at him, my brow furrowed with concern. This information was changing everything I'd attached to my identity in the last few months. I'd finally come to terms with being a mage and with having *some* fae blood. But if what she was saying was correct, I was *half* fae. That wasn't the same thing.

I knew so little about the fae, but I knew it was a big deal. I knew it changed things.

"What is it?" Luka asked.

"Your mom met my dad once," I said.

"No way," he said. "That's really great."

My lower lip trembled.

"It's not great?" He looked from me to his mom. "What is going on here?"

"She didn't know her father was fae."

"Raven, you knew you were part fae," he said.

"Yeah, a tiny bit. Not half. And I didn't know that my family was from another realm." My chest felt tight. What if I still had family? What if they were in that realm?

"Hey," Luka took my hand in his, "whatever this means, it doesn't change anything about you or who you are."

"That's not quite true," Ms. Drake said. "In fact, it changes everything about her."

"Not helping, Mom," Luka said.

"How?" I asked, looking at Ms. Drake.

"Well, for starters, your magic isn't the same as normal mage magic, I'm sure. You should be training a little differently than they are because you have access to both the elemental magic of the mages of this realm, and the fae magic of that realm."

I didn't fully understand but the first thing that came to mind was the blue flame I'd made in the past. The twins seemed perplexed by it. They weren't sure why I did it. I wondered if that was one way my magic was different.

"So if my father stayed here when they closed the gates, do you know what happened to the rest of my family?" I asked.

She shrugged. "I suppose they stayed in Faerie. They were very high up in the ranks there. I'm not sure of how they do things, but they were of some importance. Possibly even royalty."

My throat bobbed. I wanted to know more but I knew it was possible this was all I would get from her. "Do you know anything else?"

She shook her head. "I'm sorry. I can tell you that we enjoyed their company any time they came through for negotiations or for trade. For what it's worth, they were good and compassionate and they loved their people."

"Thanks," I said.

"You'll have to visit us soon," she said. "We have a whole

room of fae items that we were gifted over the years. I'm sure you'd find them fascinating."

"I'd love that," I said, surprised at my quick response. I'd gone from dreading this meeting to accepting an invitation to visit a princess of hell - in hell.

This was such a weird day.

Raven

After the whirlwind weekend of meeting everyone's parents, I was grateful for the routine of classes.

Why did it have to be gym? Of all the classes I was stuck with here, gym was by far the worst.

I tried not to wince at the sight of Coach Miller in his way too tight tank top. His muscles were extra bulgy today. Probably due to whatever he was doing to prep for some body building competition. He also looked tanner. But not in a good, healthy way. In an orange way. It was gross. On so many levels.

"It's a new semester and for some of you, it'll be your last." He grinned at us. "A few of you will pass the trials."

He stopped in front of me, and I held my breath and forced myself not to blink, as he stared me down. "Some of you will die in the trials."

Luka's hand brushed against mine. It was subtle, but I instantly felt reassured. Thank god he was here with me. Even when the coach moved us into groups based on gender, at least I knew Luka was nearby. I'd started to realize that just being in his proximity made me feel calmer.

"So my job is to get you all ready," he said.

"What if we're not taking the trials this semester?" A vampire named Marcus asked.

He was right next to Violet. I smirked as she lifted a judgmental eyebrow and took a step away from the offender. We all knew that this was easier if we just kept our mouths shut and let the coach talk.

If we got lucky, he'd talk for the whole period. When you interrupted him, you ran the risk of him sending you straight for laps. Or worse, burpees.

I joined my classmates in glaring at the vampire. He had his arms crossed over his chest and his hip popped in a sassy way. I had only had one conversation with him and now I was remembering why. He came across as someone who thought he was better than the rest of us.

"Mr. Valiou, you are not taking the trials because you failed the practice trials. Were it not for the enormous amount of money your parents donated each year, you'd get your ass kicked out of here. If it were up to me, you'd have to take the trials. And you'd be dead."

Marcus pouted and I shook my head. It was hard to watch.

"Alright everyone, since Marcus is so unprepared for the trials, I think we'll make the workout even harder today."

Everyone groaned. Someone slapped Marcus upside the head and Coach Miller looked away as if he hadn't seen it.

"What do you think it's going to be?" I whispered to Luka.

"Something terrible," he said.

"Class, I want you to meet our newest addition to the gym." Coach Miller took a few steps away from where we were gathered and gestured toward a massive set of stairs. They went up about two flights in height, came to a small platform, then went down on the other side.

"You'll all be running the stairs until the bell rings. If anyone walks, they'll join me after dinner tonight to run stairs until they throw up."

Shit. Just when I thought running and burpees were the worst he could throw at us.

We all turned toward the stairs and shuffled our way there. Nobody was in a rush to get started. *Stupid Marcus.*

"Marcus, you're first. You set the pace and if you fall below, you'll be the first to join me tonight," Coach Miller said.

I fell into line right behind Luka, dreading the next forty-five minutes.

"Ten seconds in between. Everyone runs," Coach called.

As I watched the people in front of me begin their run, I realized how tall the stairs really were. They looked even worse up close. I was going to feel this tomorrow.

"Just keep an even pace and move your arms like you're running so you always look like you're running," Luka said.

"Good advice," I said. "At least I get to look at your ass while we're running."

"Oh yeah, you got the best seat in the house." He winked, then he took off up the massive staircase.

I counted to ten, then I started up. Halfway, my calves were already burning, my pulse quickened, and my breathing got more difficult. By the time I reached the top, I was ready to bend over and catch my breath. But I knew that wasn't an option. So I tried to catch my breath - and not fall on my ass - as I took on the decline.

Having Luka setting the pace in front of me helped. And he did have a fantastic ass. Especially in his gym shorts. I was going to need alone time with him after this.

Wondering if Luka and I could squeeze in a quickie during lunch kept me distracted for the first few rounds. I followed his advice, pumping my arms as if I were running even if I had to walk a couple steps here and there.

So far, I seemed to be avoiding drawing any attention to myself. I winced as Coach Miller grabbed a couple of people and pulled them to the side before sending them back into the line. He was making good on his threat.

I did not want to spend my time after dinner on this stairway to hell. I was pretty sure I'd throw up on the first round so at least it would be over quickly, but that did not sound like a good way to start your evening.

Someone's shoe caught mine and I picked up the pace, worried I was dragging too slow.

Everything hurt.

I could feel my body wearing out. How much time had we been at this?

"Don't stop," Luka called. "I'll rub every inch of your skin down for you tonight."

I was breathing too hard to respond, but I flashed him a smile. When we got down and were waiting in line to go back up, I tapped him on the shoulder. "I'm going to hold you to that."

"I can't wait," he said, then he darted up the stairs as if he weren't tired at all.

I pouted to myself and whimpered a little as I slowly walked toward the step. As soon as I got to ten, I climbed, swinging my arms as if I was running. But the run had gone out of me. It was all acting at this point.

Suddenly, someone grabbed my leg and I went down, knocking my jaw on the step as I fell.

Pain shot through my face and I cried out as I desperately tried to regain my balance.

I failed.

My shoulder knocked against another stair as my body slid down. I landed hard. My head cracking against the wood floor.

I sat up slowly. Blackness blurred the corners of my vision and the room spun. Sounds were muted, as if they were coming from very far away.

Then, someone punched me in the face.

I fell backward to the ground again, and I'm pretty sure I lost consciousness for a second. All at once, noise surrounded me, and someone was helping me sit up.

"That's for taking more than your share," someone said in my ear. I didn't know who it was but it was a female voice.

I turned toward the speaker and saw two of the same siren snarling down at me. I narrowed my eyes, trying to steady my vision.

Finally, she returned to one figure.

"Stay away from Zach," she said. "He's taken. Stick to your demon and your wolf, selfish whore."

I sputtered out something nonsensical as I grappled with the fuzzy vision and screaming pain in my head.

"What the hell is going on over here?" Coach Miller asked.

"She stopped and I ran into her," Delores said.

"That's not true," I managed.

"It is, if she moved her lazy ass, none of this would have happened," Delores added.

"It's true, coach, I saw the whole thing," Melody, another siren said.

"No, I was moving," I said, starting to wonder if I had stopped. Nothing seemed very clear right now. Then I remembered her threat. "She was trying to hurt me."

"I'll see you both after dinner," Coach Miller said.

"Raven," Luka set his hand on my knee. "What happened?"

"I fell," I managed.

"You're bleeding," he said. "Coach, she has to go to the hospital."

"She's fine," Delores said. "I'm sure she's faking it. Mages can do all sorts of things with magic."

"This isn't magic, and you know it," Luka said.

"Down, boy," Delores said.

"Is it getting hot in here or is it just me?" Melody added.

"Get the fuck away from her," Luka said.

"Luka, I think I'm going to throw up," I said. I wasn't really following the conversation. I just knew that my head felt like someone had taken a hammer to it and the whole room was spinning.

"She's not throwing up in here," Coach Miller said. "Get her to the hospital."

Luka helped me up, and threw my arm over his shoulder, bearing most of my weight on him. "Come on, Raven."

My eyelids grew heavy and I felt my chin drop.

"Stay with me, Raven," Luka said. "No sleeping yet."

I focused on his voice, trying to stay awake. I was vaguely aware of the fact that I probably had a concussion. Leaning on him for support, Luka and I managed to make it out of the gym.

Luka

I paced the hall in front of the hospital. Fuck them and their stupid rules about no visitors.

I knew where the rule came from, of course. And I knew it was made to keep the students in there safe. But just because one rogue vampire used to use it as his own personal blood bank didn't mean the rest of us were going to try something.

Another reason to be wary of the bloodsuckers.

I heard footsteps and turned to see Ben jogging down the hall. Like this day could get any worse. Of course I was going to have to deal with Raven's other boyfriend.

I wasn't opposed to sharing, but usually sharing involved a one-time thing. And sex. Now, I was sharing my mate and I still wasn't sure what that meant in terms of how I was supposed to relate to this wolf.

"Tell me she's okay," Ben said.

To his credit, he looked pale with worry. And he didn't add in any digs at my being here. "She's probably got a concussion. There was some blood from her fall, maybe a broken nose, but they won't let me in."

"Did you tell them you're her mate?" he asked.

I blinked at him. Had he just admitted that? "No. I don't think they care."

Ben walked past me and pounded on the door. "Anyone there?"

A few seconds later, the door opened and a nurse in a crisp white dress greeted us with her hand on her hips. "I already told him. No visitors."

"But we're her mates," Ben said.

The nurse's brow furrowed briefly, then she pursed her lips. "No visitors."

"At least tell us how she's doing," I said.

She closed the door a little, but paused, as if debating how much she should say. Finally, she opened the door again and let out a heavy sigh. "I can't let you in."

"Then I'll push my way in," Ben said, moving toward the door.

I grabbed him and pulled him back. "No, you won't."

The nurse looked pissed rather than afraid. No telling what kind of supernatural she was, but I was guessing she could handle a wolf shifter if she didn't even flinch at Ben's aggression.

"Can you just give us an update?"

She glared at Ben. "Are you going to be calm?"

"Fine," he said.

She turned back to me. "She's got a concussion and a fracture in her cheek. We're healing it and keeping her tonight. She should be back to normal tomorrow."

I gently pushed Ben away from the door. "Thank you."

Ben let out a low growl.

"Hey, she's safe there and they're fixing it," I said.

The nurse closed the door and Ben's shoulders dropped. He took a few steps away, then turned back to me. "What happened?"

"Someone pushed her down the stairs, I think." I debated if I should tell him about the punch in the face. Then I realized he might already know. I wasn't sure what his bond was like with her, but I knew that he could sense her pain. How much did he know when they weren't together?

"Another female punched her when she was down," I said.

Ben's hands balled into fists. "Tell me the name."

"Raven's going to be pissed if you go vigilante, you know that, right?" I said.

His jaw tensed and I could almost feel him considering his options. He glanced back at the closed door, then looked at me. "I'll wait till I get word from her tomorrow. But if she asks me to, I'll kill the person who punched her."

"That's fair." I doubted that Raven would want that, but who was I to explain that to a pissed shifter?

"Now what?" I asked, looking toward the door again.

"What do you mean?" he asked.

"Where does this leave us?" I asked. "We've never talked about how this works. Both of us formed a mating bond with Raven."

"And today isn't the day we're going to start talking about it," Ben said. "We're not girlfriends."

"I know that," I said. "But this could be complicated."

"It's not complicated," Ben said. "You stay away from her while I'm with her."

"And when I'm with her?" I asked.

He growled.

"Yeah, I'm not a wolf. That alpha shit doesn't work on me." I crossed my arms over my chest. "When I'm with her, you stay away if you want me to return the favor. Unless you want to join in?"

"That is never happening again." He was already walking away before I could say anything else.

For a wolf shifter, it was actually a pretty touchy-feely conversation. Not one I ever thought I'd have. I was an incubus. Sharing didn't bother me, not when it came to sex at least. I wondered what Raven's thoughts were on the whole situation. We'd never discussed that night in the shower.

I watched Ben walk away and laughed to myself. My life had taken some strange turns since Raven arrived.

And I knew I wouldn't trade it for the world.

With one last glance at the door, I walked away. I might not be able to get into the hospital, but there were other ways of checking in on her.

All I needed was for her to fall asleep.

Raven

Everything was dark. Dripping sounded nearby and I turned toward it, trying to find the source of the sound. Or some light. Any light.

I worked to steady my breathing, forcing myself to stay calm. It wasn't easy. I could feel a clammy sweat on my palms.

This has to be a dream. It's only a dream.

It was a dream, wasn't it? I spun in a slow circle, afraid to move too far just in case I really was in a black room. What if there was furniture around me. Or something worse?

Was I unconscious? Was this what that felt like? I'd never

been punched before. Maybe I blacked out. Maybe this was why they called it blacking out.

Footsteps sounded and my heart raced. "Who's there?"

"Raven?" Luka's voice called into the blackness.

My shoulders dropped as relief rolled over me. If Luka was here, this had to be a dream. "I'm here. Luka, can you turn on some lights?"

A shimmer of light sparkled overhead as if the room had been painted in stardust. I held my hand up, my fingers brushing against some of the flickering lights. They seemed to move and shimmer like fireflies, not staying put in one place for long.

The dark space was illuminated now and I could see Luka walking toward me. I was happy to see him, but disappointed at the circumstances. Once again, I was in the dungeon. The same room I'd been going to in my nightmares since I was a child. Why was I always drawn to this place? And why wasn't it lit today? That was new.

Luka's fingers gently touched my arm and I smiled at him. "Thanks for coming."

"Of course," he said. "How are you doing? What did the nurse say?"

"Concussion," I said, recalling the throbbing pain in my head. "Fractured cheek. That hurt like a mother."

"I bet," Luka said. "I broke my nose once. Well, I didn't, my cousin popped me in the nose."

"Ouch," I said, reaching up to touch my own nose, then I reached for Luka's. Now that he mentioned it, I could see the slight bump on an otherwise perfect profile. I slid my fingertip over it, surprised I never noticed it before. If anything, the minor imperfection made him even more handsome.

"They told me it would make me look tough but it healed so well most people can't tell." He shrugged. "It was a long time ago. I'm worried about you right now. Not me."

"I'll be fine," I said. "At least that's what the nurse said."

"Did she use magic to heal you?" He slid his fingers through my hair, cradling the side of my head as if checking for injury.

"Yes," I said. "Don't worry so much."

He scowled for a brief second, his eyes flashing red before returning to blue. "She shouldn't have hurt you. Why did she do that?"

"Um," I fidgeted, then stepped away from his touch. "I was with someone else over the weekend."

"I know," he said.

"You know?" I asked.

He frowned. "I could smell him on you."

My cheeks heated. "Why didn't you say anything? Don't get me wrong, I'm kind of glad you didn't, but still."

"Cause I don't own you, Raven," he said. "You're my mate and I'd do anything for you, but I need you to be happy."

"Wow," I said, blinking up at him. That wasn't what I expected.

"So she hit you because you fucked her boyfriend?"

"Not exactly," I said.

"Her girlfriend?" He straightened and his lips curved. "Cause I'm on board with that just so you know. I mean, I'm good with a boyfriend too, but you and me haven't tried it with another girl yet."

"No!" I said. "It wasn't her boyfriend, it was her boyfriend's brother and I guess she's threatened."

"Ah," he said, nodding sagely. "You finally fucked one of the twins."

"How did you know?" I asked.

"Raven, I feed off sex. When you're around them, it's literally in the air."

I turned away from him and scrubbed my face with my hand. He was taking this so well and I should be thrilled, but I was still having trouble adjusting to the fact that my romantic life went from zero to …. Three. Maybe four?

Fuck.

How the hell did that happen?

I turned back to Luka. "Is it normal in this world to have multiple mates?"

He shook his head. "No. It's actually rare to even have one. But it can happen."

I swallowed. I'd heard that before but I wasn't ready to believe it based on how my luck had gone. Every one of them, even the twins, felt like part of me. I couldn't even imagine life without them. And I didn't want to know what a life without them looked like. But I had to admit, it would be simpler if I hadn't mated with three males. Probably four if I let myself be honest.

Because as we talked, I was suddenly sure that what I felt with Luka and Ben was a mating bond. And what I felt with Matt and Zach was the same thing. It felt different, but the pull was there. The lust was there. The need to have them in my life - and inside me - was there.

It was a lot to take in for someone who grew up in the human world.

Luka set his hand on my upper arm. "Want me to go?"

I shook my head. "No." Then, I grinned at him as I thought back to the last good memory I had. It was his ass in front of me climbing those stairs.

"I want you to stay. I want all of you to stay." I set my hand on his hip, then slid it around to his cock, cupping it with my hand.

"You don't have to ask me twice," he said as he wrapped his arms around me and pulled me close.

Suddenly, the room was blurring past me and I buried my face in his chest until everything stilled.

When I looked up, we were in a field of soft grass dotted with tiny white flowers. The landscape was nearly monochromatic in the light of the full moon.

A gentle breeze rustled the grass and nearby, an owl hooted softly. Crickets sang and I could taste the tang of the sea in the air.

My whole body relaxed, taking in the sweetness of the fresh air and the empty quiet of nature. It was the two of us, surrounded by the less complicated creatures of the earth.

I'd never felt so at peace or so connected to a place in my whole life. "It's beautiful."

"I thought you'd like this," he said.

"What is it? Is this a memory?" I asked.

"Of sorts," he said. "It was a place my grandmother showed me in dreams. It's a meadow in Faerie."

My chest tightened. *Faerie.* This was my heritage. Where half of my family was from. A place I'd never see in real life.

And it felt like home.

Luka

Raven's face was practically glowing with awe as she looked around at the landscape I'd created for her. I wasn't sure if she'd like it. I knew she had some fae blood and since finding that out, I'd practiced recreating this place in my own dreams until I got it as close as I could to what it looked like when my grandmother did it.

It wasn't quite the same, there was something missing in my execution, but it was made up for by the company I had.

I reached for her hand, taking it in mine as she continued to look around.

"Luka, it's perfect," she said. "It feels like our place. Like we're supposed to be here."

"I'm glad you like it," I said. "And I know of a way you can repay me for it."

She lifted an eyebrow. "Oh yeah?"

Then, I made her clothes disappear. She squealed and covered her tits for a moment before releasing them. It was as if she had fallen back into human ideas of modesty. Sometimes, I forgot just how much human influence there was in her.

She didn't seem human when the two of us were together but those brief actions reminded me of her past. It also reminded me of how fucking lucky I was that she was even here at all.

"Not fair that your clothes are still on," she said with an exaggerated pouty look.

"Sure, it is," I said. "I told you that you had to repay me. Use those wiles of yours to get my clothes off."

She set her hand on her hip. "My wiles?"

"Yes," I said, lifting my chin with cheesy bravado, "your feminine wiles."

She narrowed her eyes and pursed her lips. I nearly moaned right there just from seeing her pucker those luscious lips. "Come on, Kitten. You up for the challenge?"

"I'm going to make you beg for it," she said.

I smirked. "I hope so."

She approached me slowly, swinging her hips with each step. Her tits bounced gently as she walked and my cock responded to her movements.

"Looks like your body is already betraying you." Her eyes flicked down to the tent in my pants. Then she looked up at me through her long, dark lashes, locking those green eyes on mine.

My body heated as she kept her gaze on me while melting to the ground. She stopped on her knees, her face right in front of my fly.

"Let's see if I can turn up the heat," she said, unzipping my fly.

My erection sprung free and I could feel her hot breath on my cock. I balled my hands into fists, urging myself to hold out. I wanted this to last a while but Raven already had me ready to throw her on the ground.

Her tongue made contact with my shaft, licking from the bottom to the tip. She flicked her tongue on the tip and I groaned. When her lips surrounded my cock, her warm mouth wrapping around it, my eyes rolled back in my head.

As she worked her lips up and down my cock, my breathing grew shallow. Her mouth was like magic and with each playful flick of her tongue, my willpower was melting away.

Raven slid her hands around my hips, gripping my ass. Her breasts brushed against me as she leaned closer.

It was nearly enough to make me lose control. I grabbed her head and pulled her away. "Easy there."

She grinned up at me, wiping her mouth with the back of her hand. "I thought you wanted a challenge."

"I changed my mind," I said. "I just want to fuck you."

She stood and slid her hands under my shirt, then she lowered her hands. "This is a dream, isn't it?"

I nodded.

She grabbed a fistful of my shirt in each hand and pulled. The buttons popping from the force.

I'd never been so turned on in my life.

Quickly, I pulled off the torn remains of my shirt and tackled her to the ground.

She laughed as we landed in the grass, her mouth quickly finding mine. Her kiss was ravenous, eager, and so, so hot.

I kissed her back, pushing my lips into hers with a force I rarely used with her. We were fueled by passion and heat and something primal I couldn't identify. I didn't care. I had to have her. Every piece of her.

I bit down on her lower lip, harder than usual and tasted blood. She nipped me back and we didn't break stride. The kissing resumed even harder and hotter than it had been. We both needed this.

Using my knees, I spread her thighs apart so I could settle in between them. Then I moved my mouth to her breasts, sucking one nipple, then the other.

Her hands tangled my hair and her heavy panting only made me want her more.

Sliding my hand past her belly, I quickly found her soft mound. Without warning, I slid two fingers inside her. She was soaked and I met no resistance.

Her hips bucked, responding to my touch. I slid another finger inside her, preparing her for my cock.

She moaned as I continued to thrust in and out with my fingers. Her hips bucked wildly as her breathing continued to quicken. Her moans came faster and more frequent. Then she cried out, digging her fingers into the dirt on either side of her as she came.

I smirked down at her as I slid my fingers out of her.

She stared up at me, panting. She didn't speak but her eyes said it all. She wasn't done. And neither was I. Now it was my turn.

I leaned down, kissing her stomach as I slid my hands up to her breasts. I caressed them gently, then worked my way to her nipples, pinching them hard.

She screamed and grabbed my back, digging her fingernails into my skin as she pulled me closer. Her eyes widened in surprise for a moment before she lifted her head and pressed her lips to mine.

When she bit down on my lip, I slid my cock into her all at once. Hard.

She gasped, breaking the kiss for a heartbeat, then returning her lips to mine.

My thrusts were fast and hard, timed with my rapid breathing. Raven's legs wrapped around my back, pulling me closer to her. I could feel her hot breath on my cheek as our bodies moved together in the rhythm of my hips.

But I wasn't ready to come yet. I needed more time with her. And she felt too fucking good.

I pulled out and grabbed hold of her legs, releasing them from their grip on me. She whined but I just smirked at her. "We're not done yet. Turn over."

She lifted an eyebrow, surprised by my command. But a moment later, she rolled over to her stomach. Her back was covered in dirt from the soft ground and I brushed it away before grabbing her hips.

I pulled her to her knees, moving her hips in line with my cock. She was on all fours, her face close to the ground, ass in the air. She had the most gorgeous ass. I grabbed a handful as I slowly slid my full length into her.

She gasped and I thrusted. After only a few moments of my hips, we were back in matching rhythm. She pressed back against me as I continued to drive into her. Holding on to her hips for leverage, I went harder than usual, driving my cock into her.

Raven moaned and I felt her wetness dripping onto my thighs. With each of her cries of pleasure it was getting harder for me to hold out.

Leaning in closer, I picked up the pace again as my own climax roared through me.

Raven cried out a moment before I came.

Sweaty and satisfied, the two of us curled up together in the tall grass. The wind blew Raven's hair gently as she traced lazy circles on my chest with her finger tip.

I could almost feel the peace within her and I wished I could bring her this much happiness all the time. For now, I was going to have to settle on dreams and stolen moments.

Raven

"You have visitors," the nurse said, her lips in a tight line.

My brow furrowed as I looked up at her from my bed. I was sure that I'd misheard her. They were very clear on the whole no visitor thing.

She tugged the curtain around my bed open and two familiar males walked in. Two handsome faces, nearly identical, grinned at me.

Despite my confusion, I grinned at Matt and Zach. "So you can bribe the hospital staff."

"Not exactly," Matt said, moving to my bedside. He sat down

on the edge, his grin replaced by a look of concern. "But our mom did make a phone call. She requested that we check on the status of her ward."

His expression told me he wasn't thrilled with his mom stepping in.

Zach lingered at the end of the bed, not approaching closer. He looked tense and uncomfortable. He wasn't his usual self. "Are you alright?"

He managed a small smile. "Says the girl in the hospital bed."

"We've been worried," Matt said, taking my hand in his.

I glanced at Zach again and noticed that his jaw tightened as his eyes settled on Matt's hand on me. *Is he jealous?*

"I'm fine now," I said. "Just waiting on the all clear so I can get out of here."

The curtain opened again and the nurse walked back in. "Which you'll have in a few hours if everything still looks good." She glanced at the twins. "Which is what I told your mother."

"She can be very insistent," Matt said.

"I don't recall her checking on Ms. Winters last time she was in here," the nurse grumbled.

"Really, I'm fine," I said. There was so much more I wanted to say to both of them, but now wasn't the time.

"This is my fault," Zach said.

"How is this your fault? You weren't even there," I said.

"No, but Delores seemed to think that she and I were in a relationship and seemed to think you were a threat," he said.

"Oh, that," I said.

"Yeah, that," he said.

"So this whole thing was over a male?" The nurse tutted. "Waste of time, if you ask me."

"I set her straight, if that helps," Zach said. "Told her there's nothing between us."

My chest tightened and I felt like the wind had been knocked from my lungs. *Nothing between us?* How could he say that? It was true that I hadn't explored my relationship with him as much as I had with Matt, but now that I knew what could be, I didn't want to lose it.

"I told her she and I were never going to work. That my heart belonged elsewhere," he added.

I took a relieved breath.

"You have to let me make it up to you," he said.

"That's great, very sweet," the nurse said. "But you two are going to get me in a heap of trouble. You can make out later."

Before I even got to reply to him, the nurse shooed them both beyond the curtain.

I settled back into the bed, my mind whirring. What was I going to say to them when I got out of here? How was I supposed to handle all of this?

Part of me actually wanted them to keep me in here for a few days so I could try to work things out in my head. But I knew that wouldn't help. There wasn't any impending doom. Nobody was trying to kill me, there wasn't a mad dash to get my magic back. Things were about as normal as they could be for The Academy of the Elites.

Leave it to me to create a problem from something I should be thrilled to have. I knew I was the luckiest girl alive to be surrounded by so many males who wanted me to be happy. I knew our connection wasn't something to take lightly. But that didn't mean it was easier to navigate. I closed my eyes, hoping that maybe a nap would help me pass the time.

Soon enough, I woke to the sound of the curtain being pulled back again. The nurse walked in, alone this time.

"If your temperature and your dilation are back to normal,

you'll be able to go." She leaned down and felt my forehead with her hand. "But I do recommend you go to your own bed and rest *alone* tonight. You're still recovering."

I frowned, not trusting myself to comment. I wasn't sure how much she assumed about me. Or what she actually knew. Either way, she was probably right and a good night's sleep would be rather nice.

The nurse flashed a light into each of my eyes, then stood. She gave a satisfied nod. "You're all clear. But I recommend you don't hit your head again any time soon."

"Got it," I said, really, really hoping that nothing else dramatic or life threatening happened until the trials. Those were going to be bad enough as it was.

Taking her advice, I went straight to my room once I was discharged. A few people stared at me in the halls and I noticed whispered conversations as I walked by. It wasn't anything out of the ordinary at this point. I was getting used to being a mainstay of gossip around here. Plus, I was too tired to worry about anything other than my nice warm bed.

"You're back!" Makayla jumped up from her place on the couch in the common room as soon as I stepped off the stairs.

"Yeah, and you were right, I did have to go to the hospital again."

She grinned as she pulled me into a hug. "I hate that I'm right, but I do so love telling people *I told you so.*"

I laughed as she threw her arm around my waist and guided me toward my room.

"You need rest. I stashed some snacks in your room. Ben let me use his key," she added.

"Thanks," I said.

We paused outside of my door and she dropped her hand from me. "I'll meet you here tomorrow morning for a non-oatmeal breakfast?"

"Sounds great," I said. Then I slid my key card into the slot on my door. "See you then."

Thankfully, my room was empty. I had half expected to find Ben waiting for me. The only thing that was waiting for me was a pile of snacks on my desk as Makayla had promised. I also noticed my clothes and backpack were here too. I'd tucked those in the locker. Makayla must have gone to get them for me.

I dug through the packaged beef jerky, bags of chips, and dried fruit before I found the box of Swiss Cake Rolls. Makayla knew they were my guilty pleasure.

Tearing open the box, I grabbed a cellophane wrapped package of cakes and carried them over to my bed.

When I woke, I was laying on the unopened melted mess of cake rolls and my lights were still on. I picked up the package by a corner and tossed them in the trash can. Well, that was a first. I'd never wasted junk food before.

Glancing at the clock, I checked the time. *Five in the morning.* I was never up this early. I considered turning off the lights and crawling back in bed but I was feeling a little restless.

I wondered if Luka or Ben were awake yet. Probably not. It was hours before classes started. Was anyone up yet?

After a quick shower, I left my room and headed into the main school building. It was chilly without all the extra bodies around. I walked past the office. The lights were off and the doors closed. It was a little spooky to see.

I took a turn and wandered past the library. Surprisingly, there were a few students in there. Probably pulled an all-nighter. I hoped whatever they were cramming for wasn't something I missed while I was in the hospital yesterday.

Letting my feet lead, I continued walking around the school without a destination in mind. I came to a stop in front of the spell casting room. I'd missed the first day of my independent study yesterday. I was sure Professor Halifax was pissed about that. She'd probably tell me that a concussion wasn't a good excuse.

Something crashed to the floor beyond the door and my brow furrowed at the sound. Was Professor Halifax already in there setting up for the day?

Opening the door a crack, I peeked inside. A single emergency light in the back cast an eerie glow over the darkened space. Something rolled across the floor and I opened the door wider to see several candles still moving. They hit the desk in the center of the room and stopped.

Another crash came from the back of the room and I could see a flickering light under the crack of the back store room door. Professor Halifax was probably in there getting supplies for today's lesson.

"Hello?" I opened the door a little wider and stepped into the room.

Something clanked from the back room and the light under the door went out. I moved into the room. "Professor? Is that you?"

Silence.

I walked toward the storage closet. "Sorry I missed yesterday, are you there?"

Just as I reached for the doorknob, someone tapped me on the shoulder. I gasped and turned, my heart nearly leaping into my throat.

I blew out a relieved breath when I saw Professor Halifax standing in front of me. "It's just you." My heart raced, not getting the memo that the threat was unwarranted.

She frowned. "What are you doing here, Ms. Winters?"

"I woke up early," I said.

"So you thought you'd intrude on my prep time?" She asked.

"Um," I wasn't sure how to respond to that. I glanced over

my shoulder toward the closet where I'd heard all the noises. Now I wasn't even sure it had been real.

"Ms. Winters?" Professor Halifax asked.

I looked back at her. "I'm sorry. I came to see what I could do to make up yesterday's lesson."

She pursed her lips and her eyes flicked down then back up, as if examining me. "You seem in good health."

"I am now," I agreed.

"Good. We'll have a double lesson today. You'll stay through your lunch period." She lifted her chin toward the door. "Be off with you."

"Thanks, I'll see you later," I said, feeling super awkward. Quickly, I made my way back to my dorm. Maybe I'd just wake up Makayla and get a head start on breakfast next time I woke up early.

Raven

I spent most of my morning assuring my friends that I was fine after the head injury. I even managed to avoid making eye contact with the sirens when I got breakfast. The only good thing was hearing that Coach Miller still made Delores run the stairs after dinner. And she did throw up.

Between trying to fake smile at everyone and pay attention in class, I was wondering about what I'd expect in my independent study. What more could Professor Halifax want to teach me? I supposed that I could benefit from learning how to control my temper a bit, but that didn't seem like it needed a whole semester.

During spell casting, I kept watching her expressions, hoping for some sign of what was coming after class ended. She lectured the whole period, not even giving us a minute to talk with our partners.

While I'd lost classes with Ben, I still had spell casting with the twins. It should feel like old times. But now, I was overly aware of how close they were to me with each passing tick of the clock.

Finally, the bell rang and everyone started packing up their bags to head to lunch. I remained in my seat, dreading what was coming next.

"You coming?" Zach asked.

"I have to make up yesterday's class" I said, lifting my chin toward Professor Halifax.

"Want me to stay?" Zach asked.

"No, that's okay, no need for you to sit through it again," I said.

"I can stay," Matt said.

"She'll be fine by herself," Professor Halifax said as she stopped in front of me. "Though, I will expect you here promptly after lunch for your independent study."

Zach frowned and I could tell he didn't like the situation. I wondered if he was jealous.

The twins walked away and left me alone in the room with the professor. "So, what did I miss? Should I take notes?"

She sat down next to me. It was the most informal thing she'd ever done. Almost like she was letting her guard down. "We need to talk."

My stomach tightened. That wasn't a great phrase. It was usually followed by words like *I'm breaking up with you* or *you're fired.* "About?"

"The Yule Ball," she said. "They whisked you away to meet with your probation officer before you could even process what happened."

"That's true," I said.

"How are you doing?" She looked genuinely concerned.

I wasn't sure how to react. It had been a long time since an adult, I mean technically I was an adult, but a long time since someone in a position of authority asked me how I was doing. "I'm okay, I guess."

She frowned. "You've been through a lot in the last several months. I have a feeling you are not okay."

"Well, I don't really have a choice," I said. "I have to be okay or at the least, I have to fake it."

"Right, but your magic won't be as strong as it should be if your head isn't in the right place."

There it was. The reason she was concerned. My magic. For a moment, I thought maybe she was worried about *me*. Magic was an odd thing. And mine seemed especially curious to those around me. "I am doing my best."

"I worry about you, you know," she said, standing. "You and me aren't so different."

"We aren't?" I didn't mean to say the words out loud, but it was hard to imagine her finding similarities between us. She was so composed and sure of herself. And she was powerful.

She smiled. "There are few with fae blood in the human realm. Those of us who are left here should help one another."

"Like the magic thief helped me?" I asked.

She pursed her lips. "The magic thief didn't speak for the rest of the fae. It was a surprise to all of us to find out she was fae in the first place. Magic thieves are usually half demon, half mage."

"I'm sorry, I wasn't trying to say fae are bad," I said. "It's just that she went after me so I guess she didn't share your sentiment."

"I suppose not," she said. "Why don't you go grab some food. Meet me back here in ten minutes. I can't have you passing out on me."

I didn't wait to be told twice. I shoved my notebook in my backpack, then quickly zipped it up.

Knowing I only had a few minutes, I grabbed some fruit and a sandwich in a plastic bag, giving my friends a wistful glance before walking toward the door.

I wasn't looking where I was going and walked right into someone, dropping my sandwich. "Sorry."

I knelt down to pick up my food, grateful it was still wrapped. A familiar hand brushed against mine, grabbing the sandwich before me. I looked up to see Zach.

He grinned at me. "In a hurry?"

I stood and took the offered sandwich from him. "Yeah, she gave me a few minutes to grab food before my independent study."

He frowned briefly. "How exactly can it be an independent study when there are two of you meeting in there?"

"Zach Obscura, are you jealous?" I teased.

"Yes," he said, without flinching.

I blinked back at him, unable to hide my surprise at his words. Zach was a flirt but he had a sweet streak. Between him and his brother, he was the one I would have thought was more likely to cover for me the way Matt had.

"Speechless?" he said with a smirk. "I'll take that as a good sign. You better go. Don't want you to be late."

"Yeah, thanks." I walked away from him but turned to glance over my shoulder. He was still watching me as I walked away.

When I arrived back at Professor Halifax's class, Matt was already waiting for me. I joined him in our usual seats, setting the sandwich on my lap. "So what did you do with her yesterday?"

"Nothing, she sent me out. Said we'd start today," he said.

I frowned, wondering why she'd made me skip lunch for no reason. Though, I guess she'd convinced Matt to get here early too. I opened the sandwich wrapper and held half of it up to him. "Hungry?"

He waved it away. "I already ate."

I took a bite and considered him. "Did she ask you to come early?"

"No, but I figured you might want some company," he said.

The door opened and I looked up to see Professor Halifax walking in. She popped a stick of gum into her mouth as she crossed the room to us. "Finish up. We'll start in a minute."

She walked toward the back room where I'd heard the sounds earlier today. I wondered if she was storing an animal back there. The thought made me smile. I had a feeling it probably wasn't a puppy.

Quickly, I shoved the rest of my sandwich in my mouth and chewed. The food made me feel better, a little more in control of my life. Though, I had a feeling it was all a fallacy. Either way, I'd take the brief moment of feeling better about my life.

"You two, down here," Professor Halifax said, holding a piece of obsidian the size of her head.

I stared at the rock, my brow furrowed. What the hell was she going to do with that?

Matt and I stopped in front of her and she handed the rock to Matt. He took it wordlessly. Then she lifted her eyebrows and nodded her head toward the rock.

I took her silent cue and slid my hands under the rock, my fingers next to Matt's. The places where our skin made contact heated, warm simply from his touch. It created a stark contrast against the cool stone.

"What I said in the office was true," she said. "It is possible for you to channel the other's magic. So that's what we're going to work on."

"Why?" I asked. "I don't want Matt to be able to do this. I don't want him to get in any more trouble. Unless there is a way to make it go away. To turn it off."

"You can no more turn it off than you can choose your parents," she said. "It's part of you, and as I've said before, you must learn to control it."

"How does Matt channeling my magic help with that?" I asked, also wondering why the hell we were holding a random rock.

"If he feels you tap into your time magic, he can channel it away from you. So if you lose your temper, he might be able to cover it for you and keep it from activating."

"Oh." I supposed, given my history, that wasn't the worst idea.

"And, he can eventually learn to help you strengthen it if you ever want to use it for real," she added.

"But it's illegal," I said.

She shrugged. "It wasn't always illegal and it's good to have options."

It wasn't like I had a record of being a rule follower, but this wasn't something I wanted to mess with. "Can we just focus on getting me to stop using it?"

"If that's what you want, yes," she said.

"That's what I want," I said.

"Tell me how I can help," Matt said.

"Today's class is simple. The stone will amplify your magic. Each of you need to work on finding the source magic for the other. It's one thing to find your own, another thing to find it in a partner."

"How do we do that?" I asked.

"Focus," she said.

I stood there, feeling awkward. Matt closed his eyes and I glanced over at Professor Halifax. She nodded once.

Turning back to Matt, I closed my eyes and focused on my own magic, thinking about it until I felt the spark within me. My fingers seemed to buzz with energy. Using that, I imagined sending it toward Matt, searching within him.

To my surprise, I felt something. It was clearly magic, but it wasn't my magic. A bead of sweat rolled down my face and I could hear my heart pounding in my chest. Searching for someone else's magic was harder than I imagined it would be.

Finally, I honed in on something - a flicker. Like a tiny flame of magic that wasn't mine. As I closed in on it, I felt something squeeze me, making it harder to breathe. I opened my eyes, gasping against the sensation.

Matt opened his eyes too and he pulled the stone away from me. I dropped my arms to my side, working to catch my breath. "What was that?"

"I think I started to draw on your magic," he said. "I'm so sorry."

I wiped my forehead with the back of my hand. "That wasn't a good feeling."

"I didn't mean to," he said.

"Interesting," Professor Halifax said.

We both turned to look at her. She reached for the stone and took it from Matt. "You two did that more quickly than I expected." Her eyes narrowed, then widened as if she had an idea.

"What?" I asked.

She shook her head. "You two had sex."

Embarrassment heated my cheeks. She said it so matter of factly. Like it wasn't a big deal. I still wasn't used to the cavalier way sex was treated around here.

"Neither of you should have the ability to do what you just

did on the first try," she said. "Your consumption of your bond has made you both stronger."

"You're saying that we have more power after having sex?" It didn't really make sense.

She nodded. "In your case, your power seems to grow with your mates. Lucky girl."

"I thought that didn't work that way for mages," Matt said.

"She's not a mage," Professor Halifax said. "At least not fully."

"I know about the fae blood," he said.

"It's a lot more than a few drops of fae blood," Professor Halifax said, "isn't it?"

I nodded. "I just found out. I'm half fae."

"Interesting."

"So she gets more powerful every time she has sex?" Matt asked.

I glared at him. I did not want to discuss my sex life with my professor.

"No," Professor Halifax said. "Just when she completes the bond with her mates."

"Zach," Matt said.

My cheeks grew even hotter. We both knew I had just as much of a bond with his twin as I did with him. And now it turns out that sleeping with Zach wasn't just good for my libido. It would literally make me more powerful.

Somehow, that made me not want to jump in the sack with him. I didn't want it to be about that. Call me a romantic, but the whole thing felt cheap now. Like if I had sex with him now, it would be self-serving. Wouldn't Zach always wonder?

Besides, there was that whole getting punched in the face by Delores. And I wasn't in a hurry to experience that again.

"Yes, if she has sex with another mate and confirms the

mating bond, she'll grow in power," Professor Halifax said. "That would be something."

"I'm not going to jump in bed with someone just to see my power increase," I said.

"Why not?" Professor Halifax asked. "It's a way to see your magic grow. It might give you that missing piece to control your time magic on your own."

"I know Zach wouldn't mind," Matt said.

"I'm done with this conversation," I said. "Professor, is that all for today's lesson?"

"Yes," she said. "I'll see you both tomorrow."

I grabbed my stuff and headed toward the door, ignoring Matt calling after me.

Raven

The next few days fell into a routine, with me being overly coddled by everyone. It was like they were afraid I would crack. Even Delores was avoiding me.

It was starting to get on my nerves. Even Professor Halifax and Coach Miller seemed to be going easier on me.

Then, I got the note. Officer M was here to see me. The rest of my life was going too smoothly. Boring, even. Might as well throw in some threats and inappropriate conversations with my parole officer.

I dragged my feet to Dr. Green's office, dreading the meeting. I did get a bit of a break since I was supposed to be off on good behavior. But the fact that three of the weeks off were during a holiday made it seem like nearly yesterday since our last encounter.

Taking a deep breath, I knocked on the door.

"Come in," Officer M's voice called.

I cringed, already feeling his beady gaze on me. His unusual and gag inducing smell hit me the second I walked into the office. It was worse today than usual. As if he was rotting away while sitting there in the chair behind the massive desk.

His red face glistened with sweat, a scowl on his lips.

I kept my chin up, not wanting to give him the satisfaction of knowing how uncomfortable he made me.

Discreetly, I glanced around for Dr. Green. He wasn't anywhere in sight. I tried not to let it bother me, but this was the first time he hadn't been at least outside the office waiting for me.

I hoped that didn't mean anything. As I sat down in one of the chairs facing the desk, I started to consider what I'd do if Officer M attacked me. It was irrational to think about. The thief was gone and there wasn't any reason why I should feel unsafe, but Officer M really got under my skin.

"It feels like it's been years since I last saw you." He grinned at me, then opened the folder in front of him, taking his eyes off of me to read whatever document he had in there.

I didn't know what to say so I stayed quiet.

He looked back up. "You're on track to finish out your parole by June if you play your cards right."

"I'm following all of the rules," I assured him.

He lifted an eyebrow. "Except for the big rule. The rule that says you can't use time magic."

My brow furrowed and I tried not to blink as I stared into his watery, pale eyes. "I have no idea what you're talking about."

For once, I was telling the truth. While we'd practiced finding each other's magic, I'd never used my time magic while working with Matt and Professor Halifax.

"At the Yule ball," he said. "I know it was you."

"Matt told you that was him. And it was an accident," I said.

"I'm not buying that, dear." He leaned over the desk, getting closer to me. My skin prickled as discomfort twisted in my gut.

"You might have tricked the Obscura twins into doing your bidding, but that doesn't mean that I'm not on to you."

"I didn't trick anyone," I said.

He pursed his lips and blinked at me but didn't take his eyes off of mine. All I wanted to do was back down. To physically move away from him. But I wouldn't give him the satisfaction.

"You must be part siren or part succubus. Somehow, you have control over those boys. When I figure out what it is, I'm going to bring you down. Madeline Obscura is not the type to be messed with and once I show her that you pulled one over on her boys, she'll come after you," he said. "You might not even make it to the prison alive."

My jaw tightened as I fought back the urge to spit in his face. "You keep threatening me, and I won't back down because I didn't do anything wrong."

"You did. And I'm going to prove it. The only thing you bought yourself was less meetings with me. Which means that I'll have more time to dig into how you did it," he said.

"Maybe you should be spending your time trying to figure out how a thief was able to infiltrate so many positions of power," I spat.

He backed away from me, his whole body tensing. I'd struck a nerve. "You don't get to tell me how to do my job. I'm here to keep you on the straight and narrow."

"You're wasting your time." I crossed my arms over my chest. "I told you, I didn't do anything wrong."

"Even if I believed that, we both know it's a matter of time before you lose control," he said. "Those with time magic are like a ticking bomb. We know it's going to explode sooner or later."

"I won't use my time magic," I said. "I don't know how many times you're going to make me say it."

"Every time I see you," he said. "Until I catch you breaking that promise."

I scowled at him, my chest tight with frustration. I wanted to scream at him or slam my fist on the desk to prove a point. But I knew it was what he wanted. He was trying to get to me. Trying to break me.

He sat there, his gaze fixed on me, the smallest curl of a smirk on his lips. He was waiting for me to snap.

Suddenly, the lights flickered. Then they sizzled and the scent of burning wires filled the air.

I looked up just as they popped, sending shards of broken lightbulbs falling from the ceiling.

I jumped up from my chair, brushing off the tiny pieces of glass from the fixture above me. "What the hell?"

The room was illuminated by only the thin strips of sunlight coming from the slatted closed blinds of the corner window.

"What did you do?" Officer M was standing next to me, his red face damp with sweat, his pale eyes narrowed on me.

"I didn't do anything. I was sitting right here, next to you," I said.

Without waiting for approval, I walked to the door and opened it, peeking out into the main office. The entire room was shrouded in darkness.

I could see the silhouette of the receptionist, but she wasn't moving. "Excuse me?" I walked toward her. "What's happening here?"

No reaction.

She stared blankly ahead, no sign of concern on her expression.

Oh shit.

My heart raced.

Someone had stopped time.

Someone *else* had stopped time.

Because I certainly didn't do it. I was pissed, sure. But I hadn't felt even the slightest flare of my magic.

"What did you do?" Officer M repeated. "How did you do this?"

I turned and glared at him, my jaw set, my hands balled into fists. "Don't you dare try to pin this on me. You know damn well I didn't do anything. I was sitting in that office with you."

"You're the only time user here," he snapped. "Unless your boyfriend did this." A sick grin spread on his lips. "In which case, he'll be locked up for the rest of his life."

My stomach twisted as I stared at the fat man in front of me. He was a sad excuse for a law enforcement officer. Why hadn't I been stuck with a strong, sexy officer? You know, the kind that poses for pictures with puppies for charity calendars? Or at least a good, smart, caring officer. The kind who does his job properly.

No, I got stuck with the corrupt, bottom of the barrel officer who was doing all he could to see me fuck up. How the hell was this man still employed? Instead of *him* asking *me* what I did to get away with it, shouldn't I be asking how the hell he even had his job?

"You know damn well Matt had nothing to do with this," I said.

"Do I?" He smiled, showing me his pointed yellow teeth. "Do you have something you want to confess."

"Look." I gestured to the main office. "Whoever did this had some serious control if they were able to keep us moving and freeze the rest of the office."

His upper lip twitched and he looked like I'd just told him there was no such thing as Santa Claus.

"Sorry to ruin your fun, but I couldn't have done this either," I said. "And you know that. I don't have anywhere near this kind of control."

"I bet you wish you did," he snarled.

"Sure," I said. "So I wouldn't worry about using it on accident. I'm not stupid. I know how good I have it here. You really think I'd want to throw all this away just because I want to use some power I didn't even know I had?"

His lips parted but he didn't say anything. I'd actually rendered him speechless. Guess he'd never considered that maybe I didn't have any motive to use the power he was here to keep me from using.

"Shouldn't you be investigating this or something?" I asked, feeling emboldened by my truth bombs.

"Yeah. But you're coming with me." He wrinkled his nose. "I'm not sure I believe you didn't have anything to do with this."

I rolled my eyes, not even trying to hide my frustration. "Fine. Lead on, fearless leader."

He ignored me and started to walk toward the main office door. I followed him, my shoes crunching over broken glass from popped lights.

The hallway was eerily quiet, despite being nearly full of people. Time had stopped right during the change between classes. I hadn't even heard the bell in Dr. Green's office.

We walked past frozen mages, shifters mid-step, and vampires reaching for their friends ahead of them. Some of the students were dusted in white powder.

I looked up and noticed that the stone of the ceiling looked cracked in places. Had it always been like that or was this new? I'd never bothered to look up in the hall before.

I stopped in front of one of my classmates. Ian, a sulky stereotypical vampire in a long black coat with perfect black eyeliner under both eyes. He held one strap of his backpack on his shoulder and his shiny black nail polish and perfectly groomed black hair made the white powder stand out even more than it did on the other students.

I rubbed my fingertips on his shoulder, feeling the gritty substance. It felt like fine sand. It probably had come from the ceiling.

"What are you doing?" Officer M called.

I looked up and narrowed my eyes to find him in the dim light of the hallway. He was almost to the stairway. Quickly, I wiped my fingers on my pants and hurried to catch up to my parole officer.

We walked down the stairs, weaving around statue-like students mid-stride. It was like walking into the middle of the fucking apocalypse. If Medusa was running the show.

The only thing that made it worse, was that so far, I was stuck here alone with Officer M. Literally the last person I wanted to do anything with.

Whoever did this better fix it, fast.

Raven

As we continued down the hall, I searched for familiar faces. I wasn't sure what I'd do when I saw my friends, but I needed to see that they were here. That they were safe. Well, as safe as someone can be while frozen in time.

With each face that wasn't Ben, Luka, Matt, Zach, Makayla, or one of the other shifters I hung out with, I grew increasingly nervous.

"Looking for someone?" Officer M asked.

"Yes," I admitted, seeing no reason to hide it. "I want to make sure my friends are safe."

He seemed surprised by my response. "I thought you'd be trying to find Mr. Obscura. If he's not here, if he's not frozen, that will look bad for him."

"We're still on that?" I asked. "I thought we agreed that he wouldn't be capable of this."

"*You* agreed that he wasn't capable of this. But if you didn't do it, someone did. And while I was convinced that you were the true perpetrator at the Yule ball, I now have my doubts," he said.

I shook my head. I never got anywhere with Officer M. It was like speaking to a child. It also made finding Matt a priority before the magic wore off and everyone went back to normal.

We walked down the class hallway and I glanced inside classroom doors, most of them propped open already by students who were entering or exiting.

As we passed the astronomy classroom, I let out a relieved breath. Both Ben and Makayla were frozen on their way out of the classroom.

I stopped for a moment and pressed my palm to Ben's cheek. He was warm but I couldn't see any signs of breathing. He was here, though. And he had to be okay. He just had to be.

I set my hand on Makayla's shoulder and gave it a gentle squeeze. *Hang in there. I'm going to get you two out of this.*

"What did you find?" Officer M asked.

"Just some of my friends." I caught up to him, giving a quick backward glance at Ben and Makayla. "How are we going to fix this?"

He laughed. "You're asking me? Between the two of us, only one of us has any experience with time magic."

I frowned. "Well, even if I knew how to fix it, I wouldn't be allowed to."

He didn't respond.

Good.

The whole thing was absurd. Why the hell was this kind of

magic illegal in the first place? I mean, I guess I could see how it was dangerous. Anyone could freeze time then walk in here and do whatever they wanted.

Okay. It was hella dangerous.

All these people were sitting ducks. A bad guy could do whatever they wanted, take whatever they wanted.

Until that moment, I hadn't felt the true weight of the power I could wield. It was an overwhelming, chest crushing sensation.

Feeling slightly dizzy, I focused on moving down the hallway, looking at the faces of my classmates.

They were all so vulnerable like this. So fragile. No wonder they were terrified of this kind of magic.

Though, it was also quite beautiful in its own way. It was so quiet. So peaceful. Imagine if someone used magic like this to stop a riot or freeze the fire in a burning building.

There was so much potential for good.

But I supposed like everything, it was abused by too many. The bad apples ruined it for the rest of us.

"Maybe you were right," Officer M said.

I looked over toward his voice and laughed at the sight ahead of me. Both Matt and Zach were sitting on a bench, looking down at a book they held between them.

Not waiting for Officer M, I ran toward them and knelt down in front of them so I could see their faces. Their eyes were glued to the page, their sandy hair hanging down over their foreheads.

I pushed Matt's hair back and looked into his eyes, then I did the same with Zach. My heart ached as I saw their blank expressions. No flicker of recognition. No breath. No life.

They were both warm, they were both alive, I had to remind myself, but I suddenly felt like I was living in a tomb.

I stood quickly and turned to look at Officer M. "We have to fix this. They can't stay like this."

"I'll have to call this in. I can't fix this on my own," he said. "Back to the office."

"There's one more person I have to find," I said, knowing I wouldn't be able to go back until I saw Luka.

"They'll still be here when we get this sorted out," he said.

"Please," I said. "I just need to see one more person."

He frowned. "Fine. But I'm going to consider you a suspect if time starts again while you're away from me."

I raised my eyebrows. "Seriously? We're back to that?"

He shrugged. "I'm just doing my job."

Badly. I shook my head. "I'll meet you in the office soon. My friend had gym next, I'm just going to check there."

He lifted his chin in a weird little nod, then turned away from me.

I darted down the hall, dodging students, a couple of professors, and a rather large cat that I suspected was a student who shifted.

Finally, I made it to the gym. Luka wasn't in the hallway. Before I could think better of it, I opened the door to the men's locker room and nearly ran right into a classmate who had apparently been frozen seconds after entering the locker room.

Shimmying around him, I walked around the locker room, attempting - but not really succeeding - at keeping my eyes above the waist.

I had a lot of very good looking and well-endowed classmates.

And two who were not so well-endowed.

I bit down on my lip to keep from giggling like a twelve-year-old. The stress was starting to morph into feeling a bit punchy.

My stomach twisted into knots as worry continued to spike. I had to find him. I turned a corner and ran right into someone.

A tall someone. Who happened to be very naked.

I screamed as embarrassment burned red-hot in my cheeks.

Of all the people to run into while they were naked, Remi was last on my list. Yet here he was, with his trademark cocky grin that made him look so very much not frozen in time.

I pressed my finger into his rock hard peck. He didn't flinch. Blowing out a slow breath, I backed up so I could walk around him.

But I did glance at the package first.

And I could see why Makayla was enjoying herself. "You go, girl."

Once I was away from Remi, I saw another group of guys by another wall of lockers. One of them had his tee-shirt over his head, covering his face and most of his upper body. But I recognized that ass.

Just to be sure, I walked around to his front and lifted the shirt. Luka stared blankly back at me.

My knees went weak and I collapsed to the bench in front of the lockers. Seeing him like this was heartbreaking. They were all stuck. All frozen in time. And I didn't know how to help them.

Then, it hit me. I'd been so worried about finding my friends and proving that I hadn't stopped time that I didn't consider who really had.

Shaking, I pushed myself to standing. I had to get back to the office with Officer M. While I knew he was inept, I also knew we weren't the only people who weren't stuck frozen in time.

And the other person was likely the one who did this to us. But why? And why were we spared?

I gave Luka a quick kiss on the cheek, then made my way out of the locker room. As soon as I hit the hallway, I took off at a run for the office.

Good thing I was in such good shape now. I never realized

that all the running I did in gym would be applied so literally to the things I did here at the academy.

Officer M was hanging up the phone when I arrived back at the office. I waited for him to tell me what was going on.

He looked up at me. "The lines are dead. No calls are going in or out."

"What?" My heart raced. "Did someone cut the lines? Don't you have magic to fix that or magic to contact people?"

"I do, yes," he said. "But it appears that we're in a time bubble."

"What's a time bubble?" I asked.

"Essentially, we're totally sealed off from the outside world. Anything inside the bubble is suspended in time and anything outside the bubble is off limits to us. We can't use modern technology or magic to communicate beyond the bubble."

"Well, how do we break it?" I asked.

"You know, I have no idea," he said. "It's not exactly something they teach us since all time magic users were supposed to be dead."

An icy chill ran down my spine. "Supposed to be?"

"Not like that," he said. "I meant that you're the first we've had record of since, well, your parents."

"Right," I said. "Obviously, your people aren't very good at keeping records because clearly you've missed some."

"It seems that's the case," he said.

"I don't blame them, really," I said. "If I knew that those with time magic were being hunted and labeled by the government, I would hide my powers, too."

"You did hide your powers," he said.

"Not on purpose," I said. But for the first time in my life, I thought that maybe I understood why my alcoholic aunt in the human world had been my guardian. Who knew what would have become of me if someone in this world had raised me.

"Well, isn't this a pretty sight? A school of frozen students and a useless officer of the guild," a woman's voice said.

I turned to see Professor Halifax standing in the office doorway, her hand on her hip. "I'm guessing you don't have a plan for fixing this, do you?"

"Is it over?" I asked. "Is everyone unfrozen?"

She shook her head. "There are two rooms in this building that are magic proof. The first, as you've probably guessed is Dr. Green's office."

"Well, that explains why we weren't hit," I said. "The second?"

"The old dungeons," she said. "Obviously they didn't want people to use magic to break out prisoners."

"Like confinement?" I asked, confused.

"No, old crumbling cells. We use them for storage now. They're definitely not safe for long term stays. Thankfully, I was working on inventory." She glanced around. "Where's Dr. Green?"

"He said he had business to attend to," Officer M said.

"It's just us," I said with mock cheerfulness.

"Alright," she said. "Officer, you have any *legal* ways to break this time bubble?"

"Um…" Officer M shifted nervously.

Professor Halifax let out a frustrated breath. "I thought not."

"Please tell me you can fix this," I said.

"I can't, but you can," she said. "But in order to do that, your parole officer is going to have to turn a blind eye."

"Absolutely not," he said. "She is not going to break her parole on my watch."

Professor Halifax folded her arms over her chest. "Fine. Then we'll wait while you break the spell."

"Can't we catch whoever did this?" I asked.

"They're probably outside the school," Officer M said in a disgruntled tone. "There's no way they stayed in here."

"What's the point of all this? Why would someone do this?" I asked.

"No idea," Professor Halifax said. "But I'm sure we'll find out what the next steps of their plan are soon."

She walked over to one of the chairs in front of Dr. Green's desk and took a seat. "Might as well get comfortable. We could be here a while. Who knows how long. Hours, days, years…"

"Years?" The word came out in a squeak.

"Imagine the story when it breaks. A whole school of the most important and well connected supernatural kids taken out. The plot thickens when they find out an officer of the guild was present inside the school during the attack."

She leaned back in the chair, throwing her arm over the back. "Can you imagine what Ben Lucia's father will do to your family if his son doesn't make it out of here alive?"

"Fine. Do it. But not in here. And don't give me any details," he said.

She stood. "I need your word that you will not punish her for this."

"You have my word," he said.

"Swear it, goblin," she said.

He spit on his hand and extended it to Professor Halifax. She spit on her hand and then shook.

My nose wrinkled in disgust. Gross.

Raven

"So he's a goblin?" I asked as we walked out of the office.

"You didn't know?" Professor Halifax asked as she wiped her palm on her dress.

"No," I said. "He creeps me out."

"That's because he's untrustworthy and useless," she said. "But he'll keep his word. He has no choice."

"Do you really think I can fix this?" I asked.

She stopped walking, right next to a group of students who were frozen while shoving another student against the wall. "I hope so, but we haven't really tested what you can do."

"This is the only way, isn't it?" I asked.

"I'm afraid so," she said.

"Who do you think did this?" I asked.

She shook her head. "I wish I knew. My guess is the word is out about you and that someone else is looking for someone with your skill set."

"Another thief?" My breath caught. I didn't want to go through all of that again.

"I don't think so." She paused, as if considering. "But I'm starting to think you aren't the only one with time magic. Maybe a distant relative or something? Who knows? When you get out of here, you might even want to find whoever it was. Maybe it's not a malicious thing."

I hadn't considered that. "Freezing a whole school seems like a pretty big thing to do out of the goodness of someone's heart."

She shrugged. "Could be a show of power? Or a test? I suppose there are a lot of possibilities."

"I guess so," I said, not feeling comfortable with any of the suggestions.

"We should go to my classroom, we'll be more comfortable there." She turned and started walking away.

I looked over at the scene in front of me. One mage girl was up against the wall, her shoulders lifted up near her ears as she braced herself for impact. She looked terrified.

Three mage boys surrounded her, one had his hands on her and the other two had their arms extended. They were all laughing.

I moved next to the girl and carefully dragged her away from them, propping her against the wall nearby.

Then I shoved one of the mages so he fell against the wall and the other two were about to push him.

There were some good things about stopping time.

Quickly, I ran after Professor Halifax. She was already in

her classroom. Walking out of her back storage area with a couple of cushions in her hand. Thankfully, it was empty of students.

"You were lucky that you were in the basement," I said.

"Yes," she agreed. "Had it not been my free period, I'd be just as frozen as the rest of you. Guess it was good that Dr. Green asked me for my inventory numbers today."

"Where is he? Do you know? He's usually there for my parole meetings."

She set the cushions on the floor in the center of the room. "I'm not sure. It's not often that he leaves his office. I always thought that was partially because of the magic seal in there. If he's in there, there's always someone who is safe if there's a spell that backfires or an attack on the school."

"Why don't they just put that on the whole school to prevent that?" I asked.

She smiled. "How would you practice magic then? You can't cast spells in those rooms, either."

"That makes sense," I said.

Professor Halifax settled into one of the cushions on the ground, then patted the empty one. "Sit. We have time to unfreeze."

"Got it," I said, taking the seat next to her. "How do we do this? I've never used the time magic on purpose."

"That's not true. We practiced, remember?"

"That was containing it," I said.

"What do you think closing off a time bubble is?" She lifted an eyebrow. "You have to reverse the spell. It's exactly what we did before but on a much larger scale."

"I lit candles," I said. "I never re-started time. Even when I stopped time, it never held this long."

"You nearly opened a portal. That's far more powerful than whatever caused this. I'd wager that you're stronger than the caster who put us in this bubble. This will be an interesting test of what you're capable of."

Those seemed like impossibly big shoes to fill.

"Set your hands, palm up on your knees," she said. "Close your eyes."

I followed her instructions, opening my palms and closing my eyes.

"Now, breathe in through your nose, out through your mouth," she said.

"Like yoga class?" I asked.

"Exactly," she said. "It's calming. Centering. A way to clear your mind. You have to find the magic."

"Okay." I took a deep breath in through my nose and blew it out through my mouth. I felt ridiculous. This was never going to work. My friends were going to be frozen forever and I was going to spend the rest of my life in a creepy castle with Professor Halifax and Officer M.

A shudder ran down my spine.

I could not let that happen. No way was I going to be stuck here with him. Ugh. I tried again, focusing on breathing. Trying to empty my mind.

"Feel for the source of the magic, just like you did when you connected with Matt," Professor Halifax said. "It might be a little more difficult because you don't know the caster. And you're not bonded. But the practice is the same."

I nodded, not sure if she could see me. Either way, she didn't say anything else while I sat there, breathing and emptying my mind. Finally, feeling centered, I started to reach out for any signs of magic that wasn't mine.

It felt like I'd been there for hours and I could feel frustration creeping in around the edges of my calm. My fingers twitched and my ass was starting to hurt despite the cushion under me.

I blew out another breath, hoping for any signs of magic. In desperation, I reached out toward Professor Halifax. Her magic pulsed like a beating heart. It was pure and clean and vibrant. Not the hot spark mine was.

Then, I noticed something else. Something a little unstable, like a live electric wire. I let go of the feeling of Professor Halifax's magic and shifted my senses to the new feeling.

That was it. It had to be.

Whatever I was feeling was charged and alive. It felt similar to my magic, but it wasn't quite the same. There was a vibration to it that seemed to hum like the wings of an insect. And like an insect, it felt both fragile and powerful at the same time.

I reached out, tugging on it. My own magic flared to life, sending a rush of shockwaves across my skin. I winced, but the discomfort passed quickly.

Grabbing hold of my magic, I sent it toward the foreign magic. I needed to squash it like a bug.

Sending my magic out, I surrounded the fluttering unfamiliar magic, squeezing it with mine until I could feel it shudder in violent bursts as it struggled to stay alive. I was smothering it, extinguishing it.

The magic fought me, pushing back against mine. I felt sweat drip down my back and my pulse raced. My hands balled into fists as I fought back, containing the offending magic.

Finally, with a gasp, the other magic dissipated like smoke. I let out a breath I didn't know I was holding then my shoulders slumped in exhaustion.

I ran a hand through my hair, pushing it away from my face. It was damp with sweat. Something dripped down my face and I wiped under my nose. When I pulled my hand away, it was covered in blood.

I touched my nose with my fingertips and then looked at them. They were soaked in crimson blood.

Professor Halifax handed me a box of tissues. I hadn't even noticed her get up to grab them.

I took them from her and blotted the blood.

"You did it," she said.

That was when I noticed that there was sound outside the room. The bustle of the halls filled with people moving from one class to another.

Relief flooded through me and I laughed, surprised that I'd pulled it off.

"You did good," Professor Halifax said.

The door opened and a few students stepped inside. They all stopped as soon as they saw me.

"Are you okay?" A shifter girl, Carly, asked. "Do you need the nurse?"

"I'm fine," I said, making myself stand on wobbly legs.

"You're blocking the doorway," Professor Halifax said.

The students moved quickly, throwing curious glances my way as they took their seats.

"You should probably finish your parole meeting," she said.

"Yeah," I said. "I'm definitely looking forward to that."

"And I suggest you don't tell anyone about this," she said. "You never know when word that you used your magic could get into the wrong hands."

I nodded, not keen on the idea of hiding this, but it made sense. There was too much risk.

Ben

I frowned as Luka slid into the space next to Raven. He'd been at the lunch table, on the other side of her from me for the last couple of weeks. You'd think I'd be used to it by now but I wasn't sure it was ever going to get easier.

Since our awkward conversation, he'd kept to his word and on the nights I spent with Raven, he didn't come to her dreams. At least I didn't think so.

I didn't like thinking about what she might be doing on the nights we weren't together.

The others at the table had accepted him and laughed and

talked easily with him. I liked to pretend he was just a friend. Just part of the group. Especially since our parents were now working together.

It seemed whichever aspect of my life I was thinking about, he was going to be part of it.

I never would have imagined that I'd be stuck thinking about how to deal with an incubus who won't go away.

Raven laughed and I looked over at her. I'd been so caught up in my own head that I lost the thread of conversation.

"What did he do when he found the squid?" She leaned over the table, eating up every bit of the conversation.

"He screamed like a girl," Makayla said. "You would have died."

She tossed her head back with laughter, the whole table joining in. Jamal slapped the table with his palm and Makayla wiped a tear.

"He's never going to eat sushi again," Jessica said.

"Mages are so squeamish," Starla added.

"You got that right," Raven said. "If my sushi plate came to life, I'd freak the fuck out too."

"Hey, everyone," a male voice called. I turned to see Matt Obscura. *Great*. Just what I needed to brighten my day.

Raven and I hadn't ever talked about Matt, but until today he hadn't been a part of our usual group. Was he going to join in on the lunch table? Because it was one thing to deal with one of your girlfriend's other mates. Adding the second one was just going to push me over the edge.

"Matt, is everything okay?" Raven asked.

"Yeah, just finished my weekly parole meeting," he said.

I growled involuntary, hating that he had done something so noble for her. I wished I could have taken the fall for Raven. But I didn't share their magic. It was something that the two of them had in common that Raven and I would never share.

Sometimes I wondered if that was why she went to him some nights. Things were different for me around other shifters. They understood the call of the beast inside. They understood the need to run, the need to break free sometimes.

I never regretted what I had with Raven and I've never wished she was a shifter, but I wondered if she connected with him in a different way.

"How'd it go?" she asked.

"He said something *weird*," Matt said. "Can we talk for a second?"

"Sure," she said, already out of the seat.

I followed her with my eyes as they walked out of the cafeteria.

"What do you think that's all about?" Luka asked.

I glanced over at him. Now that Raven was gone, he was basically sitting next to me. My life had gotten odd since Raven came into it. Eating lunch with a demon. What was going to happen next? "No idea."

Though, I was pretty sure I had an idea. Raven had told me about the time stop. I suspected she told Luka, too. She said she was supposed to keep it a secret. But that's too big of a secret to hold on your own. Now, I was wondering if she never told the mage.

The corners of my lips tugged up into a smile. If she kept that from him, maybe they didn't share any extra special kind of bond.

Raven was back at the table before I could wonder any more.

"Everything okay?" Luka asked.

"Yeah. Just Officer M's usual threats," she said.

"I can't wait till you get to stop seeing that guy," Luka said.

"I agree, guy gives me the creeps," I said.

"Tell me about it," she said. "Hey, I gotta run, but I'll see you tonight still, right?"

I grinned. "I'm not going easy on you tonight."

"Well, I won't be visiting any dreams tonight," Luka said.

"He's talking about our strip poker tournament in the dungeon tonight," Raven said.

"I'm definitely not visiting your dreams," he said. "Strip poker always leads to sex."

Raven's eyes widened a little but she didn't say anything.

I laughed. "I sure hope it does."

Raven gave me a playful punch in the arm and I grabbed her fist, using it to pull her closer to me. Leaning in, I moved my lips to her ears so I could whisper. "Just wait until you see all the things I have planned for you after I get you naked."

I could feel her body heat rising from my words. She glanced at me, looked up at me through her lashes. "I'm going to hold you to that."

Grabbing her chin with my hand, I turned her face to me and then pressed my lips to hers. She kissed me back, quickly slipping her tongue into my mouth.

Then, she broke the kiss and gave me a playful grin. "You have to get me naked first. And in case you forgot, strip poker champion right here."

I laughed. She beat the pants off of me last week. "We'll see. I've been practicing."

"Well, everyone, it's been great, but there's no way in hell I'm going to be late to gym," Makayla said.

"Shit, you're right," Luka said. "Time for class."

I stood and then leaned over Raven. "See you tonight."

"I'll see all of you tonight." She lifted her eyebrows and gave a knowing nod.

My cock was hard already just thinking about getting her naked and on my bed. I was going to need to keep myself distracted for the next few hours.

"Come on, lover boy," Makayla said. "I'll walk you to class."

Raven waved, then turned back to her tray. No doubt Luka was going to walk her to her next class. At least he wouldn't be there tonight. He could have the two minute walk.

I got her all night tonight.

As soon as Makayla and I left the cafeteria someone cut us off, stopping right in front of us.

"You got a minute?" Matt Obscura asked.

I frowned. Until he started sleeping with Raven, I could never tell the two of them apart. Now, I knew which one was Matt because he always had a trace of Raven's scent on him.

"What's up?" Makayla asked.

I tensed, not happy that we were standing here with him. I tolerated Luka, but there was no way I was adding another boyfriend to our table at lunch.

"I'm worried about Raven," he said.

That got my attention but also drew suspicion. I'd just been with her. She was fine. "Why?"

"She probably didn't tell you since it's kind of a mage thing," he said.

"Spit it out," I said.

He frowned. "Though, I am guessing she told you about the time stop?"

I nodded.

"Yeah, we know," Makayla said. "I didn't know *you* knew."

"We talked about it in our independent study," he said. "Anyway, our parole officer mentioned today that there could be another magic thief."

"Raven didn't say anything about that," Makayla said.

"She didn't say anything about that to me, either," I agreed.

"I know," he said.

"Do they know for sure?" I asked.

"No," he said. "But Officer M sure seems to think there's some external sinister source that caused the time bubble."

"How does this connect to Raven?" I asked, getting impatient.

"It's her magic," he said. "Ever since she got rid of the time bubble, her magic has been weak. She's barely keeping up with her spells and there's no way she could do a spell like that again."

"Doesn't your magic recharge?" Makayla asked.

"Yeah, it's supposed to at least," he said.

"How?" I knew people like Luka needed sex. I had no idea what a mage needed.

"That's the thing, it should just happen with rest and time," he said. "But it's been a few weeks and it's still weak. I'm worried that if there is a thief and she needs to defend herself…"

"She has three boyfriends who swarm around her, I'm sure she'll have help," Makayla said.

"Like she'd let us fight for her," Matt said. "You know her. She'd charge in and put herself in danger."

"That's true," Makayla agreed.

"I don't understand what you're asking," I said, knowing this was going somewhere.

"Look, I don't like it either, but Professor Halifax mentioned that Raven might get stronger with each mating bond she forms. And there's a bond she hasn't fulfilled yet."

"You can't be serious," I said.

"Are you pimping out your brother?" Makayla asked.

"I'm just saying that maybe you two could encourage her to think about it," Matt said.

"You want us to tell her to have sex with Zach?" I asked. "Cause that is never going to happen."

"You think I want to share her with anyone else?" he asked.

I growled and he took a step back.

"Listen, Zach has no idea I'm here. He flirts with her, but he'd never make a move unless he thought she wanted him to. All I'm saying is that maybe we can encourage them to be alone together."

"I still can't believe you're trying to get us to help your brother get laid," Makayla said.

"If it recharges her magic enough, it's worth it," Matt said. "A mage with low magic isn't going to be able to defend herself properly. She's getting by okay and it's possible it'll return to full strength in a few days, but if she has the potential to be stronger, why wouldn't she take it?"

"How come she hasn't said anything to us?" I asked.

"I don't think she even notices," he said. "Magic is still pretty new to her. But I'm telling you, I can feel it. The vibration of her magic was unmatched by anyone's I'd ever felt before. Now, it's a low buzz. Pretty normal for a mage, but Raven's not normal. And if there's someone after her again…"

"Tell you what," I said. "You get them together, I won't interfere, but I'm not going to help you set it up."

Without waiting for an answer I walked away. There was no way this day could get any weirder.

Ben

I leaned in closer to Raven, placing my lips against her ears. "What if I just lose to you right now?"

She bit down on her lower lip and I could tell she was considering the offer. We were alone in the common room as everyone else was still at dinner. But I knew my window was short. If the others got here, she'd want to join in on the weekly poker game. And while I was getting used to losing to her, I was ready to skip to the good part.

Especially after that conversation with the Obscura twin. Those two thought they could have anything they wanted. Raven was a smart girl, though. She wasn't going to fall for their tricks. Well, I didn't think she would anyway.

While most of me wanted to threaten him and tell him to stay away from my girl, I knew that was the one way to piss her off to the point of never getting laid again.

Raven protected her independence fiercely. It was possibly the most sexy and most annoying thing about her.

"What about the game?" she asked.

"Let the others play," I said. "I want you to myself."

Voices floated into the common room as people filed down the stairs. I leaned back against the couch, knowing the moment was gone. She'd never leave now.

She leaned back next to me, turned slightly so her tits were pressed against my chest. I had to hold back from groaning out loud. I wanted her so bad it hurt. "You sure you don't want to leave?"

She licked my lower lip, then bit it gently. "Soon."

That made me groan. There was no holding it in that time. "Raven, you're going to make me take your clothes off right here."

"You're going to have to earn that tonight," she said.

"Oh?" I poked her in the side, making her giggle. "Are you saying I have to win your favor tonight?"

"Is that a bet anyone can make?" A male voice said.

"I'll take a piece of that," another male chimed in.

I growled, the hair on the back of my neck standing on edge at the familiar sound. "Who let the mages in here?"

Raven elbowed me. "I'm a mage."

"You're a cool mage," I said. "And Raven isn't property, you can't win her."

"I was flirting," she said.

"Right," one of the twins said.

"You two never come down here," Raven said. "What brings you to the dungeon?"

I locked my eyes on them, my upper lip twitching as they took seats across from us on the other couch. When they were together, I had no idea which was which. I couldn't pinpoint Raven's scent. Especially not with her lounging against me.

I pulled her in tighter, wanting to remind them that she was mine.

"We heard there was a game," one of them said. He pulled a stack of bills out of his pocket. "This enough to buy in?"

Raven laughed. "It's not that kind of game."

"We have different stakes down here," Makayla said as she settled into the space next to Raven.

"Oh?" The twin holding the money looked intrigued.

"Strip poker," Raven said. "Think you can handle it?"

"We aren't seriously letting them play, are we?" Starla said as she took her usual place at the table.

I glanced around the room. Everyone seemed to have arrived right after the twins. Most of the other shifters were watching them with suspicion. I didn't blame them.

Most mages treated us terribly. And aside from Raven, they never came down here.

"Why not?" Remi asked.

I looked at Remi, my eyebrows raised in surprise. He seemed like he'd be the last to accept them in our game. Shit, we only recently allowed Remi to join. And that was only because of Makayla.

Frowning, I realized that we'd set a precedent when we let Remi play. Since he was seeing Makayla, even if she still hadn't admitted it officially, he was allowed in. And as much as I hated it, one of the twins was spending time with Raven.

"You sure you two can handle it?" Raven asked. "It doesn't seem like your game."

"Oh, we can handle it," the twin with the money shoved it back in his pocket.

"What do you think, Ben?" Raven looked up at me. "Do we have room for two more?"

"I guess so," I said.

"Alright, if you're in, take your seat. I'm dealing," Starla said.

While everyone grabbed a seat around the low table, I leaned close to Raven so I could whisper. "You're still spending the night in my bed tonight."

"Of course I am," she said. "But you still need to earn me."

I'd never been so turned on by the prospect of playing poker in my life. I wanted to get her naked and then I was going to carry her over my shoulder back to my room like a cave man claiming his bride.

As we played, someone put out glasses and we passed around bottles of liquor. With each hand, the conversation grew louder and the laughter more boisterous.

Three rounds in and I was still fully clothed. Raven had lost her shoes and one of the twins, Zach I think, was down to bare feet. He was terrible, which was turning out to be entertaining to watch.

Finally, I lost a hand and pulled off my own shoes. Raven leaned in closer to me, her body pressed against mine. Feeling her warmth on me was the best thing in the world.

I had to admit, even the twins couldn't ruin the mood.

We kept playing and drinking and everyone was having friendly side conversations. To my surprise even the mages were getting along with the rest of the group. I hated to admit it, but they weren't as bad as I originally thought. Not that I felt any better about Raven spending time with them, but I supposed there were worse people she could hang out with. I'd even managed to figure out which was which. Though, if they changed places, I'd be screwed.

A few more hands and I had lost my socks and my belt. Raven had lost her pants in the last round and another loss would have her losing her shirt. A couple of the shifters had left the game and the twins were down to their tee shirts and boxers. They were in surprisingly good spirits about it.

"There was that one summer when I convinced him he could breathe under water," Zach said.

"You didn't!" Raven laughed. "What happened when he tested it?"

"He nearly drowned. It was the angriest I ever saw our dad."

"I was a kid," Matt said.

"You were thirteen," Zach said.

Everyone around the table laughed.

"Alright," Starla said. "Moment of truth."

Raven groaned as Starla turned the cards. "Shit."

"It's about to get very cold for you," Starla said. "Take it off!"

"Dammit," Raven stood up, setting her cards on the table. Then she pulled her shirt off. She was standing there in her bra and panties and I can tell you there was nothing cold about it. In fact, I felt like I was on fire.

Foreplay was over. I wasn't going to wait until she was naked.

I set my cards down on the table. "Well, it's been fun, but there's something I need to do."

I grabbed Raven and tossed her over my shoulder.

She squealed. "Ben! Put me down."

"Not till we're in my bedroom." I turned so I was facing the rest of the group, Raven hanging over my shoulder. "See you all in the morning."

Laughter, whoops, and cheers followed us down the hall

from our friends in the common room. As soon as I closed the door behind us, I set Raven on the bed. She grinned up at me.

"What do you think? Did I do enough to earn you tonight?"

"Maybe," she said. "What are you going to do with me now that you have me?"

"Everything," I said.

"I like the sound of that," she said.

Raven

It was odd how quickly things seemed to get into a normal routine. After last semester, I'd expected a bit more drama. Though I had to admit, I kind of liked it boring.

Classes took most of our time. All of my friends were planning to take the formal trials this spring so we were pretty focused on learning as much as we could before it was time.

That didn't mean we didn't have fun. Regular poker games, tumbles in the library with Luka, and the occasional study session with Matt while Zach was away had kept me busy.

The one thing in my schedule that I hated doing was going to my parole meetings.

I hadn't seen Officer M since the time bubble last month. After the incident, he hadn't said anything about what I'd done. It was as if nothing happened. I half expected him to show up today with handcuffs and charge me for using my magic that day.

When I saw Dr. Green standing in front of the door, I breathed a little easier. Officer M was usually better when the dean was around. Not that it helped much, but it made me feel better.

"Hey, Dr. Green," I said. "It's been a while. You must be busy."

"I am," he said. "Professor Halifax caught me up on what happened last month."

My brow furrowed and I realized I hadn't seen the demon around campus since returning from break. "Have you been gone all this time?"

"I had some business to attend to," he said as he opened the door.

"Okay." I walked into the office. "Well, welcome back, then, I guess."

Officer M wasn't in the chair behind the desk. In fact, he wasn't even in the room. I looked around again, wondering if I was missing something. "Am I early?"

"No, you're on time, it seems Officer M is running late." Dr. Green took his seat and folded his hands on the desk. "Why don't you have a seat."

I obliged, feeling awkward in the silent room. I looked over at the tree clock. Today, it was covered in tiny brown buds. One or two of them open to reveal pink flowers. I narrowed my eyes, studying the growth. Was the clock alive?

Once before, I'd seen the clock with things growing on it, but they'd been gold fall leaves. Nearly dead. This was new life. And it created a stark contrast with the black, lifeless looking tree.

Tick. Tick. Tick.

The clock hand moved and I stared at the gold eyes of the creepy owl. Time felt like it was moving slower in here.

I turned away from the clock, startled by my own thoughts. Then I realized that if someone did stop time in this school, Dr. Green and I wouldn't know. We'd be safe due to the magic shield in his office.

"How come there aren't other places in the school like your office?" I asked. "With the magic shield."

"There are, but they aren't used much anymore," he said.

I remembered the old dungeons Professor Halifax had told me about. "It seems like having a few more spaces like this could be helpful after the time bubble and all."

He frowned.

"Am I not allowed to talk to you about it?" I figured he knew. I also figured there wasn't really anything off the table with him.

"You can," he said. "I'm just still not happy with the lack of results around it."

"So they don't know who did it yet?" I asked.

"Do you want to know where I was?" he asked.

That wasn't what I expected at all. Dr. Green rarely told me anything. I'd gotten used to his ability to brush my questions off and get me off topic. This time, he'd moved me off topic by offering information. It wasn't his usual play. "Sure."

"I've been looking for any of your relatives that might still be alive," he said.

"Oh." I barely managed the word. It seemed an impossible thought. My shoulders slumped and I suddenly felt like my arms were too heavy. "And?"

He shook his head. "Dead ends so far, but I'm running into strange situations."

My brow furrowed and I waited in silence, worried that if I asked a specific question, he'd stop talking.

"I wasn't willing to share anything about your family with you because I wanted to have good news to share. Now, I'm starting to think that might not happen."

This was an angle I hadn't considered. I always figured he was hiding things from me, but I sort of made it more sinister in my head. "You were looking for good news?"

"Yes," he said. "You came from a large extended family so there was a good chance someone was out there. A cousin or aunt or something."

"But you can't find them?" My voice was small. I hadn't realized how much I wanted to find someone from my family until now. To have even a single person who shared a history with me would be amazing.

"Worse, when I find their trail, I keep finding that they've met the same bloody end as your parents."

My chest felt like it was being squeezed. "Because of their magic?"

"I suspect so," he said. "Time magic is illegal, but it's also rare. And we know it's inherited. I just never thought someone would target a whole family line because of it."

"How long ago?" I asked, not able to finish the sentence. I wanted to know how long ago the last member of my family had taken a breath. How long had I been as alone as I felt?

"Shortly before the thief died," he said. "Which makes me think she was the culprit."

I swallowed over the lump in my throat. That wasn't that long ago. Someone from my family had been alive after I found out I was a mage. "There's nobody else?"

"I'm not sure yet," he said. "I was following some tips I got about some of your father's relatives, but I wasn't successful finding them. I'm not sure if it's because they are gone, or if it's because they are much better at hiding than I am at seeking."

"Maybe they're out there then," I said, not sure if I believed it. I took a deep breath, hating the other thought swirling in my head. It was the selfish thought of self-preservation.

"Do you think it's over? That the thief was the one who was doing all of this? Or is there someone still out there hunting my family?" I felt terrible for asking, but I wanted to know what I was in for once I left the protective walls of the academy.

"I think it was the thief," he said. "But we can't be sure."

I nodded, not sure what else I could say or do. "This family you were tracking, were they near here?"

"No," he said. "They were supposed to be in the mountains, outside of a hidden fae settlement. None of the locals were helpful but I don't always give people the warm fuzzies when they see me."

"Maybe I could go," I said.

"You should go after you graduate. If nothing else, you can learn more about your fae heritage," he said.

I shook my head. "You've known the whole time, haven't you?"

"I told you, I didn't want to have this conversation with you without any good news."

"Yet, here we are," I said.

"I told you I didn't find the family I was looking for," he said. "I didn't tell you that I didn't have *any* good news."

I cocked an eyebrow. "Oh?"

"Your case was dismissed last week," he said.

The words didn't seem real. "Wait, what? Is that why Officer M isn't here?"

"He'll be here, but not to see you," he said. "I wasn't able to get Mr. Obscura's case dropped yet. But the council agreed that your circumstances were unique and you've been given a clean slate."

I covered my mouth with my hands as I laughed. That *was* good news. It wasn't as good as it would have been if he'd found some of my family, but it was incredible.

I lowered my hands to my lap. "So no more meetings with Officer M?"

He shook his head. "None."

I closed my eyes and leaned my head back, relishing the feeling of freedom. I'd been so worried that I'd accidentally do something wrong and end up in a prison cell.

"But you have to promise me you'll take more care in the future regarding your magic," Dr. Green said.

I opened my eyes and looked at him. "I will, I promise."

As I left the office, I felt like I was floating. This was a huge surprise and I hadn't realized just how much the parole was weighing on me until it was released.

It wasn't until I was sliding my key card into my door later that night that I realized Dr. Green didn't tell me *not* to use my magic.

And if there was one thing I'd come to learn about Dr. Green, it was that everything he did was with purpose.

Luka

Raven caught my gaze as soon as she walked into the room. I waved and then tapped the desk next to me indicating that she should join me.

She smiled, and headed toward me, dropping her backpack next to the chair before sliding into the seat. "Hey, thanks for saving me a seat."

"Any time, kitten," I said.

Coach Miller cleared his throat and the whole room fell silent. I could feel Raven's tension next to me. I slid my hand under the desk and rested it on her knee, trying to send as much reassuring energy as I could her way.

I'd been here a year longer than her and seen the trials first hand. I was ready to get out of here and move on with my life.

Raven, on the other hand, was one of only a few first year students who were going to complete the trials this spring.

"Listen up," Coach Miller said. "You are all here because you're required to take the trials three months from now. Consider this your only disclaimer warning that you could die in the trials."

"On that sunny note," Professor Halifax said, "congratulations to all of you for making it this far. If you're here today, you're here because you passed the practice trials last semester."

"Which are nothing like the real trials," Coach Miller said.

"True, the trials are more difficult and will require more individual skills, but you will be prepared by the time we reach the end of the term," Professor Halifax added.

"If you listen to us," Coach Miller said. "And don't get soft on us now."

I wanted to roll my eyes at Coach Miller. He was trying so hard to get us to freak out. But this was what we were here for. Part of our training for the trials required us to attend these mandatory meetings in the evenings leading up to the main event.

This was the first of many to come and if this was how they were going to go, I was even more ready for the trials to come so I could get out of this. Thankfully, we only had to endure six of these meetings. One this month, then they got more frequent as we got closer to the final day.

"We'll be working with you in small groups for the next few weeks," Professor Halifax said. "You've all been assigned specific times and places to meet based on your strengths. Group training will never be more than six students at a time and will focus on pushing you to improve in your weaker areas."

"Which means you're going to hate us for the next few months," Coach Miller said with a grin.

I really, really hoped I wasn't in a group with him. Though, I wasn't sure what they'd consider my weaknesses, so it was hard to tell.

Professor Halifax held up a folder. "Each of you has a folder with your unique training schedule. Traditionally, there are six meetings, including this one. This year, we've added a few additional meetings for some of you to help you prepare. Pay attention to your individual schedule and don't worry about what other people are doing. Got it?"

Affirmative murmurs sounded throughout the room as Professor Halifax and Coach Miller started passing out the folders.

I glanced around the room, looking at the familiar faces of the students I'd spent the last year and a half with. Some of them were more prepared than others. And there were one or two I was surprised to see in this room. They must have gotten very lucky during their practice test to be here today.

I caught sight of Ben and he gave me a quick nod before turning back to look at the front of the room. He'd probably been checking in on Raven.

Since our talk a few weeks back, we hadn't spoken much. We interacted on occasion at lunch or in the halls, but Raven was our buffer. With her around, we never had to have an actual conversation. Which was totally fine by me.

I tightened my grip on Raven's thigh, suddenly feeling protective of her. It was one thing to share your lover in the bedroom while you got to participate, it was another thing to let her go and enjoy someone without you. Honestly, there were times I was jealous of her and there were times I wanted her all to myself.

Having a mating bond with one person was odd. I'd always been so fluid in my attraction to others and only interested in sex as a form of entertainment and a means to an end to recharge my magic. With Raven, it was something else. It was about connection, intimacy, and love. I never knew sex could be that way.

Professor Halifax dropped a folder in front of me and handed Raven's to her. She took it and opened it. I grabbed the folder on the desk and opened mine.

I scoffed, hardly believing the group I'd been assigned to. This wasn't an accident.

"Well then," Raven said. "This isn't going to be awkward. Not at all."

I understood the sarcasm in her tone as I stared at the names. Raven and I were in the same group. With three others.

Ben, Matt, and Zach.

They'd paired her with her mates. Including the one mate I knew she still hadn't completed the bond with.

I wasn't blind to her attraction to Zach and whenever the two crossed paths, the sexual energy between them was enough to give my magic a buzz. It was only a matter of time.

Part of me wanted to encourage her to get it over with. But it wasn't my place. Unless of course, she wanted to invite me, which I was all for. Zach and his brother were two of the most handsome males I'd ever seen. I'd have no problem joining anything with either of them. Or maybe both?

"Luka?" Raven interrupted my thoughts and I turned to look at her.

"It'll be fine," I said.

"They have us scheduled to meet weekly," she said.

I glanced down at the paper again. That was unusual. "Is this during your independent study class time?"

She nodded. "I guess it's not so independent anymore."

"I guess not," I said. What was Professor Halifax getting at by doing this? I knew it was unusual for someone to have multiple mates, but it wasn't *that* unusual. It happened often enough that we weren't even a subject of gossip aside from the fact that we were dating.

"Alright, everyone. You've all been given your official warning. You might die during the trials, this is your last chance to drop out, and all that," Coach Miller said. "You begin your small group meetings based on the schedule in your folder. And some of you will be lucky enough to be working with me."

"Your group meetings count as class sessions and you're all expected to be on time and in proper uniforms," Professor Halifax added. "You're dismissed."

"Well, this will be fun," I said as I stood.

Raven gave me a weak smile. "Yeah, can't wait."

Out of the corner of my eye, I noticed movement. I turned to see Ben and both of the Obscura boys heading toward us. No surprise there. I was guessing they were even less thrilled about this set up than I was.

"Did you ask to be in a group with all of us?" Ben asked Raven.

"No," she said.

"It's probably because she's more powerful after each of the bonds with us," Matt said.

"Is that true?" I asked. That was news to me.

"Professor Halifax said something about that," she said.

"Then why haven't you hooked up with Zach yet?" I asked.

Nobody said a word.

"Seriously, if it helps you to get stronger, you should," I said. "Especially after the time bubble. Why not try everything you can?"

"I can tell you it's not from lack of trying on my end," Zach said.

"Seriously?" Raven said.

"What? I've never kept it a secret," Zach said.

"Maybe I didn't want you to feel like I was having sex with you for my own selfish reasons," she said.

"She's fine the way she is," Ben said.

"She could be stronger," I added.

"We're not having this conversation," Raven said. "I'm going to my room. Alone. I will see you all tomorrow in Professor Halifax's room."

Raven

I felt bad walking away from them when I knew all four of them mostly had my best interest in mind.

Except for Zach. I wasn't sure about him. He was harder to figure out than the others. He was such a flirt and was so upfront about sex. Plus, there was the whole thing about hooking up with his identical brother when he wasn't around.

I guess I never knew how to approach him or my feelings for him. While the attraction was there, and had been from the start, I'd held off. It was complicated enough, and I'd been able to avoid him and avoid the feelings I had for him.

But that wasn't going to work once we started having weekly meetings. Just the five of us and Professor Halifax.

What was she thinking?

I turned over in my bed and tossed the covers aside. Sleep wasn't happening tonight. I knew exactly why Professor Halifax was doing this and it was all about me. Matt was right, she all but told me to have sex with Zach to help strengthen my magic. And now she was putting the five of us together to go over things before the trials.

How was that going to work? I knew I had a mating bond with all of them. Including Zach. Being around all of them and their sexual energy was going to drive me crazy. Especially if I was still holding out for Zach.

That couldn't happen. I couldn't do that to myself or to Zach. The two of us would probably end up tearing each other's clothes off in the middle of the classroom.

I sat up, trying to tell myself that the only rational thing to do was to fuck him now. I had to. If I didn't, there was no telling what our libidos would make us do.

Plus, I'd been laying here thinking about him doing things with his tongue. And no matter what else I tried to picture in my head, he kept coming back to mind.

Determined to seduce Zach, I hopped out of bed. I wondered if I should put on something sexy. He probably didn't care what I was wearing, but I did. The tee shirt and shorts I was wearing were cute, but they weren't exactly screaming *take me, I'm yours*.

Quickly, I threw on a black lace bra and matching undies. Then I pulled on a long black jacket. It was the closest thing I had to a robe. It would have to work.

Slipping my key card into the pocket, I quietly left my room.

It was after midnight and as I crept down the hallway, I could hear the sounds of quiet music and muffled conversation from the night owls in my dorm. Thankfully, the common room was empty.

Taking the stairs two at a time, I bolted out of the dorm before Ben or anyone else could catch me. I absolutely looked like I was on a mission to get a booty call.

Probably because I was.

Keeping my head down, I walked through the halls, ignoring the occasional student I passed. Finally, I made it to the Mage dorm and started up the stairs toward the Obscura suite.

When I stopped at their floor, I discovered I wasn't alone. Standing in front of the door in a little black dress was Delores.

"Well, well, well," she said. "Someone's here for a nightcap."

"Yeah, I just had a question about something," I said, recalling the feeling of her fist in my face. I didn't want to experience that again.

She turned toward me, her hands on her hips. "I thought I told you to leave him alone."

"I'm visiting Matt, if you must know," I lied.

"Matt is out for the night." She stood there silently, her head cocked to the side.

I knew she was waiting for me to leave but I'd come here for Zach, which I was pretty sure she'd figured out. Plus, when she'd punched me, I wasn't prepared so I didn't know to defend myself or fight back. I wasn't about to make that mistake again.

I'd never thrown a punch, unless you counted my desperate clawing and scratching to get away from the men who attacked me the night I was brought here.

"I wonder how far I have to push you to get you to use your time magic," she said, taking a step closer to me. "I was hoping you'd do something after I pulled you down the stairs but that wasn't enough. Hitting you didn't work, that just knocked you out."

"You wanted to get me to use my time magic?" I knew she wanted to hurt me, but I didn't consider that she could be trying to set me up. And while I'd been officially released of my sentence, I knew they'd throw me back into meetings with Officer M at the least if I used my magic.

She shrugged. "I want you gone. Lots of us want you gone. You're causing a disruption in the way things work around here."

"I've never done anything to you," I said. "Maybe your ego is getting in the way of reality."

"You don't belong here," she said. "This school isn't just about learning your magic. It's also about alliances and networking. It's about finding partners in business and in love. And you went and snapped up a prince of hell, the gangster prince, and now you've got your sights on the crown jewel of this school. Getting in good with the Obscura family can make you set for life. Marrying one of them will keep your children and their children set for life. Get it?"

"I get it," I said. "You're a gold digger."

The door opened and I turned to see Zach. "Hey, ladies."

"Zach, tell this slut that we already have plans," she said.

"Um, I'm not sure why you're talking about my girlfriend like that," he said.

"You said you two weren't a thing," she said.

My brow furrowed. Zach and I weren't a couple. We'd never discussed it and we'd never been intimate. But something told me to keep my mouth shut here.

"Yeah, Zach's out," he said.

Delores's face turned crimson and her eyes widened. "Matt?"

I bit down on my lip to keep from saying anything. I was certain the man speaking to us was Zach.

"I thought you were out tonight?" she said.

"Maybe he's with some other girl?" Zach said.

Delores looked pissed and without a word, she turned and stomped away from us.

I held back the giggles until she was out of sight. "What did you do that for, Zach?"

Zach shrugged. "It's been a while since I pretended to be my brother."

"For a girl who says she's got a thing for you, she really can't tell you from Matt," I said.

"Most people can't tell us apart," he said.

"I don't get that. I used to have to look for the freckle on your hand but now I just know. You're not the same."

"No, we're not," he said.

"Is it really just you here tonight?" I asked, my mind going back to my original intentions.

"Yeah," he said. "Matt had to do something for our mom. He'll be back before classes start tomorrow if you want to come back then."

"I didn't come here for him," I said.

He cocked an eyebrow. "Really?"

I unbuttoned the jacket, letting it open enough that he could see that I was only wearing underwear and a bra underneath.

"You really did come for me, didn't you?" He grinned, then stepped back so I could enter the room.

As soon as I heard the door close behind me, I slid off the jacket and let it fall to the ground. Slowly, I turned to face him, a smile on my face.

"You are even more stunning without your clothes than I remember," he said.

"At least I didn't burn them off this time," I said.

"It's still early," he said, crossing the distance between us. "Give me some time to get you going. I have a feeling we'll make our own fire."

He grabbed me by the waist and a thrill of anticipation

rushed through me. A second later, his lips pressed into mine and my core instantly heated. Everything about this was right. The feel of his hands against my bare skin, the taste of his mouth on mine, the pressure building inside me, begging for release. It was as if my body had been desperately waiting for this.

Raven

Everything felt right with the world as Zach scooped me up and carried me through the room. I devoured him, my lips and his, working hungrily in unison. We'd waited too long for this and neither of us was willing to let go.

We bumped into walls a few times, but I didn't break the kiss and Zach didn't let go of me. I wrapped my legs around his waist and leaned into him more, sliding my tongue into his mouth.

He moaned against my mouth and I nearly lost control just from knowing that he was enjoying this as much as I was.

Finally, he pushed through a door and the two of us fell onto a bed in a heap of intertwined limbs. Bursts of magic trailed up my back and down my arms, sending shockwaves of tingles through me. Every touch was electric and I couldn't get enough of him.

Suddenly, I realized my panties and bra were gone. I didn't even notice Zach removing them.

My mind felt fuzzy with desire and I knew I wasn't thinking straight anymore. I'd do anything to feel him inside me.

Forcing myself to remove my lips from his, I leaned back and took a few breaths. My whole body felt like it was on fire. Everything about this was intense and holy shit I was turned on. "You're still dressed."

Zach grinned and then he climbed off the bed and stripped faster than I thought possible. We were both beyond the point of wanting foreplay and I knew it. We needed each other.

He hopped back on the bed and knocked me over while climbing on top of me. Then, he grabbed my thighs and pulled my hips to his. My ass came right up against his knees.

Leaning in, he held my legs up while positioning his hips between my thighs.

I wanted him so bad.

He didn't make me beg. In a single thrust, he was inside me fully and I cried out as the pressure of his size gave way to pleasure.

He held on to my thighs as he thrust hard and fast. I gripped the sheets with my hands, hanging on while he pounded away. Each thrust was so intense in the best possible way.

Zach lowered my legs and leaned in close so our bodies were pressed together. Slowing his rhythm, he moved his lips to mine. This kiss was slow and sensual but just as powerful.

I grabbed hold of him, keeping his chest pressed against mine as he continued to thrust. My hips joined his, moving in unison. Even though the pace had slowed, there was no easing of pleasure. On the edge of orgasm, I dug my fingers into his back, urging him to continue.

My magic was building alongside my climax. I could feel it surging through my veins, bursts of power mingling with pleasure. It was too much.

Tossing my head back, I cried out as an orgasm rippled through me in intense waves. He thickened inside me, groaning as he reached his climax. I held on to him as he stared into my eyes, the two of us panting and sweaty. Magic still thrummed in my veins, as if begging for escape. The sensation made it difficult to breathe, as if I needed another release.

Zach pulled me closer, groaning as he reached his climax. As soon as he did, my magic seemed to respond, exploding from me in a surge of power I had no control over.

Decorations fell from the walls, lightbulbs exploded, pillows burst, sending stuffing flying into the room. Then, just as quickly as the destruction began, it all froze, suspended in the air as if someone hit a pause button.

Zach climbed off of me and the two of us looked around the frozen destruction, dumbstruck.

"What's happening?" I asked.

"Did you do this?" he asked.

"I think so," I said.

My magic had built during sex and this was the result. It was destructive, everything around us was in ruins. But there was a peace to it in its frozen state. "I stopped time."

I felt trapped, like everything inside me was locked away. This wasn't happening. This couldn't be happening. I had worked so hard to contain my magic and keep it from going beyond my control.

I was too powerful to contain it. I should never have completed the mating bond with Zach.

A warm, steady hand pressed against my upper arm. "Deep

breaths." Zach turned my chin toward him and locked his gaze on mine. "Deep breaths. This is okay. You gained more magic and you lost control. It doesn't mean we can't fix it."

I nodded, surprised that he knew exactly what I was thinking. "How?"

"Whatever you did to make it happen, can you do the opposite?"

"I don't know." It felt different now. I felt different. Like the vibrations of the magic never fully went away. They seemed to call to me, connecting me to the objects that were held in suspension around us. The destruction around us.

"Did I do this or did you?" I asked. "I mean, I know the time thing was me, but broken things."

"I think it was all you," he said, taking my hand in his. "But we can fix it."

That's when I realized that *he* wasn't frozen. Every time I'd used time magic in the past, it impacted the people around me, freezing them.

"You're not hurt," I said, squeezing his hand, "and you're not frozen."

"I'm not." He grinned. "Either you spared me or the bond is keeping me safe."

I hadn't considered that. It was clear that something had shifted after we sealed our bond. My magic had changed. I let go of his hand and tiptoed to the door. Standing behind it so I could cover the fact that I was naked, I poked my head out.

Silence.

Had I frozen everyone?

I wasn't sure how far my magic could reach and I was terrified to leave the room to find out. At least the lights in the hallway and the rest of the suite were still attached to the wall. I hadn't continued the destruction beyond the bedroom.

I padded back to the bedroom where Zach was patiently waiting for me on the bed.

He extended his hand. "What if we try to fix it together? Didn't Professor Halifax say that your magic would grow with your bonds? Maybe I can help."

"Yeah, that's a good idea," I said, settling down on the bed next to him. I accepted his hand and took a deep breath. We needed to fix this.

"You take the lead, I'll send my magic in as support but you're the one who has to guide it," he said.

"Okay." My whole mouth suddenly felt super dry. I licked my lips and swallowed, trying to send the nerves away.

Taking a deep breath, I focused on finding my magic as Professor Halifax had instructed. It burned brightly within me, a raging fire instead of the usual spark. I gasped, surprised by the power I could feel in myself. It was obviously not the same as the magic I'd had prior to having sex with Zach. The bond with him had really changed me.

I just hoped it was for the better.

Using that fire, I guided it, thinking about reversing what I did. Turning back the destruction.

My lower lip trembled as I felt the power coursing through me. Zach's magic mingled with mine, sending in a boost of power. Focusing on the task, I pushed the magic forward.

Suddenly, the broken glass and stuffing receded, floating through the air until it returned to where it came from. Before my eyes, the fixtures repaired themselves, the pillows refilled with fluff and the damage was undone.

When everything was back to the way it had been, I let go of the magic, sending a wave of power from me like a ripple. I could feel it in the air, radiating away from me.

I wasn't sure what I did, but I knew I'd restarted time.

My skin tingled as the remains of the magic crawled through

me. I could feel it better than ever before. It was responding to me now, working with me instead of fighting me.

Turning to the lamp next to the bed, I sent a burst of magic and the light exploded. I called to my time magic and halted it, freezing it in an arc of shattered glass. I waited a heartbeat then called it back, rewinding time to repair the broken glass. With a twist of my wrist, I started time back to normal. I turned at looked at Zach.

He was still holding my hand, his eyes wide, lips parted. "You've got it now, don't you?"

I nodded. "I can control time."

"Yes, you can," he said, a smile on his lips.

I thought he'd be terrified. I was. This was a lot of power. Not only could I stop time, I could reverse it, which meant, I could change it.

For the first time, I fully grasped exactly how powerful and dangerous this magic was. "We just have to hope nobody felt me doing that."

"If they were frozen, they won't notice," he said.

Bang. Bang. Bang.

"Open the goddamn door, mage," someone shouted from behind the door.

Zach let go of my hand. "Stay here, I'll take care of this."

He quickly pulled on a pair of jeans and walked out of the bedroom, closing the door behind him.

I scavenged around for something to wear and ended up pulling on one of Zach's white button up shirts. Thankfully, it fit me like a dress.

"Where is she?" Ben's voice called. "Tell me she's with you."

I opened the door and walked into the living area to see Ben, red faced and tense, yelling at Zach.

"What is going on here?" I called.

Ben physically relaxed the second he saw me. He walked right past Zach toward me. "The thief must be back or there's a new one or something. Someone stopped time. I don't think it was from outside the school because I wasn't stopped and I could leave the school. Didn't you say for the bubble the exits were sealed?"

"Yes," I said.

"We have to get you somewhere safe," Ben said. "I'm sure my dad can keep you hidden."

"Ben…"

"We can't let them get you, it was too close last time," he said.

"Ben!" I shouted this time, gripping his upper arm with my hand. He finally stopped talking and looked at me. His eyes were wild, his brow lined with worry.

"Ben, it was me," I said. "I did it. I didn't mean to, but I can control it now."

He looked from me to Zach and then back to me. "You and him?"

I nodded. "Apparently it unlocked all of my magic."

"About damn time," another male voice drawled.

I looked up to see Luka standing in the open door.

"Now we don't have to worry about you so much," he said. "Though, we should probably close this door if we're going to talk about this."

Luka closed the door. "What do you need from us?"

I glanced at three of my four mates and I could feel the connection brewing between us. Their magic was calling to me, as if I could easily reach for it and take it. Completing the bond with Zach had changed everything.

"I can start time again," I said, walking toward the couch without waiting.

I sat down and closed my eyes.

"What are you doing?" Ben asked.

"Shh," Luka said. "Let her do this."

I took a deep breath and found my magic, the way I had found the magic when time was last stopped. Only, this time it was my magic, and not someone else's. This time, it was much easier to hone in on the vibrations.

And this time, I grabbed hold and commanded the magic to my will easily.

I opened my eyes, certain that I'd restarted time.

"Is it done?" Zach asked.

I nodded.

"Nobody can say anything about this," Ben said.

"Agree," Zach and Luka said at the same time.

Something felt like it changed between the three of them, too. But I couldn't put my finger on it. And I wasn't certain they were ready to accept it.

Raven

While all four of my mates seemed to be getting along for my sake, I still wasn't sure how it was going to go when the five of us were in the same room with a professor for an hour or two.

The week flew by, all of us slammed with work as our courses picked up in anticipation of the impending trials. There were still nearly three months before the trials, but if first semester was any indication, I knew the time was going to rush by.

Though, at least this semester there wasn't anyone after me. At least I hoped not. We still didn't know anything about who had caused the time bubble outside the school or why. But I was going to go with no news was good news.

Plus, I finally felt confident in my own magic. I wasn't supposed to manipulate time, but I *could*. And I might have tested it out a few times in my own room.

Whatever the ability to shatter and destroy objects was, I didn't know. As far as I knew *that* wasn't illegal. It was destructive and dangerous, just like my time magic could be, but I'd never heard of it before. That didn't mean it wasn't something equally as forbidden so I wasn't about to ask.

With the elimination of my parole meetings, I was getting a bit braver or riskier, in testing what my magic could do. I felt in control of it now and while all four of my mages urged me not to use it, I had to see what I could do. On a small scale. And never in front of anyone.

A knock sounded on my door just as I was sliding my backpack over my shoulders.

"You ready?" Ben asked.

I opened the door and stepped into the hallway. "You're going to be nice, right?"

"I'm always nice," he said.

"I mean to Luka, Matt, and Zach," I said.

He frowned.

"I'm serious, Ben," I said.

"I've never done anything to any of them, have I?" He asked.

"No, but you've also never been in a room with just them and me before, either," I said.

"Did you ask them to be nice?" He asked.

"Yes." And I had. All week. Every time I was alone with any of them, I reminded them that I wanted them to at least pretend to get along.

Since adding Zach to the mix, I'd had to be even more aware

of my time. None of them wanted to share me, which I understood because I honestly didn't want to share them.

The conversation regarding what we were never really happened. All of us just sort of fell into an uneasy understanding that I was mated with each of them and that I was going to spend time with all of them.

It would be a hell of a lot easier if they got along, though. Or if I could occasionally go out with all of them at the same time.

I'd had one awkward dinner with both Matt and Zach that ended with me leaving before dessert and bolting to my room. They were both so territorial. I was hoping it would wear down eventually.

We reached Professor Halifax's classroom without any other conversation. Knots twisted in my stomach as I tried to tell myself it was going to be fine.

Ben opened the door for me and I stepped inside to see Luka, Matt, and Zach already there.

Playing hacky sack.

And laughing.

Together.

Huh. Maybe this wouldn't be as bad as I thought.

"Want in?" Luka asked.

"No thanks," I said. "I've never had the coordination to keep it going."

Luka kicked the little bean bag to Matt. "Ben?"

"I'm good," Ben said.

I smirked, trying to picture my brooding alpha shifter playing hacky sack with a couple of mages and an incubus. It was a ridiculous image.

The ball landed on the floor and all three of them groaned.

Matt grabbed it off the ground and held it up. "Another round?"

"Toys away," Professor Halifax said. "You five are my strongest group by far and I fully expect focus and discipline from all of you. My groups don't fail the trials. You will not let me down."

"No pressure," Luka said.

"Tons of pressure," she replied, clearly not amused by his tone. "This group is made up of a prince of the underworld, the would-be princes of the mage community, a half fae, and the son of the most feared man in the supernatural world. If any group has an unfair advantage, it's you four. And I happen to know that Coach Miller will be designing a trial with you four in mind."

"Wow," Luka said. "When you put it like that we sound like the dream team of magic students."

"Because you are," she said. "This is the most elite school in the world for students with magic. And you five are the cream of the crop here. All eyes will be on you. You should expect jealousy from others."

I'd already experienced my share of jealousy. Delores had spent all week glaring at me. I knew as soon as we were alone, she was going to try to fight me again. This time, though, I would be ready.

"The competition has always been every student for themselves," Ben said. "I'm guessing something has changed?"

"Yes." Professor Halifax pursed her lips and looked at each of us in turn. "Coach Miller designs the trials. This year he has determined that it will be a team trial. You all pass, or you all fail."

"Well, good thing we've got the best team possible, right?" Luka threw his arm around Ben and Zach, pulling them close, a huge grin on his face.

Ben looked like he was about ready to slug him. Thankfully, he just shrugged him off and took a step closer to me.

Luka dropped his arms. "Seriously, though. This has to be aimed at Raven. Coach Miller has been out for her since the beginning."

"It makes it easier for her to pass with us along to help, though," Zach said.

"You haven't seen how he treats her in gym class," Luka said. "If he designed it this way, you can bet he's going to go for our weakness to try to take us out."

"So we figure out each of our weaknesses and work on it," Matt said.

"We all have the same weakness," Ben said.

"Me," I said, feeling anxiety twist in my gut. "If he wanted to make it fair, he'd have thrown us with random people."

"That's true," Professor Halifax said. "Thankfully, he's not as attuned to magic and he has no idea that the four of you together are far more powerful than he could ever imagine."

"So what's the plan?" Luka asked.

"The five of you have to learn how to be a unit. To support the whole group using all your skills. Including your magic." She put her hands on her hips. "Can everyone set aside their differences for a while to help the group?"

"Of course we can," Luka said. "We all want out of here, right?"

"Right," Matt and Zach said in unison.

"Ben?" Luka turned to the shifter. "Right, buddy?"

Ben growled. I elbowed him in the side. "Right," he said.

"So how do we do this?" I asked, hoping to get everyone distracted while they were sort of getting along.

"Magic meld," Professor Halifax said.

"Wait, what?" My eyes widened. Magic melds were dangerous. Everyone knew that.

"Not yet, but that's the goal," she said. "You four are bonded to Raven. But to be stronger, you need to connect all of your magic."

"I'm not sure I want to bond with anyone else," Ben said.

"You won't bond the same way you did with Raven," Professor Halifax said. "The mating bond is different than a magic bond."

"I don't know," Matt said. "It seems to have bonded us."

"Because you were already meant to be her mate," Professor Halifax said.

"Mages don't do that," he said.

"Fae do," I said, starting to feel uncomfortable. Were they regretting what we did? "But we didn't know I was fae then."

Matt crossed to where I was standing and stopped in front of me. He grabbed my hand and squeezed. "I'm damn grateful that you are. I don't want to undo what we have."

I nodded, appreciating how easily he could feel my thoughts.

"Alright, everyone's feelings need to be set aside. Coach Miller brought in a dragon to try to take some of you out in the practice trials. There's no telling what he'll do this time."

"Don't you have some say?" I asked.

She shook her head. "I was lucky I was able to snap up your group for private sessions. He wanted you five for himself."

I couldn't imagine what weekly sessions with Coach Miller would have looked like. Probably a whole ton of running the stairs for no reason.

"Where do we start with all this if the magic meld is the grand finale?" Luka asked.

"You need to learn each other's magic. You need to be able to sense it, feel it when it flares, and channel it with any member of your group."

"How?" Ben asked.

"We start simple," she said, walking toward the benches where we sat for class. "You boys sit."

My mates followed her instructions, sitting awkwardly with large gaps between each of them, on the front bench.

"Raven, you stand here." She pointed to a place in front of the guys, in the middle of all of them.

I took the position.

"Now, you need to use your magic and they are going to focus on what your magic feels like until they can identify it in a whole room full of mages using magic," she said.

"Okay," I said.

"Just go with a basic fire ball," she said.

I moved my hand, the fire coming to me easier than ever before. There were so many benefits to that final mating bond snapping into place.

"You four, hone in on her signature, find her magic. Memorize it," she said.

We repeated the exercise over and over. Me making fire balls, my mates staring at me. It was exhausting. As I continued the process, though, something started to change. I could feel other magic joining mine. With each round of creating fire, the tingle of magic grew, leaving an electric charge hanging heavy in the air.

I could feel all four of them.

And it was doing things to me.

As the magic grew, my face flushed and my core heated. I bit down on the inside of my lower lip, trying to keep my thoughts on the task at hand and not the growing dampness in my panties.

What was happening to me?

The more magic they sent my way, the more aroused I got. My breathing grew heavy and it wasn't from the exertion of the magic. If I wasn't careful, I was going to jump on them. Any one of them. All of them. I never wanted them so badly in my life.

Finally, we were dismissed.

I said the fastest goodbye ever to the four of them and rushed to my dorm room, closing the door behind me. Stripping my clothes off as I walked toward my bathroom, I tried to push the arousal from my mind. What the hell had just happened?

Thank god for cold showers.

Ben

Raven left so quickly that none of us got to check in with her after our session. Good thing she lived in the room next to me. And I had a key.

I should probably have knocked but she *did* give me the key for a reason. And tonight felt like a good reason. While most of me wanted to check in with her, I couldn't deny the arousal that had flared during our training session.

It didn't make sense. Usually, I was able to keep my libido in check around others but tonight it was on overdrive. I needed to make sure Raven was okay. I also just needed her. Badly.

I could hear the sound of the shower running when I stepped into her room. It was tempting to strip down and join her but last time we'd had sex in the shower we'd had company. I wasn't sure I wanted to bring that memory back to her right now. Right now, I didn't want to share her at all. I wanted her to myself. All of her.

The bathroom door opened and Raven stepped out, a towel wrapped around her. She jumped in surprise when she saw me. "Ben! You scared the shit out of me. Why didn't you knock or something?"

I held up the key.

"Right," she said. "Maybe I should ask for that thing back."

I grinned. "You don't want to do that."

She dropped the towel to the floor. "You're right. I don't."

My eyes widened. I wanted her. I came here hoping for this. But I never expected to be greeted this way.

Raven walked toward me slowly, her wet hair dripping down her naked body. She was stunning without her clothes on. Her skin was so soft and all of her curves drove me wild. I wanted to touch every inch of her.

She stopped right in front of me. "Are you going to get naked or do I have to do it for you?"

She didn't have to ask me twice. Quickly, I stripped off my clothes. Then, I grabbed her around her waist, picking her up so I could kiss her. She wrapped her legs around my hips and I stumbled forward, our lips locked together in a punishing kiss. Her fingers worked their way through my hair as the kiss deepened.

Somehow, we ended up in the bathroom and I set her down on the countertop next to the sink. Her legs were still wrapped around my waist and I was now at the perfect height to enter her.

As if she knew what was coming, she slid her hips to the

edge of the counter and then she smiled at me. It was a playful, knowing smile. As if this had been her plan the whole time.

It was enough to drive any man to his knees.

Tilting her hips up so I had better access, I entered her in one quick thrust.

She cried out in a gasp and tossed her head back, her elbows bracing against the countertop for support. Her breasts moved up and down with each thrust and her moans of pleasure were driving me wild.

I leaned down, taking one of her nipples in my mouth, slowing my thrusts. She grabbed my back and slid her palms down to my hips, encouraging me to pick up the pace. I obliged, moving my mouth to her lips, devouring her as I continued to fuck her.

Her kisses were distracted and I could tell she was already nearing climax. After a few more thrusts she pulled her mouth away from mine, gasping for breath as she reached orgasm.

I wasn't ready yet but watching her close her eyes and hearing her cry out was almost enough to push me to the edge.

As the orgasm finished, she regained some control and she reached for me again, pulling herself closer to me. Then, she laced her fingers through my hair, pulling my head closer to her. She kissed me hard then sucked my lower lip into her mouth, flicking it with her tongue.

The sensation was all I needed to get me there. I groaned into her mouth as I came.

The two of us remained there for a moment, her arms wrapped around me, as we caught our breath.

I couldn't help but think that I was the luckiest man in the world.

Luka

Raven winked at me from her place in the circle of students gathered to watch another combat session in gym. Coach Miller had taken to doing them every few days. Drawing two random students and making them battle it out. So far, I'd avoided it and so had Raven. I wasn't sure why but I was grateful.

I had a feeling Professor Halifax would have some choice words for the coach if we showed up to our training session later today with black eyes. She kind of scared the shit out of me. She was far more powerful than I realized before. But she was helping us, so I supposed that made up for a lot.

Our last two sessions with Professor Halifax had gone better, Raven was quickly learning how to adapt to finding our magic and weirdly, I was starting to feel the magic from her other mates.

I swore I could feel Ben's energy during breakfast. It was weird. Not necessarily in a bad way, but it was different. And a little hot. Every session finished with me needing a cold shower.

Raven and I had managed a few meet ups in the library the last few weeks and our encounters seemed to super charge my magic. It was wild. Just the two of us was the same amount of energy that I'd get from a whole orgy.

I sort of wondered what it would be like for my magic if she invited her other mates. It had to be something extraordinary. But I wasn't about to ask her for that. Not with Ben still glaring at me when I got too close to her. The twins might be more amenable to it.

"Luka, in the circle," Coach Miller called.

Fuck. It was a matter of time before he was going to toss me in here. Shoulders slumped, I shuffled in, using my body language to let whoever the competitor was know that I wasn't into this. With any luck, it would be someone else who would half ass it until the coach got bored.

"James," Coach Miller called. "In the circle."

I lifted my chin in greeting to the ice demon entering the circle. His dorm was on the same floor as mine and when we were first year's we'd shared booze in our rooms a few times before we got too invested in our studies. Well, before we both found girls. We hadn't talked in a while, but I knew he was a tough opponent.

"Shake hands," Coach Miller said.

I walked up to him and we shook. James looked focused, his jaw set. Guess he was going to take this fight seriously.

"No physical touch in this round," Coach Miller said. "Magic only. Let's see what a couple of demons can do."

I frowned. This had to be a trap of some sort. Or he was trying to get me to show what I could do before the trials. Based on what Professor Halifax said, Coach Miller was out to get us.

"Ready, go!" The coach shouted as he backed out of the circle.

James launched a ball of ice at me right away and I lunged to the side to avoid it. I had to think fast. The coach was expecting a show here, but I'd never fully shown my magic to anyone. Sure, I'd done the basics to pass classes and complete assignments, but I never let it all out.

And I knew my magic was charged more than it ever had been after all those library *study sessions* with Raven. I craved her touch again just thinking of it. But now wasn't the time to imagine Raven's lips on my cock.

I dodged another ice ball, and another. Noting that James already looked frustrated. I had to do something.

If he was going to throw ice, I'd throw fire. That was what was expected of me, right?

I conjured a fire ball and hurled it toward James. Of course he moved out of the way and the fire landed on the gym floor. Another student threw water on it, leaving a charred black circle that sizzled and smoked.

"That's all you got?" Someone in the crowd called.

I frowned. I didn't want to hurt him. I didn't want to use my full magic. Even Raven didn't know the true destruction I was capable of. In a weird way, my own magic wasn't all that different than Raven's. It just wasn't illegal and it wasn't pleasant.

James circled me, then sent a shimmer of ice across the floor, right under my feet.

I slipped as I tried to move away from the attack and landed on my side. My hands heated, responding to the attack involuntary. As I pushed myself to standing, my heat melted the ice into a puddle of water.

A few murmurs sounded in the group around us. They seemed to like that trick.

"Come on, man," James said. "Quit holding back."

"Oh, trust me, you want me to hold back," I said.

"I don't think you've got it," he said. "A few fire balls? What else you got? You going to seduce me to death?"

The gathered crowd laughed.

A circle of icicles rose up around me, blocking me in. I sighed. It wasn't even fair. I could melt these with a single touch.

"Come on, man," James said.

I caught Raven's eyes. She wasn't laughing. She looked like she was holding her breath.

That's when I felt it, a surge of magic rush through me that didn't belong to me. It was Raven's magic and it was wild.

It felt like a million tiny pins entered my skin at once, then as quickly as they came, the pain stopped. My magic hummed to life, embracing Raven's entangling with mine.

The icicles around me caught on fire – the ice literally burned. Stunned gasps sounded from the crowd.

I wasn't sure how I did it or what I did to cause it, but it created quite the spectacle.

With a flick of my wrist, I summoned the flames to melt the ice. Then I sent the flame in a straight line toward James.

James jumped to the side, but I was ready. The fire surrounded him, blocking his exits the way he'd done to me.

Quickly, James sent his ice to the flame, but the flame grew taller. I felt my magic grow, intensifying with every passing second.

James continued to throw ice at the fire but it didn't stop.

"You want to see what I can do?" I asked, drunk on the magic swirling through me.

James looked at me, eyes wide.

I snapped my fingers and he fell to the ground, asleep. Then, I made him stand and commanded him to walk toward the flames.

Raven could stop time and alter it.

I could command sleep and make the sleeper do what I wanted. It was a cruel gift. One I'd taken care to hide.

"Stop," Raven called.

I turned to her and suddenly, the impact of what I'd done came crashing in around me. I commanded the flames to die out and let James fall to the ground.

He laid there, unmoving, surrounded by a circle of black ash.

"Well," Coach Miller said. "You learn something new every day, don't you?"

I swallowed and kept my jaw set, not wanting to give him anything more than I already had.

"Wake him up, Demon," Coach Miller said.

I turned to James and called to my magic, using it to wake him from the very deep sleep I'd sent him into.

James sat up and looked around, groggy. It took him a minute, then he seemed to remember what had happened. He groaned. "I guess I deserved that."

I grinned, glad he was taking it well.

"Never encourage a demon," Violet said.

"Good advice," I said.

I walked over to James and offered my hand, helping him up.

"Thanks, man," he said.

"You two going to fuck next?" Coach Miller asked.

I glared at him. He was such a prick.

"Time for laps. All of you. Go. Run."

I rolled my eyes and walked away from the circle of students who were still staring at me, heading toward Raven.

She was already at the track but she was waiting for me to catch up to her. "What was that?" She started jogging.

"I think I used your magic," I said.

"That part I got," she said. "What did you do to him?"

"Put him to sleep," I said.

"And you can control him when he's asleep?" She asked.

"Yeah," I said.

"Can you do that for anyone who is asleep?" She asked.

I could see a flicker of an emotion that was hard to pinpoint in her eyes. Was she afraid of me? "I can, but I don't."

She smiled. "Looks like I'm not the only dangerous one."

Raven

"Luka." I waved to the incubus as he approached Professor Halifax's door. The others were already inside but I wanted to check on him again after this morning's gym class. He hadn't come to lunch and I was worried about him.

His brow furrowed when he saw me and he hurried over to where I was standing. "You okay?"

"That's what I was going to ask you," I said. "You didn't come to lunch."

"Sorry," he said. "I needed some space."

"From me?" I asked, surprised the words came out. They

sounded needy, like I was making it about our relationship. "From my magic, I mean?"

It had weighed heavily on me since not seeing him at lunch. Our magic had connected in gym, there was no denying that. I wasn't sure how much of what he did was because of me. I was pretty sure I'd sent him extra magic.

Watching him look so uncomfortable had sent a shockwave through me. I had to help him and while I didn't mean to send my magic, it was the result.

"No," he said. "It's just that nobody knew that I could control people like that. It's not exactly a welcome skill set."

"What about other incubi? Can they do that?" It seemed like it would be a normal thing for an incubus. They could create dreams and travel into the dream world. Being able to make people physically respond while sleeping didn't seem too far of a stretch.

"Not really," he said. "It's something my family can do, but most incubi can just use fire elemental magic and manipulate dreams. They can't transfer that to a physical body."

"But your family can?" I asked.

"Yes," he said.

"So why would anyone be surprised?" I asked.

"I guess I didn't want them to know," he said. "I know it sounds stupid, but it's not a power I enjoy. I've seen it abused. Nobody should lose their free will."

"I agree," I said. "But we know you're not going to do that."

"I did it today," he said. "I was trying to avoid it, but it just sort of happened. I lost control. I haven't done that since I was a kid."

There was more to this story than I was getting. "What happened, Luka?"

"Please don't make me talk about it now," he said.

"Help me understand then," I said. "Help me know what I can do to make you feel better."

"You can't give me access to your magic again," he said. "I can't be trusted."

"Luka, that's not true. I trust you with my life," I said.

He shook his head. "If you knew what I did, you wouldn't be saying that. Just promise me, will you? Promise me that if we have to, you share your magic with Ben or Matt or Zach. Anyone besides me. There's something unstable in me and I can't lose control around you."

My heart ached seeing him like this. I wanted to help. I wanted to heal him. Luka was usually so carefree and sarcastic. Whatever had happened in his past was something so dark that even he couldn't laugh it off. I wanted to protect him and wished that I could erase whatever was causing him pain. "Okay, Luka. If that's what it takes, I'll share magic with the others before I give it to you."

"That's not what I asked," he said.

"I can't promise that I'll never share it with you," I said. "You have to know how much you mean to me."

He nodded. "Alright, I'll take it. Life or death only."

"Agreed," I said. "Now, is there anything I can do to cheer you up?"

He grinned. "I can think of several things but we can't really do any of them in this hallway while the others are waiting for us."

"Rain check?" I offered.

"Oh, god yes," he said.

The door opened and Ben looked out at us. "Did you two forget that you have to turn the handle and push to get the door to work?"

"Aren't you funny?" I asked as I walked toward the door.

Ben tried to hide his smile. As much as he and Luka butted

heads, I had noticed them talking more often at lunch lately. It was almost like they were friends. I knew better than to push it but I had to admit, I was hoping they'd continue to get along.

"Oh good, we're all here," Professor Halifax said. "Have a seat. I have news."

The room suddenly felt very small and my legs felt heavy as I moved to the bench with the others. There was no way this was good news.

I sat down and Ben quickly sat next to me on my right side and Matt slid in next to me on the left. Luka and Zach sat next to Ben. The five of us stared up at our professor, waiting to hear whatever she had to say.

Professor Halifax's expression was grim as she walked over to the five of us. "Listen carefully. There has been a change to this year's trials."

"What kind of change?" Matt asked.

She glared at him and he pressed his lips together into a tight line. She looked away from him, taking us all in with her focused gaze. "Due to something we're not allowed to know about, they've moved up the date of the trials."

"What does that mean?" Zach asked. "*Something we're not allowed?*"

Her nostrils flared as she took a deep breath. "I don't know. They won't give the reason. But apparently there's some kind of risk or something going on so they've moved up the trials."

"To when?" I asked. This wasn't good for me. My magic was finally doing what it was supposed to do. In fact, it was stronger than most of my classmates. But I had only been here a semester. I needed more time. I wasn't ready.

"The end of the week," she said.

"What?" I blurted out.

"That's crazy," Matt said.

"Why would they do that?" Luka asked.

"That's not how it's supposed to go. Are they going to move up graduation too?" Ben asked.

"Good question," I said. "We're supposed to be here till June, right?" I wasn't ready for the outside supernatural world. I was still wrapping my head around the fact that I had four mates and that I was going to have to find something to do for a living after I finished here. But I thought I had more time.

The five of us started talking over one another, peppering Professor Halifax with questions.

She held up a hand. "Silence."

Her words echoed through me, knocking me back a little. There was magic behind that word. She'd never used magic on us before and it freaked me out enough to shut my mouth without question.

All four of my mates were silent too. They'd clearly felt the magic behind that word, too.

Professor Halifax looked tired. She closed her eyes and pinched the bridge of her nose for a moment, then opened her eyes and dropped her hand. "I tried to petition this, but I was overruled. I don't know how this will impact graduation. I just know that this will be our last session together and we didn't even touch on the things I wanted you to learn."

"The magic meld," I whispered.

She looked at me. "Yes. But you're not ready."

"Do you think we can complete the trials without it?" I asked.

"I hope so," she said. "I can't in good conscious ask you to attempt a magic meld with all of you."

She couldn't ask, but that didn't mean we couldn't try it on our own. "How dangerous would it be if we tried it?"

"Raven," Luka said.

I ignored him. "You said before that it should work, right? That it would finish our bond?"

"Yes," she said. "In theory. I don't think it would cause any harm, but you would have so much magic running through you that you might lose control."

"What would it mean if she lost control?" Matt asked.

I was glad I wasn't the only one thinking about trying it behind her back.

"I don't know," Professor Halifax said. "Best case, she breaks things."

"Worst case?" Ben asked.

I turned to look at him, shocked as hell that he seemed to be considering it.

"Worst case," Professor Halifax said. "She could create a time bubble or open a portal she didn't intend to open."

"Just from doing a magic meld?" I asked. That seemed extreme. Okay, well, maybe not the breaking things. Could I really make a time bubble, though? Or open a portal? Both of those seemed extreme.

"It's possible," she said. "But it's just theory at this point. I haven't ever seen what a half fae in a magic meld could do."

She tapped her chin with her index finger, lost in thought for a moment. Then she looked at me. "Though, since you have a mating bond with them, it should be safer than a typical meld. And you did survive the meld with the Obscura twins."

It was as if she was trying to talk herself into telling us to try it. Then she shook her head. "No, it's too risky. I can't in good conscious ask you to attempt it."

"Well, what else can we do?" Zach asked.

"Study, get some rest, make sure the five of you can communicate quickly and can rely on each other. There's not really enough time for anything else," she said.

"That's disappointing," Ben said.

"Professor, do you have anything for us to work on today or

should we work on our communication skills independently?" Matt asked.

"If you have anything you want to work on with me, now's the time, otherwise, you can prep however you'd like," she said.

"I think it's time for us to work on some strategy as a group," Matt said. "Our suite is big enough for the whole group."

"I'm in," Ben said.

"Oh no," I said. "This is a bad idea."

"We're not going to do anything crazy," Matt said.

"Yeah, maybe we'll just come up with our own hand signals to communicate faster," Zach said.

I shook my head. I knew exactly where this was going.

"I've always wanted to see the Obscura suite," Luka said.

I lifted an eyebrow and looked over at Luka. "You too?"

I was outnumbered. It was clear they wanted to attempt the magic meld. And I was pretty sure Professor Halifax wanted us to try it too. *Fuck.* I was the loose cannon here. If I didn't pull my weight and something went wrong, I wasn't going to get a second chance this time. Plus, Matt would be in the room with me and he was still having weekly meetings with Officer M.

"You sure?" I looked at all my mates.

Ben stood and offered his hand. "Come on, we've got trials to prepare for."

Raven

"So we're really doing this?" I asked, still not believing my eyes. All four of my mates were in the same room at the same time. And none of them were fighting.

It wasn't like they fought regularly, they'd just all made it clear that they didn't want to share me when it was our time. I'd had to find ways to balance being with each of them. The only exception was Luka and Ben who sat at the same table during lunch with me. Matt and Zach never joined us.

Yet, here we were, all standing in the living room of the Obscura suite as if we were getting ready for cocktails.

"I don't see what choice we have," Matt said. "If Coach Miller is trying to set you up to fail, it could be an attempt to push you to use your time magic."

"I'm getting much better at controlling that," I said.

"Not good enough," Zach said.

I bit down on my lip, recalling the moment I'd stopped time with him. The sex had been incredible and the power surging through me afterword had been nearly as good. I never realized how much of a thrill having power could be until that moment and it scared me.

"We don't know what this will do," I said. "I can't let anything bad happen to any of you."

"Raven, you can't always be the one protecting everyone else. You have to let us take care of you on occasion," Luka said.

Ben growled and I turned to him, feeling my own tension rise alongside his. "Raven, the four of us think this is best and we're willing to take the risk. What are you holding back for?"

I wasn't really sure. It should be enough that the rest of them were on the same page, but it still made me uncomfortable. I knew how strong my magic got when we were together. When Zach and I bonded, my magic temporarily went beyond my control. What would happen if I bonded with all of them that way at the same time?

"What if I lose control and hurt you?" I asked, finally realizing what my fears were.

"I don't think you will," Zach said. "Remember after our bond snapped into place and you stopped time?"

I nodded. "That's exactly what I'm afraid of."

"You're forgetting the part about me and the others not being impacted by your magic," he said.

I blinked a few times, letting his words sink in. He was right. The rest of the school seemed to have been frozen in time by my magic, but all of them had been kept safe.

"I don't think we can be harmed by your magic," Zach said. "I think it's part of the bond."

"Raven," Ben said, taking a step closer to me. "I need to see that cocky girl who beats me in poker right now."

"And the wild child who runs head-first into a dragon attack," Luka added.

"The mage who took out two grown men who tried to kill her," Zach said.

"And the woman who got this group of misfits to come together for a common goal," Matt said.

My throat stung as tears threatened. Never in a million years did I think I'd have even one man who made me feel this way. But here I was, with four. Four men who supported me and rallied with me. They believed in me. In us.

"Alright," I said. "If you all think it's for the best, I'm in."

A few minutes later, we'd pushed all the furniture against the walls, clearing a large space in the middle of the room for the five of us to sit in a circle.

Like a group of teenagers holding a seance at a sleepover, we held hands. A heavy tension hung in the air that surprisingly didn't come from the fact that my mates were holding hands.

It was coming from an impending sense of doom regarding the upcoming trials. None of us knew for sure what Coach Miller was up to with the change of date or what he'd create in the course, but we knew he was dangerous.

"So where do we start with this?" Ben asked.

I looked up and gave him a reassuring smile. He was across from me, the twins on either side of me. Since the three of us had successfully done this before, we thought it might be best to keep the connection between us and try to expand it. It was all theory, though. None of us actually knew what we were doing.

"It really isn't much different than what we were working on with Professor Halifax," Zach explained. "Only this time, instead of just sending our magic to Raven, we'll be sharing it with the whole circle."

"Try focusing on the person next to you," I suggested. I had no idea if I was right, but it felt right. "We can share our magic through our connected physical bonds, linking all of us together."

Almost instantly, I felt a surge of magic spike through me and I nearly let go of Matt and Zach's hands. They squeezed me tighter, responding to my lack of pressure. It reminded me to hold on and I squeezed back.

The room filled with a familiar charge that I'd come to associate with magic. Only this time I caught the scent of leather and smoke and pine, mingling with the electric scent.

I inhaled, realizing that the air was charged with the magic of all of us. Ben's raw energy, Luka's smoke, the pine I'd caught on Zach and Matt. It twisted and rolled through the air, taking my own electrically charged magic with it.

Magic buzzed around me, vibrated to my very core. Usually, when so much magic surged through me, it was painful. This time, it was raw and sensual. Every inch of me felt alive. As if I was suddenly hyper aware of everything around me.

I could feel the calluses on Matt's hand and noted how much rougher they were than Zach's. I could hear Ben's heart beating in time with my own. I could feel Luka's warm breath from across the circle.

Everything was on overdrive.

Including me.

Along with the rise of the magic and the sensations of the room came the rush of arousal. I'd felt it before when channeling magic with my mates. Only this time, I wasn't sure I was going to be able to turn it off.

My heart raced, my face flushed. I could feel myself losing focus as lust mixed with the influx of magic. I bit down on my lip, fighting against it. I couldn't let it take over. I had to fight against it.

We just had to finish the magic meld. I just had to make it through to the end.

I lifted my knees, squeezing my thighs together as ripples of magic shot right through my core. I pressed my lips together to keep from moaning. It was too much.

What the hell was wrong with me? Why was this happening? Was this normal? Why the hell was I so turned on?

Nearly panting, I couldn't take it anymore. I had to break contact or I was going to climax right here in front of all of them.

I tried to pull my hands away from Matt and Zach. They both held on, but I pulled harder, finally breaking free of Matt's hand.

Turning to Zach, I looked at him, silently begging for him to release his grip on my hand. Instead, he pulled me in to him and pressed his lips to mine.

Zach

Bursts of magic exploded through me, making me feel like my veins were on fire. But it wasn't painful, it was hot. Like really, really hot.

Raven's hand tugged against mine. She was trying to break free.

The urgency in her action only heightened my desire. I had to keep her. I had to claim her.

I didn't care that we weren't alone. I didn't care if that shifter ripped my arms off for taking her right here. I was going to have her and there was nobody who could stop me.

Grabbing her hand tighter, I pulled her closer to me and before she could resist, I pressed my lips to hers.

She moaned into the kiss and I could feel her practically melting into me. She wanted this as badly as I did.

I slid my hand under her shirt, half expecting resistance, but unable to control myself. She was everything. I had to have her. Without breaking the kiss, I managed to unbutton and remove her shirt. As soon as it was off, she leaned forward, knocking me to the ground.

I looked up at her, startled but pleasantly surprised by her taking control. She straddled me and quickly unhooked her bra, tossing it to the side.

Another set of hands reached around her, grabbing her breasts and I noticed that Luka had joined in. There was a momentary flare of jealousy, but it subsided quickly. It was like this was supposed to happen. We were all connected through Raven and there was an intense vibration in the room that made me think we were now connected on a deeper level.

Raven turned and pressed her lips to Luka's before turning her attention back on me. She gave me a quick kiss, then she climbed off of me and walked across the room to where Ben and Matt were standing and watching the action unfold.

She grabbed each of them by their hand and led them toward the center of the room where Luka and I were waiting.

I could feel the hesitation and the tension rolling off of Ben as if I was inside his head. I wasn't guessing on his emotions, I was feeling them. The thought made my head spin. How was that possible?

I turned to look at Luka and I could feel his arousal and his excitement. Unlike Ben, he was ready for this. He lived for this. Whatever had happened during our magic meld *had* connected us. I could tell how Raven's other mates were feeling.

While there was an overwhelming sense of hesitation coming

from Ben and Matt, there was one emotion that every male in this room had in common: lust. We were all ready to jump on Raven.

And as I watched her slide her hands up Ben's shirt and pull it off over his head, I knew she was ready too.

Raven

My skin was on fire with arousal. I needed him. I needed all of them. Ben felt the most tense out of all my mates and I had a feeling if I won him over, everything would be fine. I wasn't sure where those thoughts were coming from, but I went with it. Lust and desire were making my thoughts foggy. All I could think about was sex.

Ben didn't resist when I pulled his shirt over his head, though he remained rather stoic in his expression. I could tell he was aroused, his cock gave that away with the tent in his pants.

I pressed my breasts against his chest as I worked his zipper. It only took a few seconds of skin on skin for him to let go.

His arms were around me before I finished unzipping his fly and his lips were on mine by the time I got my thumbs hooked in his waist band. As his lips moved with mine, I slid his pants down.

His tongue darted into my mouth, massaging mine. He was just as desperate as I was now, all of his resistance was broken.

I pulled away from his kiss but grabbed his hand and dragged him with me as I walked toward Matt. Sliding my fingers through his sandy hair, I pulled his head closer to me so I could kiss him.

Matt matched my pace hungrily, his hands exploring my body, caressing my breasts, teasing my nipples.

While kissing Matt, I reached for Ben's massive cock, stroking it with my free hand. I could feel his hips working in time to my movements and knew he was enjoying the attention.

A new pair of hands joined Matt's, exploring my breasts, while another hand grabbed my ass. Someone slid a finger inside me and I moaned into Matt's mouth.

A hard cock rubbed against my ass and Matt pressed his erection against my hips. I let go of Ben and quickly helped Matt and myself out of our clothes.

The whole room felt like it was pumped full of sexual energy and I wondered if this was how Luka felt every time he fed. It was heady and it made me want to never leave this room again. I wanted to stay in here with the four of them forever.

Luka grabbed my hand and led me back to the rug in the middle of the floor, but Ben grabbed hold of my other hand. The look in his eyes was fierce and possessive and hot as hell.

Ben grabbed me and lifted me up, carrying me to one of the couches that had been moved out of the way. He sat down, positioning me so his cock was lined up between my thighs.

I braced myself with my knees, straddling him on the couch so he didn't enter too quickly. Ben was the largest of all my mates and while I enjoyed it rough from time to time, tonight wasn't like that. It wasn't fast and dirty. It was beautiful and sensual and slow.

He entered me slowly, giving me time to adjust as he did. Once he was in, I moved my hips, riding him with undulating motions. Luka was next to me again and I half expected Ben to send him away, but he ignored him, keeping his eyes locked on mine.

I grabbed Luka's hand and pulled him closer to me. With my position, I was perfectly placed to give his cock some attention with my mouth. I closed my lips around him, using my tongue to write the letters of the alphabet on his shaft. He groaned and grabbed a handful of my hair, guiding my movements.

Ben's hips moved up and down, making me moan around Luka's cock. We continued on like that for several minutes before I felt Luka's cock thicken in my mouth. He pulled out and turned away from me, his body shaking as he came.

Zach was next to me now, his cock by my shoulder. I adjusted slightly so I could take hold of it, moving my hand up and down the shaft as I bounced on Ben's cock.

Behind me, a pair of hands reached around, fondling my breasts and a cock pressed at my rear entrance. I'd only done that once before, with Ben and Luka, but I had enjoyed it. Whatever was going on with the five of us had me so relaxed that I wasn't stressed about trying it again.

I glanced behind me to see Matt preparing to enter me. He moved slowly, taking time for me to adjust as he did. I was grateful he wasn't as large as Ben. With each inch he pressed into me, I felt fuller and was surprised to find I was more aroused. I gasped as his full length slid into me and slowed my movements.

I turned to Zach and took his cock in my mouth, flicking my tongue along the head and down the shaft until he came.

After a few thrusts, Matt groaned as he came, sending me into a full body climax. Shaking and panting, I leaned into Ben, kissing him. He thrust a few more times and came with a groan.

Sweaty and exhausted, I climbed off of Ben and collapsed on the couch, snuggling into my wolf shifter. Luka sat on the other side of me, resting his head on my breasts. Matt and Zach were on the floor, on either side of my legs.

At this moment, all of us were physically connected. Each one of my mates was touching me. Even through the post sex haze, I could feel their magic working in time with mine. I could feel their satisfaction and a little bit of unease.

The meld had bonded us even stronger than we had been before it happened. And I had never been more grateful in my life.

Raven

The rest of the week flew by in a blur of classes, stolen moments with each of my mates and bouts of nervous pacing at the thoughts of the upcoming trials.

Tomorrow, everything would change.

But tonight, I wasn't going to let it get to me. Or at least I was trying not to. Makayla was propped on a pile of pillows on her bed and I sat in the squishy hot pink chair next to her bed.

Tonight was about relaxing and trying not to let the impending doom of the trials create too heavy of a fog around us.

So far, it wasn't working well. We were both wound tight, our conversations always coming back to the trials.

"Your partners aren't going to let you down, right?" I asked Makayla again. She'd been paired with two wolf shifters, a mage, and a demon. It was an odd group, though I suppose no weirder than my own.

"We'll be fine," she said. "Besides, I'm much more worried about you."

"Me?" I was surprised to hear her say that. I had told her far too many details about the last week. "I'm pretty sure I'm going to be just fine."

"You're in a unique situation, for sure," she said. "Paired with your four mates is good and all, you know they'll do anything for you but at what risk?"

"I know," I said. "We discussed that. I'm the weak link in the group."

She shook her head. "You're not the weak link. Don't ever say that. Nothing about you is weak. You're the bond that holds them all together. You're also the one the others would do some-thing stupid to protect if they don't trust you."

"They trust me," I said.

"But can they trust you to take care of yourself?" She threw a pillow at me and I caught it. "If I were in your group, I'd worry about myself and *know* that you were fine. You can take care of yourself. If they're too busy watching what you're doing because they feel like they have to swoop in and rescue you, they won't pay attention to what they're doing."

"You're right," I said. "But I think they get that. I hope."

"I hope so too," she said. "There's nobody in my group that I'm emotionally attached to. We'll help each other, sure, cause we have a vested interest in passing. Not because we care if the other survives."

"Brutal," I said, tossing the pillow back to her.

"It's the point of the trials, though." She pulled the pillow to her chest and held it tight. "To weed out the supernaturals who can't hack it. That's why they do it. It's some kind of leftover Spartan thing. But they don't put us out in the cold as babies. They wait till we're so-called adults."

"We're going to be fine," I said, not believing my own words. I knew I could count on my mates and I knew we prepared the best we could, but it still seemed overwhelming. I mean, the practice trials had a dragon. How were they going to top that? "What do you think it'll be like?"

"No idea," she said. "This is the first time they've ever moved it up or done it in groups."

A knock sounded on the door and Makayla jumped off her bed and raced to the door. I wondered if Remi was here for a booty call. She was still seeing him but still not willing to call it anything other than a casual fling.

"Anyone in the mood for a pizza?" A familiar male voice called.

I turned to see Luka standing in the doorway, a cardboard box in his hands. To my surprise, he was accompanied by Ben, Matt, and Zach.

My brow furrowed. Why were all four of them together? Without me? I wasn't sure that had ever happened before.

"Pizza?" I asked suspiciously as I walked to the door.

Makayla took it from Luka. "Thanks. But you're still not invited. Girls only tonight."

"We're not trying to intrude," Matt said. "We just wanted to drop some things off for the two of you."

"Together?" I asked, a hand on my hip.

"Well, if we're going to have to work together tomorrow, we have to be civil at least," Luka said.

"We're trying to lock down how each of us feels, you know, with the bond," Ben said.

"Oh." I nodded. That made sense. It was easy for me to grasp which of my mates I felt with the new emotional bond we'd forged, but I was mated with each of them. They weren't mated with each other. Just me. It was still a strange thing knowing they could communicate and feel each other after our magic meld.

"Offerings," Zach said, holding up a box of Swiss Cake Rolls.

I grinned. "Thank you."

Makayla took the box from him and set it on her desk next to the pizza box. Luka passed a six pack of Coke to her also.

"We'll let you two get back to makeovers and pillow fights." Luka winked.

"Right," I said. "I'll write all about it in my diary later."

Ben cracked a smile at that one and I was glad to see him letting down his guard a little.

"Sleep well," Zach said.

"You too." I felt a little wistful as Makayla closed the door. While I was glad that I didn't have to choose one of them to be with tonight, I did miss them when they weren't with me.

"You know, maybe I'm wrong about this whole boyfriend thing," she said. "I didn't realize you could get them to bring you things."

I laughed. "I didn't either."

She grabbed the food and set it on the middle of the floor. The two of us sat cross-legged on the rug and then grabbed a slice of pizza.

"You know, Remi wants me to meet his mom," she said.

"No." My mouth dropped open in surprise. "Does that mean the two of you are getting more serious?"

She shrugged. "Maybe."

For the next hour we ate junk food and giggled about boys. If it weren't for the trials tomorrow, it might have been one of the most fun nights of my life. Instead, the conversation eventually came full circle, back to the weight of tomorrow.

"I suppose we should get some sleep," she said.

"Yeah," I agreed.

We cleaned up the food and I gave her a quick hug before heading to my room.

My bed was cold and lonely tonight. I knew Luka wouldn't visit me in my dreams. We needed to be rested and prepared for tomorrow. That didn't mean I couldn't have a great dream of my own, though.

I imagined myself on an island as golden sunshine warmed my skin. Nearby, was the sound of the ocean waves lapping against the shore. I could almost smell the sunscreen I imagined Ben was rubbing on my back. Luka was blending drinks while Matt and Zach played volleyball.

Then, I imagined that we all got naked. I fell asleep before I got to the good part.

Raven

None of us knew what to expect as we waited in the men's locker room. We were the only group here right now and I knew Violet's group was after us. Makayla's group was in the women's locker room, with a start time ten minutes before ours. I wondered how she was doing.

I wasn't sure if the fact that we were only staggered ten minutes apart was good or bad. I was betting on bad.

"Remember to use the bond," Matt reminded us.

"We know," Ben said. He still sounded like he was pissed that he had to have the others in his head.

"Also remember that they're probably going to try to use me as bait or something," I said.

A rush of emotions surged through me. Mild panic mingled with anger and fear. My mates were worried about me already.

"I can take care of myself," I reminded them.

"Yes, but you can't go out there expecting to be the hero," Luka said. "You could have died last time."

"You would have," I said.

"It's time," Ms. Halifax said from the doorway. I hadn't even heard her open the door or walk in. That wasn't good. We hadn't even started yet and I was already letting my emotions distract me.

I had to stay focused.

Ben grabbed my hand and gave it a quick squeeze. "We can do this."

I nodded and tried to force down the wave of fear rising in the pit of my stomach. I had to stay calm to help them stay calm.

They would all try to protect me, but they were also counting on me. And I wasn't about to let them down. Lifting my chin, I gave Ben's hand a squeeze before letting go. "We're ready."

Professor Halifax opened the door to the gym wide for us, leaning against it to hold it open.

Beyond her was nothing.

Just darkness.

My palms felt damp already, but I forced myself forward. One foot in front of the other.

As soon as I stepped into the gym, the darkness seemed to collapse around me with crushing force. I turned back toward the locker room, intent on grabbing hold of whichever mate was nearest but the light from the door was gone.

"Ben?" I called. "Luka? Matt?"

No answer.

"Zach?"

My words echoed through what seemed like an endless expanse of nothing. I extended my arms in front of me, feeling blindly for anything. Slowly, arms still out in front of me, I turned in a slow circle.

There was nothing there.

It was just me.

Where had the others gone?

My heart pounded against my ribs as fear made my chest constrict. I was alone and in a dark empty room, similar to the recurring nightmares I'd had since I was a kid. The only thing missing was the sound of dripping water and the bars of the cell.

Only, this wasn't a dream. It was real. And it was terrifying.

I tried to relax and take a few deep breaths. My mates and I had a connection. I should be able to find my way to them through that bond. Closing my eyes, I searched for the emotional ties that bound us. I should have some kind of flicker of emotion. Some way to feel them, to reach them.

The only thing I could sense was the beating of my own heart.

I opened my eyes and tried to adjust to the dark. This shouldn't be happening. What did they do to us? Where were we and how was I cut off from them?

I suddenly felt like I was suffocating. There wasn't enough air. I dropped to my knees and took more breaths to steady myself. There had to be a way out of this. What was I supposed to do?

They told us this was a team event, but what if we were actually on our own? What if my mates were already through this? What if by sitting here, I was failing the trial?

Determined to fight through this, I forced myself to stand. Balling my hands into fists, I lifted my chin and took a few cautious steps forward. Nothing happened. The ground felt stable.

Was this just the gym with all the lights off? What kind of trial was that?

That's when I heard it.

A roar that made my hair stand on edge.

I wasn't alone.

I was in the dark with a monster.

How had the others vanished so quickly? Where did Professor Halifax go? My pulse raced and I could feel tension spreading through my body. None of this made sense. Then again, I was in a school with magic. What did I expect?

The practice trials had dragons. Honest to god, fire breathing, trying to kill me dragons.

What the fuck kind of creature could be worse?

Ben

The light went out from behind us almost instantly and I turned to see the door was closed. I couldn't sense Professor Halifax anymore. She must have gone into the locker room, leaving us alone in the dark gymnasium.

Not even the emergency lights were on, making the space feel both small and endless all at once.

I reached for where Raven should be and my fingers met with nothing but air. Brow furrowed, I took a careful step forward, reaching out with my hands.

I expected to run into someone. I did not expect to still be standing here alone. "Raven?"

No response.

"Anyone there?"

Nothing.

Fear began to build, a sensation I wasn't comfortable with. I had to be the one in control, I had to be brave at all times. That was my job. It was something I excelled at.

I wasn't used to being afraid.

But I wasn't used to having something I was afraid to lose. My own life on the line wasn't enough to cause me anxiety. It was the fear of not knowing if Raven was safe.

She'd been right here next to me. And now she was gone.

Everyone seemed to be gone.

I didn't like that I could sense the emotions of the others or that I could feel when they were near, but now I was grateful for it. I should be able to find Raven and the others based on the bond from our magic meld.

I shook out my hands and tried to clear my thoughts. Magic like this wasn't so different from what we did with the pack, but that was with wolves. And only while we were in our wolf form. While human, I couldn't feel the others.

Quietly, I waited. There should be something here. A sense of fear that wasn't mine or a flicker of hope from someone who had found a way out.

Instead, it was just me and my wolf. At least I could feel both sides of myself in this desolate darkness.

Frowning, I spun in a slow circle, looking for any light I could use as a guide. This was just the gym, after all. And if the practice trials were any indication, we simply had to get to the other side. Find the exit, win the trials.

It shouldn't be so hard.

It also shouldn't be so easy.

Because as of right now, there were no obstacles I could tell, other than the fact that it was dark and that they'd separated us from our group. So much for a group challenge. They built that up and then divided us first chance they had.

That was probably part of the plan, but we'd talked about this and we knew what to do. If anyone was separated or if we had a chance to get through on our own, we were to take it.

Though, I never intended to follow that plan solo. I always assumed I'd have Raven with me. She was the one thing that could change the plan. If I knew she was safe, I could keep going. She was strong, I knew that. But how could I cut through here without her when I didn't even know where she was?

"Raven?" I tried again, hoping she'd hear me. I just wanted some sign that she was alright.

Again, I was greeted with silence.

Shaking my head, I slowly moved forward, keeping my guard up. I had to find her. There was no way I could go for the exit until I had her with me.

Suddenly, the ground rumbled and something roared. It was a screeching kind of roar, the kind that made you wince against the sound.

I wasn't sure what it was, but it was big.

Luka

The creature screamed into the darkness, shattering the silence with its cry. I knew that sound. I would recognize it anywhere.

But how the fuck did they get a malacoda here?

The evil serpent like creatures that guarded the depths of hell were notorious for their insatiable appetites and fierceness. They could walk on two legs like men but were four times the size of a normal man. Their claws and the huge spiked tail could slice through most objects, flesh and bone included.

They were carnivores who chewed on the bones of their victims until they devoured the body whole.

These were not the creatures that you should be letting out of hell. They were not to be trusted. How did they pull this off? Did my mom send one here? If she did, what was she playing at? Even she didn't go near the malacodas unless she had a sacrifice to offer them.

And I was not in the mood to be a sacrifice.

"Raven?" I whispered her name. She had to be close. We all came through the same door. I'd been feeling around in the dark for several minutes, but none of this made sense.

What had they done to the gym to cause this separation between us? What kind of magic had they used? Whatever they did, they blocked our connection and they left no traces of magic in the air.

It was as if we were in a vacuum where magic didn't exist.

The malacoda screamed again, setting my teeth on edge. That beast made my head hurt just from its cry.

Fuck. We were in trouble.

There was no facing off against one of these beasts. Our only chance was to get past them to the exit.

"Raven?" I attempted again, not wanting to go too far from where we'd come in. I knew I should go, that was our plan. Get to the exit no matter what. But how was I supposed to leave her?

The scent of sulfur and rotten flesh filled my nostrils and though I couldn't see it, I knew the malacoda was close.

Quietly, I moved away from the smell, arms out in front of me to feel for any obstacles.

As I moved farther away from the monster, I started to feel something. It was faint and fragile, but it was there. The tiny flicker of magic that only Raven could make me feel.

She was close to me, or at least closer than she had been.

Relying on the connection we had, I continued away from the monster, adjusting my direction based on the strength of the magic I could feel.

It thrummed in my chest, calling to me.

She had to be nearby but all I could see was darkness. This was a time for faith. Faith that our connection was stronger than whatever the hell else was in this dark room.

I wished I would have learned more about the creatures that lived in hell. Silently cursing my lack of paying attention in school, I crept through the darkness. What was it about those monsters? Were they the kind that could smell fear? Did they drain magic with a single touch?

I froze, recalling something that explained a whole lot right now.

They absorbed light.

Not just breaking lights, they sucked it in, leaving a black, empty void. Much like the one we were standing in now.

So as long as the creature was alive, we were stuck in the dark. And we had no chance against this beast. Even with weapons, it was a suicide mission.

My only hope was to find Raven and get us the fuck out of here.

Matt

Frustrated, I gritted my teeth. There had to be a way to create light. I was good at this. I was good at using magic. I was a fucking fire elemental mage from one of the most powerful magic families of all time.

Any flame I made only lasted a second before fizzling out to nothing. I couldn't even see the smoke in the black expanse of nothing around me.

What the hell was this?

It wasn't the same as just turning off the lights. I wasn't an expert on darkness, but this was like a black hole or something. And apparently, I wasn't able to add any light to the room.

Whatever beast was circling the space with its eye-watering screech was clearly not something I wanted to mess with. So maybe it was for the best that I wasn't drawing attention to myself. But I couldn't feel Raven and it sent a heavy weight of dread in the pit of my stomach.

Where was she?

I was right behind her when we came in. I was right behind everyone. Yet, I was alone. I couldn't feel any of the others. Not Raven, not any of the other males. It was as if I was in some kind of vacuum where magic and light were sucked away into a void.

What the fuck was going on here?

The beast screeched again, making the floor rumble. I wrinkled my nose as the scent of something awful wafted through the air. It smelled like burning and death.

Trying not to inhale too deeply, I instinctively moved away from the smell, knowing that whatever caused it was bad news.

The only thing I did know was that I had to get out of here. And I knew that if I wandered in circles trying to find Raven, she'd be pissed at me for not getting myself out.

I laughed, thinking about how mad she'd been when I took the blame for her using her time magic.

What I wouldn't give for her to use it now. If she froze time and found some light, the five of us could walk out of here away from whatever the monster in the dark was.

But I knew she wouldn't do that.

Maybe she was already out of here?

I needed light. If I could see, I could find her. I could check and make sure she was okay. I could also find out if the awful monster noises were just Coach Miller trying to scare the shit out of us.

I could picture him doing that. Trying to make some kind of psychological terror with noise and darkness.

I wanted to believe that the threat wasn't real. But there wasn't any way to explain my inability to create fire. Or the fact that this dark wasn't normal. It was heavy and thick. The kind of darkness that could swallow you whole.

Carefully, I walked forward, my arms extended in front of me. If I could find a door, I could let in some light. It might be enough to draw the others toward me.

I just needed some light.

Zach

I thought I heard someone calling me. "Raven? Is that you?"

My voice was swallowed up by the darkness around me.

Shaking my head, I kept walking. It felt like I'd been walking for hours. How long had we been in here?

All I was doing was walking in circles, feeling for walls or people or god forbid the creatures making those horrible sounds. Making fire would be stupid. It would draw the monster to me, but it was tempting. The sinking darkness was starting to make me feel a little bit like I was at the bottom of the sea. And not in a good way. Like in the cement shoes kind of way.

My breaths grew shorter and I had to force myself to inhale and exhale slowly, calming myself. It was so claustrophobic in here. I knew we were in the gym. I knew the room was huge, but it didn't feel that way right now.

I took another step and my foot slipped on something, sending me landing on my back with a thud.

I groaned. "Fuck"

Aching and a little dazed, I rolled to my stomach and set my hand in something wet and warm.

And slimy.

It was either drool or shit from whatever creature was roaming around the room.

I had to swallow down the vomit that rose to my throat as I wiped my hands on my pants. When I got out of here, I was going straight to the shower.

Maybe I'd bring Raven with me when I found her. I kept telling myself that staying positive would help get me through this faster and there was nothing more positive than thinking about Raven naked.

The thought didn't last long through, as my feet stepped in another pile of something wet. Immediately back in the present reality, I side stepped, hoping to be free of whatever this substance was. I tried to breathe in through my mouth, afraid of smelling the goo that was all over me.

A low rumbling growl sounded from behind me, the sound making my bones rattle. I froze.

Whatever had left the fluid all over the ground was behind me. And there was no amount of breathing in through my mouth that would cover the stench of death and fire breathing down my neck.

Fear and adrenaline spiked and I knew I had two choices. I could run or I could turn and attempt to fight an unseen monster.

Running was probably the smarter choice. But sometimes I made stupid choices.

Slowly, I turned around to face the beast.

I could smell it, the rotting, putrid scent as it breathed its warm breath on my face. The creature was waiting for something. For some reason, it wasn't attacking. It didn't make one of its shrill cries. It was just standing there.

This was my chance. If I could take it down, Raven and the others had a shot to get out of here unharmed.

Fire was my best weapon. It came to me easily and it was reliable. Quickly, I called to my magic, igniting my hands. The flame rose, for a moment I could see the horrible monstrous face of the creature.

It had a huge head like a giant but the teeth were like those you'd expect to see on a tyrannosaurs rex. Its long, lanky limbs were capped by fingers and toes with massive claws. Between its naked legs was a tail lined with spikes. The creature was hideous and horrifying all at once.

Extending my hands, I commanded my fire to release. Instead, it just fizzled out.

Quickly, I called the fire again. Once again, it illuminated the monster then died before I could do anything.

It was as if the magic was being pulled away from me. What was going on?

The creature growled again, the same low rumbling that felt like someone had the bass on way too loud. It made my teeth chatter and vibrated in my bones.

There was no way that was a good sound.

I had no weapons. I had no magic. The monster in front of me was twenty feet high with claws that could take down a yeti.

I turned and I ran.

Raven

Ahead, I saw a crack of light as if there was a door in the distance. I'd been walking around here for what felt like hours, desperately trying to find my mates and avoid the monsters.

I was sure I'd walked past here before and I'd never seen a light. But then again, in the dark everything sort of looked the same. For all I knew, I'd been circling the same little area and finally turned a different direction.

Moving slowly, I walked toward the light. Hopefully, that meant someone got out. I wanted to know that Ben, Luka, Matt, and Zach were all safe. For a while now, I'd started telling myself that maybe they'd listened to me. Maybe they were all out of here already and that's why I couldn't sense them.

Maybe they were beyond the door, waiting for me to get through and join them. The thought motivated me enough for me to pick up the pace.

I moved faster, desperate to reach the light.

The closer I got, the more hopeful I felt. My chest filled with flutters of anticipation as I realized it was actually a door ahead of me. An actual way out.

This was it, I was almost done. Was I really going to finish the trials? It seemed too easy, but I didn't want to complain. I just wanted to get out of here.

The gym was scary as hell in the dark.

Reaching ahead, I felt a doorknob. Tears stung the back of my eyes. I'd never been so emotional about a door before in my life. Being alone in the dark with just the sound of monsters screaming was enough to break anyone.

I paused, my hand on the doorknob. Suddenly, I wasn't sure I should open it. What if it was a trap? What if it released more monsters? In all this darkness, there was only this one door.

A monster screeched again, the sounds making me wince in pain. It was worse than nails on a chalkboard. Whatever that thing was, it was terrible. I did not want to come face to face with it. Especially in the dark. Especially when all the magic I had tried didn't work.

We were defenseless in here. And I had a feeling that those monsters wouldn't be willing to turn on the light so I could at least know where to try to land a kick. Cause that was the only weapon I had. I could try to claw it to death, but something told me it probably had worse claws than I did.

The door was my only chance.

Holding my breath, I turned the doorknob.

A rush of air blew past me, sending my hair whipping around

my face. I had to close my eyes against the bright light for a moment, then had to squint to try to make out what was beyond the door.

The wind pulled me away from the darkness of the gym, through the open door. I fought to hold on to the door handle. I needed to keep this door open, just in case the others were still in there. If I could prop it open, they could see the light.

The wind grew stronger and I lost my grip as I was dragged away from the gym and thrown to the ground.

As soon as I was on my feet, I ran back to the door, desperate to get it open. I couldn't feel any of them. None of their magic signatures, none of their emotions. Which meant they were still in there with the monster.

I tugged on the door handle, kicked the door, pounded on it. Screaming in frustration, I shook the handle again. Nothing. It wasn't going to budge.

There had to be another way in. I raced down the hall, hoping to find one of the other entrances to the gym. I wasn't sure what I'd do if I got back in, I just knew I had to get to them.

I couldn't feel any of them, but that didn't mean they weren't in trouble. In fact, it made me worry even more. My heart pounded and awful thoughts flooded in. What if they were already dead? What if they were hurt and couldn't get out?

What the hell was Coach Miller playing at by having a monster like that in there? And what was with the dark room? You'd think there'd be some obstacles and some things we could do to show the skills we'd gained here. Instead, we'd been left as monster food.

Fueled by my anger, I ran faster down the hall, stopping at any door I found that might lead to a back entrance to the gym. None of them opened except for one that was filled with cleaning supplies.

I skidded to a halt at the end of the hallway, peering out to where my classmates were moving around the school. Maybe someone out there had an answer. An idea of how to get in, or a weapon I could borrow.

As I stared at the hallway, I realized something wasn't right.

Narrowing my eyes, I studied the figures in the hall. *No.* No, no, no. This wasn't right. This couldn't be.

None of my classmates were moving. All of them were frozen in place, mid step, mid conversation, even one mid-jump. Someone had stopped time.

Like the time it happened while I was in Dr. Green's office, I knew it wasn't my doing. There was someone else here using time magic. Last time, Officer M had told me it was someone outside the school. Was that still the case or had someone found their way in?

If they did, it was possible they were looking for me.

Hoping that the time stop had also applied to monsters, I raced toward Dr. Green's. His office was magic proofed. He might be sitting in there right now not even aware of what was going on.

I got halfway to his office when someone walked out of a room in front of me. I stopped, heart pounding as I stared at Professor Halifax.

"Thank the gods you're okay," she said. "Are your mates with you?"

"No," I said. "They're still in the gym. What's going on?"

"Time bubble," she said. "Hurry, in here."

I followed her toward her classroom. "Were you in your back room? How long has this been going on?"

As soon as I stepped into the classroom, I knew I was fucked. Staring back at me, a wide grin on her face, was the magic thief. The magic thief that was supposed to be dead.

I heard the door close behind me and everything started to come into place all at once.

Professor Halifax was the one who killed the thief, she was up and moving after the last time bubble, she'd made sure I was in a trials group with my mates. For all I knew, she was the one who moved the trials up.

All of it was a trick.

"You're supposed to be dead," I said, glaring at the thief.

"Funny, so are you," she said.

I balled my hands into fists and clenched my jaw as I stared at the fae who had killed my parents and tried to do the same to me. I wasn't going to let her win. Even if she had help, I wasn't going down easy.

Professor Halifax walked around me and stopped in front of me. She was in an emerald green tunic and black leggings with thigh high boots today. Her long hair hung loose down her back, tucked behind her pointed ears.

"Why?" If I was going to die, I at least wanted to know why.

"It's nothing personal," she said.

"I think trying to kill someone is usually personal," I said.

"You sound like a human," the thief said.

"Half human," I said. "And if not killing people is what humans are known for, I'm happy to embrace that side of myself."

"You would," she said, then she turned to Professor Halifax. "I don't understand why I can't just kill her and take her magic."

"I told you, we need her," Professor Halifax said.

The thief rolled her eyes in a very human gesture and walked over to the front row of benches. She sat down and crossed a long leg over her other leg. Leaning back in her seat, she stared at me, as if she was waiting for me to do something.

"What am I doing here?" I asked.

"You and I have been working on opening portals for months now," Professor Halifax said.

"So?" I asked.

"So, I need you to open one with me," she said.

"That's not going to happen," I said.

"Oh, I think it will," she said.

"Just open it yourself," I said.

"I'm still up for taking her magic and us doing it," the thief said.

"I've waited too long for this," Professor Halifax said. "The last time you tried to open it you just made a time bubble. I told you, killing her isn't enough anymore."

"So that's what that was," I said.

"If she's not strong enough to do it after stealing my parent's magic, I won't be strong enough. Just let me go," I said.

"You weren't strong enough," she said. "Not until you completed that bond with all of your mates."

"Seriously?" I shook my head. "That's what this was all about? That's why you moved up the trials and pushed us toward the magic meld? So I could open some stupid portal for you?"

"Stupid portal!" The thief was on her feet now, moving toward me. "What do you know about being trapped in a realm that's not your own?"

Professor Halifax intercepted, stopping the thief from moving closer to me. "Sit down, Leanna."

"That's what this is all about?" Sympathy tugged at my insides. I didn't want to feel bad for her, but I understood wanting to go home. Honestly, I would be more sympathetic if she hadn't tried to kill me.

"You just want to go back to Faerie?"

"And you're going to make it happen," the thief said.

"I don't think so," I said. "I might barely stay awake in Magical Theory, but I know enough to know that opening portals is bad news. I haven't even been using magic for a year!"

"You'll do it," Professor Halifax said. "And you'll do it correctly."

"Right, cause you threatening me is going to make me do it better."

"It will when you know the stakes," she said.

My brow furrowed. "If you're talking about me dying if I do it wrong, I'm pretty sure that's the same result if I don't do it at all with your little trigger-happy sidekick over there."

"I'm not talking about your death, though that is a possibility," she said.

My chest felt tight and I tried to hide that it suddenly felt more difficult to breathe. I already knew what she was going to say but I didn't want to hear the words.

"Your mates are trapped in a room with a malacoda. Go ahead and turn me down. I'll let her kill you, then I'll command the malacoda to eat your mates. As it is, I'm sure it's feeling frustrated that I won't let it attack."

I didn't know what a malacoda was but based on the sounds it made in the gym, I knew it was bad. I didn't have any doubts that it could eat my mates.

"Choice is yours," Professor Halifax said. "But if she loses the time bubble before you decide, I'll make the choice for you."

"I don't think I'll be able to hold it for too much longer, you might want to decide quickly," Leanna said.

"What happens after I open the portal?" I asked.

"We go through and you can close it after us," she said.

"Then you're gone?" I asked.

"You'll never see us again," she said.

"What about my mates and the monster?" I asked.

"You open the portal and I'll give you the flute I use to command it. You play each note in order and you can send it back to hell."

It sounded too good to be true. She'd be gone, the thief would be gone, the monster would be gone, and my mates would be safe.

I shook my head. "Not good enough."

"You don't really have a choice," Leanna said.

"I want the monster gone now," I said. "Send it back to hell so I know they're safe. Then I'll open your portal."

Professor Halifax smiled in a way that made me think I could have asked for more. I seemed to be playing right into her hands. "As you wish."

She pulled a small flute that looked like a whistle out of a pocket in her tunic and played a series of three notes. "It's gone."

"You're sure?" I asked. "You sent it back to hell, alone, without my mates? They're all safe in the gym?"

She nodded.

"Now they're safe, but you're about to be dead," Leanna said. "I've got maybe five minutes left on this bubble before I lose it. Please, keep talking so I can kill you. I really want to taste your magic. I'm curious if it tastes more like your mom or your dad."

It took every ounce of my willpower not to charge at her and claw her eyes out. I knew that was what she wanted. She'd win if she got to kill me. I'd win if they went through that portal and never returned.

"Tell me what you need me to do," I said.

Raven

The room vibrated with magic and we hadn't even started yet. Whatever the silver object was sitting on the floor in front of me, it was powerful.

"You'll channel all of your magic through me, but aimed at the urn," Professor Halifax said.

"Urn?" I asked, feeling a wave of nausea. It was bad enough that I was doing magic with someone who stole my own parent's magic before killing them. Adding in that I was focusing my magic on a container housing a dead person?

"It's empty," Professor Halifax said.

"It doesn't have to be empty," Leanna said. "It's not too late for me to steal her magic."

"No," Professor Halifax said. "We don't know when we'll find another time magic user."

This whole thing is because of the type of magic I have. Why couldn't I be a normal mage? A fire elemental or air elemental would be just fine with me.

There was no changing that now, though. All I had to do was help them open this portal, then I could push their asses in and let the magic fade, locking them in there. I knew opening a portal to the fae realm was illegal, but so was just about everything I could do. And at least this was useful. We'd all be better off with these two gone. "Can we get this over with?"

"Remember what I taught you," Professor Halifax said. "Focus on connecting your magic with the two of us. Just like you did with your mates. You send your magic though me as they did with you. Get it through me, to the urn. I'll worry about the spell to open the portal."

That made me feel better. At least I wasn't technically opening the portal, I was just an accessory to the crime. "I'm ready when you are."

She positioned herself between me and Leanna, which was good because if Leanna let one more comment slip, I might just risk it all to get in a good punch.

The urn vibrated more, rattling against the floor. It looked like it was about to explode. I winced, tensing as I turned sideways to position my back toward the unstable looking silver object.

"It's time," Professor Halifax said. "Through me, to the urn."

I took a deep breath and did as she commanded, sending my magic out in a rush, focusing on going through her toward the urn. I felt it flowing through me like water running down pipes. It was almost like it was draining from me and pouring into her.

Exhaustion seeped in, as if to my very bones. I had never felt my magic deplete so quickly.

"Hang on, a little more," Professor Halifax said.

In front of us, light exploded out of the urn as if someone turned on a flash bomb, but the light didn't fade. It glowed blindingly bright. I had to look away, squinting at my feet instead of looking at the urn.

Something sizzled and I could smell smoke and the familiar electric charge of my own magic.

The light stopped and so did my magic. I fell to my knees, feeling like I'd been squeezed of everything I had. Panting and sweaty I looked up at Professor Halifax. She was still looking straight ahead, unconcerned by the fact that I was a crumpled mess on the floor.

I looked back over at the urn and fell down on my ass, shocked as I blinked at the sight in front of me. There was a doorway coming out of the urn. An actual fucking doorway.

An arched opening the same size as a normal door glowed brightly. The urn right in the center. I could see trees and sunshine and fields of grass beyond the portal opening.

It was like staring outside.

A breeze blew in through the door, cooling my hot forehead and sending strands of hair whipping around my face.

We'd done it. We actually opened a portal to the fae realm.

It was achingly beautiful. I crawled toward the opening, feeling a pull to it.

"It's your home too," Professor Halifax said. "You feel it, don't you? She's calling us all."

"I do feel it," I said.

"That's what I've been feeling since I left. You'd have done it too if it was the only way home," she said.

I stopped moving, shaking off the draw of the view in front of me. "No. No, I wouldn't."

Forcing myself to stand, I turned to face her. "You tried to have me killed."

"It wasn't personal," she said.

"But it is," I said. "You can't go around killing people to get the things you want."

"I beg to differ," Leanna said, walking up next to Professor Halifax. "In fact, I'm pretty sure I still want to know if your magic tastes the same as your fae father."

She shoved Professor Halifax aside and charged me, wrapping her arms around me as she knocked me to the ground.

I pushed her off of me, startled by how slowly I was moving. I had nothing left. No energy to fight.

Leanna punched me in the face, hitting my right cheekbone and sending my head whipping to the side. I rolled to the side, trying to avoid getting hit again.

She came at me again and I blocked my face with my arms. The blow didn't come and I peeked up through my fingers to see that she was standing over me, her foot raised above my ribs, ready to crush my chest.

Desperate but moving slowly, I rolled away just in time. Forcing myself to stand, I turned to her. The room was spinning and even walking was making me feel winded. I had to get away from her.

I backed up till I hit the door, grabbing the handle behind me. It didn't budge.

"It's sealed. You're stuck in here," she said. "And this is how you'll die."

"Look out!" Professor Halifax called.

Leanna turned and I looked up just in time to see something with fur and teeth and claws grab hold of Leanna and drag her down.

I didn't wait to see what the creature was. I ran toward

Professor Halifax. If the monster followed me, maybe it would eat her first.

To my surprise, Professor Halifax grabbed me and pulled me behind her. Odd that she was choosing now to be noble, but I wasn't in any position to argue. Energy still low, I ducked behind the professor and looked over her shoulder toward the door.

Leanna was on the ground. Well, at least what was left of her was there. The monster, a horrible creature that looked like a lion with the head of an eagle was digging its bloodied beak into Leanna's torn up corpse.

I retched, turning around to spill my lunch all over the floor. Wiping my mouth with the back of my hand, I turned back to look at the creature. It was staring at me now, its black eyes staring at me. It didn't blink, it just stared.

I stood frozen as did Professor Halifax. After what felt like minutes, the creature returned to tearing pieces out of Leanna. I wanted to feel bad for her but moments before the monster burst through, she had been trying to kill me.

"Did that thing get in through the portal?" I asked.

"Yes," Professor Halifax said.

"We have to close it," I said.

"I'm going through. You can come with me or you can face the griffin on your own," she said.

Suddenly a screeching roar broke through the silence of the room and the griffin that had been happily eating stood and answered back in the same tone.

The hair on my arms stood on end. It was calling to more of them. More of those beasts on the other side of the portal.

"We have to close it," I said.

Professor Halifax shook her head. "I'm going. You're on your own."

She walked toward the portal, leaving me standing there staring at the griffin. I wasn't sure where to go. It was on all fours now, facing the portal. I was half expecting it to chase down Professor Halifax.

Another screech.

I turned toward the portal and saw a herd of griffins dotted across the field. They were moving toward the portal. Professor Halifax stopped.

"I thought you wanted to go in," I said. "Do it."

"You'd like that, wouldn't you?" she asked. "Have you forgotten all I taught you so quickly? I helped you."

"You tried to kill me," I said.

"But I decided not to," she said.

"How does that make this any better?"

Claws clicked across the stone floor and I turned to see the creature moving toward me.

It had taken out Leanna without any effort. I knew I wasn't in any position to fight it. I didn't even know it was a griffin until Professor Halifax called it that.

Quickly, I climbed up the stone bleachers, going higher up on the rows of seats, hoping it might back down if it didn't feel threatened by me.

The creature stopped in front of the first row and spread its huge wings, flapping them so hard it made my hair blow in front of my face.

I stood on the top row of seats, my hands balled into tense fists. If it came for me I was going to have to try something. But what?

Just then, the door burst open and Dr. Green exploded into the room followed by Ben, Zach, Luka, and Matt.

"Watch out!" I cried.

The griffin was already on its way to the newcomers. Dr. Green created a ball of fire in his hands and waved it in front of the monster. The creature whined and stepped back, seemingly afraid of the flames.

Zach and Matt made fire of their own, following Dr. Green's lead at coaxing the creature toward the portal.

"Get Professor Halifax away from that portal!" Dr. Green cried.

Ben and Luka ran toward the portal and grabbed Professor Halifax, who didn't even put up a fight. They dragged her away from the portal.

Matt, Zach, and Dr. Green used their fire to guide the griffin back toward the portal.

"We need to get it closed," Dr. Green said.

"Good luck with that," Professor Halifax said.

"Close it," Dr. Green said.

"No, I don't think I will." She grinned.

Now I knew why she wasn't fighting it. She thought she still won.

The griffin was back in the portal now, joining the group of others. Zach and Matt were standing in front of the opening, holding their flames out to deter the others.

"I can close it," I said.

"You don't have it in you," Professor Halifax said.

"I don't have to do it alone," I said.

Raven

Dr. Green crossed the room and grabbed hold of Professor Halifax. "Close it down."

"You won't be able to do it," she said. "The effort is going to kill you."

A rush of magic surged through me, surging through my veins with a comforting heat. My mates were already sending magic my way, recharging me and giving me the strength I needed to close the portal.

"You're wrong," I said.

"You don't even know the spell," she said.

I climbed down the rows of seats and walked over to the portal, ignoring her words.

"You'll fail and she's going to take you all down with her," she screamed. "Is this how you want to die?"

"She sure doesn't want us to do this," Luka said with a grin. "It really makes me want to do it more."

"That's because she knows we can," Matt said.

"Come on," I said, moving to a space in front of the portal. I extended my arms out on either side and felt the warm grip of Matt on one side and Zach on the other. I knew Ben and Luka were joining their hands too, sending more magic through me.

I felt alive as magic tingled across my skin. Heat and ice, strength and power. Their magic was invigorating, making me feel invincible. Blocking out the cries from Professor Halifax, I focused on the urn.

She'd told me before that was the source of the power for the portal. It had to be closed through there.

As I sent the combined magic of all five of us toward the urn, I felt a pull, like an undertow trying to drag me under. I gasped and stumbled but two strong grips pulled me back.

"We got you," Matt said.

I tightened my grip on their hands, grateful for their support. It wasn't just the magic. It was everything they provided. They believed in me. They cared for me. They were magic in the sack. These mates of mine were the best thing that ever happened to me and I wasn't going to let a portal full of monsters take them away from me.

With a scream, I sent everything I had toward the urn, urging it to close, sending the magic back to where it had come from.

A blinding light filled the room followed by a huge explosion sound. Something pushed against us, sending me flying backward. The force broke my grip on Zach and Matt and I slammed to the ground, managing to get my hands under me just in time to keep from landing flat on my back again.

"No! No!" Professor Halifax was screaming.

The light faded and my eyes adjusted as I sat up and looked around the room. Matt and Luka were on one side of me, rubbing their eyes and blinking against the loss of the bright light.

Ben and Zach were on my other side, both of them working their way to standing.

I pushed myself to my feet and offered a hand to Matt. He took it and I helped pull him up. Then I turned to look at the portal.

The urn was smoking and it looked like it had been torn apart. Professor Halifax was crying into Dr. Green's chest.

My brow furrowed as I watched the demon let her cry. He looked very uncomfortable and slightly confused.

The whole classroom was a mess but there weren't any griffins and there wasn't a portal. Aside from Leanna, there were no casualties.

I let out a long breath of relief and stumbled toward the benches, sinking down to one.

Silently, each of my mates followed and joined me on the bench.

"Are you alright?" Ben finally asked, setting his hand on mine.

"I'm fine," I said. "Or at least, I will be."

I looked at all of them, relieved that they were here and looked more or less healthy. "How did you get out of the gym?"

"Dr. Green," Ben said. "Don't fuck with him. Ever."

"I've never seen someone take out a malacoda before," Luka said. "I didn't think it could be done."

"So much drool," Zach said.

"So, so much drool," Matt echoed.

I couldn't help but grin at them. They were here and they were alive. Somehow, we'd managed to survive all of it.

"Alright, where is she?"

I looked up in time to see Officer M step right into a bloody pile of Leanna. His upper lip curled in disgust and he stepped over the remains and dragged his foot over the floor to clean his shoe. Then his eyes caught mine and he grinned, showing those yellow teeth.

"I knew I'd catch you eventually. That time bubble wasn't going to last forever," he said. "I had to wait outside until it broke, but I knew I'd find you here."

I lifted my eyebrows and stared at him, waiting for the rest of the situation to come to him.

As if on cue, he looked away from me and took in the rest of the room. "What the hell happened in here?"

"You wanted your time magic user?" Dr. Green asked. "You stepped in her."

Officer M slowly turned around and looked at the remains of Leanna. There was enough of her face left to identify her as the thief that was supposed to be dead.

"She was a lousy thief," Professor Halifax said.

"And here's your prize," Dr. Green said, dragging Professor Halifax over to Officer M. "She opened a portal to the fae realm."

"With help," Professor Halifax said, turning to look at me.

"With coercion," Dr. Green said.

Several security guards ran into the room and congregated around Officer M. He passed Professor Halifax off to them. "Take her in for processing. She's never going to see daylight again."

The security officers left the room, Professor Halifax in tow. Officer M looked at me. "You should consider a job in law enforcement. You might not be as bad as I thought you were."

"Thanks," I said, forcing a smile on my face. If I ever saw him again, it would be too soon.

Officer M walked out of the room leaving me with my mates and Dr. Green.

"You five need to get cleaned up," he said. "Even if the change of dates for the trials was a set up by Professor Halifax, you still passed the trials."

"I was yanked out before I did anything," I said.

"And you're the one who ended up killing that thing," Luka said.

Dr. Green cocked an eyebrow. "Are you five telling me you want to take the trials again?"

"No," we all said in unison.

"Then it sounds like we have a celebration to throw."

Dr. Green stepped over Leanna's remains as if he'd walked over a hundred dead bodies. Maybe he had.

Now that it was over, my body felt too heavy. The idea of walking back to my room was almost too much. But I was in desperate need of a shower and I didn't want to wait around to see if dead fae turned into angry ghosts.

Ben stood and I looked up at him. I knew I should get up, but I was so tired. He leaned over and scooped me up, throwing me over his shoulder. I squealed in surprised delight.

"Let's get you cleaned up," he said.

"There's probably nobody in the locker room," Luka said.

"I think we all need a shower," Matt said.

Raven

Large hands slid past my hips, sliding my pants down. I glanced behind me to see Zach squatting on the ground behind me. He gently lifted my foot and pulled my pants off. I went along with it, letting him undress me. It still didn't feel real that we were all in here together. Especially not after everything we'd just been through.

A second set of hands worked the buttons down my chest. I turned to see Luka giving me one of his most delicious smirks as he finished removing my shirt.

I stood there in my underwear, my skin tingling, my body on

fire with need. Last time I got to have all four of them, there was magic involved and I certainly never thought I'd get that lucky again.

In front of me, Ben and Matt stood near the large open shower area, watching with hungry expressions. I knew how they felt. I wanted them just as badly as they wanted me.

With each heartbeat, I could feel the arousal rising in the room. As if all of us were putting our desire out there for the others to feed from. It was heady and raw and sexy as hell. All I wanted was to taste and feel each of my mates.

"I can't be the only one getting naked," I said.

Luka was the first to strip off his clothes and the first to grab hold of me and press his lips to mine.

My body responded, pushing back into his kiss. I ran my fingers through his hair, then down his muscular shoulders to his back before settling my hands on his hips.

Someone tugged on my arm, pulling me away from Luka and I turned to see Ben, who was also naked. He was a head taller than Luka and while Luka was lean and graceful, Ben was rock hard muscle. He pulled me to him, then picked me up so my mouth could reach his.

His kiss was on fire tonight. Every movement of his lips sent shockwaves through me, straight to my core. We moved together but I didn't care where Ben was taking me as long as he kept kissing me.

All too soon he set me down and I gasped at the sensation of cold tile beneath my bare feet. "It's freezing in here." I covered my chest with my arms.

Luka pulled my arms down. "Don't hide from us, Kitten."

"How about we turn up the heat?" Matt asked.

Matt turned on all the shower heads in the huge group shower and steam was already rolling over the tile and filling the room in a fog.

Zach grabbed my hand and led me to one of the showers, pushing my hair away from my face as warm water rushed down me. I was instantly warmed and even more turned on than I was before.

"Warmer now?" he asked.

I nodded.

"Good." He pushed me toward the wall and leaned over, claiming me with his mouth. His hand slid down my side to my thigh and he pulled my leg up to his waist, tilting me toward him.

My body responded, my hips tilting so I was in just the right position for his cock. He thrust into me quickly, still holding my thigh against him with his large hand.

I moaned into the kiss and ran my hand through his hair, pulling him tighter to me. After a few more thrusts, the tingling in my core grew until it expanded into an orgasm that had me digging my fingers into his back.

Zach buried his face into my neck as he climaxed. He let go of my leg and spun me around so I was facing the other three.

In a heartbeat, I was surrounded and hands were everywhere on my body. Luka kissed me, then broke away from the kiss. His lips were replaced by Matt's, then Ben's mouth was on mine.

Somebody's tongue teased my nipples and a strong hand slid down my back to my ass. A finger slid into me and I leaned back against Ben's firm chest, not fully aware of who was touching which part of me.

My whole body was alive with sensation. Kisses, caresses, and firm muscles pressed against me. Every inch of my skin was on fire as ripples of pleasure rolled through me over and over.

Matt was on his knees in front of me now, his tongue doing things to my clit that made me hold my breath as another climax shook me.

Someone leaned me over so my ass was in the air and a huge

cock slid into me. I knew right away it was Ben based on his size alone. He grabbed my hair gently and pulled me back up, still thrusting with his huge cock. I moaned, leaning my head back against his chest.

Matt continued working his magic on my clit, this time with his fingers, sending me into a climax that had me seeing spots. Panting, I grabbed hold of Luka, who was next to me and pulled him closer for a breathy kiss. He caressed my breasts, making it even harder to focus.

Ben grabbed my hips, pulling me closer to him as he thrust deeper and I cried out as I climaxed again. A second later, Ben joined me, groaning as he came.

Another mouth was on mine and another cock was inside me a moment later. I didn't even have time to catch my breath before I was gasping with another orgasm.

We continued for a while, kissing, touching, moaning. The whole thing was like a dream. Until the water got cold.

As we came down from the sex induced haze post orgasm, I looked around and realized just how lucky I was. I'd fought coming to this school. I wanted nothing more than to be normal. But I wasn't normal, and neither were any of my mates. We were all amazing and being together made us even more exceptional.

Wrapped in dry towels, the five of us found seats on the benches in the locker room.

"I'm going to miss this place," Luka said. "I never thought I'd say that."

"Me too," Ben said.

I smiled, still not used to seeing them getting along so well. "I don't even know what I'm doing after I leave here, but I enjoyed it while it lasted."

"Whatever it is," Matt said, "we'll figure it out together, right?"

"Together," Luka agreed.

"Sounds good to me," Zach said.

I turned and looked at Ben. His expression blank. I held my breath, waiting for him to speak.

Finally, his lips turned upward in a smile. "Yeah, I can go along with that. Together."

I wasn't sure what my future held, but I knew that with my mates, it was going to be amazing.

To Be Continued

Unbound Magic

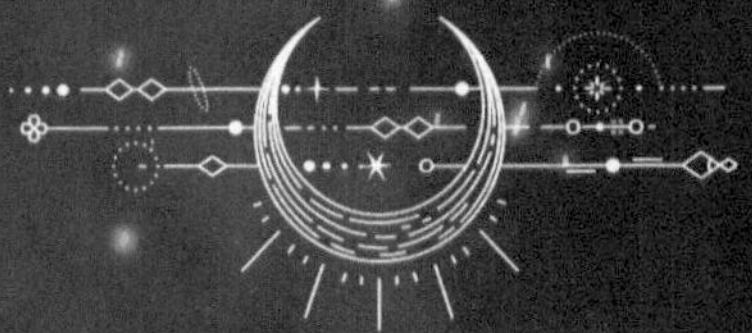

SPECIAL EDITION COLLECTION
BOOK 4

ALEXIS CALDER

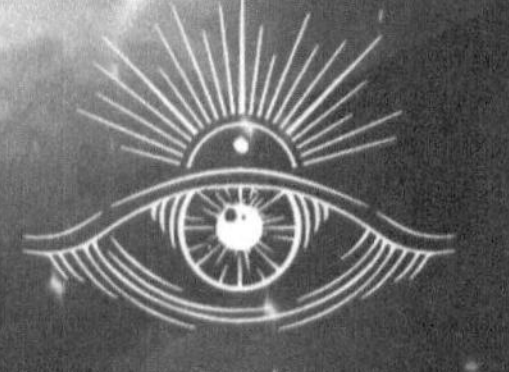

CHAPTER 1

RAVEN

The clock ticked ominously in the background. The black, dead branches of the tree showed no signs of life today. Even the yellow eyes of the carved owl were missing. It was as if the clock didn't want to be here.

I knew I didn't want to be here.

At least this time while sitting in Dr. Green's office I wasn't alone. Ben was leaning against a cabinet while Luka paced the office. Matt was in the chair next to me and Zach was looking at all the books on the shelf against the wall.

None of us said it, but we were nervous. We'd gone to bed after the trials, giddy with anticipation of what it could look like after graduation.

I was still terrified, but there was something amazing in knowing that I had their support. We'd discussed the possibility of me joining any of their family businesses, but none of the options had resulted in us staying together. I didn't have an answer for that part of our problem.

The door opened and I stopped bouncing my knees as tension spiked through me. Dr. Green's heavy footfalls sounded behind me and I caught myself holding my breath.

He cleared his throat and settled into the chair behind his desk. Luca, Zach, and Ben walked toward the seats and stood behind me. I could feel the heat of them there and it calmed me.

"I'm afraid I have some bad news," he said.

I stared at his pink face. His fangs hung over his lower lip and his jaw was set. He looked tense. That wasn't a good sign.

"What is it?" Luka asked.

"I submitted the results of the trials to the board and they rejected my recommendation to allow you all to graduate," he said.

"What?" Ben asked with a growl in his voice.

"What does that mean, exactly?" I asked.

"It means you'll have to finish the semester," he said. "They declared the trials a farce and won't certify them as official. They say to consider it a practice."

His upper lip is curled enough to show more of his fangs than usual. I can tell he's annoyed by the decision, but it seems his hands are tied.

"So all we have to do is take the actual trials in the spring and we're good to graduate?" I asked.

He nodded.

I was surprised how relieved I felt. I had no idea what I'd do when I left here and this gave me a little more time to figure it out. It was actually comforting. I had more time with my mates and with my friends. I had more time to figure out this world and where I fit.

And I had more time to try to figure out how to keep all my mates together when we left this place.

"It's not so bad," Zach said. "We didn't really get a chance to show what we have anyway, right?"

Matt blew out a breath. "I was looking forward to getting out of here, but I suppose it could be worse. What's a few more months?"

"It's more time for someone to find Raven in here and attack her," Ben said.

My stomach knotted. He was right, so far, I really hadn't been safe here.

"But also, more time for her to learn her magic so she can actually defend herself," Luka said.

"That's true," I agreed. "I'm just tapping into what my magic means. When I got here, it was untamed, but I still don't feel like I have a handle on it. Especially now that I know I'm half fae. I do need to learn how to control it."

"She's safe here," Dr. Green said.

"That's what you said before," Ben said.

"Ben, the thief is gone," I said.

"And Professor Halifax is locked up," Matt said.

I hear a low growl and I know Ben isn't happy with what they're saying. I turned and set my hand on his arm. "I'm going to be fine. Besides, I have all four of you with me. Who else can say that?"

He cracked a tiny smile. "Fine, but I'm keeping your spare room key."

"Hey, shouldn't we all get them?" Matt asks. "Just in case she needs us?"

"Nobody should have a spare room key," Dr. Green cuts in. "And we should consider moving Raven to the mage dorm."

"She can move into our room," Zach said, "we have more than enough room."

"Yeah, she'll love sharing that suite when your mom's in town visiting," Ben said.

I try to hide my smile. Ben's right. As long as it's possible for Ms. Obscura to pop in and make herself comfortable in their room, I was never going to stay there.

"Still, the mage dorm might be a better fit for her," Dr. Green said.

"I don't understand why she was in the shifter dorm to begin with," Zach said.

"It's underground," Dr. Green said.

"So?" Zach said.

"If her magic flared," Ben said. "The shifters might get hurt, but the rest of you would be safe."

"I'm not proud of it," Dr. Green said. "But I had to think of the best solution."

"Seriously?" I said. "This whole shifter hatred thing has to stop."

"I have nothing against shifters," Dr. Green said. "It was a matter of safety. There's less students down there and your magic probably would have been muted by the stone walls."

"Why didn't you just lock her up?" Ben asked.

"I'm not the monster, here," Dr. Green said. "Do you know the strings I had to pull to get her here? To keep her here?"

"Our mom did that," Zach said.

"There are so many things you don't know," he said.

"Then tell us," I said.

"I'm tired of being in the dark all the time. Don't I deserve to know?" I asked.

Dr. Green stood and took a few steps, turning away from us. He stood with his hands clasped behind his back.

"Dr. Green, what could possibly be worse than the time thief trying to get to her?" Matt asks.

"We took care of that," Luka said. "And we can't protect her if we don't know what to prepare for."

"It's never been about protecting her from the outside

world," Dr. Green said. He turned and locked his eyes on me. "It's been about protecting the outside world from *her*."

"What's that supposed to mean?" I asked.

"While I figured you were a mage, I never could pinpoint the reason why your magic was so late in showing. Now that we know you're fae, it makes more sense," he said.

"You were afraid of me?" The realization was almost amusing. When I first arrived here, I'd been terrified of him.

"She's not like Professor Halifax," Zach said.

"No, I'm not," I said quickly.

"Still, you have the ability to open portals to the fae realm and news of that is going to get out," he said.

"I'm not going to open any more portals," I said. "And the extra time here is just going to help me learn how to use my magic better."

"There's something else I want to tell you five. This doesn't leave this room," Dr. Green said. Then he looked at Matt and Zach. "Not even your mother can know this."

I was surprised to hear him say that considering how close he seemed to be with her.

"We won't say a word," Matt said.

"Our lips are sealed," Zach added.

"What is it, Dr. Green?" Luka asked.

"We've got a new spellcasting instructor on her way. And like our old one, she's fae. However, unlike Professor Halifax, she's only recently crossed into our world from the fae realm. She's going to be the best chance we have at helping Raven learn her magic," he said.

"Why are you telling us this?" Ben asked. "We never would have known this on our own."

"Raven would have figured it out eventually and I don't want her worried that this is someone intent on hurting her. Or you four jumping in and trying to be the hero over nothing," Dr. Green said.

I shifted in my chair. He was right. I could see all of us jumping to conclusions after everything we've been through.

"Does that mean more private lessons?" I asked.

"Unfortunately, it does," he said. "For all of you. After all, we now know your magic has bonded and we know Raven can channel it. I've read about it, but I never thought I'd see it happen."

"More magic bonding?" Luka asked. "I like the sound of that."

I squeezed my thighs together, my body already responding to the overwhelming feeling of being with all four of my mates. When our magic combined, it did something to us that had resulted in several very hot encounters.

The bell rang, pulling me back to the present.

"Go to class," Dr. Green said. "You've still got a trials to pass."

Raven

We'd had two full glorious days off from classes, recovering from our ordeal and planning for what we thought was graduation. Instead, it was back to the grind. And of course, it was time for gym.

I begrudgingly said goodbye to the twins and Ben and headed toward the gym with Luka.

"You know, you don't have to make any decisions yet," he said.

"Decisions?" I asked.

"About what you're going to do after the academy," he said.

I took a deep breath. This was picking up our conversation from earlier today when we'd had a few minutes alone. "I guess that's the good part about being stuck here a few more months. More time to decide what I'm going to do."

"You know, you don't have to only consider joining other people's family businesses," he said.

"Says the prince of hell," I said.

He chuckled. "I'm serious. I don't need to go back there. I could stay here with you if you'll have me."

"You're kidding, right?" I stopped walking and turned to face my handsome incubus. His messy blonde hair was covering one of his eyes.

I reached up and pushed it aside and my heart skipped a beat when my eyes found his. Those baby blues were enough to stop me in my tracks every time. I didn't think I could ever get tired of him.

"You'd give up being a prince of hell and stay here in the mortal realm?" I asked.

He shrugged. "What's the point of eternity if you're doing it alone?"

The bell rang again.

"We better hurry." Luka grabbed my hand and practically dragged me the rest of the way down the hallway.

He brought up something I hadn't considered before. I kept thinking about how I was going to insert myself into the life of one of my mates. Or even take Makayla up on her job offer. I hadn't thought about what I really wanted and asking them to follow me.

It was an interesting thought and it brought up something I wasn't prepared for. What was it that I wanted to do with my life? When I'd been living in the human world, it was survival. Just getting through to my next paycheck. The next day. The next shitty apartment. There wasn't much of a future to consider.

Now, I was nearing the end of a program of study on magic of all things. What exactly did people do when they graduated from here? They mostly all had family positions to fall into but I knew there had to be some actual jobs and industries that I could consider. I mean, there was a government system and prisons and a school board. If they had that kind of infrastructure, what else was out there?

"See you in a few," Luka called as he let go of my hand in front of the boys' dorm.

I had a minute or two before we had to be dressed and on the gym floor. Five minutes after the bell, class started. If I was late, I was going to have to deal with Coach Miller. As it was, I was expecting something from him since I'd missed the last two days.

To be honest, if I knew there was a possibility of coming back here, I might have gone to his class just to keep him happy. Then again, I hated this class enough to possibly skip and deal with the consequences. It didn't matter now. I was here and I was stuck with it till spring.

I quickly opened my locker and pulled out my clothes and changed. Jogging to the gym, I managed to join the others just as Coach Miller slithered over to us.

A shiver ran down my spine. No matter how many times I saw that man, I was going to feel totally creeped out just from looking at him.

Half man, half serpent, Coach Miller was a thing of nightmares. Add in the fact that he made us run laps and other unpleasant things that I thought I'd left behind in my high school gym class days and it made it that much worse.

"Isn't this cute," he said. "It looks like we're all back where we belong. And none of us are special enough to get a free pass out of here."

His eyes are on me then they move away and I know he's looking for Luka.

"We had to close down the gym and go through the whole mess of bringing that monster in here. There was drool everywhere. For what? For some special little fae girl to open a portal and nearly let the bad guys win?"

Someone snickers and I want to crawl into a hole and hide forever.

"None of you are special," he says. "You're all a waste of oxygen until I decide otherwise."

He was looking at me again and I stared back, forcing myself not to break eye contact. I wish I was anywhere else right now, but I wasn't. And Coach Miller was a bully. I couldn't let him know how much he got to me.

"Go run some laps, all of you," he said. "You can spend the entire class running like the cowards you are."

My jaw tensed. Coach Miller was awful. He had no idea what we'd been through and I wouldn't call myself or Luka a coward. But honestly, running laps for an hour is one of his lesser punishments so I jogged toward the track and considered myself lucky.

It could be so much worse.

"Hey, you okay?" Luka asked as he matched his pace to mine.

"I'm fine," I said. "I'll be happier when I no longer have gym class."

He smirked.

"Pick up the pace, incubus, or you'll be doing laps after dinner," Coach Miller called.

"Go," I said. "I'll see you later."

He blew a playful kiss and winked before taking off ahead of me.

"Hey, girl," Violet said, taking Luka's place. "I was pissed when I heard you were going to leave. You didn't even say goodbye."

"I wasn't out yet," I said. "And I never would have left without a goodbye. But lucky you, I'm here till the end of the term."

"I'm selfishly glad you're sticking around," she said. "Scarlett might not be as thrilled."

"That doesn't surprise me," I said with a laugh.

Violet and I fell into a comfortable pace and a comfortable conversation. It made me feel a little better about everything I'd just been through. I mean, it was terrible, but at least I got some more time here to figure all this out with my friends before I was thrown into whatever the real world was for supernaturals.

Suddenly, someone ran into me, nearly knocking me over. "Hey!"

Delores was a few steps ahead of me now and she tossed her head back to look at me. "Watch where you're going. Watch everything."

"Is that a threat?" I asked, heat filling my chest. I never got even with her after her last stunt that sent me to the hospital. I figured letting it go was the best plan, but now I wasn't so sure.

She smirked, then turned away from me and kept running. I shook my head. "I can't stand her. What is her problem?"

"Besides the fact that you scooped up four of the most eligible bachelors in the school? No idea," Violet said.

"You're supposed to be on my side," I said.

"Oh, I am," she said. "And I applaud you for pulling off what might be the best boyfriend heist of all time."

"That's not making me feel better," I said.

"Don't you know? Vampires are terrible at making people feel good," she said. "We live too long to sugar coat anything."

"I suppose that's not a bad thing. Especially in a place like this," I said.

"You definitely want vampire friends," she said. "We're the only ones who will tell you to your face if you're being an asshole."

"I'll keep it in mind," I said.

"Plus, we throw killer parties," she said. "There's a party tonight. You in?"

"Maybe," I said.

"You could use a night out," she said. "Maybe ditch the boys and go solo for a change."

"I like my boyfriends," I said, startled by the statement. Not because I was surprised about liking them, but because I'd never really said it out loud. I had four boyfriends. Four.

I sort of saw why Delores was mad. Though, I wouldn't trade any of them for the world.

"You should come, either way" Violet said. "Bring them all if you want."

"We'll see," I said.

I knew I had some things to figure out first. Like how the hell I was going to balance the next few months at school with four different men. While they were able to share from time to time, I knew they'd all want alone time. And I had to admit, I did too.

Having multiple boyfriends wasn't something I'd ever heard of in the human world. How was I supposed to do this?

"You'll figure it out," Violet said.

"Figure what out?" I asked. "Don't tell me you can read minds."

She laughed. "No, but you look awfully serious. Whatever it is, stop overthinking it already."

I laughed. "You know, it is good to have a vampire friend."

A whistle sounded. "Alright you pathetic excuses for super-naturals. Head to the showers. Don't expect tomorrow to be this easy," Coach Miller shouted.

I did not need to be dismissed twice. Violet and I jogged toward the locker room door and got at the back of the line of girls heading in.

We'd moved on to discussing music while we waited and I shuffled forward in the line. As we got closer, I realized the lights were out. "What the hell?"

I turned to Violet. "Who turned off the lights?"

She shrugged. "I can't tell but I don't see anything weird." She gave me a grin. "Another vampire perk. We can see in the dark."

I smiled then turned back to the dark locker room. "Hey, someone turn on the lights."

Inside the room, girls were screaming and laughing. Nobody seemed to care that the lights were out. I frowned, wondering if I was the only supernatural in the group who can't see in the dark. Guess the human mage half of me won in the vision department.

"I'll go find the light switch," Violet said.

Carefully, arms extended, I shuffled in slowly. I just needed to get to my locker. I should get there by the time Violet turned the lights back on.

Someone grabbed me and I screamed. It was stifled by a hand going over my mouth. I kicked and fought, trying to get out of the grip of whoever had me, but they were strong.

Hot breath from heavy breathing hit my ear and my skin crawled at how close my captor was. I tried to free myself again, twisting and fighting with everything I had. They were just too strong. Who the hell was this?

"Calm down, little mage," a male voice hissed. "You listen to me and you and your friends will be safe."

I screamed into the hand, not intending to go along with whatever the hell this was.

"Hush, now," the voice said. "You have something I want.

An old book. Bring it to me and nobody will get hurt. Library. Midnight. Come alone."

As quickly as the arms had grabbed a hold of me, they were gone. The lights flickered to life and I was left standing in the locker room, sweat covering my brow from fear.

Around me shrill cries of the other girls sprang up around the room and lockers slammed and conversation continued. Nobody else seemed to have just encountered a threat from a mysterious stranger.

Shit.

Just when I thought things were getting better.

Raven

Magical Theory class seemed to be over before I even noticed what was happening. All I could think about was the weird encounter in the locker room. My skin was crawling at the thought of some random guy getting in there while we were all changing.

Plus, there was the threat and the book to consider. I had to assume the book in question was the one that Professor Halifax gave me but that didn't make sense. Who else would know I had that book? And who in the school would want it?

If a teacher or another student asked me about it, I'd probably have handed it over. Did that mean we had another villain inside the school? What the hell was with the lack of security in this place?

I didn't see what value the book even had, but I wasn't that dumb. If someone went through all that smoke and mirrors of turning off the lights and grabbing me, the book was far more valuable than I realized.

Which meant, I couldn't give it to the stranger.

Fuck.

I just wanted to have a normal few months at this place, but I was starting to think that wasn't possible. I attracted weirdos.

"Raven, did you hear me?" Professor Hurd called.

I blinked and looked up at the old man. His huge eyes stared at me through his thick glasses.

"I'm sorry, professor," I said. "I wasn't paying attention."

He pressed his lips together into a thin line and shook his head.

"Someone thinks she's too good for this place now," someone called from behind me.

"It's not that," I said. "I'm sorry, I'll focus better."

"Well, it won't help you today as class is over, but tomorrow I want to see you paying attention," he said.

The bell rang and everyone around me stood and grabbed their bags. I was so focused on the encounter in the locker room that I hadn't even gathered my things yet.

Quickly, I packed up and slung my backpack over my shoulder. I stopped in front of Professor Hurd's desk. "Sorry about that, professor."

He lowered his glasses and looked up at me from over the frames. His eyes were now far too small for his face. It threw me off no matter how many times I saw it. "You're getting sloppy just when you should start paying more attention."

"I know, I know," I said. "The trials and everything."

He shook his head. "No, not the trials. Your magic is too strong for you. When you arrived, you had *untamed magic*. It was weak then, but still chaotic and dangerous. Now you've unlocked magic that few understand. You're a danger to yourself and those around you if you don't figure out how to use it."

My lips parted and I wanted to say something but I didn't know what. It honestly wasn't a surprise to hear there was something wrong or different or dangerous about my magic. It's what I'd been told since I arrived.

"Hopefully that new professor can help you," he said. "You need tools and training. And you damn well better pay attention."

"I will," I said.

"Now go," he said.

"See you tomorrow." I waved as I walked toward the door. My interactions with Professor Hurd had always been odd, but I think there was merit in his words. He'd been right about a lot of things regarding my magic and while I wasn't sure he liked me, he was at least tolerating me.

Aside from running to Dr. Green, there wasn't much I could do about the intruder and I'd been specifically told not to get anyone else involved. For now, I was at an impasse. Until I decided to either go meet the person or violate their strange request and tell someone.

As I walked to Spellcasting, I wondered why the person asking about the book didn't break into my room. I supposed I should be grateful for that, but the book had come to my room rather mysteriously through Professor Halifax. Did professors have keys to student rooms?

Matt and Zac waved to me as I walked into Spellcasting. They'd saved a seat between them for me and I was grateful to have them there. The creepy violated feeling of the encounter eased a little as I settled between them.

"How's your morning going?" Matt asked.

"Interesting," I said.

"What's wrong?" Zach asked.

"Whatever it is, I can feel it radiating off of you," Matt said. "Spill, Raven."

"Not now," I said. "I can't say anything here."

Zach grabbed my hand and gave it a squeeze.

"You will be silent when I speak," a woman's voice called out.

A hush fell over the class and I turned to the center of the room where a tall, silver haired woman with visibly pointed ears was standing. She was wearing a green dress that was assembled in pieces, like patchwork. Though, it had an elegance to it I didn't typically associate with a style that usually looked so bohemian. Her silver hair was pulled up in an elaborate series of twists and knots on top of her head, and around her throat she wore a necklace that reminded me of bones.

She was chilling and enthralling all at once and she was obviously not shy about showing her fae heritage. Though, I shouldn't be surprised considering Dr. Green's statement that she'd come through just to teach here. Illegally. The whole thing made me a little uncomfortable and also oddly impressed by Dr. Green's rule breaking. I didn't think he had it in him. Though, I was learning more about him with each passing week and his file would not be clean for sure.

"That's better," she said. "I am Professor Flora and I am replacing your disgraced professor. Do not expect that because she was fae and I am fae that we are the same."

There were a few gasps around the room at the truth bomb dropped by the new teacher. I grinned. It was refreshing in a school full of lies and deceit and hidden truths to have someone be upfront for once.

She turned her gaze on me and my eyes widened, my smile

faded. Her eyes were gold and reminded me of a cat. I forced myself to stare back, unblinking for as long as I could, but I couldn't hold. After I blinked, she turned away.

"I was told you focused on elemental magic last semester," she said.

"That's right, professor," Jane McCarthy said. I'd know that voice anywhere. If there was an opportunity to suck up to a teacher, Jane took it.

"I didn't ask you to speak," Professor Flora said.

I heard a stifled squeak from behind me and imagined that Jane was very red-faced right now. I'd never heard a teacher call her on her insufferable brown nosing before. I liked the new professor more every second.

"You should all be well versed in all four elements with your strengths and weaknesses by now," Professor Flora said. Her eyes narrowed and I got the feeling she was daring the class to say something. Nobody spoke.

"Which means you're ready to move on to more advanced spells," she said. "Raise your hand if you consider yourself well versed in all four elements?"

The twins raised their hands. Zach elbowed me.

I shook my head. I didn't consider myself well versed in all four elements. I was comfortable with fire, but that was about it. My studies had been limited with everything else going on.

I glanced around the room. I was the only person who didn't have their hand up. My stomach twisted and I felt hot. That was not the way to be singled out with the new professor. I nearly put my hand up just to join the crowd, but she was looking right at me now.

"Interesting," she said. "Either I have a class of geniuses, or many of you are lying. Such an odd skill that we fae do not possess. It still strikes me as a feat any time I see it performed."

She clasped her hands in front of her and began to pace in a slow circle around the auditorium. The whole class was the quietest I'd ever heard them.

"Things will be different for the remainder of the semester. My job is to prepare you for not only a fictional trials in a controlled environment, but also for the real world beyond this classroom." She stopped walking and stared out into the class. "The only way I can do that is to get you into real world situations."

I straightened. This sounded interesting. And terrifying. What could she be planning for us?

She turned and walked toward the desk in the center of the room and picked up a large top hat. I was sure it hadn't been there before. Did she just make that appear? "You'll draw a topic out of my hat." She smiled, as if waiting for the class to get the joke. Nobody said a word. I smiled despite myself.

She walked straight to where I was sitting and held up the hat. "Cheeky, right?"

"Very," I said. The fact that it was a top hat, the kind humans associated with magic didn't get lost on me, though I doubted my classmates were in on the joke. The fact that she knew this also told me she understood humans. She might have come from the fae realm, but she'd been here before. And fairly recently if she knew about top hats and magicians.

"You'll go first, my little fae." The words were endearing but her face was a mask of indifference. She was impossible to read.

I stuck my hand inside the hat and pulled out a folded piece of paper. She then moved the hat to Zach, then Matt before walking around the room to each student.

I glanced at my mates and I could tell all of us were confused by this process. Matt shrugged and then opened his paper. I looked down at my own folded paper and opened it.

Shaking my head, I folded it back up. This was not random. Nothing about this was random. I thought I was long done with this kind of magic, but apparently, it wasn't ever going away. I glared at the paper, hoping it would change into something else. Anything else.

"What does yours say?" Matt whispered.

"Portals," I said. "Yours?"

Matt blinked a few times, clearly just as startled by my paper as I was. He passed his to me and I read it. My brow furrowed and I looked back up at Matt. "What is *dream walking*?"

"Visiting people in their dreams," he said. "If you're really good at it, you can control them. But I don't think she's going to teach me how to do it. It's kind of an incubus thing."

"So maybe how to kick someone out of your dream?" I asked, thinking of all the amazing dreams I'd had with Luka. I don't think I'd ever kick him out.

"Maybe," Matt said.

"What's yours?" I asked, turning to Zach.

"Shifters," Zach said, his brow furrowing.

"Shifters?" I asked, my mind going right to Ben. Why would shifters be something covered in our Spellcasting class as a real world situation?

I looked over at our new teacher who was still passing out tasks to students. Suddenly, I wasn't so sure I liked her so much after all.

Matt

I had no idea what this new teacher was trying to do, but it sure seemed like she was setting us against non-mages. It was odd considering the fact that she was fae. Professor Hurd never let his dislike of shifters show and favored the mages, but this was something else. Unless she legitimately thought we were at risk of needing to fight demons and shifters.

The bell rang and Professor Flora called over the sound rustling and zippers. "Next class, be prepared to begin your individual study of your chosen topic. You will be tested."

"Can't wait for that," I mumbled.

Raven caught my eye. "At least yours isn't something that's possibly illegal."

"This woman is insane," Zach said under his breath.

I had to agree. We were going to have to keep an eye on her. After Professor Halifax, my trust of fae was thin. I knew Raven was half fae, but she didn't know anything about the fae. She didn't know their past or why they'd really been banned from our realm.

They were terrifying at full power. The strongest magic users there were. From what I'd heard, they weren't all that fond of humans and while the practice of stealing human children *should* be over, considering they weren't supposed to cross into our realm, I doubted that was the case. The fact there was a fae who joined us from their realm proves that theory.

Professor Flora watched us silently as we walked past her to the door. I could feel her gaze on me even after I couldn't see her anymore. A chill shivered down my spine. It was going to be a long couple of months in her class.

As soon as we were outside, I grabbed Raven and pulled her against the wall so we could get away from the stream of students pouring through the hallway. Zach noticed the action and joined us.

"Hey, what did you want to tell us before?" I asked.

Her eyes darted around and I could feel the anxiety practically rolling off of her.

"What is it?" Zach asked.

"You can tell us," I said.

She shook her head. "Not here. My room."

"Okay," I said. "Lead the way."

We went against the flow of students who were heading to the cafeteria for lunch. I tried to think of what she might be so upset over, but I couldn't figure out what it might be. She'd had two classes this morning without us, so my guess is it was something there. Were the sirens giving her shit again?

Heat filled my chest at the thought. If they were trying to hurt her again, I was going to have to do something to stop it. The last time one of them went after Raven, she'd ended up in the hospital.

The shifter dorm was quiet as we walked down the stone steps. The temperature dropped as we made our descent. I hated that she lived down here. "You know, you can still move to our room any time. At least there's sunlight in our room."

"I like my room," Raven said. "Besides, it's not for too much longer. It seems crazy to pack up and move for such a short time."

I frowned, wondering how much of her decision to stay down here was the fact that the shifter lived next door. We might tolerate each other for Raven, but I still wasn't thrilled about sharing her. Not even with my brother.

The common room was empty and Raven seemed to relax a little at the sight. Whatever it was she wanted to tell us, she really didn't want it to get out. A little thrill went through me. Maybe her and the shifter weren't as close as I thought. She was with us right now and not him to say whatever was weighing on her so heavily.

We paused outside her room while she unlocked the door and then we all filed inside. She was silent as she closed and locked the door behind her.

"What's going on, Raven?" Zach asked.

She shook her head and turned to face us. "Something really weird happened in the locker room this morning."

"Oh?" I asked, not sure if I liked where this was going.

"The lights were out and someone grabbed me," she said.

My brow furrowed. That was not what I expected her to say. "Who?"

"I don't know. Male voice, I think. Asked me to bring him a specific book at the library tonight but not tell anyone," she said.

"Which book?" Zach asked.

"I think it's this book that Professor Halifax gave me. It had some stuff about untamed magic in it. I read through it a bit but honestly I forgot about it until today." She walked over to her desk and opened a drawer. When she turned back to us, she was holding a leather-bound book.

"That's it?" I asked. "Why would someone want it? Any ideas?"

She shook her head. "He said if I didn't give it to him or if I told anyone, he'd hurt my friends."

"So that's why you needed to keep it secret," I said, reaching for the book. "Can I look at it?"

She passed it to me and I opened it. As I flipped through the pages, I skimmed the words for anything that looked like it might be of value. Of course there were so many kinds of magical objects that it might not be about the content. For all we knew the book was cursed or something.

"Let me see," Zach said.

I passed it to him, not seeing anything at first glance.

He flipped through it. "I'm not even sensing any magic in this book. I can't see why anyone would want it. Are you sure it's the right book?"

Raven shrugged. "I think so. I don't have any other books aside from my textbooks and I doubt that was what he was after."

Zach closed the book. "We need to keep this safe. Obviously, this person can't get into your room for some reason so we should keep it here. But we can't give it to them."

"I agree. Just because we can't figure out what's special about it doesn't mean we're not missing something," I said.

Raven took the book from Zach and put it back in the desk drawer.

"Want me to do a locking spell on the desk?" I asked.

"Sure," Raven said. "Don't let me have access to it. That way whoever this is can't even make me open it."

I walked over to the desk and set my palm against the drawer. I learned locking spells as a kid to mess with my brother. Once I'd locked him in the bathroom for six hours before the nanny found him and broke the spell. He didn't speak to me for days after that and kept trying to get back at me. When he finally managed to use an illusion charm to make me think there was a giant snake in the living room, I'd been so terrified that I turned and promptly fell down a flight of stairs, breaking my arm. We put the pranks to rest after that. Despite it all, we were best friends and we had each other's backs.

"Okay." I turned to Raven. "Nobody but me can get that open."

"Thanks," she said. "Now what do I do about tonight? He wants me to meet in the library at midnight. I have to go."

"You can't be serious," Zach said. "Just stay in. What's he really going to do?"

"We can't let him keep roaming the school," she said.

"You're right," I agreed. "We've got to stop him."

"How?" she asked. "I can go with a fake book but we don't even know what he looks like."

"I don't like the idea of you going as bait," Zach said.

"We don't have a choice," Raven said.

"Raven brings a different book and goes to the library alone," I said, then turned to Zach. "You and me will already be there, studying at different tables. Raven can take a seat at a table in the middle of the room and we can watch her from both sides."

"I still don't like it," Zach said.

"Me neither, but it's the best we've got," Raven said.

"We can take him down as soon as he approaches her," I said. "Plus, there's always a hundred people in the library. We'll have help once we make some noise. It won't just be us."

"That's true," Zach said. "Alright. What time does this peeping tom want you to meet him?"

"Midnight," she said.

"Could he be any more cliche?" Zach asked.

Raven grinned. "I suppose you would have preferred a nice unusual time?"

I laughed and the other two joined in. It was a good break to the tension.

"Okay, I'll find a book this afternoon," Zach said. "And we'll be at the library by ten waiting in case we see anything weird. Maybe we'll get lucky and he'll show up before you get there."

"We can get Luka and Ben to join us too," I said.

"Don't tell the others," Raven said.

My brow furrowed. As much as I loved that Raven was using us as her heroes, I could see this going better with some help.

"I don't want anyone else involved. Just in case," she said. "I almost didn't even tell you two. I don't want anyone to get hurt. But I know I can't do everything by myself."

I could feel her fear and it broke my heart. She looked cool on the outside, but this man scared her. I grabbed her arm and pulled her close to me and then wrapped my arms around her. "We're going to get this guy. Don't worry."

Raven

I stayed guarded the rest of the day, focusing on my studies and trying to keep my head down. Everything seemed to be moving in slow motion as it always does when you're waiting on something.

Faking a headache, I grabbed a paper plate of food at dinner, excusing myself from my usual meal with my friends.

"Need me to come with you?" Makayla asked.

"No," I said. "I think I'll just eat and call it an early night."

Makayla pressed her lips together, giving me a look that made me think she saw right through my lie.

"It's been a busy few days," I said.

She smiled, seeming to relax a little. "It has. And I have to tell you, I'm a terrible person because I'm glad you're sticking around for a while."

I squeezed her hand. "Same. We'll talk tomorrow, okay?"

"Okay," she said. "You sure you don't need me? I can sing to you or pet your head."

"Pet my head?" I asked, eyebrow arched.

She shrugged. "It's soothing. Maybe it's a wolf thing."

I laughed. "Goodnight, Makayla."

"Night," she said.

I turned and walked out of the cafeteria, grateful that Ben and Luka weren't there yet. They were usually later showing up for dinner so I was hoping to get in and out without being spotted. Makayla would relay my message and she could deliver my lie so much better than I could to either of them.

I didn't fully understand the bond between all of us but I knew there were certain feelings and thoughts they could sense. If there was any chance they could tell how stressed I was, there was no way they'd let me go back to my room alone.

Thankfully, I made it back to my room without being stopped. My heart was already racing as I closed the door behind me. The meeting in the library tonight was eating away at me, making my stomach twist in knots. I was afraid but I also wanted it to hurry up and get here already.

I set my paper plate on my desk and set my backpack on the ground. Then I pulled out the decoy book Matt had passed to me in the hallway earlier today and set it next to my plate. The book seemed to taunt me. I picked it up and moved it next to the door. It could wait there till it was time to go.

I walked back to my desk and settled into the chair. Since I'd skipped lunch I was starving and our cafeteria made amazing food. Tonight's dinner was the option that looked the easiest to eat in my room. Some kind of sandwich with a cup of fruit and a healthy pile of french fries. I picked up the sandwich and took a bite. It was filled with mozzarella and tomatoes. I'd made a good choice.

After a few bites I felt restless, so I stopped eating and reached for the drawer where the book was stored. As soon as I touched it, a jolt of electricity shot through my fingers.

I pulled my hand back. *Fuck.* Shaking my hand, I glared at the drawer. I'd forgotten all about Matt's locking spell but I guess it was good to know it was working.

Absentmindedly I grabbed a few fries while I wondered about the book. What could be inside of it that was so important? Or was it something else?

Professor Halifax had given me that book and never asked for it back. She didn't seem to mind that I had it. Did she know that it had some kind of value or did she not care?

It was maddening to know that I had something in my possession that was more than it seemed without being able to crack it. And the only person who could answer my question was in a prison cell somewhere for trying to kill me then use me for my magic.

I frowned at the memories of Professor Halifax. She'd seemed like she was the real deal. She'd helped me with my magic. But it was all for personal gain. If she made me more powerful, she could get me to do her bidding.

I reached for another French fry, but they were all gone so I went back to my sandwich. What I wouldn't give for a few minutes of trashy television to distract me right now.

Finished with dinner, I stood and walked over to my bed. I plopped down and reached for a book that Makayla had given me. It had a half-naked man on the cover. I hadn't started it yet but it looked promising as a distraction.

I started reading and then the light faded around me and I

was in a dark dungeon. I looked down at my hands. The book was gone. *Shit.* I had to be asleep. Gray stone walls and iron bars locked me in on all four sides. Water dripped in the background and the air felt cold.

Wake up. Wake up. I had somewhere to be. I couldn't be asleep right now.

"I was wondering if you were ever going to go to bed," Luka's voice came from all around me.

I turned in a slow circle, trying to find him. "Luka? Where are you?"

He appeared in front of me in a pair of red satin pajamas. "Hey, kitten."

I smiled. "Nice pajamas."

He stretched his arms out and lifted his chin. "I thought you might like them. Sexy, right?"

I laughed. "So sexy." Then I remembered I needed to wake up. "Luka, I wish I could stay and play with you, but I have to wake up."

He dropped his arms and his brow furrowed. "Why? Makayla said you weren't feeling well. Sleeping is exactly what you should be doing."

"I have a test," I said. "I needed to do a little more studying. Can you wake me up?"

"Want me to come to your room? I can help you study," he said.

"No!" I shouted.

His face darkened. "I get it. You're not alone."

I shook my head. "That's not it at all. I really just need to study."

"It's the twins, right? And here I thought we had so much fun together. I mean, if you're going to have a party, you could invite me too." He grinned.

"I would definitely invite you, but it's not a party," I said.

"Alright," he said. "But I can't wake you up from within the dream. That's actually really dangerous. I can wake myself up and go knock on your door."

Shit. If I didn't wake up, I could miss the meeting. "Okay, fine. But I have to tell you something first and you have to not freak out because I already have a plan."

"Um, what?" he asked. "You just said fifty words in a second."

"Something weird happened and I didn't tell you all because I am trying to protect you," I said.

He moved closer to me. "What happened?"

"Promise me you won't do anything crazy," I said.

"Promise. Now spill."

I told him the whole story about the locker room and my conversation with the twins. Then I explained the plan.

"So they're waiting in the library and you're going in as bait?" he asked.

"Yes," I said. "But we have it under control."

His jaw tensed and I swear his eyes flashed red. "Raven, you can't do things like this. How many times have we told you that you aren't in this alone?"

"I asked for help," I said, suddenly feeling small. I'd done the right thing. "I'm trying to protect you."

He shook his head. "Wait there. I'm coming to wake you up. When you go to the library, all of us will be there with you."

"Wait, *all*?" I asked.

But Luka was already gone. I sat down on the floor of my dream dungeon and pulled my knees to my chest. Somehow I had a feeling I was about to get a wake up call from not just my incubus but also a very pissed off shifter.

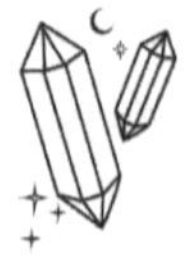

Even though I knew the wake up was coming, I wasn't prepared for it. As soon as I felt someone touching my arm, I woke with a start. Through blurry vision I saw Ben glaring down at me.

You do not want to be on the receiving end of Ben's glare.

"Hey," I managed as I rubbed my eyes.

"Thought you'd go save the world without us?" Ben asked, his expression still stern.

I sat up and looked over at Luka giving him a glare of my own. "Tattle-tale."

"Good thing he did," Ben said. "You don't know what you're dealing with. What if this stranger means to harm you? What if this isn't about the book? What if they want your magic like Professor Halifax did?"

"Right?" Luka agreed. "Did you even consider that it might be someone else who broke into our school? They have a shitty track record for security here."

I ran my hand through my hair, sure I had major bed head. "Look, he told me he'd hurt my friends if I said anything."

"So?" Ben asked. "We can take care of ourselves."

I looked at him. He was wearing a skintight white undershirt that his pecks and shoulders were practically ready to burst through. His strong jaw was tense and his eyes looked dangerous.

He looked like he could take on a monster alone.

"You're right," I said. "You can."

I looked over at my incubus, Luka. He wasn't in the red satin pajamas anymore but in a black shirt and jeans. You could still see the curve of his lean, muscular shoulders. And I knew exactly how strong he was. "So can you."

Then I turned back to Ben. "But I still don't want to put either of you - any of you - at risk."

"We know," Luka said. "But we're in this together, okay?"

I sighed. "Fine. What time is it?"

"Eleven-thirty," Luka said.

"Alright, well, I didn't miss it." I climbed off the bed and walked to the bathroom, closing the door behind me without explanation.

I appreciated them coming to my aid, but I really didn't want to see any of my mates hurt. But Luka made a good point, the same worry I'd had about lack of security at this school. I had no way of knowing if the bad guy was someone from inside our school or a new threat.

Though all of my instincts told me it wasn't a student. It just didn't make sense for it to be someone who went to school here. Especially because if I were trying to get something out of another student's room, I'd probably try to sneak into their room first.

I wasn't the only one who had found a way to pass a spare key to a friend and we did have magic here. If someone wanted to break into my room, there was probably a way to do it.

Unless that person was staying hidden and not interacting with anyone.

I splashed water on my face and ran a brush through my tangled hair. After a quick change of clothes, I finished getting ready. I paused in front of the door, my hand hovering above the doorknob.

I didn't want to do this. I wanted to finish school without threats hanging over my head all the time. But it didn't look like I was going to get what I wanted.

With a sigh, I opened the door. Both Luka and Ben were

sitting on my bed and my body heated on instinct as a shiver went straight to my core. Why couldn't we just stay here and climb in my bed together? That would be a much more fun way to spend the evening.

Ben stood. "Don't look at us like that."

Luka grinned as he stood. "Later, kitten."

I felt my cheeks heat. Was I that obvious? "You two better go first and find a place to sit. I'll give you a couple of minutes, then I'll go in with the book."

Ben growled.

I set my hands on my hips. "Don't growl at me. You know this is the best option."

Luka hit Ben lightly. "Come on. Let's go."

Ben still didn't look happy, but he moved toward my door.

"I'm going to be fine. I have all of you looking out for me," I said.

As soon as they were through the door, my confidence waned. I glanced at the book. How was I going to pull this off?

Ben

I hated walking away from Raven knowing that I was agreeing to let her be bait. I knew she could take care of herself, but I also knew there was a lot in the world of magic that she still didn't know about. Part of me wanted to let her stay sheltered from the other bad parts. I mean, getting forced to open a portal to the fae realm was bad enough, but there was more out there.

Luka was already at a table in the library when I walked in and he did a good job of ignoring me when I entered. If the creep who threatened Raven did his homework, seeing her mates in here would probably tip him off. I almost hoped it was enough to scare him away. Though, we did need to catch him. I didn't want Raven being cornered in the locker room again. My whole body tensed at the thought. Whoever this guy was, he was sneaking into a women's locker room. It wasn't right.

I grabbed a book from a random shelf and settled into a table not too far from Luka. After opening the book, I looked around the library and saw the twins seated nearby, also with books on their desks.

I knew none of us were actually reading. We were all waiting for Raven. Despite the fact that I wasn't fond of sharing her, I was grateful for her other mates right now. The twins were powerful mages. I'd heard stories about them and the things their family could do. Luka's powers were rumored to be stronger than most other demons, and I knew my wolf could be out in a heartbeat if needed.

Raven was still putting herself at more risk than I wanted her to, but we had her back. And I was glad that the four of us could be here for her.

I looked down at the book I had and couldn't help but smile. I didn't even know what it was about because it was written in what looked like ancient runes. Probably some old dwarf history.

Flipping through the pages, I skimmed the pictures. At least I could figure those out on my own.

A tingle shot through me and I knew Raven was approaching. I could feel her.

Forcing myself to stay glued to my book, I felt the hair on my arms stand on edge as I caught her scent. Out of the corner of my eye, I saw Raven take a seat at a table in the middle of the room. She had the decoy book with her and I could sense her nervousness from here.

It was probably good that she was nervous. That meant she'd be cautious. My Raven had a history of running headfirst into things without thinking and a little hesitation might keep her alive.

I glanced at the clock on the wall. It was midnight on the dot. Any second now that asshole was going to stroll in here and approach Raven. Or he'd see us and bolt. Either way, it was time to stop pretending I was reading.

Scanning the room, I looked for anyone I didn't recognize. Any signs of movement from behind the shelves drew my attention. But so far, all I saw was a handful of other students who looked like they were legitimately studying. And one couple that ducked behind a long bookshelf.

Nothing looked out of the ordinary.

The twins had also given up reading at this point. The books on their desks were closed and they were looking around the library just as I was. None of us were doing a great job of stealth but I think we were too worried about Raven to pretend we weren't here.

A sizzling sound came from above me and I glanced skyward just as the lights went out.

Surprised murmurs and a few startled cries sounded from around the library and my heart raced. This was not what we had planned.

My eyes adjusted enough that I could see the outlines of the tables and some movement but in unshifted form, my vision wasn't much better than a normal human.

Fuck it. I was not going to wait around for some asshole to come and grab my girl. "Raven?"

I stood, knocking the chair to the ground. I made my way around the table, my hands in front of me to feel for anything that might catch me off guard as I walked toward her table.

"Raven? Move toward my voice."

I bumped against other desks as I moved closer to her.

"Raven, answer him," Luka called. "I can't see you anymore. Raven? Where did you go?"

"What do you mean you can't see her?" One of the twins called, I had no idea which one, but I could hear the panic in his tone.

"Demon, you had eyes on her?" I called.

"I did, *wolf,* but she's gone now. Her table is empty," Luka said.

"Fuck," I said.

"My magic won't light," one of the twins called. "It's like the trials. I can't make fire."

"Don't tell me we've got another monster on the loose," I said, a shiver going down my spine. That thing was awful.

"No, I don't think so," Luka said. "This is something else."

Someone screamed and my wolf clawed at my insides, begging for release. The only reason I kept it at bay was that I knew the voice didn't belong to Raven. So far, she wasn't crying for our help and I couldn't sense that she was in danger. Whatever was happening either muted my connection with her or she was actually doing okay. I somehow doubted in was the latter.

I stumbled forward, following the faint scent I found in the air. Finally, I reached the table where she'd been sitting. A book sat on the table.

"He must be here," Luka said from right next to me.

I nearly jumped. "Warn a guy."

"I thought shifters could see in the dark," he said.

"When I'm a wolf, sure," I said.

"Sorry, mate," Luka said. "The decoy book is still on the table, but she's gone."

"He's here and he has her," I said.

Raven

My hands were clammy and I could feel my pulse pounding in my ears. It was time and I didn't know what to expect. All four of my mates were at tables around me. I could feel them with me and it gave me comfort. but I was still terrified.

Who was this person who'd threatened me? And why was my life always in danger? It was getting really, really annoying.

Something sizzled and I looked up, startled by the sound. Then everything went black.

Shit. This was not good.

Quickly, I called to my fire.

Nothing happened.

I tried again.

Nothing.

Fuck, no. I was not going to play this game. I stood, ready to get the hell out of here. The second I opened my mouth to call to my mates, a hand covered it. My eyes widened and I reached to pull the hand away but my arms were restrained within a heartbeat.

"Shhhh," a voice whispered in my ear.

Tears burned behind my eyes. I knew I couldn't fight this guy. I'd tried before and failed. And apparently my magic wasn't working either. For a moment, I just stood there, feeling defeated.

Then he started dragging me away from the table and every nerve fired at once. I wasn't going to let him take me anywhere. Grunting, I tried to break his grip, twisting and turning in his arms.

When that didn't work, I dug my heels into the ground, trying to plant myself in place. If I could keep myself here long enough, I was certain one of my mates would find me and help me.

He kept dragging me.

Shit.

I was running out of ideas. No matter how much I struggled, it didn't seem to slow my captor down. I had to get away from him, but how? I stopped struggling and went limp. If I showed him I wasn't going to fight, maybe he'd ease up and I could make a run for it.

I heard a door open and panic surged through me. He was taking me out of the library. I twisted again, pulling my arms and kicking my legs. I did everything I could to free myself from his grasp. I didn't budge. Who the fuck was this guy?

Then all at once, he let go of me and shoved me to the floor. I jumped to my feet and ran for the direction I thought the door was, finding the handle quickly. I turned it and it didn't budge. I pounded on the door. "Help me, please!"

I jiggled the door handle again and kept pounding. "Someone help!" I kept screaming until my throat was sore and then I pressed my forehead to the door, as utter and total defeat washed over me.

"Are you finished?" a male voice asked.

I turned and leaned against the door, staring into the darkness. Somewhere in whatever room I was in was my captor. Whatever or whoever he was, his magic was powerful. Too powerful.

"What do you want from me?" I asked.

"The book," he said.

"I brought it for you and you left it on the table," I said. "So I don't think this is about a book."

"Ah, that's where you're wrong," he said. His voice was chillingly calm. Smooth and clear and devoid of emotion. "I only want the book. That's it. You give it to me and we're done. I have no desire to harm you or any of your friends."

"I brought you the book," I said again, following through on my bluff.

"No, little liar," he said. "You brought me *a* book. Not *the* book. And you brought your mates. All four of them. Which means, you told people about us."

My skin felt like it was crawling. "There is no *us*. I don't even know who you are."

"I'm no-one to be trifled with, I'll tell you that, little liar."

"Stop calling me that," I said. I could almost hear the smile in his voice. He was enjoying this. Sick fuck.

"Oh, but you are a liar, dear girl," he said. "You are not afflicted with the burden of the truth since you are only half fae."

The words sent a shockwave through me and my whole body

tensed. He hadn't said it, but he didn't need to say it. I was dealing with a fae. My last encounter with someone from that realm had nearly gotten me killed and I wasn't keen on repeating any of that. "So, you're friends with Halifax."

"No," he said. "She and I are actually on opposite sides, though I can appreciate her handiwork with you."

"You do know I'm not going to give you what you want," I said.

He scoffed. "Why must the young always make things so much harder on themselves?"

"Let me go, asshole," I said.

"I'll give you some time to make the right choice," he said. "I warned you. If you don't do what I want, your friends will suffer. I'm guessing next time we meet, you'll be more inclined to assist me."

"Don't count on it," I said.

Something clicked. Something that sounded very much like a lock. Without turning my back on the fae, I grabbed the door handle again and turned. This time, it opened.

I flung open the door. "He's in here! Come quick!"

With a buzz the lights flickered back to life and I squinted against the unexpected brightness. I never moved from my position in front of the door but when I looked up, there was nobody in the room.

I let go of the door handle and took a step into the study room. It had a long table surrounded by chairs and a white board on the wall. There were no other exits. Just the door I came in through. I squatted down and looked under the table even though I could see that nobody was hiding under it.

I stood and walked in a slow circle around the room, feeling the walls for any seams or signs of hidden doors. It appeared empty.

"Raven!" Ben shouted.

I turned just in time for him to slam into me and pull me into an embrace.

He released me from the hug then held me out at arm's length. "Are you hurt?"

I shook my head. "No, I'm okay."

"What happened?" Matt asked as he walked into the study room.

"Was he here?" Luka asked as he joined us.

Zach walked in last, his face ashen. "I was so worried we'd lost you."

"I'm okay," I said. "But we've got a big problem on our hands."

"So he was here?" Luka asked.

I nodded. "He knew the book was a fake without even touching it. He also knew all four of you were here and that you're my mates. And he knew about Halifax."

"Don't say it, Raven," Matt said. "Don't say this is about some portal again."

"I don't think it is," I said. "I think he really just wants the book."

"Maybe we should just hand it over," Zach said.

I shook my head. "We can't do that."

"We need to figure out what's so important about it," Matt said.

"Guys, there's something you should know," I said.

All four of them looked at me and I took a deep breath. "We're dealing with a fae here. A full blooded, crazy powerful fae. And he's not going to stop until he has that book."

"How do you know?" Ben asked.

"Well, she is fae," Zach said.

"I know that, but I didn't know they had a thing where they could sense each other," Ben said.

"I don't know if we do," I said. "But he pretty much told me. Dude was obsessed with the fact that I could tell a lie."

"Oh yeah," Luka said. "They hate that."

"So what now?" Matt asked.

"Well, first I want to get out of this room. Just standing in here is giving me the creeps." I shivered.

"Come on," Ben put his arm around my shoulder and guided me out. "I'll walk you to your room. You need some rest. We can figure out our next steps tomorrow."

"I still think she'd be safer with us," Zach said.

"She's fine in her room," Ben said.

"He'll take care of her," Luka said. "You know he will."

"We could too," Zach said.

"Drop it," Luka said.

"All of you stop," I said. "I'm going to my room and I'm going to sleep. Tomorrow, we'll figure this out."

Raven

By morning, I was even more on edge than I had been the night before. The fae who threatened me didn't give me a timeline or a plan. He just said he wanted the book.

I tested the drawer and it still sent a shock through my fingertips. The book was still safe. For now.

It should have made me feel better knowing I had kept the book out of his hands, but I was wavering. The magic he already possessed was insane. He'd managed to extinguish all the light and remove my ability to do magic. How was that even possible?

Part of me wanted to give him the book to send him away.

But I knew I couldn't. If he was already that strong, what else could the book add to his magic skills? The thought was terrifying.

He'd warned me not to tell anyone, but I couldn't think of a single solution where I could outsmart him without giving in. I had to go to Dr. Green. He'd shown his cards and I was pretty sure he was on the straight and narrow. Besides, he'd never tried to kill me so he had that going for him.

It was the only option. I couldn't do this on my own, and I couldn't expect my mates to help. He already knew all of them and had managed to affect all their magic too.

Feeling determined, I slid my backpack over my shoulders and headed for a late breakfast. I had gym first, which I did not want to be late for, so Dr. Green would have to wait until lunch. I was hoping that if the fae was watching me, he'd see that I was going about my day as normal. It wasn't unheard of for me to visit Dr. Green. In fact, attending meetings in his office had been a requirement for a while.

It was a risk, but it felt like the best option.

The cafeteria was nearly empty when I arrived, but I spotted Makayla at our usual table. She stood and waved when she saw me, then sprinted over. Oddly, she was alone. It was later than I thought.

"Hey," she said. "I was starting to worry. It's not like you to skip breakfast."

"Late night," I said.

"I heard," she said.

I cocked an eyebrow. "You heard?"

She shrugged. "Ben gave me the short version. You know, Raven's life is in danger *again*. Please watch over her if I'm not around *again*."

I grinned. Of course he did. "Sorry about that.

She slid her arm into my elbow and guided me toward the

lunch line. "It's fine. I fully expect you to protect me from life or death one of these days, though. It's only fair."

"Any time," I said.

She pulled her arm away so I could grab a foil wrapped breakfast sandwich. I also picked up a bottle of water and then thanked the lunch ladies. They really did make the best food in the world and they were always so friendly.

"You sure you don't want two sandwiches, Raven?" One of them called.

"No thanks, I've got gym first," I said.

"Alright, something extra at lunch then," she said with a wink.

"Thanks," I said, giving her a wave.

I unwrapped the sandwich and ate as I walked, Makayla at my side.

"Ben didn't tell me the details as to who or what is trying to kill you this time," she said. "Care to enlighten me?"

I swallowed my bite of sandwich. "Sorry. Can't give you that."

She sighed. "I didn't think so. You will tell me when it's over, though, right?"

"Definitely," I said. "We'll have a girls night, order pizza and I'll tell you everything."

"You still owe me that to tell me about what went down at the trials. And I need the details about how the hell you managed to snag *both* of the Obscura twins," she said.

I stopped walking. "You know, you're right. Tomorrow. My room this time. Pizza and catching up."

"Deal," she said just as the bell rang. "See ya at lunch."

"Bye," I said, my mouth full.

I quickly finished the rest of the sandwich and threw the foil in the recycle bin. Then I hurried to the gym. The sooner I got this over with, the sooner I got to spill everything to Dr. Green.

As soon as I stepped into the locker room, I knew something was wrong. Tension was thick in the air and the usual conversation and laugher was missing. Most of the women in the room were sitting on benches and none of them were dressed in gym clothes. Their expressions were grim and eyes downcast. A few girls were wiping tears from their faces.

I scanned the room for Violet and didn't see her so I walked over to Megan, a mage who had always been nice to me. "What's going on?" I asked as I took a seat on the bench next to her.

She sucked in a breath and then turned to look at me. Her cheeks were red and I could see the lines from tears on her face. "You didn't hear yet?"

I shook my head. "What?"

"It's Violet," she said. "Scarlett found her this morning."

"Don't tell me she's…" I covered my mouth with my hand and my throat tightened. I couldn't even finish the sentence.

"She's in the hospital but it doesn't look good," Megan said. "She was totally drained of blood."

"Oh my god," I said. "Who does that?"

Megan shook her head. "I don't know."

"It's worse, though," someone said.

I looked over to see Delores staring down at me. "The attacker was fae. Which means it was you or that new professor."

"What? How do you know it was a fae?" I asked, ignoring her threat against me. I knew I didn't attack Violet and I was pretty sure it wasn't the new professor. But Violet was my friend and the fae who threatened me warned me not to tell anyone.

"There were traces of magic on her from the blood draining spell," Delores said. "And we all know how Luka's mom feels about vamps."

I stood, anger replacing my initial shock. "I would never hurt a friend so whatever you're implying you might want to stop."

"Or what? You going to use some of that fae magic on me? You know, they should send you back to your realm where you belong," she said.

Anger surged through, blurring my vision and without thinking it through, I pulled my arm back and punched Delores in the face.

She wasn't expecting it and I landed a blow so hard, it sent shooting pain through my hand. Delores's head turned with the impact and she flew backward until she hit the lockers behind her.

I shook my hand out and took a step back, ready for her to retaliate. She pushed herself from the lockers and blinked at me a few times, looking dazed for a second. Then she bared her teeth. "You want to play, little fae?"

I braced for impact, ready to punch her again no matter how hard my hand hurt. She came at me, screaming as she charged me, her fingers curved like claws.

I slid to the side, forcing her to change positions. Her finger-nails made contact with my cheek and she scratched the side of my face. It stung like hell but only made me angrier.

Heat rose inside and suddenly my hands were on fire. "You want to mess with me, Delores? You already tried to kill me once. If I was going to harm someone it would be you, not my friend Violet."

Delores stopped in her tracks, her shoulders moving up and down with her heavy breaths. "You want to play dirty?"

"Come at me, bitch," I said, holding my hands in front of me.

She lifted her hands and I heard popping and groaning sounds. Then, water came spraying in from the showers in a stream, guided by her hand movements.

Screaming surrounded me and I was vaguely aware of the other girls in the locker room running from our fight.

I was soaked and my fire went out. Hands still smoking, I charged her. My shoes squished over the wet floor but all I could think about was taking her down.

A body check later and she was on the ground in the puddle of water she'd created. I punched her in the face again, this time, hitting her lip. She licked the blood and her nostrils flared. Her sea green eyes glowed, turning bright green and she started to sing.

"Cover your ears," someone called.

I climbed off her and slammed my hands over my ears. It almost blocked out the sound of her voice, but it was so loud I could still hear it. It was unearthly and ethereal. I had to fight against the urge to hear it. I could feel my will power breaking with each heartbeat. I had to get away from her.

Desperate, I turned and headed toward the nearest door. It opened from the other side before I got there and Coach Miller filled the doorframe. "What the hell is going on in here?"

The singing stopped and I dropped my hands. I was soaking wet and my shirt was torn, though I couldn't remember how it happened.

Delores was bleeding and dripping. Both of us were panting.

"Confinement, both of you," he said.

Raven

I sat against the white wall staring at Delores. The room they threw us in was totally empty. It wasn't a replica of the last time I'd been here. Same white walls, and bare floor. Same blinding florescent lights. Same feel of utter dread seeping into my bones. But this time I was in a larger room and this time, I had company.

I could have done without the company.

Delores had her knees pulled up against her chest, her arms wrapped around them. Her chin rested on her knees and she was glaring at me with her sea green eyes. "This is your fault, you know."

I leaned my head against the wall. The real torture of being in here was having to spend time out with the girl I'd tried to knock out.

"We wouldn't be here if you just stayed in your place like you should," she said.

I lifted my head and stared at her, my brows furrowed. "In my place?"

"You don't belong here, we both know that," she said. "You're nobody. You didn't spend your whole life being groomed to come to this school. You didn't have to outshine all the other kids or earn the best test scores. Shit, you didn't even know how to cast a spell when you got here."

"That's what this is all about?" I asked. "That I'm not good enough for your school?"

"You're not," she said. "You shouldn't be here. It threw everything off. Years of hard work and planning."

"Years of planning what, exactly?" I asked. "Because last I checked, the thing you're the most mad about was that I got the guy."

She scoffed. "You got *all* the guys. Not just *one*. You took the four most eligible bachelors and claimed them all. I'm still not even sure how you pulled it off."

"We have a bond," I said, though I wasn't sure why I was bothering to explain anything. I didn't owe her a thing. "It wasn't planned."

"Right," she said. "You just happened to bond with those specific men."

I sighed. "You know, I don't care what you think."

"I should be impressed," she said. "I can't even pull off that kind of scam and I'm a siren. My power is literally to entrap men."

I laughed. I knew she meant it as an insult, but it struck me as amusing. How often had I been completely overwhelmed by the fact that I had *four* mates? The idea was impossible to wrap my head around at first. Yet, now that they were mine, it was the only way I could imagine my life. I was part of each of them and they were all a part of me.

It was beyond magic or enchantments. Our connection was something else that was so much deeper. Like our souls connected. We were impossible to separate.

"What's so funny?" she asked.

"You," I said. "How you actually think I went around trying to find a way to convince each of these intelligent, powerful men to follow me around or something. As if I could train them. You know them better than that. You know they're all smarter than that. Even your enchantments would wear off eventually."

She set her forehead down on her knees, hiding her face. Apparently, the conversation was over.

I stood, feeling suddenly too restless to sit. Our prison had a single door. White with a small window and a silver door handle. I walked over to it and stood on my tiptoes to peek out the small square window. Beyond our room, I could see the white hallway and an identical door across from us.

There weren't any signs of other people around, though. I lowered back to my feet and let out a sigh. How long were they going to keep us in here, anyway?

I ran a hand through my hair and started pacing the room. I wondered what was going on out in the school without me. Did all my mates already know I was here? Had any of them found out about Violet?

I stopped walking, suddenly terrified.

What if they went to Dr. Green? What if they told someone?

It was obvious that the fae who was threatening me was the

one who had hurt Violet. Had he seen her and I talking during gym class before I walked into the locker room?

I walked over to Delores and kicked her shoe.

She looked up at me with a snarl. "What?"

"Tell me what you know about Violet," I said. "And none of your bullshit accusations this time. You know damn well she's my friend and that I'd never hurt her."

Delores looked up at me, her expression hard. There was a lot of bad blood between us but none of it came from me and she knew it. I waited, keeping my eyes locked on her. I wasn't going to let her get away with silence.

After what felt like minutes, she rolled her eyes and let out a sigh. "Fine. I know you probably didn't hurt Violet."

"*Definitely* didn't hurt her," I corrected, though a wave of guilt washed through me knowing that I was still responsible. There was no way I'd tell that to Delores, though. And honestly, it was more about not getting anyone else hurt. That fae wasn't messing around and I had no idea what he was capable of. For all I knew he was listening to me right now.

I shivered, the thought unnerving. I had no idea what I was going to do about him but right now I was more concerned about Violet. "Is she going to be okay?"

Delores's brow furrowed. "You actually do care about someone other than yourself."

"I care about a lot of people," I said. "Spill."

"You pretty much know what I know. She was drained of blood, which as I'm sure you can guess isn't a good thing for a vampire," she said.

"I'm pretty sure that's not a good thing for anyone," I added.

"Touché," she said. "But it's especially dangerous for a vampire and incredibly painful as it can take days or even months for them to die from it."

"Why would someone do that?" I asked.

She shook her head. "I don't know. It's usually something that's done in torture situations. To try to get someone to talk."

Ice seemed to flow through my veins. Had that fae tortured Violet? What could he possibly have thought she'd know? Then my mind whirred right to my mates. There had to be torture methods for every supernatural that I wasn't aware of. Ways of exploiting weaknesses. Was he going after them next?

I turned away from Delores and scrubbed my face with my hand. I fucked up. Instead of keeping my cool and being the bigger person, I'd lost my temper and ended up in here where I can't help anyone. For all I knew, the fae was out there picking off my mates one at a time.

That can't happen. I cannot be stuck down here. I turned back to Delores. "We have to get out of here."

"Tell me about it," she said. "I can barely even feel my magic anymore and I have no interest in dying any time soon."

I'd almost forgotten about the deaths that were tied to time spent in confinement and here I was on round two. Well, that was another bit of disturbing information to add to my list of issues.

"You've been here longer," I said. "Any ideas on what we have to do to get out? Is it like a timed thing or is it just up to Coach Miller?"

She shrugged. "Unlike you, I've never been here. How'd you get out last time."

"A fae with a stolen face tried to kill me and they let me out after that," I said. "I wouldn't recommend we duplicate that."

"Fair," Delores said. "So all that shit is true? All that talk about you and the fae and the portal and everything?"

I wasn't in the mood to rehash my past but another peek out the window told me we weren't likely to get out anytime soon. The hallway was still empty. Not a sign of life anywhere.

I walked back to my spot against the wall and slid down to the floor. "What do you want to know?"

She cocked an eyebrow. "We're going to be here a while, why not start at the beginning?"

"Which beginning? How I accidentally murdered two dudes and wound up in here or how the fae tried to kill me and steal my magic?"

"Shit, Raven," Delores said. "You really killed two guys?"

"Yeah," I said. "But they deserved it."

"I'm sure," she said. "What did they do, try to steal your lunch money?"

I laughed even though there was nothing funny about it. "Well, they had me pinned against a wall with a gun to my throat. I didn't ask them their exact plans, but considering I tried to hand over my purse and they didn't take it I don't think it was going to end well for me."

She was silent for a moment and I wondered if the conversation was over.

"I had no idea," she said. "I assumed you just pulled strings with the Obscuras to get in here."

"They're paying my tuition," I blurted out, though I wasn't sure why I said it. "My parents were killed by the time thief that tried to kill me and I guess my mom and Ms. Obscura were friends. So there's that."

"Okay, back up," she said. "So the time thief was after you but she offed your parents first?"

I nodded. "Apparently she wanted more time magic and since that's my hidden talent, she came after me."

"So you didn't just make all this up to get on the Obsucra family's good side?" she asked.

My brows pulled together as I studied her expression. She looked like she was serious. "Why would I do that?"

"Just something I heard," she said.

"Well, then," I said. It suddenly made more sense as to why she hated me. "I don't know where you're getting your gossip, but they suck."

She laughed. "Yeah, maybe."

The door opened and we both turned to see Dr. Green standing in the doorway. He was frowning down at us. "Delores, back to your classes. Raven, we need to talk."

Delores didn't need to be told twice. She was on her feet and out the door without even saying goodbye. I wasn't sure, but something told me I'd see less issue from her from now on. Assuming I survived my next encounter with the fae.

Dr. Green stood in the doorway, as if he didn't want to enter the room. I didn't blame him. I could feel it muting my magic. It reminded me a little of what it was like in the dark room of the library. No magic at all with whatever that fae had done.

"I know you heard about Violet," Dr. Green said.

"How is she?" I asked.

"She's going to make it," he said. "But that's not why I bring it up."

I waited, wondering if he'd seen the attacker. Maybe this was good news. Maybe he'd caught the fae who attacked her.

"I have to ask you, do you know anything about her attack?" he stared at me, unblinking.

I tensed, unsure of what to say. I wasn't prepared for this. This morning, I was set on telling him everything and now that I have the chance, I can't. I know that Violet was a warning. If I tell him, someone else is going to be hurt. Because I can't give the fae the book so I have to buy myself some time.

"I have no idea," I said.

His face fell a little, disappointment showing in his expression. It broke my heart. I'd come to trust and respect Dr. Green and I hated that I couldn't be honest with him.

"Very well," he said. "Go back to class. No more fighting."

I nodded. "Thank you, sir."

He stepped away from the doorway and waited in the hall. I walked past him and without looking back, headed away from him. I needed to figure out something fast before anyone else got hurt. Only this time, I was going to have to do it alone.

Raven

The bell rang just when I made my way into the main hallway and I was surrounded by students all moving at once. I grabbed someone's shirt. "Hey, what period are we in?"

The student, a red-head with her hair pulled into two low pigtails squinted at me as if I was speaking a different language.

"I was in confinement," I said. "What period are we in now?"

She scrunched up her face and tugged her arm away from me as if my time in confinement might rub off on her. "Just finished lunch."

"Thank you," I said, not waiting for her to respond.

I pushed my way through the masses toward the cafeteria. It was already empty when I arrived. *Fuck.*

I could either go to my next class or try to hunt down all my mates and Makayla to make sure they were all safe. Considering I just spent the last couple of hours in confinement, I figured I should probably go to class.

That's when I remembered that my backpack was in the locker room still. I frowned. I did not want to go back there right now.

Worse, I realized my next class was supposed to be independent study with Professor Halifax. But Professor Halifax was currently in jail and there was a new fae here. And I was pretty sure she hated me already.

For a moment, I stood near the doors to the cafeteria, contemplating just going back to my room. Could I get away with just saying I was sick? What would they do if I just spent the rest of the day in there alone?

I ran a hand through my hair, feeling frustrated at the whole world. It wasn't like it would fix anything. Going to my room just meant I'd overthink the whole situation and probably not come up with any solutions. And I'd likely still end up having to deal with my independent study tomorrow.

None of my choices were good so I might as well get this over with. Hoping Professor Flora didn't care that my backpack was MIA, I headed toward her classroom.

As I neared her door, a familiar face greeted me. My heart fluttered and a rush of joy filled my chest. Matt was waiting outside of the Spellcasting room door. At least I knew one of them was safe. "I am so glad to see you."

He grabbed my hand as soon as I reached him and pulled me closer to him. "I heard you were in confinement. Are you okay?"

My shoulders dropped at his concern. He looked really worried and I could feel his tension. It was heavy and dark.

"I'm fine," I said. "I wasn't in there very long. I'm so glad you're alright. Did you hear about Violet?"

He nodded.

Now it was my turn to have all of my emotions go to a dark and stormy place. "It was my fault. I wasn't supposed to tell anyone."

"Don't do that to yourself," he said. "You're not the one who hurt her. *He* made that choice and that makes *him* the bad guy, not you."

I nodded, only half believing him.

"It's going to be fine. We'll figure it out together," he said.

I swallowed over a lump in my throat. That wasn't going to happen. Whatever this was, I was going to figure it out on my own. "We should go in and get this over with."

He took a deep breath. "I almost didn't come since Professor Halifax is gone but no way was I going to leave you alone with her."

"Thanks," I said. "Maybe she'll just send us away?"

"That would be nice," Matt said. "You and I haven't had any solo time in a while."

I smiled at him. Rolling around in-between the sheets sounded like exactly the kind of stress relief I needed right now. But first we had to get out of this class. "You ready?"

Squaring my shoulders, I opened the door and walked in, Matt right behind me.

"You're late," Professor Flora called.

I stopped in my tracks and faced the professor. She was in a pink dress today that looked oddly similar to a toga. I wondered if she was wearing clothing that was popular in Faerie. Her silver hair was swept up into a pile on top of her head and dozens of gems were pinned in her hair. She looked more like she was ready to go to a party than teach a class.

"Sorry, I was in confinement this morning," I said.

She pursed her lips.

I was pretty sure she didn't care.

"So we were doing this independent study with Professor Halifax to work on connecting our magic and it turned out, the whole thing was a scam. You know? She just wanted us to help her open a portal. So I'm not sure we still need this," Matt said.

Professor Flora cocked an eyebrow, making her features look even sharper than usual. "You're correct, young man. You may leave. Only Raven needs to be in attendance."

I let out a stifled squeaking sound of surprise. That was not what we were hoping for. If I was stuck doing this, I thought I'd at least be doing it with my mates.

Professor Flora's gaze was on Matt, but I was pretty sure she was smirking at me.

"Well, I can stay if it will help Raven," Matt said. "We do have a unique bond."

"I know all about her bonds," Professor Flora said. "I read her file. It's possible that I know more about her than you do."

"My file?" I asked, recalling the folder Dr. Green had when I first arrived.

Professor Flora still had her gaze set on Matt. "You are dismissed, Mr. Obscura. For now."

Matt turned to me, his expression pleading. I could tell he felt terrible.

"I'll see you at dinner," I said.

He nodded and then turned to leave.

I looked over at Professor Flora. "So, what are we working on today?"

"Remedial magic," she said.

"Uh, I know I'm still pretty new, but I did open a portal a

few days ago," I said.

"Could you do it again?" she asked.

"It's illegal to open a portal to the fae realm," I said. "So no, I wouldn't do it."

"But *could* you?" she asked. "Because I'm wondering just how much magic you are capable of on your own or how much of that was magic you channeled through your more experienced mates."

I hadn't thought of that before. All of them grew up with magic. They'd studied it before coming here. I was the one who was new to all of this. "Fair point."

"This way," she said, gesturing to the desk in the center of the circular room.

On the table there were five rocks sitting on squares of colored cloth. They were all black and smooth. While they were pretty enough, they didn't look special. But I'd been here long enough to at least know that surely wasn't the case. If she had them out for me, they were something important.

"These are element stones," she said. "All magic can be traced to one of the elements as you have likely learned in your studies."

"Yes," I said. "My strongest is fire. So I spent most of my time here thinking I was a fire mage."

"Your mother was a fire mage," she said. "Your father was … something else."

"Fae, yeah, I know," I said.

She smirked. It was unnerving. I didn't like seeing her so self-satisfied. It didn't feel like it was going to end well for me.

"Fae magic is different," she said. "We align with elements, but we also have magic from our court. In Faerie, there are five courts. Autumn, Winter, Spring, Summer, and Shadow."

I remembered reading about the courts briefly in one of the few books I'd found on the topic of Faerie. Mostly, it was just a rundown of the creatures that lived there and the million ways they could kill you. It never got into the fae themselves, though I was certain they were more deadly than any of the creatures listed in the book. "I know the names of the courts, but that's about it."

"I'm not surprised. Those who live in this realm are afraid of us," she said.

A tiny shiver ran up my spine at her words. *Us.* I was part of them, part of that realm that caused so much fear. It was difficult to imagine. Most of my life I was just Raven. A human girl trying to make it in the world.

Then, I found out I was a mage, which had been difficult enough to adjust to. Adding the fae blood was just more confusion. I still wasn't even sure I ever fully wrapped my head around being a mage.

"This will allow me to find out your court," she said. "I have my suspicions, but I want to confirm before we move on. Each court has their gifts and it's important to know what you are predisposed to with regards to your magic."

"Alright, what do you want me to do?" I asked, stepping toward the stones.

"It's simple," she said, walking to the other side of the desk so she was facing me.

She waved her hand over each stone in turn. The third stone lit up, glowing green. "See that?"

I nodded. "It's beautiful." It really was. The stone had changed color and now looked like an emerald with a green light radiating from it.

"I'm from the Spring Court, so the spring stone responds to me," she said. "Your turn."

I shook my head, not quite sure of what to expect as I lifted my hand. I waved it over the first stone, nothing happened. Then I moved to the second stone, nothing. Third stone, still nothing. I was starting to wonder if this whole thing was a big joke. Some trick she was playing on me. Or maybe it worked, but I wasn't actually fae after all.

When I waved my hand over the fourth stone, it turned molten orange and lit up in a warm glow like that of a fire. "Wow."

"Summer," she said. "Do me a favor and try that last stone."

I moved my hand away from the glowing orange stone over the final stone. As soon as my hand hovered over it, I gasped. The stone dissolved in front of my eyes, leaving a swirling cloud of black smoke. "What the hell?"

"Summer and Shadow," she said.

I set my hand down and both rocks returned to normal. "What does that mean?"

"It means you're the missing child of the youngest prince of the Summer Court. He was half summer, half shadow as his parents united their kingdoms in marriage. He came to this realm and never returned," she said.

"That's a lot to take in," I said.

"It is," she agreed. "And now I know where we have to begin."

"You make it sound so ominous," I said. "What does that even mean?" I was getting really tired of people keeping things from me.

"It means we'll start by finding out what your magic is capable of and we work with that to help you reach your full potential," she said. "But you're in no shape to be doing anything yet after that time in confinement. We'll start next week."

I wasn't going to argue with a week off of independent study sessions. "Great."

The bell rang and for the first time ever, I was grateful to go to my History of Magic class.

Raven

I felt naked without my school bag but it was going to have to wait till tomorrow. I did not want to have to go back to gym any sooner than I had to. Luckily, the student next to me let me borrow some paper and a pencil so I could at least take notes.

Professor Craft walked into the room in a flourish of flowing fabric. She had an affinity for long skirts and cloaks. Today's outfit was a navy-blue skirt dotted in silver stars. Her cloak matched and looked like it was made of enough fabric to make two cloaks.

She stopped in front of her desk and tucked a strand of gray hair behind her ear as she stared out at all of us. "Based on recent events, I think a deviation from the curriculum is appropriate."

I straightened in my seat, wondering where she was going with this. Recent events *had* to mean the fake trials Professor Halifax had set up. And I had a feeling my return to class was partially to blame for her changing her lesson. Otherwise, she'd have started whatever this detour was right after the events. Not wait until my second day back in class.

She walked over to the white board and grabbed a marker. "No notes today. This isn't exactly on the up and up. But you have a right to know."

I set my pencil down, feeling a mixture of intrigue and guilt. I also had a feeling I knew where she was going. After just coming from my lesson with Professor Flora, I was glaringly aware of the missing information regarding fae history. I also knew it wasn't officially supposed to be taught.

Professor Craft wrote a single word on the board and I knew my guess was correct.

Faerie

The word seemed to mock me. Reminding me of how out of my element I was here. I wasn't just green when it came to the world of supernaturals. I was completely unaware of how my fae heritage played into it at all.

Whispers filled the classroom and I swore I could feel the eyes of a dozen students on me. I forced myself to stare ahead, not turning back to meet their gaze. Of course the whole school knew all the details of the event in the Spellcasting room. Why wouldn't they? Gossip spread through this building faster than mono had in my high school.

"You're not taught about the fae realm because all portals were sealed between our realms," Professor Craft said. "Some fae remain with us, either by choice or because they didn't have the ability to open a portal before everything was sealed. Some are here because they are part fae. Including one of your classmates."

Professor Craft stared at me and I felt my face heat. *Fuck*. If anyone was unsure if the rumors were true, they all knew now. Thanks for that.

"The fae are not to be feared as you've been taught, though," she said.

I looked up at my professor, surprised by her statement. My classmates were clearly startled too because the whispers started back up.

"Listen," she said. "I've made a career out of studying history and while I know I don't look a day over fifty, I can tell you I've lived several human lifetimes and I have seen things."

The class was quieter now, hanging on her every word.

"Tell me," she said, walking around her desk so she was standing in front of the rows of students. "Are there no bad mages? No bad shifters? No bad humans?"

"There's bad people in every group," someone said.

"Exactly," she said. "There's always someone who ruins it and makes the rest of us look bad, right?"

"Right," several people answered.

"Let me tell you, I've heard it all. Try being a fallen angel. I'm supposed to be evil by nature, right?" She raised her eyebrows.

The class laughed and I smiled along with them. I'd been here long enough to know that the human misconceptions about supernatural creatures was very wrong. Like she said, there wasn't any good or bad group of supernaturals, just good or bad people within them.

"So do you think the fae are evil?" Professor Craft asked.

Nobody said a word.

Professor Craft hopped up on her desk, taking a seat on top

of it. She set her hands on her lap and looked out at the class, her eyes finally settling on me. "Raven? Are you evil?"

"Of course not," I blurted out.

"Of course you're not," Professor Craft agreed. "The fae were locked out because their magic is far more powerful than the magic of the supernaturals native to this realm. Some of them abused their power. Most did not. However, that was not the true reason why they were sent away."

"What was it?" I asked, totally hanging on every word by this point.

"You think they're powerful here, in their realm, their power is beyond frightening. Their power is muted in our realm to the point where some of their magic doesn't even work here. Their most deadly spells and darkest magic has to be cast in their realm. Which made it a very dangerous place to visit. It was also difficult for some to resist the temptation.

"And of course, we know the stories about what it was like in Faerie. If you eat their food or accept their drinks, you never want to leave. The magic in their very earth that grows their food is far beyond what we can comprehend or control. They can force most other creatures to do anything they want. Though, in our realm, other creatures can match them. On their home turf, none of you would stand a chance. Except for *maybe* Raven. And only because she could eat their food and probably resist their compulsion. The rest of you would be screwed."

I'd never heard the classroom so quiet before. The hair on my arms stood on edge. Every part of me felt on edge. I had no idea the fae were that powerful. And now I almost didn't blame everyone for being so afraid. They closed off that realm for a good reason. Not that it was the right call, but I could see why they made that choice out of fear.

As I replayed Professor Craft's words in my mind, I started

to wonder about the book. Here, it was nothing. But it had come from a fae and was being sought after by a fae.

My hand shot into the air.

"Yes, Ms. Winters?" Professor Craft asked.

"Do they have magical objects the way mages and others do?" I asked. "For spells or whatever."

"Of course," she said. "While their magic seems to be more quickly accessed and more inherent, it's still possible to use spells, charms, and other things similar to how mages work. Though, like mages, some fae are more powerful than others."

She turned her attention back to the class. "Now, who can tell me the four courts of Faerie?"

"Five," I said. "You mean *five*."

She smirked. "Good catch. Most often only the four high courts are taught."

"I know," one of my classmates said.

"Go ahead," Professor Craft said.

"They're named for the seasons," the girl said. "Summer, Spring, Winter, Autumn."

"Correct,' Professor Craft said. "And as Raven mentioned, there are rumors of a fifth though I have never met anyone from that court."

"Shadow," I said, unable to keep it in.

"Yes, the Shadow Court," Professor Craft said.

The whole class seemed to be holding their breath.

"The Shadow Court is a bit of a mystery," she said. "The Shadow Fae are said to be able to control light in any form. And they're said to be able to control the flow of magic itself. Closing it off or directing its path. They are said to be experts at using portals."

I could almost feel the gaze of the class on me. *Shit*. Why hadn't I just kept my mouth shut?

Though, there was some good that came from it. I was now

almost certain the fae I was dealing with was from the Shadow Court. He had closed off the lights and eliminated our magic. He literally did the two things his court was known for doing. If only I knew how to use that knowledge to my advantage.

Professor Craft hopped off her desk and walked back to the white board. She wrote down the names of the four major courts. "We'll skip Shadow since it's not usually an issue. Shadow Fae rarely leave their own court."

Under each of the courts, she wrote a few words, explaining as she went. "The Summer Court is associated with fire magic. Spring with an ability to speak to animals. Winter with a mastery of both water and air. And finally, Autumn is known for its association with earth-based magic."

A few hands shot up and students asked questions but I was so deep in thought, I had a difficult time concentrating. All I could think about was that book and why I had it and why the shadow fae wanted it.

By the time the bell rang, I realized there was only one person who could help me. And right now, she was locked in a prison cell.

Good thing I knew a demon who could travel through dreams.

Raven

I was on pins and needles my whole last period class. My idea was insane and I wasn't even sure if it would work. But it was the only one I had. If there was a chance Professor Halifax knew what was in that book, I had to find out. What if she could help me destroy it? Or send the shadow fae away?

I knew Luka was in a conjuring class last period and I had a general sense of where it was so as soon as the bell rang, I beelined it to his classroom. If I had a choice, I'd do this myself but I couldn't dreamwalk. Even if I could, my magic was still weak from the confinement room.

The hallway was teeming with happy people. The day was over and it was finally time to hang out with friends and socialize. Pockets of students were gathered in the middle of the hall or against walls. I swerved around them, glaring at them for slowing me down. Usually, I didn't mind what other people did but today, it really pissed me off. Luka was probably heading straight to the cafeteria to find me but I had to catch him first.

His classroom door was closed and I didn't see anyone milling about. My heart sank. I was too late. Shoulders slumped, I walked toward it just in case. The door swung open, nearly hitting me. I jumped out of the way as the class filed out. They got out late which meant something was going right for a change.

I waited off to the side, watching for Luka. He walked out of the room with his usual swagger and a grin on his face. His blonde hair was perfectly tousled and he cut quite the figure in his white button down shirt and fitted black slacks. If it weren't for the other things we had to do, I'd drag him right to my bedroom.

"Luka," I called.

His eyes found mine and it sent a charge through me. How he could get me going with one look, I'd never know. But it worked every time. It was either the incubus in him or it was our bond. Either way, he made my whole body feel hot.

"Hey, kitten," he said as he walked over to me. "What a nice surprise. I was worried

about you with those rumors going around, but you look okay."

"I'm fine," I said.

"Good," he said grabbing me and pulling me in for a kiss.

My lips felt hot against his and I leaned into the kiss, savoring his smoke and leather scent. After the day I had, Luka was like instant relief for my tension. His hand moved to my lower back and then slipped down to my ass. He squeezed it as he deepened the kiss.

Someone whistled as they passed us and it broke me from the temporary trance he'd caused. I pulled away from the kiss. "I needed that."

"Should we go somewhere and finish?" he asked, a mischievous glint in his eye.

I groaned. My body wanted to but I knew I couldn't fully relax till this fae thing was under control. "I need a favor."

"Anything, kitten," he said, lifting his eyebrows.

"Not that kind of favor," I said, wishing it was. "Can we talk in my room?"

"Lead the way," he said.

The halls were less crowded than they had been as we made our way to the dungeons. Luka stayed behind me, but I could feel his body heat as we walked. He was just as interested in doing other things as I was, that was for sure.

When we reached the common room, I winced and then quickly tried to cover my expression. Ben was sitting on the couch looking toward the stairs. He stood when he saw me. "I've been so worried."

While I was relieved to see him and find out that he was safe, I wasn't looking forward to kicking him out so Luka and I could do what needed done. I walked toward him and he met me in an embrace. His strong arms felt safe and comforting.

"I'm okay," I said as I pulled away from the hug. "I was only in there for a couple of hours."

"I should kill her for getting you sent there," he said with a growl.

"Not necessary," I said. "I think we actually worked everything out."

"Oh?" he asked.

"Yeah, I have a feeling she won't be bothering me anymore."

He grinned. "I heard you had a hell of a right hook."

I couldn't help but smile. "Well, that's not what made her back off, but I held my own."

"You missed lunch," he said.

"Yeah," I agreed.

"Come on, I'll buy you dinner. Your other boyfriend can join us too," he said without even looking up at Luka.

"I feel so seen," Luka said.

"I'm glad to see you two playing nice," I said. "But there's kind of something I need to do with Luka."

"He's welcome to join us," Luka said.

I glanced over at my incubus. Was he flirting with my other boyfriend? "Not that. I told you already."

"Oh, yes," he said. "It's a secret. I don't even know what she's up to."

"Just trust me on this, Ben," I said.

Ben's jaw tensed and I could feel how conflicted he was.

"I promise, if this works, I'll explain everything to you tomorrow," I said.

"I have to wait a whole night?" he asked, looking skeptical.

"Please," I said. "Tomorrow, me and you. One on one." It was a cheap trick because I knew what that meant to him. I knew he preferred to have time with just the two of us more than any of my other mates.

For a moment, I wasn't sure if he was even going to respond. Then finally, he nodded once. "You win this time, demon. But remember, I'm right next door all night long."

Luka gave him a mock salute. "You got it, boss."

Ben scowled at him, then looked back at me. "You need to eat, at least."

"He's right there," Luka agreed.

"Fine, I'll go for dinner but you two both need to promise me you'll go along with me being on my own tonight. I don't want the others to know yet. Not after Violet."

Ben's face fell. "That's what this is about again? How many times do we have to tell you that you don't have to protect us?"

"Look, if this goes the way I hope, I'll have some information and then we can all make a plan together. I promise," I said.

"Alright," Ben said. "I'll hold you to that."

Luka

Surprisingly, dinner went smoother than I thought it would. Nobody questioned Raven about wanting to get back to her room. Everyone was worried about how she was feeling from her time in confinement and turning in early seemed like a normal reaction.

When I arrived at her room after giving her a head start, I noticed that Ben's door was open a crack. I shook my head and walked over to his room and pushed the door open. "Hey."

He was laying on his bed reading a comic book and looked up at me over the top of the pages. "Hey."

"You know I can protect Raven," I said. "You aren't the only one who is strong."

He set the book down and sat up. "It's not that you can't protect her, it's that I *could* be helping."

"Maybe," I said. "I don't know what she's up to. It could be something that involves my unique skill set."

Ben narrowed his eyes.

"Not like that," I said, quickly. "But dude, you gotta get over this macho thing you do."

"I don't do a macho thing," he said.

I laughed. "You do."

He growled.

I shook my head. "Listen, if Raven was in trouble I'd ask for help."

His expression softened at that comment.

"I wouldn't sit in the room next to you and let her do something stupid. Though, we both know she's totally capable of taking care of herself."

"Most of the time," Ben said. "But this is something more. That fae wasn't messing around. He nearly killed Violet."

"I know," I said.

"I'm starting to think she should just give him what he wants. Her life isn't worth it," he said.

"Let's give her the chance to do whatever she's planning tonight before we jump to giving some crazed fae something that could very well be a weapon. He hasn't given his word that he won't hurt Raven if she gives him the book, has he? We don't know what he'd do with it."

Ben scowled. "I hadn't thought of that."

"I know," I said. "You have to trust her. And me." I took a deep breath, hating the words I was going to say next. "And the twins."

Ben shot me a look that I could practically feel. He hated the idea as much as I did. Then, he took a deep breath. "You're right."

"I know," I said with a grin. "I usually am."

Ben shook his head. "It's going to be a challenge sharing her with all of you."

"Yeah, good thing she's worth it," I said.

"She is," Ben agreed.

"And hey, I'm open to you joining in any time." I winked.

"Alright, that's your queue to leave my room," he said.

I walked out, closing the door behind me. Ben and I had a weird relationship. We weren't quite friends, but at the same time, we had a connection through Raven that almost made me feel like we understood each other better than friends would.

Raven's door was closed and I wondered if she'd been able to hear our conversation through her wall. The walls in the demon dorm were pretty thin. I'd heard things I wish I hadn't over the last few semesters.

I knocked on her door and she opened it almost instantly. Her hair was swept back in a ponytail and she'd already changed out of her uniform into black shorts and a white tee shirt. She wasn't wearing a bra and I could see her nipples through the thin fabric. My cock twitched. I wanted her so bad I could almost taste her kiss already.

"Come on in," she said, as if she wasn't aware of what she was doing to me.

When I walked past her, I caught the scent of arousal and smirked. She wanted me just as much as I wanted her. It took all my willpower to make myself not just throw her on the bed right now.

She asked me here for a reason and I would have to wait to find out what her plan was. And hope that it ended with my cock inside her.

I heard the door close behind me. "So what's this top secret plan of yours?" I asked.

"I want you to try to talk to Professor Halifax in her dreams," she said.

"I'm sorry, what?" I blinked at her, stunned. Why the hell would she want me to contact the crazy professor that nearly got us all killed?

"I think the book is from the fae realm and I want to know what it is and why he's after it. She gave me the book. She might know. Then we can find out what the deal is and maybe even find out a way to destroy it," she said.

"Um, what part of this plan helps us get rid of the fae who already took down one of our friends?" he asked.

"It's a start," she said. "We have to start somewhere."

It felt like my own conversation with Ben was coming back to get me. I'd told him to trust Raven and I needed to follow my own advice. She was right, it was a start. We didn't have any other strategies. "Alright."

She let out a breath and her shoulders dropped in relief. I could feel her tension ease. "Thank you."

I closed the distance between us and slid my hands around her waist. "It's a little early for her to be asleep so we'll need to do something to kill some time."

She cocked an eyebrow. "Oh? Did you have something in mind?"

I pressed my lips to hers and she practically melted into me, her body conforming to mine as she kissed me back. Our lips moved in unison and I deepened the kiss as I dropped my hands to the hem of her shirt.

She slid her tongue into my mouth and I slid my hands under her shirt, stopping when I got to her breasts. I groaned into her mouth as I caressed her tits and played with her hard nipples.

Raven's body was hotter than usual and I could feel her need for me in the force of her kiss. I pulled back, breaking contact long enough to remove her tee-shirt.

Her hands reached for my pants, expertly working my belt loose. She popped open the button and pulled down the zipper. Then she grinned at me as her thumbs rested in the waistband. She was making me wait. Teasing me. And it sent a rush of heat through me, making me want her even more.

After several long heartbeats, she tugged my pants down and then she dropped to her knees.

I gasped as her warm mouth closed around my cock. My eyes rolled back and I moaned as she worked her mouth up and down. Her tongue flicked at the tip before closing her mouth back around me. Every movement drove me wild.

I grabbed a fistful of her hair, guiding her head as she continued to suck me. Her mouth was incredible and with each flick of her tongue, I felt myself inching closer to climax.

Raven's hands grabbed my ass as my cock hit the back of her throat. I was nearly there, and while I wanted to take my time with her, I couldn't think clearly enough to pull away from her.

Suddenly, the pleasure reached its peak and I groaned as I thickened in her mouth, coming so hard my body convulsed.

Raven looked up at me from her knees, a smile on her face. "Was that the kind of distraction you were hoping for?"

"You are amazing," I said, taking her hand and pulling her to her feet. "My turn."

Music came through the wall, the pounding of bass and muffled words of some rock song. I glanced at Raven and laughed. "Guess I was too loud for Ben."

Her cheeks flushed crimson.

"Let's see if I can make you scream louder than his music," I said.

She laughed as I picked her up and carried her to her bed. It was my turn to make her feel good.

I could feel her body responding to every touch. She lifted her hips, making it easier for me to pull her pants off. In no time, I removed all her clothes and I stared down at her gorgeous body.

Her red hair was splayed out behind her making her look like a mermaid in the water. Her perfect tits and the curve of her hips drove me wild. I grabbed her thighs and moved in closer to her, my cock already coming back to life.

I pulled on her legs, dragging her ass off the edge of the bed. She squealed and grabbed hold of the blanket. The whole room seemed to heat as I sensed her arousal peak.

In a single thrust, I was inside her. She moaned, arching her back as I thrusted into her. Leaning down, I caught a nipple in my mouth, sucking on it. My hands explored her body while her arms wrapped around me, pulled me closer to her.

Her hips moved in rhythm with each thrust, the two of us moving in unison, our breathing getting heavier. Raven dug her fingernails into my back and cried out as she climaxed. As she tightened around me, I gasped, reaching my own climax.

I rested my head on her chest. Both of us were sweaty and breathing hard but it was perfect. Being here with her was more than I ever dreamed of. I'd do anything to see her happy. And I'd do anything to keep her safe.

14

Luka

It was odd attempting to enter someone's dreams when I knew Raven was watching me but it wasn't much different than it had been for me in school when I was a kid. I'd attended Brimstone Academy's lower school in the Underworld as a kid. Most of the students there were demons and fallen angels and other creatures that lived in that realm. The upper school wasn't exactly a place most people wanted to go. It had a population of reform students who were required to be there and a number of kids who went there when they or their parents didn't believe in mingling with people who lived in this realm.

I was fortunate that my test scores and my mom's status allowed me to come here. Especially because it led me to Raven. I took a deep breath as I tried to clear my mind, but all I could think about was staying in this realm with Raven. The idea of only going back to the underworld for holidays was actually really appealing. Whatever our future held, I hoped it was here.

Opening one eye, I peeked up at Raven. She was sitting on the bed next to me, staring at me. "You know, it's not helping with you hovering over me."

"Sorry," she said.

"Come on," I tugged on her sleeve and pulled her down next to me on the bed. She quickly settled into my chest with my arm wrapped around her. "Close your eyes. If you're calm, it might help me."

"But you said I can't let you fall asleep," she said.

It was true, I needed to be only half asleep to enter other people's dreams. If I fully fell asleep I was just as likely to fall into my own subconscious as everyone else. But I'd been doing this for years without supervision. "Nobody keeps me awake when I visit your dreams. I think I can handle it."

She yawned and nestled in closer. "Okay. Thanks, Luka."

I kissed her forehead. "Anything for you."

She was asleep in seconds and I wondered if she even slept at all last night. Feeling more relaxed with Raven in my arms, I closed my eyes and attempted to contact the in between. The place that existed between dreams and the waking world where I could travel to other people's subconscious.

After a few deep breaths, I found myself there. It was a gray space of nothing that had to be traversed based on emotions, sensations, and intuition. I thought about the magical signature I got from Raven, the part of her that I'd struggled to identify when we first met. I was pretty sure that was the fae blood. I used that to make my way through while trying to seek out

Professor Halifax. Visiting dreams wasn't an exact science, and I'd made mistakes and ended up in stranger's dreams, but I was determined to pull this off.

"Luka?" Raven's voice floated toward me.

I turned and my jaw dropped open. "What are you doing here?" Raven was standing in front of me in the inbetween. We weren't in her dream, at least I didn't think so. It was as if I'd called her to me.

"I don't know where I am," she said, sounding nervous.

"You're in the gate to the dream realm but I don't know how you got here," I said. "I've never heard of anyone besides an incubus or succubus doing this. And I've never been able to bring someone through with me."

"Maybe it's a fae thing?" she asked, sounding hopeful. "I mean, I have to admit this is better than my usual nightmare."

"That's true," I said. It broke my heart every time I met her in the dungeon in her dreams. I wasn't sure why she was always there and I'd been afraid to ask. I really hoped it wasn't a memory from her past or a premonition of the future.

"What should I do?" she asked.

I shrugged. "I guess you should come with me. If it doesn't work, you'll either go to your own dreams or wake up."

"Okay," she said. "How do we do this?"

Raven

It was an odd place, this dream gateway or whatever it was. Everything around me was in soft focus. Gray, smoky fog spanned as far as the eye could see. Under my feet was a flat gray walkway that reminded me of cement but with the texture of a cloud. It was strange. I almost felt like I was floating, but my feet were grounded. As if I weighed almost nothing. Each step felt like bouncing and I was afraid that if I jumped, I'd keep floating away forever. Did gravity even exist in this place?

"You might be able to help," Luka said, reaching for my hand. "Focus on Professor Halifax's being. Your feelings about her and the way she made you feel when you were in her presence."

"The fear part or the feelings of her being a magical badass?" I asked.

"Maybe not the fear so much as that was more about the event than her," he said.

"Alright," I said. For all she'd done to me, she had at one point, been a mentor. She'd helped me regain my magic and find out about my past. I knew she was powerful, though apparently, she had the wrong kind of magic to open a portal.

Ahead, I saw a dark archway form out of black smoke. "What's that?"

"An opening to a dream," Luka said. "Let's find out if we got the right person."

I squeezed Luka's hand, not wanting to let go as we approached the black smoke. There was nothing visible through it and a creeping sense of dread clawed at my chest. It didn't feel right. It felt like I wasn't all here. Like I was watching myself instead of actually moving through the archway.

The air felt thicker and cooler as clouds of black mist wound their way around my ankles. I held my breath as blackness took over, leaving me in what felt like a moment of freefall.

Just as I was about to panic, the smoke cleared and we were standing in a field with a long table in front of us. The table was surrounded by people in fine clothes and they appeared to be sipping tea. Trays of sweets, bowls of fruit, and towers of tiny sandwiches lined the table. Bouquets of fresh flowers dotted the center of the table and butterflies flitted around them.

A warm breeze blew a loose strand of hair, making it tickle my face. "Where are we?" I whispered.

"We're in someone's dream," Luka said.

"Professor Halifax's dream?" I asked.

"Hopefully," he said.

I scanned the gathered people, looking for a familiar face. Then I spotted her. Professor Halifax was at the head of the table, smiling down at those gathered around her.

She was in a flowing white dress and a wide brim hat. Not something I'd expect to see her in but it was rather sunny in her dream.

I pointed to her. "She's there."

"I see her," Luka said. "Here's where it gets delicate. We need to feel like we're part of the dream. It will help her stay asleep longer."

"Okay," I said.

"See what they're wearing?" he asked. "Imagine yourself in something similar so you blend in."

I looked down to see that I was still in my shorts and tee shirt that I'd gone to sleep in. Actually, I wasn't sure if I was asleep but that was a question for another time. I closed my eyes and imagined myself in a white lacy dress that might be appropriate for an occasion such as this.

When I opened my eyes, I was in a cocktail length lace sundress. *Not bad.* I turned to Luka and he was in a cream-colored linen suit. He looked *very* good in that suit.

He extended his elbow. "Shall we?"

I slid my arm through his and we casually walked to the end of the table where Professor Halifax sat. Her eyes widened when she saw us and she stood.

"Greetings, dear professor," I said as if we were old friends.

"What are you doing here?" she asked. "How did you get into Faerie? You shouldn't be here."

"Why not?" I asked. "Am I not fae?"

"Of course you are," she turned to Luka, "you. This is a dream, isn't it?"

"It is a dream of a party, isn't it?" Luka asked.

"Don't try to play me," she said. "I know you can enter

dreams but I have no idea how you got in. If this is a dream, I'm still in that shit hole prison. And you want something from me."

"I need to know about the book you gave me," I said, dropping all pretense.

She smiled. "So you figured it out, did you? Took you long enough."

"I didn't figure anything out," I said. "I locked it up. There's a shadow fae trying to take it from me."

She walked away from the table and moved close to me. "Are you sure?"

"I'm sure," I said.

She shook her head. "I was afraid of that."

"Spill, Professor," I said. "We don't have much time and he's already tried to kill at least one student."

"That book is ancient dark magic, but it only works in Faerie," she said. "I stole it when I came here so I could destroy it. Turns out, it's indestructible. But it's magic is useless in your realm. As long as it's here, it's nothing but a book. If it gets back to the other realm, though, you can kiss both our realms goodbye."

"So what do I do?" I asked. "I can't let him have it."

"It's not my problem, is it?" she asked. "I'm in prison."

"You owe me," I said.

"I don't owe you anything," she said. "I'm repaying any debt I might have owed you in this cell. My magic is gone. Drained completely and they feed us gruel. I haven't seen the sun since I arrived."

I had to admit, I felt a little bad. But then again, she did try to kill me. "You brought that on yourself."

"If you grew up in Faerie and you got trapped here, you'd understand," she said. "I don't regret anything."

"Where'd the shadow fae come from?" Luka asked.

Professor Halifax shrugged. "He must have snuck in when we had the portal open."

"It was surrounded by monsters," I said.

"Shadow fae are not like other fae," she said. "They can become the shadows, move with them, control them. He could have come through and none of us would have noticed."

"How did he know to look for the book here?" Luka asked.

I glared at Professor Halifax. It was a good question. "Why did he come through that portal?"

"I don't have to tell you all this," she said.

"Please," I said. "I know you won't help us directly but you could at least level the playing field. We've got nothing."

She pursed her lips and looked like she was considering saying something.

"Come on," Luka said. "What can you give us?"

"Fine," she said. "It might be my mate. He knew I took the book and he might have sensed me through the portal."

"Is that why you were trying to get back?" I asked. My stomach tightened. What would I do to get back to my mates? I couldn't even imagine being away from them for more than a day, let alone years. That must have been torture for her.

"I did what I had to do and now question time is over," she said.

"Wait," I said.

But the black smoke was already circling around my ankles and Professor Halifax and the tea party vanished.

I woke with a start and turned to see Luka staring back at me. "What happened?"

"She woke up," he said.

I closed my eyes and whined. "We were getting good information. We just needed a little more."

"We got everything we need," he said. "We now know that

book can't get in his hands. And we know what kind of fae we're dealing with for sure."

"What now?" I asked.

"I guess we wait till he comes around to see what his next move will be, then we make a plan," he said.

I hated it. I hated everything about this. We couldn't give the book to him and we knew how dangerous he was. How was I supposed to fight against that? What was I supposed to do when he came for me again?

"Raven," he said. "We need to tell the others."

I nodded. "Fine, but nobody else."

Raven

The next few weeks went by without so much as a whisper from the shadow fae. I wondered if he had left the school or if he somehow managed to get inside my desk without us knowing.

When I asked Zach about that, he wondered if the shadow fae was waiting for us to unlock it to check. So the drawer remained locked. And we waited.

Classes blurred into each other as the weeks dragged by. We were still preparing for the trials and all our teachers were finding new and creative ways to push us.

The one good thing that had happened was that Violet was finally out of the hospital and back to attending classes with the rest of us. Every time I saw her, I was reminded of how dangerous our situation still was even if the shadow fae hadn't shown his face again yet.

"Don't forget everyone, you have a meeting with your trials mentor tonight," Professor Craft called. "Meet in their classroom at seven."

I tensed. In all the post fake-trials craziness, I forgot all about the meetings we'd had leading up to them. My mentor was currently in a prison cell and was pretty pissed at me for that.

The sound of bags being zipped and students preparing to leave filled the room and I glanced up at the clock. The bell would ring any second. I shoved my notebook and book into my backpack just as the bell rang.

My classmates filed out and I made my way up to Professor Craft's desk.

"Ms. Winters," she said. "Did you have a question about the lesson?"

We'd moved on from fae history into the demon wars of the twelfth century. It wasn't as interesting as it sounded. "No, just about the mentor thing. My mentor is currently incarcerated."

"Ah, yes," she said. "Her replacement, Professor Flora, is taking over her students."

"Wonderful," I said. Even after a few weeks of lessons, I still didn't have much of a feel for Professor Flora. We'd taken notes and done independent research in the library so I hadn't had much time to figure out her views on the world.

I had no idea what to expect in our meeting with Professor Flora, but when we discussed it at dinner, the five of us agreed we should be prepared for anything. Which meant changing out of my black jeans and into something that moved a little freer.

Makayla and I left dinner together and walked back to our dorm room. "How's Remi?" I asked.

"He's fine," she said. "He's still convinced I'm going to move in with him after we graduate."

"Wait a minute." I grabbed her arm and stopped her from walking. "Were you going to tell me this?"

"I didn't tell you?" she asked.

I put my hand on my hip. "Makayla! That's a big deal. Why didn't you tell me?"

She shrugged. "I'm not sure if I want to move in with him. I don't even know if we're going to keep seeing each other after graduation."

"You better figure it out if he's asking about living together," I said.

She sighed. "I know. But hey, I don't see you making plans about what you're going to do with all four of your mates."

"Good point, I'll drop it," I said, resuming walking.

She walked alongside me. "Any word on what the actual trials will be like?"

I shook my head. "No idea. I just hope it isn't as awful as the fake ones."

"I am so grateful I never had to go in there," she said. "And I still can't believe all the trouble Professor Halifax went through to get you to open that portal for her."

"I know," I said. "Some days it feels like it was a hundred years ago and other days it feels like yesterday."

We reached the common room and waved to Starla and Jamal, who were curled up on a couch in a tangle of limbs. It was hard to tell where one of them started. They were a giant pretzel.

"Don't you two have a room you could go to?" Makayla asked.

"It's more comfortable here," Starla said. "Besides, I thought you'd all be out at your meetings."

I forgot they weren't taking the trials. "Not till seven."

"We'll wait till then before we get naked," Jamal said.

"I am never sitting on that couch again," Makayla said.

"You might not want to sit on any of the couches then," Starla said.

"Okay, TMI," Makayla said.

"Seriously? You have your own rooms," I said.

Jamal shrugged.

I shook my head but kept a smile on my face. "Fair warning, I'll be coming back through here in a few minutes."

"You have till seven," Jamal said.

"Come on," Makayla said. "We better hurry."

The two of us burst into laughter as we left the common room and headed to our dorms. "I am never going to look at those couches the same way again," Makayla said.

"Me neither," I agreed.

"Raven, you got a minute?" A deep voice said from behind me.

His voice sent a shiver down my spine in a good way. I turned to see Ben crossing the common room toward us.

"I won't wait up," Makayla said. "See you later."

I waved to Makayla then turned back to my shifter. "Everything okay?"

"Can we talk?" he asked.

"Sure," I said, unlocking my room. "Come on in."

I held the door open for him and he walked in. I followed, then closed the door behind me. "What's wrong?"

"I know I told Luka I'd let it go, and I'm trying. I really do trust you. I want to let you do it all on your own, but I can't stop worrying," he said.

My brow furrowed as I stared at my mate. He looked distraught and uncomfortable. The two of us usually fell into such easy understanding but that wasn't happening right now. It was heartbreaking to feel him like this. "Ben, what exactly are you talking about?"

"The whole fae thing," he said. "I don't want to bother you about it, but are you keeping things from us? I don't want you going off to be the hero. I want to help."

I let out a breath and closed the distance between us. "I'm not hiding anything. I just haven't heard from him."

Was it possible that my alpha was feeling left out? I had been spending a lot of time with the twins doing homework lately since our classes were similar. And there was my dream time with Luka. I really hadn't made much time for him in the last few weeks and I felt terrible.

I caressed his cheek, feeling the rough stubble under my palm. "Ben, thank you for worrying about me."

He grabbed my hand and pulled it to his mouth, pressing his lips against my fingertips. "You know how much you mean to me, right?"

I nodded. "And you know I feel the same about you."

The whole room seemed to heat up and I clenched my thighs together against the rush of arousal that was spreading through me. Ben's lips brushed against my fingers, one at a time, kissing as he moved along.

He took hold of my other hand and repeated the kisses. My breath hitched and I found myself internally begging for more. It felt like teasing. Giving me those gentle kisses. It was so unlike his usual aggressive nature when we were intimate.

I could sense his unease and I wanted to make him feel better. To let him know how much he meant to me. I leaned into the kiss, pushing my lips against his, harder. He met the pressure, letting his hunger for me take over.

My panties were already soaked and I wanted nothing more than to feel him inside me. I slid my hands under his shirt, feeling the rippling muscles of his abs and up to his rock hard pecks. Every inch of his skin felt like it was on fire and I knew he was responding to me.

He deepened the kiss, his usual aggressive urgency returning. I moaned into his mouth, feeling my own body temperature rising to match his. As his hands moved under my shirt, surges of electricity radiated from his touch. Everything was in overdrive. All my senses working at once. I wove my fingers though his hair, pulling his head down to kiss him harder. He responded by biting my lower lip and then sucking on it until I moaned.

Ben broke away from the kiss but his lips moved to my ear, then down my neck to my throat. He kissed the sensitive skin making me shiver with desire. I breathed out his name as pressure built in my core. "Ben, please."

He looked down at me, his expression hungry and fierce. With a low growl, he pushed me against the door. I gasped, getting even more turned on by his actions.

My wrists were in his hand now and he pinned them above me, holding them in place. His legs caged me in, keeping me trapped against the door.

With his free hand, he worked the button and zipper of my pants and I lifted my hips to help him guide them down. Then, he removed his pants and kicked them aside. Mine were still around my ankles, acting as another restraint but I didn't want to fight it. I wanted him to take me.

"Gods, you are so sexy," he said, his voice filled with lust.

"Ben." My brain was so foggy I couldn't even form words. I couldn't wait anymore. The way he looked at me, the feel of his rough hand on my stomach, his erection pressed against my hip. It was all too much. My breathing was heavy, desperate, I needed him.

He grabbed my thigh with his free hand and pulled my foot out of my pants. My panties were still on but they were already soaked. I could smell the arousal of both of us mixing in the room and all it did was make me pant harder and want him more.

Ben let go of my wrists and I threw my arms over his shoulders. My leg was around his waist now and he angled his cock toward my entrance.

With a thrust of his hips, he filled me and I tossed my head back with a moan, hitting the door. I didn't care, though. The only thing I could think about was the feel of his huge cock inside me.

Ben grunted as he pushed into me and I tightened my leg around him, forcing him in deeper. His arms went around my head, caging me in.

I raked my fingers through his hair and pulled his head toward me. Our lips met in a sizzling kiss, my lips swollen from the pressure. His stubble scratched my cheeks as his mouth moved to my neck, then lower to my breasts. I moaned as he licked each of my nipples.

Suddenly, he pulled out, leaving me panting for more. With a smirk, he grabbed me around the waist and turned me roughly so I was facing away from him. His hand slid down my back to my ass. With one hand around my waist, he pushed me down so I was bent, my ass in the air.

His fingers slid into me with ease and I gasped as pleasure surged through me. His cock rubbed against my ass while his fingers continued to bring me near orgasm. I grabbed my ankles for support, feeling lightheaded from being upside down. There was too much sensation at once. His fingers, his cock, his rough hand on my back. It all worked together to send me into a screaming orgasm.

My body was still shuddering when he slid his fingers out and replaced them with his cock.

I moaned in time with him as his hard thrusts quickly got me to the edge of orgasm again. As I cried out in pleasure, I felt him thicken. He groaned as he came. Folding on top of me, Ben slid his arms around me. He kissed my shoulders. "I love you."

"I love you too," I said.

Ben

Raven's scent lingered on me as I walked into the Spellcasting room. I knew the others would know exactly why we were a few minutes late. We had an unusual bond, the five of us. Raven's other mates wanted her to be happy just as much as I did. And I knew they'd protect her with their lives. So for that reason alone, I did my best to deal with sharing her.

Sharing wasn't exactly in my nature. But I found that the more time I spent with the others, the easier it got. Our arrangement felt less forced and more natural. Part of me wanted to fight that, but as we spent more time together doing normal things like eating lunch, it was harder to do.

We were getting used to each other. Starting to rely on each other. In a way, we were our own strange little pack.

"Sorry we're late," Raven said as she took a seat next to the others. I crossed the room and sat down next to one of the twins, Matt, I think. Surprisingly, I was making the effort to get to know who they were. Though I had no clue when they weren't next to each other.

A lithe, silver haired fae woman stood in the center of the room. Her shrewd eyes passed over our group. I hadn't yet met Professor Flora, but I'd heard enough about her to be weary of her. She seemed to make Raven and the twins a little uncomfortable and I could see why.

There wasn't even a touch of anything friendly in her expression. She looked cold and hard and stern. Like a grandmother who didn't approve of your life choices.

We just got here and I was already itching to leave.

This was going to be a long session.

"I don't know what Professor Halifax allowed you to do, but you will be on time from now on," Professor Flora said.

"Sorry," Raven said.

"The other faculty informed me about the typical nature of these trials. It is my job to ensure that the five of you are prepared," she said.

"We're prepared already," Luka said. "We're good to go."

"Are you?" Professor Flora said.

I wanted to elbow Luka to tell him to shut up but I couldn't get to him from where I was sitting.

"Your mate here has been without full use of her powers for weeks after her second trip to confinement," she said. "And none of you have done anything to help her recover."

"I didn't ask them to help me," Raven said. "But they would if I needed them to."

"You always need to be at full strength," Professor Flora said. "We can't even begin our independent study until your magic returns. And that's just academic. Suppose there was an attack or a situation where Raven needed to defend herself?"

"The school is safe," Matt said.

"That's what they said before," I grumbled. I had been prepared to dislike Professor Flora, but she was speaking my language. If Raven's magic wasn't what it was supposed to be, which she hadn't told me about, it needed fixing. And if we could help her, I was in.

"Alright, I'm guessing you want us to do something to help Raven's magic," Luka said. "Are you talking a magic meld or using our bond or what?"

"You're the smartass of the group, aren't you?" Professor Flora said.

Normally, I'd agree with her, but Luka was just trying to move us along. Besides, out of the three other mates, I was actually starting to think of Luka as a friend. "Hey, we're all supposed to be on the same side, right?"

Professor Flora frowned.

"Can we start over?" Raven asked, jumping up from her seat. "Professor Flora, I'd like to introduce you to my other two mates, Ben and Luka. They are both very talented and wonderful people. Ben and Luka, this is Professor Flora, our new Spellcasting teacher. She'll be helping me learn how to better understand my fae magic."

"That was unprofessional of me," Professor Flora said. "It's been a long time since I've had to work with a mated group like this. At the academy in Faerie, it's rare to see. Mating bonds are usually formed when we are much older."

"It's okay," Raven said. "Just let us know what you want us

to do. We want to pass the trials and graduate, right?" Raven looked at each of us in turn.

"Sure do," Matt said.

"Of course," Zach said.

"Since we have to do it again," Luka said.

Raven looked at me. I nodded. She turned back to Professor Flora. "We're ready to learn."

"Alright," she said. "Our first step is to heal your magic. You five should be using that bond in your favor. You have an advantage over anyone else in this academy but if one of you is broken, you will all feel it."

"How do we help her?" I asked.

"Each of you will need to transfer a little bit of your magic to Raven. You'll be weakened for a few hours, but yours should recover quickly. As if you used too much in a spell or as if you just shifted." She nodded to me.

I straightened. "That sounds easy enough. What are we waiting for?"

"Do we just hold hands?" Matt asked.

"Ben, get over here, I want to hold your hand," Luka said with a wink.

I shook my head but cracked a smile at his joke. "You're too much sometimes, you know that?"

"Are you looking at this like a healing spell?" Zach asked, returning the focus back to the task at hand.

"Well that is an interesting approach to it, Mr. Obscura," Professor Flora said. "How would you suggest going about it?"

Zach looked a little flushed now that all of us were looking at him. He glanced over at Raven, then looked back at the professor. "I'd probably go one at a time. Starting with the mages as our magic is more similar to hers. Then if needed, Luka and Ben could transfer some of their magic as well. But it might not be needed. And in a real-life situation, I'd rather keep some members of the group at full strength."

"That is an intelligent strategy," she said.

"Good work, Zach," Raven said, grinning.

"Mage magic will transfer most easily to Raven, as would fae," Professor Flora said. "Most often, healing magic works best when like magic is used. So it won't be as beneficial to get magic from another kind of magic user. However, I think your bond would allow for it. What are your next steps?"

"I think we should go with Zach's plan," I said.

Zach looked surprised.

"It's a good plan," I said. "A solid strategy like the professor said."

"Alright," Luka said. "You two get her fixed up. What do you need from me and Ben?"

"I guess just hang out till we know if she'll need any extra magic," Zach said.

I didn't like feeling useless, but I reminded myself that they were going to be draining some of their own magic. Which meant that Luka and I would have to step up if something bad happened.

Normally, that shouldn't be a threat outside of the trials, but given Raven's history, who knew what could happen. Especially with that shadow fae still waiting to make his return.

"I've never actually done this spell," Raven said. "I read about it in our textbook, though."

"Don't worry," Zach said. "We've done it a few times."

"You have?" she asked.

"Good way to get out of trouble when you end up breaking a bone doing something you're not supposed to do," Matt said.

"Your childhood was so different than mine," she said.

I stood and moved out of the way, Luka joining me near the door to the classroom. I felt like an outsider as I watched Matt and Zach sit down on either side of Raven. Each of them took hold of her hand and they all closed their eyes. Zach said something at a whisper I couldn't make out and Raven nodded. Whatever they were doing, it was mage magic and I wasn't part of that.

"This is much more typical," Professor Flora said.

I hadn't even noticed her approach us. Were all fae so damn sneaky? "What do you mean?"

"I've seen cases of multiple mates in Faerie, but usually only two or three. And never with other creatures. Fae usually stay with fae. But Raven is also a mage. I was surprised she'd formed a mating bond with a shifter and a demon," she said.

"Well, she did," I said, protectively.

She shrugged, then walked away.

I glared after her. In my few minutes with the professor, she had done nothing to endear herself to me.

"That's enough," Professor Flora called to Raven and the twins.

The twins let go of Raven's hands and all three of them opened their eyes. They did look like a matched set. Three elite mages from good families with exceptionally strong magic. Out of the five of us, Luka and I were the outcasts.

I'd never felt like that before, but that was probably because the twins joined as Raven's mates last. But now that they were here, would they take over? Would she rather spend more time with them because they could relate to her better?

Professor Flora set her hands on either side of Raven's head. "You feel like you're back at full strength. We can resume our independent study on Monday." She lowered her hands then looked at the twins. "Well done, gentlemen."

I frowned, back to feeling useless. Raven had been hurt and I never stopped to think about how to help her. I didn't even notice that she was so low on magic. And if it happened again, I wasn't going to be able to help her the same way the twins could. It was an uncomfortable sensation. I prided myself on being able to take care of my friends and family. And Raven was the most important person in my life.

"Good thing she's got them," Luka said. "Now we know how to help her if she goes down again."

"Yeah." I wished I could be like Luka sometimes. He was so laid back about all of this. "How do you do it?"

"Do what?" he asked.

"Go along with all of this," I said.

He shrugged. "Raven's happy, so I'm happy."

I took a deep breath and held on to that thought. It went so far against how I'd been raised. Growing up, it was take what you can get and hold on to it. Don't share. Don't give any ground. Fight for your territory. This was different. And for the first time, I realized it wasn't really a bad thing. It was a struggle to see how we could all fit together, but we really could.

Raven looked up at me and smiled. "Don't worry about me so much, Ben. I'm okay."

I shook my head. Here I was, worrying that she'd leave me behind and even while sitting between two other mates, she was picking up on how I was feeling.

"You're right, Luka," I said, slapping him on the back. "We keep Raven happy and we all win."

Zach

Magic has always come easy to me. I remember watching Matt struggle with simple spells when we were younger. He would get so frustrated. He's got it now and he's easily as good as I am. But it didn't start that way. Our mom used to say I was a natural mage, whatever the hell that meant. We were both full mages, but I guess it's like anything. I was the faster twin to learn magic and reading, but he was riding a bike weeks before I was ready to remove the training wheels.

The difference was that we always did it together. We appreciated our alone time, but when it came to the hard things, we had each other. This didn't feel like that. This felt like dividing us on purpose.

I glared at Matt and Raven, unsure of what we had in store for today's class. All we knew was that it was one on one with Professor Flora and honestly, that scared the shit out of me. After a few weeks in her class, it was obvious that she knew her stuff. But we'd done basic magic, researched our independent topic we'd drawn from the hat, and listened to lectures.

All of that had been normal. But there were signs of her power. Signs of her slightly different ways of doing things that made me wonder what to expect.

She lifted the hat again. "Your individual test times are in here. Random selection. On your test time you will come alone and wait outside the door until I call you in. If you are not scheduled to test, I expect that you're in the library preparing for your test or using your time wisely for your other studies. One of you will go today. Every other day, we'll have three per period."

Raven's fingers brushed my hand and she causally wrapped her hand around mine for a heartbeat before letting go. She was trying to comfort me. Or comfort herself. Either way, I could feel how nervous she was.

While Professor Flora had assured us that our tests were all illusions, that none of it was real, it was still a lot. Raven was going to have to face down the idea of a portal for the first time since that night with Professor Halifax. It wasn't right to put her in that situation again.

"Your turn." Professor Flora held the hat in front of the three of us. "Ladies first."

Raven dipped her hand in and pulled out a slip of paper. "Next week. Thursday."

I grabbed a paper and looked at it. Suddenly, I felt like I had a rock in my stomach. *Today.* I got to be the lucky one who went first. "Looks like I get to get it over with."

Matt took one and held it out to show the rest of us. "I'm on Monday. But you're first, figures."

I laughed. When we were kids, I liked to tell him I was the older brother. It was only a few minutes difference, but technically I was older.

"It'll be fine," Raven said. "How bad can it be? Some pretend situation we have to react to?"

"I'm sure it's exactly like the tests in our Italian classes in high school. You know, meet with the teacher and answer questions," Matt said.

"Right," I said. "I'm sure it's exactly like that."

Conversation filled the room as more and more students got their assigned times. Everyone sounded on edge and nervous. At least we were in good company. This wasn't something we usually did. Practical tests were still done in front of the whole class in other classes. I suppose in a way, this was kind of nice. If we failed spectacularly, we did it in private.

"Hey, you okay?" Raven asked.

I nodded. "I'm fine. Might as well just do it, right?"

"I kind of wish I was going today," she said. "I don't want to worry about it for two weeks."

"Well, I guess it's good that I'm going today. I'll be able to tell you what to expect."

Raven didn't look convinced. "Come find me when you're done, okay?"

I nodded. "You got it."

"Who is the lucky one who gets to go today?" Professor Flora asked as she walked back to her desk.

I held up my hand. The class was full of conversation and I could feel their eyes on me. I'm sure they were speculating what was about to happen to me.

"Alright, Mr. Obscura, you remain here. Everyone else, you're dismissed."

Raven and Matt stood and both of them faced me. Their expressions were sympathy mixed with fear. "Don't look at me like that." I stood and set a hand on each of their shoulders. "It's a test. Not death row."

Raven sighed. "Yeah, but I still worry about you."

I laughed. "Professor Flora is *not* Professor Halifax. I'll be fine."

"Alright," she said. "Good luck."

"Or should it be *break a leg* since it is a performance?" Matt asked with a grin.

"Let's stick to *good luck*," I said.

"See you soon," Raven said.

I waved to them as they left the class and watched as all of my classmates filed out. It wasn't long before the Spellcasting amphitheater was empty. And quiet. Far too quiet.

"Mr. Obscura, do you have any final questions before we begin your test?" Professor Flora asked.

"I'm either ready or I'm not," I said.

She smirked. "That's true." She crossed the room to the door and then locked it.

My pulse raced and I tried to tell myself that she wasn't trying to harm me. This was just a test. She was tough, but she was helping us learn. Besides, Dr. Green trusted her. Though, he had trusted Professor Halifax too.

Fuck. I really hoped she wasn't going to go all crazy fae on me.

"Mr. Obscura, your topic is *shifters*. I hope you prepared thoroughly. There are a variety of shifters across all the realms. In fact, some mages can even use magic to shift into other creatures," she said.

"I spent a lot of time looking into that," I said. "I even considered trying some of the spells."

"What kept you from going that route?" she asked.

"The number of poor outcomes I read about," I said. "I wasn't willing to be stuck as an animal if I couldn't pull it off."

She pursed her lips and stared at me for a few long seconds. "I have a feeling you could pull it off, but I understand not wanting to take the risk."

"Right, living the rest of my life as a snake or a raven sounds pretty terrible," I said.

"What about a wolf?" she asked.

"I guess that wouldn't be as bad, but still not ideal," I said.

Growling sounded from behind me and I turned to see a huge black wolf baring its teeth at me. I jumped and looked back to Professor Flora, but she was gone.

Shit. Apparently the test had started and I was on my own. With a wolf the size of a small horse.

I took a few steps back, sizing up the creature for possible weakness. It moved toward me with slow, graceful steps. Yellow eyes were locked on me and I knew I was in trouble.

If the beast charged me, I'd have to defend myself and I didn't want to hurt anyone. But then again, she'd said this was going to be an illusion.

This was a test.

It's just a test.

"Easy, boy," I said. It probably wasn't a good idea to jump straight into attacking a wolf. Especially if the wolf was a shifter. Killing another supernatural was a one-way ticket to jail. So if you ever went hunting, you damn well better be sure you're not hunting someone you might know.

The wolf's hackles were raised and it growled at me again, showing its sharp yellow teeth. That jaw could snap me in half.

"Hey, I don't mean you any harm." I quickly muttered a calming spell, sending what I hoped was a rush of warmth and comfort toward the angry creature.

It snapped its jaws at me, seemingly more pissed after that. Time to try another tactic.

I'd been working on a forced shifting spell for a while. It wasn't something that was usually taught and it was very controversial. But it would allow me to force a shifter back into their human form rather than have to harm them.

Quickly, I called my magic. Tiny shockwaves ran through my arms and blue sparks formed on my fingertips. I released the spell, hitting the wolf with everything I had.

To my surprise, the wolf whimpered and fell to its side, then vanished in a cloud of smoke.

I blew out a breath. It was all pretend. None of this was real.

Then, suddenly Ben was standing where the wolf had been. "What the fuck, Zach?"

"Ben?" I looked around the room. The door was still locked. Ben wasn't even in this class. Why was he here? "Are you really here or is this another illusion?'

"You need to stay away from Raven," he said, walking toward me. His steps were powerful, purposeful and he moved much in the same way the wolf did.

"You're not real. You're not here," I said. "This must be some trick of my subconscious."

"Did you hear me, mage?" He was still approaching me. "Wolves don't share. We don't like it. And now that Raven is safe, she doesn't need you. Stay away from her. She was mine first."

"Dude," I said. "Not cool. Raven chose all of us."

He growled and his eyes flashed yellow. I swore his canines were the size of fangs. *What the fuck is going on?* "If you won't back down, I'll make you back down."

Ben dissolved and all at once, I was facing another wolf. This one was gray and still huge. I stepped back away from him. *This isn't real.*

I called my magic again, sending the same spell to force his shift. The sparks came quickly and struck true. But the wolf didn't back up. Instead, he lunged for me. Claws dug into my chest as I was knocked to the ground.

I yelled as searing pain burned in my chest from the puncture. His claws were still in me as he pinned me to the ground. This wolf was heavy as hell and I struggled to breathe under the pressure.

Hot breath hit my face as the wolf's jaws snapped in front of my face. I tried to pull away but the claws tore at my skin and I screamed again. The wolf growled and snapped its jaws again.

This didn't feel like an illusion.

Pain made my vision blur but I fought against it, willing myself to call a spell. My magic flared and faded, as if it didn't want to release. I took a deep breath and screamed as I reached for the magic and held it, forcing it through.

A sphere of electricity shot from around me, sending the wolf flying off me. I pulled myself back, wincing against the searing pain. Wolf claws fucking hurt.

The creature was already on its feet, growling again. It raced toward me just as I got to standing.

Extending my hands in front of me, I called another burst of electricity and it slammed into the beast. He whined as the magic hit him, knocking him down again.

This time, in another cloud of smoke, the wolf vanished and Ben was on the ground. He was unconscious and covered in bruises. His upper lip was bleeding and one of his eyes was already black.

Had I done all that?

I ran to him and knelt down next to him. This wasn't supposed to be real. None of this was supposed to be real.

What the hell kind of test was this?

I pressed my fingers to his neck, feeling for a pulse. I'd used too much force in that last burst. Panic seeped in as I pushed my fingers in harder. I couldn't feel his heart.

Oh shit. Oh shit. Oh shit.

"Professor!" I called. Where the hell was she?

Black tendrils of smoke wrapped around my wrists and encircled Ben's fallen form. A moment later, he was swallowed by the clouds and he was gone.

I stood and stumbled backward, confused and shaken by what had just happened.

"Well done," Professor Flora's voice called. She was standing near her desk now. Or had she always been there?

"What the hell was that?" I asked. "Why would you make Ben the shifter I had to fight?"

"I didn't choose Ben," she said. "The magic was set up for you to call the shifter you most feared. It could have been anyone. But apparently, the shifter you're the most concerned about is the one who often shares a bed with your mate."

"Why?" I asked. This wasn't right. I shouldn't have had to fight him even if it wasn't real.

"I told you," she said.

"Why shifters? Why did you give me shifters?" I asked.

She shook her head. "You were there when I let you draw. You chose shifters. And you chose to fight Ben."

My nostrils flared and I clenched my jaw. It didn't make sense. Ben was supposed to be on my side. But he was a shifter. And they were known for being rash and reckless. This might have been fake, but it was a window into a possible future. What would we do if Ben ever lost control and shifted into his wolf form? I didn't think I was afraid of him, or afraid of him being around Raven. But now I had to wonder.

"Why didn't my spell work on him? The forced shifting spell?" I asked.

"He's an alpha," she said. "You can't force an alpha back to human form."

I swallowed hard. It was the one trick up my sleeve after weeks of research. It was the one thing I thought I could use in case I ever needed it. And it wouldn't work on Ben.

Professor Flora clasped her hands in front of her, as if waiting for me to say something.

I wasn't sure what to say. I thought I trusted Ben. But now I didn't know what I thought.

"Do you want to know how you did?" she asked, finally breaking the long silence.

"Sure," I said.

"You passed," she said. "Well done."

"Thanks," I said. I'd never had such mixed feelings after taking an exam.

And now I needed to decide what to tell Raven.

Raven

Zach didn't show up at dinner but Matt didn't seem concerned. It was difficult to focus on anything without knowing how he did on that test. Professor Flora was still difficult to figure out and we'd never had a test where we were put in a situation. I still wasn't even sure what that meant.

"Raven?" Makayla elbowed me. "You with us?"

"Sorry," I said. "I'm just worried about Zach." I turned to Matt. "How are you not worried?"

He shrugged. "I'm sure he's fine."

I frowned. There was no way I could concentrate until I knew he was okay. After my last experience with a fae professor - in Spellcasting no less - my mind was filled with all sorts of worst case scenarios. What if she released a shifter in the room with him and had him fight someone? What if she wasn't who she said she was and was trying something weird? Why was he the first to go? She made it look like it was random, but I knew enough about magic to know that almost nothing was an accident around here.

"I'm going to go check on him," I said.

"Does that mean you won't be finishing your French fries?" Makayla asked.

I pushed my plate over to her. "All yours."

"I'll walk with you," Matt said.

"It's okay," I said. "You finish your dinner."

"You sure?" he asked.

"I'm sure." I stood and waved to the rest of the table. Surprisingly, Ben and Luka were deep in conversation. It was nice to see them getting along but still a little alarming. I wasn't going to question it, though. Every so often, we deserved to have some good things happen, right?

The hallways were dotted with people making their way to or from dinner. Some of them were already out of uniforms and changed into party clothes. It was a Friday night and some students would make their way to town or to dorm parties. In the shifter dorm, Friday night meant poker night. Luka and the twins had even joined us recently.

Plus, there was always the option of the vampire parties that were held every few weeks. The whole school had an open invitation to those, but they had a reputation for getting wild. One of these days, I'd head back to one. But I still felt too guilty about what happened to Violet. She wasn't going to parties again yet and had a pass to miss gym until she was fully recovered. I missed her but during our visit a few days ago, she'd assured me she was improving.

The worst part was not being able to tell her why she'd been attacked. Or being able to admit to her that I was partially responsible.

That thought nagged at me as I walked through the halls toward the mage dorms. The shadow fae still hadn't shown his face and while the others kept saying that maybe he'd given up and left, I knew he was still out there. I just had no idea what he was waiting for.

I climbed the stairs to the Obscura dorm room and waved to a couple of mages I passed on the way. They were polite to me, but none of them stopped to talk. I wasn't exactly part of the mage world. Especially since finding out I was half fae. At first, it was the fact that I lived in the shifter dorm that seemed to keep other mages from connecting with me. Now, it seemed like they were all a little afraid of me.

They were probably justified, too. Especially after seeing what the shadow fae could do.

I stopped in front of Zach's door and tried to push the thought of evil fae out of my mind. The last thing I wanted to consider was that Professor Flora was up to something nefarious. I knocked on the door. "Zach? Are you in there?"

My heart hammered in my chest. If he wasn't here, where could he be? There'd been other Spellcasting classes after ours. Normally, I'd have been in that room for my independent study, but that was waiting till next week.

I knocked again. "Zach?" *Please be in there.*

The door opened and a pale, sleepy looking Zach stared down at me. He managed a weak smile. "Hey, Raven."

He looked awful. Like he'd been sick for days and hadn't left his room. Fear gripped my chest. Something was very wrong. "What happened? Do you need to see the nurse?"

"No, no nurse," he said. "I actually already went. It's why I missed class this afternoon."

"When you didn't come to dinner I was so worried," I said. "Did she hurt you?"

"No, but the test was brutal," he said. "It wasn't real, but apparently the illusions can feel real."

"What does that even mean?" I asked as I walked into his entry way.

Zach closed the door behind me and the two of us walked toward the couch. He sat down and I took the seat next to him.

"Well, I had to fight an illusion of a shifter and when it landed on me, I could feel it," he said, lifting his shirt.

I gasped as I saw the bandages on his chest. Blood was seeping through them. "That is not okay."

"I'm fine. The nurse says the wounds are real but they'll heal magically tonight since they were inflicted by a magical source or something like that," he said. "I'm not quite sure I understand it, but either way, I'm supposed to be better tomorrow."

"Want me to try to heal you?" I asked. "You did it for me. I can do it for you if you teach me."

"No," he said. "We did that to help you regain your full magic. If you heal me, you'll lose too much of yours. You're probably still recovering from confinement."

I gently touched the skin near the bandage. "It looks awful. How could she let that happen?"

"It's alright," he said. "I'm actually sort of glad I went through it. It was very eye opening and I got to practice some real-life skills. We never get that chance."

"Isn't that the point of the trials?" I asked.

"Sure, but we don't get to try anything till the trials themselves and if we fail there, we really fail, you know?"

"I guess," I said.

"Hey, I'm okay." Zach lowered his shirt and took hold of my hands in his. "I'm going to be just fine."

I sighed. "I hate seeing you in pain."

"It doesn't even hurt anymore. It's probably healing already." He leaned down and set his forehead against mine. "Try not to worry about me."

"I always worry about you," I said. "I worry about all of you."

I could feel the heat of his warm breath on my face. My breaths were timed with his, coming in unison. Our bodies were already responding to one another, the closeness sending a shiver of desire through me.

Tilting up my chin, I pressed my lips to his. That was all it took. His hands slid under my shirt and we worked to peel each other's clothes off as we kissed. I broke away from the kiss long enough to lift his shirt over his head and he pulled my shirt off. Then our lips returned to each other. His tongue slid into my mouth and I met it with mine, deepening the kiss.

Pants came off in a rush of movement. My hands were all over his firm stomach, his smooth back, his strong arms. His hands slid to my ass and he lifted me.

I threw my legs around his waist, my mouth still on his. He stumbled and nearly lost his grip, but caught me. We both laughed.

"I should probably keep my eyes open while I walk," he said.

I bit down on my lower lip, staring into his eyes. My whole body felt like it was on fire. "No more walking. Just stop here."

I wasn't even sure where *here* was, but he listened, setting me down. To my surprise we were in front of the dining room table.

"Works for me," he said.

I pulled myself up on the table and grabbed his hands, dragging him closer to me. He settled in between my thighs. I could feel the wetness spreading, begging for him.

Zach's mouth found mine again and he lowered me to the table so I was laying down, my legs still around him. He shifted just enough that I could feel his erection against my inner thigh, and it made me even wetter just knowing how excited he was.

His thumb found my clit, teasing it until I moaned into his mouth. Then a finger slipped into me, then another. I broke free of the kiss, unable to concentrate on anything other than the pleasure building inside me.

I tried to grab at the table for leverage, but my hands slipped. Instead, I dug my fingers into Zach's back. He teased my clit with one hand, while curving his fingers as he went in and out of my center.

My back arched as the pleasure built. I gasped and moaned until I couldn't take it anymore. Wetness spread as I climaxed, screaming in pleasure.

Zach removed his fingers and I stayed on the table, feeling exhausted and satisfied. Our eyes met and I knew the look he was giving me. He wasn't done yet.

I grinned. "You are amazing."

"Just wait," he said as he grabbed my legs. He pulled my hips off the edge of the table and this time, his cock was lined up with my entrance.

I held my breath in anticipation as he teased me by rubbing the head along my slit. When I felt like I couldn't take it anymore, he entered me, holding on to my hips as he thrust.

I slid on the table with each movement, each movement making me gasp. Zach repositioned my legs so my ankles were on his shoulders, making my hips angle up. I gasped as his cock hit me in a new place. A place that instantly had me crying his name. I'd never felt anything like it.

"Oh my god," I gasped. Orgasm came quickly with another

building on its heels. Zach continued to thrust and I squealed as pleasure peaked again and again.

I lost track of how many times I came and by the time Zach finished, I was gasping for air.

My legs felt like jelly when I climbed off the table. "Whatever that was, it was amazing."

"I'm never going to be able to eat at this table again without thinking of you," he said.

I laughed and covered my face in my hands. We'd just had sex on the table where I'd had lunch with his mother. It felt a little naughty. But shit, that was some of the best sex I'd ever had.

"We can clean it for them," I said. "And then maybe we can try it again next time you're alone?"

"I like the way you think," he said, leaning in for a kiss.

My hands slid up his chest and I felt the bandages, reminding me about his injury. In the heat of the moment, I hadn't stopped to think about how all that physical activity might have affected him.

I pulled away from the kiss. "How's your chest?"

He lifted off the bandage and the wound underneath wasn't bleeding anymore. In fact, it looked nearly healed.

"That was fast," he said. "I guess she was right."

"I'm glad," I said. "I don't know what I'd do if anything ever happened to you."

"I love hearing you say that," he said.

"It's true," I said.

"You know what you mean to me, don't you, Raven?" He brushed a loose strand of hair away from my face.

"I do," I said.

"I just want you to be safe," he said.

"I know," I said. "And we'll have this whole thing figured out soon."

"It's not just the fae thing," he said. "I worry about you."

I frowned. "I'm doing pretty good at taking care of myself."

"You do," he agreed. "But just don't forget to ask for help when you need it. Next time that fae shows up, promise me you'll tell me right away?"

"I promise," I said, already not sure if I could keep the promise. It was a really good thing I wasn't cursed with the fae inability to lie.

Raven

It was late by the time I slipped into my own room, a smile still on my lips from my time with Zach. He had a way of making me feel like the only woman in the whole world when I was with him.

I slipped off my clothes as I walked toward the bathroom. A quick shower would help relax me enough to get a good night's sleep. When I reached the bathroom, I flipped on the light switch and screamed as I realized I wasn't alone.

And I was naked.

Fuck me.

I covered myself as best as possible as I stared down at the shadow fae who was sitting on my bathroom counter. "How long have you been there waiting for me, creep?"

He grinned and for the first time, I could make out what he looked like. He was tall and lean, much like my professors who were fae. He had long silver hair and a square jaw. He was handsome but the elongated canines in his smiling mouth gave him a predatory look.

I grabbed my towel from the hook on the wall without taking my eyes off him. As I wrapped it around me, I noticed that his bright green eyes flicked down and up, checking me out. I wrinkled my nose. "I was not naked for your enjoyment."

"Shame," he said. "You look quite beautiful naked."

"You're disgusting. And unwelcome." I wanted to ask him what he wanted or why he was in my room. But we both knew the answer to that question and I wasn't prepared to hand over the book.

Suddenly, I was hyper aware of the fact that the book had been in my room without any protections until recently. And apparently, he could now enter my room. Had he come in before and missed the book? Or had he come in after he threatened me and looked for it?

I shuddered and goosebumps spread on my arms. I'd never felt so violated in my whole life. What if this wasn't the first time? "How'd you get in here?"

He hopped off the counter and walked toward me. He was much taller than I anticipated and his broad shoulders made me think that he was probably quite strong despite his lean frame. "Come back to the fae realm with me and learn."

"No, thank you," I said. "I'm good here."

He shrugged. "Your loss. Either way, you'll give me the book."

My brow furrowed and I narrowed my eyes as I tried to read

his expression. He'd been gone for weeks. What had he been doing? I never believed he wouldn't come back, but why now? "You know I'm not going to give you the book."

"Your magic has returned to full strength," he said. "I gave you safe passage while you recovered as a gesture of good will. Now I'm done playing nice."

"Like you played nice when you nearly killed my friend?" I asked.

"I warned you," he said. "You didn't listen."

"You're still not getting that book," I said.

"I'll have to hurt someone closer to you then," he said. "Perhaps one of your mates?"

My pulse raced and my chest tightened as fear gripped me. I could feel the muscles in my jaw fluttering as I tried to keep my face impassive. I didn't want him to know how much he was getting to me. "You're a coward."

"I am not," he said. "I would prefer a fair fight. I'd much rather just kill you and get it over with. But then I won't get the book. I've traced it to your room, but I can't find it. I need *you* to access it for me."

I swallowed hard. I was only alive because he thought I could give him the book, yet it was Zach's magic keeping it locked up. I could no more release it from its hiding place than the shadow fae. But if he knew that, I'd already be dead.

"I talked with Halifax," I said, hoping to distract him.

He straightened. "So you know what the book is."

"I do," I said, not knowing where I was going with this. All I knew was that I couldn't give him the book and I had no clue how to get him out of my room.

"So you know it belongs to me," he said. "She stole it from me."

"Because it's dangerous," I said.

He smirked and his eyes glinted. "My mate always has been the self-righteous type. I assume she was training you to follow in her footsteps?"

I had no idea how to answer that.

He shook his head. "There is no reason to have royal guard here in this wasteland. She should never have fled here. And when I have that book, all of her sacrifices will be in vain."

"I have no idea what you're talking about," I said. "She told me the book was evil. And that you were her mate."

"Yes, I am," he said. "Mating bonds can be cruel sometimes. But they did allow me to track her after she left me."

"I get the feeling you deserved being left," I said.

"You'll learn soon enough, young fae," he said. "The pull to faerie is strong. I knew she'd come back eventually. And unlike you, I could wait an eternity for her."

"You won't get the book." I gripped my towel tighter, my hands in fists. If I attacked him first, would I stand a chance? Could I defeat him? Should I call to my mates and ask for help? A million thoughts were buzzing through my mind. The only thing I was certain of, was that I wasn't going to give him the book. He was clearly unbalanced and I believed Professor Halifax's warnings despite her attempts to kill me.

"Do you know the power you'd have if you went home?" He reached for me and brushed his fingers across my cheek.

I backed up until I hit the wall. I wanted to smack his hand away but I wanted to keep the towel over me more. "Don't touch me."

He lowered his hand. "Your powers will always be weak here. Bound by mortal rules and the physics of this world. You'll grow old, and one day, you'll die.

"But in Faerie, your magic would awaken. Fully unbound, limitless, and eternal. You'll age so slowly that one day, you'll wish for death to claim you. Give in. Hand me the book, and I'll take you home."

"It's not my home," I said.

He growled and moved so fast I screamed. His arms were on either side of my head, caging me in against the wall. His chest was pressed up against me and I could feel the heat of his skin on mine.

His eyes flashed with a terrifying sliver glint and he bared his sharp teeth. "I'm done with your games, little girl. I need that book."

My lower lip trembled and I forced myself to glare at him. "Then you'll have to kill me. I can't get it for you. My mates locked it up, away from me, even. Go ahead. Kill me. See if they'll be willing to help you once I'm dead."

He groaned in frustration and then slapped me, sending a stinging pain across my cheek.

I couldn't help but grin up at him. "Checkmate."

"You think you won?" he asked.

"You can take your anger out on me or my mates, but you'll never get the book," I said.

"Then I'll start picking off students one at a time until it's just the five of you," he said. "You have one week to give me the book."

He lifted his hand and closed his fingers into a fist, then opened them. He was holding a small glass vial filled with something that was as black as night. "When you're ready to give me the book, shatter the vial and I'll come. Make sure you're alone. And you know the rules. Tell anyone, and I'll consider your time up. This time, I won't leave any blood in your friends when I hurt them. They won't be waking back up."

He passed the vial into my hand and I closed my fingers around it.

Black smoke wrapped around him in tendrils until it

completely encircled him and he vanished. I waited a few heartbeats, just to make sure he was gone, then I fell to my knees.

I had no doubt he'd make good on his threat, which meant, I was out of time. There had to be something I could do to catch him and to make sure he didn't get the book. What could I do in the next week to make this stop?

Raven

Matt set a stack of books down in front of me. "Have you seen these? I found them in a very neglected corner of the library. I had to wrestle a spider for them."

I laughed and dragged the books toward me. "Thanks, Matt. But you should be focusing on your research. You've got your test before mine."

He shrugged. "I've been studying this stuff for weeks now. And after what Zach said, it doesn't sound like she'll be quizzing us."

"No, it doesn't," I said darkly. "I still can't believe that the illusions were real enough to inflict actual injury."

"Good thing mine's a dream, right?" Matt said. "You can't get hurt in a dream for real."

"Luka did tell me something about danger if you were woken up from within a dream, though. So definitely don't do that." I pulled the top book from the stack and wiped the dust and cobwebs from it. Matt wasn't kidding when he said he'd had to wrestle spiders. Sticky webs were all over the book. Trying not to overthink it, I wiped my hands on my jeans.

"I guess I should have talked with Luka about it," Matt said. "But that felt weird."

"How come?" I asked. "I mean, you *have* seen him naked. How weird could it be?"

He shrugged. "Most of us don't want everyone to know what we're capable of fully, you know? We're taught to always hold some magic back in case we're ever attacked for real."

I remembered when Coach Miller had pushed Luka too far in gym. He'd done magic he wasn't proud of. Magic that he didn't want anyone to know about. But I was glad I knew and it helped me understand him better in a weird way.

"What are you hiding from me?" I asked Matt with a grin.

He leaned closer and his lips brushed against my ear. "Why don't you come to that corner I found and find out?"

"With the spiders?" I asked. "No, thank you."

"I'll get rid of the spiders," he said.

I cocked an eyebrow. "If you have magic that gets rid of spiders, that's something I want to see."

He stood and took hold of my hand, helping me up from my chair. I followed him through the shelves of books, past the librarian's desk. She frowned at me while eyeing me over her glasses. Her mossy green hair moved as she shook her head. The things she must see - and ignore - in here.

We wove between tables dotted with other students who

were studying for classes. Then we came to a staircase I'd never seen. "Has this always been here?"

"Who knows?" he said. "Every time I'm in here I see something different."

We went down the twisting staircase into another level of the library. It was just as large as the space above and overflowing with books. A few tables were scattered around and a couple of students were working on various things. We walked past them and through the zig-zag disarray of shelves.

In an especially dark corner we sped up to get away from the group of students who were obviously not studying. A trail of clothing led away from them like breadcrumbs.

I stifled a giggle and we kept walking. Matt tugged my arm, dragging me toward an isolated little corner that was nearly fully dark.

"Is this the place?" I asked.

"Nice, right?" he asked.

"Yeah, if you're looking for a place to build a nest for your hundreds of eggs." I shuddered. I could see the webs clinging to books. It did look abandoned. We were surrounded by shelves on four sides with only a small entry way formed by a space between two shelves. It was very much like it had been done on purpose. Whoever set the shelves up here knew what they were doing.

"Just wait," Matt said.

"You've got a minute," I said as a shiver ran through me. I could almost feel the skitter of bugs on my skin. "This place is freaking me out."

Matt let go of my hand and walked toward the center of the square space. "Watch this." He grinned as he lifted his hands and a bright light shot out from his fingertips.

I closed my eyes against the initial shock of the light and then slowly blinked them back open. When I looked again, there was a shimmering transparent dome over the two of us. It filled the space around us right up against the book shelves.

Slowly, I turned in a circle, looking at the sheer sparkling magic around us. My lips parted in surprise. "What is it?"

"It's a barrier spell," Matt said. "Nothing can get in or out."

"Oh?" I asked.

"Yes, you're my prisoner." He laughed as he walked over to me. "Most importantly, no spiders can get in."

"I like where you're going with that," I said. "What about other people? Other mages?"

"We can see out, but to anyone walking by it looks like there's nobody here," he said.

I moved closer to the barrier and brushed my fingers against it. It tingled against my skin. "How long does it last?"

"Until I call it down," he said. "I've never held one too long. Zach and I used to use it when we were kids if we wanted to get away from our nanny."

"That sounds terrible," I said.

"We weren't the nicest kids," he said.

"What happens if someone walks in here?" I asked.

"They'd feel it," he said, "but they couldn't get in."

"Can other magic users detect it?" My mind was already racing to how we could use this against the shadow fae.

"If they run into it or if they're looking for it, I suppose," he said. "But I doubt anyone is looking for us back here."

"Can you teach me this?" I asked.

"Sure," he said.

"Now, can we take a break from studying?" He slid his arms around my waist.

"Yes, please," I said, throwing my arms over his shoulders. I slid my fingers into his hair, guiding his head down. Our lips met and he kissed me. Gently at first, tender kisses. His lips were soft and he tasted like peppermint. He pulled slightly away from the kiss and sucked my lower lip into his mouth. His fingers tangled into my hear, pulling my head closer as he resumed the kiss. Deeper this time, hungrier.

I moaned and felt dampness spread between my thighs. Without breaking the kiss, I worked the buttons of his shirt until I could slide it off him. I raked my fingers over his chest, feeling his firm muscles under my touch. My hands found his pants and he dropped his hands to mine. We broke the kiss to help remove each other's pants.

Matt stood naked in front of me, his impressive erection at full attention. I knelt down in front of him and used my tongue to lick his cock from the bottom of the shaft all the way to the tip before closing my lips around it.

Matt groaned as I bobbed up and down, using my tongue to stimulate the sides. His hands guided my head until I felt him tense.

I wasn't ready for him to come yet.

Wiping off my mouth, I looked up at him. "Why don't you join me down here?"

He grinned and got on his knees. I gently guided him down so he was laying on his back before climbing on top of him.

His cock was in front of me, not yet inside me. I wanted to tease him a little first and give him some time to recover.

The cold stone floor of the library was hard against my knees but I was so far gone that all I could think about was getting more of Matt.

His hands started at my hips and slid up my waist toward my breasts. He groaned a little as he cupped them and played with my nipples. I moved my hips against his cock, teasing him.

"Raven, you have no idea what you do to me, do you?" he asked.

"I have an idea," I said. Probably the same thing he did to

me. He could turn my insides to mush with just a few words or a gentle caress.

I leaned down so I could kiss him and adjusted my hips so I was positioned with my entrance above his cock. When I broke the kiss and sat up, I lowered myself onto him.

Matt's hands moved to my hips and he groaned as I began to move my hips, undulating and gyrating against him. He lifted his hips making his cock hit my g-spot and I moaned, leaning back on him.

Setting my hands on the ground behind me, back arched, I continued to ride him. The two of us moving together, sending waves of pleasure through me.

Panting, I moved faster as my climax neared. Matt's thumb found my clit and he teased me, sending me over the edge. I cried out as orgasm exploded through me.

Matt's hands moved back to my tits and he groaned as he came.

A few seconds later, Matt had our clothes out on the ground for us and we cuddled on top of them. My head rested on his chest and he ran his hand over my hair.

I never wanted to leave.

Matt

Zach's wounds from his test were already gone. As he'd been told, the magic wore off and it was as if it had never happened. But that didn't make me feel any better about going into my own test with Professor Flora.

And of course, I had the first appointment of the day, so there wasn't even another student I could ask about how theirs went. At least Raven had a few more days before she had to go. After everything she'd been through, it wasn't fair to ask her to have to participate in something that would put her through it all again.

I stepped into the familiar classroom. For nearly two years,

I'd learned a lot in this room. Despite Professor Halifax's descent into evil, or whatever the fuck that was, she had been a good teacher.

"Mr. Obscura," Professor Flora looked up from where she was sitting behind her desk.

"Good morning, Professor." I flashed my most respectable smile.

She pursed her lips as if she wasn't impressed by me. Or maybe I was reading too much into it. She stood and walked around the desk, her long gray dress dragging behind her across the stone floor as she walked.

"I hope you prepared satisfactorily," she said.

"I've been studying since it was assigned," I said.

"We'll find out soon enough." She walked toward the door and then flipped off the light switch leaving only the faint glow of the emergency light on. "You might want to sit down, Mr. Obscura."

I walked over to the rows of benches and took my usual seat. It felt empty and strange without Zach and Raven by my side.

When I looked back to where Professor Flora had been standing, she was gone. Thankfully, Zach had warned me about her vanishing right before the wolf showed up to attack him.

I took a deep breath. The test was likely already started. I had no idea what to expect as my topic had been dream walking, which happened in sleep. And I wasn't sleeping. At least I didn't think I was.

Footsteps came from nearby and I turned to see someone I didn't recognize walking into the center of the room. He had long blonde hair that was tucked behind his ears. Both of his ears had gages in them, stretching the lobes more than usual earrings.

His face was familiar, but I couldn't place it.

"So, you're the one who has been sharing his girlfriend with my little brother," the man said. He smirked and I thought I saw a flash of red in his blue eyes.

"Who are you?" I asked.

"I'm surprised the family resemblance isn't tipping you off," he said.

I narrowed my eyes. He looked so familiar, but I couldn't place it. Then, it hit me. This was a test on dream walking, which was incubus territory. This man looked strikingly similar to the only incubus I currently associated with. And as he mentioned, I was sharing a girlfriend with. "You're Luka's brother?"

"You can call me Drake. I haven't been topside in a while," he said. "But when asked if I could come and test one of the Obscura twins?" He laughed. "There was no way I'd miss that."

"Alright, so you're giving me the test?" I asked. "How are we doing this?"

"We already started, little mage," he said.

My brow furrowed. All we'd done was talk. That wasn't much of a test so far.

"Turn around," Drake said.

I obliged and my mouth dropped open in surprise at the sight of myself sleeping on the stone bench. I looked at my hands. I was solid. I wasn't dead or anything. But this was fucking surreal. "I'm asleep?"

"Watch this," Drake said. "Stand up and dance, little mage."

I shuffled to the side as my sleeping body rose, eyes still closed, and started moving around. *What the hell?*

"What are you doing?" I asked.

"It's a gift," he said. "I can make you do whatever I want while you're sleeping."

"Put me down," I said. "What the hell is wrong with you?"

"Sit down," Drake said.

My sleeping body crumbled to the floor and I winced. I had a feeling I was going to feel that when I woke up.

"What kind of test is this? What's the point of you showing off what you can do?" I asked.

"The point is for you to regain control of yourself so you can wake up," he said.

Raven's warning came back to me. "I thought it was dangerous to wake yourself up from a dream."

He lifted an eyebrow. "You have done your research."

"So how do I stop this?" I asked.

"That's your test," Drake said.

I shook my head. None of my studies had prepared me for this. I'd learned about how dreams could be invaded and how you could fall into nightmares so deep and dark, they haunted your waking hours for the rest of your life. I read about recurring themes and favorite strategies and ways to talk yourself down if your dreams were hijacked by an incubus. I never once read about an incubus controlling you while you slept.

"Did you put me to sleep or was that Professor Flora?" I asked.

"That was me," he said, proudly. "To be honest, I'm not nearly as good at this as Luka is, but I can make your life hell just the same."

"Luka can do this too?" I asked.

"Sure," he said. "It's kind of a family trait."

Shit. What if he did that to me? Or Raven? He could just force us to sleep? How the hell did I not know that?

I walked away from Drake, trying to recall what I'd read. Nothing had prepared me for this.

"If you'd prefer, we can go with traditional dream walking," Drake said.

I looked over at the incubus just in time to see him transform into a dragon. My eyes widened as fear gripped my chest. I knew it wasn't real but *holy fuck* there was a giant dragon glaring at me.

Smoke billowed out through its nose and it opened its jaws and let out a burst of flames. I could feel the heat as I ran from the fire. I knew this was a dream, but I could feel the heat from that fire.

I climbed up the stone benches to the highest level of seats and stopped at the top. The dragon roared, the air from its cry blowing my hair around.

In all the books I'd read, I heard about how real dreams could feel, but I never realized just how real they'd be.

Drake's dragon spread its wings and flapped, lifting off the ground as it headed toward me. I scrambled back down the seats and ran toward the classroom door.

I needed to buy some time.

I pulled on the handle and the door opened. I ran into the hall and my feet sunk. That's when I realized I wasn't in the hallway at school, I was in the middle of a vast expanse of sand.

The door was gone. I was in the middle of a desert with nothing but dunes of sand in every direction.

Hot sun beat down on me and I was already sweating. *Shit.* This was the weirdest dream ever. But at least I wasn't looking at my sleeping self anymore. To be honest, that was the weirdest and possibly freakiest part.

I couldn't wake myself up, but I had to end this dream. I just had no idea how I was going to do that.

In my research, I'd read that you needed to take control of the dream. Send the bad away. Create the dream on your turf. Direct it in a happy direction so you could send away the invading incubus.

Blowing out a breath, I tried to think of better locations than a desert. Warm beaches, tranquil forests, the school's ballroom all decorated for a special occasion. Anywhere but here.

The room seemed to spin as if I was flying through space. Everything around me was blurred. It stopped all at once, leaving me standing in the middle of a forest. Birds called around me and I could feel the mist in the air. Dappled sunlight filtered in through leaves. It was warm and peaceful.

"You want to play?" A voice boomed around me and then a shriek broke the tranquility. Hundreds of birds rose up from the trees and flew away, squawking and crying.

Unease settled into the pit of my stomach like a weight and I turned toward the source of the initial sound that scared away my dream birds.

The dragon was back, crashing through the tree tops. Fire erupted from the beast, setting the trees ablaze.

I started running.

Catching myself, I remembered about taking control. Breathing in through my nose and out thorough my mouth, I worked to calm myself even as I ran over fallen branches and through bushes.

I imagined the beach. White sand, turquoise waves, Raven stretched out on a towel waiting for me to rub sunscreen on her back. The image felt so real, so vivid. I held on to it, not willing to release it.

Heat flared behind me, but I didn't look back. I could hear the flapping of the wings, the breaking of trees and the fleeing of animals ahead of me. But I didn't let go of the beach.

Suddenly, everything blurred and I was in fast-forward once again as the forest spun past me.

When it settled, I was on the beach as I had imagined. In my hand was a bottle of sunscreen.

"What took you so long?" Raven's voice sounded from behind me.

I turned to see her looking over her sunglasses at me. Her green eyes sparkled and she had a wide grin on her face.

She was also in a bikini that left absolutely zero to the imagination.

Holy shit. This was the kind of dream I wanted to have every night.

"Well? What are you waiting for?" she asked as she stretched out on the towel.

I walked over to her, unable to hold back my smile and already feeling my shorts getting tighter.

The sunscreen was warm, just like the air around us. I could taste the salt and the roaring of the waves against the shore created a calming rhythm.

I rubbed the sunscreen around in my hands, focusing on how real it felt, before starting to apply it to Raven's smooth back.

"Tan lines?" Raven said, her voice muffled by the towel under her.

I grinned, knowing exactly where she - where I - was taking this dream. Carefully, I tugged on her bikini string, untying it.

The strings fell to the side and I had an unobstructed view of her bare back. My cock ached as I rubbed the lotion on her back. This was my dream, wasn't it? Didn't that mean I could keep going with this?

I frowned at the thought. As much as I wanted to continue what I've started, I didn't want to be interrupted by a dragon.

As if called by my thoughts, Drake appeared on the beach, walking toward me in the nude.

"Seriously?" I asked, trying not to look at everything on display.

Raven pushed herself up on her elbows. "Who's there?"

"Hey, gorgeous," Drake said. "Why don't you come hang out with me?"

Raven didn't hesitate. She was on her feet so fast, I didn't even get to finish rubbing in the lotion. Her top fell to the sand and she walked right over to Drake as if transfixed.

His eyes dropped to her tits, which to be fair, are amazing. But they weren't for him.

Anger surged through me and I charged him. Suddenly, Raven was gone.

"You lost focus," Drake said as he shifted into the giant dragon.

Fuck. He was right. I had full control over my dreams until I got distracted and started wondering about him. *I* summoned him here.

Once again, I was running. Deep breaths, focused, calm. I imagined my bedroom. Empty, alone. Just me. In my bed. No distractions.

The blurring came faster this time and before the dragon even sent his first fire, I was in my room alone.

I kept my mind clear and focused by looking at the details in my room. The framed photo of me and Raven. The crystal I picked up on a family vacation. The school books and my backpack. My sweater hanging over my chair. It was bland and boring and safe.

But my mind was sharp and focused. I was a vault. No distractions.

Suddenly, everything faded and my eyes fluttered open. I was back in the Spellcasting room and Drake was grinning at me.

"Took you long enough," he said.

"You're an asshole, you know that?" I asked.

"Yeah, I do," he said.

"He is, but you passed," Professor Flora said.

"Yeah?" I asked. "Please tell me we don't have to do that again."

"Not for class, no," she said. "But you do share a mate with a demon with the same powers. You should know what he is capable of."

I swallowed. It was odd to think about what Luka could do. I never knew exactly how powerful his magic was before tonight. "But it's just a dream, right?"

"Sure," Drake said. "But if you didn't fight back, I could get anything I wanted from you in that state."

"Good point," I said. My mind whirred. It was a dangerous skill for sure. But the possibilities of how to use it were endless. The ability to find missing people and get information that was otherwise impossible to find was endless.

Though, there was the other side of it. If someone like Luka was using this power, would anyone even know? What if he was visiting Raven in her dreams? Could he be making her do things she didn't want to do?

There was good that could come from it, but I wasn't sure I liked the idea of Luka's magic when it came to Raven.

Raven

I wasn't sure what to expect from my first day back to independent study with Professor Flora. The shadow fae was weighing too heavily on my mind for me to spend any time coming up with what she might have me do. Plus, there was his comment about my magic in this realm compared to how it could be in the fae realm.

Not that I was considering leaving this realm. And I would never take him up on his offer. But I was curious about what it meant. Dr. Green's revelation regarding my placement in the shifter dorm for the safety of the other students was even more interesting now. What was I truly capable of? And was it possible to tap into that magic? To control it?

I think I finally had a handle on my time magic and I hadn't once lost control in the last month. But what else could I do?

Professor Flora was sitting on a stone bench on the front row of the amphitheater seating. She stood when I entered.

"Welcome back," she said.

"Thanks," I said. "And thanks for showing us how to get my magic back." Though, now that I knew my weakened magic was what was keeping the shadow fae away, I sort of wished I'd had more time.

"Of course," she said. "Dr. Green used a favor to get me here. I assured him I would provide you with any assistance I could to help you with your dual heritage."

That was surprising, but it explained her presence here more. Though, I wished I knew what the favor was that he'd called in. What had Dr. Green done for Professor Flora? Now wasn't the time for that question, though. And I had a perfect opening for my most pressing question.

"Can you tell me how my magic is different here than it would be in Faerie?" I asked.

She lifted her eyebrows as if my question surprised her. Then she smiled the tiniest bit. Maybe I'd asked the right question for once.

"Your magic here is prohibited by the rules of this realm," she said. "Faerie is a place of magic. It fills our air and it's in our food. The whole realm vibrates with it and it charges our magic in a way that isn't possible here."

"So as long as I'm here, my magic will be *bound*?" I tested the word, waiting for her reaction.

"You've been studying." She sounded impressed. "Yes, here

you are bound by the limits of magic in this realm. You'd need to visit Faerie to fully expand your powers."

She narrowed her eyes. "Is that what you're considering?"

I shook my head. "No. At least not now. Maybe someday."

"It is illegal to cross into Faerie," she said.

I smiled, knowing full well she'd done that very thing to get here. "I know."

"Then I have fulfilled my duty as your teacher in discouraging you from doing something illegal," she said. "Shall we move on to working with your powers?"

"Yes," I said. "I'd really like to learn more about shadow fae. What they're capable of. What it would take to fight one."

"Perhaps you are thinking of a visit?" She seemed to say the words more to herself than me. "I am not of the shadow court, but I know they work in shadows. It might be possible for you to learn how to wield some element of control over them. Though, you're only a quarter shadow fae so I'm honestly not sure."

"How would I try?" I asked.

She walked over to her desk and slid open a drawer. I heard her moving things. A moment later, she walked back to me and set a lantern down on the bench. "Sit."

I sat next to the lantern.

She lifted her hand and the lights in the room went out. "Shadow fae can remove light. I can only flip the switch."

My mind flashed back to the locker room and the library. The darkness brought by the shadow fae. Was it possible that Professor Flora knew what was going on? For a horrible moment, I considered the fact that she could be involved. What if she was helping him?

I couldn't deal with that thought. It was too much. Part of me felt like I was being naive trusting her, but my instincts were telling me she wasn't connected to the shadow fae. I had to trust that he was on his own.

Professor Flora picked up the lantern and flipped a switch. It lit up, casting a bright glow into the darkened room. She set the lantern down on the bench next to me and then sat down herself.

"Shadows are tricky to control," she said. "I can't do it, but I've seen it done. When I was a child, there was a shadow fae who would come to our village and perform for us. He'd create shadows with his hands and then direct and move the shadows. Once, I asked him to teach me. He said it was only something those from his court could do. However, he also told me he'd learned how to do this skill when he was a child. I think it's where you should start."

"Making shadow puppets?" I asked.

She nodded.

I shrugged and waved my hand in front of the light, casting a huge shadow on the wall. Then I closed my fingers to my thumb as if making a mouth, opening and closing my hand.

I felt ridiculous.

"You're not calling your magic at all," Professor Flora said. "You're just making shadow puppets."

"I have no idea what I should be doing," I said.

"How do you use your other magic?" she asked. "When you control time, you're tapping into that fae magic. What does that feel like and how do you call it?"

I thought back to the few times I'd used time magic. I'd only fully had control of it once or twice. But there was a moment when I'd called it. I made the decision to use it and I had even reset everything once. The ability to tap into it was there.

Until that moment, though, I hadn't considered how different the time magic felt from the other magic I used in classes. My regular spells and simple incantations didn't feel the same as the time magic.

I spread my fingers wide and the shadow of my hand showed

on the wall in front of me. There had to be a way to isolate that shadow. A way to make it do what I wanted.

In a way, it wasn't all that different from time magic. I was isolating a moment by taking the shadow and controlling its actions. I could make it move on its own or rewind it to where it had been if I could get it to be free of the attachment to my hand.

Focusing on what I wanted it to do, I reached for the magic I held deep within. It responded, a low humming vibration. Little sparks shot down my arms and I directed the magic toward the shadow.

A flicker of something I hadn't felt before rose within me and instead of snuffing it out, I embraced it, coaxing it along. The feeling grew and then I felt a popping sensation in my hand.

It startled me and I pulled my hand away, shaking it. Only, when I moved my hand, the shadow stayed where it was.

"Holy shit," I said.

"See if you can get it to do anything," Professor Flora said.

I lifted my hand and used my fingers to attempt to guide the shadow the way I might guide a flame I'd conjured. To my surprise, the shadow responded, moving in the direction I indicated.

Shocked, I dropped my hand to my lap and released the magic. The shadow vanished in a tendril much the same way the shadow fae had.

If I could get better at this, there had to be some way I could use it to address my shadow fae problem. But how?

The bell rang.

"That was good," Professor Flora said. "See you tomorrow."

I was a little stunned as I walked out of the classroom but for the first time since the shadow fae cornered me in the locker room, I was starting to think that I had a shot at putting an end to this whole mess.

Between the weekend in the library and my newfound shadow magic, an idea formed. And I was no longer just thinking about how to hide the book. Now, I was thinking about how to capture and stop the shadow fae. There was a little more to do, but things were finally coming together.

Raven

Matt was waiting for me when I left the Spellcasting room. I nearly forgot he had previously been attending this period with me so he was off. I wanted to go right into my thoughts about the fae, but I was more curious about his exam.

"How was your test?" I asked.

His face fell.

"That good, huh?" I asked.

"I passed," he said. "So I guess that's what counts."

"What happened?" I asked.

"Did you know that an incubus can control someone while they sleep? And even force sleep?" he asked.

My stomach twisted uncomfortably. I *did* know that but I also knew Luka didn't like that others knew. Though, I supposed it wasn't a secret anymore if Matt had found out in his test. "Not all of them."

"Right, but Luka's family can. Which probably means Luka can," he said. "Raven, has he ever forced you to sleep?"

"No!" I exclaimed. "Why would you think that?"

"How would you even know, though?" he asked. "He could make you sleep and you wouldn't even know."

"He'd never do that," I said.

"Raven, it was awful. I saw myself being controlled and I couldn't stop it," he said. "If I didn't know I was dreaming…"

"Matt, I trust Luka, and you should too." I set my hand on his chest, trying to comfort him. Whatever he'd just been though had clearly been traumatic. "Luka would never hurt us."

"What if he lost his temper? Or thought he was helping?" he asked.

I shook my head. "What if *you* lost *your* temper? Couldn't you use magic you didn't mean to? Even I've stopped time on accident."

"That's not the same," he said. "You weren't raised with it. You didn't even know you had it. And with mages, we can fight magic with magic. You can't even use magic in a dream."

"What happened, Matt?" I asked.

"I don't want to talk about it," he said. "But I don't think I like you being alone with him."

I raised my brows. "That's not your decision to make. And I told you, he'd never hurt me."

"You didn't just see what I saw," he said.

"Well, explain it to me," I said.

"I have a feeling it's not going to change your mind," he said.

"No, it won't," I said. "But maybe I can help you get over this fear."

"It's not fear," he said, shaking his head. "It's complicated."

"Matt, whatever she put you through was done on purpose as worst case scenario," I said. "And honestly, I'm starting to think it was also done on purpose to get you to not trust Luka."

Matt's brow furrowed.

"Think about it, Matt," I said. "Has Luka ever given you a reason to doubt him?"

"No," Matt said.

The bell rang and I jumped. We were now late to class but between all the distractions, it was hard to care.

"You should go," Matt said. "I don't want you getting in trouble."

"I can't go while you're like this," I said. "Besides, I have something I need to talk to you about."

"It can wait till after class," he said.

I sighed and slid my hand up to his shoulders and stood on my tiptoes so I could give him a kiss on the cheek. "It's going to be okay. Meet me in your room after last period?"

"That I can do," he said.

"Bring Zach," I said. "You should both hear this."

I waved as I darted down the hallway toward my History of Magic class.

Class was already in session when I slid into my chair but Professor Craft didn't skip a beat in her lecture as I settled in. She lifted her chin in greeting, but didn't make a fuss about my being late.

As quietly as possible, I pulled out my notebook and opened it to a blank page so I could take notes.

"If you turn to page 347 in your text, you'll see the diagram of the years the Black Plague was most active in Eastern Europe during the rise of the Blood Cult that dominated the vampire community at the time," Professor Craft said.

I dug my book out of my bag and flipped through the pages. To my surprise, there was a folded up piece of paper shoved in the book at the exact page she'd asked us to turn to. I wondered if the student who had the book before me had left their notes tucked in there.

"It was a slow rise to power until the high point of the plague," Professor Craft said.

I opened the paper and my blood ran as cold as ice. I could no longer hear my professor and I felt like I was suddenly trapped in the dark dungeon that haunted my nightmare.

It wasn't notes from a former student. It was a warning. And it was written in what looked like blood.

Four Days

The shadow fae had been in my room again. He'd left a note in my textbook in the exact place I needed to turn to. Was he here now? Was he lurking in the shadows following my every move?

Suddenly, I felt like I couldn't breathe.

How was I supposed to do this? The beginnings of a plan formed in my mind, but if I told anyone, he'd know.

I glanced around the room, suddenly feeling totally exposed. A shiver ran down my spine. What if he watched me practicing shadow magic in my lesson? What if he was in my room while I was sleeping?

This had to stop.

My mind whirred as I half listened to Professor Craft. I knew I wasn't safe and the worst part was that the people I loved weren't safe.

I was so deep in my own thoughts that I nearly jumped out of my seat when the bell rang.

Quickly, I packed up and raced out the door toward Matt and Zach's room. I was done being afraid and it was time to fix this.

Matt and Zach greeted me at the door but Zach was closer so I grabbed him and pulled him into a kiss and went right for the button on his pants.

"What the hell, Raven?" He was startled, but his cock was already forming a tent.

I stood on my tiptoes and pressed my lips to his ear. "I think I'm being watched. Please go with it."

He kissed me back, fiercely and then grabbed my hand and led me toward his bedroom.

"Um? You guys?" Matt called.

I turned and gestured for him to follow us. Thankfully, he did. As soon as the door closed behind us, I walked over to Matt and kissed him.

He didn't fight it like I expected him to, instead he moaned into my mouth, grabbing the back of my head and pulling me deeper into the kiss. I enjoyed it for a moment before pulling away.

On my tiptoes, I whispered. "Can you put us in that bubble?"

He nodded and quickly called the spell, sealing the three of us in a bubble in Zach's room.

"Are you going to explain why I'm going to have blue balls for a week?" Zach asked.

"This keeps our conversation private, right?" I asked.

"Yes," Matt said.

"Sorry for all that," I said. "I'm hoping the shadow fae isn't one to watch."

"He came back?" Zach said, his tone changing instantly to worry.

I climbed onto the bed and sat cross-legged. The twins joined me, taking a seat on either side of me.

"What happened?" Matt asked.

"Three days ago he reappeared," I said.

"Raven!" Zach shouted. "Why didn't you tell us?"

"Let me explain," I said. "He showed up in my room. Which means, he has more access to places than we realized. And he gave me a week to meet him with the book. So I've been trying to figure out what to do."

"He was in your room?" Matt said. "That's it, you're moving in with us."

"No, I'm not," I said. "I can't change anything. I need him to think we're in here having sex right now."

"Shit, you really think he's following you?" Zach asked.

I nodded and pulled the piece of paper from my textbook out of my pocket. I set it on the bed between us. "This was in my textbook during History of Magic. On the exact page the professor asked us to turn to."

"I'm going to kill him," Zach said.

"How?" I asked. "Because that's part of the problem. He's powerful and his magic is unfamiliar."

"I don't know, but I'll figure something out. He can't do this to you, Raven," Zach said.

"You said you had an idea?" Matt said.

"Yes," I said. "I want to set up a trap for him."

"I don't like where this is going," Matt said. "We tried this once before, remember?"

"I know," I said. "But we'll be smarter this time."

"What do you want us to do??" Zach asked.

"Well, first, I think we have to talk to Professor Flora. We need a better decoy book or a way to destroy the book completely," I said. "And she knows fae magic better than anyone here. If there's a way to do it, she might know."

"Okay," Matt said.

"And we're going to need everyone's help," I said. "Ben and Luka."

"No," Matt and Zach said at the same time. "This is mage business. They're unpredictable. What if they do something crazy?"

I cocked an eyebrow. "Technically, this is fae business and we've been through this. We're in this together. Whatever weird thing you're going through with them has to end."

They didn't look happy but they didn't argue. And that was good enough for me for now. "As soon as we sort out the book, we can move on with the rest of my plan."

Quickly, I described my idea.

"That could work," Matt said.

"I think it will," I said.

"But I need one of you to talk to Professor Flora for me. And try to keep it private," I said.

"I'll go tonight," Matt said.

"Thank you," I said. If there was a way to destroy the book or make a copy, we had a shot at my plan.

"Since we're here, though…" Matt said, moving a little closer to me. "Maybe we should make our distraction more believable?"

My lips parted and I tried to think of a response. It had been a while since I'd been with more than one man at a time and to be honest, I'd wanted to do it again. I just didn't think it would be with Matt and Zach.

Matt's mouth closed over mine, his kiss warm and confident. I leaned into him and slid my tongue into his mouth.

His hands went up my shirt and he pushed up my bra, freeing my breasts. He cupped each of them and played with my nipples. I moaned into his mouth.

Another set of hands slid around my waist from the back and went to work on the button of my pants. I shifted my hips, giving Zach more access. He slid my pants and panties down and I stepped out of them while continuing to kiss Matt.

Zach's hands explored my ass and then one of his hands went between my legs. His fingers found my clit and he teased me while Matt continued to caress my breasts. So many sensations at once had me bucking my hips and panting into the kiss.

Finally, I couldn't take it anymore and tossed my head back to cry out as an orgasm spiked through my core.

Zach turned my face toward and claimed my mouth with his. I turned into him and discovered that he'd removed his clothes when I pressed my hips against him. His cock pressed into my side and I reached down for it, stroking it with my hand.

He pulled away from the kiss, groaning in approval from my touch.

Matt was next to me now and he turned me back to him for another kiss. I let go of Zach and quickly stripped Matt of his clothes. He pulled my shirt off over my head in return.

He tangled his hands into my hair, gently pushing my head down. I smirked. I knew exactly what he wanted. Leaning down, I took his cock in my mouth. He groaned as I expertly worked my mouth and tongue along his erection.

Behind me, Zach's hands caressed my ass before a finger slid into my wet slit. I moaned around Matt's cock.

Zach added a finger and I moved my hips, accommodating him as the pleasure continued to grow. After another orgasm, he removed his fingers and I could feel his cock at my entrance.

It slid in easily and I moaned just as Matt pulled out of my mouth. He came hard in front of me and I grabbed hold of his hips to steady myself as Zach continued to thrust.

Pleasure was already building again and I gasped with each movement. Zach groaned and pulled my hips closer as he came.

Sweaty and still panting, I stood and kissed each of my mates in turn. The two of them had almost made me forget about the danger lurking at the academy. I was grateful for them and how well they read me. The encounter had been exactly what I needed.

After we dressed, Matt let down the bubble around us. As soon as it was down, my anxiety returned. I knew we were about to embark on a dangerous plan. I just hoped we could pull it off.

Raven

Matt didn't waste any time getting the bubble up around all of us in our training session with Professor Flora.

"What is the meaning of this?" she asked, raising her hands in the air as if she was going to cast magic.

I rushed to her and grabbed her wrists. "Please, wait. I have something I need to talk to you about."

"Raven, what the hell is going on?" Ben asked.

"All of you, just give me a minute," I said.

"Let her talk," Zach said.

"You two are in on this with her?" Ben said. "Why am I not surprised."

"First of all," I said. "I'm over the weird competition going on between the four of you. We were in a good place after the portal disaster. I need all of you. I'm not making exceptions. You four need to get it together."

My mates stared at me wide eyed.

"Thank you," I said. Then I turned to Professor Flora. "We're in here because I need your help and it's not safe out there for me to talk."

"He came back?" Ben asked.

"What did he say this time?" Luka asked.

"Who came back?" Professor Flora said. "Raven, explain yourself or I'm breaking this spell. There is no need for me to be part of you and your mates working out whatever is going on between you all."

"There's a shadow fae loose in the school and he wants something from me," I said.

Professor Flora's eyes narrowed. "Are you certain?"

I nodded. "He's visited me three times now, asking for a book that used to belong to Professor Halifax. Apparently, it has dark magic that can only be used in the fae realm."

Professor Flora scrunched up her mouth. She looked annoyed.

"Please, I need help destroying the book. Or making a passable decoy. Something to convince him I have it so we can catch him."

"Why do you want to catch him?" she asked. "Why not tell Dr. Green. This really isn't a job for students."

"Because last time I told someone and he found out, he nearly killed my friend," I said. "He's been hiding in the shadows and I'm pretty sure he's watching me."

Professor Flora shook her head. "You aren't skilled enough

to catch a shadow fae yet. Maybe with a few more weeks of study, but not now."

"You know we can bind our magic," I said, glancing around at my mates. "I think with all of us working together we can stop him. But the book is what I need help with. If it's as bad as Professor Halifax says, I don't want it around."

"She's not a professor anymore," Professor Flora said.

"True," I said. "But that doesn't make the book any less dangerous."

"If the book is what I'm thinking it is," Professor Flora said, "there's only one way to remove the magic. It can't be destroyed, though. That's not possible."

"Well, how do we remove the magic?" Zach asked.

"You transfer it," Professor Flora said. "It's not the book that has the power, the book is likely just a vessel. And the fae who is after it is likely tracking the magic. He'll know if the book is no longer holding it."

"So we move it to another object and keep it close by," Matt said.

"That doesn't stop the magic," I said. "What if he gets the new object?"

"You can't transfer it to an object in this realm," Professor Flora said.

I ran a hand through my hair as frustration tugged in my gut. We were going around in circles. It was like the only way to get rid of the shadow fae was to give him the book. But I felt an obligation to keep it out of his hands. How could we pull this off if everything I thought might work was another dead end?

"We can transfer it into a person, can't we?" Zach asked.

I looked over at Zach, noting his serious expression, then turned to Professor Flora.

She smirked. "You have been doing your homework."

"That sounds too dangerous," Luka said. "Taking magic

internally has never worked out well. There's several lost souls in the underworld who thought they could handle it."

"Would it work?" I asked.

"It would," Professor Flora said. "At least it *should*."

"No way," Ben said. "I know what you're thinking."

"I'm with Ben," Matt said. "You are not taking that kind of risk."

"There's five of us, though," I said, letting the words sink in for a minute. "I don't want to volunteer you all, but…"

"She's right," Zach said. "That kind of magic could be handled safely in a smaller dose. And if we divided it, it would be harmless without all five of us to bring it back together."

"Would that work?" Matt asked.

"I've never seen it tried," Professor Flora said.

"Do we have any other options?" I asked.

Nobody said a word. I knew it was our only choice. I hated asking my mates to do this, but I had no idea what this dark fae would do with magic like this. If we split it between ourselves, it would be eliminated from both realms.

"You need a new moon for the transfer to work," Professor Flora said.

"That's in two days," Ben said.

"Luckily, he gave me four days," I said, fishing the note out of my pocket and holding it out.

"In the meantime," Professor Flora said. "You need to work on your magic."

She lifted her hand and with a flick of her wrist, the bubble around us collapsed. "Mage tricks are no match for Fae magic."

My chest tightened. My whole plan was built on using mage magic. But what other choice did I have?

"The five of you need to learn to work together," Professor Flora said. "It's the only chance you have at passing the trials and your parlor tricks won't work."

I smiled at Professor Flora. Maybe she was on our side after all.

"You each have talents and weaknesses," she said. "You weren't given your topics on accident."

"I knew it!" Matt said.

"What topics?" Luka asked.

"I've spent the last few weeks researching dream walking," Matt said. "And your brother came and gave me a test."

"Wait, what?" Luka asked.

"Were you going to tell the rest of us that?" I asked.

"It doesn't matter right now," Matt said. "Because now I know why you did it. At first I thought you were trying to drive a wedge between us but that wasn't it, was it?"

"It is showing unfair favoritism to the group that I'm sponsoring for the trials," she said. "But I don't lose."

"Someone catch me up on this," Ben said.

"Your weakness is anti-shifting spells and your inability to control your emotions when you're in your shifted form," Zach said.

"What?" Ben asked.

"I'm telling you, I studied shifters for weeks and my exam was against you."

"You left that part out," I said, suddenly realizing why Zach had been so weird after his test.

"I wasn't proud of how I reacted," he said. "But now I know your weaknesses and your strengths. Which means, I can help you get better before the trials."

"And I suppose that means Matt is supposed to help Luka?" Ben asked.

"There is hope for all of you after all," Professor Flora said.

"What about Raven?" Ben asked.

"I have to work with Professor Flora," I said. "Is that what you were getting at?"

She nodded. "Your fae magic is both your weakness and your strength. You have to control it or you'll do something you regret."

"Like stopping time?" Zach said.

"Like that," I agreed. "Or worse."

I could feel my mates staring at me and I knew they were wondering what my words meant.

"Go ahead," Professor Flora said.

I nodded then took a deep breath. I'd been practicing the shadow magic in my room but it was still difficult to control. Calling to my magic, I pulled the shadows from the corner of the room toward me. They came to me like smoke, wrapping around my ankles like tendrils of darkness.

"Raven," Luka said, in awe. "That's amazing."

"Turns out, I'm part Shadow Fae," I said. "I'm still not sure how it can help me, but it's something I'm working on."

"How does this connect to portals?" Zach asked. "That was your topic."

I had no idea. We hadn't even gotten into portals in my independent study lessons. All of my research for that had been on my own and so far, I didn't see any connections.

"It doesn't really," Professor Flora said. "But portals are her weakness. She can control her time magic now. But until she can fully contain all her fae magic, she's at risk of doing things she shouldn't."

"Are you saying she could accidentally open a portal?" Zach asked.

"Probably not," she said. "But I know some day she might choose to and she should be able to control it."

I blinked a few times, startled by her words. That wasn't what I expected. "So it has nothing to do with the trials?"

"It has everything to do with your heritage, and your choices," she said. "No fae should be forced to stay in this realm. Even if they are half fae."

"We saw what that drove Professor Halifax to," Luka said.

"Do you want to go to the fae realm?" Ben asked.

"I don't know," I said. "I mean, I suppose it's something I've wondered about but I don't even know what I'll do when I gradate, let alone for the rest of my life."

"Wow," Zach said.

"Yeah, wow," Luka agreed.

"Hey, I'm not going anywhere right now," I said.

"We know, Raven," Matt said. "But it brings up the fact that after graduation, everything will change."

"I don't want it to change," I said. We were back at the conversation we'd had right after defeating Professor Halifax. Our futures. We'd put the topic on hold for a few weeks, but it never really went away.

"Can we focus on one thing at a time right now?" Luka suggested.

"Good idea," I said. We had a book to destroy, a shadow fae to catch, and a trials to pass.

Why was everything always so complicated?

Raven

The next two days were a blur as I went through the motions of getting my classwork done. Even Luka wasn't his normal cocky self. It was unsettling. But I kept reminding myself that once this was over, we could go back to focusing on normal school stuff. Whatever that meant at the Academy of the Elites. Because let's face it, I had yet to experience *normal*.

My independent study with Professor Flora was surprisingly helpful as I worked to harness more of my shadow magic. It was an odd skill that I was struggling to find balance with. Having the ability to wield both fire and shadow was going to come in handy for sure. But it was difficult to think too far ahead right now.

Plus, Professor Flora kept reminding me that I still had a test next week over portals. After how harrowing the tests for Matt and Zach had been, I was nervous.

I tried to shake all the nerves free as I walked into the cafeteria for dinner. Fixing a fake smile on my face, I walked over to where Makayla was waiting for me.

"You look like shit," she said.

"Wow, nice to see you too."

She laughed. "You need a night off. And you still owe me a girl's night," she said.

That was true. While I'd finally caught her up over a series of short conversations about the trials and everything that had happened that night - well, mostly everything - we hadn't had a chance for our night in yet.

I glanced over at the line waiting for cafeteria food, then looked back at Makayla. "Should we call for pizza?"

Makayla threw her arm over my shoulder. "We should."

"Hey, Raven, Makayla," Ben said as he walked toward us.

"Sorry, Ben, I'm stealing your girl away," Makayla said.

"Impromptu girl's night," I said, giving him my cheesiest smile.

He laughed. "Have fun, you two."

"Thanks," I said, as Makayla led me away.

After a quick call to the pizza place in town that was run by a family of supernaturals, we settled into my room.

"So, tell me about Remi," I said. "Any updates?"

Makayla's face turned bright red. It had been a few weeks since I heard the latest and her blush was a dead giveaway that something new was going on. "Spill."

"I finally told my parents," she said. "So I guess that means he's not just a fling."

I squealed. "And? What did they say?"

"They're looking forward to meeting him," she said. "I was surprised how well they took it, honestly. But I did wait till they got news that my youngest brother just dropped out of high school. So I look great compared to that."

I laughed. "Is that what siblings are for?"

"Of course! Save your bad news for when one of them screws up worse," she said. "Want to know the craziest part?"

"What's that?" I asked.

"My dad wants to interview him for a job," she said.

"Wow," I said. "He must think you two are serious."

She shrugged. "I guess we are."

"So you're moving in with him after graduation?" I asked.

She smiled. "Probably."

"I'm happy for you," I said.

"What about you? Going to find a cozy four bedroom house and rotate which room you sleep in?" She elbowed me playfully.

"I'm still trying to figure all of that out," I said.

A gentle knock sounded on the door and I jumped to my feet, grateful for the distraction. I opened the door, money in hand to pay the delivery guy.

Only, there wasn't anyone at the door. I looked down, just in time to see the swirls of shadow as they dissipated. An envelope sat on the ground.

I picked it up and opened it quickly, using the door to block myself from Makayla. Of course the note was from the Shadow Fae. And of course, he was reminding me of my deadline.

Only this time, he was also leaving me a more specific threat. The words on the note should have sent fear coursing through my veins. But it didn't. I was furious.

I crumbled up the note, anger making my face hot.

It's one thing to threaten me. It's another thing to threaten my mates or my classmates.

This note was worse than that.

Apparently, if I didn't get the book to him, he was going to open as many portals to the fae realm as he could and let the monsters in.

If that happened, it wasn't just going to be a few people who were hurt. Nobody in the school would stand a chance.

Tomorrow, I was going to bind that book with my mates and we were going to end this.

"Where's the pizza?" Makayla asked. "I'm starving."

"Wrong room," I said as I closed the door. "I'm sure it'll be here any minute."

I walked back into the room and settled down onto a pillow on the floor. For all I knew, the shadow fae was in the room with us right now. I wasn't sure if it would be better for him to see me ignoring his threat or if he wanted to see me upset.

"What's wrong?" Makayla asked.

"Nothing," I said. "Just worried about a big test I have tomorrow, that's all."

"The Spellcasting one?" she asked. "I keep hearing all the mages complaining about it. That new professor sounds intense."

"She is," I said, grateful for the subject change. "Hey, did you ever figure out how to get those mice to deliver messages in your class?"

She shook her head. "No, I'm probably going to fail that class. Good thing I don't see myself ever needing an animal familiar. I mean, who puts a wolf shifter into that class?"

I laughed with her. She wasn't great with the animals either but she'd been better than me.

Another knock on the door. I raced to it so fast, I nearly knocked Makayla over in the process. This time, it really was the pizza guy.

Relieved, I tipped him extra and took the pie. "Hungry?"

Makayla and I spent the rest of the evening eating and talking. For most of the night, I forgot about tomorrow. Once she left, though, I found myself in my bed awake and wondering if I could actually pull this off.

There was only one way to find out.

Raven

"Raven?"

I looked over at Ben, who was sitting next to me at dinner. His forehead was lined with concern.

"Are you alright?" he asked.

"Fine," I said. "Just distracted."

Luka and the twins had skipped dinner tonight to prepare for our big plans of the evening. While Ben had been talking with the other shifters, I'd apparently zoned out.

"You're not looking so hot," Makayla said, narrowing her eyes. "What are you hiding from me?"

I laughed. She knew me too well. "Nothing."

"Something," she said with a sigh. "Fine, tell me when you're done saving the world or whatever the hell it is you're doing."

"I've got that test coming up, that's all," I said.

Makayla shook her head, clearly not buying it tonight. But she didn't bring it up again. She passed me her plate. "More fries?"

"I'm good, thanks," I said.

Ben stood and then leaned down to kiss me on the cheek. "See you later."

"Bye," I said.

"Poker tonight?" Jamal called.

"Maybe," Ben said. "You guys start without me."

"Wait up, Ben, I'll walk with you," I called as I grabbed my plate. "Catch you later, Makayla?"

"I know what that is," Starla said. "Booty call time."

"Not everything is about sex all the time," Makayla said.

I shrugged and lifted my eyebrows. "Sometimes it is."

My friends around the table cat-called after Ben and I as we left the cafeteria. He slid his arm around my shoulders. "I wish you wouldn't have said that."

"Why not?" I asked. "Now they'll just think we got stuck in bed if we don't make it to poker."

He paused for a second and glanced at me. "Good point. But I think we should try to squeeze in some one-on-one time just for the sake of authenticity."

"I support that plan," I said. "I mean, it's for the benefit of everyone, really."

He laughed and pulled me closer. Then he started walking again. "I'm going to be so glad when this is all done and we can go back to normal."

"Me too," I said. My stomach tightened as I thought about

what the rest of the night would bring. Zach had Ben's spare key and if everything was going to plan, he was getting the book from my room right now.

Ben and I walked past the stairway to the shifter dorms and headed toward the entrance to the lower levels of the school. I'd been down there twice before. Both times for confinement.

This time, we were using something that Professor Halifax mentioned to me when the time thief had stopped time inside the school. There were a few old dungeons, mostly used for storage. From what she'd said, they were impenetrable from the outside for magic to get in.

The rest of the group was already waiting for us inside the ancient dungeon. A chill ran up my spine as Ben closed the door behind us.

I was standing in a room that looked almost identical to the place I visited in my dreams. Along the back was a wall of iron bars. Behind them was a crumbling brick wall, blocking the view of whatever used to be on the other side. The ground was cold stone and a dripping sound echoed throughout the room.

Luka grabbed my hands. "Hey, you okay?"

My lower lip was trembling but I reminded myself we had work to do. "I think so."

"What's wrong?" Matt asked. "Raven?"

"It's a dream I have sometimes," I said. "Since I was kid. It's a room that looks like this. And I'm alone and scared."

Matt and Zach stood on either side of Luka and I could feel Ben behind me. All of them moved in closer to me, wrapping me in a giant group hug.

"You're not alone, now," Ben said.

"Thank you," I said, breathing in my mates. Being here with them made everything better. The room that had haunted my nightmares wasn't so bad if I could have them along with me.

They moved away from me, Luka still holding my hands. "It's almost over."

Zach held up the book. "We follow the plan, and we set this whole mess behind us."

I nodded. "Okay, let's do this."

Zach set the book down in the center of the room and the five of us stood around it. "I'll lead," Zach said, looking at each of us in turn.

I had a general idea of how the spell would work from texts I'd read, but it wasn't a spell that was recommended for mages to do. Much like everything I seemed to be doing lately.

Zach stretched his hands out, taking hold of Luka and Ben's hands. I grabbed hold of Luka and Matt. We hoped that keeping a mage between each of the non-mages would make the spell work better. It wasn't exactly tested on other magic users.

"Ready?" Zach asked.

"Let's get this over with," Ben said.

"Agree," I said. I wanted this whole thing over with. The book, the shadow fae, everything.

Zach took a deep breath and then closed his eyes. I followed his example and blew out a breath while I waited for him to cast the spell.

A moment later, he started speaking the words. "Magic within, reveal your secret."

I kept my eyes closed as the tingle of magic filled the air like an electric charge. Zach kept speaking, his words hardly above a whisper. I was too focused on summoning the magic into me to notice what he was saying. It called to me, coming to me easily. The magic in the room seemed to want freedom.

"We offer ourselves as your keeper," Zach said.

I gasped as a burst of bright pain hit my chest and expanded outward. Luka and Matt squeezed my hands tighter and I heard them grunt against the influx of magic. Almost as soon as it started, it dissipated, leaving a warm tingle across my skin.

I opened my eyes and looked at my partners. All of them had a blue glow on their skin. My own skin held the same properties. As I looked around at my mates, the color faded, and we all returned to normal.

"I think it worked," Luka said. "At least, I hope that's what that stabbing sensation was."

"I don't know how you mages deal with this kind of magic all the time," Ben said.

"It doesn't always feel like that," Zach said, breaking his hold on the others. He knelt down and picked up the book, then dragged his fingertips over the cover. "I don't sense any magic in it anymore."

"Good," I said, reaching for it. I took the book and held it against my chest. Then with my free hand, I fished the little vial of shadows out of my pocket and held it up. "Who's ready for part two?"

All of my mates were silent for a moment. I could feel their fear and I knew they were worried about me. I swallowed against the lump in my throat. I was worried about myself. We'd have one shot at this. As soon as the shadow fae had the book in his hands, he'd know the magic was gone.

We couldn't make any mistakes.

"We'll be waiting for you," Ben said, finally, breaking the silence. "All of us."

"Yeah," Matt agreed. "We do this together, right?"

I smiled. "Right."

28

Raven

A group of students walked past me. Bursts of laughter punctuated their conversation. It was an odd contrast. Me, walking on my way to the Spellcasting room, hoping I wasn't about to die. Them, enjoying a normal night away from studies without a care in the world. I envied them but I was also glad that they were safe.

I liked this world I'd come to be a part of. I liked the magic. I liked the mystery even. I loved my mates. If I hadn't come here, I wouldn't have them. They fulfilled an empty place inside me I didn't even know existed.

As I tugged open the door to the Spellcasting room, I knew I was doing the right thing. I'd take any risk necessary to ensure that they were safe. The part I hated about all of this was involving them. I wished I could do it on my own, but I knew I needed help from time to time.

And I was grateful I had them to help and support me. Being independent was part of who I was, but they'd taught me to learn how to be part of a family.

I took a deep breath as I closed the door behind me. I wasn't sure what the outcome of this night was going to be, but it helped shed some light on where I wanted to be in the future. Wherever I ended up, I was going to be just fine if I could keep my mates with me. Together. I couldn't let us end up split up. If we survived this, I was going to figure out a way for us to all stay together as one family. Because I needed them. And they needed me.

The Spellcasting room was eerie. Empty and lit only by the emergency light near the back of the room. The circular amphitheater was filled with long shadows from the single light, making it a perfect place to hide if you could move in the shadows.

I set the book down in a corner and took a step back. After lots of trial and error, I had the shadow magic down well enough to pull the shadows over the book, hiding it from sight.

I was pretty sure the shadow fae would be able to see right through it, but I had to at least make an attempt.

Now that that part was done, I dug the vial out of my pocket. My heart pounded against my ribs and my stomach filled with nervous flutters. I was about to do something really, really stupid. And I was about to break at least one major rule.

Taking a deep breath, I stretched out my arm, holding the vial over the stone floor. Then I dropped it.

The glass shattered and a billowing cloud of shadow rose from the vial, swirling around my ankles.

I tried to step away from the dark shadows, but they locked my feet in place. *Fuck.* I did not see that coming.

Pissed at myself for not detecting that trap, I clenched my teeth and balled my hands into fists. It didn't prevent me from doing what I needed to do, but it sure made things more complicated.

I heard a hissing sound and turned toward the door in time to see gray shadows moving like smoke through the crack under the door. The shadows built on the other side, forming the rough shape of a figure. A moment later, they cleared and the shadow fae was standing there staring at me. "I see you've come to your senses."

"Or I gave up," I said. "What's with the trap?"

He shrugged, then walked toward me. He moved with the grace of a lion stalking its prey. Even his movements sent a chill down my spine. I knew enough about magic to know he was more dangerous than any of the monsters I'd encountered so far.

"You pass off the book, I'll release you and be on my way," he said.

"I hid it in this room," I said. "Let me go so I can get it."

"No need," he said, walking past me.

I twisted as best I could while my feet were glued to the ground by the swirling smoky shadows. He walked right to the corner where I'd hid the book, not even hesitating. With a wave of his hand, he cleared the shadows and picked it up.

He was grinning as he walked back toward me. "I wondered if you had any ability to access the shadow magic you had."

"I'm a fast learner," I said.

He looked down at the book and his brow furrowed. My heart pounded harder. This was it. Time was running out. Any second, he'd sense that the magic was gone.

When he looked back up at me, his upper lip was in a snarl and I could see his fangs. "What did you do to the magic?"

"Magic?" I asked innocently. "You asked me to bring you the book. I fulfilled my end of the bargain."

"You know that's not what I was after," he said.

"Are you going to go back on your word?" I asked. "You said if I gave you the book, you'd leave this place. You also said you'd release me."

"You didn't follow through," he said with a growl. "You kept part of the book for yourself." Eyes narrowed, he moved closer to me. "I can feel it. The magic is close. What did you do with it?"

I swallowed hard. "The agreement was for the book."

His hand was on my throat so fast, I didn't have a chance to call to my magic. Gasping for breath, I clawed at his huge hand, trying to pull it away from me. The edges of my vision blurred as I struggled for air.

"I will kill you," he said. "Where is the magic?"

I couldn't run, I couldn't break his grip. My head spun and I could feel myself losing consciousness.

A sound like an explosion shattered the silence of the room and he let go of his hold on me. I gasped, sucking in air as I turned toward the sound.

All four of my mates were standing in front of a pile of stone. They'd been hiding in the secret passage Ms. Obscura had shown me, waiting in case I needed them.

Suddenly, the room went dark, all light gone from the space. I knew the shadow fae was working his magic, eliminating the light.

I sucked in a breath. We'd been prepared for this. I moved my feet and they were free from the magic keeping me stuck, which meant, my theory was correct. Even his magic was gone when he turned out the lights.

"You want that magic?" I called into the dark. "You'll have to come and take it from me."

I felt the rush of air moving as he closed in, grabbing me. The shadow fae held me tight, his grip binding my arms around me.

"Where is it, little fae?" he asked. "I will kill you and and all your mates. That's a promise."

I closed my eyes and reached out toward my mates through our bond. As we hoped, I could feel them. We might not have our magic, but our connection was something stronger than that.

The chains rattled as my mates moved closer and I knew they were closing in. Fae had one major weakness. One that I wasn't afflicted with being half human.

Iron.

The shadow fae cried out, releasing me from his grasp as my mates bound him in the iron chains they'd hidden in the passageway.

All at once, the shadows cleared from the room. I bolted away from the shadow fae, giving my mates more room to wrangle him.

When I turned back to look, he was on the ground, bound by iron chains. He hissed in pain, his gaze locked on me. "You think this is over?"

Just then, Professor Flora and Dr. Green entered the room.

"Right on time," Luka said.

Dr. Green's eyebrows lifted. "How long has this been in the works?"

"Just a few weeks," I said.

He shook his head. "Things are going to be a lot less interesting around here after the five of you graduate."

The shadow fae growled. "You think you can keep me in chains?"

"Oh, maybe they can't," Professor Flora said. "But I can.

Nice to see you, Lucan."

Lucan, the shadow fae, snapped his jaws at Professor Flora. "You're just as guilty as me. You crossed here illegally. They'll come for you."

"I don't think so," she said. "But now you'll be trapped here. At least you get to join your mate."

He growled.

Several guards burst into the room, pausing at the sight of a bound man on the ground.

"Escaped fae," Dr. Green said. "Attempted to kill a student and threatened a lot worse, I'm assuming."

"Again?" One of the guards asked.

"It's been a long a semester," Dr. Green said.

The guards stared at me and I could practically feel their judgement. And I didn't blame them at all.

"You'll be able to confine him, right?" I asked.

"Not for long," he threatened.

"Yeah, yeah," the guard said. "We've got far worse than you in our prisons. You won't be going anywhere."

I watched as they dragged him away, keeping him bound in the iron chains. Adrenaline was still surging through me, making me feel hyper alert. It was hard to believe it was actually over.

"You five, my office," Dr. Green said before he turned and followed the guards out of the Spellcasting room.

"Hey, at least there's no dead bodies on the floor this time," Luka said.

I shouldn't have laughed, but I did. Having showdowns with evil fae in this room was becoming far too common.

"I take it the binding spell worked?" Professor Flora said.

I nodded.

"You five have a lot of work to do. I have no idea what that's going to do to your magic or to your bond." She turned and left the room.

Raven

Dr. Green's office was starting to feel comfortable. That wasn't a good thing. I was guessing I'd been in here more in the nearly two semesters of study than most students were during the full two years.

"Explain," he said as he settled into the chair behind his desk.

I glanced at my mates and noticed that Professor Flora was absent from the meeting.

"Raven?" he said.

I looked back over at him and sighed. "It's a long story."

"It always is," he said.

"It started with a book," Zach said. He nudged me with his elbow. "Go on."

I summarized the whole thing as quickly as I could for Dr. Green, noting the frown that didn't leave his face. I told him about the book, and the visit to Professor Halifax in her dreams. The locker room threat, and the shadow fae showing up in my bathroom. When I finally got to the note, Zach took over.

"We destroyed the book's magic the best way we could," he said.

"Honestly, if anything, we should get out of the trials after all this," Luka said. "Between the whole Professor Halifax thing and her crazy mate, anything the school throws at us is going to be a piece of cake."

Dr. Green looked at each of us in turn, finally resting his gaze on me. "If it was up to me, I'd have you all graduate if only to stop sending all the crazies to this school. In all my years here, I've never seen so much excitement."

"I assure you, I'm not asking for it," I said.

"I know, Raven," he said.

"I think you need to fire the security team, though," Matt said. "I mean, seriously?"

"Though, the new threat did come in from a portal I opened under duress," I said. "It wasn't like an outside security team could have stopped that."

"True," Matt said.

"Are we in trouble?" Ben asked.

Dr. Green smirked. "I don't know what I'm going to do with all of you."

"Hero's banquet?" Luka suggested.

I laughed. "All I want is a quiet night to rest. And a few weeks of normalcy before the trials. I don't even know what it's like to be a regular student."

"The trials are in six weeks," Dr. Green said. "You five think you can manage to stay out of trouble until then?"

"You know, I don't think we can make any promises," Luka said.

"I sure hope nothing else comes up," I said. "Is there a way to scan the school for any hiding outsiders? Make sure no other crazed fae snuck in?"

"Actually, there are some dark magic detections spells," Zach said.

"Don't worry," Dr. Green said. "The guards are already checking."

"Six weeks?" I looked at my mates. "Think we can go that long without having any extra drama?"

"We're not going to let you out of our sight," Matt said. "Are we?"

"Hell no," Ben said. "We all know you're the trouble-maker of the group."

I laughed.

The clock chimed and I looked over to see the owl's eyes wide open tonight. It was midnight. We'd made it to a new day.

"You five have class in the morning," Dr. Green said as he stood. "Don't make me call you into my office again."

He looked like he was fighting a smile while trying to maintain a stern expression. I was grateful for him. Without him at the helm, who knew what would have happened to me here.

As we walked down the hallway, the adrenaline finally wore out and I was suddenly exhausted. I stifled a yawn.

"Long day," Matt said.

Luka slid his arm around my waist and pulled me close to him. "You need some sleep."

"We all need sleep," I said.

Luka guided me away from the hallway that led to my dorm room. My brow furrowed. "Hey, wrong way."

"Nope," he said. "The twins were right. You need more protection. There's two of them in that room."

"Plus, there's room for all of us there," Ben added.

"Wait a minute." I stopped walking and looked at all of my mates. None of them were arguing. "You all agreed to this?"

"We had some words while we were waiting in the secret passage," Ben said.

"And you didn't kill each other?" I asked.

"Our differences aren't as important as making sure you're safe," Zach said.

"So we're going to have a sleepover in your dorm room?" I asked, still not believing it.

"There's room for all of us there," Ben said.

"We don't even have to share the same bed," Luka said. "Though, I'm open to it if anyone wants company. While Raven is my favorite, you're all pretty hot."

I laughed at the bright shade of pink Ben's face was. It was true, though. I'd not only managed to connect with four intelligent, amazing men, I'd hit the sexy jackpot. How the hell did I get this lucky?

Deciding I should go along with this decision while they were all getting along, I started walking again. This would be the first time all of us had shared one room. Sure, we'd shared *other* things before. But those nights had still ended up with me in my room alone.

The room was dark when we entered and Zach flipped on some lights. "I'll wait with Raven if the rest of you want to check the rooms. Just in case."

I looked at Zach with my brows raised. "You do realize the fae who was after me was literally able to turn into a shadow."

"Yeah, but he's gone," Ben said. "I'll check this way."

"I've got this side," Luka said.

"Looks like I've got the bedrooms," Matt said.

They all took off in three different directions while I stood there feeling awkward with Zach. "I'm not helpless, you know."

"We know," he said. "But do you know how helpless you made us feel? We want to help you, Raven. We have to work together when one of us needs help."

"Does that go for all of you?" I asked. "If Ben needed help, would you be willing to help him?"

He hesitated and I knew I'd caught him. I was just about to say so when he opened his mouth.

"Raven, I don't know how to explain it, but the four of us share our own bond. It's not like the bond I have with you, but yes, I would help him if he needed it. For your sake and for mine. We're connected somehow. It doesn't make sense, but that's where we are," he said.

My jaw dropped open. "I wasn't expecting that."

"Me neither," Ben said. "Place looks clear."

"Wow, that was touching, bro," Matt said.

"Sexy and sweet, Raven, this guys a keeper," Luka said.

My face heated as I felt all of them staring at me. I was surprised by Zach's comment but I shouldn't be. Every time we'd combined our magic, I could feel the bond between us. We were connected.

I walked toward the middle of the room. "You're all keepers."

My mates surrounded me now and I could almost feel the electricity sizzling between us. It made my knees weak and I had to take a deep breath to steady myself.

Ben moved closer to me and without hesitation, he held me with an arm around my back and dipped me before leaning down for a kiss. I threw my arms around his neck, matching his kiss with hunger of my own.

He lifted me and broke free of the kiss, leaving me gasping. Everything felt a little fuzzy as a lust took over. Wetness spread between my thighs as the others closed in. Excitement shot through me. Was I really getting this lucky again?

Zach slid his hand behind my head and pulled me into a kiss while someone's hands went up my skirt, sliding my panties to the side.

Zach's fingers worked the buttons of my shirt and I shimmied out of it, hardly noticing it drop to the ground. Fingers slid into me and I gasped, closing my eyes as pleasure mounted.

Someone's hand slid up my arm and fingers brushed against my neck before guiding me away from Zach. I turned to see Luka staring at me. His blue eyes hooded with lust. I cupped the side of his face with my hand then slid my fingers into his blonde hair, moving his face toward me.

He gave me a cocky smirk. The one that sent shivers down my spine. Instead of kissing my lips, he went for my neck. Kissing, nibbling, and doing something with his tongue that made me throw my head back and moan.

His hands found my breasts and he teased my sensitive nipples. From behind me I could feel a cock rubbing against my hip. Someone was ready for more. I leaned into Luka's chest, lifting my hips so my ass was in the air a little.

Glancing behind me, I saw that it was Matt who was ready for me. He slid his fingers into my slit, making me groan. Then he gently slid a finger into my ass. I gasped in surprise, startled but not in pain.

Luka's hands moved away from my breasts and he slid a finger into my mouth. I sucked, watching Luka's eyes grow wide. Getting an Incubus off was a huge turn on. I knew that out of all my mates, he was the most experienced and when I could do something to make his eyes bulge, it made me feel powerful.

He pulled his finger out of my mouth. "Raven, the things you do to me."

I grinned, a thrill rushing through me at the control I knew I had over him. But it was short lived. His hand moved to my mound, his fingers finding my clit and I melted into him, all willpower gone.

As Luka's expert fingers worked magic, Matt's cock pressed into my ass. He was slow and gentle and with Luka's distractions, I didn't feel any pain. Instead, I was gasping and moaning with each thrust as Luka slid a finger into me and continued to tease my clit. I had no idea how he was working such orgasm inducing skills. I was far too gone to pay attention. The only thing I knew was that I was screaming so loud, they could probably hear me several rooms over. I didn't even care. It all felt too good.

Another set of hands was on my breasts now and I leaned my head back, moaning as I was overcome with sensation.

Matt grunted behind me as he came and I was gasping for air from the multiple orgasms Luka's fingers had managed. Both men moved away from me, Luka with a sly grin. He knew what he did to me and *damn* it was amazing.

Still breathless, I practically fell into Ben who was now standing in front of me. He lifted me and I wrapped my legs around his waist. He carried me to the dining room table, using it as a seat. As soon as he sat down, he slid into me.

I moaned as he stretched me. Out of all of my mates, Ben was the most well-endowed. He roughly grabbed a handful of my hair and pulled my head closer to him. His mouth claimed mine, his stubble rubbing on my face as we kissed furiously. My skin felt like it was on fire.

We broke the kiss and I positioned my knees so I could ride Ben better. He leaned back as I moved my hips. His cock hit me in just the right place. My back arched and I cried out as each thrust drove me closer to another climax.

Out of the corner of my eye, I saw Zach moving closer to us. I reached out and grabbed his hand, pulling him closer to me.

His erection was at just the right height for me and I pulled him into my mouth.

He braced himself with one hand on the back of the chair and one on the arm rest. Ben grabbed my hips and lifted and guided me to continue riding him while I was licking and sucking on Zach.

Both of my mates were panting now and I could tell they were close. Another set of hands slid up my back and I knew at once it was Luka. His erection pressed against my back, then went lower. I knew where he was going and I leaned forward on Ben to help him enter me easier.

His cock pressed at my rear opening and Ben slowed for a moment, keeping me still. The fact that they were working together made me so hot. The pressure inside me was building to an explosion and as soon as Luka entered me fully, I released Zach and cried out as I came.

Using my hand, I finished Zach while another orgasm built. I was so full with Ben and Luka both inside me but the two of them found a rhythm that had me gasping for breath at each thrust.

I came again and again, losing track of what was even happening. Then, Ben grunted as he came followed by Luka.

Sweaty and exhausted, I found my way to the couch and squeezed in between Matt and Zach. The twins cuddled up with me. Luka threw a blanket over us and after he tugged on his pants, he grabbed a seat on the couch next to Matt.

Even Ben joined us.

I was still naked between the twins when I woke the next morning. I had a feeling I was going to enjoy staying with all of my mates in the same room.

Raven

Normal, it turns out, moves quickly. None of the other students knew what happened. It wasn't even a topic of gossip. Other than catching up Makayla, I hadn't even discussed the crazy weeks prior with a shadow fae after me.

It was strange how easily we all settled into a routine. Strange and wonderful. Though, it did come with the downside of having to take my turn at the Spellcasting exam.

My palms were sweaty as I stepped into the familiar room. I was here twice a day for lessons. But every time I entered, I had to shake off the ghosts of what happened in here.

Today, though, I was far more focused on what this test would bring me than what had occurred in the past. In an odd way, it was sort of comforting. It was probably the first time I was in the Spellcasting room thinking about my exams and my classes without the nagging dread of the showdowns with two different fae.

"I assume you're prepared for today's exam?" Professor Flora asked.

"I hope so," I said.

"Good," she crossed the room and set a single black stone down in front of me.

My chest tightened. Maybe I hadn't let go of the past as much as I thought I had. Memories of using the stone to help Professor Halifax open the portal flooded through me.

"What exactly are we doing?" I asked.

"First, I'm opening a portal, and you'll close it," she said. "On your own this time."

"Not to Faerie, I hope," I said.

She smiled. "No, not Faerie."

I blew out a sigh of relief. After the stories I heard about Matt and Zach's tests, this didn't seem so bad. "I think I can handle that. It's just an illusion after all."

"Not for you," she said. "The others got an illusion. Your magic needs proper training. You'll be closing a real portal. Then, you'll be opening one of your own."

"Wait," I said, my pulse racing. "I've never done that. And it's supposed to be really dangerous."

"Do you know why the time thief wanted your magic?" Professor Flora asked.

"To get stronger and open a portal," I said.

"Yes, but do you know *why*?"

"I was told it's the strongest magic there is," I said.

"Time magic is especially important with portals because when you go into another realm, you're not just opening a space, you're affecting time. Time moves differently in other realms. Spend a week in Faerie then return here to find you were only missing for an hour."

"Wow," I said. "I didn't realize."

"Your specific type of magic doesn't necessarily make it *easier* to open the portal, it makes it more accurate. Less danger-ous. It's like using a key instead of picking a lock," she said.

"So that's why she wanted it?" I asked. "It wasn't about power it was about accuracy?"

It sounded so foolish. Was it worth years of stealing magic just to make your portal?

"More than accuracy," she said. "If you open a portal and it's not stable enough to handle the time shift, it can collapse. Often with the caster inside of it."

"That's why they're so dangerous," I said.

She nodded. "Most humans and similar creatures are so focused on *power* that they ignore nuance. It's not that the stronger magic users can do this better, it's the type of magic. The ability to hone it so it's more accurate. It's a subtle art that isn't taught and isn't appreciated. It lacks the showmanship that some other magics have."

"Why is it forbidden, then?" I asked. "I mean, I get why stopping time isn't allowed. I've seen the damage it can do. But why not teach or cultivate time magic if it helps with travel between realms?"

"Because once again, it's about power. Only this time, it's about the type of power that comes with control. The ley lines and the methods of traveling between realms are heavily policed by the various government organizations. If individuals could travel between at will, they'd lose that control," she said.

"Wow." I was still new to supernatural politics but it sounded similar to what I'd experienced in the human world. "Alright. So what does that mean for me?"

"It means that you have a gift," she said. "Which I assume will come in handy considering the fact that one of your mates is from another realm."

My gut twisted uncomfortably. I didn't like to think about Luka being so far away from me. Ever. I wanted him by my side always. I wanted all of them by my side. And for the last several days, we'd all been sharing the Obscura suite. Granted, it was larger than any home I'd ever lived in so it wasn't exactly like we were on top of each other. But they were all there. I could call to any of them and they'd hear me. It was perfect and it made me feel more at peace than I ever knew I could feel.

"Alright, how do we do this?" I asked.

"That's your test," she said. "You've been studying it for weeks now. I can't tell you how to do it. You have to show me what you know."

"But this is real," I said. "What if I screw it up?"

"Then we'll learn quickly just how effective your magic is," she said.

"Let's begin."

Bursts of yellow sparks exploded from Professor Flora's fingertips and I jumped back. The sparks grew, extending toward the rock. Or maybe they were coming from the rock. Either way, the bursts of light intensified until a shimmering circle of gold light expanded into an oval shaped portal.

I could see water beyond. Angry gray waves splashing as if caught in the middle of a storm. The scent of salt hung in the air and spray from the ocean landed on my skin.

"What is that?" I asked.

"Where is that is the more appropriate question," Professor Flora said.

"Where is it?" I asked.

"The Realm of the Sea," she said. "Some humans call it Atlantis."

My jaw dropped. "Atlantis?"

The waves crashed, sending a huge surge through the portal. It splashed out onto the floor, soaking my shoes.

"Are you going to close it or will I have to fail you?" Professor Flora called over the sound of the surf.

I blew out a breath and returned myself to the task at hand, trying to clear my mind of the initial shock of the whole thing. Though, I had to admit that hearing her tell me there was a portal to Atlantis brought up a whole lot of questions.

Calling my magic, I focused on the opening in front of me. A familiar sensation bubbled up within me. Rolling through me like a comfortable old friend. My time magic was still there, waiting for me to call it. Though, this time, I wasn't trying to stop time, I was trying to close a portal. It wasn't something I even thought of doing until the conversation we just had.

My whole plan had been to destroy whatever the source of the portal was. The rock, in this case. Or disable the individual who was keeping the portal open. I never thought about trying to close it on my own.

Something else joined my time magic, something I didn't recognize. A seething, dark sort of magic that sparked and popped and sputtered like a burning fuse. It was wild and careless and it wanted out.

Adrenaline coursed through me and I grabbed hold of the new sensation, guiding it through me, letting it mingle with my time magic. This new feeling burned brighter, as if latching on to my time magic.

It felt good. It felt right.

It felt powerful.

As it surged to a peak, I channeled it through my hands,

guiding it to the portal. It flowed from me in a stream of blue light, surrounding the portal with an intense brightness that made me turn my eyes away.

As the magic enveloped the portal, it hissed then sizzled. I glanced back, squinting into the light just in time to see my magic swallow the portal whole. The lights went out in the classroom and the emergency light buzzed slightly, casting the room in its odd glow.

Breathless, I lowered my hands and stared up at Professor Flora. Her lips parted and her eyes widened.

She looked honestly surprised. I wasn't even sure that was possible. She'd always been so difficult to read. So composed.

An electric charge hung in the room, leaving the scent of magic lingering in the air. Professor Flora walked over to me and without a word, she took hold of my hands. "How did you do that?"

"Do what?" I asked. Wasn't I supposed to close the portal?"

She locked her silver eyes on me. "I haven't seen magic like that since I was home."

I wasn't sure what to say. My magic had felt different, but it felt right. Like it was supposed to be that way.

"Somehow, you tapped into your magic that has been dormant in this realm," she said. "Your fae magic is no longer untamed. It's unbound; it's free."

"How?" I asked.

She shook her head. "My guess is that whatever was in that book was strong enough to overcome the lack of magic in this realm."

I sucked in a breath. That wasn't supposed to be possible. "If that's the case, I guess it's good that we got rid of it."

"The question is, what will it do to your mates?" She looked more serious than I'd ever seen her.

"It won't hurt them, will it?" I asked.

"No," she said. "But it will impact their magic."

I swallowed hard. "What does that mean for us?"

"I don't know," she said. "But right now, we need to finish your test."

"You seriously want me to open a portal?" I asked. "I've never done it before."

"You have to find out what you're capable of," she said. "And you have to find ways besides freezing time to channel your magic."

"I can't exactly go around opening portals to other realms," I said. "I might as well just stop and start time."

"Except for the fact that opening portals isn't illegal. Stopping time is. At least in this realm," she said.

"Alright," I said, giving in. It was clear I wasn't going to win this. "Just go for it?"

She nodded and stepped away from the stone. Last time I'd opened a portal, I'd had some help from a fae who was using my magic. This time, I was on my own.

From my research, I knew the stones were attuned to the location that the portal was to open. So I already knew this portal was tuned to open in the middle of the ocean in Atlantis. Which was crazy. But that wasn't the point. The point was, it was clear that Professor Flora didn't want me to take her anywhere. Why else would she choose the middle of the sea?

It actually made me feel more comfortable knowing that the portal went basically nowhere.

Taking a deep breath, I called to my magic. It surged through me. The time magic once again mingling with the newfound magic. I felt more powerful than ever before and I felt like I understood how my magic was supposed to feel. This was the real me. The magic I had before was muted and less capable. This was a force of nature.

The magic coursed through my veins, moving like fire. Tiny

shocks burst on my skin sending a tingling across my body. I never felt more alive than I did right now.

Bright blue energy surged from my fingers, moving toward the rock. It spread upward and expanded, creating an opening like I'd seen from Professor Flora. The portal sparkled and flashed as it stabilized.

I lowered my hands a little but kept hold of the magic. In front of me the gray ocean waves crashed, sending a spray of saltwater through the portal. It coated my arms, making them damp. Laughter bubbled up from within and I cackled like a mad woman. Using my magic like this felt right. It felt like I finally had control. It felt like nobody would ever be able to hurt me again.

"Well done," Professor Flora said. "You may release it."

I nodded and then lowered my hands before closing my fingers into a fist. The magic ceased and the portal shrunk until it was gone.

"I've repaid my favor," Professor Flora said.

"What exactly was your agreement?" I asked as I wiped the water from my arms with my hands.

"I told Dr. Green I would help you until you were capable of taking care of yourself. Today, you showed me that you are ready," she said.

I grinned. I'd felt that too but it was nice to hear it from someone else. "Thanks."

"Those trials they're putting on for you in a few weeks won't be any concern for you," she said.

My stomach twisted. I wanted to believe her, but it was just one more thing standing between me and my own happily ever after. Whatever the hell that was going to look like.

"Go on," she said. "You're excused from independent study."

And just like that, I was on cloud nine again. The trials were weeks away. I could spend a few days at least basking in the extra freedom I'd gained and enjoying my newfound power.

Now, I just needed to find my friends and celebrate.

Raven

For once, I was relieved to be heading into gym. The last few days of class had been relatively normal. No bullying from Delores, no expectations, nobody after me. And on top of that, Coach Miller actually seemed to be teaching.

It was weird. But I wasn't going to argue.

I left the locker room and joined the circle of students, scanning them for Luka. Instead, I stopped on a familiar face that I hadn't seen in weeks. "Violet!"

I ran over to her and threw my arms around her. She hugged me back.

"I'm so glad you're back," I said. "I hate that they won't let people visit you."

She let go of the embrace and smiled. "I can tell you, being in the hospital for that long sucks. I don't recommend it."

"Oatmeal and broth?" I asked, then I realized she didn't eat the same food as me. "Bagged blood, maybe?"

"Cold, too," she said with a shudder. "It's almost worse that way."

"I'll have to take your word for it," I said. "But I am so glad you're here and you're okay."

"Thanks," she said. "Dr. Green told me they got the guy."

I nodded. "Yeah, they did."

"Good," she said. "I hope they do awful things to him in prison."

"Me too," I agreed.

"Violet, welcome back," Luka said, wrapping an arm over her shoulders in an awkward hug.

"Hey, thanks, demon," she said. "And thanks for the visits."

"Visits?" I asked, lifting my eyebrow.

"I took some messages from Scarlet into Violet's dreams a couple of times." He shrugged.

"Wow," I said, a little surprised. "I didn't know you took orders. I would have had you check on her for me."

"I gave you updates on her," he said.

"That's true," I said. "I just didn't realize it had been from dream visits."

"It was only a couple of times," Violet said. "And he was a gentleman if you're wondering."

I wasn't actually. I trusted Luka and we'd never really talked about him being only with me. After all, I was with four men.

Luka slid his arm around my waist and pulled me into him before planting a kiss on my cheek. "I've only got eyes for this girl."

"You two are enough to melt my little black heart," she said.

"Us?" he said. "You should have seen Scarlet pining over you. She was a mess."

Violet bit down on her lip. "Yeah, we're kind of adorable."

"Yeah, you are," Luka said.

I grinned at my friend. She was safe and happy. I was in the arms of the sexiest demon there was. And he was thoughtful, kind, and all mine. Despite everything, life was good. Better than I ever thought it could be.

"Listen up, class," Coach Miller said.

Luka lowered his arm from my waist and the three of us turned to face our teacher.

He was wearing a shirt today. I really was having the best day ever. Not having to look at his overly huge muscles and his spray tan was a nice change. "Listen up. You've got three weeks until the trials. Most of you will be taking them for real this time. This is it. No re-dos. No monsters or fae to ruin it. And I don't get a say in how it's run."

He glared at all of us as if we'd done something to personally ruin the trials for him. "After the last issue, the school board doesn't think we can handle it. So they'll be setting up the trials. I have no idea what they'll throw at you. All I can do is whip your skinny asses into shape over the next three weeks."

I shifted, waiting for the burpees. Or the stairs. What fresh hell was he going to subject us to today?

"Suicides," he called. "One-hundred of them. If you finish, you get to hold planks till the bell rings."

We all groaned. Nothing like running back and forth for an hour. He'd really been on a running kick the last few weeks.

"Oh, and I forgot," Coach Miller said.

I turned to look at him and a chill ran down my spine at the sight of his grin. He looked far too pleased for him to say anything good.

"The school board did get one thing right. You will each take the trials alone. No groups. No teamwork. Just you and whatever they decide to throw at you."

I swallowed against the lump in my throat. That changed our plans for sure.

"We should have seen that coming," Luka said.

"Thank the gods," Violet said. "I have more chance of passing on my own than I did relying on the people I was thrown into a group with."

I knew my group would have passed together and I had to admit, I was disappointed. Luka grabbed my hand and squeezed. "You'll be fine."

After my last session with Professor Flora, I knew I'd be fine. That wasn't the reason I was upset. "I was looking forward to doing it together."

"Don't worry. There's lots of things we can do together." He winked.

I grinned. He was right. At the end of the day, I still got to go home to my mates. All of them. In one room. Every day I kept waiting for them to say something about changing the living arrangements, but instead, they seemed to be getting more used to it.

The other day, the twins grabbed some snacks for the room and they picked up Ben's favorite chips and Luka's favorite soda. A week ago, that never would have happened. We had all fallen into a weird, comfortable routine. We did homework together most nights and a few times, we'd all watched movies together on the couch. It was perfect. And I never wanted it to end.

The class was lined up, ready to start our sprints. Violet pulled her hair up into a messy bun and looked over at me. "I didn't miss this class while I was in the hospital, that's for sure."

"I know you didn't," I said. "But I missed you."

"Good," she said. "Cause you're going to slow it down so you can help me not look so bad. I haven't run in weeks."

"You got it," I said.

Coach Miller blew his whistle and we took off. It felt good to move my body and let my thoughts drift. After a few minutes, I was breathing heavy. The one good thing about gym class was that it forced me to shut off my brain and just get through the task.

Though, I wasn't going to miss it when I graduated. Three weeks. Thoughts about the trials tried to force their way in, but I was too tired from running to let them win. Right now, I was just a student in gym class with no other concerns. Worrying about the trials would have to wait until later.

Raven

The gym was a buzz of conversation as we all waited to hear what was in store for us. Last time we'd gone through this, we waited in the locker rooms with our groups. This time all of the students taking the trials were here together.

I stood next to my mates, the five of us in a close huddle. Several other small groups had formed, like us, they had planned to do this together. While people like Violet were thrilled to be away from the confines of their group, not everyone felt that way.

"Hey, don't tell me you're going to just stand guard around

my girl the rest of the day," Makayla's voice came from behind me.

I turned to see her standing with her hands on her hips. "You know, not everyone is out to hurt her."

"Habit," Ben said, taking a step back.

They really were surrounding me like I was a prized possession. I suppose I didn't blame them. While I knew they trusted me to take care of myself, we'd been through a lot together and I could see why they were nervous.

"You ready?" I asked Makayla.

"Hell, yes," she said. "What could the school board really throw at us?"

"Last time the school board was in charge of running a trials, two students died," Zach said.

I glared at him. "That is not the kind of news we need to hear minutes before starting the trials."

"Hey, she asked," he said.

"Sometimes keeping that to yourself isn't a bad idea," Luka said.

"How many died last time the school hosted a trials?" Matt asked.

"None if you count the fake one that was designed just to kill us," Ben said.

"True," Matt said.

"Last year one student died," Zach said. "So I guess there's risk no matter what."

"Good thing I had two visits to confinement," I said under my breath. The rumors about confinement leading to early deaths had been circling my mind a lot lately.

"You're going to be fine," Makayla said. "You took out two scary fae. I mean, who else can say that?"

"Actually, they did most of the work," I said, looking at my mates.

"We did it together," Ben said.

"And the last one wasn't that big of a deal," I said.

"Still better than most of the students here could do," she said.

"Wait a minute." I nudged Makayla with my elbow. "Why aren't you freaked out about all this?"

"Cause I don't have to work with my group," she said. "They were going to get me killed. All I have to do is keep myself alive. That I can handle."

I frowned. "I liked my group."

"We can't all be as lucky as you," she said.

"Hey, babe." Remi walked over to us and wrapped his arm around Makayla. Her face went beet red.

"Hi guys, Raven," Remi said.

It was still a little weird playing nice with Remi, but he'd slowly been let into our group. Though, watching him and Makayla made it easier to accept him. It was clear they were crazy about each other and he spoiled her. Which I fully approved of. If anyone deserved a man to wait on her hand and foot, it was Makayla. She wasn't the type to take advantage of it and Remi loved doing little sweet things for her. Who knew he was just a big softie?

"You all ready for this?" Remi asked with a grin.

"We're ready," I said, not feeling my words.

"Can you believe we're all going to be graduating next week?" he asked.

"I am so ready to get out of here," Makayla said.

I wasn't sure how to respond. Things had been so good with my mates that I hadn't brought up the plans for what we were going to do when we left. Now certainly wasn't the time.

A whistle sounded and I blew out a relieved breath. Then I remembered that the whistle meant it was time for the trials. My pulse raced and my palms were sweaty already and I didn't even know what we were facing yet.

Coach Miller slithered to the front of the group. He was accompanied by three women in suits and Dr. Green.

"Welcome, students," Dr. Green said. "And honored members of the school board." He nodded to the three women, then turned to us.

"You have all been waiting for today since the first day you stepped foot in our doors. Today you will put your years of practice, training, and lessons to the test in real life situations. Nothing you encounter today is an illusion. Everything is life or death."

The words hung in the air. Nobody moved and I was pretty sure we were all holding our breath.

"The trials are an ancient tradition dating back to the first supernaturals competing in the Olympic Games. In those days, it was for promoting peace. Today, we use them as a way to determine that you have enough control and cunning to call yourself a graduate from this prestigious institution.

"The Academy of the Elites is the best school for supernaturals in the world. And we have a reputation to uphold. If you fail these trials, you will not earn your diploma."

"If you fail the trials, you will likely die," Coach Miller added.

Dr. Green nodded. "The trials are dangerous. There is no way out once you begin. You must finish."

"Or die," Coach Miller added.

Dr. Green seemed to ignore him. "You'll have three hours. Coach Miller, will you do the honors?"

Coach Miller's chest expanded as he straightened his shoulders. He was clearly enjoying his moment in the spotlight. "The school board has outdone themselves this year. You are all getting one of the most interesting and dangerous trials I've ever seen. Even I'm impressed."

"Thank you, Coach," one of the women said.

He nodded toward her then turned back to us. "They created a course that's loaded with things that want to hurt you." He slithered along the gathered group of students and stopped in front of me. I tried not to shudder at how close he was.

"All you have to do is get through it. You finish, you graduate," he said. "Questions?"

The room was silent.

"Walk," Coach Miller said. "Outside, all of you."

As we passed through the doors of the gym, I expected to be met with spring sunshine. Instead, I was greeted by a tunnel made of vines and leaves. "What the?"

Ahead, the tunnel split off into two directions. Coach Miller waited for us at the fork. "Two minutes between each of you. I better not find anyone waiting for someone to catch up. Remember, this is a solo trial. I don't want to spoil the surprise for you, but I'm pretty sure the board put in some extra surprises just for people who try to go in groups."

"This should be fun," Luka said.

"Can't wait," Ben said.

"Just think, when we finish, we're done," Zach said.

"I'll meet you all at the end?" I asked.

"We'll be waiting for you," Ben said.

"Probably not, I'm guessing she'll be waiting for us," Matt said.

"I appreciate the vote of confidence," I said.

"Remi," Coach Miller called. "You're up first."

The buzz of conversation around us ceased in a heartbeat. The wait was over. It was time to go.

Remi gave Makayla a kiss on the cheek. "I'll see you out there."

"Good luck," she called to him.

My stomach twisted into knots as I watched Remi disappear into the darkness beyond the door.

"Ms. Winters," Coach Miller called.

My heart raced. I thought I was ready for this but now that it was my turn, I wasn't so sure. "Yes?"

"Your turn," he said.

I blew out a breath. "Might as well get it over with, right?"

"Good luck," Makayla and Luka said in unison.

"You got this," Zach said.

"Don't over think it," Ben said. "Use your instincts."

"We'll see you at the end," Matt said.

I walked to the front of the group of students and stood in front of Coach Miller. "I'm ready."

"I doubt that," he said. "But you might as well go, anyway. Pick a side. Stay alive."

I resisted rolling my eyes. He was so dramatic. How bad could it be? I stepped up toward the entry and dropped my guard, letting my magic flow through me. To the right, I felt nothing. No magic. To the left there was something else. Something that made the air feel charged with energy. It was a magical signature for sure. But to what?

Just because one side didn't feel like it had magic, didn't mean that side was better. There were lots of ways to make our life hell without magic. Monsters, booby traps, more monsters…

Deciding I'd take my chance with the magical elements, I turned toward the electrical buzzing in the air. With a deep breath, I walked into the maze, away from Coach Miller and all the other students.

As I walked through the dark tunnel, I realized I'd never really done anything on my own. There'd always been someone there to help me or bail me out. This was my chance to see what I could do on my own.

My feet sank into soft mossy ground and I breathed in the scent of a garden. If not for the tingle of magic around me or the heavy sense of dread weighing in my gut, this would be nice.

Light filtered in through cracks in the canopy above. Areas where the vines weren't quite as thick as the rest of the tunnel. It was just light enough to see where I was going without using magic to guide my way. Which was a good thing as I wanted to save all my strength just in case something came at me.

The feeling of magic intensified, growing stronger with each step. Whatever I'd chosen to encounter was coming up fast.

Ahead, I saw a slight shimmer in the air. I wasn't sure what it was, but I knew it was the source of the magic I'd detected. Stretching out my arm, I brushed my fingers over the shimmer. My hand met resistance, like glass.

It was a barrier of some kind, blocking off my path. I smirked. This was so much better than a monster.

Calling to my magic, I spread my fingers wide, reaching toward the shield. I sent a pulse of energy forward and it hit the shimmering air, spreading outward like ripples in a lake.

The shield sputtered and shattered, falling like glitter to the ground. *First obstacle done.* I walked through, feeling more confident with each step. So far, this wasn't anything to worry about. And if this was a sample of what the trials had in store, I was going to be just fine.

I reached another fork and peered down the two paths. One was dirt and lined with bare, brown branches. The other path was the same moss I'd been walking on and the tunnel was made of the green, twisting vines. *Interesting.* They'd even changed the appearance this time.

Once again, I felt for magic. As I breathed in, sending my senses outward, I heard a roar that made me open my eyes wide. A chill ran down my spine. I'd had too many encounters with monsters to walk toward one. Ever. Not going to happen.

I held my breath, waiting to see if the creature revealed itself again.

Another loud roar. I felt it vibrating in my bones. More importantly, I knew it was coming from the dirt trail.

Without hesitation, I turned and walked onto the mossy trail in front of me. I'd take any magic they could throw at me over a monster any day. I was tired of fighting off creatures.

This time, the trial grew colder with each step and I could see frost forming on the leaves. I shivered and goosebumps rose on my bare arms. Rubbing my hands over my arms, I continued forward, unsure of what I was going to find.

My breath came out in clouds and my teeth chattered. Maybe I would have been better off with the monster. It was as cold as the walk-in freezer at the restaurant I'd worked at.

Shivering, I continued forward. Was this the whole challenge of this part? Just getting through the cold? I wondered if I should turn back and chance the path with the monster. Just as I contemplated lighting a fire in my hands for warmth, I heard a rustling noise behind me.

About time I ran into a classmate. It was getting too quiet in here. I turned to see who had caught up to me.

I gasped. It wasn't a classmate. It was the walls closing up behind me. Vines grew over the path I'd just taken, closing me in. No option to go back now.

Taking a deep breath, I rubbed my arms again and moved forward. After a few more steps, I realized I wasn't feeling so cold anymore. Either the air was warming up or I was getting used to it. I wasn't sure which was worse.

It was darker ahead, but I thought I could make out a circular space that appeared to have multiple pathways. At least I could get away from the weird closing walls.

I emerged into the opening and stopped walking. There were five different doors in front of me. None of them were open as

I'd seen in the past. I had a feeling that some of those doors were more dangerous than others.

Moving closer, I reached out to see if I could sense anything behind them. With a creak, one of the doors opened. I jumped back, wondering which of my classmates ended up here.

The person who stepped through the door wasn't a classmate. It felt like ice was running through my veins as dread seeped into every cell in my body.

"This is impossible," I said. "You have to be an illusion. You're in prison. They took you away."

"Little fae, you didn't think their prison would keep me locked up, did you? I'm not like your old teacher." The shadow fae smiled at me.

"Your mate, you mean?" I asked. "You left her there?"

"She might be my mate, but she betrayed me. She deserves what she's getting." He took a step toward me. "You know who else betrayed me? You. And it's your turn to pay."

I glanced behind me, wondering if I should run. The trail I'd come through no longer existed.

I was trapped and alone.

Luka

I glared at Coach Miller. He was calling off names one at a time, purposefully leaving me until the end. The twins went through a few people after Raven and then Ben had gone. He just really hated me. With each student that went after Raven, it was more distance between the two of us.

He knew what he was doing. He split up all the friends. Makayla was still waiting with me. Finally, he called her. She glanced over at me. "I'm sure she's fine."

"Right." With each passing second, I was feeling more and more anxious. Usually, I was able to calm my nerves. These things didn't get to me. But today, there was something nagging at me that made me feel on edge.

Two more students went after Makayla and I moved closer to the front. There were only three of us left.

"Demon," Coach Miller called.

I glared at him. He rarely used my name and he wasn't calling me *demon* as a term of endearment.

"You're up, lover boy," he said.

Clenching my teeth, I walked past him, not giving him the satisfaction of a response. Finally, I could see if I could catch up to Raven. I didn't care what he said about working together. I knew Raven could take care of herself but I'd feel better if I could be close to her.

I followed her scent, easily turning at each fork toward the direction I knew she went. Ever since the night we bound the book to ourselves, I'd felt like all my skills were heightened. It was as if everything had been amplified by the magic I'd taken inside me.

Right now, I was grateful for it because it was taking me straight to Raven. Everything inside me was telling me to get to her. It didn't make sense. I trusted Raven and I knew she was powerful in her own right. And this was just a test. Despite the dire warnings, I never really worried about any of us finishing it. But there was something wrong. I could feel it.

The air grew colder and I ignored it, hardly phased by the change. My demon blood ran hot and while I disliked the cold, I could block it out. In the dim light of the tunnel, it looked like I was headed toward a dead end.

I stopped walking and reached out for the bond with Raven. She was nearby and I was going to trust my instincts.

Walking forward, I stopped at a wall of vines. I couldn't explain it, but I knew she was behind the barrier and I was going to get to her.

The worst part was that I could sense that she wasn't alone.

I reached out, tugging on the vines. As I expected, they didn't budge. I could feel the magic coursing through them. It felt dark and heavy. Not like the magic I usually experienced at the academy.

This wasn't a job for a demon. My magic wasn't strong enough.

Whatever was happening to Raven wasn't part of the trials. I was sure of it. Closing my eyes, I took a deep breath and used my magic to reach out toward the other three. We'd developed an unusual bond during our magic meld. Raven wasn't the only one I could sense.

Their magic was weaker than hers and I could tell they were farther away. But I knew I needed them here. Raven needed them.

I sent a burst of my own magic out through our connection, trying to share my location. *Raven's in danger.*

A surge of anger rolled through me that didn't belong to me. Adrenaline spiked and I knew the others were responding. They heard my call and they were on their way.

I only had to wait a minute before one of the twins showed up. He was breathless and his shirt had a hole burned in it. I glanced at the hole then looked back up at him.

"Fire breathing lizard," he said. "Don't ask. Where's Raven?"

"I think she's through here," I said. "It's sealed with magic. I can't break it."

"Where's Raven?" Another voice asked.

Ben had arrived, his whole body tense. I could almost feel the anger vibrating off of him.

"Through here, I think," I said. "Don't shift on us yet."

He growled. "I can't hold it much longer. They tried to force a shift down that trail." He lifted his chin in the direction he came from.

"Deep breaths, bro," the twin said. "We're going to get her out."

"Hey, why am I last to the party?" The second twin arrived. He looked in better shape than his brother.

"Last again, Matt," the twin who I now knew was Zach said.

"Yeah, yeah," he said. "What are we doing here? If Raven's in trouble, we need to move."

"She's through here," Zach said.

The twins moved closer to the wall of vines and I stepped back to let them do their thing. This really was their area of expertise.

"I can feel her," Matt said.

"It's a shield barrier," Zach said. "We can take it down. Be ready for when it falls."

"We're right behind you," Ben said, his teeth bared.

I was pretty sure we were going to have a full-fledged were-wolf on our hands any second. Hopefully he'd wait till we were through.

"Hey, Ben," Matt said. "If your wolf can help Raven, don't hold back. We'll move out of your way."

"We do this together," Ben said. "But I will shift if needed."

Matt nodded, then turned back to the barrier. He and Zach lifted their hands toward it and I could feel the vibrations of the magic they were creating. I didn't know enough about spells and mages to know what they were doing, but I trusted them.

And it dawned on me that they trusted me too. I told them Raven was in danger and without question, they came.

We were an odd group. But we were all in this together, no matter what happened next.

Raven

"How did you even get out?" I asked, hoping he'd go into an elaborate bad-guy speech. I had no idea what I was going to do and I needed time.

He grinned, showing his fangs. "I control light. I am the shadows. There is no prison that can keep me."

My stomach twisted into knots as I thought about what I should do. This wasn't about getting something from me. This was about taking me out. And I was not going to go down today.

It dawned on me that he had yet to call his shadow magic.

Whatever his plans were, he'd kept the lights on. I had to attack first.

Quickly, I called to my magic and it surged through me, rising up in response to the fear gripping me. I lifted my hands and launched fire at the fae.

When the flames cleared, he was gone. But I knew he wasn't actually gone. In the darkness of the vine covered enclosure, there were too many shadows. "Where are you?"

"Everywhere," his voice filled the air around me, ethereal and echoing through the space. "Nowhere."

I shivered, turning in a slow circle as I looked for anything that stood out. "Leave me alone. Just go away."

"After what you did to me?" His voice was more solid now.

I turned toward it and saw him standing in front of me again. "You have no chance against me." He clicked his tongue. "And to think, I offered to take you back with me."

"You had no good intentions," I said. "That book was dangerous in your hands."

"And who put those ideas in your head?" he asked. "My old love, perhaps? The one who betrayed me before you?"

"It doesn't matter," I said. "I made my choice."

"You made a poor choice, taking her side," he said.

This time, when he used his shadows, I could see them. They slithered toward me like tentacles, reaching for me.

I darted away from them, my skin already crawling at the thought of him getting his shadows on me.

The shadows moved slowly, swirling like smoke. They adjusted, slithering toward me.

I wasn't going to be able to outrun them. Lifting my hands, I called the fae magic. I'd had limited success so far, but I had some shadow powers of my own. I grabbed hold of his shadows and tugged on them. They resisted my magic, still fighting to come toward me.

I wasn't able to send them away as I hoped, but I had enough in me to keep them from coming closer.

"You're learning some," he said. "Too bad it's not enough."

Sweat formed on my brow and I struggled to hold the shadows at bay. I didn't know what would happen if he won, but I wasn't willing to find out.

I pushed against the shadows, using everything I had to send them back to him. My magic hummed within, rising up to force the shadows back. The new magic I'd gained seemed to be waiting in the distance, unwilling to give me a boost.

The shadows gained ground, one of them slipping past me. It wrapped its way around my ankle and tugged. I stumbled, nearly losing my hold on the other shadows.

This wasn't working. There had to be something else I could do. While holding off the shadows, I called to the new magic. The magic that gave me the boost when I was opening the portals. It felt different, but it wanted out. I could tell it was ready.

I grabbed hold of the new magic, forcing it through. I had to control these shadows. With a scream, I threw everything I had at the shadow fae, going right for the source.

A burst of white light exploded from me, sending all the shadows away and leaving me standing in a circle of light.

The shadow fae growled and quickly rallied. He sent his shadows toward me again, but they stopped short, unable to pass the light around me.

He pulled his shadows back.

"I've won, your shadows can't hurt me anymore," I said.

He smirked. "You forget. I control the light too."

A moment later, everything went black. The light around me, the dim light from the gaps in the vines. It was all gone.

But so was our magic.

If he was desperate enough to cut off his own magic, he was

afraid of me. At least I had that going for me. Because it looked like I was about to be stuck in hand to hand combat with a dude who was twice my size.

"You play dirty," I yelled. I didn't even care anymore. At this point, it wasn't looking good for me. Who gave a fuck if I riled him up? "You have to pull out all your tricks to take down a girl with a year of magic training under her belt? You're a fucking coward."

The hit came hard and fast, knocking me to the ground and knocking my breath out with it.

I gasped for air as I quickly got to my feet, swinging wildly to attempt to land a blow of my own. All I hit was air.

He really was going to do this. Just hit me while I was blind until he took me out.

"Come on, at least make it a fair fight," I called into the darkness.

"If you'd been raised in Faerie, that would have been one of your first lessons," he said. "There's no such thing as a fair fight."

A fist hit the side of my face, sending my head back. My cheekbone made a sickening cracking sound and my eye swelled closed almost right away. Searing pain spread through my face into my head and the metallic tang of blood filled my mouth.

Stumbling forward, I moved away from where the hit had come from. Tears streamed down my face. The punch hurt like a mother fucker. I was angry and terrified. How the hell was I going to survive this?

I held my breath, trying to ignore the burning pain in my face. If I could hear him, maybe I could attack. Maybe I could take him by surprise.

Silence answered me.

I'd never felt so alone in my life.

As the seconds ticked by, the darkness seemed to deepen and I wondered if this was it. Was this how I was going to die?

After everything I'd been though, it didn't seem right. I'd suffered too much. And there were my mates. The thought of leaving them made my heart hurt worse than my face.

I couldn't leave them.

I needed them.

We were part of each other. Part of something larger than ourselves.

As I thought about each of them in turn, something shifted. It was as if I could sense them.

Of course I could sense them.

They'd been telling me to be more aware. More open to the bond. More in tune with our connection.

I wasn't ready to leave them.

Closing my eyes, I took a deep breath and focused on my mates. Their scents, the way their magic felt when we connected, the taste of their kisses, the feel of their skin against mine. The way my heart leaped out of my chest at the sight of them. The way they could comfort me with a word or a touch.

My memories were so sharp it was almost like they were here with me.

Magic ignited somewhere inside me like a song that had to be sung. It called to me, it called to them. I could feel it, one chord of a larger composition. A piece of a whole.

And it wanted the other members of the ensemble.

I could feel them, as if their hearts were beating inside me. As if we were one. They were so close to me.

Ignoring everything else, I walked forward into the darkness, guided only by my intuition, by this new magic that was begging for release.

My fingers brushed over a wall of vines. I set my hand on the foliage and spread my fingers wide. I knew they were there on the other side. I could feel their magic breathing to life through the barrier.

It just needed a little help.

Summoning the new power, I sent it toward them.

A blue light radiated from my hand, moving quickly like lightning until it had illuminated each leaf of each vine. I removed my hand and looked around at my prison.

The whole circular space was glowing and against the opposite wall, stood the shadow fae.

His teeth were bared and he looked like he was ready to fight.

I wasn't scared anymore.

I didn't need to look behind me to know they were with me. "Welcome to the fight, boys."

"We should have known you'd try to have all the fun by yourself," Zach said.

"We're not worried about sending him back to jail this time, right?" Luka asked.

"Oh, hell no," Ben said.

The shadow fae lifted his hands and dropped them, quenching the light I'd created and sending us all into darkness.

Only this time, I didn't feel my magic fade. Not all of it anyway. The new magic, the magic that called out to my mates was stronger than ever.

I reached for them, my hands easily finding two of theirs. I couldn't explain what was happening, but the magic inside me was calling to them and theirs was calling to mine.

We were connected as one. The magic inside me bubbled to the surface and spread through me, shooting through my arms into my hands. A bright white light exploded from me and I could see all of us hand in hand.

The shadow fae was in front of us and he turned away from the light, shielding his face.

Letting out a scream, I sent everything I had at him. The light intensified, blinding me so I had to close my eyes.

When it settled, the normal dim light of the trials was around us, the light restored.

A pile of gray ash sat on the ground where the shadow fae had stood. My eyes widened at the sight.

We'd taken him out.

Whatever our magic did together, it was far more powerful than I could have ever imagined.

"What just happened?" I asked.

"We each have a piece of the magic from that book," Zach said. "I think we found a way to access it together."

"Shit," Luka said. "Good thing we didn't let him have it."

"Good riddance," Ben said.

"Is he really gone?" I asked.

Matt walked over to the pile of ash and touched it with his toe. "I don't think there's any coming back from this."

"He did try to kill us, I guess," I said, guilt swirling inside me.

"Don't do that to yourself," Ben said. "He was here to kill you."

"How the hell did he even get here?" Matt asked.

"He broke out of the prison," I said.

"Then we really had no choice," Zach said. "He would have kept coming."

"Hey, this is supposed to be a solo test," a voice called. "Even when they split you all up you find each other."

I turned and smiled at the familiar voice. "Hey, Violet."

"You five better split up," she said. "I'm pretty sure they've set some traps for groups that linger together. I passed a couple of kids in a pit back there."

It was hard to believe that after everything we'd just done, we were still in the middle of the trials.

"You heard her," Luka said. "Ladies first. Raven, we'll be right behind you."

"Good luck," Violet said. She tugged on one of the doors and it opened without issue. She disappeared behind it, closing it after her.

"Well, what are we waiting for?" Matt said. "We've got a trials to complete."

It still didn't feel right, but I blew out a breath and reached for the door nearest to me. "I'll see you all at the end."

"We'll be there," Ben said. "All of us."

I glanced at my mates again, feeling an overwhelming sense of appreciation for all of them. We were about to be thrown head first into our future but I no longer worried about it. I know we'd all end up together.

Raven

The rest of the trials seemed sedated compared to facing down a shadow fae. I had to cross a field of poisonous thistles, make it through a dark tunnel, and climb a wall. I was pretty sure the wall was Coach Miller's handiwork.

In the end, none of it felt difficult. I attacked each challenge with confidence. By the time I saw the light ahead that showed me the way out of the maze, I realized that I was no longer worried about how to use my magic. I didn't feel like I was behind or unqualified.

When I walked into the sunlight, I felt different. Empowered.

Free.

The good feeling faded as soon as Dr. Green came running over to me. "Ms. Winters, I need you to get inside right now."

"That's a hell of a congratulations," I said. Even his panicked expression wasn't enough to take me down right now.

"The shadow fae escaped," he said.

"I know," I said.

"You know?" he asked.

"You remember how I ended up here?" I asked. I didn't like thinking about it, but I'd started my journey here with a body count. I supposed it was fitting that it ended that way as well.

"He was in there?" Dr. Green asked.

"Not anymore," I said. "I'm afraid there's not even a body to show for it."

Dr. Green smiled, then quickly cleared his throat and forced his expression into one of indifference. "Well, I suppose we'll never know what happened to him. I will report to the authorities that we didn't see him at the academy."

He started walking away, then turned back to me. "Congratulations, Raven. I knew you had it in you."

"Thanks, Dr. Green," I said.

"Raven!" Makayla ran toward me, Remi right behind her. Her shirt was torn in half and she had what might be scorch marks on her pants. But she was here and she was smiling. Remi actually looked worse. But they'd both made it.

I ran toward her and we met in a hug, both of us bursting into a fit of giggles.

"Can you believe we finally did it?" she asked. "We're going to graduate. And neither of us died."

I laughed harder. There were too many times during my short tenure here that I wasn't sure I was going to make it. "I'm glad you didn't die."

"Same, girl," she said.

Someone else put their arms around me, squishing me in-between Makayla and the newcomer. I recognized his smoke and leather scent right away. "Luka! You made it!"

"Of course I did, Kitten," he said.

"Get in here," Luka said, dragging Remi into the hug. He piled on, grabbing on to Makayla.

Out of the corner of my eye, I saw Ben and Zach walking toward us. Behind them I saw a frazzled looking Matt. He'd clearly encountered something rough as his face was smeared with dirt and his hair was a mess. But he was safe.

They were all safe.

And a moment later, they all joined in the group hug.

It didn't take long for a few other students to join in. Violet and Scarlet, and even some kids I rarely talked to. It was a giant pile of love.

Everyone was just happy to be alive.

Finally, we all broke apart and waited for the last few students to find their way through.

We didn't have to wait long. When the last student came through, Coach Miller blew a whistle.

"I officially call the Trials of the Academy of the Elites to an end," he said. "And for the first time in six years, every student who participated completed the trials. Zero casualties."

We all cheered.

"It's party time, now, right?" Luka asked.

"The celebration will be in the ballroom at nightfall," Dr. Green said. "Congratulations to all of you."

Last time I'd been in the ballroom for a party, it hadn't gone as I hoped. Makayla and I walked in together, hand in hand, both of us haunted by that night.

The party was in full swing when we arrived. Colored lights flashed and a disco ball hung in the middle of the room, adding to the effect. Loud bass vibrated up through my feet from the DJ spinning in the corner.

Students were already on the dance floor, their bodies moving and grinding to the music.

I looked over at Makayla and smiled. Her eyes sparkled with joy and the tension she had walking in seemed to be gone.

"We deserve this," she said.

"Yes we do," I agreed.

"I'm going to get trashed," she said, laughing.

"Lead the way to the bar, my friend," I said.

The two of us linked elbows and wove our way through the crowd toward the bar near the DJ. We sipped drinks and caught up on the last few weeks. I told her about the shadow fae during the trials and she lifted her glass. "Here's to my best friend, the most kick ass woman in the world."

I laughed and knocked my glass against hers. "Thanks."

Remi walked up to us. "Can I borrow my girlfriend for a dance?"

"She's all yours," I said, lifting my glass.

Makayla knocked back the rest of her drink and winked at me. "See ya later."

"Have fun, you two," I said.

They cut through the crowd to the middle of the dance floor. As I watched them, I caught sight of my men. All four of them, walking toward me.

The sight of them still sent a shiver of desire through me. Especially the way they were all looking at me.

They made their way through the crowd and stopped in front

of me. All four of them, together. It wasn't something I saw happen often.

"We had an idea," Zach said.

"Oh?" I took a drink. "What kind of idea?"

"About us, after graduation," he said.

My stomach twisted. I was feeling more confident about finding a way to keep them all with me, but I hadn't yet nailed down what that would look like. "And?"

"I turned down my title," Luka said.

My brow furrowed.

"Us too," Zach said. "Well, we're stepping away from the family business."

"I already had," Ben said. "But I would have left again if I could."

"Okay," I said, feeling uneasy. "Where is this going?"

"We have something special between us," Zach said.

"That magic we used isn't normal," Luka added. "We'd be crazy not to use it."

"And crazy to split up," Matt added.

"I agree with that," I said. "But I have no idea where you're going with this."

"We can use it," Zach said. "Years ago, there were organizations you could hire to hunt down dark magic or help find missing people. They haven't been as prevalent lately. I think it's time that makes a comeback."

"Like private investigators? Or like vigilantes?" I asked.

"Maybe a little of both," Luka said. "Either way, we start our own business. The five of us. And we use this magic to help people."

"And if we happen to find out what happened to your family along the way, even better," Matt added.

"What do you think?" Luka asked.

My heart was so full just looking at my mates. I didn't have words for how I felt. They wanted to stay together. To use our magic to help people. What more could I ask for?

I set my glass down on the bar and walked closer to them and then spread my arms wide. "I think I'm the luckiest girl in the whole world."

They moved in for the embrace. The five of us were all connected. We completed each other. And though they had struggled with sharing, we found a way to make it work.

"Come on," Luka said, breaking away from the group hug. "Let's go dance."

I followed them all toward the dance floor, fully prepared to have the most fun night of my life.

I'd survived the trials, I'd passed the Academy of the Elites. I was about to be a graduate. And I was going to stay with all my mates.

I'd been through so much in the last year but I wouldn't trade any of it. Because in the end, it was worth it to begin my life after the Academy like this.

The End

A NOTE FROM THE AUTHOR

Thank you so much for reading Academy of the Elites, Books 1-4. I truly hope you have enjoyed reading it. If you have, please show your support by leaving a review. It only takes few moments.

Just visit the series page!
Amazon.com/gp/product/B07ZF8FPHG

For the latest news about new releases, sales, upcoming books, giveaways, and more join my newsletter today!

https://landing.mailerlite.com/webforms/landing/k4t1u0

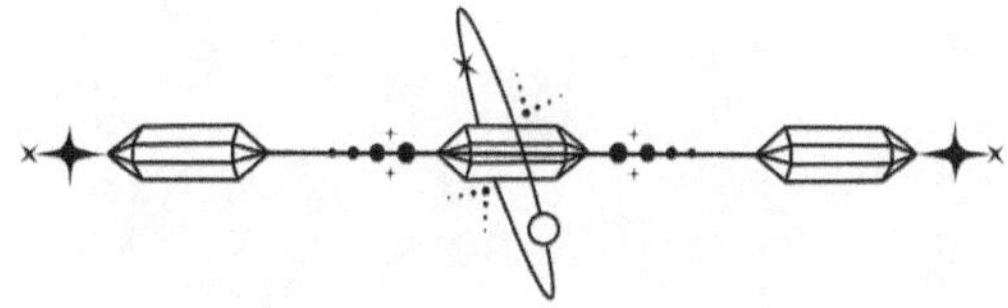

ABOUT THE AUTHOR

Alexis Calder writes sassy heroines and sexy heroes with a sprinkle of sarcasm. She lives in the Rockies and drinks far too much coffee and just the right amount of wine.

ABOUT THE AUTHOR

For more awesomeness check out my website
www.alexiscalder.com

And don't forget to follow me!

Amazon: https://www.amazon.com/stores/Alexis-Calder/author/
B07TP5VCGZ
Goodreads: https://www.goodreads.com/author/show/19382078.
Alexis_Calder
Bookbub: https://www.bookbub.com/authors/alexis-calder
Facebook: https://www.facebook.com/AuthorAlexisCalder
Instagram: https://www.instagram.com/author_alexiscalder/
TikTok: @authoralexiscalder
Twitter: @alexiscalder1

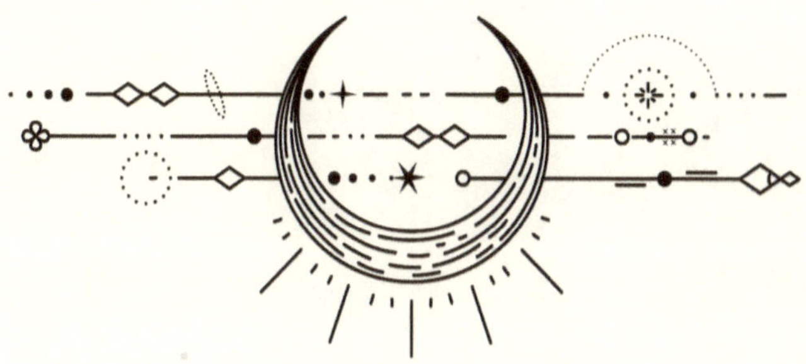

Get a Free Bonus Scene!

https://landing.mailerlite.com/webforms/landing/k4t1u0

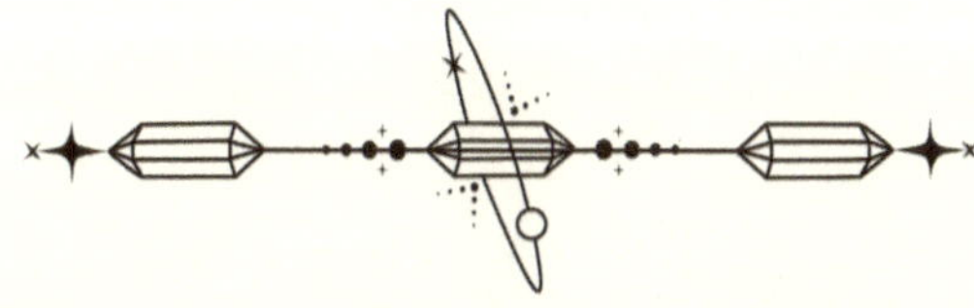